Andrea Barrett

lives in Rochester, New York. She is the author of four previous novels, while her most recent book, *Ship Fever & Other Stories* won the National Book Award for fiction in 1996.

From the British and American reviews of *The Voyage of the Narwhal*:

'Andrea Barrett takes in her sweep the great intellectual and ethical imperatives of the time – questions of race, slavery, evolution; Barrett's big, arcing themes are handled with such deftness and unshowy confidence. Her prose is steady and restrained, but the images of the icescape dazzle and scorch the mind's eye. She makes us feel most eloquently how it is easier to investigate thousands of miles of frozen tundra than it is to explore the private sea of one's being.' GINNY DOUGARY, *Independent on Sunday*

'Barrett's main characters are fictional but her account is rivetingly authentic, told in a nineteenth-century narrative style worthy of Dickens. Enthralling ... a ripping yarn for twenty-first-century readers.' SARAH HURST, *Literary Review*

'Andrea Barrett recreates the intellectual universe of the mid-nineteenth-century naturalist as brilliantly, as convincingly, as she conjures up the northern landscape. Her writing is erudite and evocative, dense with period and geographical detail.' MARGARET WALTERS, *TLS*

'In *The Voyage of the Narwhal* Andrea Barrett re-imagines the great polar expeditions of the nineteenth century, and shows the rare gift of making the familiar striking and strange. The book holds the reader by the serene spaciousness of its imagination and by the clarity of its human portraits.' MAGGIE GEE, *Daily Telegraph*

'An old-fashioned adventure novel ... immaculately researched. An odyssey round the human heart.' *Tatler*

Further reviews overleaf

ALSO BY ANDREA BARRETT

THE VOYAGE OF THE
NARWHAL

ANDREA BARRETT

Flamingo
An Imprint of HarperCollinsPublishers

For Carol Houck Smith

Flamingo
An Imprint of HarperCollins*Publishers*
77–85 Fulham Palace Road,
Hammersmith, London W6 8JB

www.**fire**and**water**.com

Flamingo is a registered trademark of HarperCollins Publishers Limited

Published by Flamingo 2000
9 8 7 6 5 4

First published in Great Britain by
Flamingo 1999

First published in the USA by Norton 1998

This novel is entirely a work of fiction. The names,
characters and incidents portrayed in it are the work of the
author's imagination. Any resemblance to actual persons,
living or dead, events or localities is entirely coincidental.

Photograph of Andrea Barrett by Barry Goldstein

Map by Jacques Chazaud

ISBN 0 655141 6

Printed and bound in Great Britain by
Clays Ltd, St Ives plc

Contents

ILLUSTRATIONS

The Winter quarters of the Narwhal

C. Agatha
C. Violet
Jensen Point
Fletcher Lamb
Bay
C. Laurel
Rensselaer Harbor
Ahoatok
Etah

ELLESMERE IS.

Smith Sound

Kane Basin

Jones Sound

Coburg I.

C. Atholl
C. York

BAFFIN BAY

Beechey I.
Devon Island

Barrow Str.
Lancaster Sound

Somerset Island

Bylot I.

Peel Sound

Prince of Wales I.

Bellot Str.

Boothia Pen.

Gulf of Boothia

Baffin Island

William I.

Back's Great Fish R.

The Voyage of the Narwhal

1855–1856

Chazaud

Melville Bay

Upernavik

GREENLAND

Disko I.

Godhavn

Davis Strait

NOTE: *The sites named along the coast of Ellesmere now bear the names assigned to them by Dr. Kane and later explorers.*

I hate travelling and explorers. . . . Amazonia, Tibet and Africa fill the bookshops in the form of travelogues, accounts of expeditions and collections of photographs, in all of which the desire to impress is so dominant as to make it impossible for the reader to assess the value of the evidence put before him. Instead of having his critical faculties stimulated, he asks for more such pabulum and swallows prodigious quantities of it. Nowadays, being an explorer is a trade, which consists not, as one might think, in discovering hitherto unknown facts after years of study, but in covering a great many miles and assembling lantern-slides or motion pictures, preferably in color, so as to fill a hall with an audience for several days in succession. For this audience, platitudes and commonplaces seem to have been miraculously transmuted into revelations by the sole fact that their author, instead of doing his plagiarizing at home, has supposedly sanctified it by covering some twenty thousand miles. . . . Journeys, those magic caskets full of dreamlike promises, will never again yield up their treasures untarnished. A proliferating and overexcited civilization has broken the silence of the seas once and for all. The perfumes of the tropics and the pristine freshness of human beings have been corrupted by a busyness with dubious implications, which mortifies our desires and dooms us to acquire only contaminated memories. . . . So I can understand the mad passion for travel books and their deceptiveness. They create the illusion of something which no longer exists but still should exist, if we were to have any hope of avoiding the overwhelming conclusion that the history of the past twenty thousand years is irrevocable.

—CLAUDE LEVI-STRAUSS, *Tristes Tropiques (1955)*

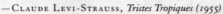

PART I

LOSSING—BARRIT SC

His Lists

(May 1855)

I try in vain to be persuaded that the pole is the seat of frost and desolation; it ever presents itself to my imagination as the region of beauty and delight. There . . . the sun is for ever visible; its broad disk just skirting the horizon, and diffusing a perpetual splendor. There . . . snow and frost are banished; and, sailing over a calm sea, we may be wafted to a land surpassing in wonders and in beauty every region hitherto discovered on the habitable globe . . . What may not be expected in a country of eternal light?

— MARY SHELLEY, *Frankenstein* (1818)

*H*e was standing on the wharf, peering down at the Delaware River while the sun beat on his shoulders. A mild breeze, the smells of tar and copper. A few yards away the *Narwhal* loomed, but he was looking instead at the partial reflection trapped between hull and pilings. The way the planks wavered, the railing bent, the boom appeared then disappeared; the way the image filled the surface without concealing the complicated life below. He saw, beneath the transparent shadow, what his father had taught him to see: the schools of minnows, the eels and algae, the mussels burrowing into the silt; the diatoms and desmids and insect larvae sweeping past hydrazoans and infant snails. *The oyster,* his father once said, *is impregnated by the dew; the pregnant shells give birth to pearls conceived from the sky. If the dew is pure, the pearls are brilliant; if cloudy, the pearls are dull.* Far above him, but mirrored as well, long strands of cloud moved one way and gliding gulls another.

In the water the *Narwhal* sat solid and dark among the surrounding fleet. Everyone headed somewhere, Erasmus thought. England, Africa, California; stony islands alive with seals; the coast of Florida. Yet no one, among all those travelers, who might offer him advice. He turned back to his work. Where was this mound of supplies to go? An untidy package yielded, beneath its waterproof wrappings, a dozen plum puddings that brought him near to tears. Each time he arranged part of the hold more of these parcels appeared: a crate of damson plums in syrup from an old woman in Conshohocken who'd read about their voyage in the newspaper and wanted to contribute her bit. A case of brandy from a Wilmington banker, volumes of Thackeray from a schoolmaster in Doylestown, heaps of hand-knitted socks. His hands bristled with lists, each only partly checked-off: never mind those puddings, he thought. Where were the last two

hundred pounds of pemmican? How had half the meat biscuit
been stowed with the candles and the lamp oil? And where were
the last members of the crew? In his pocket he had another list,
the final roster:

ZECHARIAH VOORHEES, *Commander*   AMOS TYLER, *Sailing Master*
COLIN TAGLIABEAU, *First Officer*   GEORGE FRANCIS, *Second Officer*
JAN BOERHAAVE, *Surgeon*   ERASMUS D. WELLS, *Naturalist*
FREDERICK SCHUESSELE, *Cook*
THOMAS FORBES, *Carpenter*
Seamen:
ISAAC BOND, NILS JENSEN, ROBERT CAREY,
BARTON DESOUZA, IVAN HRUSKA,
FLETCHER LAMB, SEAN HAMILTON

Fifteen of them, all hands counted. Captain Tyler, Mr. Tagliabeau, and Mr. Francis, who together would have charge of the
ship's daily operations, were experienced whaling men. Dr. Boerhaave had a medical degree from Edinburgh; Schuessele had
been cook for a New York packet line; Forbes was an Ohio farm
boy who'd never been to sea, but who could fashion anything
from a few odd scraps of wood. Of the seven unevenly trained
seamen, Bond had reported for duty drunk, and Hruska and
Hamilton were still missing.

Their companions, invisible in the hold, waited for directions—waited, Erasmus feared, for him to fail. He was forty
years old and had a history of failure; he'd sailed, when hardly
more than a boy, on a voyage so thwarted it became a national
joke. Since then his life's work had come to almost nothing. No
wife, no children, no truly close friends; a sister in a difficult situation. What he had now was this pile of goods, and a second
chance.

Still pondering the puddings, he heard laughter and looked

up to see Zeke hanging from the rigging like a flag. His long arms were stretched above a thatch of golden hair; as he laughed his teeth were gleaming in his mouth; he was twenty-six and made Erasmus feel like a fossil. Everything about this moment was tied to Zeke. The hermaphrodite brig about to become their home had once been part of Zeke's family's packet line; with his father's money, Zeke had ordered oak sheathing spiked to her sides as protection against the ice, iron plates wrapped around her bows, tarred felt layered between the double-planked decks. In charge of the expedition—and hence, Erasmus reminded himself, of him—Zeke had chosen Erasmus to gather the equipment and stores surrounding him now in such bewildering heaps.

Where was all this to go? Salt beef and pork and barrels of malt, knives and needles for barter with the Esquimaux, guns and ammunition, coal and wood, tents and cooking lamps and woolen clothing, buffalo skins, a library, enough wooden boards to house over the deck in an emergency. And what about the spirit thermometers, or the four chronometers, the microscope, and all the stores for his specimens: spirits of wine, loose gauze, prenumbered labels and glass jars, arsenical soap for preserving bird skins, camphor and pillboxes for preserving insects, dissecting scissors, watch glasses, pins, string, glass tubes and sealing wax, bungs and soaked bladders, brain hooks and blowpipes and egg drills, a sweeping net . . . too many things.

Erasmus stroked the wolf skins his youngest brother had sent from the Utah mountains. Just then he would have given anything for an hour's conversation with Copernicus, who understood what it meant to leave a life. But Copernicus was gone, still, again, and the wolf skins were handsome, but where would they fit? The sledges, specially constructed after Zeke's own design, had arrived two weeks late and wouldn't fit into the space Erasmus had planned for them; and he couldn't arrange the scientific equipment in any reasonable way. Every inch of the cabin was full, and they were not yet in it.

On the *Narwhal* Zeke slipped his feet from the stay, hung by one hand for a second, and then dropped lightly to the deck. Soon he joined Erasmus among the wharf's clutter, moving the theodolite and uncovering a crate of onions. "These look nice," he said. "Do we have enough?"

While they went over the provision lists yet again, Mr. Tagliabeau walked up with the news that their cook had deserted. He'd last been seen two days earlier, Mr. Tagliabeau reported. In the company of a red-headed woman who'd been haunting the docks.

Zeke, his hands deep in onions, only laughed. "I saw that hussy," he said. "What a flashing eye she had! But that it should be Schuessele who got her, with that monstrous beard of his. . ."

The wind tore one of Erasmus's lists away and sent it spinning through the masts. "We're leaving in three days!" he shouted. Later he'd remember this display with embarrassment. "*Three days*. Where are we going to find another cook?"

"There's no need to get excited," Zeke said. "The world is full of cooks. Mr. Tagliabeau, if you'd be so kind as to take a small recruiting tour among the taverns . . ."

"Wonderful," Erasmus said. "Do find us some criminal, some drunken sot."

They might have quarreled had not a group of young men dressed in Lincoln-green frock coats, white pantaloons, and straw hats trailing black ostrich feathers come dancing up the wharf. The United Toxophilites, Erasmus saw, making a surprise farewell to Zeke. The sight made him groan. Once he'd been part of this group of archers; once this had all seemed charming. Resurrecting the old sport of archery, flourishing the arrows retrieved from those first, magical trips to the Plains—as a boy, he'd participated in a meet that drew two thousand guests.

But he'd lost his taste for such diversions after the Exploring Expedition, and he'd let his association with the Toxies lapse. Zeke, though, was part of the new young crowd that had taken over the club.

"Voorhees!" the Toxies cried. All around them, crews from other ships stared. "Voorhees! Voorhees!"

They gave Zeke three great cheers, hauled him down the length of the wharf, and formed a circle around him. Erasmus received courteous nods but no recognition. He listened to the mocking, high-spirited speeches, which likened Zeke to a great Indian chief setting off on a buffalo hunt. One youngster with a shock of red hair presented Zeke with a chalice; an elflike boy offered a patent-leather belt from which dangled a grease box and a tassel. Zeke accepted his gifts with a smile and a handshake, thanking each man by name and showing the poise that had made Erasmus's sister call him a natural leader.

Yet what had Zeke done? So very little, Erasmus thought as he eyed the grease box. A few years of sailing from Philadelphia to Dublin and Hull on the ships of his father's packet line, investigating currents and ocean creatures, although often, as he'd admitted to Erasmus, he'd been too seasick to work. Other than that all his learning came from books. As a boy he'd insinuated his way into Erasmus's family, through their fathers' friendship and an interest in natural history. Now they were further bound by Lavinia. But that Erasmus should be standing in Zeke's shadow, setting off for the arctic under the command of this untried youth—again he was amazed by his decision.

Zeke, as if he heard what Erasmus was thinking, broke through the circle of green-coated men, seized Erasmus's arm, and drew him into the center. "I couldn't do this without Erasmus Darwin Wells," he cried. "Three cheers for our chief naturalist, my right hand!"

Erasmus blushed. Was this what he wanted? A kind of worship, mixed with disdain; as if Zeke wanted to emulate him, but without his flaws. But exactly this grudging caution had stranded him alone in midlife, and he pushed the thought aside. When the Toxies presented their green-and-gold pennant, he grasped the end marked with a merry archer and smiled at Zeke. Zeke made a speech of thanks; Erasmus made a shorter one, not mentioning that he'd known the club's founders or that he'd learned to shoot a bow when some of these men were still children. As he spoke he saw Captain Tyler hanging over the *Narwhal*'s rail, gazing curiously at them. His face, Erasmus thought, was the size and color of a ham.

The Toxies departed, Zeke climbed back on the *Narwhal*, and Erasmus was once more alone. He folded the pennant and tucked it into the wolf skins. Then he reconsidered the stowing of the sledges: back to front in a line down the center of the hold? or piled in a tight tower near the bow? He worked quietly for an hour, pushing down his worries by the repeated checking of items against his lists. Mr. Tagliabeau interrupted him, returning to the wharf in the company of a fresh-faced, dark-haired, blue-eyed boy.

"Ned Kynd," Mr. Tagliabeau said. "Twenty years of age." Zeke hopped down to investigate. After making introductions all around, Mr. Tagliabeau added, "Ned would like to join our expedition."

Zeke, hovering once more near the mound of supplies, looked Ned over. "You've had experience cooking?"

"In three places," the boy said shyly. As he listed them, all in the rough area by the wharves, Erasmus noted his heavy Irish accent.

"And have you been to sea?" Zeke asked.

Ned blushed. "Just once, sir. When I made my crossing."

"But the sea suits you?"

"My . . . circumstances then were not such that anyone could have enjoyed them. But I believe I would have, if I'd had work and meals and a place to sleep. I enjoyed being on deck very much. I like to watch the birds and fish."

"You'd be cooking for fifteen men," Erasmus said. "You're capable of that?"

"I wouldn't like to boast, but many a night I've cooked for three or four times that number. I was at a logging camp in the Adirondacks for some time, before I made my way to this city. Loggers are hungry men."

Zeke laid a hand on Erasmus's shoulder. "If he can feed loggers, he can surely feed us."

"You'd be bunking in the forecastle," Erasmus said. "With the seamen. They can be a bit rough."

"Not rougher than loggers, I wouldn't guess."

"Done, then," Zeke said. "And welcome. Gather your things and say your good-byes, we leave in three days." Off he went, bounding down the wharf like an antelope.

And so it was that Ned, hastily engaged to fill Schuessele's shoes, came to join the expedition. Later Erasmus would think many times how little might have steered Ned away. Mr. Tagliabeau might not have bumped into him beneath the chandler's awning; the Toxies' ostrich-feathered hats might have spooked him had he arrived but a few minutes earlier; Zeke might not have been there to interview him had he arrived but a little later. Any small coincidence might have done.

THAT NIGHT ERASMUS was sleepless again. In the Repository, his family's little natural history museum, he rose and paced the floors and tried to understand what he'd been doing. For twelve years he'd been camped out here, his world contracted to display cabinets stuffed with dead animals, boxes of seeds and trays of fossils, the occasional stray beam of light shining through the windows like a message from another planet. Framed engravings of eminent naturalists leaned down from the bookshelves, watching benignly as he bent to work that wasn't work, and went nowhere. Who could understand that life? Or how he'd decided, finally, to leave it?

Across the garden loomed the house he hadn't slept in for more than a decade. Everything showed his father's hand, from the carved ferns on the moldings to his own name. He was Erasmus Darwin for the British naturalist, grandfather to the young man who'd set off on the *Beagle*; his brothers were named after Copernicus, Linnaeus, and Alexander von Humboldt. Four boys gaping up at their father like nestlings waiting for worms. An engraver and printer by trade, Frank Wells's passion had been natural history and his truest friends the Peales and the Bartrams, Thomas Nuttall and Thomas Say, Audubon of the beautiful birds and poor peculiar Rafinesque, who'd died in a garret downtown.

On summer evenings, down by the creek, Mr. Wells had read Pliny's *Natural History* to his sons. Pliny the Elder had died of his scientific curiosity, he'd said; the fumes of Vesuvius had choked him when he'd lingered to watch the smoke and lava. But before that he'd compiled a remarkable collection of what he'd believed to be facts. Some true, some false—but even the false still useful for the beauty with which they were expressed, and for what they said about the ways men conceived of each other, and of the world. Sometimes pacing, sometimes sitting on a tuft of grass, Erasmus's father had passed down Pliny's descriptions of extraordinary peoples living beyond the edge of the known. *A race of nomads with legs like snakes; a race of forest dwellers running swiftly on feet pointed backward; a single-legged race who move by hopping and then rest by lying on their backs and raising their singular feet above their heads, like small umbrellas.* Stories, not science—but useful as a way of thinking about the great variety and mutability of human nature. How easily, he'd said, might we not exist at all. How easily might we be transformed into something wholly different.

In those old stories, he'd said, were lessons about gossip and the imagination and the perils of not observing the world directly. Yet although he was a great collector of explorers' tales he'd traveled very little himself; Erasmus had never known what his father would most like to have seen. As a counterpoint to Pliny he'd offered his sons the living, breathing science of his friends. They'd helped design the Repository and delighted Erasmus and his brothers with accounts of their travels. When Lavinia was born, they'd named her after her dying mother and tried to distract their friend from his grief with bones and feathers.

Now Erasmus followed the tracks of those men across the polished floor. He stopped at a wooden case holding trays of fossil teeth. Beneath the third tray was a false bottom, which only he knew about; in the secret space below the molars was a woman's black calf walking boot. His mother's; once he'd had a pair. Before the servants took her clothes away, to be given piece by piece to the poor, he'd stolen the boots she'd worn most often. For years he'd hidden them in his room, sometimes running his hands up the buttons as another boy might have fingered a rosary. Later, about to leave on his ill-fated first trip, he'd given Lavinia the left boot after swearing her to secrecy. This other he'd buried. Had it always been so small? The sole was hardly longer than his hand, the leather was cracking, the buttons loose. Where Lavinia's was he had no idea.

Four years ago, when his father died, he'd received the house, the Repository, a small income, and the care of Lavinia until she married. Which meant, he thought, that he'd inherited all the responsibility and none of the freedom or even the solid work. Was it his fault he hadn't known what to do? The family firm had gone to his middle brothers, who'd settled side by side down-town, within walking distance of their work: two moons, circling a planet that didn't interest him. Meanwhile Copernicus had headed west as soon as he received his share of the estate. Out there, among the Indians, he painted buffalo hunts and vast land-scapes while Erasmus and Lavinia, left behind, leaned against each other in his absence.

Copernicus sent paintings back, some of which had already been shown at the Academy of Fine Arts. And sometimes—when he remembered, when he could be bothered—he sent packets of seeds, shaken from random plants that had caught his eye. His afterthoughts, which had become Erasmus's chief occu-pation. Erasmus had examined, classified, labeled, cataloged, added them to his lists. He filed them in tall wooden towers of tiny drawers, alongside the seeds his father's friends had brought back from China and the Yucatan and the Malay Archipelago, and those he'd salvaged—stolen, really—from the collections of the Exploring Expedition. When his eyes grew strained and his skin felt moldy, he retreated out back, between the house and the river and behind the Repository, planting samples in oblong plots and noting every characteristic of the seedlings.

But all that was over now. He put the boot away and returned to bed. *In Africa*, his father had said, *are a tribe of people who have no heads, but have mouths and eyes attached to their chests.* Sleep eluded him yet again and his lists bobbed behind his lids. In Ger-mantown and along the Wissahickon, people sent him socks and marmalade and then dreamed of this expedition. Vicarious trav-elers, sleeping while he could not and conjuring up a generic exotic land. Lavinia had friends like this, for whom Darwin's Tierra del Fuego and Cook's Tahiti had merged with Parry's Igloolik and d'Urville's Antarctica until a place arose in which ice cliffs coexisted with acres of pampas, through which Tongan sav-ages chased ostriches chasing camels. Those people sent six candles encased in brown paper but couldn't keep north and south straight in their minds, placing penguins and Esquimaux in the same confused ice and pleating a continent into a frozen sea.

None of them grasped the drudgery of such a voyage. Not just the planning and buying and stowing but the months sitting idly on the decks of a ship, the long stretches when nothing happened except that one's ties to home were imperceptibly dissolved and one became a stranger to one's life. No one knew how frightened he was, or the mental lists he made of all he dreaded. Ridiculous things, ignoble things. His bunk would be too short or too narrow or damp or drafty; his comrades would snore or twitch or moan; he'd be overcome by longing for women; he'd never sleep. Sleepless, he would grow short-tempered; short-tempered, he'd say something wrong to Zeke and make an enemy. The coarse food would upset his stomach and dyspepsia would upset his brain; what if he forgot how to think? His hands would be cold, they were always cold; he'd slice a specimen or stab himself. His joints would ache, his back would hurt, they'd run out of coffee, on which he relied; a storm would snap the masts in half, a whale would ram the ship. They'd get lost, they'd find nothing, they'd fail.

Giving up on sleep, he lit a candle and reached for his journal. On his earlier voyage this had been his constant, sometimes sole, companion, but tonight it let him down. Pen, inkpot, words on white paper; an inkstain on his thumb. He couldn't convey clearly the scene at the wharf. He gazed at his first messy attempt and then added:

Why is it so difficult simply to capture what was there? That old problem of trying to show things both sequentially, and simultaneously. If I drew that scene I'd show everything happening all at once, everyone present and every place visible, from the bottom of the river to the clouds. But when I describe it in words one thing follows another and everything's shaped by my single pair of eyes, my single voice. I wish I could show it as if through a fan of eyes. Widening out from my single perspective to several viewpoints, then many, so the whole picture might appear and not just my version of it. As if I weren't there. The river as the fish saw it, the ship as it looked to the men, Zeke as he looked to young Ned Kynd, the Toxies as they appeared to Captain Tyler: all those things, at once. So someone else might experience those hours for himself.

Irritated, he put down his pen. Even here, he thought, even in these pages meant only for his own eyes, he wasn't honest. He'd left out the first mate's self-important strut; the appalling sight of his own hands, which amid the onions had suddenly looked just like his father's; and the sense that they were all *posturing* in front of each other, perhaps for the benefit of the green-coated boys. He rubbed at the stain on his thumb. Nor was it true, or not wholly true, that he wanted to paint the scene as if he weren't in it. He *did* want his own point of view to count, even as he also wanted to be invisible. Such a liar, he thought. Although chiefly he lied to himself. He'd wrapped himself in a cloud. Beyond it the world pulsed and streamed but he was cut off; people loved and sorrowed without him. When had that cloud arrived?

STILL THEY WEREN'T ready to leave. Captain Tyler banished Zeke and Erasmus the next afternoon, while the men tore out and then rebuilt the bulkheads in the hold. The sledges hadn't fit after all, in any configuration; the wood took more space than planned and the measurements on Zeke's sketch had turned out to be wrong. A clock ticked in Erasmus's chest: two days, two days, two days. They could leave no later, they were already late, the season for arctic navigation was short and the newspaper reporters and expedition's donors were ready to send them off on Thursday. Did he have enough socks? The right charts, enough pencils?

He was wild with anxiety and stuck here at home, with Zeke

and Lavinia and her friend Alexandra Copeland. They were in the front parlor, all four of them working. Maps and charts and drawings spread everywhere. Without explanation he rose and ran to the Repository, which he ransacked in search of Scoresby's work on the polar ice.

He rolled the ladder along the shelves; the book was gone, yet he couldn't remember packing it. And couldn't bear the thought of explaining why it had suddenly seemed so crucial. The wry face Alexandra had made as he bolted embarrassed him. Yet her presence had been his idea—Lavinia couldn't stay alone, with only the servants for company, and she hadn't wanted to join Linnaeus or Humboldt. "A companion," he'd proposed. "Who'd like to share our home, in return for room and board and a modest payment."

Lavinia had chosen Alexandra, who'd accepted a pair of rooms on the second floor. When Linnaeus and Humboldt, unexpectedly generous, offered work hand-coloring the engravings they were printing for an entomology book, Alexandra had accepted that as well and made herself at home. Now there was no escaping her; sometimes she even followed him into the Repository. But she was good for Lavinia, he reminded himself. The way she pulled Lavinia into her work was wonderful. He took a breath and headed back.

At the parlor doorway he paused to watch his sister, who was frowning with concentration and shifting her gaze from the original painting pinned above her desk to the engraved copy she was coloring with Alexandra's help. Caught up, he thought, as she'd never been helping him with his seeds. The plates showed four tropical beetles. The sun lit the brushes, the water jars, and the ruffled pinafores so dabbed with gold and rust and blue that the beetles seemed to have leapt from the plates to the women's legs. "Has anyone seen my copy of Scoresby?" he asked.

"I've been reading it upstairs," Alexandra said. She touched her brush to the paper, leaving three tiny golden dots. "I didn't know you needed it."

Erasmus, admitting his foolishness, said, "It's not as if I have room for one more thing."

"I'll get it." As Alexandra put down her brush and moved away, Lavinia called for tea and leaned over the table on which Erasmus and Zeke had spread their papers: rather too close to Zeke's shoulder, Erasmus thought. As if she were pulled by the fragrance of Zeke's skin; as if she did not have the sense to resist the almost farcical beauty that made women stare at Zeke on the street and men hum with envy. It pained him to watch her betrayed by her body's yearnings. To him she was lovely, with her wide hazel eyes and rounded chin, now charmingly smudged with blue. Yet he suspected that to the gaze of others—perhaps even Zeke—she was merely pleasant-looking. She seemed to know that herself, as she knew that among her monthly meetings of earnest young women, gathered to discuss Goethe and Swedenborg and Fourier, she was valued more for her sensibility than for her brilliance. One by one those women had married and disappeared from the meetings, leaving behind only Alexandra and her. Once, when he'd been voicing his concerns about Zeke, she'd said, "I know I love him more than he loves me. It doesn't bother me." Then had flushed so darkly he'd wanted to pick her up and pace her around the floor, as he'd done when she was an infant and needed comforting.

As Lavinia traced their planned route with her index finger, past Devon and Cornwallis and Beechey Island, where Franklin's winter camp had been found, then south along Boothia Peninsula and King William Land, Erasmus thought how maps showed only two things, land and water. To someone who hadn't traveled, their journey over that arctic map might seem a simple thing. Turn left, turn right, go north or south, steer by this headland or that bay. He and Zeke, who'd pored over their predecessors' accounts, knew otherwise. Ice, both fluid and solid, appeared and disappeared with consistent inconsistency; one year an inlet might be open, the next walled shut. Lavinia, unaware of this, traced the route backward and said with satisfaction, "It's not so very far. You'll be home before October."

"I hope," Zeke said. "But you mustn't worry if we're not—many expeditions have to winter over. We've provisioned for a full eighteen months, in case we're frozen in."

While Lavinia gazed at the deceitful map, Alexandra returned with Erasmus's book and then asked the question Lavinia might have been framing in her mind. "I haven't understood this all spring," she said. "If you take this route, which you say concentrates most efficiently on the areas in which you have some evidence of Franklin's presence, how can you also search for signs of an open polar sea? De Haven and Penny reported Jones Sound clogged with ice when they were there." She smoothed her paint-stained garment. "Ross found most of Barrow Strait frozen, and Peel Sound as well. Even if you manage to approach the region of Rae's discoveries, which lies south of all those areas, surely you can't also simultaneously head north?"

Erasmus lifted his head in surprise. The same question had worried him for months, but he'd pushed it aside; Zeke hadn't mentioned his desire to find an open polar sea since the evening that had launched them all on this path. Lavinia's twenty-sixth birthday party, back in November; Alexandra had been present that night as well, although Erasmus had hardly noticed her. He'd been full of hope that Lavinia was about to get what she most desired.

He'd spared no expense, dressing the Repository's windows with greenery and lining the sills with candles, scrubbing the dissecting table and shrouding it with crisp linen, on which he'd spread biscuits, a roasted ham, a turkey and a salmon in aspic. Lavinia had rejected her first three suitors—too dull, she'd said.

Too weak, not smart enough. While her friends married and produced their first children she'd held out for Zeke and somehow won him. Erasmus had been terrified for her during her long campaign, then relieved, then worried again: his own fault. Zeke had asked for her hand but been vague about the details, and Erasmus had failed to press him. His father would have known better, he thought. His father wouldn't have permitted Lavinia to bind herself for an uncertain length of time. The damage was done, but secretly Erasmus had hoped Zeke might choose the party to announce a wedding date.

In the kind light of the candles Lavinia might have been a candle herself, radiant in white silk trimmed with blue ribbons. She stood perfectly still when Zeke, just as Erasmus had hoped, silenced the room and said, "I have an announcement!"

Erasmus had sighed with relief, not noticing that Lavinia looked confused. Zeke rested his elbow on a case that held a bird-of-paradise. "You've all heard the news announced by John Rae earlier this month," he said. He stood with his chin up, his chest out, one hand dancing in the air. "No doubt you share both my sorrow at what appears to have been the fate of Franklin's expedition, and my relief that some news—however fragmentary, and possibly incorrect—has been obtained."

He went on about the tragic disappearance of Franklin and his men, the many rescue attempts, the details of what Rae had discovered—old news to Erasmus, who'd followed every newspaper article. His guests listened, glasses in hands, among them women who would have listened with equal interest had Zeke been reciting the agricultural products of China; anything, Erasmus imagined them thinking, for this chance to gaze at Zeke blamelessly. Yet his own sister was the woman Zeke had chosen. "Perhaps you also feel, as I do," Zeke added, "that now that the area has been defined, someone has to search further for any possible survivors."

A guest stepped sideways then, so that Erasmus caught sight of Lavinia's face. She looked as puzzled as he felt.

"To that end," Zeke continued, "I've been able to obtain the backing of a number of our leading merchants for another expedition. Our valiant Dr. Kane has been searching for Franklin in the wrong area, and although we're all worried about him—and although I'd be the first to go in search of him if a relief expedition wasn't already being organized—something more is needed. I propose to set forth this spring, to search more thoroughly for Franklin in the areas below Lancaster Sound. While I'm there, I also propose to study the region, and to further investigate the possibility of an open polar sea."

Everyone had cheered. Erasmus had stretched his lips in something like a smile, hoping no one would notice his surprise. What merchants, when, how . . . did everyone know about this but him? Lavinia, even, who might have hidden her knowledge—but she wore a smile as forced as his own. Zeke must have made these arrangements in secret, taking pleasure in presenting his plan only when it was complete.

After the flurry of congratulations, after the first buzz of questions about where Zeke might go, and how he might get there, and what sort of ship and crew he envisioned, Zeke took Lavinia's hands. She beamed as if his announcement were the ideal birthday present, and when a guest sat down at the piano and began to play, she and Zeke led the crowd to the floor.

Erasmus went outside to have a cigar and calm the storm in his chest. He was watching the smoke rise through the still night air when Zeke appeared with two glasses and a bottle. He had to ask questions, Erasmus thought. Fatherly questions, although that role still felt odd: what this meant in terms of the engagement, whether Zeke wanted to marry Lavinia before he left—or release her, perhaps, until he returned.

Leaning against one of the fluted porch columns, Zeke filled the glasses and lit a cigar for himself. Erasmus opened his mouth to speak, and Zeke said, "Erasmus—you must come with me. When are you going to get another chance like this?"

Erasmus choked, coughing so hard he bent double. All the expeditions he'd already missed—was this what he'd been waiting for? Even Elisha Kent Kane had spurned him, sailing off with a crew of Philadelphians younger but no smarter than himself. Perhaps Zeke sensed his discouragement, and the extent of his wounded vanity.

"You're ideal for this," he said. "Where could I find anyone else as knowledgeable about the natural history of the polar regions? Or as familiar with the hardships of such a journey?"

The idea of serving under a man so much younger than himself was preposterous, but it seemed to him that Zeke was looking for a partner, not a subordinate. Surely Zeke wouldn't ask for his help if he didn't regard him as an equal, even—naturally—a superior? Erasmus said, "You're kind to think of me. But you might have asked me earlier—I have responsibilities here, and of course my own work . . ."

Zeke bounded from the porch to the grass below. "Of course!" he said, pacing before the columns. "It's a huge imposition— I wouldn't think of asking you if your work weren't so *invaluable* . . . but that's why you're the right person. I didn't want to bother you until I was sure I had backing for the expedition. Think of what we'll see!"

Somewhere in those icy waters, Franklin and his men might still be trapped in the *Erebus* and the *Terror*. Even if they couldn't be found, many new species, even new lands, were there to be discovered. Erasmus thought of being free, this time, to investigate everything without the noxious Navy discipline. He thought of northern sights to parallel, even exceed, his brief experience in the Antarctic; of discoveries in natural history that might prove extraordinarily important. Then he thought of his sister, who appeared on the porch with her white dress foaming like a spray of catalpa blossom.

"You should go in," she said to Zeke. "All the guests are longing to talk with you."

He leapt up the steps and she steered him inside. With a swirl of skirts she turned to Erasmus.

"Will you go?" she said.

Eavesdropping, he thought. Again. She'd done this since she was a little girl, as if this were the only way she could keep track of her brothers.

"Please? You have to go with him."

He had his *own* reasons, Erasmus thought. For going, or staying. "Did he keep this secret from you?"

"He *had* to, he said he needed . . ."

"Doesn't that worry you?"

"As if *you* ever tell me anything," she said. "And who are you to criticize him? Especially since Father died: all you do is mope around, sorting your seeds—do you think I haven't seen you at eleven in the morning still in bed? So Linnaeus and Humboldt can run the business without you. So you haven't found anyone to fall in love with since Sarah Louise."

Sarah Louise, he thought. Still the simple sound of her name made him feel like he'd swallowed a stone. A dull ache, which never quite left him. As Lavinia knew.

"Copernicus isn't married either," she continued, "but you don't see Copernicus moping around, you don't see *Copernicus* wasting his life . . . I *need* you."

A snarl of guilt and tenderness caught at him. As children, he and his brothers used to bolt for the woods and return hours later, to find Lavinia waiting by a window with an unread book in her lap. He'd been the one she looked up to, the one who tied her shoes and taught her to read. Sometimes, when the other boys weren't around and he'd remembered not just that her birth had cost him his mother, but that she'd never *had* a mother, they'd drawn very close. Then his brothers would tumble in and he'd abandon her again. Back and forth, oldest and youngest. He had failed her often enough.

She drew him inside, to a corner behind a case of stuffed finches. "*This is who I love*," she said fiercely. "Do you understand? Do you remember what that feels like? What if something happens to him? You have to take care of him for me."

"Lavinia," he said. Her hands, squeezing his left arm, were very hot. Once, after Zeke had been describing the shipwreck that made him a local hero, Erasmus had found her weeping in the garden. Not with delayed fear over what might have happened to Zeke, not with hysteria—but with longing, she'd managed to make him understand. A boundless desire for Zeke. When he'd tried to remind her that Zeke had flaws as well as virtues, she'd said, "I know, I *know*. But it doesn't matter. What matters is the way I feel when he touches my hand, or when we dance and I smell the skin on his neck." The strength of her feelings had embarrassed him.

"You know this means waiting even longer," he said. "Has he mentioned a date?" His fault, he thought again. Why hadn't he asked Zeke himself?

"Not exactly. But when he gets home, I know he'll want to settle down."

Of course he wanted her to marry Zeke, not just to ease his own responsibilities but because he wanted her happy. Didn't he? She'd cared first for their father and then him. "You're sure . . ." he said. "You feel sure of his feelings for you?"

"He loves me," she said passionately. "In his own way—I know he does."

A blinding headache had seized him then, blurring the rest of the party. And through a process he still didn't understand, he'd been led to this table and Alexandra's pointed questions; to the fact that, in two days, he'd be sailing north in the company of a young man he'd known for ages yet couldn't imagine accepting orders from.

One of the maids came in with the tea tray: Agnes? Ellen? The servants were Lavinia's province; as long as meals appeared on time Erasmus didn't notice who did the work. He thought they didn't know this, although Lavinia sometimes reproached him. And although once he'd overheard the staff in the kitchen referring to "the seedy-man" and then laughing furiously. Now he avoided the eyes of the girl with the tray and drew a breath, waiting to hear what Zeke would say about the open polar sea.

"You read a lot," Zeke said to Alexandra. If he was startled that she'd remembered his comment at the party, it didn't show. "I've noticed that. So you must have learned about the stretches of open water persisting all winter and recurring in the same places every year. What the Russians call *polynyas*. Inglefield found open water in Smith Sound. Birds have been seen migrating northward from Canada. A warm current flows northward beneath the surface, several people have observed it—suppose it leads to a temperate ocean, free from ice, surrounding the North Pole beyond a frozen barrier?"

"Suppose," Alexandra said. Her right hand sketched an arc in the air, as if she were still holding her paintbrush.

"When Dr. Kane left," Zeke continued, "he said he was going to look for signs of this phenomenon if he could. So there's nothing so strange in my wanting to look as well."

Many times in the months since the party Erasmus had sat in the offices of wealthy men, while Zeke proposed their search for Franklin. A portrait of Franklin in full-dress uniform hung in the *Narwhal*'s cabin—Franklin, Franklin, Zeke had said, as he asked the men for money. It made sense that he concentrated on this aspect of the voyage—how proud the merchants were, contributing to such a good cause! In Zeke, Erasmus thought, they saw a young man who could succeed at anything. The man they'd dreamed of being, the man they hoped their sons might be. Other expeditions might have failed, but Zeke's would not.

"It's a theory," Zeke told Alexandra now. "An interesting theory. In the arctic one can never predict where the ice will allow one to go, nor one's speed, nor even always one's direction. My plan is to follow this route and search for Franklin. But were conditions to be unexpectedly good—were one of the northern channels to be open, say—it's possible we'd do some exploring."

"Possible," Alexandra said. "Hence you provision for eighteen months?"

"For safety's sake," Zeke said. He stroked his eyebrows, taming the springy golden tufts; perhaps aware that Lavinia followed the gesture intently. And perhaps, Erasmus thought, a bit annoyed that Alexandra didn't. A sensible woman, she seemed immune to Zeke's charms.

Lavinia, tearing her eyes from Zeke's hand, said, "I don't see here on the maps where you'd head north at all."

"Only if he were *driven* to it," Alexandra said. "Were he to raise this money to search for Franklin, and then purposefully head in another direction, that would be quite wrong."

Zeke gazed steadily at her, and she gazed as steadily back. "The maps never tell us what we need," he said, turning toward Lavinia. "That's part of the reason we go."

Later Erasmus would realize that for all his alertness to Zeke's gestures and the women's responses he hadn't been paying sufficient attention. The lamps were lit, the sun was setting, they were munching delicious chocolate cake; the maps beckoned and he was dreaming of glory. His own glory, his own desires. They might find survivors of Franklin's expedition; or if not, surely better evidence of what had happened than Rae's dispiriting tale. With any luck they'd find other things as well. All sorts of specimens, not just plants but seaweeds, fishes, birds—he would write a book. He'd sketch his specimens and write their descriptions; his talent was for drawing from nature, capturing the salient features as only a trained observer could. Copernicus, so skilled with color and light, would turn the sketches into paintings; Linnaeus and Humboldt would prepare the plates. Together they'd make something beautiful. For years, in the light of his disappointments, he'd pretended to himself that he wasn't ambitious—but he was, he was. And lucky beyond belief to be part of this voyage. A blaze of excitement blinded him.

"And you, Erasmus," Alexandra said. "What do you think of all this?"

"In the polar regions," he said, "it's true that one must be flexible, and take what opportunities are offered."

He looked down at the volume she'd relinquished. He would bring it, after all. Surely there was room for one small book. "Zeke and I will respond to what we find, and decide accordingly."

THAT NIGHT, IN her diary, Alexandra wrote:

It's not Lavinia's fault her brothers underestimate her. I know she'll be different once the men leave and we're on our own; her mind dissolves in Zeke's presence. I'll be glad when we can be ourselves. This house is so beautiful, so spacious—what would my parents think, I wonder, if they were alive to see me in these two gorgeous rooms I now call my own? The window over my bed looks down on a planting of dwarf trees. My bed-linen is changed weekly, by someone other than me. And this painting is such a pleasure, so much more satisfying than needlework. So much better paid. Beneath the lining of my sewing box I've already tucked a surprising sum. Soon I'll be able to purchase some books of my own, an extravagance when I have the Repository shelves to browse through, once the men leave . . . I'm impatient for them to go, I am. And wish that, like Erasmus, I might have the luxury of sleeping out there.

Does he know that he rocks the toe of his boot in the air whenever Zeke speaks? I wonder what Erasmus was like as a boy. Before he grew so frozen, before he sat with his chin tucked into his collar like that, and his right hand wringing his left so strongly one wonders he doesn't break the bones. Lavinia says that when she was a girl he was fond of beetles and moths, and teased the succession of governesses who raised her. I can't imagine him teasing anyone.

THE *NARWHAL* SET sail on May 28, in such a wild flurry that everything important seemed still undone and nothing Erasmus meant to say got said. He and Zeke stood on the deck in their new gray uniforms, waving their handkerchiefs. Above them the Toxophilites' pennant streamed in the wind, snapping straight out then beginning to droop, snapping straight out again. Terns hung motionless in the high currents, and Erasmus felt as though he himself were hanging between two worlds.

The acquaintances of the *Narwhal*'s crew gathered in little knots close to shore, followed by the cheering Toxies in their green outfits. Dotting the wharf in separate clusters were Zeke's and Erasmus's relatives and friends, their clothing splayed into wide colored planes by the wind whipping across the river. Alexandra had brought her entire family—her sisters, Emily and Jane; her brother, Browning; and Browning's wife and infant son—all of them huddled so tightly that it was as if even here, in the open air, they couldn't expand beyond the confines of the tiny house they'd shared since their parents' deaths. They were small, neat, and yet somehow fierce-looking; abolitionists, serious young people. They dressed in the colors of sparrows and doves but more closely resembled, Erasmus thought, a family of saw-whet owls. Browning had a Bible in his hands.

Later, Alexandra would write in her diary about the argument she and Browning had over the verses he read out loud. Later she'd sketch a portrait of Erasmus during these last minutes, which showed his hand clasped nervously around a stay, his graying hair curled beneath a cap that made him look oddly boyish, the tip of his long, thin nose sniffing at the wind. But for now she only stood silently, watching him watch everyone. In the oily water around the pilings wood shavings swirled and tossed.

To the left of Alexandra's family stood a group of employees from the engraving firm and some representatives from the Voorhees packet line; beyond them were Linnaeus and Humboldt, as plump and glossy as beavers, and Lavinia, leaning on both of them, overdressed in swirls of blue and green and flashing in the sun like a trout. At the tip of the wharf, befitting their support of the expedition, came Zeke's family. His father stood suave and proud, his still-thick thatch of ruddy hair moving in the wind and revealing his massive eyebrows and the lynxlike tufts on his ears. His mother, shrouded in black for the death of an aunt, was weeping. Not surprising, Erasmus thought; she was famous for the way she coddled her only son. Flanking her were Zeke's sisters, Violet and Laurel, beautifully dressed and seemingly contemptuous of their merchant husbands, who weren't sailing north.

They waved; the water opened between the wharf and the ship; the tune piped by the Toxies' piccolo player shattered in the breeze until the separate and unrelated notes merged with the calls of the gulls. *Behind the mountains and beyond the north wind,* Erasmus's father had once read to him, *past the cave where the cold arises, live a race of people called Hyperboreans. Here are the hinges on which the world turns and the limits of the circuits of the stars. Here there is no disharmony and sorrow is unknown.* The figures on the wharf began to shrink. Everyone, except the dead, whom Erasmus had ever loved; every person who might be proud of him or admire his courage or worry over his fate. The faces faded, and then disappeared.

2

Past the Cave
Where the Cold Arises

(June–July 1855)

Of the inanimate productions of Greenland, none perhaps excites so much interest and astonishment in a stranger, as the ice in its great abundance and variety. The stupendous masses, known by the name of *Ice-Islands*, *Floating-Mountains*, or *Icebergs*, common to Davis' Straits and sometimes met with here, from their height, various forms, and the depth of water in which they ground, are calculated to strike the beholder with wonder; yet the *fields* of ice, more peculiar to Greenland, are not less astonishing. Their deficiency in elevation, is sufficiently compensated by their amazing extent of surface. Some of them have been observed near a hundred miles in length, and more than half that in breadth; each consisting of a single sheet of ice, having its surface raised in general four or six feet above the level of the water, and its base depressed to the depth of near twenty feet beneath.

The ice in general, is designated by a variety of appellations, distinguishing it according to the size or number of pieces, their form of aggregation, thickness, transparency, &c. I perhaps cannot better explain the terms in common acceptation amongst the whale-fishers, than by marking the disruption of a field. The thickest and strongest field cannot resist the power of a heavy swell; indeed, such are much less capable of bending without being dissevered, than the thinner ice which is more pliable. When a field, by the set of the current, drives to the southward, and being deserted by the loose ice, becomes exposed to the effects of a grown swell, it presently breaks into a great many pieces, few of which will exceed forty or fifty yards in diameter. Now, such a number of the pieces collected together in close contact, so that they cannot, from the top of the ship's mast, be seen over, are termed a *pack*.

When the collection of pieces can be seen across, if it assume a circular or polygonal form, the name of *patch* is applied, and it is called a *stream* when its shape is more of an oblong, how narrow soever it may be, provided the continuity of the pieces is preserved.

Pieces of very large dimensions, but smaller than fields, are called *floes*; thus, a *field* may be compared to a *pack*, and a *floe* to a *patch*, as regards their size and external form. Small pieces which break off, and are separated from the larger masses by the effect of attrition, are called *brash-ice*, and may be collected into streams or patches. Ice is said to be *loose* or *open*, when the pieces are so far separated as to allow a ship to sail freely amongst them; this has likewise been called *drift ice*. A *hummock* is a protuberance raised upon any plane of ice above the common level. It is frequently produced by pressure, where one piece is squeezed upon another, often set up on its edge, and in that position cemented by the frost. Hummocks are likewise formed, by pieces of ice mutually crushing each other, the wreck being coacervated upon one or both of them. To hummocks, the ice is indebted for the variety of fanciful shapes, and its picturesque appearance. They occur in great numbers in heavy packs, on the edges and occasionally in the middle of fields and floes. They often attain the height of thirty feet or upwards. . .

A *bight* signifies a bay or sinuosity, on the border of any large mass or body of ice. It is supposed to be called *bight* from the low word *bite*, to take in, or entrap; because, in this situation, ships are sometimes so caught by a change of wind, that the ice cannot be cleared on either tack; and in some cases, a total loss has been the consequence.

— WILLIAM SCORESBY, *The Polar Ice* (1815)

Zeke started heaving over the *Narwhal*'s rail before they cleared the bay. He had mentioned, Erasmus remembered, some seasickness on his father's ships—but this was no spasm, a few hours' illness and a night's recovery. This was endless retching and a white-faced speechless headache. As they passed New York and surged ahead of the ship heading off to search for Dr. Kane, the elation Erasmus might have felt was squelched by worry over Zeke's condition.

"Why didn't you warn me?" he asked. Around him the crew hovered, disdainfully watching Zeke respond to the slightest swells.

"I thought it would be different this time," Zeke whispered.

Erasmus, contemplating Zeke's falsehood, remembered an image he'd long forgotten. A pale, frail, yellow-haired boy reading mounds of natural history books and explorers' journals in a deep chair piled with pillows—that had been Zeke, aged thirteen or fourteen.

His own father, Erasmus remembered, had acted as a sort of uncle to Zeke during Mr. Voorhees's business trips: an antidote to a houseful of women. He'd brought armfuls of books during the year Zeke spent in bed after a bout of typhus, and had later welcomed Zeke's visits to the Repository. Erasmus, just back from the Exploring Expedition then, had been only vaguely aware that Zeke regarded him as some sort of hero. But after Zeke finished reading the journals of Franklin's first voyage, Erasmus had heard him say to his father, "This is how I want to live, Mr. Wells—like Franklin and his men, like Erasmus. I want to *explore*. How can anyone bear to live and die without accomplishing something remarkable?"

Erasmus had dismissed those words as boyish fantasies, watching unsurprised as Zeke was funneled into his family's business. He worked in the warehouse, he sat in the office, he traveled on the ships of the packet line; he complained he had no time for his own studies, yet acted like his father's right hand. Then a lightning bolt struck a ship he was on, burning it to the waterline and killing some of the crew. Flames shooting into the night, shattered spars, the cries of the lost; Zeke had saved twenty-six passengers, herding them toward the floating debris and caring for them until their rescue. His descriptions of the incident, Erasmus believed, had made Lavinia fall in love with him. Afterward Mr. Voorhees, as a kind of reward, had allowed Zeke a certain amount of time for his scientific investigations on each voyage.

Erasmus, thinking those investigations were just a hobby, had expected Zeke to mature into a merchant captain. Yet Zeke kept reading and planning and making notes—dreaming, while no one paid attention, of a quest that would make his name. Until finally, at Lavinia's birthday party, he'd surprised them all.

"In the water," Zeke had once told Erasmus, "while I was floating there, knowing I might easily die, I understood I would *not* die. I was *not* sickly, I was very strong; I could keep my head in an emergency. I was destined—I am destined—to do something remarkable. Men have made themselves famous solely by mastering a subject which others have not yet seen to be important. And I have mastered the literature of arctic exploration."

That mastery was of little use during the first ten days of the voyage, which Zeke spent flat on his back, flounder pale, his oddly large palms and short, blunt fingers dangling over the side of his berth. Erasmus cared for him as well as he could, remembering his promise to his sister and his own early misreadings of Zeke's character. Unpleasant work: yet for all his worry, there was still the great pleasure of being at sea again. The wind tearing the clouds to shreds, tearing his old dull life to shreds. In his journal he wrote:

*How could I have forgotten what this was like? Thirteen years since I
was last on a ship, waking to the sounds of halyards cracking against the
masts, water rushing past the hull; and each day the sense of time stretching out before me as rich and vast as the ocean. I think about things I've
forgotten for years. Outwardly this is much like my last voyage: the
watches changing, the ship's bell ringing, the routine of meals and duties.
Yet in other ways so different. No military men, no military discipline;
just the small group of us, gathered for a common cause. And me with
all the time in the world to stand on the deck at night and watch the stars
whirling overhead.*

RAIN, FOUR DAYS in a row. Erasmus stayed in the cabin for
much of that time, besotted with his new home. Between the
bulkhead separating the cabin from the forecastle, and the equipment shelves surrounding the stepladder leading to the deck,
everything else was squeezed: hinged table and wooden stools;
lockers, hanging lamp and stove; and, stacked in tiers of three
along the sides, six berths. Mr. Tagliabeau, Captain Tyler, and
Mr. Francis occupied the starboard berths. On the port side, Dr.
Boerhaave had the bottom, Zeke the middle, and Erasmus the
upper berth, which was lined and curtained off with India rub-
ber cloth. The rats creeping up from the hold at night might have
seen the officers arranged like cheeses along their shelves and, on
the opposite side of the bulkhead, the seamen swaying in their
netted hammocks.

Yet physical discomforts didn't seem to matter. With his curtain drawn, Erasmus could almost pretend he was alone; almost
forget that Zeke lay just a few inches below him, Mr. Tagliabeau a few feet across from him. Two wooden shelves held his
books, his journal, a reading lamp, his pens and drawing supplies. Compass, pocket-sextant and watch hung from particular
pegs; rifle, flask, and pouch from others. Order, sweet order.
Everything under his control, in a space hardly bigger than a

coffin yet warm and dry and lit. As the rain tapered off on the fourth day he read and wrote in there, happy until he heard Zeke vomiting.

Delirious from lack of food, Zeke whimpered and called for his mother and sometimes for Lavinia. That boy in the invalid's chair was still apparent in his eyes, although he'd already managed to make it clear that he resented whoever helped him. Erasmus opened his curtain, fetched a clean basin, soothed Zeke's face with a damp cloth. Perhaps, he thought, Zeke wouldn't remember this day or hold these acts against him. When Dr. Boerhaave, still a stranger, said, "Let me see what I can do," and opened his medicine chest, Erasmus left Zeke in the doctor's hands and went to get some fresh air. Low swells, a crisp breeze, the rain-washed sails still dripping and the clouds parting like tufts of carded wool. Beneath that sky the deck was dotted with men picking oakum. Which was Isaac, which was Ivan? Erasmus had made a resolution, after watching Alexandra's ease with the same servants whose names he still forgot. On the *Narwhal*, he'd promised himself, he'd pay attention to everyone, not just the officers.

That was Robert, he thought. On that coil of rope. Sean, by the sturdy capstan. And in the galley, cooking as if he were dancing, Ned Kynd. A glance at the simmering carrots, a stir of the chicken fricassee, then a few quick kneads of the biscuit dough on a floured board.

Erasmus dipped a spoon in the stew pot and tasted the gravy. "Delicious," he said, thinking with pleasure of the live chickens still penned on the deck. Fresh food for another several weeks; he knew, as Zeke and perhaps even Ned did not, how much this was to be relished. "You're doing a fine job."

"It's a pleasure," Ned said. "A pleasure to have such a tidy place to cook in. And then the sea—isn't it lovely?"

"It is," Erasmus agreed. They spoke briefly about menus and the state of their provisions; then about Ned's quarters, which he claimed were fine. Never sick, always cheerful and prompt, Ned seemed to have made himself at home. Already he'd adopted the seamen's bright neckerchiefs and was growing a spotty beard. After a few minutes' chat about the weather and a spell of comfortable silence, Ned said, "May I ask you a question?"

"Of course," Erasmus said, praying it wouldn't be about Zeke.

"Could you tell me about this Franklin we're looking for? Who he is?"

Erasmus stared at him, a piece of carrot still in his mouth. "Didn't Commander Voorhees explain all this to you, when you signed on?"

Ned cut biscuits. "That Franklin was lost," he said. "That we were to go and search for him . . . but not much more than that."

Where had Ned been these last years? While Ned slipped the biscuits onto a tin, Erasmus leaned against the water barrel and tried to summarize the story that had riveted everyone else's attention.

"Sir John Franklin was, is, English," he said. "A famous explorer, who'd already been on three earlier arctic voyages."

The chicken simmered as Erasmus explained how Franklin had set off with over a hundred of the British Navy's finest men. For ships he had James Ross's old *Erebus* and *Terror*, refitted with hot-water heating systems and experimental screw propellers. Black-hulled, white-masted, the ships had left England in the spring of 1845, provisioned for three years. Each had taken along a library of some twelve hundred books and a hand organ, which played fifty tunes. The weather was remarkably fine that summer, and hopes for a swift journey high. Toward the end of that July they were seen by a whaler, moored to an iceberg at the mouth of Lancaster Sound; after that they disappeared.

"Disappeared?" Ned said. His hands cut lard into flour for a pie crust.

"Vanished," Erasmus replied. Everyone knew this part of the

story, he thought: not just himself and Zeke, but Lavinia and all her acquaintances, even his cook and his groom. "How did you miss this?"

"There was starvation in Ireland," Ned said sharply. "How did you miss *that*? I had other things on my mind."

The chronology of these two events fell into line. Ned, Erasmus realized, must have been part of the great wave of Irish emigrants fleeing the famine. He was still just a boy, he could almost have been Erasmus's son. "Forgive me," he said. He knew nothing of Ned's history, as he'd known nothing of his servants' lives at home. "That was stupid of me." Of course the events in Ireland had shaped Ned's life more than the stories of noble Franklin, unaccountably lost; or noble Jane, his wife, who by the time Zeke proposed their voyage had organized more than a dozen expeditions in search of her husband.

Ned sliced apples so swiftly they seemed to leap away from his knife, and Erasmus, after an awkward pause, explained how ships had converged from the east and west on the areas in which Franklin was presumed to be lost, while other expeditions traveled overland. All had made important geographical discoveries, but despite the rockets fired, the kites and balloons sent adrift in the air, the foxes tagged with messages and released, no one had found Franklin. Erasmus's fellow Philadelphian, Dr. Kane, had been with the fleet that reached Beechey Island during the summer of 1851, finding tantalizing traces of a winter camp.

Erasmus tried, without frightening Ned, to describe what that fleet had seen. Three of Franklin's seamen lying beneath three mounds; and also sailcloth, paper fragments and blankets, and six hundred preserved-meat tins, emptied of their contents and refilled with pebbles. But no note, nor any indication of which direction the party had headed on departing. Subsequent expeditions hadn't found a single clue as to Franklin's whereabouts.

The Admiralty had given up the search a year ago, declaring Franklin and his men dead.

"Why would Commander Voorhees want to do this, then?" Ned asked. "If the men are dead?"

"There was news," Erasmus said. "Surprising news."

In the fall, just as Zeke had said at Lavinia's party, John Rae of the Hudson's Bay Company had startled everyone. Exploring the arctic coastline west of Repulse Bay, not in search of Franklin at all but purely for geographical interest, he'd come across some Esquimaux. A group of thirty or forty white men had starved to death some years before, they said, at the mouth of a large river. They wouldn't lead Rae to the bodies, and Rae had thought the season too far advanced to embark on a search himself. But the Esquimaux had relics: Rae purchased a gold watch, a surgeon's knife, a bit of an undervest; silver forks and spoons marked with Franklin's crest; a golden band from a cap.

"The part that set everyone talking, though," Erasmus said, "was the last story the Esquimaux told Dr. Rae."

Three pies were taking shape; he filched some apple slices. Was it wrong, he wondered, to bring up the subject of starvation with a boy who might have seen it directly? Was it wrong to talk so freely with a subordinate? But Ned, crimping the crusts together, said, "Well, *tell* me."

Erasmus, leaving out the worst parts, described the Esquimaux tale of mutilated corpses and human parts found in cooking kettles. There could be no doubt, Rae had said, that his countrymen had been driven to cannibalism as a last resort.

"What an uproar Rae caused!" Erasmus said. He registered Ned's pallor, but he was caught in his own momentum now. "You'd have thought he killed the men himself, from the public's response. The Admiralty dismissed his findings and said Englishmen don't eat Englishmen. But they declared the fate of

Franklin's expedition resolved, despite the fact that Rae's story accounted for less than a third of the crew."

"You look for the rest, then?" Ned asked.

"*We* look."

He wound up with the facts that had set them off on their own quest. Although the Admiralty had given up, Lady Franklin persisted, bombarding the press with pleas for further, private expeditions.

"Until the ships are found," Erasmus said, "there's no proof that all the men are dead. Dr. Kane is still searching for them, but he headed for Smith Sound before Rae's return. Franklin might have reached that area if he'd headed north through Wellington Channel, but now we know he went southwest and that Kane's a thousand miles from the right place. We have all the facts Dr. Kane was missing, and our job is to search in the area Rae insufficiently explored."

Ned finished the pies and then looked up. "Commander Voorhees made it sound as if we were going to rescue *survivors*," he said. "Yet it seems we're only going after corpses."

"Not exactly," Erasmus said, flustered. "There may be some survivors, we hope there are. We go in search of them, and of news."

He left the galley feeling uneasy, a biscuit in his hand. He'd imagined that the ship's crew shared his and Zeke's thoughts: the story of Franklin clear in their minds, the goals of the voyage sharply defined and their own tasks understood. Now he wondered if they were like Ned, signed on for their own reasons, occupied with their own concerns, hardly aware of the facts. One was thinking, perhaps, about a belled cow walking high on a hill. Another about a pond and four locust trees, or about drinking whiskey or shoeing a horse, what he might buy when he was paid off, a young woman, an old quarrel, a sleigh's runners slicing the snow.

* * *

THE LAST TIME Ned had sailed on a ship, he'd been sick and stunned and hadn't known how to read or write. This time he'd do it differently; this time he'd keep a record. Before leaving Philadelphia he'd bought a lined copybook, of the sort boys used in school. That night he wrote:

The apple pies were very good. But Commander Voorhees still hasn't eaten a mouthful, nothing I make tempts him. Today I saw a large school of bluefish. Mr. Wells came to visit while I made dinner and told me about the explorer we're searching for. Except he is dead, also all his men I think. Not only frozen but starved. When he told me about the men eating each other I thought about home, and all this evening I've been remembering Denis and Nora and our voyage over, and all the others dead at home, and Mr. Wickersham who taught me to read and write, and everyone. I get along well enough with the seamen I bunk with, but don't yet have a special friend among them and wish I did. Although I've heard Mr. Wells asking the other seamen for details of their lives, he didn't ask me one thing about the famine years nor how or when I arrived in this country. Nor how it was that I happened to be free, with less than a dollar in my pocket, on the very afternoon Mr. Tagliabeau came looking for a replacement cook. Only he seemed surprised that I hadn't heard about the famous Englishman. If I hadn't tried to stop the fight between the two Spaniards that afternoon, and been fired for my pains and denied my last week's wages, I wouldn't have leapt at the chance for this position. When we return to Philadelphia in October I wonder if he'd help me find work away from the docks, perhaps in one of the inns out Germantown way.

OFF ST. JOHN'S, the scattered icebergs—pure white, impossibly huge, entirely covered with snow—cured Zeke like a drug. Captain Tyler, Mr. Tagliabeau, and Mr. Francis viewed them calmly, after their many whaling voyages. Erasmus, who'd seen similar bergs off Antarctica, restrained his excitement for the sake of appearances. But the men who hadn't been north before gaped openly, and Zeke was overcome.

"Look! Look!" he shouted, racing about the deck and then diving into the cabin for his journal. His first entry, dated June 15, 1855, was a series of hasty sketches captioned with rough measurements: *The largest iceberg is a quarter-mile across.* Nils Jensen, who couldn't read but had remarkable calculating skills, leaned over the drawing and murmured some numbers suggesting the berg's volume and area. Other excited men crowded around, but perhaps only Erasmus saw, behind the hamlike shoulders of huge Sean Hamilton, the officers exchanging glances and sarcastic smiles.

That night, with Zeke up on deck and not heaving into a basin, Erasmus slept soundly for the first time and so missed the actual collision. One great thump; by the time he woke and ran up on deck the *Narwhal* was moving backward, rebounding from a slope-sided iceberg and shorn of her dolphin striker and martingales. Past him ran Mr. Francis and Mr. Tagliabeau, Thomas Forbes on their heels with a sack of carpenter's tools. Shouts and calls and terse instructions; what was damaged, what intact; a dark figure draped over the bowsprit, investigating, anchored by hands on his ankles and a rope at his waist. Erasmus rubbed sleep from his eyes and tried to stay out of the way. Captain Tyler, standing next to Zeke as his crew worked, turned and said, "Had you taken the course I *suggested . . .*"

"This course is fine!" Zeke exclaimed. "The man in the crow's nest must have been sleeping. You there!" He tilted his head back and hollered at the figure on the masthead: Barton DeSouza, Erasmus saw. Was that Barton? "You look sharp there!"

The moon was full and the berg gleamed silvery off the *Narwhal's* bow. Barton muttered something Erasmus couldn't hear. A hammer beat against a doubled wall of wood as Thomas and his helpers began repairing the damage. Nothing serious, Mr. Tagliabeau called back.

"It's late," Zeke pointed out. "They could do that tomorrow."

"Better to do it now," Captain Tyler said. "Suppose a squall were to strike in the next few hours?"

He turned his back, he called out orders, figures moved in response to his words. Zeke retreated—just when he should have asserted his authority, Erasmus thought. The men had instinctively looked to Captain Tyler during Zeke's illness, reverting to what they knew; on the fishing and whaling ships where they'd served before, the captain was the sole authority. Here, with an expedition commander who couldn't set a sail somehow in charge of the ship's captain, they were all uneasy. Erasmus overheard them now and again, a grumpy Greek chorus: *He's never been north of New York; he doesn't know how to roll a hammock; he changes his shirt twice a week*—Sean Hamilton, Ivan Hruska, Fletcher Lamb. Each time Zeke gave an order they turned to the captain and waited for his nod before obeying.

Erasmus saw all this, but couldn't fix it. For the next few days he focused instead on trying out the dredge and the tow nets. Already he could see that Zeke wouldn't share his scientific work; after all he was to be alone, as he'd been on his first voyage. He tied knots, adjusted shackles, replaced a poorly threaded pin, remembering how shyly his young self had hung back from his companions. While he was working up the courage to be friendly, everyone else had been pairing off, or clumping in groups of three or four from which he was excluded. Everyone had been courteous but he'd been left with no particular friend; and at times he'd thought he might die of loneliness.

He was older now, he was used to it. Yet still he felt grateful when Dr. Boerhaave, who'd been reading near the galley, edged up and broke his solitude. "Those little purple-tinted shrimps," he said, "are they *Crangon boreas*?"

Later, Erasmus would gain a clearer picture of Dr. Boerhaave's face. For now, what he first noticed was his mind: quick and shining, sharp but deep, moving through a sea of thought like a giant silver salmon. Dr. Boerhaave, Erasmus learned quickly, knew as much natural history as he did. Although he was the better botanist, Dr. Boerhaave was the better zoologist and was especially knowledgeable about marine invertebrates.

As they probed their captives, Dr. Boerhaave said he'd been raised in the port of Gothenberg, but educated in Paris and Edinburgh. His excellent English he attributed to his years at sea. Over a group of elegant little medusae captured in their tow net—"*Ptychogastria polaris*," Dr. Boerhaave said—he described his trips as ship's surgeon aboard Scottish whalers and Norwegian walrus-hunters.

"I was curious," he said. "I liked Edinburgh very much, but I didn't want to set up a practice there and see the same people for the next forty years. And the idea of returning permanently to Sweden . . ." He shrugged.

Erasmus, embalming a medusa, said, "Commander Voorhees told me you'd been twice to the high arctic. With whalers? Or were those more formal expeditions?"

"The latter," Dr. Boerhaave said. "On the Swedish exploring expedition I accompanied, we went up the west coast of Spitzbergen to Hakluyt's Headland—not as far as Parry got, but we saw some of the same places that Franklin and Beechey explored with the *Dorothea* and the *Trent*."

Franklin's first voyage, so long ago. For a minute Erasmus thought how that had led, by an unexpected web of events, to their own voyage.

"Later I went with a Russian expedition to Kamchatka Peninsula and the Pribilof and Aleutian Islands, then into the Bering Straits. We'd hoped to reach Wrangel Island but were stopped by icepack in the Beaufort Sea."

He drew an equatorial projection of the medusa before them, revealing the convoluted edges of the eight gastric folds. He had excellent pencils, Erasmus observed. The line they made was both darker and sharper than his own.

"What about you?" Dr. Boerhaave said. "Your own earlier journey—I read all five volumes of Wilkes's narrative of the Exploring Expedition, it was very popular when the first copies arrived in Europe. But I don't remember seeing your name mentioned. How is that so?"

Erasmus flushed and directed Dr. Boerhaave's attention to some questionable seals on the preserving jars. "It's a long story," he said. "I'll tell you another time. How did you decide to join us?"

"I thought it would round out my picture of the high arctic," Dr. Boerhaave said. "Different ice, different flora and fauna. Anyway I was already on this side of the ocean. I came to America several years ago, to visit some of your New England philosophers. Emerson, Brownson and the others—it interests me, what they've done with the ideas of Kant and Hegel. You know this young Henry Thoreau?"

"I don't," Erasmus said.

"I met him and some of his friends in Boston, which was delightful. But all along I also hoped to do some exploring, either out west or in the arctic. At a dinner party I ran into Professor Agassiz, whom I'd once met in Scotland—we share an interest in fossil fishes. He put me in touch with some members of your Academy of Sciences, which is how I learned your expedition needed a surgeon. The position was just what I'd been hoping for."

"Was it?" Erasmus said thoughtfully. "You might just as easily have had mine—you're better trained. I expect you did both jobs at once on your other trips."

Dr. Boerhaave looked down at his drawing. "Differently trained, that's all. And in a way it's a relief simply to be responsible for the health of the crew and to have someone else in charge of the zoological and botanical reports. I've always thought both jobs were too much for one man to do well."

"But we must be partners, then," Erasmus said. "Real colleagues. May we do that?"

"Or course," Dr. Boerhaave said. With his pencil he drew a delicate tentacle.

DR. BOERHAAVE WROTE to William Greenstone, an Edinburgh classmate who was now a geologist of some repute:

Although we're not to Greenland yet, we've not been idle. I've examined all the men, so as to have an accurate point from which to assess their later health. On a journey this short, and with ample opportunities to acquire fresh food, there won't be signs of scurvy, but the alternation in day length and the sleep deprivation may cause changes.

It's an unusual situation for me, having an official naturalist on board. I worried that he—his name is Erasmus Wells—might be jealous of his position and equipment, and that I might have few opportunities for collecting and examining specimens. Yet in fact Mr. Wells is quite congenial and seems willing to let me share in his investigations. So far we've found nothing exciting but are in heavily traveled waters where everything we capture is well known. Yesterday we took a Cyclopterus spinosus *though: not quite two inches long, covered with the typical conical spines, and very like those I saw off Spitzbergen; I was surprised to see it this far south.*

I think I'll like my new companion. He's somewhat fussy and tends to be melancholy, but he's intelligent and well traveled. His formal education is spotty by our standards, but he's read widely and seems more—I don't know, more complicated *than the usual run of Americans. Not quite so blindly optimistic, nor so convinced that one can make the world into what one wishes. Perhaps because he's older. Except for him and me and the ship's captain, the others are hardly more than children. I packed the bottom sampler you gave me care-*

fully, and once we enter Baffin's Bay I'll do my best to obtain samples of the seafloor for you.

HERE WAS THE arctic, Erasmus thought, as the *Narwhal* moved through Davis Strait and the night began to disappear. Or at least its true beginning: here, here, here.

His eyes burned from trying to take in everything at once. Whales with their baleen-laden mouths broke the water, sometimes as many as forty a day. Belugas slipped by white and radiant and the sky was alive with birds. The men cheered the first narwhals as guardian spirits and crowded around Erasmus as he sketched. With one of Dr. Boerhaave's excellent pencils he tried to capture the grooved spike jutting from the males' upper jaws and the smooth dark curves of their backs. Nils Jensen, out on the bowsprit, watched intently as each surfaced to breathe and called back measurements—ten feet long, twelve and half—which Erasmus noted on his drawings.

One day the coast of Greenland appeared, the peak of Sukkertoppen rising above the fog and flickering past as they sailed to Disko Island. A flock of dovekies sailed through the rigging, and when Robert Carey knocked one to the deck Erasmus remembered how, as a little boy, he'd glimpsed three of these tiny birds in a creek near his home, bobbing exhausted where they'd been driven after a great northeaster. This one looked like a black-and-white quail in his hand. Bending over the rail to release it, he saw fronds of seaweed waving through ten fathoms of transparent water. As soon as they anchored at Godhavn he and Dr. Boerhaave sampled the shallows, finding nullipores, mussels, and small crustaceans. Then they saw people, floating on the water and looking back at them.

In tiny, skin-covered kayaks the strangers darted among the icebergs; their legs were hidden inside the boats, their arms extended by two-bladed paddles. Flash, flash: into the ocean and out again, water streaming silver from the blades. The paddles led to tight hooded jackets; the jackets merged into oval skirts connecting the men at their waists to the boats—like centaurs, Erasmus thought. Boat men, male boats. It was all a blur, he couldn't see their faces.

Sean Hamilton tossed them bits of biscuit and Erasmus revised his first opinion: *This* was where the journey began, with this first sight of the arctic men he'd read about for so long. That these Greenlanders had traded with whalers for two centuries, been colonized by the Danes and converted by Moravian and Lutheran missionaries, made them less strange: but they were still new to him. On the first night in port, over a dinner of eider ducks at the huge-chimneyed home of the Danish inspector, he looked alternately at a bad engraving of four Greenlanders captured near Godthaab and brought to Copenhagen and, out the window next to the portrait, at the jumble of wooden huts and sealskin tents into which the mysterious strangers disappeared.

ON THE *NARWHAL* the crew made their final preparations. Thomas Forbes, Erasmus saw, kept his carpenter's bench in perfect order. Ivan Hruska's hammock had a hole in it, which he repaired beautifully. Mr. Francis appeared to regard the boatswain's locker as a treasure chest, keeping close track of every marlinspike and bit of spun yarn he passed out. All this bustle pleased Erasmus. This was their last chance to ready the brig for her encounters with the pack, and finally, he thought, the men had been infected with the sense of urgency he'd had for months.

He and Zeke, equally busy, acquired sixteen ill-mannered Esquimaux dogs, a stock of dried codfish, bales of seal and caribou skins, full Esquimaux outfits for all the crew, and an interpreter, Johann Schwartzberg. After sharing a walk with him, Erasmus wrote:

He's a Moravian missionary—an extremely interesting man. He's lived among the Esquimaux both here and in Labrador, and he knows their language as well as Danish, English, and German. He'll be invaluable if we meet Esquimaux around King William Land. When Zeke approached him, we learned that he'd followed the news of Franklin's expedition avidly and had already heard about Rae's discoveries. He seems genuinely thrilled to join us. The men call him Joe, and already I can see that he's sensible, mild-tempered, good-humored, and handy.

It was Joe who determined how many knives and needles and iron bars they should barter for the fish and the furs, and Joe who examined each Esquimaux outfit for proper fit. Zeke asked Mr. Tagliabeau and Mr. Francis to work with the dogs; when they tangled the traces and crashed the sledge and fumbled helplessly, it was Joe who demonstrated how to control them. Buff and brown and white and black, long-haired, demonic, and curly-tailed, the dogs were nothing like the well-mannered hounds Zeke kept at home. With a peculiar turn of the wrist, Joe directed the whip toward the head of the most recalcitrant creature and clipped off a piece of its ear.

Zeke, watching this with Erasmus, caught his breath and said, "Oh, how cruel!"

Mr. Francis shot a contemptuous glance back over his shoulder. "Perhaps you'd like to reason with them?" There was something weasel-like about him, Erasmus thought. That narrow chest; the thick hair growing low on his forehead and shading his deep-set eyes. "Maybe you can *persuade* them," Mr. Francis added.

"Would you take over?" Zeke asked Joe. He pulled Erasmus away. "A good commander recognizes those things that are abhorrent to him, or which he does badly, and gives others charge of them," he said. "Don't you think? Joe's a fine teacher, and Mr. Tagliabeau and Mr. Francis are coarse enough to be good drivers."

Joe also knew how to build a snow house and how to repair a sledge. And it was Joe who helped Erasmus overcome his initial discomfort around the short men with their glossy hair and unreadable eyes. *Hyperboreans*, Erasmus thought, recalling his father's tales. Was it Pliny who'd claimed they lived to a ripe old age and passed down marvelous stories? But his unease was grounded in experience, not myth. At Malolo in western Fiji, he'd seen savages murder two of the Exploring Expedition's men with no apparent provocation. In Naloa Bay he'd watched a native calmly gnaw the flesh of a cooked human head, which Wilkes had later purchased for their collection.

Yet the Esquimaux weren't violent, only a little sullen. Joe said, "You need to understand that they're doing us a favor—it hasn't been a good year for seals, and they don't have many spare skins. They're trading with us because the Danish inspector is sympathetic to Commander Voorhees's mission, and he ordered them to. You might give the men who bring you the best skins some extra token."

Erasmus offered small metal mirrors and was rewarded with smiles, which made him more comfortable. When he sketched the strangers, emerging from the skin tents scattered at the edge of the mission or rolling their delicate boats upside down and then righting them with a touch of their paddles, the orderly shapes he made on paper ordered his feelings as well.

After a last dinner at the home of the Danish inspector, the crew slept and then made sail early the following morning. Their wildly barking dogs were answered by the dogs on shore. Even that sound pleased Erasmus. They'd made good time so far and now, on this first day of July, they were finally ready. His lists had been worthwhile after all, and all the worry, all the fuss.

* * *

LATER, WHEN HE'D try to tell his story to the one person who might most want to hear it, he'd puzzle over how to recount the events of the next few weeks. The incidents had no shape, he would think. They were simply incidents, which piled one atop the other but always had to do with a set of men on a ship, moving fitfully from one patch of water to the next. At the rails he and Dr. Boerhaave gaped at the broken, drifting floes of sheet ice Captain Tyler called "the middle pack." A few inches thick, twelve feet thick; the size of a boat or of downtown Philadelphia; between these were the leads, the openings that sustained them. Without a sense of their passage through the pack, nothing that came later could be fully understood.

They saw the ice through a haze induced by the dogs, whose howling made sleep and even conversation impossible. No one knew what to do with them, nor how to manage their ravenous appetites; the loose ones broke into a barrel of seal flippers and gorged themselves until two died. Nothing was safe from them, and no one could control them but Joe. The constant noise and the lack of sleep made everyone nervous, and in the cramped officers' cabin Erasmus felt a split, which perhaps had been there all along, begin to widen. He and Dr. Boerhaave found themselves allied with Zeke, while Mr. Francis and Mr. Tagliabeau always lined up with Captain Tyler, as if the arrangement of their berths marked emotional as well as physical territory. Joe, who slept in the forecastle with the seamen, maintained a careful neutrality. When the dogs tried to eat a new litter of puppies, Joe rescued them, raising an eyebrow but saying nothing when Zeke took one for himself.

"Wissy," Zeke said, holding the squirming creature by the neck. "After the Wissahickon." He ran his hand over her fluffy, fawn-colored head, her white front feet, the black spot on her back, withdrawing it when she turned and nipped him.

"It's a river," Erasmus explained to Joe. "Back home." To Zeke he said, "Are you sure you want to keep her? They aren't bred to be pets."

"I don't think Captain Tyler appreciates having her in the cabin," Joe added.

But Zeke was adamant, working patiently to break her habit of chewing on everyone and everything, and she was by his side as they reached Upernavik. Nils Jensen counted the icebergs, cracked and grottoed or blue-green and crystalline, while Captain Tyler disagreed with Zeke about their route. A zigzag, west-trending lead had opened through the pack, and Zeke argued that they should try to force a passage directly west, as Parry had once done.

"The traditional route through Melville Bay to the North Water is longer in distance," Captain Tyler said, kicking Wissy away from his ankles. "But ultimately it's always quicker. Why don't you *discipline* this creature?"

Finally, as the lead narrowed and then disappeared, Zeke agreed to Captain Tyler's route and they slipped through the steadily thickening fog into the long and gentle curve of Melville Bay. Trying to describe this place to Copernicus later, Erasmus would seize a heavy mirror and drop it flat on its back from the height of his waist, so it shattered without scattering. Heavy floes grinding against each other on one side; against the land a hummocked barrier thick with grounded bergs and upended floes— and in between, their fragile ship.

In this mirror land they were all alone. "No surprise," Captain Tyler said irritably, after the lookout reported the absence of ships. "The whalers always take the pack in May or June, when there's less danger of being caught by an early winter."

"We left Philadelphia as soon as we could," Zeke told him. "You know that. It's not my fault."

Meanwhile the seamen told stories of ships destroyed when wind drove the drifting pack against the coast. There was a reason, they said, why Melville Bay was called the breaking-up yard. Ships crushed like hazelnuts, they said, or locked in the ice for months: as if saying it would keep it from happening. *We should have started sooner; we shouldn't be here at all; I knew four men who died here—* Isaac Bond, Robert Carey, Barton DeSouza. Even as they grumbled, half-aware that Erasmus listened, the open water vanished.

Captain Tyler ordered the sails furled and sent a man to the masthead, where he could call down the positions of the ice. For two days, while the wind was dead but a slim lead was open, they tracked the ship. On the land-fast ice they passed canvas straps over their shoulders and chests, then fastened their harnesses to the towline. Plodding heavily, they towed the brig as a team of horses might pull heavy equipment across a field. Erasmus, who'd volunteered to help, could stop when he was exhausted, or when his hands froze or his feet blistered; here he felt for the first time how much older he was than everyone but Captain Tyler. Zeke, so much younger, would always pull longer but never finished a full watch. The men pulled until their watch was complete, and for all that, on a good day, they might make six miles.

On bad days, when the channel disappeared, they warped the brig like a wedge between the consolidated floes. Two men with an iron chisel cut a hole near the edge of a likely crack and drove in an anchor; a hawser was fastened to the anchor and the other end wound around the ship's winch. Everyone took his turn at the capstan bars. By the pressure of their bodies against the bars, the winch rotated, the hawser shivered, the ice began to groan. If the hawser didn't break, nor the anchor pull loose, the brig inched forward into the little crack. For hours they worked and got nowhere; an inch, a foot, the length of the ship.

THOSE DAYS BLURRED in Erasmus's mind. The great cliffs looming above him, the drifting bergs and shifting ice; brief bouts of sailing interspersed with long bouts of warping and tracking; the fog and wind and the brutal labor and the snatched, troubled bits of sleep; their wet clothes and hasty meals and Captain Tyler, red-faced, shouting at the men and occasionally whacking one with a fist or the end of a rope. Mr. Tagliabeau was somewhat less brutal with the men than the captain; Mr. Francis was worse.

"You have to do something about this," Erasmus said to Zeke one day. He was sweating horribly, itching from the wool next to his skin, and he thought he knew just how the men, working three times as hard as he was, felt. Fletcher Lamb had walked away from the towline after tearing the skin off his wrist, and Mr. Francis had hit him on the side of his head and chased him back.

Zeke shrugged. "What can I do? We have to make our way through this place, and there's no other way but to work the men as hard as they can stand. I promise things will be different when we reach the North Water."

It was like a single long nightmare, in which time passed too quickly and then, especially when they were bent to the capstan bars, refused to pass at all. The continuous light made things worse, not better: white, white, white tinged with blue, with gold, with green; white; more white. Their eyes burned, and as the sun looped around the sky, to the east in the morning, then south then west then finally in the north at night, with them still working, horribly sunburned, they began to yearn for the colors they never saw: sweet rich reds, the green of leaves. In their blurry sleepless state, with their bodies strained and aching, Erasmus wasn't surprised that they should lose sight of what had brought them there. It was all the crew could do to keep the brig moving and out of danger.

Zeke tried to keep the goals of the expedition alive by telling stories about Franklin; a way, he told Erasmus privately, of motivating the men. Off duty, they sprawled on the hatch covers or leaned against the boats while Zeke paced among them, describing Franklin's three earlier voyages. Franklin as a young lieutenant, seeking the North Pole by way of Spitzbergen, turned back by ice and returning to England with badly damaged ships. Franklin commanding an expedition through Rupert's Land, across the tundra to the mouth of the Coppermine River and exploring the coastline eastward in tiny canoes; Franklin in the arctic yet again, traveling down the MacKenzie River and exploring the coastline westward, nearly reaching Kotzebue Sound. In their winter camp on Great Bear Lake, Zeke said, Franklin had taught his men to read and Dr. Richardson, his naturalist companion, had lectured on the natural history of the region. After that last trip, Franklin had been knighted.

Zeke spoke as if he were transmitting the great tradition of arctic exploration, of which they were now a part. As if the stories would heal the crew's wounds and furies. But Erasmus noticed that Zeke never repeated these in the presence of Captain Tyler and the two mates. In a similar way, he was careful, himself, not to mention his disturbing dreams. Always he was sitting with his brothers at their father's knee, with Zeke, transformed into a boy their own age, hovering in the doorway and looking longingly at their family circle. Always his father was telling marvelous tales, as if he'd never taught them real science. *In ancient times*, his father said, *it was recorded that the sky rained milk and blood and flesh and iron; once the sky was said to rain wool and another time to rain bricks. It is always best to observe things for yourself.*

Erasmus tried not to think too much about what those dreams meant, or about the quarrels brewing. He shot burgomaster gulls and two species of loon, which the ravenous dogs tried to eat. Whenever they were stuck for a while, Joe tried to calm the dogs by unchaining them and letting them romp on the ice. They barked as if they'd gone insane and often proved difficult to retrieve; Zeke was forced to leave a pair behind when a berg suddenly sailed away from the brig. After that he no longer let Wissy run with the others but kept her tied to him by an improvised leash.

Ivan Hruska nearly drowned; a floe cracked as he was fixing an ice anchor, tossing him into the surging water. It wasn't true, as Erasmus had once believed, that immersion in this frigid fluid killed a man right away. Ivan was retrieved numb and blue and breathless, but alive. Fingers were caught between railings and lines, ribs were banged against capstan bars, skin was torn from palms and toes were broken by falling chisels. Dr. Boerhaave was kept busy attending to their injuries and preparing daily sick lists, which Zeke and Captain Tyler were forced to ignore:

Seaman Bond: abrasions to distal phalanges, left

Seaman Carey: two cracked ribs

Seaman DeSouza: asthma, aggravated by excessive labor

Seaman Hruska: bronchitis after immersion

Seaman Jensen: avulsed tip of right forefinger

Seaman Lamb: complaints of abdominal pain (earlier blow to liver?)

Seaman Hamilton: suppurating dermatitis, inner aspect of both thighs

Unromantic ailments, never mentioned in Zeke's tales. Meanwhile Joe tried to cheer the men. In Greenland, Erasmus learned, Joe had held services among his Esquimaux converts, during which he accompanied their singing with a zither. Now he plucked and strummed and taught the men songs, singing with them while they hauled.

A WEEK INTO Melville Bay, they were finishing their evening meal when the ice began to close in on them.

"If we cut a dock here," Captain Tyler said, indicating an indented portion of the large berg near them, "we should be safe, even if the drift ice closes full in to the shore."

"There's no time," Zeke said. "Suppose we make harbor inside this berg, and the floes seal off our exit? We could be here for weeks. And we've got the wind with us, for the moment."

They sailed on, with the men waiting tensely for orders. On deck, near the chained dogs, Erasmus and Zeke watched in silence. Soon the lead closed entirely and forced them to tie up to a floe. A second floe, which Nils Jensen estimated at some three-quarters of a mile in diameter and five feet deep, sailed past their sheltering chunk of ice, sheared half of it away without taking the brig, and proceeded serenely to shore. As it reached the land-fast ice, it rose in a stiff wave and shattered with a noise like thunder.

"Would you get out of the *way*!" Mr. Francis said, shoving Erasmus in his exasperation. Erasmus pulled back against the rail.

While Captain Tyler and Mr. Francis shouted and the men ran about with boathooks and pieces of lumber, a third floe pressed the *Narwhal* into the land-fast ice. Ned Kynd, his face as white as the ice, said, "We're going to be crushed."

He pressed into the rail beside Erasmus, who silently agreed with him. The ice on one side drove them into the ice on the other; the brig groaned, then screamed; her sides seemed to be giving way and the deck timbers began to arch. The seams between the deck planks opened. Zeke leaned toward Ned: two young men, one blond, one dark; one calm and one afraid.

"Don't worry so," Zeke said. He tapped Ned's shoulder and smiled at Erasmus. "I wouldn't let anything happen to us. Our bows are reinforced to withstand just this kind of pressure."

As if his words had been a spell the brig began to rise, tilting until the hawser snapped and they shot backward and across the floes like a seed pinched by a giant pair of fingers. For several hours they balanced on heaped-up ice cakes, until the wind changed and pulled the ice away and set them afloat once more with a dismal splash.

Zeke ordered rum for all the men and thanked them for their labor. To Captain Tyler he said, "You don't understand how well we've designed this ship to resist the ice. This is not your common whaler."

"If we had cut a dock," Captain Tyler said in a choked voice. His face was mottled, red on his fleshy nostrils and chin, white along his broad forehead and down the sharp bridge of his nose. His hands, Erasmus noticed, were hugely knotted at the joints. "If we had . . ." Abruptly he turned the watch over to Mr. Tagliabeau and retired below, where he wrapped his head in a blanket.

Later, perched on the hatch cover, Dr. Boerhaave whispered to Erasmus that he'd feared their skipper might suffer an apoplexy. They looked out at the ice, too wound up to sleep and longing to talk: not about what had just happened, but anything else. They were still a little awkward with each other. Dr. Boerhaave said, "This is very different from the other expeditions I was on. Do you find it so? I'm curious about your earlier trip."

"I was twenty-three the last time I did anything like this," Erasmus said, watching the ice pieces spin in the tide. Twenty-three, barely older than Ned Kynd; often he'd been frightened half to death. When had his commander ever taken a minute to reassure him? The sky was lit like morning, although it was past ten o'clock; how delicious it was to be alive, under the shimmering clouds! Had the brig been shattered here, some of the crew would be dead by now and the rest drifting south on the fragments. He was alive, he was safe and warm. What was the point of keeping secret his time with the Exploring Expedition?

"When you asked why you never saw my name in Wilkes's

book," he said, "there were nine civilians listed as 'Scientifics' among all those Navy men; I was the tenth. Wilkes never listed me because I joined the expedition at the last minute and didn't receive a salary."

He swallowed. Two floes touched and then parted, as if finishing a dance. "My father arranged it," he admitted. "The young woman to whom I was engaged"—*Sarah Louise Bettlesman*, he thought; still he could see her face, and remember her touch—"her lungs were weak, she died six months before we were to be married. I couldn't get back on my feet after that, and my father was worried. He pulled some strings, and after promising Wilkes he'd pay my keep for the voyage, he landed me a berth as Titian Peale's assistant."

"I am so sorry," Dr. Boerhaave said gently. "But I'm sure Wilkes felt lucky to have you."

While the ice waltzed around the bow and the clouds cavorted overhead, Erasmus told the rest of the story that had preoccupied him as he sorted and sifted his seeds.

The six ships of the Exploring Expedition had left Virginia in 1838. For the next four years they'd cruised the Pacific, from South America to the Fiji Islands, New Zealand and New Holland, the Sandwich Islands, the Oregon territory and more. Although Erasmus had been lonely, out of place, and often lost, he'd seen things he couldn't have imagined: cannibals, volcanic calderas, sixty-pound medusoids; the *meke wau*, or club dance, of the Fiji natives—natural wonders and also, always, Wilkes's brutality toward his men and his constant disregard of the needs of the Scientifics. The naval men had called the Scientifics bug catchers, clam diggers, and Wilkes had blocked their way at every turn.

They weren't allowed to work on deck, because of naval regulations and the bustle required to sail a ship. Below decks there was little light and less fresh air, and Wilkes forbade dissections there, as he found the odors distasteful and believed they spread disease. Their primary goal was surveying, Wilkes said, and he let nothing interfere with that. Day after day, Erasmus and his companions had watched the golden hours slip by while the naval men took topographical measurements of whatever island or coast was before them. Amazing plants and animals, always just out of reach. They'd set scoop nets when they could, consoling themselves with invertebrate treasures. When they thought they might expire from heat and anger, they threw themselves over the rail and into the swimming basin the men had made from a sail hung in the water. In early 1840, as they set off to explore the Antarctic waters and search for a landmass beneath the ice, Wilkes arranged to leave all the Scientifics behind at New Zealand and New Holland, so that whatever geographical discoveries he made need not be shared but might be wholly to the glory of the Navy.

He left all except Erasmus, too insignificant to worry about. On a shabby, poorly equipped ship, Erasmus and the sailors had nearly frozen to death. But they'd seen ice islands several hundred feet high and half a mile long, with gigantic arches leading into caverns crowned with bluffs and fissures. Ice rafts, some carrying boulders the size of a house. The sea had been luminous, lit like silver, and the tracks they left across it looked like lightning. Their boots leaked so badly they had to wrap their feet in blankets; their pea jackets might have been made of muslin; their gun ports failed to shut out the sea. Erasmus had been awed, and very cold, the night two midshipmen first caught sight of the Antarctic continent. Climbing up the rigging to join them, he'd seen the mountains for himself and then the wall of ice that almost shattered their ship. From that journey had come Wilkes's famous map, charting the Antarctic coast.

Everything after that was sordid; how could he tell Dr. Boerhaave? The quarrels among Wilkes and his junior officers, one ship wrecked and another sunk with all hands; crewmen massacred by the Fiji Islanders and then the retaliatory raids; floggings and a near mutiny and so many specimens lost. He fell silent for a minute. "The real point," he finally said, "isn't what we discovered but what happened when we returned. Everyone ignored us. Or mocked us."

"That's not in Wilkes's *Narrative*," Dr. Boerhaave said.

"It's not," Erasmus agreed. "Who ever writes about the failures?"

Yet this was the part he couldn't get past, the part that had twisted all the years since. Wilkes court-martialed on eleven charges and then, in a fury of wounded pride, impounding all the diaries and logbooks and journals and charts, and all the specimens.

"He took our *notes*," Erasmus said. "Our drawings, our paintings—he took them all."

Back in Washington, the specimens that hadn't been lost in transit disappeared like melting ice. Wilkes had compelled the Scientifics to work on what was left there in Washington, although all the good comparative collections and libraries were in Philadelphia. Then he'd ruined what work they completed. They'd come back to a country in the midst of a depression; what the men in Congress wanted wasn't science but maps and guides to new sealing and whaling grounds. Wilkes, with his endless charts, had satisfied the politicians. But meanwhile he delayed the expedition's scientific reports again and again.

"And then," Erasmus said, "after Titian Peale and I had spent years working on the mammals and birds and writing up our volume, Wilkes said it wasn't any good, and he blocked its publication."

He stopped; he couldn't imagine telling Dr. Boerhaave how he'd retreated from Washington to the safety of the Repository, turning finally to his seeds. Half living at home, half not; most of the privacy he'd required, without the fuss of having to set up an independent household. When he desired the kind of company he wouldn't want his family to meet, he visited certain establishments downtown or returned to Washington for a few days. Small comforts, but they were all he'd had as he wasted the prime of his young manhood. Although there were days when he'd deluded himself into thinking he might still salvage something resembling science from that voyage, in the end it was only Wilkes who'd triumphed. Despite his setbacks he'd had the great success of his *Narrative*. Even Dr. Boerhaave, across the ocean, had read it.

"It's such a *bad* book," Erasmus exclaimed. "Anyone knowing the people involved can see the pastiche of styles—the outright plagiarism of his subordinates' diaries and logbooks. Wilkes made those volumes with scissors and paste, and an utter lack of honor. He stole the book, then had copyright assigned to him and reprinted it privately. It made him rich."

"There's a certain unevenness of style," Dr. Boerhaave agreed. He picked at a frayed bit of whipping on a line. "I'm sorry. I didn't know—that's a terrible story." The string unraveled in his hand. "It's to your credit you've put that voyage behind you and joined up with Commander Voorhees."

"It's not a question of credit," Erasmus said. Although he felt a wonderful sense of pardon, hearing those words. "Only—I want the chance to have one voyage go *well*. I want to discover things Wilkes can't ruin. And—you know, don't you, that my sister is engaged to marry Zeke?"

"I didn't," Dr. Boerhaave said. "I had no idea. Commander Voorhees never mentioned . . . you'll be brothers-in-law?"

"I suppose," Erasmus said. "Of course." He picked up the scrap of string, unsure whether he should speak so personally. "My sister's very dear to me," he said. "Even though she's so much younger—our mother died when she was born, I helped raise her. I came on this voyage partly because she wanted me to watch over Zeke. He's so young, sometimes he's a bit . . . impulsive."

"So he is," Dr. Boerhaave said. "You're a kind brother."

Was that kindness? He'd lost the person he loved; he wanted to spare Lavinia that. Surely that was his simple duty. He asked, "Do you have brothers and sisters, yourself?"

Dr. Boerhaave smiled wryly. "One of each," he said. "Both in Sweden, both married—excellent but completely unremarkable people. They've never been able to understand why I wanted to travel, or why I should be so entranced by the arctic. We write letters, but almost never see each other. They're very good about looking after our parents."

He was cut off, Erasmus thought. Cut off from home; or free from ties to home. What did that feel like? "And in Edinburgh," he asked, ". . . does someone wait for you there? A woman friend?"

"Friends," Dr. Boerhaave said. Not boastingly, or in any indelicate way; just a simple statement. "Now and then, between trips, I've grown close to someone, and I stay in touch with them all. But every few years I go off like this, and it never seemed fair to get too entangled with any one woman, and then ask her to wait. I've been alone for so long it's come to seem normal."

He turned his head to follow a string of murres spangling, black and white, across the bow. "I love those birds," he said. "The sound their wings make. What about you? Are you . . . does someone wait for *you* at home?"

"No one but my family—not since my fiancée passed on."

"Such a pair of bachelors!" Dr. Boerhaave said.

There was a moment, then, as the murres continued pouring past them, in which anything might have been asked and answered. Erasmus might have asked what Dr. Boerhaave really meant by "alone"—with whom he shared that aloneness, and on what terms. Dr. Boerhaave might have asked Erasmus what he'd done since Sarah Louise's death for love and companionship: surely Erasmus hadn't dried up completely? But the moment passed and the two shy men asked nothing further of each other. Erasmus didn't have to say that he'd lived like a monk, except for brief entanglements that had left him feeling lonelier than before; that he'd not been able to move past the feeling that if he couldn't have Sarah Louise, he wanted no one. Or that, despite his love for his family, he'd often felt trapped living at home but hadn't been able to move. Where would he move to? Every place seemed equally possible, equally impossible. His father had tried to be patient with him but once, irritated by an attack of shingles, he'd spoken sharply. Erasmus, he'd said, was like a walking embodiment of Newton's Third Law of Motion. Set moving, he moved until someone stopped him; stopped, he was stuck until pushed again. Just like you, Erasmus had wanted to say. But hadn't.

THAT NIGHT HE lay in his bunk, mulling over what he'd revealed. Perhaps he shouldn't have mentioned that voyage at all—yet how could Dr. Boerhaave know him if he didn't share the biggest fact of his life? All those wasted days. While he'd been stalled a host of other, younger men had thrown themselves into the search for Franklin. Now that search was also his.

Back home he'd resisted the frenzy surrounding any mention of Franklin's name. That men sold cheap engravings of Franklin's portrait on the streets, or that because of Franklin he and Zeke had been interviewed in the newspapers and had gifts pressed in their hands, had nothing to do with him. The syrupy letters of a Mrs. Myers, saying she lived on a widow's mite but wanted to donate three goose-down pillows to aid in their search; the way, when he ordered socks in a shop, clerks came out from behind their counters to ask questions in breathless voices, as if not only Franklin and his men were heroes but so were he and Zeke—that puffery had made him uneasy. He'd focused on the practical, the everyday. Still there might be men alive, living off the land or among the Esquimaux; he and Zeke searched for them, not just for Franklin.

As he'd told Dr. Boerhaave the story of his earlier voyage, he'd seen how different it was from his present journey. This one was worthwhile. This one *meant* something. And when he finally slept, he dreamed he saw a column of men walking away from a ship. The ship was sinking, slowly and silently; the men turned their backs to it. Erasmus could see faces. A blond man with a broken nose, a short man with dark eyes and a mole on his chin. But not Franklin, nor any of the officers; no one whose portrait had been reproduced in the newspapers. Simply a group of strangers, waiting for help.

The dream both embarrassed and delighted him. Since the days of his first expedition, he'd not let himself admire anyone, nor been willing to bend his life to follow something greater. But he woke rejuvenated, feeling as if a great hand had reached down and brushed him from an eddy back into the current.

As they continued to struggle through Melville Bay, Zeke rolled off the names of the headlands they passed and said wistfully, "Wouldn't you like to have your name on something here?" Around his berth he'd built a rodent's nest of maps and papers. "Wouldn't it be wonderful to discover something altogether new?"

At night he pored over the accounts of Parry and Ross and Scoresby, sometimes reading passages aloud to the men while he paced the decks and they worked. He showed little interest in the amphipods Erasmus found clinging to the warping lines, or the snow geese and terns and ivory gulls that swooped and sailed above them. Nor was he interested in the miraculous refractions, which painted images in the sky near the sun. Sometimes whole bergs seemed to lift themselves above the horizon and float on nothingness, but Zeke no longer raptured over them. And Erasmus noticed that Zeke's journal—a handsome volume, bound in green silk, which Lavinia had given him—showed only a few scrappy entries.

"You've had no time?" Erasmus asked.

Zeke shook his head. "I keep meaning to," he said. "Lavinia made me promise I'd write in here, for her to read when we get back. But it's so large, and water spots the cover—and anyway I have this."

He showed Erasmus another notebook; he'd been keeping it for several years, he said, under his pillow at night and in his pocket during the day. Erasmus stared at the battered black volume, troubled that he hadn't known about it before.

"I started it when I began wishing I could do something to find Franklin," Zeke said. "It's where I keep notes on things I've read, little reminders to myself, and so forth."

He held it out and Erasmus read the pages where it fell open. The titles of four books Zeke meant to read and seven he'd recently read, a letter to the Philadelphia paper praising Jane Franklin's continued quest for her husband, some thoughts about scurvy and its prevention (*FRESH MEAT*, underlined twice. *In the men, watch for bleeding gums, spots and swollenness of lower limbs, opening of old sores and wounds)*, a recipe for pemmican, a drawing of a sledge runner, a Philadelphia merchant's quoted price for enough tobacco to supply the crew for eighteen months.

"Interesting," Erasmus said, although he was taken aback by this hodgepodge. Where was the urgency of their quest? "I can see this is where you kept track of what you learned while we were planning the trip. But what about now? Don't you—

describe things? Write about what you've seen each day, and the progress we're making?"

"That's not important," Zeke said. On the cabin table a candle burned, casting improbable shadows. "Or not as important as planning ahead for what's to come. I like to use this for *thinking*, writing down what's really significant. Captain Tyler may run this brig on a daily basis. But I'm the one with the vision. I'm the one who has to keep us on track in the largest sense."

"I could do the mundane part," Erasmus offered. "Keep a record of our daily life, I mean. Then you'd be free to keep a more personal account."

"Why don't you take this?" Zeke said, indicating Lavinia's gift. "It's a good size, you'll have plenty of room." He lifted a stack of pages and let them slip along his thumb: a whirring noise, like wing beats. "When we get home, we can tell Lavinia we worked on it together."

THE WIND GREW fierce again. Not far from Cape York, Zeke gave in to Captain Tyler's wishes and ordered a dock cut in the land-fast ice, where they might shelter until the gale passed. Above them a glacier poured between two cliffs crowded with nesting murres: black rock streaked with streams of droppings, the clean white river of ice; more soiled rock secreting waves of ammonia and an astonishing squawking noise. As birds left their eggs to seek fish in the cracks between the floes, a hunting party fired at them. Dr. Boerhaave, perched on a boulder, stayed behind to examine the parasites in the slaughtered birds' feathers. Zeke and Erasmus and Joe headed up the glacier's tongue.

They climbed joined by a long rope, which Joe looped around their waists as protection against the crevasses. Wissy, attached to Zeke by a separate rope, led; then Zeke and behind him Erasmus, who kept listing to the glacier's edge where it met the cliff, and where plants grew in the rocky, sheltered hollows. Chickweeds and sorrel and saxifrages, willows hardly bigger than his hand—but Zeke pulled on him like a farmer tugging a reluctant cow. In the rear Joe called out instructions when he detected a weakness in the ice. The lichens alone, Erasmus thought, would have repaid a week's visit; he didn't have a minute with them. The heaps of envelopes he'd brought for seeds were useless. The white bells of arctic heather like dwarfed lilies of the valley, the inch-high tangle of rhizomes, everything spreading vegetatively in a season too short for most plants to set seeds—he should be taking notes, copious notes, but they were moving too fast.

What was Zeke pulling him toward? A rough, craggy object half-embedded in the ice; he was missing his chance with the cliffside plants for the sake of a rock. By the time he caught up to Zeke, about to complain, Zeke was digging out one side of the boulder, assisted by Wissy's frantic paws. "What's so interesting?" Erasmus asked.

"I don't know," Zeke said. "It caught my eye, it looked so out of place—what is this doing here?"

Erasmus bent and saw that the side of the boulder opposite his hands was chipped and fractured in a way that suggested human interference. Elsewhere was a crust he recognized. "It's a meteorite," he told Zeke, annoyed that he hadn't discovered it himself.

Joe caught up to them, out of breath, and inspected the chipped side. "One of the iron stones!" he exclaimed.

"Why do you call it that?" Erasmus asked. He could feel where flakes the size of fingernails were missing.

"There are Esquimaux around here," Joe said. "The ones Ross called Arctic Highlanders. Even as far south as Godhavn we've heard stories of how they use the odd rocks stuck in the glaciers. They chip harpoon heads from them."

Erasmus inspected the rock more closely and probed it with his knife: a siderite, he decided, metallic iron alloyed with nickel.

A similar specimen had fallen in Gloucestershire in 1835—but how remarkable to find one here! And for Joe to know the story that made sense of it. "Ever since Ross explored this area, people have been wondering about the source of the northern tribe's iron," he said to Zeke. "They must have been getting it from this stone, or from others like it."

Joe nodded. "Somewhere near here are supposed to be three large ones, which the Esquimaux have named. And perhaps smaller ones like this as well."

Zeke tapped the lumpy, dull-colored rock. "We can't leave such an important discovery here."

"You can't *take* it," Joe exclaimed. "The natives need these. They call them *saviksue*, they believe they have a soul."

Erasmus looked at Joe, at Zeke, at the rock. He couldn't help himself, he coveted it.

"Them," Zeke said. "You acknowledge yourself that there are others. I'm only taking this small one."

Over Joe's protests Zeke and Erasmus chipped the ice away with their knives, until the rock was free. It was as heavy as a man. "Just help us roll it to the ship," Zeke begged; and Joe finally agreed.

In the eerie pink light they sweated and struggled and pushed, all the time hearing the distant gunshots and the indignant roar of the birds. Erasmus, as the angle of the glacier grew steeper, slipped near a patch of meltwater and fell. Joe and Zeke, roped on either side of him, tumbled seconds later. The meteorite, free of their hands, rolled clumsily as they untied the knots that tangled them. It gathered speed and lurched down slantwise, leaping over a last ridge of ice to plunge into the gap where the glacier had pulled away from the side of the cliff.

Erasmus heard it shatter and leapt to his feet. Running after it, too late to save it, stumbling and slipping and hoping, still, that he might retrieve a piece, he stayed upright most of the way down the glacier but skidded off the last, lowest ledge. He was flying; his eyes were open. He was arcing over the stony shore, heading for the ice, praying that he'd die quickly. He saw a patch of darkness the size of a dining-room table, an open pool in the ice; then he was underwater. Then under ice.

The water burned him like fire and scoured his mouth and eyes, but even as he thrashed and struggled and felt his limbs numb he saw the fish schooling around his legs, and the murres serenely swimming like fish, and the cool, green, glowing underside of the ice. He had a few minutes, he thought, remembering Ivan's near drowning. No more. Something shimmered white: belugas? He fainted, or froze, or drowned. When he came to himself again he was looking up at Dr. Boerhaave's anxious face.

"Am I alive?" he asked.

"Just barely," Dr. Boerhaave said. "Ned pulled you out."

"Did you see the meteorite?"

Dr. Boerhaave shook his head.

THEY COULDN'T RECOVER even a single piece of the stone before Captain Tyler hurried the *Narwhal* into a suddenly open lead. In his berth, recovering from his chilly bath, Erasmus rested for a day. When he felt better he thanked Ned.

"It was nothing," Ned said. "I was gutting a fish, looking right at the hole in the ice where you landed. All I did was run over with the boat hook."

With Dr. Boerhaave's help, Erasmus wrote up a description of the meteorite to send to Edinburgh. The weather grew fine— warm during the day; just below freezing during the gleaming north light that was as close as they came to night—and as Erasmus wrote to Dr. Boerhaave's friend he noted the odd combination of summer and winter features: cool air, hot sun; black cliffs, white ice. On the cloudless day when they reached the

North Water, he felt as though he were home during harvest-time.

The air was warm, the water gleaming like steel and the icebergs elevated against the horizon. The men had stripped off most of their clothes. Mr. Tagliabeau was urging them on at the capstan bars when the lookout shouted, "We're here!" and the brig broke into open water. All hands stopped work and gave three cheers. Mr. Tagliabeau and Captain Tyler embraced one another and then, to Erasmus's astonishment, shook Zeke's hand. Joe broke out his zither and played several cheerful tunes; Captain Tyler ordered the sails set; and they were free of the pack.

3

A RIOT OF OBJECTS

(JULY–AUGUST 1855)

*It was homeward bound one night on the deep
Swinging in my hammock I fell asleep.
I dreamed a dream and thought it true
Concerning Franklin and his gallant crew.*

*With a hundred seamen he sailed away
To the frozen ocean in the month of May
To seek that passage around the pole
Where we poor sailors do sometimes go.*

*In Baffin's Bay where the whalefish blow
The fate of Franklin no man may know.
The fate of Franklin no tongue can tell
Franklin and his men do dwell.*

Through cruel hardships they vainly strove.
Their ships on mountains of ice was drove
Where the eskimo in his skin canoe
Was the only man to ever come through.

And now my hardship it brings me pain.
For my long lost Franklin I'd plow the main.
Ten thousand pounds would I freely give
To know on earth if Franklin do live.

—"LADY FRANKLIN'S LAMENT"
(TRADITIONAL BALLAD)

*I*n her diary, Alexandra wrote:

On the calendar Lavinia keeps by our desks, she not only crosses off each passing day but counts the days remaining until October. She's embarrassed when I catch her doing this, embarrassed to catch herself doing it. When we visit Zeke's family, she wraps her arms around Zeke's black dogs and buries her nose in their fur; the smell reminds her of him, she claims, his clothes often carried a faint odor of dog. But otherwise she puts up a brave front and tries not to talk about her worries.

Still, I can see how distracted she is and how hard she finds it to concentrate. Apart from her anxieties, she's not used to sustained periods of work. I remind myself that at least I had my parents throughout my childhood, while she had no mother at all: of course this has shaped her, as has life with her brothers. On Tuesday, while we were trying to mix a difficult shade of greenish blue, she told me she was often invited to join in when their father read to them—if she wasn't taking drawing lessons, or piano lessons, or being instructed in cookery or the management of the household—but she listened with only half an ear, sure she'd never use that knowledge. Erasmus and Copernicus would travel; Linnaeus and Humboldt would learn to engrave the plates and print the books that resulted from other men's travels. But always, she said, always I knew I'd be left at home. So why bother to learn those lessons well?

Because, I wanted to say. Because there is something in the learning; and because we can never tell what we may someday need. Instead I pointed to our paints. When you were taking drawing lessons, I said, did you ever think we'd be doing this? It is my hope to distract her with the pleasures of our task.

We completed the plates of the annelids today and then Lavinia worked on her trousseau, arranging piles of embroidered white lawn and ribbon-threaded muslin. Waists and knickers, nightgowns and petticoats—most made by two young sisters, half-French, from Chester. Her own stitching is clumsy, but she's good enough not to ask me for help *even though she knows I've sometimes supported myself by sewing. I told her something she <u>didn't</u> know about me—in her back issues of the* Lady's Book, *which she saves religiously, I pointed out the plates I colored by hand for Mr. Godey. A gown in green and yellow, not so different from a beetle's wing covers, made her smile. "You could do this," I told her. "If you don't like working with plants and animals, I could help you find work coloring fashion plates when we're done with the book." She told me her brothers would think that frivolous work, especially as she has no need to earn her living.*

We have two pair of cardinals nesting in the mock-orange near my window. A cecropia moth hatched from the cocoon Erasmus left on the windowseat. Last night my family came for dinner, and after we talked about the antislavery speeches Emily attended in Germantown, Harriet took me aside to whisper that she is with child again. Then Browning clumsily asked if we'd had any news. Of course this upset Lavinia. No mail, I answered quickly. Not yet. But it's too soon for the whalers with whom the brig might cross paths to have returned to port.

After they left we read out loud to each other, as we do most evenings. Lavinia reads from Mary Shelley's tale of Frankenstein and his monster; I read from Parry's journal. The journal of the first voyage, when Parry was hardly older than Zeke and when his men were all in their early twenties; the one during which everything went right. Fine weather, remarkable explorations, good hunting, starry skies. This is how Zeke and Erasmus are faring, I said.

But later, after we went to our separate rooms, I read secretly in the journal of Parry's second voyage. I never raise the subject of the Winter Island and Igloolik Esquimaux with Lavinia; if she knew what Parry hinted at about the women and their relationships with his men, she'd worry about this too. I lie in the dark and dream about that place and those people. I'd give anything to be with Zeke and Erasmus. Anything. I'm grateful for this position but sometimes I feel so <u>confined</u>—why can't my life be larger? I imagine those Esquimaux befriended by Parry and his crew: the feasts and games, the fur suits, the pairs of women tattooing each other, gravely passing a needle and a thread coated with *lampblack and oil under the skin of their faces and breasts. I dream about them. I dream about the ice, the snow, the ice, the snow.*

SURROUNDED BY THAT ice and snow, Erasmus dreamed of home—less and less often, though, as the brig passed down Lancaster Sound. Around him were breeding terns and gulls, snow geese and murres, eiders and dovekies; the water thick with whales and seals and scattered plates of floe ice; a sky from which birds dropped like arrows, piercing the water's skin. Sometimes narwhals tusked through the skin from the other side, as if sniffing at the solitary ship. They hadn't seen another ship since passing a few whalers at Pond's Bay, yet Erasmus was far from lonely. Dazzled, he looked at the cliffs, and knew Dr. Boerhaave shared his dazzlement.

"Anchor," he begged Zeke. "Let us have some time up there."

But Zeke said their schedule didn't leave a minute to spare. Finally, when they tied up to an iceberg to take on fresh water, Erasmus was granted four hours. Ned and Sean Hamilton rowed him and Dr. Boerhaave to the base of a kittiwake rookery.

"We'll climb," Erasmus told Dr. Boerhaave. He was trembling, longing to split himself into a hundred selves who might see a hundred sights. "Straight up, and gather what we can." To Ned and Sean, wandering along the bouldered shore, he handed a small cloth bag. "Put plants in here," he said. "If you see anything interesting, while you're walking . . ." Then he and Dr. Boerhaave began their ascent up the bird-plastered rock, guns and nets strapped to their backs.

Four hours, which passed like a sneeze. They brought back adult birds, eggs, dead chicks, and nests. On the *Narwhal*, Ned added the cloth bag to their treasures. "We walked east for a while," he said. "We found a little field." He reached into the specimen bag and spread handfuls of vegetation on the deck. "I brought you these," he said. "Are they what you wanted?"

Erasmus turned over the bits; Ned had picked leaves and branches and single flowers, rather than carefully gathering whole plants complete with the roots. Back home Erasmus had barked at the maid when she dared to move his drying plants; here he blamed the mess on himself. He hadn't realized anyone wouldn't know how to take a proper specimen. Still he and Dr. Boerhaave were able to identify the little gold-petaled poppies and four varieties of saxifrage. Ned, Erasmus saw with some chagrin, had found a regular arctic meadow, which he himself had missed.

"You did wonderfully," Erasmus said. "Thank you for these. Let me just show you the way scientists like to collect a plant."

Briefly he explained to Ned about root and stem and leaf and flower and fruiting body. Later, Ned wrote down Erasmus's words almost verbatim, along with a sketch of a proper specimen and some definitions:

Herbarium is the name for a collection of dried plant specimens, mounted and arranged systematically. The object with the flat boards and the straps is a press. Mr. Wells means to preserve samples of each interesting plant, to name those he can by comparing them against his books, and to keep a list: that is his job here. Dr. Boerhaave helps him. I may help too, they say, if I learn what they show me. It's like learning to read a different language—pistil, stamen, pinnate, palmate—not so hard but who would have thought a man could spend his life on this? I made salad from a red-leaved plant he calls Oxyria, *which looks like the sheep sorrel at home. He was surprised that it tasted so good.*

WHERE BEFORE THEY'D been in waters familiar to Captain Tyler and the mates, and where Zeke was at a disadvantage, now they were in places none of them knew. Zeke had the charts of the explorers preceding him; Zeke had done his reading. It gave him a kind of power, Erasmus saw. For the first time, the other officers were dependent on Zeke's knowledge. It no longer mattered that Zeke had never been in the arctic before, nor that all his knowledge came from books. Ice was ice, islands were islands; channels showed up where he predicted. Book knowledge was all they had, and for a while Captain Tyler and the mates were rendered docile by their lack of it. No one argued with Zeke's orders.

Thousands of narwhals accompanied the brig up the ice-speckled strait, filling the air with their heavy, spooky exhalations—as if, Erasmus thought, the sea itself were breathing. Animal company was the only sort they had. In place of the great fleet filling the Sound four years ago, during Dr. Kane's first voyage, were those long-tusked little whales, and seals and walrus, and belugas everywhere. Extraordinarily beautiful, he thought. Smaller than he'd expected, a uniform creamy smoothness over bulging muscles, moving like swift white birds through the dark water.

Barrow Strait was empty as well. The stark and radiant landscape flashed by so fast that Erasmus found himself making strange, clutching movements with his hands, as if he might seize the sights that were denied him. Even when they reached the cairns on Cape Riley and then, on Beechey Island, the graves of three of Franklin's seamen and the relics of their first winter quarters, they lingered only briefly. These were, Erasmus and Zeke agreed, the very sites that Dr. Kane and the others had discovered in '51. From the water the gray gravel sloped gently upward, stopping at jagged cliffs. Against the background of those cliffs, the grave mounds and headstones were very small. Erasmus, Dr. Boerhaave, Zeke, and Ned examined the limestone slabs tessellated over two of the graves, and the little row of flat stones set like a fence around each mound.

"If we exhumed them," Dr. Boerhaave said, "even one, and could determine what he died from, we might gain some clues to the expedition's fate."

Zeke stepped back from the mounds. A tremor passed from his hands up his arms and shoulders and then rippled across his face. "We're not graverobbers," he said. "Nor resurrection men. Those are Englishmen, men like our own crew. They're entitled to lie in peace. And what would we learn from violating them?"

"Suppose they were starving?" Dr. Boerhaave said. "Already, that first winter. In this cold, enough . . . remains would be left that we might determine that."

"If that was me in there," Zeke said, "if that was you—bad enough they've been left here all alone. Nothing you'd learn would tell us anything about where the expedition went."

He gazed down at the graves and then back at Dr. Boerhaave. "When you were in medical school," he said, "did you . . . ?"

"Well, of *course*," Dr. Boerhaave said. As Zeke shook his head and walked away, Dr. Boerhaave smiled at Erasmus, who smiled back at his friend.

After the three of them left, Ned lingered behind for a minute, placing a stone on each grave and saying a prayer. He told no one of the strange hallucination that seized him later. As he rinsed salt meat in water from the stream that trickled above the graves, he imagined that water seeping into the coffins, easing around the seamen's bodies, who had been young, like him. Beneath the first layers of gravel the ground was frozen, it never melted, and he saw the bodies frozen too, preserved forever; cherished, honored. The vision comforted him, yet also angered him. In Ireland he'd seen corpses stacked like firewood or tossed loosely into giant pits. Here, where no one might ever have seen them, three young Englishmen had each been given a careful and singular grave, a headstone chiseled with verses, a little fence.

TIME PRESSED ON them even more sharply after that first glimpse of the lost expedition. As the sails filled, bellied out in the brisk breeze, Zeke said, "Franklin must have turned the *Erebus* and the *Terror* down Peel Sound after leaving Beechey Island. The ice is so heavy to the west, and when you think about Rae's report—where else could he have gone? It's the only place the earlier ships didn't look. They were all sure he'd gone north somehow, after finding the route blocked to the west. But how could any of his men have reached a place even close to King William Land, if not by way of Peel Sound?"

Simple logic, Erasmus thought. And so it must be true. Even Captain Tyler shrugged and agreed with Zeke. They turned south, sure they were following Franklin's trail. After thirty-five miles of hard sailing, fighting against the encroaching ice, the *Narwhal* was finally turned back by solid pack. No time for regrets, Zeke said. He retraced their route, rounding the walls and ravines of North Somerset and sailing down the east coast as far as Bellot Strait. Through here, Zeke hoped to pass back into Peel Sound.

Bellot Strait was completely choked with ice. The men stood mashed together on the bow, muttering with disappointment: "God damn this ice!" Captain Tyler said, before disappearing below. Their last chance to reach King William Land by water had just disappeared, Erasmus knew, and with it any chance of finding Franklin's ships. But they might still find traces of the expedition by land, as Rae had done. On Zeke's order they continued southward, along the massive hills and into the Gulf of Boothia.

Zeke grew cool and distant, hardly speaking except to give orders and treating Captain Tyler as if he were the skipper of a ferryboat. He allowed no stops, neither for the men to hunt nor for Erasmus to gather specimens. The winds and currents here seemed to concentrate the ice, which poured into the bay from the north and then swirled and massed, several times almost crushing the brig. The men grew nervous and muttered among themselves. Out here, far from the traditional whaling grounds, they seemed to wake as a group from a dream. Why had they come? Because they needed work, Erasmus slowly understood; not because they were inspired by the expedition's goals but because they'd needed jobs back in the spring, when Zeke was recruiting men. They'd signed on because the wages were good and because, despite all Zeke's stories, they had not really been able to imagine their task. The men who'd never been to sea before had had no useful information, no way to imagine what lay before them; those with whaling experience must have imagined that searching for Franklin would be like searching for whales.

The idea of moving just for the sake of moving, pressing deeper and deeper into the ice with no assurance of reward, was as strange to them, Erasmus thought, as flensing a bowhead would have been to him. Every order Zeke gave brought a grumble: *we should have anchored in Cresswell Bay; the men need fresh meat; the floes are scraping away the siding*—Mr. Francis, Ned Kynd, Mr. Tagliabeau.

Fletcher Lamb, who was stropping his razor when they crashed into one of the monstrous bergs, jolted his hand and cut off the tip of his left ring finger. Two of the dogs, knocked to their feet, turned on each other and filled the air with chunks of fur and a spray of blood; a kettle slipped overboard. When the *Narwhal* was finally forced to stop, separated from King William Land by the full width of Boothia, the men began clamoring to turn around the same day they dropped anchor.

Discouraged, Erasmus stared at the charts. They'd not discovered even the smallest scrap of new coastline; the excellent map of the Rosses detailed every cove they saw. Yet here, no matter what the crew thought, they might begin their real search for any traces of Franklin and his men. This was the place, Erasmus thought: the true beginning after all. What began, instead, was the death of the dogs.

The dozen left after the earlier mishaps tore around the ship, raising and lowering their heads and tails and all the while barking furiously at some invisible threat. The lead dog, enormous and black, fell first: a damp heap at the base of the mainmast. His white-footed consort followed, then two of the puppies Joe had earlier saved: red-eyed, fevered, frothing. They turned on Zeke and Erasmus and Dr. Boerhaave, who worked frantically to help them. Dr. Boerhaave wrote:

Why did I never make time for some veterinary training? In my autopsies I've found nothing more than livers that appear to be mildly enlarged, but I can't be sure of this: what does a healthy dog's liver look like? At Godhavn we heard rumors of a mysterious disease among the dogs of southern Greenland, but our own appeared to be in perfect health and continued so throughout Lancaster Sound. I should have been paying more attention. I'm not sure of the course of rabies in canines but was forced to consider this, and when four fell on their sides, pawing at their jaws, I ordered them shot to prevent the spread of disease. Commander Voorhees, who is sentimental about animals, was furious with me and we had an argument—he can't seem to grasp the idea that the sick dogs may endanger the men. In any event my efforts weren't successful: we lost the last adult today and only Wissy and one other puppy are left. I'm grateful none of us were bitten. On dissection I found no apparent brain inflammation, nor anything unusual in the spinal cord or nerves. Why didn't I think to bring along a book of veterinary medicine?

The flesh on Fletcher Lamb's injured finger has begun to mortify beneath the bandage I applied. I've debrided and irrigated the wound, but remain worried.

ZEKE HAD BEEN keeping Wissy in the cabin, where he hoped she might be safe, but the day after the other remaining puppy died she began running about, crashing off the bunks and the walls. Zeke held her in his arms, despite her mad strength; he tried to feed her tidbits and wouldn't let Dr. Boerhaave touch her. She squirmed and bit and then lay still, her head thrown back and her eyes blankly staring. Above her a tern cut through the rigging, back and forth and around the shrouds.

"You know what we have to do," Dr. Boerhaave said.

Zeke handed her to Robert Carey, who'd proved his skill with a gun by obtaining numerous birds on Beechey Island. Afterward Zeke wouldn't look at Dr. Boerhaave and nothing Erasmus said could console him. Dr. Boerhaave retreated to a corner on deck, turning a skull around in his long fingers and staring at his notes as if he might bring the dogs back to life. Caught between the two men, Erasmus wondered what the dogs' deaths meant.

Here they were, he thought, blocked from further sailing by ice, and blocked from overland travel by the lack of it. The snow on the land was mostly gone, except high on the hills and in hidden hollows; the land-fast ice was heaved and cracked and waterlogged. Even if they could cross Boothia, the strait between its far side and King William Land could no longer be frozen solid, but must be a mass of loose and shifting floes. Sledging was impossible; sledge travel was meant for spring, when the sun had returned but the ice was smooth and solid everywhere. Why, then, had they brought dogs and sledges in the first place?

But he knew the answer. Ever since they'd acquired the dogs, he'd worried that Zeke meant to overwinter somewhere if the brig failed to reach its destination. Some of the crew must have guessed this as well, but they'd all wanted to believe the dogs wouldn't be needed. Then, after every stage of their desired route had been blocked, Ned had seized Erasmus's arm and said, "Some of the men say we won't go home this summer now. That we'll stay all winter, in the ice—is it true?"

Erasmus hadn't known what to say. He'd seen Zeke take out a new set of maps and scribble in his little black book; but now the dogs were gone. Once, but only once, Zeke leaned his head against the mast and said, "I wonder if someone poisoned them."

"You know that's not true," Erasmus said gently. Everyone else pretended not to hear him.

Joe, perhaps wishing to deflect attention from the dead dogs and Zeke's foul mood, told stories that caused a different kind of uneasiness. The West Greenlanders among whom he'd lived, he said, had wonderfully designed harpoons and winter houses made of stone and turf with seal-intestine windows and seal-blubber lamps. How warm those houses could be in winter! So warm, he said, packed with bodies and lamps, that the women wore only fox-skin knickers unless they had visitors.

A hush fell over the men. For a moment, in that silence, they visualized warm, curved flesh decorated with those flirtatious frills. In Melville Bay they'd traded tales of the women who'd taken up with members of both Parry's and Franklin's earlier expeditions, and Ivan Hruska and Robert Carey had talked about Esquimaux men who'd brought their wives aboard the visiting ships and offered them in trade for knives and wood. Perhaps they'd all hoped for a similar chance.

"Of course we forbade this kind of display among our converts," Joe said. "No nakedness, we told them. And no exchanging wives." Afterward Erasmus, who'd overheard part of his story and seen the men's faces, spoke sharply to him.

EVERYONE WAS TIRED and hungry for fresh meat; with Zeke still sulking over the dogs, Erasmus took matters into his own hands and went ashore July 28 with Isaac Bond. The first caribou he'd ever seen bolted across the boggy ground, fleeing before the swarms of insects and then before Isaac, who shot four times and brought down two. They peeled the skins off carefully. In their hindquarters, Erasmus found freshly laid eggs of the warble fly and, in the hides, hundreds of holes where the larvae of a previous year's infestation had eaten their way out. Isaac, wielding a long knife, regarded the skinned purple carcasses and said they weren't so different from the deer he'd hunted as a boy. He cut off the heads, took out the tongues; peeled off the flesh, set the skulls aside.

Side by side they crowned a rock, antlers branching above white bone and lidless eyes. Erasmus, under their gaze, knelt and pointed out the joints most easily severed. Left went the knife, and right and left and down: intestines steaming, a large smooth liver, stomach pouring out masses of green paste. In another pile ribs and shoulders, haunches and loins and tongues. They wrapped the meat in the skins and Erasmus hefted his end of one bloody bundle and then froze at the sight of his own reflection in the eyes. The thread of their voyage had broken, he thought, the plot unraveled, the point disappeared; nothing was left but the texture of each moment and the feeling of his soul unfurling after years in a small dark box.

"Are you all right?" Isaac said. "Is this too heavy?"

The caribou were watching themselves being carried away. "Let's try to drag the bundles," Erasmus said. "Down to the boat."

The odd humming feeling persisted in his head. And when he and Isaac climbed aboard the *Narwhal* and found Zeke standing on the quarterdeck with Joe, talking to three Esquimaux while the crew gawked from the bow, at first Erasmus thought he'd hallucinated them.

"They're so *short*," Isaac whispered.

He stepped back toward the railing, and Erasmus involuntarily squeezed the meat in his arms. What if these strangers were dangerous? Or if the crew members did something to anger them? Zeke and Joe had no weapons; Erasmus, leaving Isaac to deal with the bloody mass, hurried to Zeke's side.

Joe and the Esquimaux spoke at some length. Then the

Esquimaux stood quietly while Joe explained that these people, very different in dress and habits from those they'd met at God-havn, wandered inland each summer in small family groups, searching for caribou. The camp of this particular group, Joe said, was several miles away, out of sight of the ship—they'd seen the hunting party, and had sent a delegation to investigate. "They invite our leaders to their camp," Joe said. "Three of us, to go with the three of them."

Zeke said, "You and me, of course." He was silent for a minute. "And Captain Tyler," he added.

Erasmus felt a little thrill at the idea that his figure, crouched near the skulls, had been the sight that drew the Esquimaux; then a fierce disappointment that he should not be included in the delegation. When he took Zeke's arm and begged to come, Zeke shook him off and said he couldn't ignore Captain Tyler's rank.

The crew watched in silence as the six men dropped down the side of the brig, rowed to shore, and disappeared over a low hill. Three and three, dressed entirely differently, Zeke's pale hair glowing behind the darker heads. The crew murmured behind them: *suppose they're murderers; suppose they're cannibals; suppose they're plotting to return with a great crowd and take over the ship—* Fletcher Lamb with his bandaged hand, Barton DeSouza, Robert Carey.

Out loud, over the muttered comments, Dr. Boerhaave said, "What if they don't come back?"

"There's no point in even thinking like that," Erasmus said. Although he was worried himself; if something happened to Zeke, how would he explain to Lavinia that he'd stayed safely on the brig?

"Shall we look at the bones from the mergansers?" Dr. Boer-haave said. "I finished the other set while you were hunting."

From the sea he pulled a dripping sack. The water was boiling with *Cancer nugax*; he and Erasmus had learned to take advantage of the little shrimps' hunger, hanging their roughly cleaned skeletons over the side in a fine-mesh net. Erasmus, still distracted, opened the sack to find that the voracious creatures had cleaned everything perfectly. The sight of the disarticulated bones calmed him a bit.

Dr. Boerhaave, making notes, said, "I'm ashamed to admit this, but—don't you sometimes experience the search for Franklin's remains as just . . . distraction? I wish our only task was simply to observe this amazing place and its creatures." In the breeze his soft brown hair with its streaks of gray lifted from his forehead and fell and lifted again, like partridge feathers.

"But it's not," Erasmus said, clutching a fistful of wing bones. He looked down at the beautiful planes and knobs in his hands. Zeke would be fine, he had Joe to help him; the Esquimaux had seemed quite friendly. "But I know what you mean. Would you pass me that wire?"

When he looked up again it was early evening, and Zeke and Joe and Captain Tyler were hopping back onto the deck unharmed. Erasmus followed Zeke down into the empty cabin, a jawbone still in his hand.

"Tell me," he said. "Tell me everything."

"It went well," Zeke said. "Joe didn't have much trouble interpreting—he says the dialect is similar to that of the West Greenlanders. They liked our gifts."

Up on deck, Captain Tyler began lashing down everything movable. "Esquimaux will steal anything," Erasmus heard him tell the men. "Everything. And you can be sure they'll be visiting now that they know we're here."

"But—what were they like?" Erasmus asked Zeke. "What were they wearing? What were they eating? What do their dwellings look like inside?"

"Interesting," Zeke said. "Different. I was concentrating on the conversation with our host. Don't you want to know if I heard any news of Franklin?" A huge smile split his face. "I've been waiting years for this," he said. "Don't you understand? Ever since I was a boy reading your father's books."

Suddenly he looked like that boy again, and Erasmus was reminded of something Lavinia had told him a few days after her birthday party. "How can I discourage him from this trip?" she'd said. "We fell in love talking about Franklin, you don't know how many hours I've spent listening to his stories and plans. He cherishes that in me, he says he loves the way I listen." Erasmus had asked her if she truly shared Zeke's enthusiasm, and she'd sworn she did. Or at least one part of it: "I admire Franklin's wife," she'd said. "Her steadfastness."

"I'm sorry," Erasmus said, abashed. "Of course I want to know."

"I asked the oldest man point-blank if he'd ever seen a ship frozen in the ice, or white men marching anywhere around here," Zeke said. "He said no but I thought I saw him exchange a look with the man sitting next to him. They've asked us to return tomorrow. Will you come?"

OF COURSE ERASMUS went, as did Ned, Mr. Tagliabeau, Thomas Forbes, several other men, and Joe—still their only interpreter, despite all the evenings Zeke had spent with him, transcribing into his black book Joe's version of the Esquimaux names for things. This time Captain Tyler, Mr. Francis, and a small detachment stayed behind to guard the ship. Dr. Boerhaave nearly stayed behind as well; Fletcher Lamb had returned to his hammock, complaining of shooting pains in his limbs and face, and Dr. Boerhaave was worried. But there was nothing he could do for Fletcher after giving him a few drops of laudanum, and so he joined the delegation.

They carried offerings of duff and dried apples, as well as knives and needles and files and beads to barter. Over the hills they went, into a rough and scrubby land bare of trees and veiled by a light drizzle. As they walked Erasmus listened to Joe, who was trying to teach Zeke some things about this group called the Netsilik. Now and then Erasmus bent to gather pebbles; he'd been lax, he felt, about examining the area's geological structure.

"You might want to be a bit more . . . cautious," Joe was saying to Zeke. "About asking directly for information; it's not these people's nature to respond to pointed questions, they dislike being cross-examined. And if I could let them know that we'll barter for everything they tell us, that they'll be rewarded?"

"Fine," Zeke said impatiently. "Fine, fine, fine."

Erasmus and the others could hardly keep up with him. In the treeless, featureless landscape, the six tents forming the camp stood out starkly. A bunch of dogs, tied away from the tents, howled like wolves.

"They'd eat the tents in an instant if they were free," Joe said as they approached. All around, on the rough stony ground, were dog carcasses, bits of rotted meat and blubber, and broken bones. Thomas Forbes tripped over something and Dr. Boerhaave, bending down, said, "I believe that's a human femur." The bone was still shrouded in bits of leathery skin.

Thomas leaped backward, stumbling on the shallow pit in which the bone had been interred. The flat pieces of limestone meant to cover the body were small and quite light, Erasmus saw, and had clearly been pushed aside by a hungry fox or a dog. Thomas cursed and then bent over, very pale.

Joe said, "It's not what you think. It's not that they disrespect their dead: but they believe that a heavy weight placed upon the deceased's body hinders the spirit from moving on. Of course the dogs uncover them, the dogs are always hungry."

"Savages," Thomas said. Later he would disappear for a day in the company of a young Netsilik woman, recently widowed, whatever discomfort he felt with the tribe's habits apparently overcome. But now Erasmus saw Thomas look with dislike on the man who emerged from a strong-smelling tent to greet them. The stranger had a sparse moustache and a tuft of hair between his chin and his lower lip; the bottom of his nose was bent to one side, as if it had been broken but not set. When he spoke, Erasmus heard the word *kabloona*.

"White man," Joe translated. In the light rain they stared at each other. The tent, Erasmus saw, was too small for them all to sit inside. They seated themselves on stones just in front of its opening.

Everything smelled of caribou. Behind him Erasmus could see how the rain saturated the hides, which hung heavily on the poles; how the rain dripped through the tiny holes drilled by warble flies when the animals had still been alive. Here too there were animal skulls, scores of skulls, jaws and eye sockets tilted among rocks and lichens. Zeke and the man who'd welcomed them—Oonali, he called himself—did all the talking, with Joe acting as interpreter. In return for the clasp knives and tobacco Zeke offered, and after Zeke had made it clear that he'd be honored to see Oonali's hunting outfit, Oonali brought out a bow and some arrows that Zeke admired.

"I'd love to bring these home to the Toxophilites," he said to Erasmus. "Wouldn't that be something?"

Erasmus was scratching steadily in Lavinia's journal—he couldn't write fast enough, he couldn't get down all the details. He sketched the bow: fir strengthened with bone and made more elastic by cunning springs of plaited sinew. He didn't sketch the curiously twisted bowstring or the slate-headed arrows, as Zeke had by then arranged to trade a pair of axe heads for the entire outfit. Next to him Dr. Boerhaave scribbled similarly, while Ned, who'd stuck his head beneath the door flap, turned his head slowly from one view to the next. Whalebone vessels and walrus-tusk knives, spoons made from what looked to be hollowed-out bones.

The camp was almost empty that afternoon: "The men are out hunting," Joe explained. But soon three women gathered around Oonali's tent and stood shyly gazing at Erasmus and the others. They were comely, Erasmus thought, despite the tattoos on their cheeks and hands. Less than five feet tall and plump, with tiny hands and glossy hair. He tried to sketch the black patterns twining up their arms while the women crowded around and laughed at his efforts. Zeke rose and offered each a steel needle.

The women made noises that seemed to indicate pleasure, promptly depositing the needles in little bags attached to their breeches. Each bag was made from the skin of a bird's foot with the claws still attached: charming, Erasmus thought. As he turned to ask Joe's help in bartering for one, the women reached toward Zeke and fingered his brass jacket buttons.

When Zeke pulled back, the women bent to Erasmus, still seated on his stone. He froze while the hands played over his chest. The slightest tugging, much more gentle than the crowding Fiji Islanders of his youth; it was the buttons they coveted, he realized, even more than the needles. Back in the brig, thanks to all his lists, he had a large tin of spares. With his knife he sliced off his three lower buttons and offered one to each woman.

Zeke frowned at him—but it was the buttons, Erasmus thought, that turned the tide of the afternoon. Four little boys pushed up to him, reaching for his journal and stroking the smooth white paper so insistently that he finally tore two blank pages from the back and handed them over. The boys grinned and ran away with their treasure; from the corner of his eye Erasmus saw them crowded on a stone cairn some way from the tents, tossing shreds that spun in the breeze like butterflies.

The women brewed vats of tea, which they served in bowls.

Dr. Boerhaave, turning one round in his hand, said, "I believe this is made of the base of a musk-ox horn." As he bent and sniffed at the horn with his long, square-tipped nose, hair drifted from the tent and into everyone's tea, catching in their teeth as they drank. An older woman with heavily tattooed hands arrived, bearing a dish of boiled caribou. Erasmus made a strangled noise when she offered him a portion on a metal spoon.

"*Quiet,*" Zeke said.

He reached for the spoon and examined it: silver, shapely, as alien here as a palm tree. To Joe he said, "Tell Oonali that yesterday, I asked if he'd ever seen white men's ships. And he said no. Ask him if perhaps he's forgotten to tell me something?"

Oonali said nothing at first. Joe stood to one side, translating, while Zeke asked quick questions, his anger ill-concealed. Had they seen any white men? Had they seen two ships? Where had the spoon come from? Did they have more like it? Had they ever met a *kabloona* named Dr. Rae, who'd traveled east of here several years earlier, and who'd bought spoons and other white men's goods from some Esquimaux?

Joe struggled to keep up with the flow of Zeke's words and made, Erasmus thought, conciliating gestures toward Oonali as he translated. Then Oonali, who had been calmly eating, spoke.

"We have not seen such ships," he said, or so Joe translated his words. "But we have heard a story, from some Inuit we met hunting seal several winters ago. These men told us that, during the previous winter, they found a ship abandoned in the ice. They climbed on this ship but found no one there, only one dead man on the deck. They wished to see into the spaces below, but the passages to the lower part"—here Joe paused, looked at Zeke, and said, "Hatchways? Must be hatchways"— "were sealed over. These men told us that one side of the ship was wounded, and that they pulled wood away from there until they'd made a hole. Inside they found many useful tools and much iron, which they took so it wouldn't go to waste. They had many spoons, like this one. I traded two good hides for this."

"But you didn't see the ship yourself?" Zeke said.

"No ship," Oonali replied.

"You haven't seen any white men?"

"I have never met one, although I have heard about them. You are my first to talk with."

Zeke, excited now, drew his copy of the Rosses' map from his jacket. "We're here," he said, indicating the bay where they were anchored. "This is the Great Fish River, here"—he asked if Joe knew the Esquimaux name for the river, which he did—"and this is the western shore. Can you indicate where the ship was seen?"

Erasmus and his companions leaned around Zeke and Joe and Oonali, forming a circle. They all knew Parry's and Ross's tales of men who could outline long stretches of coast with remarkable accuracy. Esquimaux traced maps in the snow, carved them in wood, built them from little piles of pebbles. Drew them when offered pencil and paper. "I'll give you a knife," Zeke said. "If you can show us anything."

Oonali gazed at the paper. "Where the seals are good," Joe translated, as Oonali touched a finger to a bay and spoke.

Oonali touched an inlet, then the mouth of a river. "Where my friend was lost. Where the fish are caught in the rocks."

With his thumb Oonali pressed the edge of the map, which showed the east coast of King William Land butted up against the border. He moved his thumb off the paper and a few inches into the air, where the west coast might have been had the map been larger, and the west coast charted.

"This is where the ship is sunk."

"Sunk?" Zeke said.

Erasmus didn't know whether to watch Oonali or Joe, whose face was so surprised that he could hardly form words.

"Underwater," Joe translated. "Those Inuit, they did not at first take all the goods they found, but piled them on the deck to carry back later. Then they went hunting. The hunting was good that winter. When they returned the ice had begun to break up, and the ship was gone except for the tops of the three tall poles, which pierced the water. The things on the deck had disappeared. It is thought that taking the wood away from the wound in the side caused the water to pour in."

"Is there anything left?" Zeke said. "Anything for us to see?"

"There is nothing," Oonali said. "The men who told me this story, they took from the shores all the things that floated in. Nothing is left."

THAT NIGHT, WHEN they returned to the *Narwhal* with their bow and arrows, the musk-ox bowls Dr. Boerhaave had traded for, and their precious silver spoon, Zeke gathered the entire crew and told them what he'd learned. He meant the men to be impressed, Erasmus thought, to be seized with the knowledge that they were close to the site where at least one of Franklin's ships had been. But Sean Hamilton said, "This Oonali—he didn't actually *see* the ship? And the ship is gone? And all we have to show for this story is a spoon?"

"The spoon has a crest on it," Zeke said angrily. "We'll undoubtedly be able to show exactly which of the officers it belonged to."

Sean shrugged. "I don't see how that's more than what your Dr. Rae came home with. All this way, and you've got a story told by a lying Esquimau."

"When are we leaving?" Isaac Bond asked.

Erasmus reached over and rapped the spoon in exasperation. "Aren't you *curious*? Aren't any of you one bit curious as to how this got here?"

"We're curious to know how we're going to get home," Barton DeSouza muttered. "And when."

Later Ned, alone in the galley, wrote to a friend in the mountains of northern New York. Erasmus came in for some hot water just as Ned went out to relieve himself, and he leaned over the sheet of paper on the table.

Commander Voorhees is having a difficult time. Hard luck seems to plague him. Today I thought we'd discovered something important, but now it seems that the story the Esquimaux told us means little after all. One of the two ships sank, perhaps. But where are the men? Our men are all against the commander, even Captain Tyler, and it makes me sad to hear them talking as if the commander is a fool. The more the others say he is young and inexperienced and gullible, the more I like him for his enthusiasm. I think he's only a few years older than me. But he's the one who knew enough to press this Oonali, and so got him to reveal the story of Franklin's ship. Perhaps this is all we can expect: it is ten years now since Franklin's ships left England.

A good heart, Erasmus thought; Ned had come a long way from his first response to the story of Franklin, his loyalty to Zeke and their mission seeming to grow in inverse proportion to their luck. He was pleased to see Ned sticking close to Zeke over the next few days, while Zeke pored over his maps and fondled his new bow. The other men, during their hours off, wandered toward the Esquimaux camp in an ill-concealed search for feminine companionship.

Had it not been for this distraction, which Zeke seemed powerless to discourage, Erasmus wondered whether they could have prevented an open mutiny. The men wanted to leave at once: it was clear they couldn't reach King William Land at this time of year, and that even if they did they'd find no ship. But Zeke wasn't ready to leave. Again and again he told Erasmus he felt sure there must be other traces of the expedition, and although he had no clues he wouldn't move. They were trapped, too, by Fletcher Lamb's condition. On the night they returned from the Esquimaux camp he'd developed violent spasms, and a stiffness of the jaw that grew worse hourly.

"It's lockjaw," Dr. Boerhaave told Zeke. "There's nothing I can do for him but try to keep him comfortable."

The other men shunned their sick companion and returned from their forays bright-eyed and flushed. They'd hidden spirits, Erasmus guessed, which they were now sharing with their new friends. Robert Carey and Ivan Hruska, considerably inebriated, came to blows over the favors of one young woman. All Zeke did was to growl at Captain Tyler and order him to restrain his men.

Hourly Zeke, along with Dr. Boerhaave, visited Fletcher Lamb; when Fletcher died Zeke read the service over him and then crouched in the crow's nest and wouldn't come down. As if, Erasmus thought, he were watching over Fletcher's grave. Thomas Forbes constructed a coffin, but the ground was stony and after hours with a pickaxe and shovels still the grave was not as deep as they would have liked and there were foxes everywhere. Ned set palm-sized pieces of flat stone around it, as if that boundary would shelter Fletcher's bones.

NINE DAYS AFTER their first meeting, Barton DeSouza spotted a group of Esquimaux hunters returning to camp. Their dogs carried the meat, some with the front half of a caribou draped around them, ribs curving around the dogs' backs; some pulling heaps of meat lashed to pairs of poles. Later two hunters came to the ship and invited the *Narwhal*'s crew to a feast. The Esquimaux were sick of them, Erasmus knew. The seamen were hunting their caribou, distracting their children, disappearing with their women; he was disgusted with them himself. Although he and Dr. Boerhaave never spoke of it, he thought the doctor shared his feelings. The men's behavior made Erasmus restless and filled him with longings. When he retreated to the cabin, Zeke's strange, sulky paralysis drove him away again. Although the hunters didn't say it, Erasmus understood that they wished this to be a farewell feast. He hoped that Zeke would also see it that way.

Only Mr. Francis stayed behind to guard the brig. On the way to the feast the others chattered, carrying gifts of biscuits and tea and leaving a space around Zeke, who was silent even when Erasmus pointed out the lemmings slipping over the ground. Great kettles of food were stewing over fires as they arrived, but the atmosphere was strangely subdued with the hunters back in camp. Each hunter gathered his family about him, closely watching the *Narwhal*'s crew; the men's easy camaraderie with the women and children vanished. Joe strummed his zither. A few men tried to dance but their feet stuttered under those watchful eyes; the Esquimaux wouldn't dance at all and Joe soon fell silent.

Erasmus and his companions ate until they were full and then watched the Esquimaux continue eating. When they finished Joe, still trying to knit the two groups together, persuaded some of the hunters to demonstrate their skill with their bows. Their arrows flew into the distance, piercing with uncanny precision the sheets of paper Erasmus tore from Lavinia's journal and offered as targets, but the only people smiling were the little boys who seized the targets as soon as the shooting was done. Once more they ran away, shredding the paper as they ran; once more, Erasmus saw, they clustered on the stone cairn and set the shreds flying in gusts of wind, as if trying to imitate insects or small white birds. While he pondered the children's game, some of the women upended the cooking kettles and began scraping off the dense layers of soot. It was Ned who saw the first flash of copper.

"Look," he said, pulling the bunch of twigs from a woman's

hands and scrubbing furiously. Metal, copper. Erasmus ran to the other kettles: copper, copper, copper. A film seemed to drop from his eyes, and he looked around and saw that the wooden tray on which some of the meat had lain could not have been made from any of the scrubby vegetation here; that in fact it resembled a part of a writing desk. Tent poles suddenly resembled oars, wooden spoons might have been shaped from gunwales, parts of spears and knives might have come from barrels.

"They've found a *boat*!" Zeke exulted. "These things come from a ship's boat." He seized Joe's arm and said, "Tell them I know."

"Know what?"

"Just tell them I know."

As Joe translated, Zeke seized a copper pot in one hand and a stirring stick that might have been made from an ash oar in the other. A hush fell over the camp. Oonali stepped forward.

"These things are from a *kabloona* boat," Zeke said. "Why didn't you tell us before that you had found one?"

Oonali shrugged as Joe put Zeke's questions to him. "You asked about ships," he said through Joe. Joe looked mortified, as if he'd been the one caught lying. "And about the land across from the coast. Not a small boat found on an island."

"What island?"

Oonali said something Joe couldn't translate. After Zeke took out another of his maps, Oonali pressed his thumb down on a large island at the mouth of Back's Great Fish River.

"Were there men?" Zeke said. "You told us we were the first white men you'd met."

"I did not meet them," Oonali said calmly. "They could not be met. They were dead."

By now all the Esquimaux, and all the brig's men, were pressed in a circle around Zeke and Oonali and Joe. Zeke offered axes, barrel staves, beads, and knives in return for any other items they might have picked up at the boat. In return for the story of how they'd found it.

Oonali said, "This happened some winters ago. On the island we found a wooden boat which was sheathed with this metal. Also the bodies of thirty or so men."

There had been guns, Joe translated, just one or two, and a metal box with some papers in it, some clothes, some things they'd not known the names of. They had taken many of these things, guessing they'd someday find a use for them.

"Show me," Zeke demanded. For a minute Erasmus thought all was lost. But Joe must have softened Zeke's words and framed them courteously, because Oonali, after considering for a moment, spoke to the other Esquimaux gathered around. Some ducked into the tents, returning with full hands.

A prayer book, a treatise on steam engines, a snowshoe, and two pairs of scissors. More silver spoons and some forks. Dr. Boerhaave, holding out his hands, received a mahogany barometer case, and Erasmus's hands filled with chisels and chain hooks and scraps of rope. Zeke stood open-mouthed, turning a broken handsaw end over end over end. "The boat?" he said. "Is the boat still where you found it?"

"We cut it up," Oonali said. "It was of no use to those men. We cut it up and took all the wood and useful things. Some things we have cached at our other camps."

"The bodies?" Zeke said.

"The sand has buried them. This was"—he paused to consult with two middle-aged men—"six winters ago. Or seven. We have visited this island since, and nothing is left of those men."

Erasmus wrote down everything, piecing the story together as fast as he could scribble the words. Thirty men, at least one boat, a winter that might be either 1848 or 1849; an island some two hundred miles from the point at which Franklin's ships had supposedly been beset. The men must have dragged the boat all that distance, perhaps on one of their sledges: and who were "they," and had they been the only ones left? And how had they thought to get that boat up the river's fierce rapids? In his rush Erasmus spotted his journal with caribou grease.

Someone sneezed, delicately; he looked up to see Oonali's wife. The three young women who'd served him tea during his first visit had turned out to be Oonali's daughters; this woman, their mother, had stood off to the side then, and he'd noticed her only when Joe pointed her out. She had a fine white scar running from the outside corner of her left eye into the hair at her temple, worn teeth, shy eyes. She was holding out something to him in her closed hand.

"For me?" he asked. But of course she couldn't understand his words. She had her back to everyone else and her gesture was furtive. He tore off the last of his jacket buttons and offered it on his open palm. With one hand she scooped the button up, holding the other hand over his palm and then spreading her fingers. A scrap of dried and hardened leather, spiked through with bits of metal, dropped into his hand.

He thanked her, put down the scrap, and kept writing. Then a few minutes later thought to pick it up again. Once more that film seemed to drop from his eyes: part of a boot sole, he saw, the front part, from the toes to the ball of the foot. Seven short, wide-headed screws had been driven through it, from the inside out— a line of two, at the tips of the toes, then a line of three and another line of two. Wood screws, the sort one might use to fasten a cleat or an oarlock to a boat. The heads had been countersunk, set flush with the inner layer; the tips of the screws protruded perhaps a quarter of an inch.

Staring at those broken, rusted tips, Erasmus imagined the rest of the sole, the worn heel, the broken-down upper. The broken-down man who, trying to walk across the ice, perhaps pulling a sledge or a boat behind him, might have studded his shoes for a better grip. Without thinking he slipped the scrap into his jacket pocket.

Across from him Zeke purchased every item brought for his inspection, naming each so Erasmus could note it in his journal. A riot of objects, an orgy of objects. Dr. Boerhaave bent over a mildewed black notebook. When he opened it, Erasmus saw it was only a shell, two covers with just a few pages remaining, all the rest torn out. "It could have been someone's journal," Dr. Boerhaave said. "Even Franklin's." But the pages still caught in the binding were blank, and Erasmus saw where the rest had gone: little boys, given this as a toy, had ripped the sheets out one by one. What could have been the words of one of Franklin's crew sent sailing on the breeze. He stared, then turned back to his own journal: tidy notes, long columns aligned. Everything listed except that bit of boot.

Finally, with everything piled and noted, Oonali said, "Perhaps you will return to your own place now. We have given you everything we have."

"I would like to buy some of your dogs," Zeke said. "All your dogs, if you'll part with them."

The land between here and the river was a soupy, pond-riddled, hazardous place, nearly impossible to cross at this time of year; Zeke, Erasmus saw, could only have one thing in mind. He meant, if he could obtain enough dogs, to stay here through the winter and then travel, if not to King William Land, then across the frozen strait to the island. For a moment Erasmus gave in to a vision: he and Zeke walking side by side into the Academy of Sciences, bearing these relics and full of stories. How much more glorious their entrance would be were they to say: *We saw men from Franklin's ships. We gave them proper burial.*

"It is impossible," Oonali said. "We need the dogs to carry our tents and other things. We leave tomorrow. Already we must begin packing."

As if to demonstrate, a woman began piling skins and clothes on a dog. The dog grimaced and drooped his tail, then turned to bark at a raven stealing some bits of fat.

"Let me have just a dozen," Zeke begged.

"Impossible," Oonali said.

FOR ANOTHER DAY Zeke wrestled with himself, writing and writing in his black book, talking and talking to Erasmus and Dr. Boerhaave, as he tried to figure out a way to explore more territory and find clearer signs of the lost expedition. The following morning he rose, stared at his coffee, and then said into the dim cabin, "He who does not see the hand of God in all this is blind."

Captain Tyler and Mr. Tagliabeau exchanged a glance, as did Dr. Boerhaave and Erasmus. Zeke turned and faced into his bunk, his arms spread above his head and his hands grasping the supports. As he spoke he swayed slightly, leaning into the bunk and then back out, against the air, while a white figure barked at him from a tub of ice in the corner: the little white fox Ned had trapped, which Zeke had appropriated as a pet to replace his lost Wissy. She ate from Zeke's plate; he had named her Sabine.

"I read the dogs' death as a bad omen," he said. "Or even an act of sabotage. Especially Wissy's. But it was not, it was an illness pure and simple. That we could not penetrate Peel Sound, and that Bellot Strait was closed to us, also seemed to signal the failure of our expedition. Fletcher Lamb's death, for which no one would have wished, delayed us when we might have departed. Yet in fact all these events have conspired to place us exactly here, at exactly this time, where we could meet precisely this group of Esquimaux. *We* are the favored ones. We've uncovered much more than did Dr. Rae. That we can't pursue this further is a sign that what we've found is sufficient. More than sufficient.

Through patience and persistence we've twice seen past the Esquimaux deceitfulness and uncovered the true story. I was tempted to winter here—but those men are dead, and we know where they died. We'll leave as soon as we can ready the ship."

The men cheered when Zeke announced his decision. Erasmus, listening to them bustle about as they prepared the *Narwhal* for the last leg of her voyage, considered their accomplishments. While they hadn't seen either bodies or ships, their evidence was much more direct than Dr. Rae's. They'd dined with people who'd seen bodies and carved up one of Franklin's boats. They'd eaten soup with Franklin's silver spoons and lost only a single member of their own crew. He looked forward to arriving home in triumph, bearing his neatly written journal in its green silk dress. After dusting the grease spots with salt, he wrote:

I try to set my feelings aside; I try to record here simply what I saw, what I heard, what has happened. But I admit I've found these days exciting. These are very different Esquimaux from the civilized tribes of southern Greenland. And it was thrilling to delve below their superficial deceit and uncover the crucial story about the boat. I feel as though my small role—keeping Zeke steady and providing a sympathetic ear, while maintaining all the scientific observations—has contributed much to our success. Is it ridiculous to hope I may return home as a sort of hero: the steady, older naturalist who has been of inestimable aid to the commander, and made all the important observations? Lavinia will be so proud of Zeke. Of us.

Although there was no possibility of sending letters for some weeks, Dr. Boerhaave wrote to his English friend Thomas Cholmondelay:

Do you remember the story I told you, about Mr. Thoreau's pilgrimage to Fire Island and his attempt to gather up the relics of Margaret Fuller's

drowning? It sticks in my mind: how he found that shift with her initials
embroidered on it; her husband's coat, from which he took a button; her
infant's petticoat. The relics we've uncovered here—I append a list that
will sadden your heart—put me in mind of that other shipwreck. There
is something so terribly personal about these small objects.

We've had a death on our own ship as well: a pleasant young man
named Fletcher Lamb, who succumbed to lockjaw after cutting himself
with a razor. The smallest of accidents; it too meaningless in itself. Yet by
that act our tiny crew is reduced by one. I kept him as comfortable as
possible but could do nothing to avert the end. He died quietly, after
having said his prayers and dictating a brief note of farewell to his
mother and sisters. I've lost patients before, of course. But this death, so
needless, hurt more than most. And it is disturbing that our commander
reads into the delay caused by that death a form of divine intervention,
which allowed us to make our discoveries. Are you well?

THEY SET SAIL on August 9. From the shrouds hung seven
caribou, which, along with the clusters of birds suspended in the
rigging, gave the *Narwhal* the appearance of a butcher shop
under sail. Sabine, chained to her tub of ice beneath the dead
wildlife, watched the bustle curiously.

"Don't you think I'm doing well with her?" Zeke asked Erasmus. He slipped Sabine a morsel of bread, while Captain Tyler
called out the sequence of orders that would set them moving
again. "She was so shy when Ned brought her in, but I think
she's becoming quite civilized."

She was half grown or perhaps a bit more, four pounds of
energy with a coat resembling that of a fancy cat. As they began
to move she stood and howled to her relatives back on shore.

4

A Little Detour

(August–September 1855)

I have no fancies about equality on board ship. It is a thing out of the question, and certainly, in the present state of mankind, not to be desired. I never knew a sailor who found fault with the orders and ranks of the service; and if I expected to pass the rest of my life before the mast, I would not wish to have the power of the captain diminished an iota. It is absolutely necessary that there should be one head and one voice, to control everything, and be responsible for everything. There are emergencies which require the instant exercise of extreme power. These emergencies do not allow of consultation; and they who would be the captain's constituted advisers might be the very men over whom he would be called upon to exert his authority. It has been found necessary to vest in every government, even the most democratic, some extraordinary and, at first sight, alarming powers; trusting in public opinion, and subsequent accountability to modify the exercise of them. These are provided to meet exigencies, which all hope may never occur, but which yet by possibility may occur, and if they should, and there were no power to meet them instantly, there would be an end put to the government at once. So it is with the authority of the shipmaster.

— RICHARD DANA, *Two Years Before the Mast* (1840)

At first the voyage home was much like the voyage out, except for the intensity of the deep, enveloping light. The light was like silver, like crystal, like oil—but not, really, like anything else; Erasmus could find no comparison, he gave up. The light was like itself. Under it, in Lancaster Sound, he could imagine the promise of Baffin's Bay: ships and mail and company and, a few weeks beyond that, home. At first the weather was calm, and so were the men.

Erasmus's only sleep came in little catnaps but he slept deeply during those stretches and woke refreshed. In between he spent hours with Dr. Boerhaave over their specimens. He made lists and schedules, crossing off each item accomplished: these bird skins dried and packed and labeled, these plants identified. All immensely satisfying. One day he woke in the grip of an unfamiliar feeling—a compound of anticipation and physical well-being, all he'd accomplished in the previous days balanced with all he was eager to do that day. This was happiness, he thought with surprise. The sky hung above him like a gigantic glowing bowl.

On sunlit nights, when sleep seemed such a waste of time, Erasmus thumbed through his battered copy of Hooker's *Botany of the Antarctic Voyage of the Erebus and the Terror in the Years 1839-1843,* not only because those same ships had later carried Franklin, but also because it reminded him of what he might have done on his own first voyage, had Wilkes not blocked him. Now he believed he might put together an arctic volume that would stand as a companion to Hooker's. Next to him Dr. Boerhaave re-read Parry's journals, assessing the descriptions of the Esquimaux. Collating his own notes, he talked about writing an account of the Netsilik similar to Parry's famed Appendix.

"All the arctic peoples build a culture around the available food sources," he mused. "And those cultures may be very different. Yet the tribes share racial characteristics. Just as the plants and animals recur across the arctic zone so do the people, uniquely adapted to this environment. More and more it seems to me they must have been created here . . ."

"Why must they have been?" Erasmus said affectionately. He'd grown very fond of the way his friend talked: one cerebral, slightly stilted sentence linked to the next, whole paragraphs unfurling. He'd never asked, he realized, if Dr. Boerhaave still thought in Swedish, translating mentally before he talked; or if he now thought in English. And where did his French and German fit in, and when had he learned all those languages? His grandparents, he'd once mentioned, had been Dutch. "That doesn't follow."

"You're so old-fashioned," Dr. Boerhaave said. "All the leading naturalists, and all the most progressive philosophers, lean toward this idea of separate, successive creations—why do you resist it so? Why does it seem so improbable to you that man, like the other animals, might have been created multiply in separate zoological provinces?"

"I just don't believe it," Erasmus said. And held up his hands in surrender, and laughed. Whenever they discussed the geographical distribution of plants and animals, they always parted company at the final step of the hypothesis—that just as the arctic supported a white bear rather than black or grizzly bears, murres and dovekies rather than penguins, so too might the Esquimaux differ at a species level from the men in other places.

The idea seemed wrong to Erasmus—not just theologically unorthodox, but scientifically unsound. One practical definition of a species was the ability to interbreed; everyone knew matings of all the races of men produced fertile offspring. Canadian voyageurs and Coppermine Indians, Parry's crews and Esquimaux, plantation owners and their slaves: that no one wanted to discuss these conjunctions didn't make them less true. Erasmus thought of the botanist Asa Gray, whose work he admired. That idea of varieties moving toward species over time—if man was part of nature as a whole, subject to the same physical laws that governed other organisms . . .

"Separate," Dr. Boerhaave said, "does not mean inferior."

"Differentiation always implies ranking," Erasmus said. They smiled and left the subject, returning to the books before them.

Ned listened in on these conversations, occasionally asking questions of his own and practicing what the two older men taught him about the preparation of specimens. At first he worked on birds. In his lined copybook he wrote:

Remember to measure everything before beginning to remove the skin; record color of eyes and other soft parts; if possible make an outline of the entire bird on a large sheet of paper before skinning, otherwise sketch overall shape and stance. Break the wings as close to the body as possible, then cut the skin down the center of the breast to the vent. For the head, stretch the skin gradually until the ears are reached; cut through the skin there close to the bone; then cut carefully around the eye, making sure not to cut the eyelids. Sever the head from the neck and pull out the brain with the hook; remove eyes from sockets, cut out the tongue, and remove all flesh from the skull. Poison the skin with powdered arsenic and alum or arsenical soap.

If prepared carefully, Mr. Wells says, the skins will stay in perfect shape until we return home and will be of much use to scientists. Or they may be softened and mounted in a lifelike shape, so others will have a chance to examine what we've seen. Ever since I pulled Mr. Wells from the water at the base of the cliff he has treated me very kindly; who could imagine I'd find another man willing to help me like this? I have a gift for this work, he says. I might make a living from it someday, if I wanted—in museums, he claims, are assistants with no more formal education than me, who do the initial work on all the specimens. My father would have laughed and thought this no better than undertaker's work. But that was there, and this is another country.

* * *

PART OF ERASMUS'S well-being came from the sense that he was teaching Ned something useful. As Ned's hands moved among skins and bones, Erasmus was reminded of his own boyish efforts—a squirrel, he thought, had been his first preparation—and he watched happily. On his other side Dr. Boerhaave, busy himself with an ivory gull, asked Ned, "How is it you read and write so well?"

"I was lucky," Ned said, comparing the spinal column in his palm to the sketch before him. "A man who took me in one winter taught me."

They were interrupted by the lookout calling, "Drift ice ahead!" As they leapt to their feet and stared, the ice turned into a herd of beluga whales, glimmering white in the water. After gaping at them, Ned told Erasmus and Dr. Boerhaave how he'd gotten his education.

He had left Ireland in '47, he said, at the height of the potato famine. All his family had died but his brother Denis and his older sister, Nora; the three of them had taken passage on one of the overcrowded emigrant ships bound for Quebec. But Nora had sickened on the ship, and at the quarantine station of Grosse Isle, downriver from Quebec city, Nora had been taken from them.

"We were starving," Ned said, gazing out at the water. "And Denis and I were sick ourselves, though we didn't know it yet. Nora was almost dead. These men carried her off the ship and said she had to go into the hospital on the island. Me and Denis were forced onto another, smaller ship, crammed full of Irish like us, and they sent us upriver to Montreal. We never saw Nora again."

In Montreal, he said, there were already so many sick with the fever that the residents had forced them along to Kingston. In Kingston, Denis had died.

"How old were you then?" Dr. Boerhaave asked.

"Twelve," Ned said. "I turned thirteen there."

He touched only briefly on the terrible years when, after being left for dead in a pauper's hospital, and then wandering the streets, homeless and thieving, he'd been taken in by some farmers who worked him hard. Soon after turning sixteen, he'd run away.

"All I wanted," he said, "was to be out of that cruel country. I thought that if I could just get to America, my whole life would be different."

He'd crossed the St. Lawrence into New York State and drifted from Cape Vincent to Chaumont to Watertown; then, hearing tales of logging work to be had in the Brown's Tract wilderness, he'd made the hazardous journey through the north woods. Deep in the forests near Saranac Lake he'd found work in a logging camp, though not as a logger. The men, immigrants like himself, had laughed at his slight physique but had been willing to hire him as cook's helper.

Midway through his second season, the cook had left and Ned had taken on the duties of feeding the entire camp. That year, while picking up groceries on Lower Saranac Lake, he'd met a pale Boston lawyer who planned to winter there in the hope of curing his consumption. The lawyer was building a cabin in the woods and hiring a staff. He'd engaged Ned as his cook.

All that winter, while the lawyer lay wrapped in blankets on a porch facing south, simultaneously basking in the sun and freezing in the subzero wind, he'd taught Ned his letters, so that Ned could read to him and eventually take dictation. During Ned's second winter a new cook had been hired, so that Ned might spend all his time with the lawyer and his books.

"It was a great thing he did for me," Ned said. "I'll always be grateful to him."

"Why did you leave?" Erasmus asked.

"He died," Ned said.

He was twenty, and in an hour's conversation he'd said, *they died, she died, he died, he died.* Rising to return to the galley, Ned explained in a few more sentences how he'd drifted south to Philadelphia, been unable to find any clerical work, and ended up cooking at the wharfside tavern where Mr. Tagliabeau had found him. He said nothing about the fight that had led to his dismissal.

"I couldn't seem to settle down," he said. "Everywhere I went, I missed my family." He paused for a moment, not sure how to say what he meant. What could where he traveled matter, when he had no hope of ever seeing Nora or Denis again? In a way, wandering like this was what gave him hope; he'd seen Denis die with his own eyes but Nora had simply disappeared, and if he kept moving it somehow seemed possible that she wasn't dead. That she might be wandering, like him.

"It's a strange thing," he said, "knowing you don't have a single living relative in all the world—how can you pick a place to live, when you're a stranger everywhere?"

Dr. Boerhaave smiled, as if he knew exactly what Ned meant. Both of them, Erasmus thought, had cut their ties to home in a way he still couldn't imagine.

"One thing I liked about the wharves was that all the men who came in were strangers too," Ned continued. "I was beginning to think about shipping out on a merchant ship and seeing the world, since I had no ties to anyplace. But then you all showed up, and look how well everything worked out. Commander Voorhees took me on, and here I am: in a place where hardly anyone has ever been. Where we're all strangers, except to each other."

THEY *HAD* BEEN strangers, Erasmus would think later. Even to each other. But he forgot that for a while in the blinding light.

Outside the sun shone and shone, and inside the relics obtained from the Netsilik, neatly boxed and stowed in the hold, shed a quiet radiance. Filled with purpose and caught up in his work, Erasmus was slow to register the mood of the men around him. They were fifteen people, isolated except for their brief time among the Netsilik, and they'd begun to tire of each other. Small habits loomed large: the way, for instance, that Zeke fed Sabine from his fork at the dinner table. Or Zeke's bored, superior gaze when Erasmus tried to tell him what he'd learned about Ned.

"Well, of course," Zeke said. Sabine sat on the chair beside him, following his hand alertly as it hovered over the plate. "Ned told me all of this ages ago." When had that happened? Erasmus wondered. When Zeke was brooding over Fletcher Lamb's death? Lately Zeke had seemed even more secretive than usual.

Several of the crew who'd quarreled at Boothia over women nursed those rivalries into fire again. On the voyage out, it had often been Joe who was best able to cheer and calm the men, entertaining them with his zither and his stories. But Joe had been glum since their departure from Boothia: so glum that, when a fistfight broke out between Sean Hamilton and Ivan Hruska, Joe left them to Mr. Francis's harsh discipline and came above, to hang listlessly over the rail where Erasmus was perched with his sketchpad.

"They'll get over it," Erasmus said. "They're restless, they're all thinking of home. Really we've been incredibly lucky so far. Everything we learned from those Esquimaux . . ."

The biscuit Joe tossed over the rail was caught in midair by a fulmar. "What makes you think those Esquimaux were telling us everything they knew?"

"Because—they *didn't* tell us, at first," Erasmus said, startled. The fulmar flapped away with its prize. "We had to dig out the truth for ourselves. We had to pry it out of them. If Ned hadn't seen those cooking kettles . . ."

Joe made a disgusted sound. "They told that story for their own reasons," he said. "To get the ship to go away, and the men to stop hunting their caribou and preying on their women. Couldn't you see that? They told us what we wanted to hear. And if Commander Voorhees hadn't been so blinded by his own anger and his desire to find something, he would have realized just how ambiguous the situation was."

"You're saying they *lied?*" Erasmus thought back to the look on Joe's face when he'd translated Oonali's revelations about the ship's boat. He'd assumed, then, that Joe was simply mortified by the earlier deceptions.

"Not lied," Joe said crossly. "There was surely truth in what they told us. But they knew what we were looking for, and what it would take to satisfy us, and so perhaps they bent the truth a little. Shaped the story to our desires."

"But you're the *interpreter*," Erasmus said. "It was your job to figure that out, and convey to us what was accurate, and what misleading."

"I shouldn't have to interpret gestures," Joe said. His hands, brown and broken-nailed, clamped on the rail. "If Commander Voorhees had looked more closely at Oonali, instead of at me—if he'd paid any attention to Oonali at all—he would have understood how to weigh the information."

Oonali, Erasmus recalled, had pushed two girl children behind him as he spoke at the feast, and shooed others away from the gathering of the men. Uneasily he said, "What did Oonali say, that you didn't tell us?"

"It's not what he said—it's the way he said it. It's the context in which he said it. I translated every word as accurately as I could. But I was also paying attention to other things. And you were not. Commander Voorhees was not. If you were in a negotiation with your people back home, you'd notice other things besides the words."

"Do you think there was no boat, then?" Erasmus asked. "But where did they get those kettles, the pieces of wood—everything?"

"Of course they found a boat. Dead sailors, too. What I'm not so sure of is that all the traces of them are actually gone. But they had every reason to discourage us from overwintering there, and from searching the island in the spring. Who knows what we might have found, if we hadn't been satisfied so easily with their tale?"

He paused and picked at the dry skin around his thumbnails. "Oonali's wife told me something awful," he admitted. "When we were standing apart from the others for a minute. She said at that boat, near the dead sailors—they found human parts that had been . . . interfered with. Bones with the marks of saws and knives. Skulls with holes smashed in them."

"Dr. Rae's report," Erasmus murmured, remembering the story he'd told Ned at the start of their voyage. "That's just what the Esquimaux he met told him."

"These stories are worse," Joe said. "Oonali's wife told me she found a sailor's boot, which someone had been using as a kind of bowl. There were pieces of boiled human flesh in it."

In his bunk, beneath his bookshelf, Erasmus had driven a tack and then wedged his secret scrap of leather between it and the shelf's lower side. The one thing he'd kept for himself; still no one knew he had it, not even Dr. Boerhaave. Later, perhaps when they were home, he might offer this as a last surprise to seal their friendship. Something separate from Zeke, and from the goals of the expedition, which only the two of them would share. Until now that scrap of leather had seemed like a symbol of courage, a weary foot moving across the ice no matter how tired. Yet perhaps Oonali's wife had meant it to signal something quite different. Perhaps it was the sole of the same boot she'd told Joe about . . . or perhaps these tales were horrible lies, and all Joe's worries unjustified.

"You should be telling Commander Voorhees this," Erasmus said. He decided not to show his treasure to Joe; it would only make Joe feel worse about what the Esquimaux might not have admitted. "Not me."

"You think I didn't try? I tried to tell him the night before we sailed. And he said, he said"—here Joe drew himself up and tucked in his chin—"'*I* have always read that the Esquimaux pride themselves on their excellent memories, and the faithfulness of their storytelling. I think we may have absolute confidence in what we've been told.'"

With that Joe headed up to the crow's nest, leaving Erasmus to ponder the eerie accuracy with which Joe had caught the inflections of Zeke's voice.

Later, napping briefly, Erasmus dreamed that Joe had turned into an Esquimau boy, indistinguishable from the children at the hunting camp. Then he dreamed that he was himself a tiny boy, listening to his father read. *Not far from the cave where the north wind rises live people who have a single eye centered in their foreheads. In Africa is a race who make in their bodies a poison deadly to snakes. On a mountain in India live men with dogs' heads, who bark instead of talking. Near the source of the Ganges are mouthless people, who subsist on the odors they breathe; beyond them live pygmies in houses of feathers and eggshells.*

He woke still within the enchanted circle of his father's words, and then blinked to see where he was. What had his father meant to do, reading those tales to his small sons? He and his brothers had soaked up those words, which had lit their own experiments. Cutting open a little green snake, they'd been equally ready to see eggs or infant snakes or three-headed monsters. *Try to see what you* see, his father had said. *Then integrate it with what you've already read and heard.* Still Erasmus felt a kind of pity for him. At thirteen his father had gone to work in the firm his own father founded; after that he'd read in snatches, always standing at a printing press or setting type or inking it, lugging bales of paper or bundles of pages, always on the move and starved for time. Once he'd taken over the firm he'd been busy in other ways. *I wanted things to be different for you boys*, he'd said. *For you not to have to work so hard. For you to be able to learn in peace, and travel wherever you wanted—especially after your mother died, I could never leave home for more than a few days.*

How could Erasmus not be grateful for all he'd been given? The next morning he made what amends he could to Joe, offering the heap of little disks he found in the stomach of a bearded seal. "Specimens of the operculum from the large whelk snail," he said.

Joe, who seemed to have recovered his good humor, examined them with interest and then butchered the carcass when Erasmus finished his dissection. Somewhere during those hours, both of them up to the elbows in blood, Erasmus said, "I'm sorry. You're right—I should have been paying more attention. But what can we do about it now?"

"Nothing," Joe said. "We must be thankful for what we did learn. And the Netsilik can be thankful that we're gone; and I can be thankful that we didn't do any more damage than we did."

NOTHING SHONE SO brightly for Erasmus after that. It rained for three days, windy squalls that made work difficult and left him too much time to think about what Joe had said. Then Zeke appeared on deck one afternoon and asked the crew to report to him in the cabin after their evening meal. As Captain Tyler started to ask a question, Zeke said, "I would like to see all the officers together, now."

They crowded around the cabin table in their usual formation: Zeke at one end, flanked by Erasmus and Dr. Boerhaave; Mr.

Tagliabeau and Mr. Francis and Captain Tyler clumped together, as separate from Zeke as was possible in such a tiny space; Sabine annoyingly underfoot. Zeke placed a sheet of paper on the table.

"I should have taken care of this before," he said. The paper was densely written over, in his clear hand. "And I apologize for my tardiness. This is quite standard, something that most expedition leaders require their crews to sign, and I would appreciate it if you'd attend to it now."

"May I?" Dr. Boerhaave said. Zeke nodded and pushed the paper over. Dr. Boerhaave read for a minute, before handing the document to Erasmus.

The undersigned accept Zechariah Voorhees as sole commander of this expedition, and pledge to aid him to achieve the goals of the expedition in every way possible, as deemed best by said Commander Voorhees'.

The contract, stilted and formal, went on to state that, should something happen to Zeke, the expedition would then be under the shared command of Captain Tyler and Erasmus, with the captain responsible for the safe return of the ship, and Erasmus responsible for fulfilling the expedition's goals. Erasmus had no quarrel with this: he was Zeke's right hand and this seemed a simple formality. But a more disturbing paragraph followed, stating that all members of the crew—not exempting Erasmus, nor Dr. Boerhaave—promised to turn their journals and logs over to Zeke at the conclusion of the expedition, and further promised to refrain from lecturing or writing about their observations for a period of one year after the journey's end.

Where had this come from? The blood hummed in Erasmus's temples, and when Sabine draped herself over his instep he nudged her aside more sharply than he meant to. Zeke had been distant since Fletcher Lamb's death but still Erasmus hadn't sensed how far they'd drifted apart. They were meant to be brothers; who would impose on a brother like this? When he knew he could control his voice he passed the contract to Mr. Tagliabeau and said to Zeke, "I'm sorry to disagree with you, but I think this is *outrageous*. You never said a word of this to me before. You're acting the way Wilkes did on the Exploring Expedition and I object to it, I object to it strongly . . ."

Zeke raised a hand to silence him. "It's a formality," he said. "But surely you can see the need to present our findings quickly, and in concert; not to contradict each other. Of course I'll expect all of you to help with the initial announcement of what we've learned, and I would fully acknowledge any material I draw from your notebooks."

Looking straight at Erasmus, and ignoring the whispers of the captain and the mates, Zeke said, "It's to *avoid* what happened with Wilkes's expedition that I do this. We must have no quarrels among ourselves, no results thrown into question by any appearance of disunity among us."

"Why should Mr. Wells share command with me, in your absence?" Captain Tyler said angrily. "He knows nothing about this ship."

"He shares my goals for the expedition," Zeke said. "I must be sure that if something happened to me, someone would take charge of delivering the relics and our scientific observations. As well as safely delivering the ship and its men."

Dr. Boerhaave, who'd said nothing yet, drew the paper from Captain Tyler's hand, took the pen Zeke had prepared, and signed. Then he rose. "Of course I will assist you in any way I can," he said. "As I have always done. But I'm offended that you feel a need for this. If you'll excuse me."

He nodded stiffly and went up on deck. Erasmus, left behind, stared at the paper that blocked his dream of lecturing by himself. But he'd be *with* Zeke, he thought. They'd be striding into the Academy of Sciences together—and already they were sharing the journal Lavinia had meant for Zeke. Their observations would be fused together, into a single narrative that Erasmus might write himself; Zeke disliked the act of composition and preferred to toss out broad ideas and let others shape them. This contract was the act of a young man, still nervous about his position. Surely Erasmus, so much older, could afford to give in here and work out the details later? Zeke would never prevent him writing a few articles purely about the natural history of the area, with no reference to Franklin or their Esquimaux companions.

"I won't sign this," Captain Tyler said. "In your absence, Mr. Tagliabeau would naturally be my second-in-command. Not Mr. Wells."

"I'm sorry you feel that way," Zeke said. "But if you don't sign, I'll be forced to relieve you of command."

Then everyone was shouting. In his awkward position, Erasmus felt he shouldn't speak—but all this quarreling had the effect of diverting his attention away from the paragraphs about the journals, and to the question of the succession of command. Perhaps Zeke counted on this. He wore down the captain, finally suggesting that the balance of the crew's payment for the expedition, due on their return, might be withheld if he refused to sign.

Captain Tyler signed, and then Mr. Francis and Mr. Tagliabeau; they flung themselves up the ladder and Erasmus could hear shouting from the deck. The captain—who was he talking to?—said, "I would never have taken this command if there'd been anything better around. This is no fit job for a whaling skipper, this bobbing around the arctic . . ."

"And you?" Zeke said to Erasmus once they'd left. Sabine hopped into his lap. "My trusted friend?"

Erasmus signed and shook Zeke's hand. When Zeke asked Erasmus to help him explain the contract to the men trickling into the cabin, Erasmus did that too. He inscribed the names of those who couldn't write and showed them where to make their mark. Both Nils Jensen and Isaac Bond said, "But Captain Tyler would still be in charge, if something happened?"

"Absolutely," Zeke said. "Nothing has changed."

Ned, ever amiable, read and signed the contract himself without a murmur. Joe, the last to arrive, said, "I'll want to make a report on the Netsilik to the Moravian missionaries in Greenland. Would that be permitted?"

"It wouldn't go outside the church?"

"No. But they might want to establish a mission in the area at some point, and my observations could be of use to them."

Zeke gave his permission, and Joe signed.

All throughout that evening, Sabine remained in Zeke's lap with her delicate paws on the table, peering at the contract as if she were about to sign it herself. Now and then Zeke fed her morsels and then pointed out the neat way in which she wiped her lips.

"Isn't she charming?" he said to Barton DeSouza, just as Erasmus was explaining the second paragraph of the contract. Barton looked disconcerted, the more so when Sabine turned, looked lovingly up into Zeke's face, and barked.

On deck, in the shelter of one of the boats, Dr. Boerhaave stared for a long time at his journal but closed it without writing anything. Then he took out his letter case and wrote furiously to his friend William in Edinburgh:

I've enjoyed this expedition very much but am coming to despise our commander. He lives in a world of his own making, only aware of his own thoughts and fantasies: a boy still, for all his bulk and bluster. On Boothia, he could not see the Netsilik except as agents of his own glory, and although I tried to gather information about their customs I was never granted enough time to do so, nor to gather and prepare plant and animal specimens, and he has no appreciation for the fossils I gathered; and now this: all the notes I managed to take despite him are to be his, so *that he may construct a narrative of the last days of Franklin and his men from the slight evidence he has gathered—which is slight, do not mistake this, I append a list of relics but in themselves they don't tell us more than we knew before from Dr. Rae's explorations and what we really learned, or might have learned, is something about this glorious place and its people, but he will make no use of that—<u>a whole year.</u> Of course he hasn't the least understanding that priority is granted to the naming and description of new species not by their date of discovery but by the date of published description.*

Erasmus, the following morning, made a note about a fish in his journal and then flipped through the pages, assessing his earlier entries. Had he been too personal? He drew some scales and listed the fish's stomach contents but longed to describe how he felt. He began a long letter to Copernicus. It could not be sent; there was no way to send it, and no one to receive it; Copernicus was still out west somewhere, painting canyons and Indians. But Erasmus felt the bond between them, across the length and breadth of the continent, somehow strengthened by Zeke's act.

ON AUGUST 20 they entered the waters of Baffin's Bay. They'd planned to turn north and then east here, sailing around the upper edge of the pack and retracing the great arc back to Greenland, but Isaac Bond called down from the masthead and reported a ship. Zeke, the captain, and the mates took their turns with the glass: a large ship, they agreed, caught in the ice a few miles south of them, apparently abandoned and adrift. Zeke ordered the *Narwhal* brought as close to the ship as possible. The ice loomed before them like land.

"I can't risk getting us caught in the pack," Captain Tyler said. "Not this late in the season. And not when we're so close to home."

"It's not your ship to risk," Zeke said coolly. He pushed the spyglass toward the captain and pointed out the black hull marked with a band of white. "British naval vessels are all painted like that," he said. "They're impossible to tell apart from a distance. That could be the second of Franklin's ships. The Esquimaux told us about *one* ship sinking. Only one."

Captain Tyler scanned the distant ship. "If it were . . . but there's so little chance of that. And you can see it's deserted—why should we risk ourselves?"

"Because I tell you to," Zeke said.

He turned his back and went below: as if a show of confidence that his orders would be followed would ensure that they were. Captain Tyler cracked his knuckles but worked the brig south through the ice, until they were finally blocked a few hundred feet from the other ship by a long, hummocked floe. The possibility that this *was* Franklin's ship made Erasmus tremble with excitement. To his surprise, Zeke named as the boarding party only himself, Erasmus, Dr. Boerhaave, and Ned.

"I need everyone else on hand to work the brig, in case we're nipped," Zeke said.

"Take Forbes, at least," Captain Tyler grumbled. "You may need a carpenter."

"We'll be fine," Zeke said.

They lowered themselves to the ice, picked their way gingerly across the cracks, and approached the ship. Zeke said, "If this were the ship, one of the ships, if we were fated after all to find this final sign, it would be such excellent confirmation of what we've already learned . . ."

The ship was fast in the ice. Zeke shouted as they approached, but no one answered. As they clambered aboard Erasmus's skin prickled, and he knew they all feared the same thing: that they'd find bodies inside, frozen or starved to death. The deck was in order, lines properly coiled and sails stowed, but empty of people.

Zeke pointed out the motto on the brass plate over the helm: *England expects every man to do his duty.* "Could it be the *Erebus?*" he said. "Or the *Terror?*"

As they descended into the cabin, Zeke was already talking about how they might free the ship and tow it home. Erasmus had to remind himself to breathe. If this were one of Franklin's ships, if, if, if . . . already he could imagine the newspaper headlines. They entered the dark and musty cabin. In a writing desk, Dr. Boerhaave found the logbook. He lifted it; he blew off the dust. Erasmus stared at the fine black hairs on the back of his friend's hands.

Dr. Boerhaave opened the book. "The *Resolute*," he announced.

And there they were, in a cold, dark ship that for a minute was only a ship. Then it was something else, though still not glorious. They'd all heard about this ship; it belonged to Edward Belcher's expedition, which had been frozen in during the winter of '53 and '54. Belcher, Erasmus knew, had abandoned his fleet that May, a thousand miles west of them. As he and Zeke were planning their own voyage, they'd heard the gossip about Belcher's return to England on a rescue ship. He'd been court-martialed for his poor judgment, and barely acquitted; there'd been little reason to think his vessels wouldn't be free come summer, and no one understood why he'd left them.

Zeke's face sagged as they recollected the squalid story. They stood in one of Belcher's ships, which had broken free and made the long journey eastward by itself. A discovery, but hardly an earthshaking one.

"Should we try to tow her out?" Erasmus asked.

"Let someone else salvage her," Zeke said. "It's not our job to repair that man's mistakes." He took the logbook but left the *Resolute* to continue drifting southward with the pack.

Back across Lancaster Sound again, then along the coast of

North Devon; Zeke sullen with the knowledge that their detour had come to nothing. From Jones Sound the water stretched east and north nearly free of ice, a sight that made everyone smile: all of them dreaming of home. Erasmus dreamed of his narrow bed in the Repository, his orderly specimen cases and shelves; of the cook bringing into his dining room a dish of roasted veal and glazed carrots. Dr. Boerhaave was looking forward to a trip to Boston; the men spoke of sweethearts and things they might buy with their wages; Captain Tyler said he missed his wife. Perhaps Zeke dreamed of Lavinia. Or perhaps he dreamed of other things.

In Philadelphia, women dreamed that the *Narwhal* was sailing toward them. Alexandra wrote:

Just another six or eight weeks, if all goes well. I thought I'd look forward to the end of this time, but in fact I'll miss being here: a retreat from the noise and crowding of my family's house. I've come to love my hours in the Repository and have grown very attached to Lavinia. We've completed the plates for the entomology book, but Linnaeus and Humboldt have no more hand-coloring work. They offered me a small stipend simply to continue as Lavinia's companion, but I've persuaded them to let me—and Lavinia too, I said; she needs to stay occupied—take engraving lessons from one of their employees in lieu of a salary. I have a substantial nest egg in my sewing box now. What I need is a skill I may take with me when I leave. If this is the life I am to lead—here in this city, unattached, dependent on my brother—I must do what I can to make the best of it.

The brothers objected on the usual grounds but I cited the example of Thomas Say's wife, Lucy. As their father helped arrange her election as the first woman member of the Academy of Sciences, this made them think. Lavinia made them look at Mrs. Hale's book, which she brought back from town: "Women's Record, or Sketches of All Distinguished Women from 'The Beginning' till A.D. 1850. Arranged in Four

Eras. With Selections from Female Writers of Every Age." *I mean to be an advanced woman, she told her brothers. Like those women. Isn't that what you want for me?*

We started last week. Mr. Archibault, one of the Wells's master engravers, comes to us in the Repository, bearing burins and needles and steel plates spoiled by the apprentices, which would otherwise be scrapped. More broad-minded than the brothers, he remarks that both Helen Dawson and the Maverick sisters did excellent engravings; and so anything, he supposes, may be possible. Straight lines, curved lines, incomplete lines, and dots—I have much to learn, and little time. I gashed myself several times with the burin.

LATER, ERASMUS WOULD wonder if Zeke's disappointment over the *Resolute* was responsible for what happened next. Or if Joe's earlier comments about Oonali had finally sunk in, until Zeke doubted the worth of their relics. At the point where they all expected to turn east, Zeke called the crew together on deck.

"We have four days yet of August," Zeke said. "And can look forward to several weeks of good sailing in September. The weather's excellent and the season is far from over. Your hard work has already brought this expedition much success. And I know you'll be willing to delay our return just a few more weeks, so we might bring back not only our news of Franklin's expedition, but some significant geographical findings as well."

Erasmus, sketching the strata of a distant cliff, turned to stare at Zeke as Sean Hamilton blurted, *"What?"* Two seals popped their heads from the water and stared at the ship.

"We'll head into Smith Sound," Zeke continued, "testing the boundaries of the open water. A little detour. The bulk of the drifting ice is south of us; you can see for yourselves that there's no loose pack north of us. A swift, concerted probe through the Sound might bring us far before we have to turn back. We'll make as much northing as we can in ten days, chart as much new territory as we can, and then make a quick run for Godhavn. I promise we'll be there in less than four weeks."

"No!" Captain Tyler said. He grasped a shroud, squeezing until his swollen knuckles stood out like walnuts. "This is out of the question, you can't consider it."

Mr. Francis and Mr. Tagliabeau backed him up and others also raised their voices: *my mother is waiting; the season's too late; this isn't what you told us when we signed on*—Isaac Bond, Nils Jensen, Ivan Hruska. Zeke brought out his maps, talking about his theory of polynya formation and why there *should* be open water north of the constriction of Smith Sound.

"Please," Erasmus said in his ear. "What about Lavinia?"

But Zeke shook him off and did what Erasmus had dreaded from his first words. "You've pledged to support me," he said, waving the contract. "This brief exploration is part of our goals, as I have determined them, and you must support me in this. You must."

Sabine, perched on his shoulder like a white epaulet, regarded the crowd and barked.

THE ICEBERG'S FACE was sheer and as high as their mastheads, but Nils Jensen and Robert Carey managed to scale it. They were trying to anchor the *Narwhal* to the berg's lee side, where they might find some protection from the crushing ice. Nils drove the anchor in; Robert adjusted the lines. Just as they began their scramble back to the ship, the berg split in two with a noise like a cannon shot. Robert leapt for the water, and although he was nearly frozen to death Dr. Boerhaave was able to save him. But while his companions watched, unable to help him, Nils toppled into the chasm between the berg's two halves. Later this sight recurred in Erasmus's dreams and he'd wake with his throat closed, imagining what Nils must have felt when the larger half sighed and rolled in the water, grinding a submerged tongue into the smaller half and obliterating the chasm. They did not find even a scrap of Nils's clothing.

For Erasmus this scene came to stand for the twenty-three days during which they battled the ice beyond the twin capes guarding Smith Sound. As they sailed into the great basin, he'd talked himself into sharing some of Zeke's enthusiasm. But by September 3 thin ice was already forming around the *Narwhal* at night, bridging the floes that kept them pressed against Ellesmere and prevented them from crossing to the Greenland side of the sound. Joe gazed at the floes with a long face; any part of Greenland, even this far north where he'd never been, counted as home to him. The distant shores teased him terribly.

"I joined you to look for Franklin," he said to Erasmus, chipping at the ice on deck. "Not for this."

Meanwhile Ned cooked as if he'd never stop, rushing hot soup and coffee and biscuits to the frozen men. He made dried-apple pudding again and again, a food much beloved by Fletcher Lamb and Nils Jensen, who were gone. Although he'd not grieved openly for Fletcher when he died, now that Nils was also gone he set places at the table for the dead men, unable to stop until Erasmus gently reproached him.

Nils was killed on September 6. By September 8 drift ice surrounded them and foot-long icicles hung from the rigging; by September 10 they were confronted by solid pack; by the eleventh they knew that an open polar sea, if it existed at all, lay beyond this barrier of ice. Beyond their reach.

Zeke was stunned by Nils Jensen's death, and disappointed by their failure to sail farther north, but he told the crew they'd done well. "We've charted a long new stretch of coastline," he said, showing them the maps he'd drawn and the features he'd christened. Cape Laurel, Cape Violet, Cape Agatha—his sisters, his mother; but also, and more to the crew's pleasure, Fletcher Lamb Bay and Jensen Point. What pleased them most was Zeke's order that they turn and head for home.

But on September 14 they found their route to the south walled off by a dense mass of ice that had floated in since they'd entered the basin. A stiff wind jammed the ice against the brig and her against the coast; they sailed through hail and snow and freezing rain, which glazed the deck and the rigging. They probed the pack, searching for a passage south but blocked again and again. Plates of ice swept toward the shore, grinding over the gravel and tossing boulders aside before being crushed and heaved by other floes; the rumblings and sudden, explosive cracks made the men feel as if they'd been caught in a giant mouth, which was chewing on the landscape. Their area of movement decreased each hour, until Zeke, who'd stopped eating during the five days of their frenzied oscillation, finally conceded defeat and began to look for a suitable harbor.

Later Erasmus would wish he'd thought to remind Zeke of the advantages of a site that looked southward and eastward. But he was exhausted and so was Zeke, and so were all the men; hail was beating against their faces and they could hardly see what lay before them. From the gloom rose a towering triangular point, backed by smaller pyramids; they swept around it, forced by the wind, and to their great relief found a cove bitten into the point's back side. Sharp walls loomed over them, blocking their view of Greenland, across the Sound, but in the harbor's southeast corner was a small gravel beach and a bit of lumpy ground.

Still it was a poor choice, Erasmus thought, when the sky cleared the next morning. The cove opened to the northwest, the coldest prospect. As they warped the brig closer to the beach, three icebergs swept around the point and grounded on a reef, partially blocking the mouth of the cove and plugging them in like a ship in a bottle.

PART II

5

THE ICE IN ITS GREAT ABUNDANCE

(OCTOBER 1855–MARCH 1856)

The intense beauty of the Arctic firmament can hardly be imagined. It looked close above our heads, with its stars magnified in glory and the very planets twinkling so much as to baffle the observations of our astronomer. I am afraid to speak of some of these night-scenes. I have trodden the deck and the floes, when the life of the earth seemed suspended, its movements, its sounds, its coloring, its companionships; and as I looked on the radiant hemisphere, circling above me as if rendering worship to the unseen Centre of light, I have ejaculated in humility of spirit, "Lord, what is man that thou art mindful of him?" And then I have thought of the kindly world we had left, with its revolving sunshine and shadow, and the other stars that gladden it in their changes, and the hearts that warmed to us there; till I lost myself in memories of those who are not;—and they bore me back to the stars again.

—ELISHA KENT KANE, *Arctic Explorations: The Second Grinnell Expedition in Search of Sir John Franklin, 1853, '54,'55* (1856)

*I*n Philadelphia it was beautifully clear and warm, the chrysanthemums rust and gold in the gardens and the leaves of the sweet gum radiant on the grass. Alexandra, secure in her spacious rooms, kept her diary faithfully. It was a form of discipline, she thought. A record of her education as well as a way of honoring her parents. Her first diary, smooth black leather with gilt thistles, had been a gift from them. *Today I am eight*, she had written. *I got a box of pencils, a Bible, this book to write in. A promise from Emily not to touch my paints. I have a bad cold.* Seventeen volumes now, one for each year since then; the only gap some months from her fifteenth year, when her parents were killed and she could say nothing. She wrote:

I've finished my engraving of the Passaic smelt. Lavinia stopped after three lessons, she hated cutting up her hands; but I have a gift for this, I do. Even Mr. Archibault admits that my line is expressive and clear and that I have a fine touch with light and shadow. In a way I didn't expect it's much more than copying; more like re-making, re-creating. When I'm working everything else drops away and I enter the scene I'm engraving. As if I've entered a larger life.

I meant to start on a copy of the hand's nerves and tendons but the news set us in an uproar. First we heard that the abandoned British ship Resolute *was found floating in Baffin's Bay. A crew from an American whaler sailed her down to New London; we had hopes they might have met the* Narwhal *and have mail for us, but apparently not. Then Saturday the papers here carried the story of Dr. Kane's rescue. No one can talk about anything else—such enormous good luck, the way the rescue squadron, driven back from Smith Sound, met Esquimaux who'd spent time with Kane's party and been aboard the frozen-in ship.*

Learning that Kane and his men had abandoned their ship and gone south on foot, Lt. Hartstene made his way to Godhavn and discovered the party there, just as they were about to board a Danish brig. The front page of the paper was filled with Dr. Kane's report. Sledge trips, news of Esquimaux living farther north than anyone suspected; long stretches of coastline discovered on both the Greenland and the American sides of Smith Sound; he claims two of his men have viewed an open polar sea. Having endured extraordinary cold and starvation, and a long journey by sledge and small boat, he lost only three members of his Expedition and is now a great hero. Against this his father's behavior stands out even more despicably.

Emily, who visited yesterday with Jane, is as angry as I've ever seen her. Despite the efforts of the Ladies Anti-Slavery Society and others, Judge Kane committed Williamson to prison on Friday, for failing to produce the runaway slaves he's sheltered. One of the antislavery papers notes that 'such a man can surely be no relative of the noble-hearted explorer. His opinion makes every state a slave state. . . . He is the Columbus of the new world of slave-whips and shackles which he has just annexed.' The slaves are safe, Emily says—I'm not sure whether she has direct knowledge of this—but the abolitionists who aided them may be in prison a long time. The decision has caused a split in the city, and at every social gathering. Lavinia sides with me and Emily on this, but when Emily asked if she'd be willing to let her committee meet here she declined; her brother and Zeke, she said, might be back any day, and the house must be ready for them. Later I found her crying. She's not been sleeping, though she tries to hide this.

I can't blame her for worrying. That Dr. Kane is home, while we have as yet no word of Zeke and Erasmus; that Dr. Kane is lionized for discovering the open sea Zeke hoped to find—we can only hope, Lavinia says, that Zeke and Erasmus are safe and have found some traces of Franklin. The truth, when one looks past the headlines, is that while Dr. Kane did remarkable things, he was in the wrong place; he didn't learn until reaching Upernavik of Rae's discoveries a thousand miles south and west of where he'd been. Also he lost his ship. But he is a hero nonetheless; and is not responsible for his father's detestable decision; and will be in Philadelphia shortly. Lavinia has asked her brothers to seek an *appointment with him, to find out if he's seen any evidence of the* Nar-whal. *But apparently he's seeing few people.*

LATER ERASMUS AND the rest of the crew would learn that their cove was only a corner of a bay previously named by Kane; their home only the width of Smith Sound from Kane's winter quarters. Later Erasmus would lay out calendar pages and his journal entries and the newspaper stories of Kane's return, matching up days and trying to understand how the *Narwhal* had failed to cross paths with Kane's retreat party. They'd missed each other so narrowly it seemed only fate could have kept them apart. But he'd remind himself, then, that it had never been their charge to find Kane. Even as they'd been loading the *Narwhal*, the Navy had outfitted two rescue ships, which had left New York as the *Narwhal* left Philadelphia. Everyone had understood that they'd head directly toward Smith Sound, in search of Kane, while the *Narwhal* would head for King William Land, in search of Franklin. A simple division of labor.

The *Narwhal* had arrived in Smith Sound so late in the season, and so unexpectedly, that when Erasmus thought of Dr. Kane at all, he felt sure he'd already been found. By October, though, Erasmus couldn't spare even a thought for his fellow Philadelphian. Only once, when he was adding to his growing letter to Copernicus, did he wonder if Dr. Kane had reached this far north. He wrote:

Do you ever feel this in your travels out west? That all the unexplored parts of the world are closing their doors; that so many of us, traveling so far, cannot avoid crossing each other's paths and repeating each other's discoveries? Perhaps you've passed the Absaroka Mountains, into the Wind River Valley or Jackson's Hole, and wondered what it would have been like to be the first one there. I wish I could pretend to be another

Meriwether Lewis, but those days are half a century behind us. Some-
times I have such a feeling of people crowding the world. Up here all is
emptiness, we see no human beings; yet we can't know for sure that we're
the first ones here. I have no idea where you are. You have no idea where
I am. I would give anything to know what you're doing this very night.

Then he returned to work, ashamed of having stolen even a
moment. Although there were men weeping in odd corners;
although those who couldn't write crept up to Ned and Dr. Boerhaave and asked for help drafting last testaments; although Captain Tyler disappeared periodically and was of little help; still
Erasmus tried not to give in to despair. But the *Narwhal* wasn't
yet ready for winter, and the ice thickened with each tide.

He did whatever Zeke asked, helping the men dismantle the
upper masts and lashing the lower yards fore and aft amidships.
Around that framework they laid planks, which housed in most
of the upper deck, and a thick layer of insulating felt. Boats and
spars and rigging and sails they stowed in a shed hurriedly built
on shore, along with all their coal, the supplies from the hold, and
most of the plant and animal specimens. Alongside the storehouse they built another hut in which Zeke set up the meteorological instruments.

Through a wavering cloud of frost smoke, Erasmus glimpsed
the full moon gleaming. The thermometer read ten degrees, then
zero, then ten below; cold hands, cold feet, shoulders hunched
against the wind. All the men complained and swore they
couldn't get used to it, then did. When the weather permitted,
Joe went hunting in the brief slots between the parenthetical twilights. No dovekies, no murres, no ptarmigan; but before the
other animals disappeared he shot two musk oxen, seven caribou,
and many hares. Erasmus made lists of the meals these might
provide, along with their initial store of provisions and the salted
fish Zeke had purchased at Godhavn. He might have made

another list—on one side Zeke's impulsive maneuvers, which had stranded them here; on the other Zeke's foresight with the supplies that fed and sheltered them. With the help of Joe and Dr. Boerhaave, he dug out the Esquimaux furs Zeke had purchased and fitted each man with a suit.

Later Dr. Boerhaave wrote to his friend William:

I couldn't even tell who it was at first; two furry figures huddled over a moaning third. But it was Isaac, who was careless and exploded his powder box; his hand is in danger. I extracted several shards of metal and sluiced out as much of the powder as I could. A poultice of yeast and charcoal may draw out the rest.

Everyone's cold. This place—in the morning, when the sun is low in the east, the peninsula shadows us. In the afternoon we're shadowed by the hills to our south, later by the three grounded icebergs; Commander Voorhees couldn't have chosen a colder place. Away from him the men refer to the icebergs sarcastically as "Zeke's Follies." Some folly. I meant to be back in Edinburgh by now, writing up papers and arguing happily with you and the others: walking, talking, drinking, thinking. Instead I have only Mr. Wells; but I've grown fond of him. If it were not for him and the work we do together, I think I would feel desperate.

THERE WAS NO point, Zeke said, in trying to maintain separate messes for men and officers. Their fuel was limited, they must conserve. Ned and Sean Hamilton moved the galley to a spot under the main hatch. Then Zeke rearranged the sleeping quarters, setting Thomas Forbes to remove the bulkhead between the men's forecastle and the officers' cabin.

"You'd never see this on a whaling ship," Captain Tyler grumbled. "How are you going to maintain discipline, if we're all mixed together?"

"I'm not doing this to be democratic," Zeke retorted. The previous night several of the men's bedclothes had frozen about their feet. "Just to be practical. We have only the one small stove besides the galley stove, and the best way to keep everyone warm is to allow the heated air to circulate."

As a concession to Captain Tyler, Zeke had Thomas build two shoulder-high partitions, each of which stretched from one side of the hull toward the midline, where the stove was set, and stopped a few feet short of it. From this common island the stove radiated warmth impartially fore and aft. Air flowed not only around the stove but also over the partitions, and although sound traveled freely between the men's and the officers' bunks, when the crew lay down they were hidden. When they pulled their stools close to the stove for warmth, the half-ring of officers aft and the half-ring of men forward could see each other, and talk if desired, yet were separated at least by the stove and its pipes. The division was more symbolic than real, yet it served, Zeke argued. By a judicious lowering of the voices and averting of the eyes, the officers might preserve an illusion of privacy. More importantly, they were warm.

Zeke took great pride in this, Erasmus saw, as he did in every aspect of their housekeeping arrangements. Otherwise Erasmus couldn't guess what Zeke was thinking. The mistakes that had lodged them here, the families anxiously waiting for them back home, the true nature of the relics they'd brought from Boothia—if any of these worried Zeke, he gave no sign. Mostly he seemed pleased with himself: that he'd had the good sense to bring the planks and felted cloth that sheltered them, the furs that warmed them, the extra fish to supplement their diet. That he'd had the sense to find Joe, who was so much help. Perhaps he was also pleased that Captain Tyler and the mates had no real function, now that the *Narwhal* was a cramped but stable household, and not a sailing ship.

"What do they know?" Zeke asked Erasmus one afternoon, as they paced the walk along the shore. Well within sight of the ship, for safety's sake, yet far enough away for privacy, Zeke had measured out a promenade and had the men mark it off with wooden wands. Another innovation he was pleased with.

"The whaler's whole being is oriented toward fishing successfully and then getting home before winter sets in," he said. "Captain Tyler did well enough transporting us where we needed to go, but he knows nothing about the physical and emotional demands of surviving an arctic winter and keeping a crew healthy and cheerful. Have you noticed how sullen he is after dinner? I'm beginning to wonder if he's sick."

"He's foul-tempered enough," Erasmus said. "Should we ask Dr. Boerhaave to examine him?"

"I'll take care of it," Zeke said.

But he was busy with other things—bubbling with ideas, always cheerful, endlessly energetic. By himself he built a latrine of ice; then, while the men watched curiously, a low wall around it to cut the wind. Ned and Barton joined him when he began a walled lane from the ship to the promenade; Robert Carey, with Zeke's laughing encouragement, built a little watchtower overlooking the lane, which Zeke crowned with a roughly carved woman's head. How clever he was, Erasmus thought. Zeke never asked for help, or explained what he was doing. He simply busied himself within sight of the crew and made what he was doing look like fun, until those who lagged behind felt left out. Erasmus was reminded of Zeke's resourcefulness, one of the qualities Lavinia loved.

He was drawn in himself—the last two weeks of October, before the sun disappeared entirely, were filled with giddy play. Miniature ice cottages rose on the floes, and ice castles, palaces, gated walls. To the growing village Erasmus added a model of his father's house, building another, larger and finer, when the ice shifted and crumbled the walls. Dr. Boerhaave built a version of the castle in Edinburgh, and Zeke one of Independence Hall. Mr.

Francis and Mr. Tagliabeau jointly sculpted a whale, overwhelming Dr. Boerhaave's moat. Foolish acts, grown men shaping ice like children raising sandcastles—yet the intent was far from casual. Erasmus noted the men's lifted spirits, the renewed sense of camaraderie, and was filled with admiration for Zeke's instincts. Perhaps, after all, Zeke knew what he was doing.

ALTHOUGH ERASMUS NO longer put anything in Lavinia's green journal except for purely scientific observations, in his bulging letter to Copernicus he wrote:

Let me sketch one day for you, and let it stand for the whole of our autumn. Half past seven and we rise to the ship's bell, tidying ourselves and our bunks. Some of us tend to the fires; Ned cooks and we breakfast at half past eight. Then the men turn to under the direction of the mates. Clearing the decks, filling and polishing the lamps, measuring out the day's allowance of coal and fussing over our precious stoves, banking snow along the hull, chunking ice from the nearest berg for water, hanging wet clothes from the rigging on washdays—all these duties are finished by lunch. After lunch the men pace the promenade briskly, as ordered by Zeke for their health. Sometimes they play games on the ice. When there was still a bit of light, Zeke and I and Dr. Boerhaave and Joe often went out with our rifles, hoping to shoot a bear or a seal to supplement our diminishing supply of fresh meat. The light was so dim we were seldom successful, but the hunt gave us an excuse to be away from the others for a while. Sometimes we stumbled on Esquimaux artifacts; while we've as yet seen no Esquimaux, we've found remains of ancient encampments: ruins of stone huts, a part of an old sledge, pieces of a stone lamp, harpoon tips. Surrounding these, the bones of walrus and bear.

Later in the afternoon, while the men nap or whittle, play cards or repair their clothing, and while Zeke pores over his maps and books or tends to his instruments, Dr. Boerhaave and I catalog the specimens we collected earlier. We talk about what we've seen—how nature, in this place and season, is reduced to her bones. In the tropical places I visited with the Exploring Expedition all was lushness, and much obscured by overwhelming detail, but here each thing stands singly and strong. It is so, so beautiful here, despite the danger, despite the discomfort; I would never have chosen to winter here yet it's as if I was waiting my whole life to see this. I stand on the ice, I watch and watch until the dinner bell rings at six. Afterward, in hours I've come to love, we have our school.

Close the hatches, open the hatches, dry the bedding, melt ice. Cook, sleep, hunt, study, sleep. This is how my days are shaped. Joe, Ned, and I killed a bear two days ago, huge and dirty and yellow-white. Before we killed it, it almost killed us. The sun disappeared for good yesterday, October 30, but this doesn't mean, as I once imagined, that we're in continuous night. Instead the nights are black, like our nights at home, but during the days we have twilight—a few minutes less each day but even when the solstice arrives we should still have that glow at noon. The sky is like no sky I've ever seen before. Our masts and shrouds, entirely coated with ice, glimmer against that blue-gray cloth.

Zeke said, "We should use our evenings profitably. Let each of us teach what he knows."

Dr. Boerhaave began teaching the men who couldn't read their letters; Ned assisted him, wonderfully patient because he'd learned to read so recently himself. When Zeke complimented him, he said, "May I teach one of the men to cook? So we might take turns, so I'd have more time to help Erasmus and Dr. Boerhaave with their work?"

When Zeke agreed, Ned chose Barton DeSouza. During Barton's apprenticeship the crew swallowed beans as hard as pebbles, but Barton, whose beard was oddly chopped after part of it froze to his hood, took the jibes good-humoredly and soon grew competent.

Sean Hamilton gave a brief course in butchery; Dr. Boerhaave, using the same frozen carcasses, taught basic anatomy. Erasmus found it delightful to see Thomas Forbes, usually so quiet, arguing with Robert Carey over whether the bone on the table between them was a femur or a fibula. Twice a week Erasmus spread before the men samples of all he'd gathered.

"Fucus," he said, showing them fronds from Godhavn. Isaac Bond was surprisingly interested in the different seaweeds and where they grew.

"Auk," he said. "From Lancaster Sound." Barton DeSouza was fascinated by the structure of the feathers and the quills.

As the men, in turn, taught Erasmus the whalers' names for seals and salmon and cod, he understood that theirs was a different sort of knowledge, but no less valuable than his. He began to know them one by one, and not just as the group of men who did the unpleasant tasks. Sean Hamilton was very quick; Robert Carey was slower but persistent and steady. Ivan Hruska had a wonderful, cheering laugh; Barton DeSouza, who had trouble reading, drew quickly and accurately.

Joe told stories from the Bible, rendered simple and vivid by his long practice preaching to the Esquimaux; he mingled these with tales about the tribes among whom he'd worked. He also gave Zeke language lessons and helped him compile a simple dictionary. In his tattered black book—which still, Erasmus saw, housed the most remarkable hodgepodge of scribbles and extracts and sketches and plans—Zeke noted down words and their English equivalents: *idgloo* = a house; *nanoq* = a bear; *bennesoak* = a deer when it is without its antlers. *Okipok* = the season of fast ice.

Even Captain Tyler and the mates, who usually held themselves separate, were drawn into those pleasant evenings. Mr. Francis demonstrated a whole array of seamen's knots, while Captain Tyler taught some basic navigation. In the darkness Mr. Tagliabeau, who had a wonderful eye for the stars, led groups to the tops of the icebergs. In air so cold their breath formed clouds of snow crystals, he pointed out the whirling constellations.

The second time he did this Erasmus left his outer mitts off for too long while he sketched: November 29, at eight P.M. He froze all but the little finger on his left hand, and the next day woke to find giant blood blisters extending from the tips past the second joints. The blisters ruptured a few days later, rendering his cracked and bloody hands useless for more than a week. But he was lucky, Dr. Boerhaave said; the flesh never blackened or died. Zeke held Erasmus's hands up before the men, pointing out the oozing blood and enormous swelling.

"This is what you must guard against," Zeke said. "This is what happens when you're careless."

Zeke lectured on the open polar sea. Erasmus thought the men would resent this, since the search for it was what had trapped them here. Yet they seemed interested. During their whaling days they'd all seen the open patches of water persisting strangely amid the ice and swarming with fish and sea creatures. Both Ivan Hruska and Captain Tyler had, on earlier trips, seen narwhals crowded into a small polynya, with their horns pointed straight up in the air as their bodies were crammed together.

"The theory of an open polar sea stems from ancient times," Zeke told them. In the lamplight, with his beard shining and his cheekbones flushed, he looked like a young soldier. He made his own heat, he was often sweating. In the cabin he opened his shirt to the waist while others huddled in their jackets.

He held up a diagram of ocean currents. "Parry and others have shown that there are two sites of maximum cold on the globe, one for each hemisphere, both situated near the eightieth parallel. The isothermals projected around these points make it seem likely that, within an encircling barrier of ice, the sea remains perpetually open around the region of the pole." Sabine barked, a tiny exclamation point. By then Erasmus had grown so used to her presence that he hardly registered her bounding over the shelves while Zeke talked, or standing on the table and sniffing at the cracks around the bull's-eye, or sitting, tiny and bright-eyed and white, on Zeke's shoulders as he paced the room.

The men's spirits were good, he thought. Their days and nights were full, and their imaginations were fed by their studies, so that they seldom felt bored. Dr. Boerhaave brought out Agassiz's *Poissons fossiles* and toured the crew through the plates, translating key portions of the text for them as they gawked at the bony relics.

"Nature," he said, "is not random but is the product of thought, planning, and intelligence. The entire history of creation has been wisely ordained."

From extinct fishes he leapt to Thoreau; a great collector of turtles and trout, Dr. Boerhaave said. An avid reader of explorers' accounts, and a good friend of Agassiz's. Erasmus was the one who suggested he share with the men the contents of the books and essays he'd collected in Concord. On the night when Dr. Boerhaave lectured on Thoreau's essay on civil disobedience, Erasmus saw attention on every face.

"There is a higher law than civil law," Dr. Boerhaave said. "The law of conscience. When these laws are in conflict, Thoreau argues that it is our duty to obey the voice of God within rather than that of external authority." He held a tattered magazine in his hand: *Aesthetic Papers*. The first and only issue. Robert Carey raised his hand. "What is 'aesthetic'?" he said.

LATER, ERASMUS WOULD look back on those calm months and wonder what had brought an end to them. Just hardship, he would think. Enough hardship to disrupt the balance of any small community. As the solstice approached the weather bit at them. Routinely it was twenty-five degrees below zero, then thirty below, then colder, with a wind that licked through clothes and walls.

Pacing with Dr. Boerhaave on Zeke's promenade, Erasmus would watch his friend's beard, eyebrows, and lashes grow a crisp white frost, while icicles hung from his moustache and lower lip. They talked to keep their minds off the cold. Not of home, nor their friends and families, nor women—what would have been the point? Better to avoid any topic that would have drowned them in homesickness. They explored each other's minds. In the light of the stars and the moon, the landscape glimmered indistinctly and edges disappeared, until they could imagine themselves at the moment of Creation. Could it be, Dr. Boerhaave asked, that the earth and stars and the planets and their moons had all condensed from swirling clouds of gas? And that these condensations developed constantly toward man?

The intricate joints of the hand, Erasmus said. The amazing complexities of the eye. From such everyday miracles one might infer a Creator. The hand and eye are but manifestations, Dr. Boerhaave replied. The Creator and the great design are the ultimate reality.

Their old difference rose again. A species, Erasmus said, was the collection of all individuals resembling each other more than they resemble others, and producing fertile offspring; presumably all descending from a single individual. A species, said Dr. Boerhaave as he whirled his arms in circles, was a thought in the mind of God. Everything on earth was just as God had created it, during the biblical six days and again in subsequent, successive creations after catastrophes similar to the biblical flood. Each new set of living beings was progressively more complex.

"Look at Cuvier," he said.

"Look at Lyell," Erasmus retorted.

Talking grew difficult; their beards froze to their neckerchiefs and saliva sealed their lips. The wind tore tears from their eyes and froze their lids together.

On December 21, all they saw of the sun was a red glow at noon. The cabin walls began to drip moisture; the men's furs, dusted with snow and ice, drooped damply when they came inside and stiffened when they went out again. The weakest of the men—Robert Carey, who'd never completely recovered from the dunking that had killed Nils Jensen; Ivan Hruska, who'd always had the stunted look of an undernourished boy—grew reluctant to leave their bunks in the morning and claimed an assortment of aches and congestions. The night school fell apart.

They were hungry, Erasmus thought. Or not so much hungry as filled with violent lusts for all they couldn't have. The meat in the rigging was gone by then, and Joe could find nothing to shoot. Ned and Barton tried their hardest to make appetizing meals, but everything began to taste alike. Dr. Boerhaave took Erasmus aside and said, "You know, you're remarkably pale. Are you feeling all right?"

Erasmus stared at his friend's face, as white as a boiled potato, then looked around at the others. Each complexion was waxy and pale, except where the cold had bitten crusty sores. Four of the men complained of shortness of breath.

"With your permission," Dr. Boerhaave said to Zeke, "I'd like to make a brief medical inspection of the crew each Sunday."

"No one's sick," Zeke said, frowning. "We're doing well."

"No one's sick," Dr. Boerhaave agreed. "Yet. But as ship's surgeon I'd like to take this extra precaution, so nothing gets hidden until it's serious."

"I don't want to encourage malingering," Zeke said. "We can't coddle ourselves up here."

Dr. Boerhaave pressed his lips together. "I simply think it's wise to check them regularly." Zeke shook his head.

Although Erasmus agreed with Dr. Boerhaave's caution, he

understood Zeke's reluctance as well; any acknowledgment of sickness made the men nervous. So did the darkness, and the daily task of scraping from bunks and bulkheads the frost that formed from their breath while they slept. It was disturbing, Erasmus thought, to watch the air that had lived inside their lungs turn into buckets of dirty ice. Tossing the shavings over the side, he felt as if he were discarding parts of himself.

SABINE THE FOX was cleaning herself in the tub of snow Zeke kept on deck for her delight. Even those who disliked having her in the cabin were charmed by her habit of burrowing her nose into the snow, tossing it over her back and hindquarters, and then rubbing herself with her paws. She was watching, unconcerned, as Sean and Ivan lugged a scuttle of ice to the melting funnel on the day before Christmas. Then Sean tripped, dropping his side of the scuttle, and Ivan slipped on the spilled ice and fell, thrashing his arms and his legs just as Barton emerged through the hatchway. Ivan's arm knocked Sabine from her tub and hurled her through the air: and in an instant she'd bounced off Barton's thighs and tumbled down the hatch.

She broke both hind legs. Zeke, who rushed from his bunk at the sound of her howls, was too busy comforting her to be of any practical help. Although Erasmus knew he should wring her neck right then, Zeke talked him and Dr. Boerhaave into splinting her bones and then dribbled water from a spoon down her mouth all day. Still he couldn't save her. He wrapped her in a length of gray flannel and buried her under a pile of stones near the promenade. He squatted next to the stones; he wouldn't come in. Erasmus had to go out after him.

"Zeke?" he said. "They've made dinner for us, Christmas Eve dinner. You can't let them down . . ."

Zeke brushed his outstretched hand aside. "Can't I simply

have a minute alone?" He exhaled a cloud of frost, shaking his head as he rose. "All right," he said. "Let's go be *cheerful*."

Joe had hidden seven ptarmigan, which he roasted with the help of Ned: half a bird to a man, a splendid change from salt pork. Isaac, Thomas, Robert, and Barton had secreted a portion of their flour and lard rations for the past several weeks, and with these supplies, and the dried cherries and raisins Sean contributed, they made a delicious duff. Erasmus brought out two of the plum puddings donated by a neighbor at home; Dr. Boerhaave prescribed from the medical stores two bottles of cognac, to protect them all from indigestion.

They ate and drank with good humor, despite Zeke sitting glum at the head of the table, and despite the silence falling after a memorial toast to Nils Jensen and Fletcher Lamb. Isaac pulled himself together and elbowed Barton. "A joke!" he cried. "Every man must tell a joke!"

Barton shook himself and told a coarse story about a one-legged man and a singer. Thomas responded with a joke about a carpenter and a cow. Around the table they went, all except Zeke; when silence fell again Mr. Francis and Mr. Tagliabeau led a round of whaler's songs. Then Ivan flourished his napkin and said to the officers, "Please take your seats in the theater."

Up on deck, under the housing, the men had arranged meat casks and boxes for seats and marked off a stage with a row of candles. In great secrecy they'd gotten up a little skit for the officers, prancing about in the freezing air with their fur jackets tied about their waists like skirts, and their shirts pulled open and tucked down to form flounces around their hairy bosoms. Bulky Sean played a young beauty; Ivan and Barton her jealous older sisters; serious Thomas her mother; and Robert and Isaac the two suitors competing for the beauty's hand as they fended off the sisters' advances. As the melodrama concluded with the duel of Robert and Isaac, frowning and slashing the air with their jack-knives, Sean stood on a candle box and shrieked so shrilly that Erasmus could hardly see for laughing.

Afterward Captain Tyler and the mates brought out the last surprise—three bottles of excellent port. Even as the men fell on it gratefully, and as Erasmus sipped his own delicious ration, he wondered where it had come from. Captain Tyler's bleary-eyed mornings, his snoring deep sleep—had he a private supply of spirits? Erasmus saw Zeke look down at the cup he'd just held to his lips and come to the same realization.

"Captain Tyler," he said coldly. "What is the meaning of this?"

"It's Christmas," the captain said, grinning and waving one of the bottles. "Relax yourself a bit. Celebrate. It is very fine port, is it not?"

"We are carrying no port."

Captain Tyler shrugged. "No ship's captain would travel without a small private stock," he said. "What I do with it is my own business. And what I choose to do with it tonight is share it with our fine crew."

"You are in on this?" Zeke said, turning to Mr. Francis and Mr. Tagliabeau. "I object to this. Very, very strongly."

"More music!" Mr. Francis said. Gathering the men on the makeshift stage, he started up a sailor's hornpipe. Joe played his zither, the men sang and danced, Captain Tyler joined them. Erasmus followed Zeke outside, where they gazed at one another and then at the moon. A complete halo hung around it, with the arc of another perched on top of the first like a crescent headdress.

"More snow on the way," Zeke said gloomily.

Erasmus wished he could join the frolicking men. The invisible ice crystals filling the air and bending the moon's rays made Zeke's face look ghastly; Erasmus turned his eyes back to the sky.

"Homesick?" he asked. "Lavinia should be lighting the candles on the tree about now. Serving eggnog, and those little gin-ger cookies our mother used to make. Maybe the rest of the family is there and someone's playing the piano . . ."

"Torture yourself," Zeke said. "Go ahead."

"SHOW HIM YOUR gums," Dr. Boerhaave said, standing Sean and Barton in front of Zeke one January Sunday.

Obediently they opened their mouths. "See that?" Dr. Boerhaave said. Zeke leaned toward Sean. "How puffy and red the gums are in the back?"

"And I have a loose tooth," Barton said, reaching up with his right hand. "Here."

Zeke shook his head. "I know," he said. "We need fresh meat. Joe's been out looking for bear every day this week but he's seen nothing yet." Then he returned to his charts. He was making elaborate maps of the coastline, naming every wrinkle.

"My knees and shoulders are aching badly," Dr. Boerhaave said to Erasmus later. "How are yours?"

"Not bad." But he lifted his shirt to show Dr. Boerhaave the dark, bruiselike discoloration spreading down his left side.

"Ned has patches like that all over his arms," Dr. Boerhaave said. "Ivan's old harpoon scar is beginning to ooze. I fear we're in for real trouble." He and Erasmus went through the storehouse and suggested to Zeke that small portions of the few remaining raw potatoes and a little lime juice be added to the daily rations. They worried that everything was running short.

Erasmus counted items again and again, comparing what was left against his lists. All his work and planning, and still he'd miscalculated. Already the candles were almost finished, as was the lamp oil. Joe had made some Esquimaux lamps, which he fueled with the blubber he'd put down in the fall; these helped stretch the candles but were smoky and covered everything with soot. The coal was low enough that they had to ration it and could no longer keep the cabin so comfortably warm. Erasmus found plenty of beans and salt beef and pork, but Dr. Boerhaave said these were exactly the worst things for men beginning to suffer from the scurvy. They needed fresh food, and couldn't get it.

When Erasmus showed Zeke a detailed accounting of their stores, Zeke blamed the shortages on him. "All those days you were fretting in Philadelphia," he said. "How could we have ended up like this?"

Erasmus couldn't answer him. The obvious answer—that they hadn't meant to overwinter—he'd long since realized wasn't true; more and more he understood that Zeke had plotted since the beginning to search for an open polar sea. Only living members of Franklin's expedition could have kept him from this ambition. Zeke had insisted they stock the ship *as if* they might have to overwinter, *as if* they might need these supplies in an emergency, and Erasmus couldn't blame their present straits on ignorance. Somehow, despite all his lists, he'd made mistakes. He hadn't realized how ravenous the cold and the boredom and the physical labor would make them, or how little they could depend on hunting.

Dr. Boerhaave joined Erasmus in the storehouse one dark morning when he was counting the tinned soups for the third time. "This isn't your fault," he said.

Erasmus shook his head. "Then whose fault is it? If I'd planned better . . ."

"Blame Commander Voorhees," Dr. Boerhaave said. "It's *his* expedition, as he never fails to remind us." With his mittened hands he pushed aside a sack of flour and sat on a crate of salt beef.

Erasmus looked down at the array of tins. "I can't . . . don't put me in that position."

"I'm sorry," Dr. Boerhaave said. "I admire your loyalty—I just don't like to see you blaming yourself. He doesn't listen to anyone, he's so preoccupied with his own ambitions that he doesn't think things through. If he'd told us from the beginning we were going to winter up here . . . how could you know what to plan for, if he didn't tell you?"

Erasmus fiddled with the smoking wick in the lamp. "I have to do the best I can," he said. "I promised my sister." One end of the wick sank in the melted blubber, reducing the light to a flicker. "But why *didn't* he just tell me?" he burst out.

"Why indeed?" Dr. Boerhaave said. In the gloom something scuttled along the wall; perhaps a rat. "He sits in there with his papers and leaves you to sort out his mistakes."

Erasmus tried to think of something positive. "In the fall," he pointed out, "he was wonderful about organizing the men."

"And since Sabine's death," Dr. Boerhaave said, "he's been lost in his own world again."

IT WAS TRUE what Dr. Boerhaave had said; some days Zeke seemed to have abandoned his command. Yet even with this to worry about, Erasmus was sometimes peculiarly, privately happy. The animals had disappeared and the landscape was empty: not a plant, not a creature, not an insect or a particle of mold. The only living things he saw besides the men were the rats infesting the brig and the storehouse, further diminishing their supplies. But one day he stood with Dr. Boerhaave and saw sheets of light undulating like seaweeds in the sky. The ice where they stood was bluish gray, the immobilized icebergs a darker gray, the hills in the distance a friendly, velvety black. As he and Dr. Boerhaave discussed what they saw, the arctic's simultaneous sparseness and richness seemed to unfold. In his mind the long journey they'd made, and the plants and animals they'd collected, fell into a beautiful pattern. The dwarfed low willows and birches, hugging the ground to evade the blasting winds; the great masses of mosses and lichens and the sorrel growing like tiny rhubarbs; the small rodents skilled at burrowing—"It all forms a kind of rhythm," Erasmus said, and Dr. Boerhaave agreed. The fact that they didn't fit into it made it no less beautiful.

In Lavinia's journal—what could Zeke's contract mean now?—Erasmus began making extensive notes for a natural history book. Meanwhile Dr. Boerhaave wrote in his medical log:

These signs of scurvy so far—
Captain Tyler: abdominal pains, swollen liver, gout in right foot. Mr. Francis: tubercles on three finger joints, accompanied by pain and stiffness. Mr. Tagliabeau: right premolar lost, other teeth loose, bleeding gums. Seaman Bond: purpurae on forearms. Seaman Carey: left knee grossly swollen; reports a sprain there as a child. Seaman Forbes: bleeding gums. Seaman Hruska: serous discharge from old lance wound. Ned Kynd: excoriated tongue, bruises on both arms.

Mr. Wells has those bruises on his side; now I have a few myself. Our lime juice is almost exhausted. I've been prescribing vinegar, sauerkraut, and a dilute solution of hydrochloric acid: all I have left by way of antiscorbutics. Our commander, who has no symptoms at all, prescribes daily exercise on the promenade. And a cheerful attitude.

He closed the log and picked up his journal. Still he loved to touch it; a smooth tan spine, with elegant marbled paper on the boards. He'd brought it with him all the way from Edinburgh. Whatever he put here Zeke would read; he couldn't put anything he meant: he copied into it six pages of Thoreau's essay "A Winter Walk," just for the pleasure of hearing the words in his head, shaping them with his pen. He put his head down on the cover, amid creamy moons haloed with red and green swirls, and slept.

ROBERT CAREY WAS crying. Erasmus found him wedged between two crates, his knees tucked under his chin as tears rolled down his face. To Erasmus's gentle questions he said nothing. Hours later, when he still wouldn't stop crying, Dr. Boerhaave gave him some laudanum and carried him to bed. Then Ivan Hruska said no one ever paid attention to him, that his fellow seamen ganged up on him and teased him mercilessly. Everyone preferred Robert, Ivan said, everyone coddled him; he rolled himself in his hammock and refused food until Dr. Boerhaave threatened to put a tube down his throat. Sean and Thomas got into a fistfight. Barton let the galley fire go out. There were arguments, then long tense silences.

One night Erasmus, alone in the cabin, heard from the other side of the stove an unfamiliar, nasty, muffled laughter. He stepped through the gap in the partitions to investigate and came upon a reprise of the Christmas skit, transposed into a coarser key. Isaac, as the successful suitor, had opened his fly and was waving his thick erect penis at Sean, who was rolling his eyes in maidenly shock. In the background Barton, as one of the jealous sisters, was swishing his hips. "Give *me* some of that," he was hissing, while Isaac gasped with laughter. "Let *me* . . ." He fell silent when Sean, who saw Erasmus first, elbowed him in the chest.

"Just having a little fun," Isaac said. He tucked himself back in his pants. "Can't hold that against us, can you?"

Erasmus didn't know what to say. Between the cold and the stress and the hunger his own penis felt like a tired leather tube, shrinking away from his hand each time he tried to urinate. What was all this urgent flesh? Before he had time to wonder if the playacting was play, or something more serious, Zeke stepped around the stove and joined him.

"What's going on?" he said. He blinked as if he'd just awakened.

The men were silent, apparently abashed.

"Nothing," Erasmus said. "Just a little . . . a little quarrel." Clumsy lie.

"I won't have that," Zeke said. "We're all uncomfortable. But we must stick together, we must be cheerful." When he turned his back, Isaac grabbed his crotch mockingly.

ON JANUARY 24 the southern horizon glowed reddish orange, before fading away in a violet haze. This hint that the sun would return seemed to rouse Zeke at last, although not in a way Erasmus would have chosen.

At dinner Zeke said, "We'll have sun in another month and a half, but we won't be able to free the brig until July, at the earliest. I propose we occupy the spring months with sledge trips north. It's unfortunate about the dogs. But we can pull the sledges ourselves, and the ice belt along the shore will be in excellent shape in April and May. We can examine the coastline north of here, we can follow the trend of the Sound and look for the open polar sea."

Captain Tyler laughed wildly. "If you think we're going to pull sledges like draft horses, that we'll go one inch further north with you . . ."

"You will go where I say," Zeke said. And left the cabin, to walk the promenade in the dark.

Erasmus threw on all his clothes and followed him, too angry to feel the cold although the thermometer outside the observatory read fifty below. "Why did you do *that*?" he shouted, even before he'd reached Zeke. "You couldn't have made the men more anxious if you'd tried."

Zeke continued pacing, leaving a fog trail behind him.

"What is it you *want*?"

Zeke stopped and turned to face him. "What do you think?" As he spoke his face disappeared inside the cloud his breath created. "I want my *name* on something," he called. "Something *big*—is that so hard to understand? I want my name on the map. Your father would have understood."

"My father is dead!" Erasmus called back. "Why would you want to endanger yourself and the rest of us more than you already have?"

Zeke shook his head and his face disappeared again. "Don't turn against me," he said. "Everyone else is—don't you know how much you and your family mean to me?" When the cloud blew away his eyebrows jutted out, entirely white. "Your house was where I grew up," Zeke said more quietly. Now Erasmus stood by his side. "Where I learned everything important. You and your father . . ."

"If something happened to you," Erasmus said, "Lavinia would die. Don't you worry about her?"

"Of course," Zeke said. "About her, and you and your brothers, and what you think of me—I've always wanted to be part of your family, for all of you to be proud of me. If I led a successful sledge trip north, everyone would see what I can do."

"Lavinia loves you no matter what," Erasmus said. What was all this talk about his family? A man in love, a man engaged, might be a little more romantic. "Surely you understand that?"

Zeke's frosted eyebrows drew together. "The men need to get used to the idea," he said. "We're going north."

ERASMUS THOUGHT HE had several months to talk Zeke out of his useless plan; meanwhile he must do what he could to lift the men's spirits. When the sun approached during the second week of February, he and Joe and Dr. Boerhaave took a party out to meet it. They clambered up the hill behind the brig, up and over the two beyond. An arc of light split the horizon, violet and lavender merging into rich brown clouds. Then the shining disk broke free, perched on an icy range. They opened their jackets, the briefest moment, the pale rays touching their throats. Barton cried at the sight, and Isaac pointed at the giant shadows they cast on the snow.

It cheered them, Erasmus thought. He was cheered himself and afterward saw mirages for hours, blue and green and pink balls of light. That night they all ate in some semblance of harmony.

When he woke at three A.M. and heard a faint noise, Erasmus thought at first that he was dreaming. The cabin was dark but for the gleam of one tiny blubber lamp. The fire was banked in the stove; Mr. Francis, who had the watch, had fallen asleep at the table. The curtain to his bunk was open but the others were closed and appeared undisturbed. Erasmus couldn't see beyond the stove, but he heard no sound from the men's quarters. The noise was above him, distinctly above him. He put on his boots and his furs and made his way up the ladder.

The noise ceased before he came out on deck. It was completely dark under the housing, much colder than in the cabin but not nearly so cold as it must be outside, where the wind was singing in the shrouds. He hadn't brought a lantern with him, and he would have slipped back down had he not heard another noise just then: a sort of snort or gasp.

"Who's that?" he said sharply.

Someone laughed.

"Speak up," Erasmus said. "Who's out here?"

More laughter, from more than one voice. Then, "Me. Isaac." And "Robert." And "Ivan."

A scuffle, some whispers, a giggle. "All *right*. Me, too—Thomas."

"You're sitting in the dark?" Erasmus said. "What are you doing?" He had a horrid memory of Isaac prancing around, half-clothed. "Who else is here?"

"Me" came a voice from the bow. "Barton."

And Robert—it was Robert who couldn't stop giggling—said, "Sean and Ned are here too."

"Ned?" Erasmus said. Sensible Ned. "Are you trying to kill yourselves?"

"Ssh," Ned said, from behind him. "Whisper."

He lit a candle stub, revealing the men in the feeble light. Bundled up in their fur suits and further wrapped in buffalo robes, they were huddled against the rough plank walls, far too sick and worn for any prancing. They'd been telling stories instead, Erasmus guessed, reliving memories from what seemed like another life. Some had had adventures on Boothia, which Erasmus had envied even through his disapproval: *I spent a night in a tent with a young widow; the breasts of mine were tattooed; mine was warm, warm, warm*—Thomas Forbes, Sean Hamilton, Ivan Hruska. Erasmus moved among them, coming to rest against the stovepipe housing.

"We're warming ourselves," Barton said. "And celebrating the return of the sun."

He held out a teacup with a broken handle, into which Erasmus peered. Water. He sipped, choked, sipped again: raw alcohol. Not Captain Tyler's port, nor Zeke's whiskey, nor Dr. Boerhaave's medicinal Madeira or cognac, which were in any case kept carefully locked away. He looked at the faces, scabby and marked by scurvy spots, bleary-eyed, relaxed. "Where did you get *this*?"

Robert laughed so hard he fell against Ivan. "It's what you put the fishes in!" he said. "The fishes and the little things you bring up from the seafloor."

"I took it," Sean admitted. "From the cabinet, last night." He held up an old oil bottle, half full of Erasmus's preserving alcohol.

"You drained it from my specimens?" Erasmus said. "Once you break the seals and drain off the alcohol the specimens are ruined, just *ruined* . . ."

"We wouldn't do that," Ned said. "Sean took one of the unused bottles of spirits."

"Lucky me," Erasmus said. He sipped again; the strong spirits burned the sores on his tongue.

"Lucky us, I'd say," Barton added. "Who wants to drink essence of dead fish?"

The men writhed with stifled laughter. "This is so bad for you," Erasmus said. "Never mind what Commander Voorhees would say if he caught you—alcohol only makes you *feel* warm, you'll all get frostbite." He took the candle from Ned and moved toward Ivan. "Let me see your hands and your face."

Ivan pushed his hood back and held out his hands. His left little finger and the flesh below it were waxy white, and another dead-white patch shone beside his nose. Erasmus groaned. "Look at this." He passed the candle to Sean. "Each of you look at your neighbor and see if anyone else has frozen spots."

Only Isaac did, a patch at the base of one thumb. Erasmus told Ned to hold his hand over Isaac's, while he placed his own on Ivan's frozen flesh. Still they were all speaking quietly; and still everyone but him was sipping from the teacup and the bottle. "We must all go down now," Erasmus said. "I'll decide whether to tell Commander Voorhees about this in the morning."

"It's only a little celebration," Ned said in his ear. "We have small enough chance for it . . ."

And this was true, Erasmus knew. The men were smiling; their quarrels forgotten, their bad humor gone. Was it so bad, what they'd done? He'd been unable to sleep himself, bored and cabin-sick below, and up here where the air was fresher and no one was fighting it was amazingly pleasant. He lifted his hands; Ivan's frozen spots seemed to have thawed without damage.

"Couldn't we stay a bit longer?" Barton wheedled. "You're welcome to stay with us."

He knew he shouldn't; he knew he ought to order them below, or discipline them, or at least not condone what they were doing by his presence. But he felt as if he'd stepped outside time for a minute, as if all the pressures of the last few months had dropped away. He sat; he took the offered teacup. He listened without comment as the men mocked Zeke and his plans for sledge trips, and he told himself that by doing so he was letting them blow off steam. He felt warmer after the teacup passed his way. Ned sat beside him and spread a buffalo robe over both of them, so that his legs warmed and his face radiated against the cool air. Barton passed around some pemmican—where had he gotten this? It was hidden in the storehouse, deep in a cask, only for use on sledge trips—and Erasmus chewed dreamily.

The men spoke about other trips, whales and seals they'd taken, bad captains and good. Ned told about his travels in the Adirondack Mountains, and Barton about a trip to Portugal. It was cold, Erasmus knew it was cold, but he was warm and every time he meant to rise and lead them into the cabin someone was telling a story, which he didn't want to interrupt. The candle burned out and they sat in darkness, listening to each other. Each, despite the shape of his story, saying the same thing: *I am here. I am here, I am here.*

When the hatch door popped open, the sound was as shocking as the lamplight flooding out. Zeke, showing first his hair and then his face and torso and legs, a rifle cradled in his arms, rose among them as if from a grave.

"What's going on?" he said. "Visitors? Are there Esquimaux?" His yellow hair was matted with sleep; his jacket was open and his boots unlaced.

Erasmus stood, surprised at his own unsteadiness. "Everything's fine," he said soothingly. "None of the men could sleep, so they came up here where their talk wouldn't disturb the rest of us. I woke a while ago and came up to make sure they were all right."

Zeke held the lantern high, scanning Erasmus's face; then he bent and swung it before the sitting men. Barton's eyes were swollen, Sean's cheeks were red, Ivan still had the bottle in his hand. "You're *drinking*!" he said. "Without permission, in the middle of the night . . ." He spun toward Erasmus again. "Even you," he said. "Even you."

Erasmus was looking down at his boots when Zeke's rifle, slashing horizontally through the air, caught him square in the gut. He fell against the rail, unable to catch his breath.

"What is *wrong* with you?" Zeke shouted. "I try and try to take care of you, to keep us all safe and in shape to accomplish something in the spring, and while I'm sleeping you sneak off like thieves. Wait until Captain Tyler sees this, what our laxity has come to . . ." He hurled himself back down the ladder and returned a minute later, even angrier.

"Mr. Francis is asleep at his post," he said to Erasmus. "Or passed out; his breath stinks of wine. Captain Tyler is lying in his bunk in a drunken stupor and can't even raise his head—was this your idea? Or did Tyler and Francis set out to corrupt you all? I *knew* they were drinking . . ."

"I," Erasmus gasped, still unable to catch his breath. "I . . ."

"We had nothing to do with the captain," Barton interrupted. "That's the captain's own supply, he only shares now and then . . ."

"You're hateful," Zeke said. "All of you. You can't be trusted with anything, you have no pride, no discipline, no sense of *esprit de corps*."

"It was the sun they were celebrating," Erasmus said. "They shouldn't have taken the alcohol but it was harmless, really, and I'd just about persuaded them to return to bed when you arrived."

"You," Zeke said.

He lowered himself a few steps down the ladder. "If I could I'd toss you all outside on the ice," he said. "But that would make me a murderer. You'll not see your beds for the remainder of the night, though. You like it so much up here, you stay here till breakfast." He slammed the hatch cover behind him, bolting it from the inside.

The men laughed drunkenly, amused at Zeke's display of temper and aware, Erasmus thought, of Zeke's temporary powerlessness. Up here all the traditional punishments were useless. They were already on short rations, and Zeke couldn't reduce them further without risking their lives; they couldn't be set on the shore in solitude, or confined on the brig any more than they were; they couldn't be mastheaded or set extra tasks outside: it was impossibly cold. They straddled such a fine line between life and death that they were, paradoxically, safe. Or so they seemed to think.

"We have four hours until breakfast," Erasmus said. "And it's well below freezing." He clutched his tender middle with one hand. "We have to keep moving. "

He made everyone rise. They paced the deck in a languid oval, slowing as the liquor wore off and exhaustion overtook them. Barton dropped out of the line surreptitiously, propped himself against one of the lifeboats, and snoozed. Ivan kept walking but stopped swinging his arms; Sean lost a mitten. By the time the breakfast bell rang and Mr. Francis, sheepfaced and sullen, unbolted the hatch, they'd all been frostnipped: a heel, some fingers; lips, cheeks, a chin.

Later Zeke railed at them and then demanded that Erasmus turn over all his preserving alcohol, and Dr. Boerhaave all his medicinal brandy and Madeira. These he locked ostentatiously away. From Captain Tyler he demanded all his private supplies, but although the captain produced a half-case of port, no one but Zeke believed this was all he had.

"I'm *sorry*," Erasmus said to Zeke: on the promenade, in the cabin, outside the latrine. Was Zeke going to hold a grudge forever?

Zeke gazed at him stonily. "You betrayed my trust."

"I was trying to *help* you," Erasmus said.

Still Zeke shunned him, speaking to him only when absolutely necessary. At night, inside the cabin, the air was hazed with tension. Joe, who'd slept through the disastrous party, pitched a caribou-skin tent beneath the plank housing and began sleeping there. Dr. Boerhaave began reading a chapter of *David Copperfield* out loud each night—a way, he told Erasmus, of binding everyone together and lightening the mood. But only Ned, ashamed of his role and frightened by Zeke's frigid mood, joined Erasmus in apologizing outright.

TIRED, HUNGRY, SCURVY-ridden, they moved through March in a pale imitation of their old routine. The sun, now hanging a few degrees above the horizon and gilding the mountains, cheered them despite the continued cold. They ate pickled cabbage, hardtack, salt pork and beef; all their fresh meat was gone. Zeke continued to draw up plans for sledge trips and Ned, somewhat shamefaced, helped him, thawing casks of pemmican and repacking it into small bags. He no longer helped Erasmus and Dr. Boerhaave with their work; Zeke kept him busy all the time, assisting with the meteorological records as well as the travel preparations.

One morning Zeke took Ned to determine the condition of the ice belt north of them. As soon as they left, the mood lightened on the brig. Joe trapped two foxes that afternoon, which Erasmus and Dr. Boerhaave were helping him skin and butcher. Everyone was looking forward to dinner when Zeke and Ned returned, carrying with them a human skull.

"We found an Esquimaux grave," Zeke said, resting the skull on the capstan like a prize. "Three mummified bodies wrapped in skins, and this—isn't it something?"

Erasmus, easing a fox hide from its tricky attachment over the heel, looked at Dr. Boerhaave, who was blotting the blood. Only months ago, Zeke had refused to touch the graves of Franklin's crew. Dr. Boerhaave, as if he heard what Erasmus was thinking, raised an eyebrow. Those had been the graves of Englishmen.

Joe stuck his knife into one of the fox haunches and examined the skull: brown, stained, old. "You broke open a grave?"

"It was already open," Zeke said. "Some bears had pushed away the rocks at the foot."

"And you moved the rest," Joe said.

Zeke rested his hand on the skull, looking away from the fox parts. Yet he would eat with the rest of them, Erasmus knew. No matter how sharply he remembered Sabine. He would have to eat.

"We did," Zeke said. "What was the harm in that? When we try out our sledges, I mean to bring one of those mummies back, for the museum at home."

"It's *wrong*," Joe said. "The spirits of these people can't rest if their graves are disturbed."

Joe stared at Zeke and Zeke stared back, until Joe left the deck.

Ned picked up Joe's knife and Joe's task, trying to shape pieces that would be appetizing and not resemble fox. Afterward he stood silently at the stove, although he would rather have helped Erasmus prepare the skins. *Sew up from the inside any bullet or knife holes*, Erasmus had taught him. He'd made notes. *Rub on the inside of the skin as much of the mixture of alum and arsenic as will stick there. Wrap a little oakum around the bones of each leg, to keep them away from the skin.*

But Erasmus was working away without him, not even asking if he wanted to help. After supper, though, Erasmus joined him on his nightly walk to fetch clean ice from the Follies. "I appreciate what you're trying to do," Erasmus said.

"Do you even *know*?" Ned asked.

"I know you're trying to keep Commander Voorhees company," Erasmus said. "Make him feel less isolated. He's still angry at me, he won't confide in me. I know you're trying to take up the slack."

"Something's wrong with him," Ned said. "He talked all day while we were out, he feels like everyone's against him. Someone has to listen to him."

They'd reached the first iceberg; together they began prying off chunks and heaving them into the washbasin. "My father got like this," Ned said. "Living on dreams, cut off from everyone. Flailing out at anyone around the minute he was criticized."

"It helps us all, what you do," Erasmus said. "Whatever you can do to calm him."

Ned made a face. Each time Ned did something like this, Erasmus realized, even a day's walk with Zeke, he set himself off both from the other men and from Captain Tyler and the mates. Soon he'd be stranded. As they dragged the ice back to the brig, Erasmus reminded himself that he and Dr. Boerhaave must be particularly careful to include Ned in their activities.

Inside the cabin Captain Tyler, who used to sit almost on top of the stove, positioned halfway between the men and the officers, glanced slyly at Erasmus and shifted his stool all the way to the men's side of the partitions. He'd been doing this for weeks: murmuring, murmuring—what was he saying?

"Can you hear him?" Erasmus whispered to Ned.

"I can't," Ned said. He packed the ice more tightly in the melting funnel. "He never does that when I'm in there."

Erasmus strained his ears, pretending unconcern when Mr. Francis and Mr. Tagliabeau slipped through the gap as well. Zeke was pacing the promenade, guarding the brig against nothing and no one with his rifle in his arms—unaware, Erasmus thought, that his command was slipping away. There would be no sledge trips, Erasmus heard Captain Tyler telling the men. Was that what he heard? We'll be out of here the instant the ice breaks up. Low laughter followed. Only when Dr. Boerhaave came in and said, "Are you feeling sick?" did Erasmus realize he was clutching his stomach.

Later, after everyone else had gone to bed, Erasmus and Dr. Boerhaave sat at the cabin table by the sputtering light of a salt-pork lamp. They couldn't talk about what was going on; anyone might be awake and listening.

"Try to do some work," Dr. Boerhaave said. "You'll feel better."

For a second he rested his hand on Erasmus's forearm. He was breathing slowly and deeply: in, out, in, out, looking into Erasmus's eyes. Erasmus felt his own breathing steady into a rhythm that matched his friend's. He took out his letter case and wrote to Copernicus about that skull, so delicate and troubling; halfway through, he found himself writing instead about Ned's attempts to calm Zeke. Dr. Boerhaave opened his volume of Thoreau's *A Week on the Concord and Merrimack Rivers*. Since Zeke's punishment of the drinking men, he'd begun using his journal solely to record passages from his reading. Now he copied:

"But continued traveling is far from productive. It begins with wearing away the soles of the shoes, and making the feet sore, and ere long it will wear a man clean up, after making his heart sore into the bargain. I have observed that the after life of those who have traveled much is very pathetic. True and sincere traveling is no pastime, but it is as serious as the grave, or any part of the human journey, and it requires a long probation to be broken into it."

He turned the journal so Erasmus could read what he'd written. "Thoreau gave me this copy himself," he said. "He published it at his own expense."

Erasmus, puzzled, said, "And you copy his words out because . . . ?"

"Because they're worth learning." He cast his eyes in the direction of Zeke's bunk, and for the first time Erasmus understood that Dr. Boerhaave's journal had become an act of covert rebellion.

BARTON COLLAPSED FIRST, then Ivan, then Isaac; Sean and Thomas were very weak and after Mr. Francis fell down the ladder, tearing a chunk of flesh from his knee, the wound refused to heal and he too was confined to bed. Those who could keep to their feet nursed the others, preparing and serving meals and emptying slops and laundering bandages, drawn together again by their common crisis. They weren't starving, exactly: they still had food, although it was the wrong sort. Joe stalked a bear but lost it. There were walrus, he suspected, south of the brig, but as yet he'd seen none. He'd had no luck trapping since that anomalous pair of foxes.

Erasmus, moving among the sick as Dr. Boerhaave's chief assistant, was shocked at how quickly Mr. Francis deteriorated. The wound bled, suppurated, refused to close, deepened; in a week the bone was exposed. Captain Tyler sat with him for hours, and Erasmus was touched by this kindness until the afternoon when, bending over Mr. Francis shortly after the captain left him, he smelled brandy and realized his stupor was not just the result of infection.

Outside, far from Zeke, Erasmus seized Captain Tyler by the arms and shook him. "What are you doing?" he said. "Drink yourself to death, for all I care—but how can you give that poor man spirits? It's the worst thing for him, the very worst thing."

Captain Tyler pulled away with a growl. "Lay hands on me again," he said. "Touch me like that again and . . . Mr. Francis is a dead man. Why shouldn't he have some comfort in his last days? Dr. Boerhaave spares the laudanum—for you, for his *friends*, we're all going to die up here and he wants to make sure your last days are peaceful. The brandy eases my friend."

Two days later Mr. Francis died in his sleep. Thomas was too sick to work, but Ned and Robert managed to put together a rough coffin. Captain Tyler, Mr. Tagliabeau, Erasmus, and Zeke carried the body to the storehouse, and Zeke read the service for the burial of the dead, although they couldn't bury him. Later Erasmus, packing up Mr. Francis's effects, looked briefly at his journal before handing it over to Zeke.

March 2: Snow and fog. I have no energy.
March 3: More snow. Slept all day.
March 4: Wind, very much wind. Could not sleep and felt tired all day.
March 5: Snow and wind. Much pain in my knee.
March 6: Clear sky, very cold. The knee is worse and there is a smell.
March 7: Colder. Fainted when Dr. B. changed my dressings.
March 8: Felt very bad.
March 9: Felt very bad. If I could only see Ellen . . .

THE DAY AFTER that bleak ceremony, Erasmus was chopping ice when five figures appeared near the tip of the point. By the time he'd raced into the cabin, alerted everyone, and gathered those who could move on the bow, the figures had reached the brig and were peering gravely up at them. Zeke greeted the Esquimaux in their own language, although he still needed Joe's help in interpreting their responses.

Ootuniah was the name of one of the men; Awahtok another. Erasmus couldn't catch the names of the three younger men, who hung behind the first pair and seemed hardly more than boys. All five were dressed in fur jackets and breeches, with high boots made from the leg skins of white bears. The men's feet, Erasmus saw, were sheltered by the bears' feet, with claws protruding like overgrown human toenails. Walking, the men left bear prints on the snow.

"They'd like to come up," Joe said, after speaking with them for a minute.

"It's too risky to let them all aboard at once," Zeke said. "Tell them one, the oldest one, may come. The others must remain outside for now."

Inside the deckhouse Ootuniah fingered Joe's tent approvingly. He opened the flap and stuck his head inside, then said something that made Joe laugh. Joe opened the hatch and led the way down the ladder, which Erasmus thought Ootuniah might find unfamiliar. But Ootuniah descended as calmly as if he'd been using ladders all his life. Inside, he opened the bunk curtains, picked up the books, fondled the stove. Erasmus saw him slip a wooden cooking spoon into his jacket.

Ootuniah squeezed between the stove and the partitions before anyone could stop him. But Dr. Boerhaave, who'd darted belowdecks as soon as he sensed what was going on, had managed to move the sick men onto stools and chests, so that they were sitting upright when Ootuniah saw them. Ootuniah smiled and said some words of greeting, which Joe translated. Then Joe added, for the men's benefit, "Don't be frightened, he's friendly."

Was he? Nothing seemed to surprise their visitor, Erasmus thought. Not the *Narwhal* itself, nor the number or condition of the crew. Dr. Boerhaave whispered to him, "What do you think of this? It's almost as if they've been keeping watch on us, and took Mr. Francis's death for a sign that we're weak enough to be approached safely."

Behind Ootuniah's back, Dr. Boerhaave signaled the men to sit up straight and smile. But when Ootuniah finally sat down at the table, the first thing he said, as Joe translated it, was, "Your people are sick. Do you have meat?"

Before him was a plate of salt pork and beans and bread, which Zeke had asked Ned to prepare. Ootuniah poked the food with his finger and then ignored it. "Only this food," Zeke said, and then translated his own words slowly. He looked up at Joe. "Did I say that right?"

Joe nodded. "Tell him," Zeke added, "or tell me how to tell him: 'We would like to trade with you for meat. We have needles and beads and cask staves. Do you have meat to spare?'"

Joe spoke to Ootuniah and listened to his response. "They have some walrus meat," he reported to Zeke. "Ootuniah says if you will allow the others aboard, he'll trade with us."

Zeke thought for a moment. "Not in here. But we'll receive them in the deckhouse."

Ootuniah shrugged when Joe spoke to him, then rose, went up on deck, and spoke to the group below. They ran across the ice floes, disappearing behind a line of hummocks to return with a heavily laden sledge drawn by eight dogs. They couldn't have been hiding there for long, Erasmus thought. But they might have spent days farther off, on the other side of the point—what an odd feeling, to think that the brig had been under observation!

The Esquimaux scrambled into the deckhouse, bearing great lumps of blubber and walrus meat. Erasmus and Dr. Boerhaave led the sick men up one by one, leaning them like bundles against the bulwarks. Ned and Sean put a handful of precious coal in the deck stove and brought up an iron cooking pot. In exchange for five cask staves the Esquimaux offered some chunks of meat, which Ned quickly boiled. They ate and ate, the crew slurping the hot broth and tearing at the parboiled flesh, the Esquimaux taking their own portions raw, alternating slices of meat and blubber. Zeke, after the first frenzy, said in a low voice to Joe, "See if they'd trade those dogs as well."

"They won't," Joe said after some discussion. Erasmus thought there'd been a lot said in Ootuniah's language to yield these few words in English. Yet Zeke, who claimed to understand many words now, didn't seem uncomfortable.

"It's been a hard winter, and many of their dogs have died," Joe continued. "They can't spare this team." He talked with Ootuniah more, and also with Awahtok. Wiping his mouth, he said to Zeke, "This is a hunting party; they come from across Smith Sound, from a small village called 'Anoatok,' I think. They must bring the sledge and the dogs and the walrus back to their families."

"How far away is their home?" Zeke asked. "Why haven't we seen them before?"

"It's some days' journey across the Sound," Joe said. "They believe no Inuit live on this side—they come here only to hunt."

Ootuniah spoke again, at some length, and Joe's face grew still. He asked something brief, then repeated it. Ootuniah said a word Erasmus thought he recognized, and when Joe turned back to Zeke, his eyes were round.

"They ask if we are friends with 'Docto Kayen.' "

"What?" Zeke said, leaping to his feet.

"That's what he said. He says last winter, and the winter before, they knew white men on the other side of the Sound. Dr. Kane, and his men. They lived in what he calls a 'wooden *idgloo*,' like this one. And had no luck hunting, and grew very sick. Ootuniah hunted for them, and traded with them. Last spring the party abandoned their ship and went south."

Zeke stared down at his feet for a long time. It would take weeks, Erasmus understood later, before Zeke would really absorb this information or what it meant. For now, he made only a calm proposal.

"I'd like to make a treaty with them," Zeke said. "If they'll continue to bring us food, and perhaps some dogs, we'll trade them iron and wood and other things they need. I need their help and the loan of sledges and dogs. In return I'll help them in every way I can. Like Kane did. Tell them I'm a friend of Kane's, and wish to be their friend as well."

There was more conversation, some of which Zeke seemed to understand but most of which Joe had to translate. "They thank you for this offer of friendship," Joe said. "They'll leave us half their walrus meat as a token of peace. And will discuss your proposal with their families. For now they say they must go home. They wish us well."

Zeke gave them all gifts of pocketknives. In return, Ootuniah gave Zeke an ivory-handled knife he'd concealed in his boot.

"He must have made the blade from one of Kane's cask hoops," Zeke said, turning the knife in his hand. "How do we know they haven't murdered Kane's entire party?"

Joe shook his head. "If they'd wanted to," he said, "they could have murdered all of us. Instead they've given us walrus, when I can't find any to save my life. Why would you think they're hostile?"

In the flurry of leave-taking, the iron cooking pot disappeared, and two spoons, a lantern, and a large piece of wood from the railing. The next day, when Erasmus went out to the storehouse, he found the door pried open. Only an axe and a barrel of blubber were missing—but Mr. Francis's coffin had been moved a few inches. As if, Erasmus thought, the Esquimaux crowding around it and peering down had bumped it gently and in unison with their bear-clawed toes.

6

Who Hears the Fishes
When They Cry?

(April–August 1856)

Unfortunately, many things have been omitted which should have been recorded in our journal; for though we made it a rule to set down all our experiences therein, yet such a resolution is very hard to keep, for the important experience rarely allows us to remember such obligations, and so indifferent things get recorded, while that is frequently neglected. It is not easy to write in a journal what interests us at any time, because to write it is not what interests us.

— Henry David Thoreau, *A Week on the Concord and Merrimack Rivers* (1849)

*E*rasmus held a caribou skin in his lap, scanning it in the dim light until he found one of the telltale scars. He set his thumbnails on either side of the perforation. "Like this?" he asked. Across from him, on another cask, Dr. Boerhaave sat surrounded by the heaps of skins they'd obtained from the Netsilik. Their knees were almost touching; beyond the yellow circle cast by the oil lamp, the rest of the storehouse was dark.

Dr. Boerhaave framed a similar wound with his thumbs. "Richardson did this during Franklin's expedition to the Barren Grounds. Or so my friend William Greenstone claims. Let's try."

They dug in their nails, squeezing inward as if to express pus from a wound. Both were rewarded by the sudden appearance of a fat white grub, the shape and size of a little bean.

Dr. Boerhaave peered at his. "That's it," he said. "The third instar of the warble fly."

"Shall we?" Erasmus said.

"Richardson claimed they tasted like gooseberries."

They popped the grubs in their mouths. "It's rather good," Dr. Boerhaave said, after some tentative chewing. "Fresh-tasting, a little sweet."

Erasmus swallowed. "The Indians of the Coppermine River eat these?"

"Richardson claimed they treasure them. As we should. After all they are a form of fresh meat. And they saved Richardson and some of the other men from starvation. Really the man is an admirable naturalist."

Erasmus popped another from its hiding place and ate with more relish. One skin at a time, they searched for the wounds the larvae had bored before settling in for their sleepy winter's growth. As they worked they talked about other, pleasanter times, hunting larger game. Dr. Boerhaave recalled grouse on the Scottish moors and the seals of Spitzbergen. Erasmus said,

"Spearing fish is very nice—I used to do it with my brothers, as a boy."

"Yes?" Dr. Boerhaave said. "How?"

Erasmus counted his little white treasures: eighteen, nineteen, twenty. "We went early in the spring, just after the ice melts and before the water weeds grow," he said. "When the fish are crowded together in the shallow warmer water. They're like us, then—still half-asleep from the winter, slow moving. We'd patch up the seams of our boat, and repair our spears and gather pitch-pine roots, then launch the boat at a small lake near our house."

He tucked his cold hands inside his fur jacket. "My brother Copernicus made an iron fire crate, which hung out over the water from the bow. On a still evening, very late, we'd light a fire in the crate and push off into the lake."

He was silent for a moment then, remembering the secret beauties of those nights. Where was Copernicus now?

"The fire lit the water," he continued. "A circle of light all around the boat, which let us see several feet down. Some of the fish hung with their bellies turned up to us. Others swam the way they do in summer. There were eels, turtles—the fish were so easy to spear that I felt like a criminal. When our fuel burned out we'd paddle home by the stars. A great fish roast for breakfast— what I wouldn't give for a grilled perch right now!"

Dr. Boerhaave, arranging the grubs on a tin plate, made a wry face. "Fish murderer," he said. "One of the things that made me want to meet Thoreau was an early essay he wrote about the joys of fish spearing; and then the way he grumbled later about the fate of fishes. Somewhere he talks about fish as if they have souls. About their virtues, and their hard destiny, and the possibilities of a secret fish civilization we don't appreciate. 'Who hears the fishes when they cry?' he wrote. He worries about the strangest things."

"All these interesting people you know," Erasmus said.

"Thoreau, Agassiz, Emerson, some of them so famous—did you ever want to be famous yourself?"

Dr. Boerhaave ate another grub. "You mean the way Commander Voorhees does?"

"I . . ." Erasmus said guiltily. "I guess I do mean that."

Dr. Boerhaave shook his head. "I don't think about it. Somehow I always knew I wasn't cut out for that—I'm lucky, in a way. I never wanted anything more than the chance to do some useful work. It matters to me that I contribute my bit to our knowledge of the natural world. But not that people *recognize* me. I suppose I was cut out to be a kind of foot soldier—it always seemed like those of us in the background have the time and privacy to get the real work done. What about you?" He smiled fondly. "Do you hunger for glory?"

"I hunger for roast beef," Erasmus said, returning his friend's smile. "But glory—I don't know, I suppose I'm like you. I'd like my *work* to be admired, but I hate my *self* to be singled out. Shall we bring in our treats?"

They brought the plate belowdecks, where more than half the men were confined. Sean, picking at his gums, had brought out a chunk of what he thought was old food but which turned out to be his own flesh. Ivan and Robert had both lost teeth and could chew only with difficulty; Mr. Tagliabeau had been seized with biliary colic and Captain Tyler was recovering from a urinary obstruction, which had tortured him until he passed a large stone. Almost everyone suffered from hemorrhoids, which made them bad-tempered; and they were hungry as well as riddled with scurvy.

"We have something good for you," Dr. Boerhaave announced.

Joe, who was still on his feet, looked at the tin plate. "Oh, good," he said. "From the hides? I've heard about these, I should have thought of this myself." He took two and passed the plate to Sean and Ivan.

"What are they?" Sean asked.

"It's not important," Joe said. "Just eat them."

"Nothing goes in my mouth without I know what it is," Sean grumbled. When Dr. Boerhaave finally explained, most of the men refused to touch the grubs. Zeke ate heartily, Joe calmly and steadily; Ned, after some persuasion, also ate a few. Erasmus and Dr. Boerhaave ate the rest and then returned to the storehouse.

"It's a good idea," Dr. Boerhaave said. "But useless if we can't get them into the men who most need them. We could ask Ned to smuggle them into some soup, but cooking will destroy their value."

They gathered a few more skins and returned to work. "If the ice would just open up enough for the seals," Erasmus said.

"All the animals will be back before long," Dr. Boerhaave said. "We just have to hang on a few more weeks."

But on April 13 Zeke announced that he was done with waiting. "If the Esquimaux won't come to us," he said, "we'll go to them. We must have help hunting. We must have dogs."

On the table he spread Inglefield's flawed map of lower Smith Sound; then he abutted his own charts of the Ellesmere coast, up to the point where they were frozen in. "The crossing party will be composed of myself, Dr. Boerhaave, Joe, and Ned." While Erasmus and Dr. Boerhaave stared at each other, Zeke added, "It's thirty or forty miles across the Sound to Greenland, and the village the Esquimaux described can't be far. We'll take the middle-sized sledge, so we can bring back as much meat as possible. With luck we'll have dogs to pull it on the return trip."

"The composition of the traveling party," Erasmus said. "Surely . . ."

"I must have Joe," Zeke said. "For his skill with a rifle, as well as his knowledge of the language. I'd prefer not to leave you without the services of a surgeon, but we'll be in more danger and so Dr. Boerhaave must come. You're needed here, as Captain Tyler and Mr. Tagliabeau are both sick."

But this was a punishment, Erasmus thought with dismay, as much as a practical decision. He was being punished for that night in the deckhouse with the drinking men. Separated, purposefully, from his friend. "Let *me* come," he said. "Instead of Ned." He touched Dr. Boerhaave's shoulder.

"You can't," Zeke said. "Why can't you understand that? I need you here, taking care of the men."

Dr. Boerhaave stepped forward. "If Erasmus has to stay," he argued, "why not leave Ned to help him care for the sick? We don't need a cook while we're out on the ice—wouldn't it make more sense to take one of the larger, sturdier men?"

"I need someone I can trust," Zeke said. "Someone who'll accept direction without questioning me."

My fault, Erasmus thought. If he'd managed to placate Zeke, Zeke wouldn't have turned to Ned.

Ned squared his shoulders. "I'll go," he said. "I'd be glad to go."

"I'm afraid to go," Dr. Boerhaave confessed to Erasmus later. "I don't want to, but it's my duty. What if something happens to Joe or Ned?"

They left the brig on April 16. Zeke made a speech to the men left behind; Ned pressed Erasmus's hands; Dr. Boerhaave embraced him and whispered in his ear, "Shall a man go and hang himself because he belongs to the race of pygmies, and not be the biggest pygmy that he can?" While Erasmus puzzled over that cryptic comment, the crossing party harnessed themselves to the sledge, heading for the place they'd only heard named once: Anoatok.

IN THEIR ABSENCE, Erasmus bent his energies toward improving the health of his companions. He was stronger than anyone else—perhaps from the grubs, which he ate every day for the rest of April, although no one else would touch them. Each time he ate he thought of Dr. Boerhaave. He let himself elaborate on the daydream he'd had for months: that somehow, when they finally reached Philadelphia, he might persuade his friend to settle there. Just across the creek from his home, a small stone house had been sitting vacant for several years. Dr. Boerhaave might live there, he thought—privately, yet just a short stroll from the Repository. Erasmus would give him a key. They might meet there daily; they might work on their specimens together. Sometimes they might dine together and sit by the fire afterward, reading companionably and drinking soft red wine. Nothing would separate them then.

He decorated that small stone house in his mind: the most comfortable armchairs, the neatest linen. Then suddenly there was wildlife around, and he dropped his daydreams and hunted with a passion and accuracy he'd never known before. He shot a burgomaster gull, three ptarmigan, and two caribou—the first since October. The men ate the venison gratefully and grew stronger. Ivan, the first to recover, helped Erasmus shoot a seal at a newly exposed breathing hole. One seal, then crowds of them climbing out to bask in the sun; Sean and Barton caught two more. Barton, who'd twice worked on a Newfoundland sealing ship, taught the others to eat the dark, oily flesh with slices of fresh blubber, disconcertingly sweet and delicious.

The succulent beef of the first musk ox Erasmus shot roused the last of the men. They cleaned the winter's accumulation of soot from the beams and walls, aired the squalid corners, laundered bedding and socks and shirts. Only Captain Tyler and Mr. Tagliabeau remained in their bunks. *When exhausted by sickness*, Erasmus remembered his father saying, *elephants will lie on their backs and throw grass toward the sky, as though beseeching the earth to answer their prayers. The elephant is honest, sensible, just, and respectful of the stars, the sun, and the moon—qualities rarely appar-*

ent even in man. Just then Erasmus would have happily traded Captain Tyler and Mr. Tagliabeau for a pair of useful pachyderms. He tried alternately to bully and coddle them, but they would not be moved.

Since Zeke's departure they'd collapsed entirely, as if finally giving in to their grief over the loss of Mr. Francis. Or as if they no longer believed they wouldn't share his fate, despite the vibrant signs of spring. In his bunk, above his pillow, Captain Tyler had pinned a small sheet of paper. On it he'd drawn the outline of a gravestone and written:

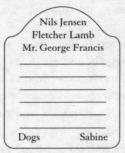

Nils Jensen
Fletcher Lamb
Mr. George Francis

Dogs   Sabine

He and Mr. Tagliabeau wouldn't hunt, or work on repairing the brig, or pace the promenade. They lay in their bunks, openly drinking and reading as if this might somehow save them. Mr. Tagliabeau burrowed into a copy of *Pendennis*; Captain Tyler into Dr. Boerhaave's *David Copperfield*, picking up where the doctor had left off reading aloud during the worst days of winter. When the men came by their bunks and said, "What should we do? What are your orders?" Captain Tyler and Mr. Tagliabeau shrugged and said, "Do what you want. What Mr. Wells says. It won't make any difference."

MAY 5, 10, 15. Still the sledge party didn't return. Erasmus worried about them—but only for their own sake; whatever meat they brought back from the Esquimaux would now be superfluous. The weather stopped chewing at them and twice the temperature rose above freezing. The light made it feel warmer; the light made up for everything. When Erasmus woke and first stepped outside, the dazzling whiteness pierced his eyes and made his head swim until he treasured the nights, when the sun sat lower in the sky and lent shades of red and yellow to the clouds. A soft mist hovered over the hills and the falling snow was heavy and wet, like spring snow back home. Home, where he might one day live in the company of his friend. *What would it mean,* he imagined asking Dr. Boerhaave, *to grow up hearing stories in which truth and falsehood are mingled like the minerals in granite?* To which Dr. Boerhaave might reply, *It could mean you were being taught to understand that anything you can imagine is possible.*

The brig was still frozen in solidly, but trickles of water seeped down the sides of the icebergs and the floes were bare of snow, sometimes wet on the surface. The broad strip of land-fast ice began to crack as the tides nibbled away at the base, and rocks tumbled down upon it from the cliffs above. Nothing like a lead opened in the solid sea ice of their cove, not even a crack appeared, but the signs of breaking up were everywhere.

Erasmus gathered the men on May 17. He was in charge now; he accepted it. Dismissing entirely Zeke's dreams of heading north, giddy with sun and the birds in the sky, he said, "I propose we break up the storehouse. The ice might begin to open any day now, and we should be prepared to stow the brig swiftly."

"Then we can go the minute a lead opens up," Isaac agreed.

They made heaps and towers on the ice and then slowly began moving the things they were least likely to need back into the hold. Erasmus, Sean, and Barton, with the guidance of Thomas, tore down half the deckhouse and closed off the remainder roughly. Erasmus began sleeping in that breezy shanty, and soon the men abandoned their stuffy quarters and joined him, leaving only Captain Tyler and Mr. Tagliabeau below.

Thomas said, "Should we rebuild the bulkhead? We're not so dependent on the stoves anymore, and Commander Voorhees will surely want the regular arrangements restored for our voyage back."

"Leave it for now," Erasmus said. "It's a day's work; we can wait and see what he wants to do when he returns."

As their spirits rose they knocked down the remains of their autumn ice village and rebuilt it more elaborately. A Greek temple rose white and elegant, next to a model of the Boston library and diagonally across from a miniature tavern which, Thomas swore, was just like the one nearest the wharf from which the *Narwhal* had sailed. Sean built a railway station and Barton, not to be outdone, built an imitation Japanese garden. Erasmus thought the men built even more gleefully and skillfully than they had in the presence of Zeke, perhaps because they knew each building raised was temporary. Not something they'd have to regard all winter, soiled and slumped and covered with snow, but a living, glistening thing that might dissolve in a few weeks. To their efforts he added a boathouse, with a little river carved before it and curving toward home.

A DISTANT SOUND woke Erasmus during the night of May 21. He threw on his clothes and ran outside, into the pearly, improbable midnight light: two figures, dark against the ice, were creeping toward him. No matter how quickly he moved, how he halved the distance between himself and the figures and halved it again, still there were only two. Two. Ned, bent forward but still upright, resting a long moment before each step; and leaning against him, almost being carried by him, Zeke.

"Wait," Erasmus said to the blackened, bloody faces. "Only a minute more." Before he touched them, before even determining how far behind them Joe and Dr. Boerhaave might be, he flew back to the brig, rounded up Barton and Sean and Isaac, and tossed down the smallest sledge. Ned and Zeke, weighed down by the lumpy packages tied to their backs, had crumpled to the ice by the time the crew reached them. Zeke was unconscious and Ned hardly better, but Erasmus bent close to Ned's ear.

"How far back are they?" he asked urgently. "Can you tell us where to start looking? Are they with the sledge?"

Ned twisted his head into Erasmus's face.

"Can you talk?" Erasmus asked, pulling back. "You're almost home, we'll have you inside in five minutes—are they far?"

"Joe left us," Ned groaned. "He stayed in Greenland. Dr. Boerhaave . . ." He banged his cheekbone into Erasmus's mouth, hard enough to split Erasmus's lower lip. Joe in Greenland? How could that be? Once more Erasmus pulled his head away.

"Under," Ned whispered. "Under. We were, he was blind from the snow, we stopped. Zeke and I, we unharnessed ourselves, we left him in the traces while we were unloading the sledge to camp, we were, we were—it was safer to leave him tied in for a minute we thought, so he wouldn't wander, he couldn't see—we were unloading."

"Unloading," Erasmus repeated. He put a hand to his streaming lip. How could he be bleeding when time had stopped?

"It cracked," Ned whispered. "The floe, right under the sledge. There was ice and then there wasn't. The sledge went in and it pulled him. So fast. I couldn't even touch his hand before he was gone."

ZEKE REMAINED UNCONSCIOUS for eleven days and was weak for a fortnight after that; brain fever, Erasmus thought. Ned was in better shape physically, but too exhausted and brokenhearted to talk. In their sleeping sacks Erasmus found some clues from which he tried to piece together the story.

Before the sledge had vanished, Ned had unloaded those sacks, most of their supplies, and Dr. Boerhaave's small medicine chest and oilskin-wrapped journal; he'd carried home both despite his weakness. Erasmus went through the chest's contents, not mourning his dead friend—not yet, he couldn't admit that Dr. Boerhaave was truly gone—but searching for remedies for the survivors. Ointments, plasters, a few canisters of pills, oiled silk, lint, bandages, scalpels. Many small bottles and vials: tartar emetic, mercurous chloride, syrup of squill, tincture of opium. Not much use to Erasmus, but he heard Dr. Boerhaave's voice as he read those names aloud. When he retreated to his bunk after tending to the invalids, he browsed through Dr. Boerhaave's journal. Before leaving the *Narwhal* Dr. Boerhaave had written:

The last pages of my acquaintance's Walden *continue to comfort me. "Is it the source of the Nile, or the Niger, or the Mississippi, or a North-west Passage around this continent, that we would find?" Thoreau writes. "Are these the problems which most concern mankind? Is Franklin the only man who is lost, that his wife should be so earnest to find him? Does Mr. Grinnell know where he himself is? Be rather the Mungo Park, the Lewis and Clarke and Frobisher, of your own streams and oceans; explore your own higher latitudes—with shiploads of pre-served meats to support you, if they be necessary, and pile the empty cans sky-high for a sign. . . . What was the meaning of that South-Sea Exploring Expedition, with all its parade and expense, but an indirect recognition of the fact, that there are continents and seas in the moral world, to which every man is an isthmus or an inlet, yet unexplored by him, but that it is easier to sail many thousand miles through cold and storm and cannibals, in a government ship, with five hundred men and boys to assist one, than it is to explore the private sea, the Atlantic and Pacific Ocean of one's being alone."*

Those words made Erasmus weep. A message for him, he thought: that Exploring Expedition was the one he'd been on as a youth, that search for Franklin had sent him here. If he and Dr. Boerhaave had truly heeded those words they might be safe in Philadelphia, comparing notes on crustaceans. Instead Dr. Boerhaave had crossed the Sound.

He'd written nothing during the crossing itself. His next entry read:

How difficult that was! Ridges of hummocks, barricades blocking our way again and again; I've never suffered such bodily pains. Yet we're safe, finally. Ned's snow blindness seems to have responded to treatment. For the last two days of our crossing I washed out his eyes with solution of boric acid, then put in morphine drops and bandaged his eyes shut; we pulled him on the sledge. A terrible trip.

The birds have been remarkable: snow buntings, a passerine that is probably the Lappland longspur, hoary redpolls, the American pipit (surely this is the extreme north of its range?), wheatears. Red-throated loons, ivory gulls, a white gyrfalcon. The pipits fly high then flutter down, repeating their song faster and faster as they approach the ground. How these songbirds change the barren landscape! Suddenly everything seems alive. The dovekies are the most numerous; our hosts slaughter great flocks of them. We join their feasts gratefully.

Campions, cochlearia, and lichens are beginning their growth beneath the snow. In a sheltered pocket, where an ice crust had formed, a purple saxifrage was flowering and a cinquefoil was greening. On some dry stones, from which the snow had already melted, I found two spiders.

And that was all. Not a word about the disappearance of Joe, the nature of the Greenland Esquimaux, the response to Zeke's requests for dogs and help. Not a word, of course, about his own trials on the journey back.

He was blind, Erasmus thought, staring out into the harsh

morning light. Not just blind but in pain. On what day had that happened? And why had he been walking blind, harnessed like a dog to the sledge? Why wasn't he being pulled on the sledge, as Ned had been pulled on the journey over?

DURING THE MONTH that Zeke was laid up, Erasmus tried to prepare the brig for their departure. Ned still couldn't or wouldn't talk. To the men, who clamored for explanations about the disappearances of Joe and Dr. Boerhaave, Erasmus could say only what Ned had whispered before his collapse: that Joe had left them, and that Dr. Boerhaave had died in an accident on the ice. Erasmus grieved for Dr. Boerhaave constantly, and was consumed with questions about his end—but there was work to do, so much work to do, and Captain Tyler and Mr. Tagliabeau continued to shirk their duties. Leaning into Captain Tyler's bunk and shouting at him that he must get up, they were so short-handed, Erasmus saw that Dr. Boerhaave's name had been added to the paper gravestone. After that he left the captain alone.

He gave orders, made lists, split the duties of nursing the sick among the well, and assigned hunting teams. He waited impatiently for Zeke's recovery, but it was Ned who recovered first and Ned, leaning on his arm while they paced the promenade, who first told Erasmus what had happened.

The ice in Smith Sound had been murderous, Ned said, like nothing they'd ever seen before: great tumbled blocks, amid which the sledge crashed like a toy. Sleeping had been almost impossible and they'd walked for twenty hours some days, half-blinded by the glare. Ned's eyes were the worst. For ten or eleven days they'd wandered, finally reaching the coast with still no idea of where they were. But Dr. Boerhaave found tracks, Ned said, the faint tracks of a sledge, and Joe steered by them to a small settlement.

How lucky they'd felt then! For there were Ootuniah and Awahtok and the three other Esquimaux who'd visited the *Narwhal*; also a few other men, four women, and a handful of children. They were feasting on walrus, and although they seemed startled by the arrival of their guests they shared their food freely and took them into their hut—a large dormitory, built of stone and lined outside with sods, very different from the tents of the Netsilik. Around a blubber fire their wet furs steamed.

For two weeks, these people had sheltered the four pale men. While Ned recovered his eyesight, Joe and Zeke and Dr. Boerhaave hunted with their hosts, capturing birds, seals, and two more walrus, which they afterward ate in the warm hut. Zeke had asked Ootuniah for dogs and men to help him journey north—he needed help, he said. And would pay for it generously. Or so Ned understood from what Joe told him.

Much of what Ned knew he'd gathered only by asking Joe. On their arrival Joe had begun to interpret, as always, but Zeke had ordered him to stop. He didn't need Joe's interpreting skills after all, he said; he'd studied hard and now he could understand the Esquimaux language himself.

"I'm not sure about this," Ned told Erasmus. "How much he understood—but he seemed to be doing well enough, and he really didn't want Joe to help him. He said he couldn't establish true friendships with these people if Joe always interposed himself between them and him. You're to be quiet, Zeke said. So Joe had time to interpret things for me. And time to talk with Ootuniah alone and listen to his stories. He told me some, they were like Esquimaux fairy tales."

The hunting trips, Ned thought, were where Joe and Ootuniah had grown friendly: he knew no more than that. On their last night in Anoatok, when Ootuniah finally, firmly, denied all Zeke's requests and said that they could spare no dogs or men, and that Zeke shouldn't travel north at this time of year, Joe slipped away. Ned and Zeke and Dr. Boerhaave woke the next morning to find that Ootuniah and his companions had loaded Zeke's sledge with a huge heap of walrus meat, but that Joe was gone.

Zeke had translated Ootuniah's explanations for Ned and Dr. Boerhaave, his face stricken as he did so. "This land is your friend's homeland," Zeke repeated. His face twisted, as though the words were sour on his tongue. "Although his own people live far south of here. He has borrowed a sledge and dogs from us and headed there. We wish him well in his journey, as we wish you well in yours. All this meat, it is for you and your men. Your friend has gone home."

Ned and Dr. Boerhaave hadn't been surprised; they'd both seen how tired Joe was of Zeke. Zeke's demands and requests and posturings, Zeke's plans and questions and maps; many times Ned had seen Joe and Ootuniah together, talking and laughing and sharing food. "It was Commander Voorhees's moodiness that drove Joe away," Ned said. "His carelessness— Joe was our most valuable crew member, and now he's gone. I could almost feel what Joe was feeling: he was in Greenland, even if so far north, and among Esquimaux, even if not a tribe he knew—and he had a chance to get away from us. Of course he took it. If I had a way to go home, I'd do the same."

Ned and Zeke and Dr. Boerhaave had been forced to travel back without Joe, loaded with precious walrus meat but with none of the things that Zeke had most desired. That trip was worse than the first, Ned said; the pack was shifting and the floes heaved beneath them. After a brief stretch of smooth, clear ice, they'd run into a maze of pressure ridges, ten-foot blocks heaped in snaking walls that forced them backward and then in circles. Zeke refused to lighten the sledge by discarding any of the meat. It was all they had to show for their trip, he said, and the *Narwhal*'s crew needed it.

"Although you didn't," Ned said bitterly. "How could we not have understood that if the Esquimaux were finding food, you would be too?"

On the fourth day, Dr. Boerhaave's eyes had given out completely. A vast confusion of rain and snow and glaring sun, wild winds and sudden sharp cold; their furs were soaked through and they had to keep moving to stay warm. Were Dr. Boerhaave to ride on the sledge, Zeke said, he would surely freeze to death. He must keep walking. Perhaps that was true. But it was also true that the sledge was already almost too heavy to pull. Dr. Boerhaave couldn't possibly lie atop that heap of meat and Zeke wouldn't discard his sole prize.

Zeke arranged the traces so that Dr. Boerhaave was harnessed next to the sledge, with Ned and Zeke himself a few feet before him, at the points of an equilateral triangle. Another set of ropes ran from Dr. Boerhaave's waist to Ned's and Zeke's, forming the triangle's sides, so that Dr. Boerhaave could then walk forward guided by the gentle pressure. And it had worked, Ned admitted. It was horrible the way Dr. Boerhaave stumbled over the ridges and mounds, the way his sightless face grimaced and colored—yet perhaps only the constant movement had kept him alive.

Or perhaps if Zeke had emptied the sled, packed Dr. Boerhaave on it wrapped in all their furs, he might be alive even now. Or if they hadn't untied the ropes connecting them to Dr. Boerhaave before unloading the sledge for their brief rest, or if they'd chosen any other place, any other time to stop . . .

"The waist ropes weren't long enough," Ned said, staring out at the white plain. Erasmus was sweating beneath his jacket, moisture trickling down his sides as if his arms were weeping. That Dr. Boerhaave had had to endure this . . . "We couldn't unload the sledge while we were still tied in," Ned continued. "Just a few minutes we weren't tied to him—how could the ice have opened just then?"

Erasmus remembered his first impression of his friend: Dr. Boerhaave's quick and shining mind, flashing like a silver salmon. Did a soul survive? His body moved among the fish but perhaps his soul had floated free. One fine idea in the mind of God, which might express itself in another form.

"It wasn't your fault," Erasmus said. And it wasn't; nor was it, exactly, Zeke's. Yet if Joe had been there it wouldn't have happened, Joe would have understood what to do: and who was to blame for Joe's desertion, if not Zeke? The sweat congealed on his chest. It could have been Zeke, sinking through that ice. It *should* have been Zeke. Behind that flare of rage was a bleaker thought. If he hadn't shared that one night with the men—if Zeke hadn't caught him drinking—he might have been there himself to save Dr. Boerhaave.

By June 15 Zeke was well enough to rise and resume command of the ship. He gathered all the men on deck, even Captain Tyler and Mr. Tagliabeau, and thanked them for their good work during his absence and subsequent illness. Erasmus stood next to him, his hands jammed in his pockets, trying to listen without shouting. Dr. Boerhaave was dead and here was Zeke. His sister's love, the leader of all these men, everyone needed him—*if I struck him*, Erasmus thought, with the calm of real hysteria; *if he fell and hit his head* . . . but Zeke's death wouldn't help anyone except, very briefly, him. He dug his fingers through the cloth and into his thighs as Sean said, "But what really happened to Joe and Dr. Boerhaave?"

Zeke told a story that resembled what Ned had told Erasmus, but was somehow quite different. In his version, Joe was unhelpful on the crossing to Greenland, and once there poisoned Zeke's relationship with the Esquimaux. Because of Joe the Esquimaux, initially willing to supply Zeke with dogs, and perhaps even accompany him on some travels north, had turned against him. There was a woman involved, Zeke hinted; he suspected that Joe had formed a relationship with one of the Anoatok women, deserting so he might meet her later.

The tragic journey back, Zeke said, had also been Joe's fault. In his absence the sledge was too heavy for three men; they'd struggled heroically, wanting to bring fresh meat to the *Narwhal*'s crew, but they'd grown overtired and it was this that had beaten them. Had Joe been there, Dr. Boerhaave might still have fallen—that was fate, no one could help it—but a third pair of hands might have been enough to haul out him and the sledge.

"This is what happens," Zeke said frostily. "When a team breaks down, when commands are ignored. A weak link in the chain imperils us all."

In the silence Erasmus chewed his lips and watched Zeke gaze toward the plain surrounding the ship, dotted with ice buildings and heaps of supplies. A pyramid of barrels holding their beef and pork, quadrangles of flour and dried apples and beans, a little tower of bottled horseradish, twelve bottles to the case. "Who gave the orders to break up the storehouse?" Zeke asked.

"I did," Erasmus said, amazed that he could still speak. Two long-tailed ducks passed by, heading for their breeding grounds farther north. How Dr. Boerhaave would have enjoyed a glimpse of them. "I thought you'd want to be ready the moment the ice opened."

"Your diligence is admirable," Zeke said. "But I hope you haven't stowed the pemmican, or any of the other traveling supplies." Everyone stared at him. "The Esquimaux have promised to visit us in a few weeks," Zeke continued. "A few men, and a team of dogs for our sledge. They'll help us make a quick trip north, while we wait for the ice to break up."

"I never heard that," Ned blurted. "When did they promise that?"

"You don't understand their language," Zeke said. "You only heard what Joe told you. They'll be here shortly. Then a party of us will head north."

The men said nothing; they stood still and then disappeared below—as if, Erasmus thought, Zeke's announcement was so absurd they'd all agreed not to hear it. For a while he couldn't speak himself. Later that night, still wondering if he'd heard correctly, he was turning the pages of Dr. Boerhaave's journal when Zeke crept up on him. He tried to shield the pages with his hand before he spoke. "Why are you still talking about this trip?" he said. Why hadn't he asked this right away? "It's ridiculous, it's such a bad idea."

"So you've said," Zeke replied. "So you've been saying since January, you could hardly be less enthusiastic. Yet the success of our whole voyage turns on this."

"What *success?*" Erasmus closed the precious volume. "Nils and Fletcher and Mr. Francis already dead and now Dr. Boerhaave, Dr. Boerhaave, Dr. . . ." He dashed away what was spurting from his eyes.

"I'll take that," Zeke said, bending over the spotted book.

"No!" Erasmus said. "Please—it should be mine."

Zeke pushed his hands aside. "It's a part of the expedition's records now," he said. "Hence mine."

DURING THOSE LAST weeks of June, Alexandra wrote:

That my life would change like this; it's so extraordinary, my fate turning because of Mr. Archibault's crippled hands, me profiting by his problems—what am I to make of this?

He arrives each evening with his secret parcels and we work long into the night. We've taken over Erasmus's Repository, lighting it as best we can; a far cry from the sunlit space of the Wellses' engraving room. They work in teams there, several men to each plate; one engraves the land-

scape, another the animals, another the human figures. Here it's just the two of us, doing the best we can.

All this has come about because Dr. Kane drives himself so mercilessly—or is driven by his publisher, we can't be sure which. The facts I piece together are these. In the months since Dr. Kane's return he's generated almost nine hundred pages of text, much taken directly from his journals but some newly written; only the Preface and Appendix remain undone. Meanwhile Mr. Hamilton, who renders from Dr. Kane's pen-and-ink sketches the beautiful paintings on which the engravings are based, has been living in Dr. Kane's own rooms that they might work day and night.

Mr. Childs, his publisher, began printing the early chapters even while Dr. Kane continued writing, and he's given specimen pages to the newspapers as a way of drumming up publicity. Mr. Childs chose the title—Arctic Explorations: The Second Grinnell Expedition in Search of Sir John Franklin, 1853, '54, '55—and plans to publish in September, but the engravings are far behind schedule. It's this frenzy that has been my great blessing. Mr. Archibault's team is the farthest behind; no one knows but me that something has happened to his wrists. When he bears down with his graver, pains shoot up from his wrists and his fingers lose their strength and grow numb; he's lost almost all control of them.

He spends his days directing the other members of his team, who engrave views of the cliffs, the sky, the ship, and the human figures. He checks the plates at each stage, he points out mistakes and calls for corrections. He's supposed to be doing the animals—his particular gift—but claims he can't concentrate while supervising everyone else and must do his own work at night. Then he sneaks the plates and their corresponding paintings out of the building and here, to me. He has a wife, six children, a widowed mother living with him, and no other income beyond his salary.

Neither of us can quite believe this is happening. That he should be so dependent on a woman still in training; that I should be given the chance, so early, to work on the plates for an important book—it's difficult for both of us. We both know I'm not ready for this. And how exasperating it is that he can't correct my mistakes directly. He paces back *and forth, cold compresses on his wrists, and can do no more than say, "Lightly, lightly." Or, "Carve deeper there, a little more pressure," or "Can't you see the way Hamilton's angled the jawbone?" I've never worked so hard. Some of what I do is good, I can see it. Sometimes I can match my line both to Hamilton's intent and to the work of the others who've already marked the plate. But sometimes my clumsiness shows. Partly I long for my work to be recognized. Partly I'm glad no one will ever know how I've served out my apprenticeship in public.*

Caught in our strange union, Mr. Archibault and I try to be kind to one another. But twice he's arrived here pale with distress, and has let me know that Linnaeus, looking over a plate, has expressed dissatisfaction. Mr. Archibault's job rests on what I do, as does the firm's reputation. Yet it's no use to think of this, I can only do my best.

I still haven't met Dr. Kane, on whose behalf an army works day and night. This man who's changed my life and made a hell of Lavinia's. Why is he *here? she asks. And not Zeke and Erasmus? She rages; then chides herself for being irrational. I find her asleep in odd corners, in the middle of the day, and when I wake her she weeps and twists her skirt in her hands. She knows my secret and doesn't hold my work against me, even tries to encourage me now and then but can do no work herself. Nothing I do seems to help her.*

Still—still, still, still—we have no word of Zeke and Erasmus. Though whalers now make their way into upper Baffin's Bay, no one reports sighting the Narwhal.

"OUR ACQUAINTANCES HAVE deceived us," Zeke said when he returned. He'd been gone for three days, exploring the far side of the point in search of the Esquimaux. His face was sunburnt and above it his hair, sweaty and rumpled, looked almost white.

Ned, who was standing next to Erasmus and sorting handfuls of scurvy grass, said, "You saw the Esquimaux?"

"I saw no one," Zeke said curtly. "The pack in the Sound is beginning to move, there are big leads everywhere and there's no possibility of travel across it. As the Esquimaux must have known when they sent us home. They never had any intention of helping us, they just meant to get rid of us. And so they have. We have no way of communicating with them now for the rest of the season."

"Why *would* they come here?" Ned said. "All they ever want to do is get away from us."

"Your opinion," Zeke retorted. "Which you may keep to yourself."

Ned turned and busied himself with the stove. Captain Tyler and Mr. Tagliabeau, still idle but well enough to sit in the sun wrapped in blankets, looked up at Zeke. "But this is good news," Captain Tyler said. "Isn't it? If the ice is breaking up in the Sound, surely we'll be freed soon . . ."

"I don't think so," Zeke replied. "I went south along the ice belt, looking for open water. The straits aren't open anywhere, they're only heaving and breaking. The ice on our side is completely solid between us and the North Water."

Mr. Tagliabeau groaned and put his head on his knees.

"We have at least six weeks before there's even the possibility of breaking out," Zeke said. "And there's no point wasting this precious time. So we don't have dogs. So the movement in the Sound blocks us from travel to the east. There's no reason we can't head north, exploring the coast. We'll break into two parties, one to guard the brig and ready it for our departure, and another to travel. Volunteers?"

No one said a word.

Zeke looked from face to face. Erasmus shifted his eyes when Zeke's gaze reached him.

"Some enthusiasm would be welcome," Zeke said. "I'll post a sheet of paper in the deckhouse tomorrow morning, and I expect six of you to sign up for the exploring party. Work it out among yourselves."

* * *

TUESDAY AND WEDNESDAY, the sheet remained blank. Ned took Erasmus aside, while Zeke rummaged through the supplies on the ice. "No one's going to sign up," he said. "Of course no one is. After what happened—I'll never go anywhere with him again. And neither will anyone else. I've talked to the men."

He looked Erasmus squarely in the eye, and Erasmus understood that, beyond the rebuilt bulkhead, Ned had been telling the crew his version of the trip to Anoatok, which must have won out over Zeke's.

On Thursday, Zeke sat down to dinner with an armful of charts. "Well?" he asked. "Who is joining me?"

"We must stay with the ship," Captain Tyler said. "Mr. Tagliabeau and I—it's our duty to guard the ship, and ready it for our departure."

The seven crewmen rose from the table as one. Ned stepped forward and spoke for them. "It's too risky," he said. Brave boy, Erasmus thought. "There's nothing to be gained. The ice may break up before you think, and we must be here when it does."

Zeke's face turned white, but he clenched his hand around his charts and said to Erasmus, "It's just you and me then, my old friend. But we'll move more swiftly without these malingerers. Shall we leave on Saturday?"

For a minute Erasmus struggled with himself. His duty toward Zeke and Lavinia, his duty toward Ned and the rest of these men—no matter what he decided, he'd fail someone. "It's a bad idea," he said. "I can't support you in this. I vote to stay."

Zeke rose, scattering papers. "This isn't a *vote*. Who said anything about *voting*?"

"I'm staying here," Erasmus said, hoping he sounded as firm as Ned had.

"You can't do this," Zeke said to him. He turned, faced the others, and repeated himself; then added, "You'll all regret this."

"We've followed you wherever you wanted," Captain Tyler said. "Look where it's brought us."

Mr. Tagliabeau said, "We might now consider this ship a wreck, since it has no power to move. Under maritime law, the commander of a ship has no further powers once a ship is wrecked."

Ned took a breath and steadied himself. "The *Narwhal* isn't a ship anymore," he said. "Maybe it's not a wreck like Mr. Tagliabeau says, but it's not a ship. It's our home, even if it feels like a prison."

Was this mutiny? Erasmus wondered. If Zeke started hurling orders at them, if he threatened them and still they refused . . .

"I'll give you all another chance to act like men," Zeke said, beginning to pace. "We'll meet here tomorrow at noon, and I'll ask each of you to state for the record your decision to support me in a journey north. Perhaps a party of six is excessive, given our reduced numbers. I need only three of you. Any three."

He left the cabin, clambered down onto the ice, and did not return. No one slept in the cabin that night. Erasmus tossed in the deckhouse, aware that below him, Captain Tyler and Mr. Tagliabeau had abandoned their bunks to join the men in the forecastle. He heard voices deep into the night, although only a few phrases floated clearly: *when a whaling ship's frozen in like this, the captain is bound to release the men; the boats should be at our disposal; if he won't do that we might confine him*—Barton DeSouza, Robert Carey, Isaac Bond. Erasmus longed for Dr. Boerhaave, who might have guided him.

At noon, they waited for fifteen minutes before they heard Zeke climb up on deck and then descend among them. From the shelf behind his bunk he took the small metal box in which he kept his charts and his journal and also, since their deaths, Mr. Francis's official log and Dr. Boerhaave's journal. He opened Mr.

Francis's log. One by one, in a steady voice, he called out the crew members' names. One by one they said, "Stay." He entered each vote, turning last to Erasmus.

"I'm sorry," Erasmus said. "But I must also stay."

"Well, then," Zeke said. "So you reveal yourselves." He wrote a few more lines in the log and then locked it inside the box. "I'll be gone four weeks," he said, squaring his shoulders. "The ice won't open before August fifteenth, almost surely later. I'll be back before August fifth."

"You're going alone?" Ned said. "You're still going?"

"Of *course* I'm going," Zeke said. "Why would I return home without taking advantage of our excellent situation here? Dr. Kane may have preceded us to the Greenland side of Smith Sound, and may have befriended our fickle Esquimaux before us, but who's to say how far north he traveled? The open polar sea may be less than a hundred miles away, and I won't give up this chance to find it because of you."

He turned to Erasmus. "I'm very disappointed in you," he said. For a second, Erasmus was reminded of his own father. "But under the terms of the contract you signed, I leave you and Captain Tyler in shared command until I return."

He left the brig again, headed for the three guardian icebergs. Erasmus followed a few minutes later, cursing as he crossed the spongy white plain and looped around the turquoise puddles of meltwater spread so deceptively everywhere. Like windows into the open sea but shallow, just a few inches deep, all lies. He waded through them, soaking his boots, panting as Zeke's figure disappeared. His own feet disappeared in the water; how could the ice be so wet on the surface, so solid below, so obstinate in refusing to release them? At the first berg he stopped and rested against the slumping contours. Around the back of the third, largest berg, he found Zeke.

"Please," he said, still panting. "Don't go off alone."

"You're the one making me do it," Zeke said.

"I can't leave the men. Not after all that happened this winter."

Zeke made a sound of disgust. "They're not *your* responsibility—they're mine. And I know they'll be fine."

"But I'm responsible for *you*." Had he admitted this before? "Lavinia made me promise I'd look after you."

"As if I'm a child?" He stepped back from Erasmus, into a puddle; his feet disappeared and he seemed to be walking on water. "As if I need the protection of a woman, of you—why would I want to marry her, if she's like *you*?"

"Because you *love* her," Erasmus shouted. Then stood with his mouth still open. He leaned back against the largest of Zeke's Follies.

"I can't think about her up here. I can't think about anything except what I have to do." Zeke looked down at the blue pool obscuring his feet. "You could still change your mind," he said softly. "Come with me—I'd put everything that's happened behind us, we could still discover something wonderful. Be like brothers."

"It was Dr. Boerhaave who was like a brother to me," Erasmus said. "And now he's dead."

Again Zeke made that noise of disgust, clicking his tongue on the roof of his mouth: *tchik, tchik, tchik.* "Noted," he said. A string of eider ducks whirred by, their harsh cries shocking in the silence. "You've made your feelings perfectly clear all along. If your father could see what you've become . . ." He turned and walked off across the film of water.

Alone, without dogs or human companions, he couldn't pull a sledge. He left two days later on foot, with a spare pair of boots, a rifle, a good deal of ammunition, and provisions strapped in an unwieldy bedroll to his back.

SOMETIMES THEY WERE ashamed. Or Erasmus was, and Ned as well; perhaps some of the others: because their lives, through the rest of July and early August, were almost easy. Each day, while their ice structures dripped and consolidated into glassy mounds, they dismantled another heap of the *Narwhal*'s stores and repacked the items carefully in the hold. Pleasant work, under the warm sun. And with each trip to the hold and back, the men could examine the tiny, heartening gap, like a mouth beginning to open, where the dark hull met the ice.

Erasmus, checking new lists against the old, found more efficient arrangements for their remaining supplies. Now that the candles were gone, and most of the wood and much of the preserved food, he was able to convert part of the hold aft of the mainmast into storage for the specimens he and Dr. Boerhaave had collected. The crates of bird skins in one neat tower; fossils matched part to counterpart, neatly labeled and layered with hides; bottles crammed with floating invertebrates swathed in dried grasses and then wedged in boxes—only now, given some room and time, was he able to see how much he had. There was enough here to keep him occupied for the rest of his life, and he would have been happy if he weren't worried about Zeke, and if Dr. Boerhaave had been present. He packed his friend's books in a case he built next to the fossils, keeping out only a few for the shelf in his bunk.

On the gravel beach smoke hung in the air; the men had developed a passion for preparing caribou skins, and hides depended like flags from scaffolds of poles raised near little fires. Erasmus asked Ned, who seemed to be directing the efforts, what this was all about. Flushed and pink-cheeked, Ned was bent over a skin, scraping the fascia away with a piece of iron pipe. Next to him Barton was arranging a white skin some distance from a fire, while on deck Isaac and Ivan and Robert were sitting cross-legged amid a pile of skins already smoked and dried.

Ned said, "You don't mind, do you? I thought it was a good

idea, a way to keep us all busy. The suits we've been wearing all winter are worn out and they smell bad—each of us decided to make a complete suit for himself, from the inside out. A sort of souvenir, for when we get home. The things you taught me helped me prepare the skins. Joe showed me the basic pattern of the garments last fall. Ivan worked as a tailor on a sealing ship when he was a boy, and he showed us all how to cut out the pieces."

"It's fine," Erasmus said. "I suppose. We don't need the skins for anything else."

"Have you seen the underwear?" Ned said. "It's wonderful." He showed Erasmus the shirt, drawers, and socks he'd almost completed. "These are from the skin of a calf a few months old," he said. "Very supple and delicate. You make them with the fur side in. Then these"—he held up a hooded coat, trousers, and mittens—"these we make from a yearling, with the fur side out."

Erasmus saw a wrinkle and several pleats where the hood of Ned's coat met the back. Something was wrong, too, with the way the sleeve met the armhole, and there were patches where the fur ran backward. It was touching, really. The eager clumsiness, the attempt to keep alive the fragments of Esquimaux lore Joe had passed along. "You're using sinew?"

Ned shook his head. "None of us can manage it. But we found some waxed button thread in the chest with the extra wool cloth . . . was it all right to take that?"

"It's fine," Erasmus said. "But maybe you could keep track of how many spools you use, and let me know."

"Of course," Ned agreed. Looking down at the garments, he said, "Ivan and I have been getting along faster than the others. So we're also making a suit for you, which we hope you'll like."

"That's very kind," Erasmus said. "But it isn't necessary. Everything that Dr. Boerhaave and I gathered, I have enough souvenirs for a lifetime."

Ned cleared his throat. "It comforts the men," he said. "If you know what I mean."

Puzzled, Erasmus said, "I don't."

"Because . . . we tell each other we're making these to bring home and show our relatives, but also some of the men worry about how late in the season it's getting, and how the ice still hasn't opened, and they dread getting stuck here again. We don't want to be caught so ill-prepared as we were last winter."

Erasmus felt his face stiffen. "It's just in *case*," Ned said hastily. "It's not that anyone questions your orders or thinks you're doing the wrong thing. But just in *case*, you know. The same way that Barton and I have been packing down some seal meat with blubber on the ice belt, where it's still cool."

"It's a good idea," Erasmus said. Was this something Zeke would have thought of, had Zeke been here? During the bright nighttime hours, when he should have been sleeping, he sometimes walked a mile or two north from the brig, trying to imagine what Zeke was doing. What he was seeing, what he might have discovered. How his provisions were lasting and whether he'd been able to feed himself solely by his luck with a rifle. He'd been proud of how well he was managing in Zeke's absence. He should have anticipated the men's worries, he knew; but he hadn't been able even to consider the idea that they might remain trapped here another year.

"We'll get out in August," Erasmus said. "We will. But if it relieves the men's anxiety to make these preparations, if it makes everyone more comfortable . . ." Abruptly he turned and walked away.

THE FOLLOWING WEEK, Erasmus walked the length and breadth of their ice-bound cove: puddles, hollows, soggy mounds, but not a single crack. Yet the North Water of Baffin's

Bay must be expanding, he thought; and beyond the protection of the headland that sheltered their cove, the currents must be heaving the ice. What was wrong, what had always been wrong, was the site Zeke had chosen for their home. Erasmus studied the patterns of shadow cast by the hills around them. The brig bobbed in a tiny pool of water, where the refracted heat from her hull had parted the lips of ice for two feet all around.

"If we could get to the mouth of the cove," he said to the men that night, "past the icebergs, we'd be ready to move when the bay opens."

"But we can do that," Captain Tyler exclaimed. "We have tools." The sense of being afloat again seemed to cure both him and Mr. Tagliabeau, who claimed to know every trick of the ice saws and powder canisters Erasmus had purchased more than a year ago.

Suddenly the pair were fitting pieces of metal together, calculating charges, giving orders to the men. All their sullen lethargy vanished. On August 1 they began sawing parallel channels through the ice, extending forward from the bit of open water under the bowsprit. The exploding canisters heaved and cracked fifty square yards of ice; the men sawed the slabs into smaller chunks and hauled them from the water, until the *Narwhal* occupied a tiny, jagged pool, three ship-lengths long but only a few feet broader than her beam. Flat on his stomach and sopping wet, Erasmus watched in wonder as tiny wavelets lapped at the edges of the pool. Each wavelet wore away a few more particles of ice. If they couldn't carve a canal all the way out to the Sound, still every cut weakened the ice. A little more open water and a swell might arise, the tides might be felt.

They sawed and blasted, sawed and blasted; they crept up on Zeke's Follies and then were beside them, almost in line with the tip of the point. Captain Tyler anchored the *Narwhal* to the stable ice, so it wouldn't snake down the canal until they were fully loaded. Although Smith Sound was still far away, although they hadn't yet dug themselves out of their cove, never mind into the larger bay, the long black ribbon stretching before the brig was immensely cheering.

August 5 passed without signs of Zeke, but no one discussed this. Zeke knew the margin of safety; that he might be a week, even ten days late, and still reach the brig before it was freed. Surely he was only exploring as long as possible. They worked around the clock, in delirious daylight, expecting Zeke every moment. On August 10, Captain Tyler set up the cables and the capstans.

Taking turns at the capstan bars, sweating and heaving to the tune of Sean's whaling songs, the crew warped the *Narwhal* to the far end of the canal. After they anchored, Ned and Barton cooked a special feast, which they ate perched on crates along the thread of water. Their condition hadn't really changed, Erasmus thought, tearing at a succulent ptarmigan leg. The brig had been one place and now was another, but the white plain still stretched around them, marked only by the line they'd carved across it. Still, the view was subtly changed, and this made an amazing difference. The hills they'd gazed at for almost a year loomed down at a new angle. The ice belt bound to the base of the cliffs was half a mile off their stern, almost beautiful in the distance. The three icebergs were right beside them, shrunken and bordered by rings of water. And the rock cairn beside the storehouse, beneath which they'd interred the remains of Mr. Francis, was no longer visible.

STILL ZEKE DIDN'T return. The temperature dropped and the sun sank toward the horizon; not night, not quite yet, but there were real twilights. On August 16 the temperature dipped below freezing and an inch of young ice formed on the canal. Perfectly smooth, Erasmus saw. Glassy and terrifying. Some slabs they'd sawed out but not yet removed were frozen into the delicate plain. The noon sun melted the ice, but on the seventeenth, when the sun set for the first time, a clear cold descended and the air grew still. The following morning Mr. Tagliabeau, long-faced, stood on the new ice and didn't fall in. That day they sawed more old ice, with less enthusiasm, and on the nineteenth found that all their efforts had been undone while they slept.

The men came to Erasmus after he'd already lain down to sleep. They stood in a half-circle around the pallet he'd made on deck: Ned, Barton, Isaac, Robert, Ivan, Thomas, and Sean. Captain Tyler and Mr. Tagliabeau, for reasons Erasmus soon understood, stayed belowdecks in their bunks. When Erasmus sat up, rubbing his eyes, Ned stepped forward from the circle.

"Commander Voorhees is lost," Ned said, after clearing his throat twice. "We all know it—we knew when he left this would happen. He's two weeks late and we have to admit that he's dead."

"He's not *dead*," Erasmus said. Although he'd been fearing just this for a week. "He's late. Anything could have happened to him, he could be near us right now."

"He's dead," Barton said, behind Ned's shoulder. "He's been trying to kill us all since the day we left home. And the ice isn't opening, and the young ice gets thicker every day . . ."

"And we're not going to be able to free the *Narwhal*," Isaac chimed in.

"We're stuck," said Ivan.

"Again," Sean said.

"There's so little fuel left," Thomas added. "Our supplies— you know, you have the lists. We can't make it through another winter."

A fog seemed to hover over Erasmus's head. He was tired, he hadn't been sleeping well. He could almost hear the new ice forming. He could almost hear the beat of wings as the birds gathered for their journeys south, almost hear hooves ringing as the ground hardened and the caribou fled. His eyes felt full of cinders. Hadn't he *wished* Zeke dead, if only for a moment?

"What is it you want?" he asked. "I don't know what's happened to Commander Voorhees any more than you do. I can't keep the ice from forming, and I can't do much about our supplies. We can assign more hunting parties if you'd like, keep half of us working at breaking up the ice and half stockpiling game; that's a good idea, perhaps we'll start that tomorrow . . ."

Ned stepped back, twisted around, and picked up something from the deck. The others mimicked his movements, and when they stood and faced Erasmus again, he saw that each held a stack of neatly folded fur clothing. "We have these," Ned said. "Each of us. And we want to leave."

For the rest of the night, and all through the following day, the men ground down Erasmus's objections. Captain Tyler and Mr. Tagliabeau kept working on the canal, punctuating the men's comments with explosions and the crack of shattering ice. The officers couldn't address the subject directly, Ned told Erasmus. It would be inappropriate given their positions; they couldn't give orders to abandon the brig. But apparently they were willing to join a retreat led by Erasmus.

The men had maps, Erasmus learned. Maps, plans, lists of their own, detailed strategies. How long had they been discussing this without him? Since the moment of Zeke's departure, perhaps; those fur suits, he now realized, had always been meant for this trip. The men had never believed that Zeke would return. And although they'd hoped that the *Narwhal* might be freed, they'd found it sensible to make an alternate plan. Among them they had a surprising wealth of knowledge.

Sean and Barton had worked out a possible route. They'd load the whaleboat onto the large sledge and drag it from their cove around the point and to the mouth of the bay; then along the ice belt to Cape Sabine, or perhaps a bit farther south. After that they'd head diagonally southeast across the Sound, dragging the boat over the solid floes and rowing across any cracks. Somewhere south of Cape Alexander, perhaps fifty or sixty miles from the *Narwhal*, they might hope to find open water or at least navigable pack ice; they'd launch the boat and work past Cape York to the inshore lead of Melville Bay. They might still hope to find whalers there; failing that, they might hope to sail to Upernavik.

"But we'd need weeks to pack everything and prepare the boat," Erasmus said. "And we'd never get far enough along before the pack closes for the season."

Then he learned that chopping out the channel, even as it refroze at night, hadn't been the only situation that resembled the work of Penelope. While he'd been—what? Sleeping, he supposed, or hunting, or scouting; apparently they'd used each moment—Ned had led the men in a secretive effort down in the hold. Remarkable nerve, Erasmus thought, for someone only recently turned twenty-one; he wasn't sure whether he felt more admiration or anger. Under Ned's direction, the men had broken neatly into his boxes, shifting contents until the labels no longer bore any relationship to what was inside. He'd heard them moving around in there; they'd told him they were hunting down the rats.

They'd calculated what they'd need for their journey: so much pemmican per man per day, so much biscuit and molasses and coffee; so much blubber for the stoves; so much powder and shot and so many percussion caps; so many sleeping sacks. All repacked and grouped together, ready to be fitted into the whaleboat. Isaac and Ivan had sewn sailcloth provision bags, made watertight with tar and pitch. And each man had already assembled a tiny sack of personal belongings.

"Thomas has taken care of the boat," Ned added.

He led Erasmus to the whaleboat resting innocently under its tarpaulin. Under that cover, Thomas had fixed a false keel to the flat bottom and built up the bulwarks with planks and canvas. Those wood shavings, Erasmus thought. Earlier, when he'd noticed them, Thomas had claimed to be making standard repairs in anticipation of Zeke's return. The large sledge, which they'd never used, had been fitted with a cradle to carry the boat. Isaac had made sturdy sets of traces, with which they might haul the loaded sledge. And Ned had made a diagram, showing where they'd fit in the cramped boat and how the provisions might be stowed; he'd thought of everything. All they needed, Ned said, was Erasmus to lead them.

"Captain Tyler and Mr. Tagliabeau cede command to you," Ned said. "If you'll only give the order, we could leave in two days."

Erasmus agonized for another thirty-six hours. If Dr. Boerhaave were here, they could have decided together what to do— but Dr. Boerhaave was gone. And it was impossible that he should leave this place that had taken his friend's bones; impossible that he should abandon the brig and Zeke. On the sodden ice he saw everywhere the Zeke he'd known as a boy: Zeke and Copernicus stringing together a reptile's skeleton; Zeke tagging along to the creek to listen to Mr. Wells read Pliny; Zeke rolling across the Repository shelves wondering what to borrow next. Wanting so badly to be taken seriously; moving beyond Erasmus's distracted gaze and then reappearing after a few years' work at his father's firm, transformed into a man they all *had* to take seriously. Erasmus could still hear his father saying, *You should give him more credit. He behaves oddly sometimes. But his mind is sharp.*

Was sharp. Is, was—how could he leave Zeke behind, even if he were only leaving Zeke's body? Yet it was equally impossible that he should condemn the crew to another winter here. They couldn't survive it, and the *Narwhal* couldn't be moved. The only possible compromise was to send Ned and the others off in the boat while he stayed with the brig, hoping for Zeke's eventual return. He might survive, with luck hunting and perhaps some help from the vanished Esquimaux.

"It would be mutiny," Ned argued. "Without you. The contract said the brig was to be under Captain Tyler's command, but you were to head the expedition. And the brig might as well be sunk. You're in charge now."

"You take the men," Erasmus said to Captain Tyler and Mr. Tagliabeau. "I'll stay here and wait for Commander Voorhees."

Captain Tyler stared at him with frank dislike. "I will not," he said. "The chain of command is clear. If you give the order to go south I'll aid you in any way possible. But I'll not take responsibility for this without you. If I made it home somehow, having abandoned the brig and you and Commander Voorhees, my reputation wouldn't be worth a penny."

"Nor mine," Mr. Tagliabeau said.

"Whatever happens, then," Erasmus said, "it will be on my head. Is that what you want?"

"It's not what *we* want," Mr. Tagliabeau said. "It's simply your duty. Your choice."

ERASMUS PACKED SOME instruments, his fur suit, and Lavinia's green silk journal. He took Dr. Boerhaave's medicine chest, both because it had belonged to his friend and because he was now the closest thing the men had to a doctor. From the relics they'd obtained on Boothia he made a painful selection: the small copper cooking pot, the prayer book and the treatise on steam engines, the silver spoons and forks and the mahogany barometer case Dr. Boerhaave had once held in his hands. The rest he had to leave behind, but he hoped that these, and the careful account in his journal, would be enough to confirm Dr. Rae's findings and their own contact with the Esquimaux who'd seen the last of Franklin's expedition. He packed the smaller items in the copper pot and sealed it with a piece of walrus hide.

From the hold he removed his specimens, too heavy to ferry home. Unwilling to let them sink when the *Narwhal* was eventually crushed by the ice, he returned them to the storehouse. He made a list of all he'd consigned there, and in a tin box he placed that, his own journal, one of Dr. Boerhaave's precious volumes of Thoreau, and Agassiz's work on the fossil fishes. He added the studded bit of boot sole, which had spent all this time lying flat and silent beneath his bookshelf: one little relic of his own. Then he broke into Zeke's private box and stole Dr. Boerhaave's journal, leaving Zeke's black volume behind. Zeke was dead, he must be dead. That frail boy with the vibrant eyes was gone and now he must look after Ned. Lavinia—he put Lavinia from his mind.

He added Dr. Boerhaave's journal to his own tin box and prepared to solder it closed. At the last minute, he took down the portrait of Franklin and stowed that as well. In Captain Tyler's bunk, he saw, everything had been removed except for the paper gravestone, on which the names of their lost companions had been inscribed. Zeke's name now occupied the bottom of the list.

He had the men clean the ship, and he left behind enough provisions to support Zeke in case a miracle brought him back. He wrote out a careful statement, explaining the situation that had driven them to leave and their proposed route; he noted the crates of specimens in the storehouse and the provisions left on board. *We leave this brig August 26, 1856.* In the season called *aosok*, he thought, remembering the word Joe had taught him. The short interval between complete thaw and reconsolidation of the ice. For their long, improbable journey they had, at most, until the end of September. Not nearly enough time.

While the men began the laborious process of hauling the boat across the level plain, toward the point that blocked them from the Sound and onto the ice belt attached to the cliffs, he checked over every inch of the *Narwhal*. Then he nailed his statement to the mast and walked onto the ice.

7

THE GOBLINS KNOWN AS
Innersuit

(AUGUST–OCTOBER 1856)

Enterprises of great pith and moment command our admiration, sympathy, and emulation with the varied force which the quality of their motives and objects deserves. The agility and courage of a rope-dancer on his perilous balance do not affect us in the same way as the generous daring displayed by a fireman in the rescue of a child from a burning house. There is natural nobleness enough in anybody to feel the difference between a hard day's journey on an errand of benevolence, and the feat of walking a hundred successive hours for a wager. A novelist, an orator, or a player, may work upon the sympathetic emotions of virtue until our heart-strings answer like echoes to his touch; but we are not deceived nor cheated into an admiration unworthy of ourselves. We were not made in the Divine image to take seemings for things. Our instincts stand by the real interests of the world and of the universe, and we will not meanly surrender our souls to any imposture. We say to every man who challenges our admiration for his deeds, "Stop! worship touches the life of the worshiper. If your objects are nothings, expect nothing for them: if your motives are selfish, pay yourself for them. We will not make fools of ourselves: we will settle the account justly to you and honorably to us."

— WILLIAM ELDER, *Biography of Elisha Kent Kane* (1858)

*L*ater, different scenes from the boat journey would float back to each of them. So much work, so much pain; so little rest or food or hope. What happened when? What happened in fact, and what was only imagined, or misremembered? Erasmus made no diary entries, nor did Ned or the other men. Of the days when they were out on the ice, heaving against the harnesses and rowing through lanes of ice-choked water, or sleeping packed like a litter of piglets inside the canvas-covered boat, nothing remained but a blur of impressions.

From their cove down the ice belt to Cape Sabine, then across the broken, heaving Sound to a point slightly north of Cape Hatherton: pack ice, water, old ice, hummocks, thin ice, pressure ridges. Always pulling, except for the wearying, exasperating times when their way was blocked by an open channel and they must unload everything, remove the boat from the sledge, ferry across, reload, and begin the whole process again. Their shoulders and hands were rubbed raw by the ropes, and Ivan would remember the acid burn of vomit on his lips; they all threw up, they were pulling too much weight. Near the leads the ice was covered with slush and often they sank above their knees. Sean would remember how his ankles ballooned, forcing him to slit his boots and finally cut them off entirely, so that he made the rest of the journey with his feet wrapped in caribou hides. Robert would remember his persistent, burning diarrhea, and the humiliation of soiling his pants when he strained against the weight of the sledge.

Erasmus would pause one day after skidding helplessly on the ice, and then he'd think of the bit of boot sole sealed in his box and wonder why they hadn't all thought to stud their boots similarly. In what seemed to him now like another life, his boots had shot him off the face of a cliff—and still he hadn't learned. But it was too late now, they had no screws; they fell and stumbled and were relieved only once, when the ice field was smooth and the wind blew from the northwest. That day they set the sails and glided for eight miles: a great blessing, never repeated, which Barton would dream about for years.

From a high point of land on the Greenland side of Smith Sound, Captain Tyler and Mr. Tagliabeau saw more ice south of them, but also, in the distance, an open channel between the land-fast ice and the pack ice slicing southward. Isaac, blinded by the snow, would not remember this sight, but the others would; and Thomas would remember his frantic rush, at night when he was already exhausted, to caulk the boat's seams and repair the holes. And how anxious he'd felt when Erasmus told him they all depended on his ability to keep the boat together with no proper supplies.

At the Littleton Islands the ice field thinned, abraded from beneath by the currents from a nearby river. Barton would remember inching forward the last few miles, sounding the ice with a boat hook at every step and eying the eddies gurgling just below his feet. And then breaking through, despite his precautions: one side of the sledge crashing under, the sickening lurch and the scramble to firmer ice. Ivan remembered that moment— always, always—because he'd been tied in closest to the sledge and, as his companions heaved, had lost his footing and been pulled into the water, to bob briefly under the edge of the ice. By the time Erasmus pulled him out by the hair, he'd broken two fingers and seen blood pour from a gash in Erasmus's forehead. In the ice-choked water Erasmus floundered, scrambling for the provision bags slithering out of the boat as the sea slithered over the sides. The copper pot containing the Franklin relics slipped out too, but the air beneath the walrus skin kept it floating low in the water and at first Erasmus thought he might retrieve it. Under the broken floe it sailed, the floe that had nearly claimed

Ivan; and although Erasmus pressed his shoulder against the edge and swept with his arms and then a paddle, finally lowering his head beneath the ice, the pot disappeared. That night a hard wind blew from the northeast, nearly freezing the wet men to death.

Erasmus would remember this because it was here that he lost the evidence of their search for Franklin's remains, and also because, although he could never be sure, he suspected that here began the process of freezing and constriction and infection that would later cause him to lose his toes. He should have been resting, with his boots removed and his feet wrapped in dry furs. But instead, that night he and Captain Tyler, with whom he'd been arguing since they left the brig, stood screaming at each other in front of the men and nearly came to blows. Each blamed the other for the accident and the loss of the relics—as each had blamed the other for every wrong turn taken, bad camping site chosen, failure hunting—and Captain Tyler had slashed the air with a boathook and said, "I despise you." A moment that Mr. Tagliabeau, never more than a few feet from his captain but less and less certain that his loyalty was justified, would also always remember. He'd longed to turn his back and say, "I despise you both," but had said nothing; on this journey he learned that he was both a coward and a complainer.

Not long after that accident, though, they stood on a high mound and saw a lane of open water spreading before them. With much effort they made their way to a rocky beach, and then unloaded the boat for the last time and sank it for a day to swell the seams. Not long enough, Thomas would remember thinking. The surf was beating against the cliffs; was it his fault the boat still leaked when it was finally, properly launched? They were ten men in a whaleboat made for six, with too much baggage. Trembling inches above the water they rowed, and felt like they were swimming. Under reefed sails, in a fresh breeze, they rounded Cape Alexander.

Ned would remember the mock sun that appeared in the sky that evening; a perfect parhelion—Dr. Boerhaave had taught him that word—with a point of light on either side. But neither Ned nor anyone else would be haunted by the sight of Dr. Boerhaave's head, which in the months since his drowning had been severed from his body by a passing grampus and then swept south in the currents, coming to rest face up on the rubble below a cliff. Among the rounded rocks his head was invisible to his friends, and the singing noise made by the wind passing over his jaw bones was lost in the roar of the waves.

Sutherland Island, where they'd hoped to land, was barricaded by ice. They bobbed all night in irregular winds and a violent freezing rain, and Ned would remember this place for the weather and the onset of his fever, which caused this journey to be jumbled forever after in his mind with his two earlier crossings of Smith Sound. Eastward with Joe and Dr. Boerhaave and Zeke he'd gone; westward with only Zeke. He remembered that. Pushing like an animal against the harness, pulling the sledge sunk into the soft surface—those journeys, or this journey?

Once the worst of the fever hit and he lay helpless among his companions, he repeated to himself the stories Joe had told him as they pulled another sledge, in another month. The stories that, once they reached Anoatok, Joe had translated for him around the fire. They'd lain on a platform inside the hut, mashed in a crowd of Esquimaux and sharing walrus steaks. Meat was piled along the ice belt and walrus skulls glared eyeless from the snowbanks. A mighty spirit called *Tonarsuk*, Joe had said, spearing a morsel from the soup pot. In whom these Esquimaux believe. And many minor supernatural beings, chief among them the goblins known as *innersuit*, who live among the fjords and have no noses. The *innersuit* hide behind the rocks, waiting to capture a passing man so they may cut off his nose and force him to join their tribe. Should the victim escape their clutches, his nose may be returned to him by the intercession of a skillful wizard, or *angekok*. The nose may come back, Joe had said; he'd been translating Ootuniah's words for Ned and Dr. Boerhaave, as they steamed companionably in the hut. The nose may come flying through the sky, and settle down in its former place; but the man once captured by the *innersuit* will always be known by the scar across his face.

Ned's fever, or frostbite, or something putrid he ate, had caused his own nose to erupt in pustules that leaked yellow fluid and then crusted over and cracked and bled. He would remember dreading his whole nose might disappear. And then thinking it *should* disappear—along with his face, his entire body: Who was to blame for all this, if not him? He had lied to Erasmus; he'd made those fur suits and shifted supplies like a thief; he'd planned this trip and organized the men. On Boothia, he'd pointed out the copper kettles that had set everything else in motion; on his earlier crossing of the Sound, he'd failed to save Dr. Boerhaave. As they passed fjords and glaciers he heard singing—not Dr. Boerhaave, but someone else—and begged the man against whose knee he was pressed to guard him from the goblins. The *innersuit* cause much trouble, Ootuniah had said. They plague many a journey. Weeping with guilt and fear, his hands cupped over his nose, Ned remembered his grandmother's tales back in Ireland. Malicious spirits who made porridge burn, toast fall buttered side down, cows lose their calves. Perhaps it was the *innersuit* who'd haunted this journey and brought the fickle, difficult weather.

Perhaps, he told Erasmus one night—perhaps it was the *innersuit* who were to blame for their bad luck. They pushed through half-solid water, around icebergs and currents of drift ice. One night they anchored in a crack as a gale struck from the northwest, watching helplessly as a floe on the far side of the channel broke off, spun on an iceberg like a pivot, and closed upon their resting place. When it hit the corner of their small dock the floe shattered, their haven shattered, everything around them rose and crushed and tumbled. The boat was tossed like a walnut shell into a boiling slurry of crushed ice and water, and Robert would remember this more sharply than the other accidents, because it was here that he dislocated his shoulder. Captain Tyler held him down while Erasmus torqued his arm back into place, and Robert would remember being amazed, even through the blinding pain, that the pair had worked in concert.

On Hakluyt Island they found birds, but failed to shoot any. A seal they shot near an iceberg sank before they could retrieve it. They ran out of food, for a week eating only a few ounces of bread dust and pemmican each day with all of them feverish, all of them weak, and Ned muttered that perhaps the *innersuit* had stolen Joe from them, and tipped Dr. Boerhaave into the water. Erasmus would remember this comment and how sharply it pained him. Despite his worry for Ned, and for the others who didn't understand how weak they'd grown but were each day less capable, still the mention of Dr. Boerhaave could make his mind freeze up. He never thought about Zeke, the thought was impossible; he hardly thought about what was happening to his feet, although they were oozing and stinking and numb; he focused on getting them all through each day, pushing forward and cooking and eating and resting and pushing again, putting the miles behind them. But when Ned muttered about goblins and Dr. Boerhaave, Erasmus had to fight to keep his concentration.

Northumberland Island, Whale Sound, Cape Parry. The sea was covered with drifting pack ice, which poured from Whale Sound in a constant stream. At night thin ice formed in the open patches, and Erasmus would remember the panic this caused him. If they were caught here they would never survive; and Ned would be the first to go. Ned was delirious, and when Robert and

Ivan shot a heap of dovekies, Ned sat upright, his nose a bloody, eroded mass, and babbled. Something about a great hunt: he and Joe and Dr. Boerhaave joining the Esquimaux on the cliffs where the dovekies were breeding. Sweeping the birds from the air with nets at the end of long narwhal tusks; thousands caught as easily as one might pick peas and the bodies boiling in huge soap-stone pots, the children sucking on bird skins and tearing raw birds limb from limb, their faces buried in feathers and blood smeared over their cheeks. But Ned wouldn't eat these other birds, he couldn't bear to bring food near his nose. He said names, only some of which Erasmus knew—Awahtok, Metek, Ootuniah; Myouk, Egurk, Nualik, Nessark—and later, when those names and the people behind them would return to haunt Erasmus, he'd remember envying Ned all he'd seen on that trip, and wishing yet again that he'd been present: Dr. Boerhaave might still be alive.

Erasmus both heard and didn't hear Ned as he forced the boat farther south. Captain Tyler and Mr. Tagliabeau contradicted his every order, more and more confident as they passed Hoppner Point and Granville Bay and it began to seem that, if they could just beat the final freezing-in, they might actually reach the whaling grounds. They were racing, racing, the temperature dropping each day and the new ice forming, the pack consolidating, the narrow channel closing: yet despite the urgency Captain Tyler argued over every tack and turn. These were his waters, Erasmus would remember him saying; they were in his country now and Erasmus must cede command to him. Here he knew what was best for the expedition.

Erasmus had unlaced his boots that morning, unable to resist confirming by eye what he could already feel; eight of his toes were black and dead. In Dr. Boerhaave's medicine chest were amputating knives, still sharp and gleaming, but it was impossible that he should use them on himself. It was also now impossible that he should walk any distance if the ice closed around them, but no one knew that yet. Or maybe Captain Tyler did know; he seemed to sense Erasmus's growing weakness.

"You refused to lead the men earlier," Erasmus would remember saying to the captain. "When the men most needed you, you'd do nothing. Now that there's a chance we might reach safety you want command, you want the credit." The rifles and powder and shot were scattered throughout the boat, but he had all the percussion caps and felt secure. "I'll shoot you if you disobey me," he said.

All the men would remember that: how nearly they'd come to having to choose sides, how only a waving gun had saved them. For the last few days, creeping around Cape Dudley Digges and then through a narrow lead at the base of the ice foot, no one spoke except to give or respond to orders. Every night the temperature dropped below freezing, although it was still warm at noon. Sometimes it snowed. They rowed through a dense sludge that dripped from the oars like porridge, and when at last they doubled Cape York they dreaded the emptiness. October 3, Melville Bay. Upernavik, on the far side of the breaking-up yard, was still so many miles away.

WHAT GREETED ERASMUS in Melville Bay was dense pack ice, broken only by small, irregular leads; he'd expected this. What he didn't expect were the dark specks on the horizon. A cluster of specks and threads of something that, wavering and wafting upward, made his heart leap. Smoke? By now he'd long been familiar with the way the blank ice shifted perspective and perception—how what looked like a bear, far away, might turn out to be a hare nearby; how a nearby gentle hill might resolve into a distant, mighty range. At first he couldn't believe that the smoke was smoke. The specks, which seemed far away and large, might be closer, might be Esquimaux hunting. But the upright lines among the smoke threads were really masts, and those were truly ships. Seventeen ships, the men told each other, counting as they smashed the thin ice blocking their way and spun in a frantic, looping course through the seams around the floes. The ships appeared to be frozen in; a mile from the cluster their boat was stopped as well. They'd already burned the sledge for fuel and were too weak to haul the boat onto the solid ice.

"I'll go," Captain Tyler said. "I'll walk to the first ship and bring back enough men to help."

"No," Erasmus said. "Too many of us are broken down, I need you here with me. The wind could change in a minute, and if the floes separate we could drift very quickly." He longed to go himself, but knew he couldn't walk more than a few steps. "Whoever is strongest and can move fastest must go. Barton, I think."

Barton leapt to his feet. "I'll run," he said. "I'll run the whole way."

Four hours later he returned with with a crew of startled Shetland Islanders from a Dundee whaler. It was snowing and dark and very cold, and the ice was grinding beneath their feet. Erasmus greeted the sailors briefly, saying only that their ship was lost and they needed help. When he saw the pity on the sailors' faces, he understood how ragged and worn they must look. "Can you help us back to your ship? Can you take us in?"

The sailors, so strong and healthy, made short work of the task. They hauled the boat up on the ice, attached the drag lines, unloaded everything but the men's personal belongings and then, after a quick examination of the *Narwhal*'s crew, sat Ned, Erasmus, and Ivan on the thwarts. Twelve of them dragged the boat, as if it weighed nothing, across the ice, while the others supported the men who could still walk. Thomas cringed at the sound of the keel splintering and grinding away.

Their way was lit by the moon, and by several fires. As they drew closer, Erasmus saw that these weren't bonfires, or cooking fires, but the remains of two ships burning. Nipped by the ice, they'd been sliced all the way through and partially sunk. Only the decking above the waterline remained. "It's the custom," one of the Shetland men said when Erasmus questioned him. "Among us whalers. When a ship is stove in, suchlike, we burn her remains." By the firelight Erasmus saw masts scattered over the ice, broken whaleboats, and a whole ship lying broadside, her keel exposed forlornly.

"Twenty vessels caught here," said the Shetland man. Magna Abernathy, or so Erasmus understood; his accent was very thick. "Three lost so far. Their crews have been taken in by the other ships, but we still have some room. Our captain started preparing for you as soon as your messenger arrived."

Then a bark loomed before them like a castle. The *Harmony*, of Dundee, Magna announced. Captained by Alec Sturrock. Between the time Magna bolted up the planks and returned with his captain, Erasmus took in the cranes and whaleboats and the scarred, oily hull. After that everything happened so fast. Erasmus and his companions were carried, pushed, washed, tidied, bandaged, clothed; shown to newly hung hammocks where their belongings were stowed and then whisked away again. In the cabin they were blinded by the light of clean-burning lamps and stunned by the smell of baking bread. Ned was taken away by the ship's surgeon, who was worried by his fever and the condition of his nose, but Erasmus was allowed to stay with the others; no one had yet seen his feet.

Inside the *Harmony*, pressed hard to port by the ice, everything was tilted but the table had been leveled. Chairs were drawn up for them, plates set before them and wine, small glasses of red glowing wine. Only after they'd chewed and swallowed in silence for several minutes did Captain Sturrock ask, "How was your ship lost? How long have you been out in that boat?"

Erasmus leaned forward, ready to speak, but Captain Tyler spoke first. "Amos Tyler, of New London," he said. "I've captained whaling ships for twenty years." A quick exchange of places and names followed; the two captains hadn't met before, but had sailed the same waters and knew many people in common. Immediately Erasmus felt the balance of power shift like the bubble in a spirit level.

"Which was your brig?" Captain Sturrock asked. "We didn't see you among the fleet earlier in the season."

Captain Tyler curled his lip. "Not this season, indeed," he said. Holding his glass out for more wine, he told Captain Sturrock his version of what had happened. How not this season, but last, he'd accepted a position as Sailing Master for an expedition in search of Sir John Franklin; how everything went wrong and they got stuck in the ice, because the expedition's commander wouldn't follow his advice. The eager questions about the fate of the Franklin expedition he answered briefly, impatiently. Then he went on and on and on, through all their own trials and the dark hopeless winter and their eventual escape. Erasmus tried to interrupt him, but couldn't. He was dizzy, sweating; the room was horribly close after their weeks in the open air and it was so hot, there were so many smells. "The *Narwhal* will never be freed," Captain Tyler concluded.

"And your commander?" asked the other captain. He looked around the cabin.

"Dead," Captain Tyler said. "As are several others."

Turning to Erasmus, he said, "This is the *Narwhal*'s naturalist, Erasmus Wells, a friend of Commander Voorhees. Commander Voorhees delegated to him responsibility for the expedition's goals in his absence, and it was his decision to abandon the brig and organize our boat journey. I merely navigated us through the ice."

Not his decision, Erasmus thought. But Ned's. Even this he

couldn't take credit for. He must let them know that Zeke wasn't surely dead, only possibly dead, that there might still be hope. When he stood to speak, the floor tilted under him and the lamps merged into one gold ball and then disappeared. He was on the floor, flat on his back. Someone had undone his boots. Captain Sturrock and his surgeon and two other men were looking down at him, talking among themselves. The surgeon touched his toes, as Dr. Boerhaave might have done. "They'll have to come off," he said.

AFTERWARD, RECOVERING IN the first mate's cabin, Erasmus heard the story of how the *Harmony* had been trapped. He and Ned lay side by side, too weak to talk but able to listen.

In July the *Harmony*, along with ships from Hull and Aberdeen and Kirkcaldy and Newcastle, New Bedford, Nantucket, and Newfoundland, had crept through the heavy ice in Melville Bay. When the fleet had finally escaped into the North Water they'd crossed quickly to Pond's Bay and then had found their route to the south blocked by fields of drifting ice. An easterly wind had driven ice into the bay, sealing the fleet inside; they'd seen no whales at all. For weeks they'd waited, anxious and bored, only to find the route south still blocked when the wind finally shifted and released them.

They'd tried to return to Upernavik; reaching Cape York again they'd found Melville Bay still choked with icebergs and heavy pack ice. Back to the west they'd gone, to be stopped again; back once more to Melville Bay, where the ice was even denser; back and forth a third time, twenty ships unable to find a safe route south. Strong winds from the southeast had crowded the fleet together, then pressed them against the ice trapped in the curve south of Cape York.

With the jib-boom of one ship overlapping the taffrail of the next they'd towed the ships through the narrow cracks until the wind closed the ice around them. The *Alexander* of New London had been crushed, and the *Union* of Hull; the *Swan* had been heaved on her side, where Erasmus had seen her. Since September 15 the fleet had been stuck here. And now, said Mr. Haslas—the surgeon, who visited Erasmus and Ned several times daily, and chattered while he examined them—now they could only hope that the ice might part once more. A strong wind from the northwest might still separate the floes, and if they could beat their way free before the young ice sealed the open water they might yet reach Upernavik.

The crews visited back and forth, held great gatherings on the ice, made music and gambled and danced; meanwhile the officers entertained each other, holding long dinners in their cabins. Captain Tyler and Mr. Tagliabeau went from one ship to the next, feted everywhere for their courage and wisdom. Or so Erasmus heard when, occasionally, one of the men tore himself away from the festivities and dropped by to see him and Ned. It was Thomas, after a visit to a New Bedford ship, who brought news of Dr. Kane.

"He left his ship in the ice," Thomas said. "Just like the Esquimaux told us. He and his crew made a journey like ours, in three small boats but earlier in the season. They crossed all the way to Upernavik and then were carried by a Danish ship to Godhavn, where they met up with the rescue expedition. They reached New York last October, and the men who told me this said it was in all the newspapers. Dr. Kane is a great hero now. Even though he was looking in completely the wrong place for Franklin."

He gazed dreamily past Erasmus's ruined feet. "Maybe we'll be heroes too," he said. "When we get home, maybe everyone will be thrilled to see us."

Erasmus looked over at Ned, lying a few feet from him and

listening intently. Mr. Haslas had debrided his nose and applied poultices. But the soft flare of his left nostril had corroded away, as if it had been burned; scar tissue, tight and misshapen, replaced the normal flesh. Instead of a neat round hole, his nose had a dark narrow slit on that side. His own deformity, Erasmus thought, could at least be hidden inside his boots—how had this happened to Ned, so young and handsome?

"Do you think?" Ned said. "Will it be like that? Or will everyone blame us for abandoning the *Narwhal*, and for failing to bring back any evidence of what happened to Franklin?"

Thomas turned to him, waving his scarred hands. "Dr. Kane left *his* ship," he said. "He had to, and so did we."

Ned turned his face away, and Erasmus knew what he was thinking: that Dr. Kane had left no one behind except the surely dead.

A FEW NIGHTS later a great snowstorm descended, and with it a gale that shifted slowly from southwest to west to northwest. Erasmus and Ned heard the rush of feet on the deck above, excited chatter all night long as the ship shifted beneath them and their tilted world slowly leveled. Early the next morning Captain Sturrock rushed into their cabin, his hair sticking up and his eyes dark with excitement.

"The wind has opened the floes," he said. "We're afloat, all the ships are afloat, and we're going to try to head south through the leads. If we could have just a few days of this, before the new ice cements everything—I've spoken to Captain Nicholson, of the *Sarah Billopp*. If we're successful he's agreed to take you to his home at Marblehead."

"Marblehead?" Erasmus said. Captain Tyler and Mr. Tagliabeau squeezed in through the door, both looking as if they'd been up all night. "We won't stay with you?"

"Of course not," Captain Sturrock said. "You wish to return to Philadelphia, don't you? And that's as close as anyone in the fleet can get you."

Erasmus turned to Captain Tyler. "Do you agree that we should join the Marblehead ship?"

"You should, certainly," Captain Tyler said. "And Ned, and whoever else wants to join you. Ivan for sure, his fingers haven't healed correctly. But Mr. Tagliabeau and Robert and Sean and I are staying on with the *Harmony*."

"Why would you want to go to Scotland?" Erasmus said. "I don't think we should split up."

"The *Harmony* isn't heading home," Captain Sturrock said. "Not right away—our holds are empty, we have nothing to show for our voyage and no way to pay off the crew. We've decided to head for Newfoundland, in company with Captain Bowring. He tells me that if we overwinter there we can head out beyond the Strait of Belle Isle in March with the sealing fleet, and take on a load of furs before we go home."

"You don't want to go home?" Erasmus said to Captain Tyler. "After all this time?"

"Of course I *want* to," Captain Tyler said scornfully. "But what will I live on? Do you think I'll ever see the rest of the money Commander Voorhees owes me for the voyage? I'm not like you discovery men, I have to make a living. The trip will be a waste for me, if I don't make up for the lost wages somehow. If we do well sealing, my share will be enough to send me home with at least something."

By his side Mr. Tagliabeau nodded away. This whole trip, Erasmus thought, all the man had done was nod. Never an opinion of his own, never an idea.

"What are 'discovery men'?" Ned asked.

Captain Tyler and Mr. Tagliabeau snorted. Before either of them could speak, Captain Sturrock answered, looking at Erasmus as he spoke.

"It's what we call you arctic exploring types," he said. "All you men who go off on exploring expeditions, with funding and fanfare and special clothes, thinking you'll discover something. When every place you go some whaling ship has already been. We know more about the land and the currents and the winds than you ever will, and more about the habits of the whales and seals and walruses. I've met Russian discovery ships, and English, and French, and never known them to discover much of anything. What is it you *discovered* on your voyage?"

"New coastline," Erasmus said. "We charted a good deal of new coast, north of Smith Sound. And we found relics from Franklin's expedition, just as I told you—that they're lost is surely not our fault."

"That's what discovery men do," Captain Sturrock said. "Get lost. Lose things. Franklin is lost, and his ships and his men, and Dr. Kane's ship is lost, and yours and all your precious relics and specimens. If the captain of a whaling ship ever lost things at the rate you do, he wouldn't be long employed."

"If I had known," Captain Tyler said. "If I had ever known . . ."

"At least American discovery ships take note of whales and seals on their voyages, and report back when they arrive home," Captain Sturrock continued. "*Our* discovery men apparently think whales are beneath them; they never so much as mention them when they return to England and write their fancy books. They're jealous of us is what it is. On the west side of Baffin's Bay, all the points and bays were named by whalers, not by discovery men."

"That British discovery ship we saw?" Captain Tyler added. "The *Resolute*, the one that set Commander Voorhees to thinking he should go north in the first place—all we did was look at it, but I heard an American whaler brought it home. It was cleaned and given back to the British government."

"We could have done that," Mr. Tagliabeau said. "That could have been us."

SEAN AND ROBERT stayed on the *Harmony* with Captain Tyler and Mr. Tagliabeau. On the *Sarah Billopp*, small and cramped, Captain Nicholson made room for Erasmus, Ned, Ivan, Barton, Isaac, and Thomas. Six men only, Erasmus thought. Out of the fifteen who'd left Philadelphia. He couldn't imagine arriving home with such a small remnant of the expedition. He couldn't imagine what he'd say to the families of the men who'd been lost or even the families of those who'd survived but who, because the expedition had so failed to achieve its goals, were headed off for another half a year, slaughtering seals. Partly he couldn't imagine these things because he couldn't truly imagine he was headed home. Yet as if the goblins had fallen asleep, the weather stayed fine just long enough for them to escape. Slipping through the ice-choked water, the fleet made its way to Upernavik, then quickly to Godhavn. There the ships went their separate ways.

The *Sarah Billopp*'s surgeon assured Erasmus that his feet were healing and that he'd be able to walk again someday. And it was only afterward, with some of the ships heading around the tip of Greenland while the *Harmony* carried Captain Tyler and Mr. Tagliabeau and Sean and Robert away from him, that Erasmus really understood all he'd lost. Ships turned east, ships turned west, and the shell in which he'd enclosed himself so he could bring the men to safety split like a sprouting seed.

He lay in his bunk, weeping. His toes were nothing. The failed goals of the expedition were not exactly nothing, but they'd always been Zeke's goals, not his. He'd lost the glorious collection of specimens he and Dr. Boerhaave had made together: all the birds and insects and flowers and ferns, the skins and scales and fossils and bones—gone, gone, gone. And with them his hope of

writing a natural history of the arctic. Yet those losses were misfortune, which anyone might learn to accept.

But the *Narwhal* had lost half her crew, and he'd lost Dr. Boerhaave, the only true friend he'd ever had. He'd lost him, he'd lost
Zeke, he'd lost his sister's chance at happiness. Lavinia waiting so
patiently at home—how could he face her? He thought of her
life, stripped of Zeke. And of his own, stripped of everything
he'd ever wanted. Next to his head was the skin of the ship, a
wall of wood; and beyond that waves, water, wind, creatures flying and swimming and breathing, the world spinning and stars
whirling around the fixed pole to the north. Years from now, so
much later, he would remember wanting to punch through that
wall and dive into the waiting water.

PART III

8

Toodlamik,
Skin and Bones

(November 1856–March 1857)

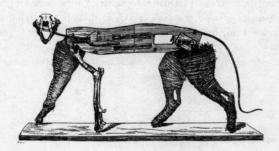

... There is a manifest progress in the succession of beings on the surface of the earth. This progress consists in an increasing similarity to the living fauna, and among the vertebrates, especially, in their increasing resemblance to Man. But this connection is not the consequence of a direct lineage between the fauna of different ages. There is nothing like parental descent connecting them. The fishes of the Palaeozoic age are in no respect the ancestors of the reptiles of the Secondary age, nor does Man descend from the mammals which preceded him in the Tertiary age. The link by which they are connected is of a higher and immaterial nature; and their connection is to be sought in the view of the Creator himself, whose aim, in forming the earth, in allowing it to undergo the successive changes which Geology has pointed out, and in creating successively all the different types of animals which have passed away, was to introduce Man upon the surface of our globe. Man is the end towards which all the animal creation has tended, from the first appearance of the first Palaeozoic fishes. In the beginning His plan was formed, and from it He has never swerved in any particular. . . . To study, in this view, the succession of animals in time, and their distribution in space, is, therefore, to become acquainted with the ideas of God himself. . . . It is only as it contemplates, at the same time, matter and mind, that Natural History rises to its true character and dignity, and leads to its worthiest end, by indicating to us, in Creation, the execution of a plan fully matured in the beginning, and undeviatingly pursued; the work of a God infinitely wise, regulating Nature according to immutable laws, which He has himself imposed on her.

— LOUIS AGASSIZ AND A.A. GOULD, *Principles of Zoology* (1851)

*T*he engravings were beautiful, Alexandra thought: even those on which she'd worked. Again she pursed her lips and blew a gentle stream of air. Again the sheet of tissue folded back, revealing the image below. Dr. Kane's *Arctic Explorations*, which Mr. Archibault had given to her; she could hardly believe she'd had a hand in its creation. Her gaze moved between the volumes and the advertisement Mr. Archibault had also brought:

WASHINGTON IRVING says—

You ask my opinion of his work. What can I say that has not been already said by more competent critics? I do not pretend to critical acumen; being too much influenced by my feelings: still I may give some opinion in this department of literature, having from childhood had a passion for voyages of discovery, and I know of none that ever more thoroughly interested and delighted me than this of Dr. Kane. While I read the work I had the author continually in my "mind's eye." I was present when he lectured in the Smithsonian Institution in 1853, on the Arctic Expedition, which he had already made; when we all wondered that one of a physique apparently so slight and fragile, having once gone through such perils and hardships, should have the daring spirit to encounter them again. I saw him after his return from that second Expedition, a broken down man, broken down in all but intellect, about to embark for Europe, in the vain hope of bracing up a shattered constitution.

It was this image of the author, continually before me, that made me read his narrative, so simply, truthfully, and ably written, with continued wonder and admiration. His Expedition, and his narrative of it, form one of the most extraordinary instances of the triumphs of mental energy and enthusiasm over a frail physical organization that I have ever known. His name, like that of Henry Grinnell, will remain an honor to his country.

Hon. EDWARD EVERETT says—

"It does the author equal credit as a man of science, and an energetic, skillful and courageous adventurer, and a true-hearted philanthropist. In conjunction with his former publication, it will secure him an abiding-place on the rolls of honest fame among the heroes of humanity. The style of typography and illustration is of superior excellence."

G. P. R. JAMES, the Novelist, says—

"I read the two volumes with deeper interest than I ever felt in any work in my life; and I concluded them with love and admiration for the man who wrote them. I only wish there were a dozen volumes more."

Gen. LEWIS CASS says—

"The expedition is a monument of human energy and endurance, originating in the most honorable and commendable motives, and conducted with rare courage, sagacity and perseverance. To the severity of truth it adds the romantic interest of perilous adventure and of the extremity of exposure and suffering. I never read a narrative which took firmer hold of my feelings, nor which excited to a higher degree my commiseration for the heroic men whose terrible calamities it records, nor my admiration for the fortitude with which these were met. It was a contest between man and nature—between the stern power of an Arctic winter and the human frame to resist it. And it is wonderful to see that in their worst extremity the objects of the expedition were never abandoned by the hardy explorers, but they seemed to triumph over the icy desolation whose broad expanse was marked by no animated being but themselves. All other life had fled before its power of destruction."

Hon. CHARLES SUMNER says—

"It is a book of rarest interest and instruction; written with simplicity, ease and directness; possessing all the attractions of romantic adventure elevated by scientific discovery, and, as we sit at our warm firesides, bringing under our eyes a distant portion of the globe, which, throughout all time until now, has slumbered unknown, locked in primeval ice."

Prof. LOUIS AGASSIZ says—

"It will give me the greatest pleasure to write a scientific review of Dr. Kane's last expedition, which I have read with the deepest interest, mingled with admiration for his energy and the warmest sympathy for his sufferings."

2

Caught up in the work itself, she hadn't imagined the results. She hadn't imagined everyone reading and discussing the book, leaving her to feel like such a liar. And she hadn't imagined its effect on Erasmus, because she'd believed him dead.

When the bulk of the whaling fleet returned in September, with no reports of the *Narwhal*, everything she'd learned about the arctic from her earlier reading had convinced her the expedition must be lost. Zeke's father had begun organizing a rescue expedition for the following summer, but although she'd reassured Lavinia constantly that the men were alive, she'd lost hope herself. Then a whaling ship had hobbled into Marblehead, miraculously bearing Erasmus and a fraction of his crew.

The newspapers had been writing about Dr. Kane's voyage to England and his glorious book; perhaps weary of praising so much, they'd leaped to blame Erasmus for abandoning Zeke and the brig. They wrote as if a mutiny had taken place, or at least acts of fatal misjudgment; they hummed with indignation and questioned the fates of Captain Tyler and the others who'd splintered off from Erasmus's command. For that boy with the ruined face, and Erasmus himself with his ruined feet, they seemed to have no pity. Erasmus had offered his journal and a piece of a boot he claimed had belonged to one of Franklin's men; the reporters had scorned him and all but called him an outright liar. Linnaeus and Humboldt, who'd brought Erasmus home, had tried to keep the worst of the press from him. But they hadn't been able to keep Lavinia from calling him a murderer. Nor could they keep him from learning that everyone, everywhere, compared him unfavorably to Dr. Kane.

Even now, staying on at his house far beyond the time she'd planned, even with Erasmus recuperating in the Repository and Lavinia confined to her bed upstairs, Alexandra couldn't make sense of this astonishing conflation of events. She tried to distract

Erasmus with her copy of *Arctic Explorations*, but as he thumbed through the two blue volumes he groaned over the coincidences between his and Kane's voyage. He looked up from the pages one afternoon, as if noticing her for the first time, and said, "What are you doing here?"

She couldn't say that this was her job now. Linnaeus and Humboldt had begged her to stay, at least until Lavinia was able to leave her bed. But she couldn't repeat the way Humboldt had said, "There are things the servants can't do," or the way Linnaeus had added, "And you've been such a friend to the family. We'd be glad to pay you the wages of a housekeeper." Closets and cupboards and linen presses had loomed in her mind, and the faces of the cook, the maids, the groom. She'd thought of herself as repaying a family's kindness, not as a paid servant. "More than those wages," Humboldt had added, seeing her face. "We wouldn't want you to do any actual housework; if you need more help just let us know."

She couldn't repeat this uneasy conversation to Erasmus. Instead she said, "Your brothers have been kind enough to allow me to stay here, and to continue my education while providing some companionship for your sister. And for you, if that's agreeable."

The portrait of Franklin looked down from the wall; on a table lay a battered medicine chest; on the bed was a metal box. Erasmus hid the contents of the box from her, but she'd glimpsed a letter case, a handful of books, and the journal Lavinia had sent off with Zeke, now stained and worn. "I write a clear hand," she said. "Perhaps I could help you with some of the papers you brought back?"

In a new book, plain black covers with a red leather spine, Erasmus wrote:

I try to take comfort in what's around me, I try to be grateful to be back home, to see what's here to see. Outside my window the sky is a dark rich gray, shot through with occasional bolts of sun, the leaves alight then mysteriously dimmed, then alight again: golden leaves. Through them move a red cardinal, a black crow, a horde of crows swirling to roost in the big oak. As darkness falls they flock in from all over the city, birds crowding every branch and all of them speaking all at once, amazing noise: are you there? I am here. Are you there? I am here. Good night, good night, good night. Why can't I simply enjoy them?

After all the time I spent dreaming of home, now I dream nightly that I'm in my bunk on the Narwhal, *with the crew intact around me. Lavinia blames me, everyone blames me, for returning without Zeke. I blame myself. I knew, as much as anyone could, what dangers we might face; those years on the Exploring Expedition let me imagine the arctic without the blur of romance. But why didn't I see the great failure of Zeke's imagination? None of his reading taught him the crucial thing. He could imagine the hardships faced by the explorers preceding us; but not that anything bad might happen to <u>himself</u>. Always he thought of himself as charmed. A boy's belief.*

What I want is to talk with my companions, but they've scattered. Thomas, who dreamed we'd all be heroes, was so ashamed of what the newspapers wrote that he signed on with a merchant ship and has already left for California. Ivan and Isaac went home to their families. Barton found work on a farm. I'm all alone. Are you there? I am here; no one's there.

This week I finally started doing the things I should have done the minute I got back. I wrote to Lady Franklin, enclosing a list of the relics and a version of Oonali's account of the sunken ship. I wrote to the families of Captain Tyler, Mr. Tagliabeau, Robert, and Sean, enclosing the letters they entrusted to me when we parted and promising to inquire into the status of the unpaid portions of their wages. I wrote to Ned Kynd, who sent a letter from the Adirondack Mountains; I paid him from my own pocket, and offered whatever help he needs.

He says his nose is healed, but is permanently deformed. I told him my stumps are almost healed, and that I'd give anything for his wounds to be mine.

The saddest task has been writing to Dr. Boerhaave's friends. In his writing case were several thick letters to William Greenstone in Edinburgh, and one to a Thomas Cholmondelay in London. I made a packet for each, enclosing the letters and my own account of Dr. Boerhaave's contributions to our expedition. How much he learned, how much he taught us all. How he died. Ned's version, not Zeke's; and even Ned's I softened. He died, I said, on a trip to gather data about the Smith Sound Esquimaux and the flora and fauna supporting them. How bitter it is to refer them for further details to Dr. Kane's book.

Kane visited almost every place we went; almost all the coastline Zeke laid down Kane shows on his map, with his own names; the very sea to the north of us—the sea whose coastline Zeke left us to explore—shows up as "Kane Basin." For descriptions of the Smith Sound Esquimaux I need only refer Dr. Boerhaave's friends to the appropriate pages in Kane's volumes; for illustrations of the people Dr. Boerhaave last saw I point to the engravings. And so forth and so on; unbearable. Even the Esquimaux names Ned muttered in his delirium are here. I wish I could compare experiences with Dr. Kane, but he's gone to England: his health ruined by his arctic experience and the exertions of writing so much so fast. To William Greenstone I offered one personal note; that our lives were saved by the little white grubs in the caribou skins, which indirectly he taught us to eat. I didn't tell him I have Dr. Boerhaave's journal. I can't stand to let it out of my hands.

WHEN ZEKE'S SISTERS visited in December, Alexandra led them to the Repository. Both were taller than Alexandra, blond and impeccably groomed, and as she drew up chairs she couldn't help comparing their rich, sleek, black dresses with her own tired poplin frock. Despite the money squirreled away in her sewing box she'd spent nothing on clothes and still had only this lilac, her brown silk, and the gray with a few fresh trimmings. Her clothes hadn't mattered when she'd spent her days wrapped in a long tan painter's smock. The chairs disappeared beneath the sisters' swishing skirts as Erasmus propped himself up.

"How is your health?" Violet asked. She gestured at the bed, where the box keeping the bedclothes off his feet made an awkward bulge.

"Better," Erasmus said. He'd seen no one from Zeke's family since his first days back in Philadelphia. "The doctor says I may be able to start walking after Christmas."

Laurel nodded. "Alexandra," she said. "It's good to see you again. You're enjoying your stay here?"

"I keep busy," Alexandra said. "I'm glad to be able to help Lavinia."

"She's still . . . ?" Violet said.

"Still," Alexandra said.

Then no one knew what to say. Zeke's parents, when they emerged from their first month of mourning, had commissioned the building of a ship for the study of marine biology, in honor of their lost hero; the keel of the *Zechariah Voorhees* had already been laid. Dignified grief, a family behaving well. Although they still avoided Erasmus they'd sent their daughters. Yet their example hadn't swayed Lavinia. Lavinia refused their invitations; she hid upstairs and wouldn't come down and seemed to be doing her best to emulate Lady Franklin. Incoherent letters poured from her pen—to the newspapers, the Smithsonian Institution, members of Congress. Someone must organize another expedition to search for Zeke's bones. Papers, papers; she gave them to Linnaeus, who promised to post them but hid them in his office safe instead.

Alexandra poured coffee and offered macaroons. In the silence Laurel finally said to Erasmus, "Our father sent some addresses for you—the families of the crewmen you asked about. And says to tell you he wrote to them himself, the first week you were back." A folded sheet of paper emerged from somewhere in the mass of black silk.

"Thank you," Erasmus said. "I appreciate that."

More silence. Alexandra felt Zeke in the room, as if he'd come through the window along with the sun and was standing there smiling and raising his tufty eyebrows. They all wanted to talk about him, and couldn't or wouldn't, she thought. His sisters were longing for something that would help them envision his last days; Erasmus was praying they wouldn't ask a single question; and she herself was caught in the stillness . . . she rose and walked to the window and back.

"I've been learning to engrave on copper and steel," she said, not knowing what else to talk about. "Did you know that? Lavinia and I began taking engraving lessons last summer from one of the Wellses' master engravers. I'm still taking them, it's very interesting."

Violet swiveled her head on her neck, like a large swan. "You were always artistic," she said. "Do you remember our lessons with Mr. Peale? One of your sisters came with you, I think."

"Emily," Alexandra said. "She hated painting, she hated those mornings."

"And Lavinia," Laurel added. "And the van Ostade girls, and the Winslows, and the three little Peale cousins. But you were always the best. When we did the flower paintings, yours were the only ones that looked like flowers growing. The still life with the dead rabbit, the one that made Martha van Ostade so sick; I still remember yours. You always had a flair. Do you like the engraving?"

"I do," said Alexandra. "Very much."

She had a sudden sharp memory of those Saturday classes in Mr. Peale's atelier. In a high-ceilinged room lit by oblong sky-

lights the girls had gathered around their easels, frowning seriously at a stuffed bird or a heap of fruit and crooking their
thumbs on their palettes. For those hours it hadn't mattered
whose family was wealthy and whose was not. Later, as they
turned eighteen and nineteen, Violet and Laurel would disappear into a world of dances and social events closed to Alexandra
after her parents' accident. But in the atelier Mr. Peale had
encouraged them all equally, correcting shadows and skewed
perspectives, teaching them to represent the real. Round objects
onto flat paper: leaves, lizards, roses, pots. Sometimes they'd
posed for each other, draped in bunting or wreathed with ivy,
allegorically arranged and fully clothed. Never a naked human
form—but how to learn the basic facts of anatomy? Secretly, at
home, Alexandra had drawn her own limbs before a candlelit
mirror.

Violet and Laurel were smiling now and had a little color in
their faces, as if the chatter about their shared girlhood had loos-
ened something in them. To Erasmus, who'd been staring at the
sheet of paper, Violet said, "We don't blame you, you know.
Some do, but not us."

"You must forgive our parents," Laurel added. "They don't
blame you either, not exactly—but this has been so terrible for
them, Father isn't ready to see you yet. But he knows we're
here."

"That's . . . kind of him." Everyone was looking away from
everyone else. Through the windows the leafless trees were black
against the sky. "It's so cold," Erasmus said, pulling the quilt
higher on his chest.

The stove was glowing, but the women looked at each other
and nodded. "We should go," Violet said. "You'll give our regards
to Lavinia? We'd be glad to see her, when she feels ready."

"I'll tell her that," Alexandra said.

When they were gone she stood a few feet from Erasmus's

bed, puzzled by his reticence. "Why didn't you tell them something about what Zeke was like up there? How he was, something good he did . . ."

"Something good he did," Erasmus repeated.

She waited, but he added nothing. In his first days home, during his bouts of fever, he'd spouted wild tales about Zeke. She hadn't known what to make of these—what had happened between the two friends up there, amid the ice and darkness?

"I feel like all I'm doing is waiting," Erasmus said. "Waiting to heal, waiting to learn how to walk without toes, waiting to see what shape my life will take now."

Alexandra lit the other lamps and fiddled with the stove until the room was warm and bright. "What did you think your life would be like?"

Erasmus leaned toward the stove. "Like my father's life," he said. "Only more so. Like the lives of his friends, who did this as more than a hobby. This little building," he said, waving at the space around him. "If you could have seen what it was like when I was a boy—half zoo and half museum, my father let us do anything we wanted. For a while we had a big tree in the corner, with live birds roosting in it. Aquariums, and an ant colony, and turtles and salamanders; and jars of preserved specimens everywhere, big slabs of fossil-bearing rock and mastodon bones and a plant press, books open on all the tables. A wonderful, fertile clutter."

Alexandra looked around the Repository, which still seemed cluttered to her. So many books and specimens, so much equipment—the microscope, the dissecting table set before the window; shelves and saucers and little zinc labels; heaps of unbound books and pages ripped from pamphlets. But it was true there wasn't a single living creature.

"Almost every fine day," Erasmus said, "we'd gather at breakfast, the four of us boys and our father, and tell him our plans before he went off to work."

Where was Lavinia? Alexandra thought. While the boys were making plans?

"We'd pick some field or stream and go gather specimens. When we returned, three of us would work at mounting or dissecting what we'd gathered and the fourth would read aloud. Embryology, ichthyology, paleontology; it was all so exciting. Sometimes we'd visit Peale's museum and study the mammoth bones and the sea serpents. At night our father would join us and examine what we'd gathered and ask us what we'd learned. Then he'd look at our notebooks."

"You kept those even as little boys?" Perhaps Lavinia had kept one too. Or perhaps she'd simply watched her world shrink and shrink, while her brothers' worlds expanded.

"Always," Erasmus said. "It was part of our father's plan for educating us. We must read French and German and Latin, and learn how to draw accurately. We were to keep notebooks of all our observations, illustrated ourselves."

"I'd love to have seen those," Alexandra said, thinking of her own sketchbooks. In Browning's house she'd had only a cubicle off the parlor to herself, and almost no privacy. Always, though, she'd had a small locked trunk of her own. In it she'd kept— still kept, the trunk was under her bed—the sketchbooks in which she drew herself and her sisters, and whatever else came to hand.

"Look under E in the bookshelves," Erasmus said. "I believe you'll find them there. If you'd bring them to me . . ."

She pushed the rolling ladder into place. Between a book about ferns and a description of the invertebrates of the Orinoco River region she found five buckram-bound books with red spines and no titles.

"I started the first when I was ten," he said, when she returned with them. "The last ends the day before I left on the Exploring Expedition." He opened one. "See? This is what we did."

She peered at a drawing of a wasp's nest. The whole nest, from the outside; an interior view after a side had been cut away; larvae and full-grown wasps in various positions. The drawings, done in black ink with a light wash, were clumsy but vivid, labeled in a boyish, somewhat crooked hand.

"That's from when I was twelve," Erasmus said. "Copernicus's are much nicer, he was always the real artist in the family. Linnaeus's and Humboldt's are more orderly, and the drawings are probably better, but they're less detailed—keeping the notebooks was always a chore for them, they never liked it as much as I did. Even when I was a boy, I was sure I wanted to be a naturalist."

"They're charming," Alexandra said, with her hand poised to turn the page. "May I?"

Erasmus nodded, and she flipped through the volume: bones, fish, birds' organs, worms, spiders, pupae, lichens. Suddenly she had tears in her eyes. Lying there so worn and beaten, Erasmus had seemed old to her since his return although there was less than fifteen years between them; he was forty-two, she thought. His hair had thinned and faded; he'd lost weight and his face was drawn, with deep lines on his forehead. His attitude of defeat had aged him further. But in these pages she could see the hopeful boy he'd been.

"That Exploring Expedition," he said. "Everything that happened after we got home, it broke something in me. But this voyage was like another chance."

For a minute he spoke about Dr. Boerhaave—all they'd collected, their good conversations, all they'd shared—and Alexandra felt a pang of envy.

"I was going to write a book about the arctic," he concluded. "Perhaps a wonderful book."

"You could still do that."

Erasmus shrugged. "No one wants to hear about our expedition. The big failure, the big anticlimax. With Zeke dead and the brig abandoned, what is there to say? What is there to write about that Dr. Kane hasn't already covered?"

"But a natural history of the arctic," Alexandra said. "Not a travel book, not a book of memoir and adventure like Dr. Kane's, but something about the area's botany and zoology?"

"That's what I meant to do, really," Erasmus said. "But all my specimens are gone, and Dr. Kane printed those long compilations of plants and animals in his Appendix. All I have left are the lists I brought home, and some notes in my journal. And my friend's journal, I have that too."

He didn't offer to show her these, Alexandra noticed. She could look at his childhood notebooks but not at what was most important to him, not what he'd done recently.

A FEW DAYS later she entered the Repository to find the tin box open and Erasmus reading something with a mottled cover. Heaped on the bed beside him were Agassiz's books about fossil fish, and near those the worn journal that Lavinia had once pressed into Zeke's hands. Alexandra expected Erasmus to bury the books in the bedclothes, as he'd done before when she interrupted his secret researches. But he left everything open this time, drawing back his hands as she approached.

"You see what I do?" he said. "This is what I do with my time these days. I paw through my own journal"—here he touched the green volume—"Zeke wasn't using this, he let me have it." With his other hand he touched the speckled volume. "Then I read in here. This belonged to my friend. I was just looking at a passage he'd written about some fossil fish, and I was comparing his description with Agassiz's plates—these books were Dr.

Boerhaave's too, I can hardly believe I managed to get them home. Do you know them?"

"Only by reputation," Alexandra murmured. "You didn't have a copy here."

"The plates are extraordinary," Erasmus said. "Copernicus can do things like this, but I never could." He flipped through the pages for a minute and consulted Dr. Boerhaave's journal. "My friend was acquainted with Agassiz," he told Alexandra. "They met when Agassiz was visiting the Scottish Highlands, looking at the fossil fishes in the Old Red Sandstone. He was recollecting that trip, and he mentioned a fish I was trying to find—here."

He pointed out a chromolithograph of an odd-looking creature, all spines and overlapping plates. Alexandra gazed at the subtle hues and textures. "That's gorgeous," she said. "Really remarkable. Work like this—it makes me see how important illustration can be, how it's truly one of a naturalist's tools."

"It is," Erasmus said. "With accurate drawings, one can compare specimens from all over the world without having to rummage in the cabinets of museums and individual collectors. It's as if I'm holding the fossil right here in my hands."

"I heard Agassiz lecture when he visited Philadelphia," Alexandra said. "Fascinating."

"I did too!" Erasmus said. "But you must have been only a child."

"Not quite—I was fifteen or sixteen."

They smiled at each other, and then Alexandra remembered the stories her sister Emily had told her. "What Agassiz is doing now," she said, "he's such an interesting thinker, and yet—have you read the essay he contributed to Nott and Glidden's *Types of Mankind*?"

"I haven't," Erasmus said. "It came out just as Zeke and I were getting ready to leave, and I never had time to look at it."

"You should," Alexandra said. "You've been among the

Esquimaux yourself now, you'd be a better judge. He extends his argument about separate, successive creations of life in different geographical centers to man. The races of man correspond to the great zoological regions, he says, and perhaps they're *autoch-thonoi*, like plants, originating where they're found. Eight primary human types, each originating in and inhabiting a specific zoological province—one of his types is Arctic man, your Esquimaux. He seems almost to be arguing that his types are separate species."

"I . . ." Erasmus said. He paused for half a minute. A white moth fluttered before him, released from a cocoon behind the books. "It's wonderful to have you around, for me to have someone to discuss books and ideas with. I appreciate all the time you spend with me. But . . ."

To Alexandra's horror, tears slid down the bony slopes of his nose.

"Forgive me," he whispered. "I'm so tired, still. I don't know what I think about anything, and Lavinia hates me and I miss Dr. Boerhaave so much—how can I know what I think about some foolishness Agassiz has written? All I can think is that he was my friend's friend, and that my friend is lost, everything is lost." He reached up, closed his hand around the moth, peered at it, and then released it.

Alexandra turned toward the window while he recovered himself. Across the garden Lavinia's window was visible, the blinds drawn although the sky was still light. Whenever she urged Lavinia to rise, Lavinia turned her head and said, "How can you understand? You were always so clever, you can do anything. But without Zeke, what am I? Zeke was the only one who really loved me."

"You should write your book," she said, turning back to Erasmus. "It's the best way to honor Dr. Boerhaave. And Zeke, and the whole expedition."

"How?" Erasmus said. "With what? All my specimens are gone."

"Thomas Say had all his notebooks stolen on his first western trip. His notes on the Indians, all his descriptions of animal species, everything. But he still managed to keep working." She picked up his journal. "May I?"

It was better than she could have hoped; on almost every page, among the descriptions and narrative passages, were sketches of birds and bones and cliffs, a tusk found in a creek.

"Say was still a young man when he died," Erasmus said, following the movements of her hands. "He died before he lost hope."

She reached for Dr. Boerhaave's journal: more sketches, in more detail. "Dr. Kane had nothing more than such notes and sketches when he got home," she said. "But from them all the paintings for his book were made and then engraved."

"I'm no artist," Erasmus said glumly. "Copernicus is the one who can paint."

"I'm not bad at drawing and painting." Alexandra looked down at her capable hands. "With your sketches, with you correcting everything, telling me the colors and what details you remember, I might be able to make something reasonable."

As if he could not stop the process, Erasmus's eyebrows knotted and his lips curled, blowing out a little derogatory puff of air. Alexandra dropped the journal and turned from him.

"I'm sorry," he said. "I didn't mean to imply, it's just—what do you really know about this?"

Alexandra seized Dr. Kane's *Arctic Explorations*, opening the second volume to one of her engravings. Before she could think about what she was doing, she stuck it under Erasmus's nose. "*I* did this, or most of it. And this." She turned to another plate. "And this, and the background to this, and this seal . . ." In her hurry she tore the tissue overlying one of the plates.

She described Mr. Archibault's injured wrists and their secret sessions. "No one knows," she said, smoothing the edges of the tissue back together. "No one can ever know, Mr. Archibault would lose his job and your brothers would be furious, you can't tell anyone. But I could help *you*, if you weren't so stubborn . . ." She could help herself as well, she thought. Together they might work on a project she could claim partly as her own.

"You worked on *his* book?" Erasmus exclaimed. "How could you betray our family like that?"

Bewildered, she pressed the volume to her chest. "Your own brothers directed the engraving for the plates."

"That was business!" Erasmus said. "They had no idea Zeke and I were in the same area as Dr. Kane. They thought I was dead, they didn't know I was coming back."

"And how would *I* have known that?"

"Would you just leave?" Erasmus said.

He turned his back and pulled his pillow over his head. After he heard the door close he fell asleep—he slept so much now, he couldn't help it—and he woke thick-headed, with the sun beginning to color the sky. He reached for his journal and wrote:

Dr. Kane's narrative of the First Grinnell Expedition was a boy's romp, an adventure story—but this new book is so good I can't bear to look at it. If he and I had become friends, if I'd gone on his expedition rather than Zeke's; but he didn't even consider me. Everyone has passed me. Maury's published his Physical Geography of the Sea, *supporting Kane's findings about the open polar basin. Ringgold's already written up some of his work from the North Pacific Expedition: another expedition that might have included me. He found small shelled animals on the bottom of the Coral Sea, two and a half miles down—a very important discovery, proving that there's no azoic zone. No place where the great weight of water prevents a plumb line from passing, creatures from living. My father used to tell me that, below a certain depth, nothing could sink and drowned bodies and wrecked ships floated far off the bottom in*

*layers related to their weight. That's what I feel like myself. As if I'm
floating below the surface, above the bottom, suspended in fluid as thick
as mercury. Why hasn't Lady Franklin written me back?*

AFTER THAT QUARREL, Alexandra avoided him and spent
more time with Lavinia. They'd seen each other tired, crabby,
partially dressed; sullen, excited, impatient, broken: although
Lavinia was difficult to be around these days, Alexandra thought
of her as another sister. The sight of Lavinia's uncoiled hair, matted around her shoulders, pained her. So did the scraps of paper
drifting around Lavinia's bed: letters pleading that people find
Zeke's body, rescue Zeke's relics, discover new seas in the name
of Zeke. None of which would ever be sent. The sight of her
brothers made her weep, the doctor annoyed her, and nothing
Alexandra said seemed to help. Sitting useless by Lavinia's bed,
Alexandra thought of calling on Browning. Everyone in their
neighborhood turned to him; despite a certain humorlessness he
had a rare talent for comforting the bereaved and once had
soothed a widow who'd locked herself in her attic after losing her
children in a skating accident. Berating herself for not thinking
of this before, she asked for his help.

For the next few weeks, Browning visited Lavinia frequently, gliding dark-suited up to her room with his Bible and
a handful of other books. Although Alexandra wasn't privy to
their conversations she could see how much they helped.
Lavinia stopped writing letters and began to come downstairs
for a few hours each day; she dressed and ate and took some
interest in the workings of the household. What had Browning
said? With his guidance she'd begun to pray again, Lavinia
revealed. As she had as a girl; it comforted her. When Linnaeus and Humboldt proposed a family Christmas dinner, she
agreed.

"I can't make the arrangements," she said. "But if Alexandra is willing . . ."

"Of course," Alexandra said. "It would be my pleasure."

"Let's have both families, then," Lavinia said. "Ours, and yours—would your brother come, do you think? I would like that."

Alexandra chose the menu, consulted with the cook, directed the housecleaning and supervised the decorating of the tree. The house was beautiful and no one minded how much she spent. On Christmas day they gathered around the huge mahogany table, with all the leaves inserted and chairs borrowed from every room. Linnaeus and Lucy and their daughter; Humboldt and Ellen and their little son; Alexandra's sisters, Emily and Jane; Browning and Harriet and Nicholas, who was almost three. Harriet, expecting another child in January, sat in an armchair with a pillow behind her back. Lavinia sat at the foot of the table, presiding over all that Alexandra had arranged. Alexandra sat to her right, where she might remind Lavinia unobtrusively of some forgotten dish or ritual. Far away, at the head of the table, was Erasmus in his wheeled chair. A turkey at one end, a ham at the other; white porcelain dishes of vegetables steaming beneath their covers; relishes and sauces and gravies and condiments; a forest of stemware, a sea of silver.

The candles sparked a confusing network of reflections from the shining surfaces, and during Browning's long prayer Alexandra saw flames in wine and faces in spoons. "So much has been taken from us," Browning said. "Yet so much remains." Then something about thanking the Lord for the bounty before them and the family remaining to them, and a long loop through the Lord's mysterious ways. How hard it is, Browning said, to accept the accidents that befall us. The ferry exploding on the river, which had taken from him and his sisters their parents; the childbed fever that had taken Mrs. Wells from her children when they were still so young—we have these losses in common, he said. They bind our families. As does this accident in the unknown regions of the north. Zechariah is gone from us, but we are grateful for the return of Erasmus.

Throughout all this, Alexandra saw, Lavinia stared straight ahead. Straight at Erasmus, her right hand tucked in her lap while her left turned a silver spoon back to front, front to back, the reflections melting, re-forming, and melting again. When Browning said, "Amen," Lavinia said softly, "I forgive you." Everyone knew she was speaking to Erasmus. "I understand that you did your best."

"I did," said Erasmus. His end of the table was so far from hers. "I did everything I could."

There was a precarious moment of silence. Then Nicholas tipped over a dish of pickles, Humboldt's little William laughed delightedly, Harriet began to scold her son and was stopped by Browning's quiet hand on hers. Dinner passed, almost festive, everyone chattering while Lavinia and Erasmus regarded each other and Alexandra thought, *Have they made up, then?* Between them she'd felt pulled so thin that light might shine through her lungs. Perhaps Browning had repeated to Lavinia the words he'd spoken after their own parents' deaths—how, in a family with no parents, they must each stand as guardians and protectors of one another.

They ate and drank, plates came and went; Lavinia directed the servants convincingly. "I'm so glad you could do this," Alexandra said. "This is wonderful."

"You did most of the work," Lavinia replied. There were gray circles beneath her eyes, and she wasn't eating. But that she was here at all was a miracle.

Somewhere else, at other Christmas dinners, people were discussing Dr. Kane and his book, the continuing searches for Franklin, the arctic in general: anything to avoid the discussions of politics and slavery that fractured families and friends. But here the topic on which everyone else fell back was also forbidden, and they struggled, and talked about books. Jane and Lucy found common ground in *The Wide, Wide World*, agreeing that they both still coveted the mahogany desk given to the novel's heroine in its most famous scene.

"That little ivory knife," Jane said, "and the four colors of sealing wax, and the pounce box and the silver pencil!"

With a pang Alexandra thought of Jane's bare bedroom in Browning's house, and the gate-legged table that served as her desk. Harriet, who also had no desk of her own, brought up a few more cherished scenes. And Emily added, "Men make fun of it, I know you all do. You like tales of adventure, in which the hero truly explores that wide world. But the novel is about tyranny, really; the tyranny of family and circumstances, and how one survives when running away isn't an option. Which it never is for women like us."

Browning raised his eyebrows and turned the conversation toward more serious books. Coffee and the puddings and pies arrived, and by the time Alexandra could pay attention again Browning and Linnaeus were discussing the relative merits of *Uncle Tom's Cabin* and Mrs. Hentz's rebuttal of it in *The Planter's Northern Bride*. Then Emily was telling Linnaeus and Lucy about her work with runaway slaves who'd made their way to the city. Perhaps she'd drunk too much of the Wellses' lovely claret.

Linnaeus said, "That's all very admirable. But can you answer the argument Mrs. Stowe has St. Clare make to Miss Ophelia? Are we in the North willing to elevate and educate the floods of freed slaves that must arrive here on emancipation? I think we won't; we can't. They're so essentially *different* from us."

Humboldt leaned into the conversation. "Are they not," he said, "even a separate species from us? In the same way that Catlin thinks the Indian tribes he painted out west are indigenous, and extremely ancient—their languages resemble no other group, they must have been created there. And Agassiz and others have argued . . ."

"Agassiz's idea of centers of creation is simple sacrilege," Browning said sharply. "This position that species are created in their proper places and don't migrate far, this thing he calls 'polygenism': to argue that human races are different species, descended from different Adams who were created separately in different zoological regions—this is to argue that scripture is allegorical rather than literal. And I don't accept that. We all descend from Adam and Eve, a singular creation. Human races have degenerated differently from that original pair."

Erasmus, Alexandra saw, was flicking his thumbnail against his front teeth. Lavinia looked up when Emily began to contradict Browning.

"Never mind that," Emily said. "It's not the theology that's important—Agassiz's polygenism is harmful because of the ammunition it provides to the proponents of slavery. And anyway he's a horrid man. He didn't come here just to give those lectures; he wanted to see Dr. Morton's collection of skulls and gather more data for his theories. I was working among the Negro servants at the hotel he stayed at, trying to convince them to provide shelter for escaped slaves passing through, and I saw him there, in the hall. One of the maids was trying to give him a message from someone who'd come by looking for him. She spoke perfectly clearly but he stood there like a big ox, pretending he didn't understand her and asking her again and again to repeat the same phrases. The look on his face—he was frightened of her. Revolted by her. How can you trust the science of a man like that?"

Erasmus flicked his thumbnail again and then spoke for the first time since he'd finished carving the ham. "Is that true?" he said. "About Agassiz?"

"As far as I know," Emily said. "He makes no secret of his attitude toward other races. No more than did Dr. Morton."

Erasmus shook his head. "Morton did good work at the Academy," he said. "But that necropolis he kept in his office—for all the time I was acquainted with him, I managed to avoid seeing the cabinet. None of us ever saw it." Linnaeus and Humboldt agreed.

"Such an awful obsession," Erasmus continued. "Hundreds of Indian crania, hundreds more from the Egyptian tombs and men all over the world robbing graves to send skulls back to him— but I don't remember any connection to Agassiz, I just remember the lectures Agassiz gave. And all the dinners feting him." He was silent for a moment. "Can't we talk about pleasanter things?" He pushed his chair away from the table and rolled in the direction of the parlor.

ERASMUS DIDN'T SAY he hadn't met Agassiz because he wasn't invited to the dinners. In the aftermath of the Exploring Expedition his reputation as a naturalist had been so slight that, despite his father's connections, no one had thought to include him. Yet what did this matter now? Most of his attention was taken up by fittings for his new shoes with the little pads that replaced his lost toes and cushioned his stumps. Late one night, when he was sure he wouldn't be interrupted, he opened his tin box and then the fossil cabinet with the hidden compartment. His nostrils filled with the smell of leather as he lined the footwear along his bed: one tiny antique woman's boot, one new man's shoe, one piece of boot sole. The fragment he'd brought home from Boothia was distinctly larger than the corresponding portion of his new shoes; his shoes now matched his mother's.

He practiced moving on his dwarfed feet, aided by a pair of walking sticks. For a while this occupied him entirely. Later, as he grew more confident but still was trapped inside by the freak snowfalls and bitter cold, the Christmas conversation began to nag at him. He read Agassiz's essay in *Types of Mankind* and studied the chart linking the world's zoological provinces and their human inhabitants. The arctic column showed a polar bear, a walrus, a Greenland seal, a reindeer, a right whale, an eider duck. Then the face and skull of what Agassiz termed a Hyperborean. The features, which looked like no person Erasmus had ever seen, might have been imagined from Pliny's description. The races of man, Agassiz had written, differed from each other more than monkeys considered separate species within the same genus.

Browsing through the long passages of biblical exegesis and the essays on geology and paleontology, Erasmus saw that the point was an attack on the unity of races, an attempt to prove their separate creation. A messy compendium, the drawings distorted—whether willfully or unconsciously—to make a point. The Esquimaux looked like misshapen gnomes and the Negroes like chimpanzees; how could anyone who'd traveled the world take this seriously? Yet he knew there were clergymen shouting that the book cast contempt on the word of God. He was no judge of theology, but he thought it was bad science to deny that humans were part of nature and all one species. He had the feet of a pygmy now, but he was still himself.

He longed, as always, for Dr. Boerhaave, with whom he might have had a proper discussion. What is life, where did it come from? Species may be placed in groups related to one another in structure—but where did that relationship originate? He and Dr. Boerhaave would have laughed as they argued. He was grateful for that memory—and grateful, too, that the horrid stretch during which he'd been able to hear his friend's voice but couldn't see his face had passed.

Bit by bit his friend had returned to him. As he lay sleepless he'd seen first Dr. Boerhaave's leafy brown hair, striped with white, perfectly straight and flopping in the wind. His long chunky nose with that charming square tip appeared next; then his narrow eyes, slightly too close together; his wide, thin-lipped, mobile mouth; and the long-fingered hands which, gesturing so fluidly, had seemed like outposts of his mind. *The world has a pattern*, he'd said. *Our minds are made to perceive that pattern laid down by the Lord.* With those words humming in his ears, Erasmus searched the shelves for his father's old copy of Morton's *Crania Americana*.

Tiny steps; he felt like a deer, balanced on pointed hooves. He propped the volume open on the table and copied out Morton's interpretation of the cranial capacity of three Esquimaux skulls:

"The Greenland esquimaux are crafty, sensual, ungrateful, obstinate and unfeeling, and much of their affection for their children may be traced to purely selfish motives. They devour the most disgusting aliments uncooked and uncleaned, and seem to have no ideas beyond providing for the present moment. . . . In gluttony, selfishness and ingratitude, they are perhaps unequalled by any other nation of people."

Certainly those people had seemed alien, but this wasn't the way he remembered them. Nor was this the way—or not solely the way—that Dr. Kane portrayed them in his book. Which Alexandra had worked on; and it was her sister who'd brought up this side of Agassiz. How could that philosophical idealism, which Dr. Boerhaave shared with Agassiz and Thoreau, have these consequences? He wanted his friend's face shining clearly; he'd almost lost that precious memory.

All of this was confusing. On his desk lay something else confusing, his first response to the letters he'd sent to the families of the three dead crewmen. Fletcher Lamb's mother had sent a bitter letter, pencil on lined paper:

I had two sons. The oldest went off on a whaling ship and was drowned to death and I forbade Fletcher to go to sea. He ran away to you. And

*now this. What am I to do without him? What am I to live on, without
a son to support me? I had hoped you'd include the balance of Fletcher's
wages. I am in urgent need of funds.*

He would pay her himself and sort out the details with Zeke's
father later; he'd do the same for Nils Jensen's mother and Mr.
Francis's wife. But the money wouldn't make things right. He'd
mishandled everything.

Every corner of his life was confused. After the Christmas dinner Alexandra, out of the blue, had asked Linnaeus and Humboldt for some engraving work. She hadn't admitted her work
on Dr. Kane's book; her glance at Erasmus had entreated him not
to betray her. She'd said only that Mr. Archibault believed her
efforts promising.

His brothers had stalled but agreed to consult Mr. Archibault;
and Erasmus had understood, as they had not, that Mr.
Archibault would support her. Almost a form of blackmail, Erasmus thought. Doubly so, as his brothers couldn't afford to cross
her; if she left they'd have to make other arrangements for the
care of him and Lavinia. Later that week they'd agreed to sub-
contract a small set of botanical engravings to Alexandra and had
arranged a work space in her rooms, but Erasmus knew they
blamed him. They were waiting for him to take charge of the
household, so they could dismiss Alexandra.

Which would leave him, he thought, alone with Lavinia. How
would they live together? She came downstairs each day and
dined with him each night, but it was Alexandra who made conversation, finding the neutral topics that got them through meals.
Only once had they approached the topic of Zeke. "If you knew
how much I miss him," Lavinia had said. "How hard it is for me
to imagine the rest of my life . . ."

"I know," he'd said. "I would have done anything not to have
it be this way." Liar, he'd thought. What a liar.

And there they sat. Her mouth said she'd forgiven him, her body at the table signaled a truce, but her gaze eluded him. She seemed to have grown a set of translucent second eyelids, like a cat's nictitating membranes. Behind that film she raged with loss. Had she been able to choose, he thought, he would be dead and not Zeke. "I'm sorry," he'd said. Again, again. "So sorry." The servants swirled around, pretending not to notice the anguish behind their words: Agnes the housemaid, Mrs. Parkins the cook, Cardoza the groundskeeper, Benton the groom. Two years ago he'd hardly been able to tell them apart; now he knew all their names, as he knew their habits and moods and troubles. He had to know them; he depended on them, and on Alexandra. Together they helped him and Lavinia return to the world that had become so strange to both of them.

ALL OVER PHILADELPHIA, merchants and tavern keepers had picked up on the craze for Kane's book. Shops displayed white fur muffs and seal-trimmed jackets *a la Esquimaux*; hairdressers styled tresses in casual topknots emulating the Greenland belles. By the wharves one might order a dish called "Dr. Kane's Relief," which appeared crowned with a tiny wooden spear. A hot brandy drink was called "Ice and Darkness," an ale "Kane's Dew," a towering dessert with almond paste "Tennyson's Monument," after the striking engraving in Kane's book. No one mentioned Erasmus and his expedition, but there was still talk of Franklin.

In England Lady Franklin pressed for another expedition to leave next summer, heading for Boothia and King William Land and perhaps employing the *Resolute*, which had safely reached Portsmouth. *The most recent American expedition*, she'd said in a speech—meaning his own, Erasmus thought with a pang—*may have failed. But apparently they saw evidence of my husband's ships as clearly as did Dr. Rae. While we sorrow over their losses, we are* *grateful for their efforts. It is imperative that a <u>British</u> ship examine this site.*

She might have written him directly, Erasmus thought. Even the smallest word of thanks, acknowledging receipt of his list. Instead she'd ignored him and taken her facts from the newspapers, never asking him to confirm or deny them. The 'apparently' stung.

Then he learned from Linnaeus what everyone else in Philadelphia already knew—that Dr. Kane had left London in mid-November, sailing for Havana in the hope that a warmer climate might cure his persistent fever. On the passage from St. Thomas to Cuba he'd suffered an apoplexy and now lay in Havana partially paralyzed and missing much of his memory.

Erasmus hobbled down to the creek after he heard this, on his first solo trip outside. At his feet the rushing brown current swept twigs and litter past the tulip trees and deposited a shingle, like a little hat, on a tuft of dried grass.

"YOUR FEET ARE much improved," Alexandra said. "It's time we got you out of here."

She threw open two of the Repository's windows; spring was in the air and the trees were unfurling small green leaves. The lists strewn over Erasmus's work table curled in the humid breeze.

"I'd like to visit the Academy of Sciences," she said. "It would help me with the engravings if I could consult some of the thallophytes there. And I can't very well go by myself—but if you were willing, we could pretend these were specimens *you* wanted to inspect. Would you come?" She had an idea that Erasmus might rouse himself if she could make him feel that he was helping her, rather than that she was helping him.

He frowned. "Do you really need to?"

"It would be an immense help," she said. "And it might be useful to you as well. You could compare the arctic specimens in the herbarium to your lists."

"I could," he said. "And it's such a lovely day. Would Lavinia join us, do you think?"

"Not today," Alexandra said. "I asked her at breakfast, but she wants to spend some time with the gardener."

"That's good," Erasmus said. "Isn't that good, that she's interested in the gardens again?"

"It is," Alexandra agreed.

The drive along the river was beautiful, the banks filmed by a haze of green and sheets of flowering blue squill spreading like water beneath the beeches. At the Academy they sat in the carriage for ten minutes while Erasmus examined the altered facade. "It's too peculiar," he said. "When I was away on the Exploring Expedition the Academy moved from the old Swedenborgian meeting house on Twelfth Street to here. I came back to find this big new building, everything moved and changed so I couldn't find anything—and now this."

"What's so different?" Alexandra asked.

"The extra *story*," Erasmus said. "It's twenty or thirty feet taller than it used to be, there's a whole extra story added on."

As she guided him inside, slowing her steps so she was at his elbow, she caught only fragments of his continual mutter. The lecture room fronting on Broad Street was now part of the library; the old meeting room was now full of shelves; all the specimens had been rearranged. There were people about, but no one Erasmus knew from the old days. The young man working in the library probably meant nothing unkind when, after Erasmus introduced himself, he said, "Of course I've heard of you. I imagine you'd like to see the collections from Dr. Kane's first trip north."

"It's . . ." Erasmus said. "I didn't have in mind those specifically, there's a set of thallophytes I'd like to see, and also all the arctic specimens. I don't know where anything is anymore."

"Let me show you," the young man said. He led them into a room lined with shallow drawers and smelling of earth and mold. "All the herbarium sheets are here. Most of the specimens came from Dr. Kane, as I'm sure you know."

"Indeed," Erasmus said faintly. At the far end of the room a stuffed dog was mounted on a pedestal, ears erect and tail curled springily over its back. Beside it stood a dog's articulated skeleton, posed the same way. "Where did you get *those?*" he asked. He drew Alexandra closer to the mount and the skeleton.

"That's Toodlamik," the young man said proudly. "Skin and bones. Dr. Kane's faithful companion on the sledge journeys, whom he managed to bring home. He sickened over the summer, while Dr. Kane was finishing his book, and when he died Dr. Kane brought him here to the taxidermist. We're so pleased to have him."

"Very lifelike," Alexandra murmured. She glanced at Erasmus, hoping this wouldn't upset him. None of this was what she'd intended; she'd meant only to ease him back into the scientific world. She'd imagined them bending over sheets of lycopodium and sphagnum, which would get him thinking about his own work. She was touched when Erasmus squared his walking sticks under him, lifted his chin, and said, "An excellent preparation. I had similar dogs myself. Now if we could look at the herbarium sheets, I'd like to compare some of the specimens with my own lists from the area."

"Of course," the young man said. "Anything you can confirm as having seen in a similar area, or perhaps if you note having seen something in a different place—your explorations didn't entirely overlap Dr. Kane's, did they?"

"They did not."

"We'd welcome your observations." He turned to leave but Erasmus moved in another direction.

Beyond the two versions of Toodlamik an open door led to another room. More bones, Alexandra saw, as she followed Erasmus. Bones and bones and bones. Erasmus moved toward the shelves. Human skulls, cheekbone to cheekbone, rows upon rows. And the skulls of bear and deer and squirrel and mouse; hundreds of bird skulls and fishes and snakes and two hippopotamus skulls.

"Dr. Morton's entire collection," the young man announced. "After his death, his friends raised funds to purchase the collection from his widow, and they presented it to us. There are over sixteen hundred crania, almost a thousand human and the rest from other species. You must have known Dr. Morton?"

"I did," Erasmus said. "But I wasn't aware you'd acquired these." He searched the shelves, peering at the labels. "Weren't there some Esquimaux skulls?"

"Those were only loaned to Dr. Morton, by a friend," the young man said. "The collection really isn't complete without them and it's too bad his friend took them back. If we could acquire even one or two specimens . . ." He paused. "You didn't happen to collect any? That you'd consider donating?"

Erasmus shook his head and the young men disappeared. Without a word Erasmus hobbled back to the herbarium, turned from Toodlamik, and went to work.

They spent the day making notes and comparing one sheet to another, all the sheets to what Erasmus remembered. Alexandra fetched and carried, making encouraging comments and diverting Erasmus's attention from the strangers who appeared at the doorway, gazed curiously at them, and then disappeared. This was his place, she thought. He had as much right to be here as any naturalist in Philadelphia, and she was proud of the way he kept his attention on his task. If people were staring at him, and whispering in the hallways—they'd stare at her too, if they knew of the work she'd done on Dr. Kane's book. The quarrel between them seemed to have vanished, and as they worked in the shadows of Dr. Kane's dog she felt very close to him. At the end of the day, when although she hadn't glimpsed the thallophytes she thanked him for accompanying her, he said, "It is I who thank you."

FOR A FEW weeks, Erasmus's dreams were haunted by Toodlamik—bones and body, eyes and sockets, versions of the living and the dead. Then letters arrived, which chased the dogs away. Captain Tyler's family wrote, wanting to know what had happened to the balance of his salary. This Erasmus forwarded to Zeke's father. After that, Copernicus's letter limped in stained and travel-worn:

Humboldt's message finally reached me. Do you know how glad I am to have you back? I can't wait to tell you everything. At the Canyon de Chelly I saw the Anasazi ruins. Hopi villages, pueblo kivas; I've been all over California. In the Salinas Valley, not far from Soledad, I painted in a place that was scorched by the sun. About the time you were beating through the ice in your little boat, I was toiling along on a mule, in temperatures over 110 degrees. We'll have a lot to talk about, won't we? I can't wait to see you, am heading home immediately, hope you are recovering. Humboldt says there's been some trouble but whatever it is hold on, I'll be there soon. I am bringing you some seeds.

The next day a letter came from Thomas Cholmondelay, Dr. Boerhaave's friend in London, expressing his appreciation for the packet Erasmus had sent. A portion was eerily out of date; he wrote about seeing Dr. Kane in London—*your fellow arctic traveler*—how much he'd been celebrated, how sad Lady Franklin and everyone else had been when Kane departed and how worried they all were about his health. On the heels of that, a letter arrived from William Greenstone in Edinburgh:

How can I thank you for forwarding Jan's last letters to me, despite your own difficulties? He was lucky to have you as his friend, and all of us who knew Jan are grateful to you and wish you a speedy recovery from your injuries. It was Jan's great wish to make another voyage north and I'm glad he saw so much before his terrible accident.

I think of him often—not just among our familiar Edinburgh places but whenever I hear any interesting news. Among our literary and scientific men, as I imagine among yours, there is much discussion of Mr. Wallace's "Sarawak Law" regarding the succession of species. Wallace remains in Borneo, but Lyell, Darwin, Hooker and others are in a flurry over Wallace's insights into animal distribution. There can no longer be much question, I think, of varieties representing separate, special acts of Creation—though I know Jan, influenced by Agassiz, leaned toward that view. I'd give a great deal to be able to argue with him over this. Meanwhile I thank you again for this gift of his words and also, belatedly, for your description of the Greenland meteorite.

He called him "Jan," Erasmus thought, looking from the letter to his friend's notebook. To each other they'd been Jan and William. Whereas he—despite all they'd shared together, they'd parted as Dr. Boerhaave and Mr. Wells.

ON MARCH 14, Erasmus and Alexandra stood at the three tall windows of her family home: Emily with them on the left; Browning and Harriet and their new daughter, Miriam, in the center; Jane and little Nicholas on the right, gazing from the second floor down onto Walnut Street. There were neighbors below them, strangers above them, more strangers up on the roof— Browning had rented out these viewing spots for a fee—but everyone was silent and the street itself was empty. Erasmus could hear the drums, but the procession hadn't yet come into sight. A light rain, falling all morning, had soaked the crepe hanging from the balconies of every house; in windows people huddled against the wind while on the rooftops black umbrellas sprouted.

The street looked like an endless dark tunnel. And beyond it, Erasmus knew, the entire route was similarly shrouded. He was cold and his toes hurt, or the place where his toes would have been. Behind him, on a small cherry table, a stack of newspapers detailed the journey of Dr. Kane's body across America. In his imagination Erasmus saw all the routes preceding this final one, spreading like a jet-black labyrinth across the country.

From Havana, where Kane had died, to New Orleans by packet boat; the casket had lain in state in City Hall. For a week, while a steamboat conveyed the casket up the Mississippi and the Ohio to Louisville, people had stood on levees and wharves to watch Kane pass. In Louisville Kane's arrival had been announced by the tolling of bells and the firing of guns; more formal ceremonies, another procession; a lying-in at Mozart Hall. Halfway to Cincinnati the steamboat was met by another boat, crowded with memorial-committee members wearing mourner's badges. In Cincinnati the procession had wound from the wharf to the railway station; at Xenia people had swarmed the tracks, delaying the train's slow progress; all throughout that afternoon and night, crowds had waited silently at every stop. At Columbus Kane's body lay in the capitol building, silent focus of more long speeches. In the smaller cities of Ohio and West Virginia, where the casket remained on the train, people had gathered at railway stations while more bells tolled. In Baltimore there had been huge crowds and the grandest procession until today's.

On Monday the funeral car had arrived in Philadelphia, where it was met by a guard of honor: city police, an artillery company, and a dozen memorial committees from various civic groups, none of which had included Erasmus. The hearse had been accompanied by eight of Kane's companions, who'd spread the flag of the lost *Advance* over her commander's coffin and then, at Independence Hall, added Kane's ceremonial sword and a mound of flowers. Until this morning, people had streamed through the hall to pay their respects. Now, at last, the procession was coming into sight.

Policemen, more policemen, then the companies of the First Brigade and, flanking the hearse itself, the Philadelphia City Calvary. The sight of the horsemen so excited young Nicholas that he wriggled halfway out the open sash and had to be pulled back and scolded by his aunt. The funeral car, Erasmus saw, was marked at the corners by golden spears bearing flags. Above the casket a black domed canopy kept off the rain; the silk ribbons that stretched to the spears drooped and the horses shone with moisture. Emily said, "There's that horrid father of his," but Browning murmured, "Not today."

The drums beat, the car moved slowly, waves of people marched. Erasmus crumpled the newspaper's guide to the procession in his hand. Almost every Philadelphian of distinction had been invited, from Kane's companions to the mayor and the aldermen, the members of the Philosophical Society, the medical faculty and students of the University of Pennsylvania, the Odd Fellows, the Fire Department and more, so many more.

"The Corn Exchange?" Browning said. "Why would they ask the members of the Corn Exchange?"

Erasmus had no answer. In all this great crowd, he thought, no place had been made for him. Nor for any of his companions: none of the living and nothing to honor the memory of the dead. At least the Toxophilites, he'd heard, honored Zeke at each monthly meeting.

Alexandra pressed his arm and he reached over and squeezed her hand gratefully. She was all he had to lean on; his brothers were comforting Lavinia, who'd refused to leave the house since Kane's body entered the city. Her presence at the procession, she'd said, would be an act of disloyalty to Zeke.

As if she knew what Erasmus was thinking, Alexandra said, "I'm sure it was only a wish to protect your health that kept the committee from asking you to join them. For you to walk so far, in this weather and with such a crowd . . ."

Erasmus looked down at his cunning shoes. "I manage very well with the walking sticks," he said. "As you know."

The funeral car was almost out of sight; below him were the members of the Hibernian Society and the St. Andrews and Scots Thistle Societies. They would pass for hours, he thought. At the church the procession would march past the casket, set up on a bier on the stone steps, and then all who could would crowd inside to hear the service. Words and words about Kane's goodness and glory and skills. As if Kane had not also lost a ship; as if his voyage had not also been marked by strife and rebellion. Someone, he noted from the program, would sing a Mozart anthem. One prominent minister would give an invocation and another the eulogy, which would be printed in the paper tomorrow but which Erasmus could already hear:

"We are assembled, my friends, to perform such comely though sad duties in honor of a man who, within the short lifetime of thirty-five years, under the combined impulses of humanity and science, has traversed nearly the whole of the planet in its most inaccessible places. . . . Death discloses the human estimate of character. That mournful pageant which for days past has been wending its way hither, across the solemn main, along our mighty rivers, through cities clad in habiliments of grief, with the learned, the noble, and the good mingling in its train, is but the honest tribute of hearts that could have no motive but respect and love."

More prayers, more singing; a dirge and then a benediction. The arctic coastline Dr. Kane had explored and named, the ice he'd fought and the Esquimaux he'd discovered; the dark winters of his entrapment and the heroic journey by which he'd brought most of his men to safety—all of this was admirable and yet why should it have eclipsed Erasmus's own journey? He'd brought men home himself, he had done what he could, he had tried . . . he pulled his hand from Alexandra's.

"Lavinia was right to stay home," he said. "I can't bear to watch any more."

He withdrew from the window, moving cautiously to the davenport. In the damp lines of his palms he found the visions he'd been fending off since his return: Zeke dying, Zeke dead, all alone in that vast white space. Death coming violent or quiet or both—a bear, a slipped razor, a fall through the ice; tumbling iceberg or slow starvation; fury or resignation. He heard the ice cracking beneath Zeke's feet; he saw Zeke searching for a hand to grab, a line to grasp, where there was nothing but a field of fractured floes. Then Zeke looking up into the sky and sinking, his arms at his side. Above there was no one to rescue him, no one even to watch. Just a fulmar, perched on a walrus's skull and regarding the bubbles of his last breaths and the skin of ice beginning to seal the hole.

Against this great mourning for Kane stood Zeke's unwitnessed final days. *I should have been there*, Erasmus thought. *Somehow, I should have been with him.*

9

A Big Stone Slipped
from His Grasp

(April–August 1857)

If a person asked my advice, before undertaking a long voyage, my answer would depend upon his possessing a decided taste for some branch of knowledge, which could by this means be advanced. No doubt it is a high satisfaction to behold various countries and the many races of mankind, but the pleasures gained at the time do not counterbalance the evils. It is necessary to look forward to a harvest, however distant that may be, when some fruit will be reaped, some good effected. Many of the losses which must be experienced are obvious; such as that of the society of every old friend, and of the sight of those places with which every dearest remembrance is so intimately connected. These losses, however, are at the time partly relieved by the exhaustless delight of anticipating the long wished-for day of return. . . .

Of individual objects, perhaps nothing is more certain to create astonishment than the first sight in his native haunt of a barbarian—of man in his lowest and most savage state. One's mind hurries back over past centuries, and then asks—could our progenitors have been men like these?—men, whose very signs and expressions are less intelligible to us than those of the domesticated animals; men, who do not possess the instinct of those animals, nor yet appear to boast of human reason, or at least of arts consequent on that reason. . . . In conclusion, it appears to me that nothing can be more improving to a young naturalist, than a journey in distant countries. It both sharpens, and partly allays that want and craving which, as Sir J. Herschel remarks, a man experiences although every corporeal sense be fully satisfied.

— CHARLES DARWIN, *The Voyage of the* Beagle (1839)

Ruddy and bearded and long-haired, Copernicus swept into the Repository and threw his arms around his brother, squeezing so tightly he lifted Erasmus from his shoes.

"Oh, be careful!" Alexandra cried.

Copernicus shot her a startled glance, then followed her gaze to his brother's feet. Quickly he lowered Erasmus into a chair.

"I'm sorry," he said. "But I'm so glad to see you!" He bent and grasped Erasmus's right ankle, then ran his hand along the foot: tarsals, metatarsals—but most of the phalanges gone. "Do they hurt?"

"No," Erasmus said, smiling in a way Alexandra had forgotten. "Say hello to Alexandra Copeland."

"Humboldt wrote me about you," Copernicus said. "What a help you've been with Lavinia, and what a good friend to our family. I'm delighted to meet you." As if, Alexandra thought, he'd forgotten all the times they'd met when she and Lavinia were girls. He clasped her hand and then spun around and said, "But where's Lavinia? I'm longing to see her."

"Let me go fetch her," Alexandra said, hoping Lavinia was up and dressed.

Later, as Copernicus unpacked the crates piled along the garden paths, she would see his paintings: Pikes Peak and the Grand Tetons and the Rocky Mountains; the Great Salt Lake, where the breeze had blown his floating body about as if he were a sailboat; alkali deserts and the Humboldt Mountains; the Yosemite Valley and El Capitan and the Indians he'd met in each place. Astonishing paintings, flooded with light and dazzling color. But for the moment she saw only the smile on Erasmus's face, and the possibility of Lavinia similarly transformed.

*   *   *

HAVING COPERNICUS HOME was a comfort, Lavinia confided to Alexandra. After all he was her favorite brother. She began to plan the household meals again: roast lamb with herbs and carrots, chicken bathed in cream. Nothing but Copernicus's favorites, she said. He'd been away so long. When her work was done, she and Alexandra sometimes joined the brothers as they sat exchanging stories of their adventures.

Each of Copernicus's paintings had a tale behind it, and a trail that could be followed through his sketchbook. A sort of visual diary, Alexandra saw, during those warm lazy afternoons. Fort Wallah Wallah on one page and a herd of buffalo on another; a group of men drying and pounding buffalo meat for pemmican. Delaware and Shawnee and Osage Indians; Kickapoos, Witchetaws, Wacos. Mormons. The black-tailed deer of the Rocky Mountains. Thousands of sketches and just a few words of description, the obverse of Erasmus's journal.

In turn Erasmus offered his own pages, Dr. Boerhaave's papers, and the long letter he'd written to Copernicus during the voyage. The papers cast shadows, Alexandra saw. Sometimes Erasmus would have to retire abruptly, leaving Copernicus alone. Sometimes, when she came down to breakfast, Erasmus would look as if he hadn't slept and later, in the Repository, he'd admit that all this talking brought him nightmares. Zeke haunted his dreams, he said. In the ice, nailed to the frozen ship, was a list of the dead in the shape of a headstone that he saw again and again. Still, the more the brothers talked, the more excited Erasmus grew. Copernicus showed Erasmus a sketch of the footwear that had protected him during a winter crossing of the Rockies: buffalo-skin boots over buckskin moccasins over thick squares of blanket over woolen socks. Erasmus showed Copernicus the tattered fur suit Ned had made for him and said, "I might write a book."

It would not be, as Dr. Kane's effort had been, an adventure tale built from transcribed journal entries, but neither would it be a simple description of the arctic. Rather, Erasmus said, the narrative would pull his readers along on a journey, as an imaginary ship moved from place to place and through the seasons. On the flagstone patio beyond the solarium, he described a sequence of verbal portraits, a natural history that caught each place at a particular time of the year. He wouldn't be in the story, Erasmus said. He'd be erased, he'd be invisible. It would be as if readers gazed at a series of detailed landscape paintings. As if they were making the journey themselves, but without discomfort or discord.

"Why not include some color plates?" Copernicus said. "I could do the paintings myself." From Erasmus's sketches and descriptions, and his own knowledge of glaciers and light—what if he were to make a series of paintings introducing the sections? Each could combine all the important features of one region, all the representative animals and plants—imaginary, and yet a portrait truer than simple fact.

Erasmus reached into his pocket and pulled out a withered slab of leather wrapped in a handkerchief. He unfolded the cloth. "Paintings like this?" he said. "That stand for a whole set of things?"

"What *is* that?"

Erasmus told him about his last day among the Boothian Esquimaux, and how the wife of the tribe's leader had slipped him this relic. He didn't say where he'd hidden it; nor what Joe had told him about the boot from which it might have come.

"Have you shown it to anyone?"

"Just some reporters," Erasmus said. "When I first got back, and everyone was asking questions and I was trying to explain what happened and what we'd found. Even if all the other things were lost, I said, this was one real bit of evidence that we'd uncovered from Franklin's voyage. But no one believed me." He paused for a second. "That's not true; Alexandra and

Linnaeus and Humboldt saw it. They believed me, I think. I'm not sure, I was so sick. I don't remember much from those first few weeks."

Copernicus balanced the relic on his palm. "But it's *real*," he said. The tips of the rusty, broken screws raised the leather off his skin, so that this thing which had once sheltered a foot now seemed to balance on little feet of its own. "It's right here."

Two big blotches rose on Erasmus's cheeks. "It's my own fault," he said. "I didn't include it on my list of the items we found, because I wanted to keep it secret, for myself. I stole it, really. And now there's no one who witnessed me finding it, no written evidence of how I got it. One of the reporters accused me of manufacturing it. Another said I could have found it anywhere, and that it might be anything. A bit from a sailor's boot, picked up in Greenland. Or a remnant from Kane's expedition, found at Smith Sound."

"There's nothing that marks it surely as belonging to one of Franklin's men?"

"Just the context," Erasmus said. "Just where I found it, and who gave it to me."

Once more, as he had for months, he berated himself for having kept this secret from Dr. Boerhaave. He'd withheld this part of himself, failed to share every corner of his heart with the man who'd been his friend—why had he done that? What had he been waiting for?

The outline of the seven screws fit exactly within Copernicus's left palm. "It's too bad," he said. "This ought to have been the one thing that would make everyone understand all you found. But I understand what you mean: it's almost as if I can see the man this belonged to, and the entire expedition. And that *is* what I mean by these paintings: sometimes one scene can capture . . . everything. The *feel* of a place."

* * *

THE BROTHERS' PLANS delighted Alexandra, but also made her feel it was time to leave. Lavinia was more serene than she used to be, more thoughtful, more reserved; but perfectly capable of running the household and seemingly at ease with Erasmus now that Copernicus mediated between them. Meanwhile her own family could use her help, Browning said. They were grateful for the money she contributed each month, but how much longer could she count on that?

To this she had no answer; she was halfway done with her botanical plates and no more had been promised. Yet, as Browning pointed out, there were scores of ways she could help her family. A dense net of obligations, which she sometimes longed to shed . . . but no one was ever free of them. Lavinia was tied here with her brothers, perhaps forever. And she herself must be similarly tied to her siblings; she would never marry, she could feel it. Passing a mirror, she would glimpse herself in her gray frock, with her hair pulled tightly back, and think how invisible she must be to anyone who didn't know her.

"Your feet are healed," she said to Erasmus one day. "And you and Copernicus have so much work to do, you don't need me here anymore."

"But you can't go," he said, seizing her hand. "Not *now*."

"We do need you," Copernicus said.

"*I* need you," Erasmus added. "The paintings Copernicus plans to make—those are just the general portraits. Chapter headings, in a way. But we must have hundreds of detailed drawings of the plants and animals and their parts, just like the ones you're working on now. Won't you be our partner in this?"

"It's not as if I'm *replacing* you," Copernicus added. Although she'd assumed that he was.

"The way we've been working these past weeks," Erasmus said. "I thought we'd just continue. We work so well together."

Erasmus in one corner, writing steadily except when he leapt up to offer suggestions; she with pen and ink in another corner, drawing sedges and seaweeds and gulls; Copernicus already painting in blue and green and gold and white, icebergs calving from a glacier above Melville Bay—they *did* work well together, but she'd assumed this was just for a few weeks until Copernicus took over her work and her responsibility for Erasmus. But perhaps things didn't have to go that way. Neither of the brothers had said a word about money, though.

"Let me think about it," she said. "Let me talk to my family."

IN LATE MAY, Copernicus took Erasmus to visit two fellow painters who shared an attic studio. Under the skylights they drank red wine and chatted gaily—a pleasure, Erasmus thought. He went out so seldom; he'd missed the company of other men. Afterward he tapped along Sansom Street with his walking sticks, delighted with the day and with his own increasing stamina. He smelled lilacs, the sharp green odor of sumacs, freshly scrubbed paving stones. He was moving across the stones—not as swiftly as Copernicus, who kept darting ahead, and then looping back to him—but still he was moving. The sweet air poured into his lungs. Those painters had liked him. Found him interesting. They'd asked him questions about his book.

At Broad Street they caught the empty omnibus. Past them sailed storefronts, window displays, pigeons rising and falling as if all attached to the same rippling sheet. Copernicus pointed out the shadow rippling beneath the flock; Erasmus asked about the shadows water cast on ice. At their stop they were talking happily when the driver interrupted them.

"Would you be Erasmus Wells?" he asked, staring at Erasmus's feet. Erasmus nodded, still thinking about what Copernicus had explained. Water cast a shadow *up* . . . "My name's

Godfrey," the driver said. At first the name meant nothing.

"William Godfrey," he added. "*Kane's* Godfrey."

William Godfrey, the deserter and traitor Kane had written about so bitterly in *Arctic Explorations*! Erasmus caught his brother's eye. "This is my last run of the day," Godfrey said. "I'd like to talk with you, if you could give me a few minutes . . ."

They agreed to meet in half an hour, at a nearby tavern. What harm could it do? On a bench by the tavern's front window, Erasmus looked out at a catalpa tree covered with foamy white blossoms and wondered what this stranger might have to say to him. "It's a good idea," Copernicus said, and Erasmus agreed. "You can compare notes."

Soon Godfrey slid in next to them. "Buy me a drink," he said. "A couple of drinks. You can afford it." A whiff of horse dung rose from his shoes.

While Copernicus fetched a round, Erasmus started to ask Godfrey about the sights they'd shared. "The Esquimaux," he said. "The ones that helped you . . ."

Godfrey leaned in too close to him, seizing the glass of beer Copernicus offered. "What was Commander Voorhees like?" he asked abruptly. Before Erasmus could answer, Godfrey said, "As bad as Kane? Was he that bad? You know, what *I* went through up there . . ."

Dr. Kane lied, he said. His book was a lie, much of what had really happened glossed over; he himself no mutineer but rather a hero who'd saved Kane's life several times. "*I* pulled him from the water when the sledge fell in," Godfrey said. His voice shot up and people turned to look at them. "*I* shot the bear he missed, the one that charged him . . ."

A carriage passed by the window, two beautiful chestnut horses and behind them, half-hidden, a woman in a blue silk dress much like one Erasmus remembered on his mother. Still Godfrey was talking: lowbrowed, pockmarked, seeming more unpleasant by the minute.

"And what did I get?" Godfrey continued, gulping at his beer. He held out his glass for a refill. "Nothing. Worse than nothing. Kane ruined my reputation, no one will hire me: look at me, driving men like you through the streets."

"I'm sorry," Erasmus offered, but Godfrey trampled over his words. Why he'd opposed Kane's orders, why part of the crew had set off on their own . . . the beer was sour and that, or Godfrey's complaints, made Erasmus queasy. That droning voice dissolved the pleasures of the day and cast him back to the dark winter, the paper headstone pinned to Captain Tyler's bunk and the names of the dead, the list that always grew longer. Erasmus was about to make an excuse and leave when Godfrey said, "You know, if anyone does, what it is to be falsely accused. And how the arctic can drive men mad."

He bent toward Erasmus and squinted. "Tell me the truth— did you kill him?"

Was that what people thought? Not just that he had abandoned Zeke, but that he'd murdered him? Erasmus rose but Copernicus pushed him down.

"How dare you!" Copernicus said. "My brother *saved* that expedition, he's the one who got everyone safely home. Zeke made his own decisions, what happened to him was his choice and you have no right . . ."

Godfrey drained his second glass and set it down. "Well, excuse me," he said to Erasmus. "Excuse me for making assumptions. But, you know—Kane's account of our voyage is so different from what actually happened . . . all I know about you is what I've read in the papers. How would *I* know what you really did?"

"I did everything I could," Erasmus said. "Believe that or not, as you choose." He rose again, sure that everyone in the tavern was looking at them. "We have to go."

Godfrey grasped his arm. "Don't," he said. "I know you despise me, everyone does—but you and I have things in common."

More carriages rolled by, a stream of handsome, well-dressed people talking and laughing, making plans, doing whatever it is people do. What did they do? They passed, leaving Erasmus cut off once more from the simple stream of dailiness. He and Godfrey had nothing in common, he thought. Nothing at all.

"I deserve a hearing too," Godfrey continued. "A fair and impartial hearing before the American public—I'm writing a book, *my* version. Will you help me? I need money. Surely you among all men can sympathize . . ."

If he would stop talking; if this awful man would just stop talking . . . Erasmus dug in his pockets, dropped a few bills on the table, and fled with Copernicus. His dismay stayed with him long after they'd reached home, and that evening he wrote in his journal:

What a horrid man! Yet something in Godfrey's account makes me wonder if our two voyages were so different. Perhaps I've been making a mistake in comparing what I did with what others claimed in print to have done. Godfrey said Kane's anger was boundless when the eight crew members seceded and set off on their boat journey; and that four months later, Kane was vindictive when the frozen men straggled back to the ship. According to Godfrey there was no saintly welcome; Kane was an iron-willed tyrant who grudgingly saved his crewmen only when their wills were broken. Godfrey boils with resentment and self-interest; yet some of what he says may be true.

If Kane was less of a hero than we all believe, am I less of a failure? The world knows Kane's version of that expedition, not Godfrey's; as it knew Wilkes's version of the Exploring Expedition and no one else's— and as it might have known Zeke's version of our own journey, had he not been lost.

Copernicus says we ought to try to talk with him again, this time without beer; he may have observed things on his side of Smith Sound I never saw, which might contribute to our portrait of the area. But I can't bear to see him again, I can't bear to think of anyone drawing a parallel between us. How can I write one word about the arctic when a person such as Godfrey is also writing a book, one that says me, me, me, me me?

COPERNICUS'S FIRST PAINTING grew, it was radiant. When his dealer visited the Repository to collect a group of the western paintings, Copernicus showed him the unfinished picture of Melville Bay and the dealer's breath whistled in his throat. "It's one of a set," Copernicus said. "For a book my brother's writing."

"When you finish them," the dealer said, "after the color plates have been made, if you'd let me sell them as a group . . ."

"We'll discuss it later," Copernicus said. "After the work is done."

He talked about the book as if it already existed, and so Erasmus wrote on. He took courage not only from his brother but from the presence of Alexandra, who turned out one handsome drawing after another. At night he fell asleep thinking about her face, her hands, the ink on her hands, the way her arms merged pale and strong into the sleeves of her smock. At the back of her neck, beneath the coil of smooth, straight, oak-brown hair, small strands escaped and whispered over the bumps of her vertebrae. He hadn't found her plain for a long time now.

On the *Narwhal* sex had been something he seldom thought about, after the first summer; perpetually too cold, too worn, too hungry, so worried he'd barely remembered the feel of skin on skin, which had seemed like something from another life. And before that, when he was still healthy and energetic, the cabin was always full of men coming and going, the light had been endless, there was no privacy. A few times, landing on the shoreline to hunt or left briefly alone on Boothia, he'd touched himself in the shelter of some rocks—but he'd thought of a red-haired woman in Washington then, a woman on Front Street, the flowery faces of Lavinia's friends. Now he lay in his lonely bed imagining Alexandra.

Thinking all the heat flowed from him, Erasmus was unaware of Alexandra's humming confusion. It was the presence of both brothers, she thought, that made her feel so strange. Copernicus's strong, broad body, his easy good humor and the way he rested his hand on her shoulder; Erasmus's focused attention, the way he followed her hands and looked into her eyes and spoke as if they were equals: which was it she wanted? Both, perhaps. Although she was aware even then that the affection she felt beaming from Copernicus was part of his general affection for the world. Perhaps it was only the delirious early summer weather that made her toss and turn in her sheets and stare at herself naked in the mirror. One lit candle, the gleam off her flank slipping into the glass and out as she imagined how she might look to another set of eyes. At night someone appeared in her dreams who was neither Erasmus nor Copernicus but both of them. During the day when she wasn't working she sat with Lavinia and talked about transplanting the irises.

All this made her blush when finally, reluctantly, she spoke to Erasmus about her financial situation. He looked so startled, even ashamed—did he never need to think about money? "I have an income," he said quickly. "More than I need. It was foolish of me not to realize that Linnaeus and Humboldt had stopped paying you. The three of us are full partners on this project, and it's only fair you should receive a salary for your efforts."

IN THE GARDEN the four of them sat, eating strawberry-rhubarb pie and listening to Erasmus read. The bleeding hearts were still in bloom, the weather had been cool; the lawn stretched soft and green between the wicker chairs and the drive. Along the drive the peonies planted so long ago rose in great clumps covered with flowers. Erasmus turned the pages on his lap. Lavinia nodded her head thoughtfully when Erasmus read a passage about the fevered coming of summer to Disko Island. It was a gift, she said. She could almost see the cliffs and ice floes sailing toward her. Even if Erasmus wasn't writing directly about Zeke, he was letting her see the last things Zeke might have seen, and she was grateful for that. Erasmus read on. A carriage appeared at the end of the drive and a man got out. After that everything happened as if in a dream.

Money changed hands and boxes were dropped onto the grass. Then another, smaller figure stepped down from the carriage, bundled in unfamiliar clothes. The figure lifted out a child; the pair sat, when the man pointed, on one of the boxes. The man began to walk up the drive, between the rows of peonies. Pink globes, creamy globes, the man touching the globes as he passed; Erasmus rose from his chair without his sticks and toppled to the ground. Then Lavinia was running toward the man, stumbling over the hem of her dress, and Copernicus and Alexandra were bending over Erasmus.

Alexandra would never be able to sort out the next few minutes. How Zeke and Lavinia got from their embrace halfway down the drive to the solarium; how Copernicus got Erasmus to his feet and into the shelter of the Repository; how she herself made her way to the mound of boxes and the two figures sitting there, so out of place—all this jumbled in her mind. One minute she was standing over the strangers—one was a woman, an Esquimau woman, and the smaller figure a little boy—and saying, as she would to anyone, "Won't you come inside?" The next she was leading them into the house and giving orders to the bewildered servants.

Zeke was a ghost, but Zeke was here; he had his arms around Lavinia, who couldn't stop weeping, but he was also calmly greeting Alexandra and asking if his companions could stay here.

Lavinia touched his arm, his neck, his face. "Yes," she said. "Anything you want."

"This is Annie," Zeke said. "And Tom. They come from Greenland." He pressed Lavinia's hand to his cheek. "They have other names, Esquimaux names, but these are the ones they use with me." He kissed Lavinia's fingers. "They speak English, I taught them how. Annie saved my life."

For a while, as Alexandra glided automatically up the stairs, that was all she knew. She turned halfway up and found no one behind her. The visitors stood at the bottom, clinging to the bannister and testing the first step as if checking the thickness of ice. Annie wore breeches, a hooded shirt, soft boots even in this heat— all made from some sort of hide, deer or seal, something Alexandra couldn't name. Tom was dressed in a similar suit and the hides smelled, or perhaps the smell came from the people. She lifted her skirts above her ankles so Annie and Tom could see her feet; she took the steps slowly and let them see how each step was safe.

In the spare room across the hall from Copernicus's room she said to Annie, "You will stay here, with your . . ."

"It is my son," Annie said. "Called Tom." She seemed to understand Alexandra perfectly.

Alexandra went to her own room, where she gathered undergarments and her gray dress. When she returned Annie and Tom were at the window, pressing their palms to the glass as if trying to reach the outside air. Alexandra opened the sash and Annie pressed her palm against the air where the glass had been, and then smiled. She shook her head at the gray dress Alexandra held to her shoulders.

"You'll be more comfortable," Alexandra said. "In this heat." Tom stuck his upper body through the window and Annie joined him. "Annie!" Alexandra said. She touched the woman's jacket and Annie pulled away and frowned. Alexandra left the dress on the bed.

Downstairs, she tried not to stare at Zeke. There were sharp lines carved around his eyes and his hands were battered and scarred; part of his left ear was gone. His clothes were patched and torn and stained. Slowly she recognized the remnants of the elegant gray uniform once worn by all the *Narwhal*'s crew.

"I put them in the second guest room," she said, hypnotized by the way Zeke's hand moved over Lavinia's back and shoulders. What was he doing here, how was he alive? Where had Erasmus gone? "I brought Annie one of my dresses, but she won't put it on."

"I'll take care of it," Zeke said. He rose. "Stay here. I'll be right back."

Alexandra took his place on the sofa, sitting still while Lavinia leaned against her shoulder and wept. Later, when Zeke went out to the Repository, Lavinia pulled Alexandra upstairs. They found Annie seated on the floor with Tom in her lap, her head resting on the windowsill and her body draped in Alexandra's dress. Best not to think what Zeke had said or done to get her into it. The bodice was loose, the sleeves too long. The white collar set off her shining dark skin. When they entered she swiveled her head and looked at them without interest. "Tseke?" she said. "Where is Tseke?"

I DIDN'T KILL HIM, Erasmus thought. That moment in the garden, when he'd tumbled to the ground: what was the name for the feeling that had toppled him? Guilt, shock, horror all mingled with joy, with relief—*I didn't kill him*.

He stood near the herbarium case, supported by his sticks and finding it difficult to breathe. Copernicus sat by the window and Zeke orbited the Repository, gazing at what was new among all that had once been familiar. "I thought you were dead," Erasmus said.

"Well, I'm not," Zeke said. "As you see."

He looked much older, Erasmus saw. Stronger, more contained. And frighteningly calm. Why didn't Zeke embrace him, or strike him, or demand an explanation or offer one of his own? Not a word; he turned to Copernicus and said, "When did you get back?"

"Two months ago," Copernicus said. "I headed home as soon as I heard about Erasmus."

"I waited as long as I could," Erasmus said. How could he explain himself? "All the men were sure you were dead and they were frightened about spending another winter there. They made a plan without me—they said I had to lead them south, because you'd left me in charge. I had to take them, I thought you were dead."

"I'm sure you did," Zeke said. "I'm sure you did everything you could. I had news of you in Godhavn. I heard you got at least some of our men home safely."

"All of them," Erasmus said, more sharply now. "All that *chose*—the four that split off, I couldn't stop them from going."

"As you say," Zeke said. "Anyway I forgive you. Whatever you did, I'm sure it was the best you could do. It turned out to be a blessing. To be *alone*, the way that I was alone—I know things about myself now. Things you'll never understand."

"Tell me," Erasmus said.

"Why should I?"

Zeke's face was clenched. After a long silence, Erasmus thinking every second, *Hit me. Get it over with*, Zeke said, "Why would I tell you anything, ever again?"

Copernicus cleared his throat. "But where were you? How did you survive?"

"That," Zeke said, "is a long story."

Apparently he wasn't going to tell it now. He wandered around the Repository, peering at a drawing of a fossil Alexandra

had left pinned to her easel, ignoring Copernicus's draped painting, looking down at the books open on the long table. He
touched Dr. Boerhaave's journal, then the green silk volume
Lavinia had once given him. "I wondered what had happened to
these," he said. "When I got back to the *Narwhal*, and found my
box broken into and Dr. Boerhaave's journal gone, I was very . . .
curious."

"I thought you were dead," Erasmus said. "I wanted to preserve what I could." He couldn't bear the questions on his
brother's face. "Who are these people you've brought with you?"

"Who are you to criticize what I do?" Zeke asked. "You abandoned me."

"I'm not *criticizing*," Erasmus said. "Only asking."

"Would you have had me spend the winter with no comfort?
In a place where it's an insult to refuse what's offered? Annie's
family took me in." Zeke turned to the pile of manuscript pages.
"You're writing something? A little memoir?"

"Not a memoir," Erasmus said. What did that mean: *Annie's
family took me in*? "Something different."

"You agreed not to write anything for a year after the voyage,"
Zeke said. "And to turn the journals over to me."

"It's already *been* a year," Erasmus said. Then was appalled at
the tone of his voice; and still couldn't stop himself. "You were
gone. And anyway, anyway—this isn't a book about our journey,
there's nothing in it about you or me or the Franklin relics, or
what happened to any of us. It's about the *place*—a natural history of the place through the seasons."

"Write if it pleases you," Zeke said. "It's hard to believe anyone will want to read such a thing, though. Not when they see
what I have to say, the story I have to tell."

From his pocket he took the black notebook Erasmus had seen
so often during their journey. "It's all in here," he said, tapping
the worn cover. With each tap, Erasmus felt a part of himself dis-

solve and re-form as a version of William Godfrey. "My journey north and all I discovered, what happened to me after I got back to the ship and found you gone, my life among the Esquimaux—everything."

Tap, tap, tap. "I'm going to marry Lavinia," he added. "The minute I can arrange it. I'm tired of being alone. What happened to your feet?"

"I lost my toes," Erasmus said. At least Lavinia would be happy; at least there was that. "Frostbite. What happened to your ear?"

"Polar bear."

Erasmus couldn't take his eyes off the black book. Zeke hadn't taken it north; he'd left it behind; *I have to travel light*, he'd said. When Erasmus broke into Zeke's locked box to retrieve Dr. Boerhaave's journal, he'd seen Zeke's black notebook waiting there.

THE EXTRACTS APPEARED in the Philadelphia paper two weeks later, appended to a reporter's brief introduction and beneath a curious set of headlines:

EXPLORER RETRACES MUCH OF KANE'S ROUTE
ABANDONED BY HIS MEN
RESCUED BY WIZARD'S PROPHECY
DETAILED ACCOUNT OF LIFE AMONG KANE'S ESQUIMAUX
ESQUIMAUX SPECIMENS HERE IN PHILADELPHIA

Zechariah Voorhees, given up for lost since the arrival here in November of the battered survivors of his expedition, has returned to us safe and well in the company of two of Dr. Kane's Esquimaux. I spoke with Commander Voorhees at his parents' home, where he greeted me cheerfully. Asked the question on everyone's lips, he responded, "My men did the right thing. When I set off on my journey north, I set a date by which I would return. Three weeks after that date elapsed, the officers to whom I had delegated responsibility determined that the safety of the group demanded they attempt a retreat. That's exactly what I would have wanted them to do. They had no way of knowing I was alive."

He was alive though, remarkably. And has much to report. To his companions' revelations about the discoveries on Boothia, among the Esquimaux possessing relics of Franklin's ships, he has nothing to add—the account provided earlier by Mr. Erasmus Wells is true and accurate, he says. As is the account of the expedition's winter in the ice. But since his men's escape to safety he has passed an astonishing year among the Smith Sound Esquimaux discovered by our own much-missed Dr. Kane.

These kind people delivered him to Upernavik in May, where he learned of Dr. Kane's tragic demise and was given a copy of *Arctic Explorations* by a Danish trader. Having read this aboard the ship that brought him home, he notes that Dr. Kane's descriptions of the western side of Kane's Basin are accurate in outline, but that his own explorations have added more detail to these areas. A corrected version of Dr. Kane's map follows on Page 3. Commander Voorhees is already at work on a narrative of his stay with the Esquimaux in the most northerly settlement of Greenland. In the meantime, as a kindness to our readers, he's generously provided a few extracts from his daily journal.

* * * * * * * * * * * * *

AUGUST 30, 1856. The men are gone; I can't believe I missed them. The *Narwhal* lies frozen in a useless canal. Heartbreaking to see how hard they worked but I must be glad they failed; here is my winter home. Everything aboard is scrupulously clean, provisions were set aside against my possible return, Mr. Wells left a note explaining what happened. I'm grateful but—four days! I missed them by so little, yet those days mean another winter here in the ice. I begin work today. I'll spend part of my time boxing off a small section of the cabin, insulating it with moss and peat so it can be efficiently heated, and stripping siding for fuel. The rest of the time I must hunt as I've never hunted, trying to cache enough food for the winter. It's an excellent time for walrus, if I can manage to take them by myself. The seals are fat, so are the musk oxen, and hares abound. I made a mistake last year, spending this month in a frantic struggle to escape rather than stockpiling supplies: a mistake I can't afford again.

I'm here for the winter, there's no denying it. The thing to do is face it. Make the best of it. Enjoy it even, learn from it. This is my chance to live, as nearly as possible, the way the Esquimaux live. To prove that a man willing to learn the ways of the north may live in relative comfort here. I have books, food, shelter; maps to make, a journal to keep. I may be a regular Robinson Crusoe.

OCTOBER 10, 1856. I rebuilt the partition, farther aft this time. I lined the bunk with fresh skins, I built a new entrance, I built what deckhouse I could with the wood they left me. I tore off the sheathing down to the waterline on the port side and chopped and stacked it. I put meat down in barrels and filled casks with blubber and oil. I cleaned the guns and moved all the ammunition into one dry place and counted every round; I'm growing short. I made new boots and a new jacket. I fixed the stove. Everything is perfectly snug. My tiny apartment belowdecks is easily heated and all is arranged in the most convenient and efficient way. With only myself to look after, no disagreements or moody men or those who pretend to be sick to avoid hard work, everything's been easy. The body of the sun is gone, but the sky shines red and yellow and blue and the ice glows green and violet. And the hunting has been so fine it's as if the animals give themselves freely to me. I'm ready for the winter, ready for everything.

OCTOBER 21, 1856. One minute nothing, the next a sledge track; it was like seeing a footprint in the sand. They appeared as I was cooking my supper—three of them, camped on the deck as I write this: Nessark, Marumah, and Nessark's wife. Nessark was among the hunters we met on our visit to Anoatok but the other two are new to me. All three spent time with Dr. Kane two years ago and the woman, who is lively and intelligent, learned some English from him and his men. She calls herself Annie, and between her English and what Joe taught me we talk fairly easily. They've come to take me to their winter settlement, she says. They don't want me in danger. I don't know how they knew I was here.

I told them I was safe, I was fine, I appreciated their offer but I could care for myself. They withdrew for a long discussion, then returned and let Annie speak for all. She says they—I—have no choice. They've been sent here by their *angekok*—the word they use for their tribal wizard. This angekok had a vision, she explained. Some children among them sickened recently and two died. The angekok determined that this was because of me.

She asks if I remember Ootuniah, who visited us last year and befriended Joe during our stay in Anoatok. I do remember him very sharply. I felt he didn't have our best interests at heart despite his gifts and this was proved when he loaned Joe the sledge and dogs I needed for myself. Now it appears that Joe told Ootuniah about the meteorite I found, the one he told me not to touch. When the angekok heard it had been destroyed, he decided I'd disturbed the iron stone's spirit. Their children sicken, he says, because that spirit is angry I'm still in this country.

What was I to say? It was a stone, I told Annie. A big stone, which slipped from my grasp. I meant no harm. She says no one blames me, it's understood that this was an accident and I'm not to be punished. Still, reparations must be made. The message the angekok sends is this: that I may pacify the spirit of the stone by making to them a free gift of all the iron that may be easily removed from the ship and transported on their sledges across the Sound. And by returning to their village with them, and allowing them to care for me. If I die here, the angekok says, I'll pollute the land somehow. Thus I must allow them to guard me.

Take the iron, I told them. Take anything you want, all the fittings, I can't use them anymore. But apparently this isn't enough. The two men seem prepared to carry me off bodily if I refuse. And so I am to go. Perhaps it's not a bad thing. They mean me no harm, I think; and I'll have warmth and company and food for the winter; and who else has lived among the Esquimaux like this? I may see things no one's seen before, live in this part of the world as no white man has. Annie does her best to make her tribe's offer attractive—we welcome you, she says.

Meanwhile Nessark and Marumah are loading their sledges with hoops and hardware they tear from the brig. On top of the iron the men pile meat from my caches; I want to go to their village as a strong hunter, not a beggar. Also I'm bringing two of the smaller sails as a gift. Everything else must stay here but my personal belongings. I pray the Franklin relics Erasmus took with him have reached home safely. That the men have reached home. We leave in a few hours.

DECEMBER 23, 1856. Anoatok is much changed since my first visit. During this season the Esquimaux usually move to Etah, where Dr. Kane visited them, but since my arrival the hunting has been unusually good and several extended families have stayed on after repairing and expanding the huts. Fresh seal-skins cover the walls, a bear skin warms the floor, the blubber lamps burn steadily. The angekok, Annie says, has determined that my presence is drawing the animals. By their rescue of me, and their continued care—I sleep with Nessark, Annie, their little boy, Annie's parents, and her two young brothers—the spirit of the iron stone has been pacified.

The traps yield foxes, and despite the darkness we've harpooned many seals. We take bears as well—although I'd assumed they all disappeared at this time of year, it isn't so. On Monday the moon was full, we were hunting seal. Suddenly an iceberg near us began to tip and shift position—and a huge bear clambered out of the snow alongside it, disturbed in his rest. Our dogs pursued him and mine was the first shot. By tradition I'm credited with the kill and the skin is mine, but it was Nessark whose spear finished him—and lucky for me, the bear was upon me. I'm now missing most of the fleshy portion of my left ear. The wound is healing and the pain isn't bad. Nessark stopped the bleeding with snow and showed me how to slice the bear's skin from the body and fold it into a shape like a sled, then how to carve out legs, ribs, backbone, and shoulder blades and set each chunk to freeze on the ice. We pulled the meat home on the frozen skin.

JANUARY 28, 1857. A most remarkable event yesterday. The Esquimaux call it *saugssat* or so it sounds to my ear. A high tide two days ago, combined with a strong wind, opened a large lead in the cove. Into it poured hundreds of narwhals in search of breathing space and food. When the end of the lead froze over again the animals were trapped. It was horrible to see them thrashing around in the ever smaller hole, pushing each other underwater as they struggled for air, pulled tighter and tighter until their tusks projected above the surface like a forest of clashing spears. Yet wonderful, too, that it should happen so near to us.

Annie's little boy spotted them first and ran home nearly

speechless with excitement—he's very clever, I've taught him much English and call him Tom. We all gathered our weapons and followed him, everyone rushing before a crack opened and freed the desperate creatures. But luck was with us not them. We stood around the edges of the pool, needing only to thrust the harpoons into the nearest animals and haul them up. Even in this we were aided, as the thrashing survivors heaved the carcasses upward.

Twenty-seven narwhals! Such a celebration we had. Tom is a hero and so, somehow, am I. Not for anything I do but because this season has been so generous. There hasn't been a saugssat here for seven years, nor such successful winter hunting. My presence—or more accurately my survival among them—is thought to have caused this good fortune. So I am pampered, fussed over, Annie makes me pants from my polar bear skin and an undershirt from the skins of murres while her mother feeds me dovekies cached since the summer in a sealskin bag. The birds, permeated with blubber, are a great delicacy. Nessark has also been most generous and begrudges me no hospitality. They're generous not only with material things but with their time and knowledge; men and women alike spend hours with me, answering my questions.

MARCH 14, 1857. I leave with both reluctance and excitement. The food caches are empty, it's time to move to new hunting grounds, we have sun for nearly twelve hours daily and the dogs are strong. It's the best time of year to make a long sledge journey and the whole encampment has decided to accompany me to Upernavik. They would move now anyway, Annie tells me. But not so far, never so far—they do this, as everything else, on the advice of the angekok. He never speaks to me directly but only through Annie. The winter has been so good, he says, and everyone so healthy, because all the elements of his vision dream were satisfied. Yet he believes the spirits will still turn against them unless they convey me safely to Upernavik—which they've only heard about, where no one of them has ever been—and hence out of their country. Annie tells me this as if ashamed. I suppose they all assume I'd want to stay here forever. And how can I tell them nothing could be luckier for me than this—that they should bend their energies, their time and skills and dogs and sledges, to bringing me just where I want to go, and likely couldn't reach myself.

I've had time, these last months, to consider all the mistakes I made my first year here. One was certainly my failure to cultivate these people more fully when they first visited us. Because Dr. Kane's ship was frozen in on this side of the Sound, he was in more immediate contact with them. Always they aided him; and might have aided us had I pressed them more last winter. Perhaps we might have escaped with their help last spring. Instead we saw them only twice; our great loss. Now it seems clear that some-thing one of my crew said or did—I won't speculate as to whom—gave these people the impression we were evil and to be avoided. Only after I was alone did they approach again, giving me the chance to adapt myself to their habits. The white man can only survive comfortably here by living as the Esquimaux do. Almost all the things we brought with us are useless. Esquimaux clothes, hunting techniques, eating habits are what make life pos-sible. I imagine that Dr. Kane also discovered this—but he never lived among them, as I've done for six months now.

APRIL 30, 1857. Upernavik, at last! The Danish traders wel-comed me and gave me news of Dr. Kane—how tragic, this unexpected death after escaping the arctic! Also they tell me my men arrived here safely and are thought to be home. The walrus are streaming north and my Esquimaux must follow them; they're uncomfortable here, they've had no previous contact with the natives of this settlement and their customs are very different. I've given each a parting gift: a knife or a packet of needles, the last of my flannel shirts cut into pocket squares for the children.

Two remain behind as the sledges head north again. Annie and her son, Tom, have agreed to accompany me home, despite the hardship of leaving their family behind. They're excellent representatives of their race, intelligent and agreeable; fine ambassadors to the civilized world. With their help I can convey to others the interest and wonders of their culture. And together we may teach other travelers how best to prepare for future journeys of discovery in the arctic.

HUNCHED OVER HIS work table, Erasmus read those columns with his stomach lurching and heaving. *Trump this*, he could almost hear Zeke saying. *You collected bones and twigs, and then lost them; you and your friend. I've brought back people. Not skulls, not brains in a jar: living, breathing people.*

He read through the columns again. Which parts of Zeke's account were true, and which were not? He'd glimpsed Zeke's notebook a few times, when Zeke was pointing out things to Lavinia; the pages were clean, no more tattered than when Erasmus had last seen the notebook in the box. No grease stains, watermarks, drops of blood or food or filth. Perhaps he'd written it all in the spring, during his journey to Upernavik. Perhaps he'd written it all on the ship that carried him home. Or perhaps only the entries regarding his journey on foot were faked, and the others were true.

He longed to ask Annie and Tom about their time with Zeke. A few times, when Zeke was off giving interviews or had gone home to sleep, Erasmus had approached the Esquimaux. Each time Lavinia had hovered. "You mustn't tire them," she'd said. Not leaving him alone with them for a single minute; equally unwilling to spend a minute alone with him herself.

From the Repository he watched strangers moving in his house.

His eyes were sore, his head ached, something hurt at the base of his ribs; he drank brandy, hoping for comfort and warmth, but it only made him dizzy. He hid for the next few days, unable to eat or sleep. He could not remember ever feeling so sick, he was sure he had a fever. A figure appeared on the flagstones, crossed the garden, opened the Repository door: Zeke. He came ostensibly to ask if Erasmus felt all right but then said, in a calm dry voice, that Erasmus was upsetting his sister. "It makes her unhappy to have you around," he said. "Especially when you behave like this."

Erasmus touched a glass of water to his parched lips. "I can't talk," he said. "I'm sick."

When Zeke left, he slipped from his chair and lay under the table. It was true that Lavinia shrank from his gaze; he'd come upon her and Zeke embracing in the solarium, holding hands in the garden, pressed against each other's shoulders. Always she looked happy until, catching sight of him, her lips would tighten and the color rise in her cheeks. Zeke, he thought, must have told her stories. Stories so ugly that she no longer trusted her own brother and could not enjoy her new happiness in his presence.

He wrapped his head in pillowcases wrung out in cold water—where had he gotten this fever? Finally, when he felt better, he dressed in clean clothes and joined the others for dinner. Candles, flowers, Alexandra quiet at one end of the table and Lavinia glowing at the other; Copernicus and Zeke between them. He sat, after a murmured apology, and confronted a platter of sauteed calf liver: the food he hated most in the world, as Lavinia had always known. Not once had she ever served it to him. The slabs gleamed at him, sending out an evil smell. Why wouldn't Zeke stay at his parents' house, where he belonged? His Esquimaux were still upstairs; he rested his arm on Lavinia's chair; his papers were scattered everywhere. He ate the liver greedily, once more asking after Erasmus's health.

Erasmus pushed away from the table, trembling and queasy.

When he stood, the surface of the table dipped and swam, shimmered and danced, the glasses waltzing with the spoons. Chasing the meteorite that had been the instrument of Zeke's salvation, he'd dropped through a hole in the ice just the size of this table. In the moment before he lost consciousness he'd opened his eyes and seen murres racing and darting around him, swift as fish, amazingly graceful. They were clumsy in the air but flew like angels through the water, and suddenly he'd seen why they were built as they were: the water was their natural home, as with walruses or whales. Now he saw that he'd misjudged Zeke in the same way. This house was the home Zeke had always craved; he'd slipped into it the minute Erasmus lost his place.

"Lavinia," Erasmus said. She glanced up at him, her eyes glazed with that translucent film. He cleared his throat and steadied his walking sticks beneath him. All he'd ever wanted for her was that she have the chance to live with the person she loved, as he had not. And if he couldn't bear the way she became around Zeke . . . "Would you excuse me?" he said.

THE FOLLOWING WEEK he made arrangements to move out of the Repository until Lavinia and Zeke were married and settled into a home of their own. "I *know* it's my house," he told Copernicus, who tried to talk him out of his decision. "I know it's a bad idea, but I'm angry all the time and I can't stand to be around Zeke like this, and I'm sick and I don't want to fight with Lavinia . . ."

"One meal," Copernicus said gently. "She ordered it because Zeke likes liver. So do I, for that matter."

Erasmus held out the folds of cloth hanging from his belt. "It's weeks," he said. "I didn't want to worry you. But I can't keep anything down."

Alexandra was equally bewildered. "*I* have to move," she said.

"Of course I do, Lavinia doesn't need me anymore. But *you* don't have to."

"I can't think," he said. "I can't work, I can't sleep, I can't eat." She frowned but helped him pack a few things. Erasmus moved slowly, deliberately, hoping that Lavinia might walk in and interrupt him. Might rest her hand on his and say, "Where are you going? Why don't you stay?"

She hid in her room, saying nothing. He hesitated near her door, wanting to knock, afraid to knock. Then, almost as an afterthought, he stopped at the room farther down the hall to take his leave of Zeke's Esquimaux. He'd seen little of them; Zeke prepared their meals, which they ate here. Zeke took them for walks each day, and at night, when he returned to his parents' house, he locked them in their room and asked Copernicus— *Copernicus*, Erasmus thought, *not me*—to check on them.

Their room looked like the inside of a summer tent; skins were hung on the walls and spread on the floor. Annie was crouched in front of the window with Tom in her lap, a plate of boiled chicken, barely touched, on the floor beside her. "Where is Tseke?" she asked. "When does he return?"

"With his parents," Erasmus said. Though he knew that was just for the afternoon. "He'll be back soon." He had no idea if Annie understood Zeke's relationship to Lavinia, or the oddness of his own position.

"I'm going away for a while," he said. What difference could this make to her? "I wanted to say good-bye to you and your son." Just as he was thinking he could never know anything about her, a dusty tan moth emerged from the fur near her knee.

"Good-bye," she echoed. She caught the moth with an absentminded gesture. As he watched she opened a crack in her fist, peered at the fluttering creature, and then released it. Exactly as he would have done. Why shouldn't they talk?

"Why did you come here?" he asked. "Did Zeke force you?"

"It was necessary," she explained. Her eyes followed the moth's path: window, ceiling, window, closet, window, window, window. "He says, 'I am a kind of angekok—did I not bring you the iron, the bears, the narwhals? Did not all the children stay well while I am with you? But I need you to come home with me and meet my people, so they will understand where I have been.' "

Her voice, repeating this, mimicked the pitch and rhythm of Zeke's in an uncanny way. The moth bounced against a row of books: *pfft, pfft, pfft.* Then soared up to the ceiling and into the window again. "He must bring me home to meet his people or my tribe will suffer. He said your ship had a spirit also, and was angry at being left behind in the ice. I must come here to where the ship is born, so the spirit does not punish my people. He says it is the same as with the spirit of the *saviksue* he disturbed."

Her English was remarkable, Erasmus thought. Zeke had taught her so much. "Did you believe that?" he asked.

As she shrugged, Tom slipped off her lap and hid beneath the caribou skin that had earlier sheltered the moth. She might have answered the question Erasmus didn't ask: *Why did you all want Zeke to leave?* They'd kept Zeke alive because the angekok ordered it, and their efforts had been rewarded. But he couldn't stay with them once winter lifted; he had no sense of his place and could only bring them ill luck. Her tribe was one great person, each of them a limb, an organ, a bone. Onto the hand her family formed, Zeke had come like an extra finger. They'd welcomed him, but he'd had no understanding of the way they were joined together. He saw himself as a singular being, a delusion they'd found laughable and terrifying all at once. When he strutted around, it was as if one of the fingers of that hand had torn itself loose, risen up, and tottered over the snow.

She might have tried to explain all this, but instead she shrugged again, eloquent shoulders in Alexandra's ill-fitting dress. "I understood he wouldn't leave without me; he said he *couldn't*. This is why my family let me go."

ERASMUS RETREATED TO Linnaeus's house. He might have rented pleasant rooms, might even have bought a house—but this was temporary, he thought. He needed to catch his breath and longed for some familial comfort while he did so. Still, he wondered if he'd made the right choice. His books and clothes barely fit into the small guest room allotted to him; the only maid frowned when she came for his chamberpot in the morning and disturbed the papers he left on the tiny desk. He missed Alexandra, who'd returned to Browning's house the same day he'd left home. He missed Copernicus; he missed especially the long days during which the three of them had worked together. Yet somehow everyone seemed to think he had brought this on himself.

He sat in the small, hot room, watching the flies hurl themselves at the window. Day after day slipping by, and now this, the worst of all. Zeke and Lavinia were being married this afternoon, at his own house. A small ceremony, only Zeke's parents, his sisters and their families; Erasmus's brothers and their families. Everyone but him. Lavinia had sent a note:

Why are you acting like this? It's your house still, and I won't keep you from it. I would like you to be with me on my wedding day. But not if you come in a spirit of bitterness. If Zeke can forgive you, if I can forgive you—why can't you accept our new lives together?

To Linnaeus he'd said, "What choice do I have?" Linnaeus, looking uneasily at the heap of books piled near Erasmus's bed, had said, "You must do what you think best."

Erasmus had sent a silver tea set and instructed Linnaeus to tell everyone his fever had returned. Now, as if his untruth had brought

it on, he had a terrible headache. The maid brought him a pot of coffee, too strong, and forgot the sugar bowl. When she returned with
the bowl but no spoon, he said, "Kate—why are you doing this?"

"Doing what?"

Her broad face, covered with freckles, reminded Erasmus of
Ned Kynd; a hint of Ireland was still in her voice although she'd
been here since she was a girl. Hard-working, intelligent, usually
good-humored; only sullen when she was alone with him. He
said, "You know."

"Didn't I bring exactly what you asked for?" But she knew what
she'd done, she'd done it on purpose. "Is there anything else?"

"Just go," he said.

After scooping sugar into his cup with a twist of paper he settled
down to write a letter to Ned. Such a confusion, he couldn't imagine
where to begin. He started with this room—the desk, the bed, the
flies—and wrote out from there. About all that had happened since
Zeke's return home, the two Esquimaux camped in his house while
he was sequestered here; about the wedding he couldn't attend.
About the newspaper article, which, although it hadn't criticized
him directly, had turned the whole city against him. He folded up
the three long pages of newsprint he was including, and then confessed his theft of Dr. Boerhaave's journal and the related glimpse of
Zeke's black book. Six pages, eight pages. His hand grew tired.

After a pause he wrote to Ned about the party the United Toxophilites had thrown for Zeke. Part welcome-home party, part
bachelor party; all the Toxies in full regalia.

*You may remember those suits. From the day Mr. Tagliabeau signed you
on; all those men in green coats and white pants, with their bows and
arrows. They're an archery club. I used to belong.*

He told Ned about the speech Zeke had given, regretting that
the Esquimaux bow and arrows he'd obtained for the club on

Boothia had been lost through no fault of his own. And the drinking, the wild toasts, the dancing women and the arrows presented to Zeke with jokes about his aim on his wedding night. He wrote about the work he and Alexandra and Copernicus had done on his book before they were stalled. Then he found himself longing to write about the lonely nights here in this room.

The walls were tissue thin, and on Sunday nights—always, but only, Sunday nights—he could hear Linnaeus and Lucy making love. Those squeals, those little groans. He couldn't imagine Lucy with her hair down, her mouth unpursed, the things she must do to make his brother make those sounds—they wanted another child, he knew. Perhaps that was the reason for their clocklike regularity. As for the way their noises made him think of Zeke and Lavinia, finally together . . . He kept himself from writing about any of this, describing instead his strange meeting with William Godfrey. Eighteen pages, twenty-one. At the end he wrote:

This is how everyone sees me now; as if I'm just like him.

IN BROWNING'S KITCHEN, the night after the wedding, Alexandra brooded as she cooked. *Dismissed*, she thought, as she lifted biscuits from the oven. She and Lavinia had never been equals, not really. What they'd done was wait together, and wait and wait and wait; and although this had bound them as survivors of a disaster were bound, so that they'd always have a connection, still she'd been Lavinia's paid companion, never exactly a chosen friend. As Lavinia had made quite clear. The instant Zeke came back, Lavinia had turned from her. "You've been so good for me," she'd said, when Alexandra proposed returning to Browning's house. "But of course you'll want to get back to your own work, now that you've managed to *establish* yourself."

Their time together was over; she'd learned a great deal and must be grateful for that. And she was determined not to lose her relationship with Erasmus. Working together, she'd felt them building what she'd always imagined a friendship might be. They'd shared thoughts, work, reading, interests; they confided in each other but also respected each other's privacy. She missed him every day.

On the tray before her she arranged the food she'd prepared for the Percy sisters: boiled chicken in jelly, the hot biscuits, butter, plum jam, lemonade. Browning had taken on the care of the two elderly women who lived across the street, and somehow they'd become Alexandra's responsibility as well. They weren't crazy, not exactly, but they were ancient and isolated and for the last six months had been convinced that people were trying to poison them. They'd take food only from Browning's hands, and eat it only in his presence. Morning and evening he brought food that had once been cooked by Harriet but which now Alexandra prepared. Then he sat patiently with them while they ate.

The texture of his life, Alexandra thought. Which was becoming the texture of hers. A crowd of people needing help, among which he spread himself and his wife and his sisters willingly but too thinly. Already she was tired of the way Browning assumed he could direct her.

Yet no matter how many hours she spent preparing meals, or helping out with the children or the family projects, there had to be some fragments of time left to her. If she slept less, perhaps. If she rose very early, even before Browning rose to prepare his classes; if she could steal an hour or two for her own work before her family began their demands: then she could feel as if she still had a life of her own. She could do what was asked of her with good grace, if she could have this time alone. The thing was not to give in completely.

As she cleaned up the kitchen and prepared to make yet another meal, she decided to retrieve the tools and materials she'd left behind at the Repository. She'd seen Erasmus only twice since her hurried departure; he was very low and didn't seem to be working at all. But despite their altered circumstances they could work secretly, she thought. Quietly, in stolen hours and stolen rooms. Still they might do something worthwhile. She stirred Browning's favorite soup, and then went to tell him she'd be away from home all the following day, and that he must do without her.

COPERNICUS WAS PAINTING in the garden. With Zeke and Lavinia gone on a brief wedding trip, he was taking advantage of his freedom; his loose muslin shirt was open over his chest and his forearms were smeared with paint. Blue streaked his hair and daubed his sweating face.

"Alexandra," he said. "What a nice surprise." He darkened a shadow, then stepped back to see the effect. Pinned to a second easel beside him were sketches he'd copied from the notebooks of Erasmus and Dr. Boerhaave. "What brings you here?"

She fanned herself; even the flagstones were sticky in this heat. "I left some drawing materials in the Repository," she said. "But I can't imagine we'll be working in there again. I thought I'd take them home, and see if I can do something there."

"You won't work here again," he agreed. "Nor will I." He wiped his hands on a rag and gestured toward his painting: icebergs, huge and luminous. In the foreground he'd recently added a stump of broken mast and a ringed seal. "As soon as this one's done, I'm moving."

"Where will you go?"

"I have friends at a boardinghouse on Sansom Street—I'm going to take a room there and share the studio on the top floor. I can't work here, it's too odd being around Zeke and Lavinia."

He led her toward the Repository. "You won't believe this," he said. "Don't be shocked."

Yet she was, when she passed through the high double doors. Inside it was so dim that for a minute, blinded after the glare outside, she could see nothing. Two huge black dogs bounded up to her, bumping their heads against her thighs and licking at her hands—"Zeke's," Copernicus said. "He brought them over the day of the wedding." She wiped her hands on her skirt. Why was it so dark in here? There were skins blocking most of the windows. On the floor Annie and Tom lay in a mass of linen that resembled a pile of sails. Why were there people lying on the floor?

"Hello," Alexandra said hesitantly. "I'm sorry, I didn't mean to intrude. I didn't know you were staying in here."

Annie had lost weight, and her hair was dirty. "Tseke gave us this as our home," she said. The dogs loped over and flopped down beside her. "Where is Tseke?"

"He'll be back in a few days," Copernicus said. "I promise." He bent over one of the basins on the floor, dipped a rag in the water, and wiped Annie's face. "Does that help?" he said. "Is that better?"

"I feel burning," Annie said mournfully. "So hot."

Tom coughed and spat. Stains and wet spots and the dogs' round-toed tracks marked the smooth polished wood; drifts of hair rolled under the furniture.

"Are they sick?" Alexandra whispered to Copernicus. "What's happened?" Her supplies had been pushed against one set of shelves; Erasmus's books were scattered and nothing remained of Copernicus's working area but a stack of crates. By the library table, someone had cast loose herbarium sheets that curled forlornly in the stink sent off by a full chamberpot.

"Zeke moved them as soon as you and Erasmus left," Copernicus said, close to her ear. "I suppose he thought they'd be better off here than in the house. But they keep shifting from spot to spot, trying to get comfortable. Nothing seems to help but the cold water. They both have fever—I'm not sure whether it's a reaction to this weather, or something more serious."

"They're to stay here?" she asked. "Permanently?"

Copernicus shrugged. "If I had anyplace to take them to, if I had anything at all to say about this—but I don't, they're in Zeke's care."

In air so foul she could hardly breathe she gathered her things together; her brushes, which she'd arranged carefully, had been jammed upright in a jar and the tips were spoiled. There were dirty fingerprints on the folder containing her drawings, but the drawings themselves seemed intact. Copernicus found a small box for her pens.

They worked without speaking, amid Tom's cough and Annie's rough breathing and the heavy panting of the dogs. Once they stepped outside again, Copernicus said, "I don't know what Zeke is thinking. I really don't. This is no place for them, they're miserable here. And the Repository is being ruined. If Erasmus saw this . . . as soon as Zeke returns, I'm leaving."

"Where did they go?"

"Washington," Copernicus said. "Zeke is meeting a group of people at the Smithsonian Institution. They're making a little party for him there, celebrating his discoveries, and he thought Lavinia would enjoy that. They only went for four days, because of Annie and Tom. Meanwhile *I'm* supposed to be the perfect person to take care of Zeke's Esquimaux. As if I'd know what to do with them, just because I've had some experience with the Indians out west. But Annie and Tom have different habits and different temperaments from any tribe I ever met—I don't know what to feed them. I don't know how to help them, or how to make them comfortable."

"I'm sorry," she said. "Is there anything I can do to help?"

"Not unless you know how to nurse them," he said. "Not unless you know something they'd like to eat. They don't like the meat I bring them. Annie wants some green plant she says will make her feel better."

"Some herbs?" Alexandra suggested.

Copernicus spread his hands. "If there's something you know. I'll try anything."

"There's some tansy and mint in the perennial border." She led him there and asked for his handkerchief. Side by side they gathered leaves in the burning sun.

"I'll miss this place," Copernicus said. "I never imagined, when I came back home, that I wouldn't have a home anymore."

The bruised leaves released a scent that began to cleanse the fumes of the Repository from Alexandra's head. "Is this—is this permanent?" she asked. "You and Erasmus would really let Lavinia take over the house for good?"

"It's just for a year or so," Copernicus said. "I think. Zeke's father has promised to build them a new house, on a plot of land he owns near Fairmount Park. But they have to draw up plans, and then build it—who knows how long that will take. Meanwhile what can we do but humor Lavinia? She's been through so much."

"You and Erasmus have been through a lot as well," Alexandra pointed out.

They knelt side by side in the border. She could smell paint, and the mint they were crushing, and the faint scents of his body and his breath. What would it be like to have him seize her, as Zeke had seized Lavinia on his return? Just as she was thinking this, he reached for a sprig and his forearm drew across her wrist like an arrow across a bow. She froze, thinking how easily she might move her hand a few inches, place her fingers in his palm. Anything might happen after that. He liked her, she knew. Even found her attractive. But he liked everyone; he made no secret of the Indian and Mexican women he'd kept company with out west, nor of the women he met in the theaters here. What she wanted, when she let herself imagine wanting anyone, was someone who might be wholly hers.

"I'm going to try to get Erasmus working on the book again," she said, rising and brushing her skirt. "And myself as well. Can I count on you? If he knew you were still painting, and supported what he was doing . . ."

"I do support him," Copernicus said, sounding surprised.

"I know. But . . ." She turned her eyes from his sun-browned throat and squinted at the garden. He was strong and good-hearted, yet perhaps not really reliable. "You've been gone for almost five years and maybe you'll want to travel again. And there's nothing wrong with helping your sister's husband while he's away. But once he returns—Erasmus needs your help more."

"I *will* help," Copernicus said. "I said I would, and I will. As soon as they return I'll let Zeke take care of his Esquimaux and I'll work on the paintings full-time."

Alexandra folded the handkerchief over the pile of fragrant leaves. "Steep these for ten minutes in a quart of boiling water," she said. "Have Annie and Tom drink the tea while it's hot, it will bring out a cleansing sweat."

She stepped into the Repository again, laying her hand on Annie's hot forehead and then on Tom's. "Zeke will be back soon," she said. She gazed at the chaos around her and moved quickly back into the light.

NED KYND RECEIVED Erasmus's letter late one July night, as he was cleaning up after a long stint cooking for a dozen boisterous hunters. Rabbit stew and porcupine pie and sauteed trout; wild mushrooms and venison filet. He had a reliable stove, good supplies, a grateful employer. The patrons called out loud compliments, and if one grew overenthusiastic and came back to the kitchen and then recoiled at Ned's face, he could claim he'd had a hunting accident and be believed. In these North Woods his was just another legend. "A she-bear tore off that half of my nose," he'd say. "Then left me for dead. I was lucky."

And he *was* lucky, he thought, washing his hands with strong brown soap. Lucky to have landed here. Behind the hotel the mountains rose in solid ranks, cliffs and ledges jutting like bones through the fur of trees and stars shining, sharp and violent, as bright as those in the arctic. In Philadelphia there'd been nothing for him, only more bad jobs in taverns near the wharves. Only the lowest sort would consider him, because of his face. Some asked if he had leprosy, and if he told them what had really happened they stared at him blankly. On an impulse he'd made his way back to the Adirondack Mountains, to a village mentioned by a man he'd known at the lumber camp: Keene Flats, on the eastern side of the highest peaks. A place, his friend had said, where a few hotels catered to city men eager for a wilderness experience.

The noise from the dining hall diminished; the hunters shambled off to their beds. After hanging up his apron and changing his shoes, Ned began the long walk along the Ausable River, to the cabin he'd rented near John's Brook.

Inside he lit the stove and a pair of candles, then opened the envelope from Philadelphia. He wrote back to Erasmus that same night:

Your letter reached me with little trouble though I've moved since you last wrote—this is a small place, and everyone knows everyone else. Your news disturbed me. I've gotten settled here, it's a kind of new life. I hoped you might have one as well.

For Commander Voorhees to show up like this—I didn't wish him dead, I'm glad he's alive but don't see why you must suffer for it. You only did what we asked you to, you led us all to safety and should be honored. Those newspaper pages sounded more as if Commander Voorhees is making up an adventure tale than reporting what he saw. Why should he get to say what he wants, and be believed? I know what *he did with that meteorite, despite Joe's advice, yet it seems he was rewarded for his errors. I remember Nessark from my stay at Anoatok, and he didn't strike me as someone who'd willingly let a family member go. Do you suppose Commander Voorhees deceived them in some way? It's the Esquimaux who make him a hero—without them he'd have nothing more than you do, just his story. It's the Esquimaux who set him off from you and me, from Dr. Kane—and I think he knows this, I think he <u>had</u> to bring them back. All this makes me suspicious.*

I feel that if you're patient your reputation will be restored in time, as will your family's affections. Perhaps it would be helpful if you left that place for a while. Up here, no one talks about us or any other expedition, they're busy taming this wild place and no one requires explanations.

My job as cook is not exciting, but it's good enough. On my days off, I still practice what you taught me; some of the hunters wish to bring home the skins of the animals they've shot, and I do what I can to prepare them. My big triumph lately has been with deer—finally I've mastered removing that leaf-shaped piece of cartilage from the ear while keeping the skin intact. For my own amusement I've prepared some small skeletons: a bat, a fox, a salamander. You're a better man than Commander Voorhees. I'm not surprised he's taken those two Esquimaux from their homes, I always thought he'd do something like this. I wish he'd lost more than his ear. Should you need me you can reach me care of the hotel, at least for the remainder of the season.

"I'm glad he's all right," Alexandra said to Erasmus, when they met in early August by the Schuylkill River. She folded the pages of Ned's letter neatly. "I was worried about him when you first came back—his poor face. But he's right that you're a better man than Zeke. And I agree with both of you about that diary, I had the same reaction when I read the sections in the newspaper. Everything I saw of Zeke before I left—he just seems *false* to me somehow. Even the way he is with Lavinia. I don't understand him. I never trusted him, not from the beginning."

Erasmus looked out at the ducks paddling in the eddies behind the rocks. When the Esquimaux at Disko Bay had tipped and rolled their delicate kayaks, the crew of the *Narwhal* had tossed them scraps of food, as strollers here might feed these creatures.

"He's already got a name for his book," Alexandra added. *"The Voyage of the* Narwhal—aping the famous works of exploration, I suppose. Copernicus told me he's written a hundred pages."

Erasmus shook his head. As if sensing that he'd not done a stroke of work since Lavinia's wedding, she'd asked him to bring some new pages and promised she'd bring some drawings. He had nothing to exchange for the detail of a whale's mouth she now spread on the bench between them.

"That's good," he said. "It's really quite close. If you could shade the baleen plates a bit more . . ."

Her face fell. "I knew I wouldn't get it right without you," she said. "And it's the only one I've been able to work on, it's so hard to get time at home."

"At least you've done something. I can't work at all."

"There must be someplace," she said. "Someplace we can go."

"We might be able to use the Repository as a studio," he said. "If we didn't bother Lavinia, if I didn't have to see Zeke . . ." Beneath the hem of her dress, one of Alexandra's shoes inscribed an arc in the dirt. "You don't think that's a good idea?"

"Have you talked to Copernicus?"

"What do you mean?" She looked so unhappy that, despite his own misery, he felt sorry for her.

"Probably he didn't want to upset you," she said. "But you should know."

She told him, then, how Zeke had converted the Repository into a kind of camp for Annie and Tom. He tried to envision it, but failed—bales of skins and puddles of water and dogs lurching against the tables. The precious books and specimens disturbed, and Annie and Tom both ill. Zeke had known and cherished that place as a boy.

"I'm sorry," Alexandra said.

"My father must be rolling in his grave. But it can't be helped, can it?"

"You could go back," she pointed out. "It *is* your house."

"There's something . . ." he said. "I can't explain it, but I know as surely as I've ever known anything that Lavinia can't be happy with Zeke in my presence. She thinks I'm judging her, she doesn't understand it's *him*, that I don't trust *him*."

"Then we have to live like this for a while," Alexandra said. "I suppose. They're building a house of their own, they'll be gone in time."

"In time for what?" He thought of Annie and her little boy. "Are they really sick?"

"They didn't look well," she said. "But I don't know what's wrong with them."

"Zeke," he said. "Zeke . . . Copernicus offered to let us work at his new studio, but really there isn't room without crowding his friends. He said that when Zeke got back from Washington, he was all puffed up from meeting politicians and members of the Smithsonian Institution, and that everyone was pressing him to exhibit Annie and Tom. A sort of lecture tour around the lyceum halls of the Northeast. One night a ventriloquist or a phrenologist, the next some itinerant professor giving lessons in physiology or showing wax models of Egyptian ruins. The next Zeke in his polar-bear pants, exhibiting Annie like another Hottentot Venus. It's such a dreadful idea, but Copernicus says he's going to do it. He's going to hold the first exhibition right here in Philadelphia. But if they're already sick . . ."

"Do you think that will stop him?"

"Nothing stops him," Erasmus said. "Nothing ever does. If he gives a lecture here, will you go with me? I have to see what he does."

"If you want," Alexandra said. "Of course I'll come. And I was thinking, in the meantime—what about asking Linnaeus and Humboldt for some space at the engraving firm? All we'd need are two desks near each other. There must be a corner they could spare."

She was looking at the river, not at him, but he could see the longing on her face. "I can't live like this," she said. "Not after having a chance to do real work. I can't stand this."

"I'll ask them," he promised. "If it doesn't work out, I'll rent us a workroom someplace else."

He let his fingers creep over her knuckles. Her hands were smooth and white, the fingernails clipped short; although her palms were small her fingers were unusually long and her nails, he saw, were deeply arched.

Later he'd think of this as the first moment he saw himself back in the arctic. Not a dark dream, like those he'd had during his first days home, but a bright waking vision: the muddy Schuylkill turned into a glacial stream; the ducks turned into murres and dovekies; the limp, moist foliage dwarfed into a crisp tangle of willows. Beside him Alexandra, who'd had only his stories from which to build her vision, dreamed in less detail. But she imagined a ship passing through dense ice, both of them scouting a route from the bow as the floes glided past.

10

SPECIMENS OF THE
NATIVE TRIBES

(SEPTEMBER 1857)

Miserable, yet happy wretches, without one thought for the future, fighting against care when it comes unbidden, and enjoying to the full their scanty measures of present good! As a beast, the Esquimaux is a most sensible beast, worth a thousand Calibans, and certainly ahead of his cousin the Polar bear, from whom he borrows his pantaloons.

— ELISHA KENT KANE, *Arctic Explorations: The*
Second Grinnell Expedition in Search of Sir
John Franklin, 1853, '54, '55 (1856)

*H*ere in the theater's gallery, near the prostitutes scattered like iridescent fish through the shoals of dark-clothed men, Alexandra felt drab in her brown silk dress. Two seats down from her, a woman in a chartreuse gown with lemon-trimmed flounces was striking a deal with a pleasant-looking man. They would meet on the landing, Alexandra heard them agree. Directly after the lecture. The man's voice dropped and the woman shook her head, shivering the egret feathers woven into her hair. "Twenty dollars," she said. The man nodded and disappeared, leaving Alexandra to marvel at the transaction.

"There must be a thousand people," Erasmus said, scanning the crowd. "Maybe more."

"It's frightening," she said. "How good Zeke is at promoting himself."

All around the city, on lampposts and tavern doors, in merchants' windows and omnibuses, posters advertised the exhibition. A clumsy woodcut showed Zeke holding a harpoon and Annie a string of fish, Tom peeping out from behind her flared boots. In the background were mountains cut by a fjord, and above those a banner headline: MY LIFE AMONG THE ESQUIMAUX. A caption touted the remarkable discoveries made by Zechariah Voorhees:

Two Fine Specimens of the Native Tribes!
More Exotic than the Sioux and Fox Indians Exhibited by George Catlin in London and Paris!
See the Esquimaux Demonstrate Their Customs!

Zeke had run a smaller version in the newspaper and mailed invitations to hundreds of his family's friends and business associates—organizing this first exhibition, Alexandra thought, like a military campaign. Ahead of him lay Baltimore,

Washington, Richmond, New York, Providence, Albany, Boston.

Erasmus said, "Can you see Lavinia?" and Alexandra, scouting the boxes on the second tier, finally spotted her dead center, flanked by Linnaeus and Humboldt and Zeke's parents and sisters. She was touching her hair then her cheek then her brooch then her nose, turning her head from side to side as if the mood of the entire audience were expressing itself through her. Everyone, Alexandra thought, made nervous by this month's chain of disasters. Across the ocean, off the coast of Ireland, the telegraph cable being laid with such fanfare had broken. Two trains had crashed south of Philadelphia, killing several passengers; last week a steamship on its way to New York from Cuba had sunk. Each of these seemed to heighten the financial panic set off by a bank failure in Ohio. Banks were closing everywhere; the stock exchange was in an uproar. The papers were full of news about bankrupt merchants and brokers. Alexandra's own family, who had no money to lose, hadn't been touched so far, and the engraving firm seemed stable. But Erasmus, whose income came primarily from his father's investments, had suffered some losses. And Zeke's father's firm was in trouble, which suddenly made Zeke's future—and Lavinia's as well—uncertain. Suddenly it mattered what Zeke charged for the exhibition tickets, and how many tickets were sold. The theater was full of people desperate for distraction.

In the glow of the gaslights Zeke strode out in full Esquimaux regalia, adjusted the position of two large crates, and took his place at the podium. The roar of applause was startling, as was the ease with which he spoke. If he had notes, Alexandra couldn't see them. Swiftly, eloquently, he sketched for the audience an outline of the voyage of the *Narwhal*, making of the confused first months a spare, dramatic narrative.

Their first sights of Melville Bay and Lancaster Sound, their encounters with the Netsilik and their retrieval of the Franklin relics; the discovery of the *Resolute* and their stormy passage up Ellesmere until they were frozen in; their long winter and the visit of Ootuniah and his companions; the first trip to Anoatok. No mention, Alexandra noticed, of Dr. Boerhaave's death, nor of the other men who'd died: nor of Erasmus. It was "I" all the time, "I" and "me" and "mine"; occasionally "we" or "my men." No names, only him. Beside her, Erasmus fidgeted.

Twenty minutes, she guessed. Twenty minutes for the part of the voyage involving the crew; then another fifteen for Zeke's solo trip north on foot and his return to the empty ship. "Now," Zeke was saying, "now began the most interesting part of my experience in the arctic. I was all alone, and winter was coming. I had to prepare myself."

From the crates he began to pull things. His hunting rifle, sealskins, a tin of ship's biscuit, a jar of dried peas. His black notebook, the sight of which made Erasmus groan. Into his talk he wove some stray lines from that, and then read aloud the section about the arrival of Annie and Nessark and Marumah. "The *angekok* is the tribe's general counselor and advisor," he explained. "As well as its wizard. His chief job is to determine the reason for any misfortune visiting the tribe—and the *angekok* of Annie's tribe determined that the cause of their children's sickness was me. So was my life changed by a superstition. From the day these people arrived I entered into a new life."

He described the journey to Anoatok and his first days there. Then he said, "But you must meet some of the people among whom I stayed." He stepped back from the podium and whistled.

There was rattling backstage, and the crack of a whip. Two dogs appeared—not his huge black hunting dogs but beagles, ludicrous in their harnesses, gamely trotting side by side. Apparently Zeke would not subject his own pets to this. Behind them they pulled a small sledge on wheels, with Tom crouched on the crossbars and Annie grasping the uprights and waving a little whip. Both Annie and Tom wore fur jackets with the hoods pulled up and shadowing their faces. When the sledge reached the front of the podium, Zeke gave a sharp command that stopped the beagles. They sat, drooling eagerly as Zeke held out bits of biscuit, and then lay down in their traces with their chins on their paws. Their eyes followed Zeke as he moved around the stage, but Annie and Tom stared straight out at the audience, shielding their eyes against the glare.

"These are two of the people who rescued me," Zeke said. "The names they use among us are Annie and Tom."

While they stood still he recited some facts. Annie and Tom belonged to the group of people John Ross had discovered in 1818 and called Arctic Highlanders—there were just a few hundred of them, he said, scattered from Cape York to Etah. Fewer each year; their lives were hard and their children sickened; he feared they were dying out. They moved nomadically throughout the seasons, among clusters of huts a day's journey apart and near good hunting sites. All food was shared among them, as if they were one large family. Because no driftwood reached their isolated shores, they had no bows and arrows, nor kayaks, and in this they differed from the Esquimaux of Boothia and southern Greenland. They'd developed their own ways, substituting bone for wood—bone harpoon shafts and sledge parts and tent poles. "A true sledge," Zeke said, "would have bone crosspieces lashed to the runners with thongs, and ivory strips fastened to the runners." He went on to explain how they subsisted largely on animals from the sea.

"The term 'Esquimaux' is French and means 'raw meat eaters,'" Zeke said. "But there's nothing disgusting in this, the body in that violent climate craves blood and the juices of uncooked food." From the nearest crate he took a paper bundle, which he unwrapped to reveal a Delaware shad. A few strokes of a knife yielded three small squares of flesh. Two he held out to Annie and Tom, keeping the third for himself. The beagles whined. Zeke popped the flesh in his mouth and chewed, while Annie and Tom did the same on either side of him. The audience gasped, and Alexandra could see this pleased Zeke enormously.

"With the help of my two friends," he said, "I would like to demonstrate for you some of the elements of daily life among these remarkable people."

Now Alexandra saw the bulk of what the crates contained. Certainly he hadn't carried all these objects home with him; he must have made some here, with Annie's help and whatever supplies he could find. There was a long-handled net, which Tom seized and carried to the top of one crate. He made darting and swooping motions as Zeke described capturing dovekies. "These arrive by the million," Zeke said. "When the hunter's net is full, he kills each bird by pressing its chest with his fingers, until the heart stops."

A soapstone lamp—where had this come from?—with a wick made from moss; Zeke filled it with whale oil and had Annie light it with a sliver of wood he first lit with a match, telling the audience they must imagine lumps of blubber slowly melting. In the huts, he said, with these lamps giving off heat and light, with food cooking and wet clothes drying and children frolicking, it had been warm no matter what the outside temperature. He brought out more hides and had Annie demonstrate how the women of her tribe scraped off the inner layers to make the hides pliable. "This crescent-shaped knife is an *ulo*," he said, and Annie sat on her knees with her feet tucked beneath her thighs and the skin spread before her, rubbing it with the blade. Beside Alexandra, Erasmus pressed both hands to his ribs.

"Are you all right?" she said. She couldn't take her eyes from the stage.

"That's exactly the way I soften a dried skin before I mount it," Erasmus said. "I have a drawshave I use like her *ulo*."

Zeke said, "The women chew every inch after it's dried, to make it soft," and Annie put a bit of the hide in her mouth and ground her teeth. "I can't show you the threads, which are made from sinews," he said. "But the needles are kept in these charming cases." Annie held up an ivory cylinder, through which passed a bit of hide bristling with needles.

Zeke took Tom's hand and seized a pair of harpoons; then he and Tom lay down and pretended to be inching up on a seal's blowhole, waiting for the seal to surface. As they mimicked the strike Zeke spoke loudly, a flow of vivid words that had the crowd leaning forward. They were seeing what Zeke wanted them to see, Alexandra thought. Not what was really there: not a rickety makeshift sledge, two floppy-eared beagles, a tired woman and a nervous boy moved like mannequins by the force of Zeke's voice. Not them, or a man needing to make a living, but the arctic in all its mystery: unknown landscapes and animals and another race of people.

Her face was wet; was she weeping? As Zeke's antics continued Alexandra found herself thinking of her parents and the last day she'd seen them. Pulling away from the ferry dock, waving good-bye, sure they'd be reunited in a week. Then the noise, the terrible shocking noise. Great plumes of steam and smoke and cinders spinning down to the water—and her parents, everyone, gone. Simply gone.

She turned to Erasmus, who had his face in his hands. Gently she touched him and said, "You have to look."

He raised his head for a second but then returned his gaze to his shoes. "I won't," he said passionately. "I hate this. All my life the thing I've hated most is being *looked at*. I can't bear it when people stare at me. I know just how she feels, all of us peering down at her. It's disgusting. It's worse than disgusting. People stared at me like this when I returned from the Exploring Expedition, and again when I came back without Zeke. Now we're doing the same thing to her."

Had she known this about him? She looked away from him, back at the stage; she felt a shameful pleasure, herself, in regarding Annie and Tom. She longed to draw them.

Annie had pushed her hood back from her sweating face, while Tom had stretched out on the sledge and was pulling at one of the beagle's ears. From his crate Zeke took a wooden figure clothed in a miniature jacket and pants. "The children play with dolls," Zeke said. "Just as ours do." Tom released the beagle's ear, seizing the doll and pressing it to his chest. Then Zeke was winding string around Annie's fingers, saying, "Among this tribe, a favorite game with the women and children is called *ajarorpok*, which is much like our child's game of cat's cradle, only more complicated."

He said something to Annie and stepped away. Annie's hands darted like birds and paused, holding up a shapely web. "This represents a caribou," Zeke said.

Alexandra tried to see a creature in the loops and whorls, not knowing that, for Annie, it was as if the stage had suddenly filled with beautiful animals. Not knowing that for Annie this evening moved as if the *angekok* who'd brought Zeke to them had bewitched her, putting her into a trance in which she both was and was not on this stage. The *angekok* had shared with her the secret fire that let him see in the dark, to the heart of things. For her Zeke's bird net wasn't a broomstick and knotted cotton but a narwhal's tusk and plaited sinews; on her fingers she felt the fat she'd scraped from the seal. She was home, and she was also here, doing what she'd been told in a dream to do.

She was to watch these people, ranged in tiers above her, and commit them to memory, so that she could bring a vision of them to her people back home. Their pointed faces and bird-colored garments; the way they gathered in great crowds but didn't touch each other or share their food. Their tools, their cooking implements, their huts that couldn't be moved when the weather changed. In a dream she'd heard her mother's voice, singing the song that had risen from her tribe's first sight of the white men.

Her mother had been a small girl on the summer day when floating islands with white wings had appeared by the narrow edge of ice off Cape York. From the islands hung little boats, which were lowered to the water; these spat out sickly men in blue garments, who couldn't make themselves understood but who offered bits of something that looked like ice, which held the image of human faces; round dry tasteless things to eat; parts of their garments, which weren't made of skins.

"At first," her mother had said, "we thought the spirits of the air had come to us." On the floating island her mother had seen a fat, pink, hairless animal, a man with eyes concealed behind ovals of unmelting ice, bulky objects on which to sit, something like a frozen arm, with which to hit something like a needle. The two men who'd stepped first on the ice had worn hats shaped like cooking pots. Through them, her people had learned they weren't alone in the world.

Much later, when Annie was grown, she'd had her mother's experience to guide her when the other strangers arrived. Kane and his men had taught Annie to understand their ungainly speech, and Annie had learned that the world was larger than she'd understood, though much of it was unfortunate, even cursed. Elsewhere, these visitors said, were lands with no seals, no walrus, no bears; no sheets of colored light singing across the sky. She couldn't understand how these people survived. They'd been like children, dependent on her tribe for clothes, food, sledges, dogs; surrounded by things which were of no use to them and bereft of women. Like children they gave their names to the landscape, pretending to discover places her people had known for generations.

From them she'd gained words for the visions of her mother's childhood: a country called England and another called America; men called officers; ships, sails, mirrors, biscuits, cloth, pig, eyeglasses, chair. Wood, which came from a giant version of the tiny shrubs they knew. Hammer and nails. Later she'd added the words Zeke had taught her while he lived with them; then the names for the vast array of unfamiliar things she'd encountered here. In the dream her mother had given her this task: to look closely at all around her, and to remember everything. To do this while guarding her son.

Her hands darted and formed another shape, which Zeke claimed represented ponds amid hills but in which she saw her home. She felt the warm liver of the freshly killed seal, she tasted sweet blood in her mouth. In the gaslights she saw the moon and the sun, brother and sister who'd quarreled and now chased each other across the sky. At first her mother had thought the strangers must come from these sources of light. Her hands flew in the air.

"Can you see what she's doing?" Alexandra whispered to Erasmus. "I can't see what she's making."

"I have to go," Erasmus said. "We have to go. Can we go?"

HE HADN'T EXPECTED the exhibition to pain him so much. Back at Linnaeus's house, Lucy said, "Well, of course I wish he'd mentioned *you*. But still it was interesting, wasn't it? You should have stayed until the end, he had Annie and Tom sing some Esquimaux songs. The way she ate the raw fish . . ." Lucy shuddered, yet she was smiling.

"She's sick," Erasmus said. "She's miserable. Zeke has no right to show her off like that, like a trained bear . . ."

"It was the stage lights that were making her perspire," Linnaeus said. "And I think he does Annie's people a service, as well as himself. The more people see what Esquimaux life is like, the more they'll respect their ways. How can that be anything but good for her and her tribe?"

Erasmus retreated to his stuffy room, where he tossed and turned and dreamed about the copper kettle packed with relics, which had slipped beneath the ice. In his dream the prayer book and the treatise on steam engines, the silver cutlery and the mahogany barometer case had all sprouted eyes and were staring at him; the kettle was staring; the walrus skin sealing the top was staring. Annie, across that crowded space, was staring directly into his eyes, as Lavinia had stared when she was a girl of ten and he'd left, bereft and barely aware of her, to join his first expedition.

Only Annie had met his eyes in that theater, he thought as he woke. Only Annie—as only Annie knew if Zeke's stories were true. He'd gone to the exhibition hoping her behavior might give him a clue; hoping, perhaps, that she'd interrupt the flow of Zeke's words and say, "But it wasn't like *that*." Instead she'd performed in silence, gazing across the hall at him.

For a week he tried to resist what he knew he should do. He visited Copernicus, who had settled into his new place and begun another painting, this one of Lancaster Sound in mid-July. Into the vista he was crowding everything Erasmus had described to him, the whales and belugas and seals and walrus churning through the water, the fulmars and guillemots whirring and diving, the murres and kittiwakes guarding their eggs from the foxes. Everywhere life, vibrant and massed, and the streaming, improbable light.

"I should go to Baltimore," Erasmus said.

"What can you do for them?" Copernicus said. "No matter how much you disapprove, you can't stop Zeke—everyone loved his talk, he's having a huge success. And he needs the money now."

He added a blue shadow to the flank of a beluga. Erasmus found the painting beautiful, but he kept seeing Annie in that landscape and soon he left.

He tried to work. He tried not to think, over the weekend, about Zeke and Annie and Tom in Baltimore; when the newspaper reported another huge crowd he tried not to see Annie's face. He went to the engraving firm on Monday and met Alexandra at the pair of desks placed back to back, which Linnaeus and Humboldt had grudgingly granted them. Six square feet for her and six for him, in the dead space in the center of the storage room. The light was terrible. From the pages of Dr. Boerhaave's journal, and the sketchier notes of his own, he was trying to build a description of some peculiar fossils they'd found before winter had confined them to the ship. A jawbone that seemed almost crocodilian; leaf casts resembling gingkos. Alexandra was drawing one of these.

"How could such a fossil be in that place?" she asked. "Where now there are no trees?"

"I don't know," Erasmus said, looking from his dead friend's sketches to his new friend's drawing. "It must have been *warm* there once. At Tierra del Fuego, years ago, I saw the fossil remains of a whale on top of a mountain."

"You could argue," Alexandra said, "that it was left behind by the Noachian Deluge. That these leaves ended up in the arctic the same way."

"You could," he said. "If you didn't believe any of the geological evidence Lyell's assembled. All of which suggests that the earth and these fossils are millions of years old."

In England, he knew, even as Lyell and Darwin and Hooker discussed the mutability of species and the nature of geological change, a respected clergyman had put forth a theory that the surface of the earth had never changed, and that life forms never altered or developed. He said, "A man in London argues seriously that when the act of creation took place, the earth sprang into being complete with all its fossils and other suggestions of an earlier life. It's a test, this man says. Another version of the tree in paradise. God hid the fossils in the rocks to tempt us into questioning the truths revealed in the Bible. Supposedly the fossils aren't even the relics left by the Flood but just—I don't know, just *decorations*."

"Do you believe that?" Alexandra said. She picked up one of the leaf casts and regarded the symmetrical veins.

"I don't know what I believe anymore," he replied. "About anything. In Germany, there's a man who says the fossil-bearing rocks fell to earth as meteorites. And so the fossils represent beings from other worlds." He looked down at the loops and whorls of Dr. Boerhaave's writing, and then closed the journal and stood.

"I can't stay here," he said. His father had coaxed him into joining Wilkes's expedition; Zeke and Lavinia had lured him north; Ned had dragged him away from the *Narwhal*; Alexandra had steered him toward his book. But this one small decision might be his. "I have to talk with Annie. If Zeke's forcing her somehow to perform like this—I'm going to go to Washington. Maybe she'll tell me what Zeke really did up there. Maybe I can make him cancel the rest of the tour."

HIS TIMING WAS bad—as always, he thought. Off by a year, a month, a day; in this case by just a few hours. He hadn't allowed for his new feet, which slowed every stage of his journey. He couldn't have predicted that the biggest bank in Philadelphia would close its doors and that depositors anxious to get to other banks would be crowding every form of transportation. And he'd forgotten what Washington was like in September, so hot and humid that the Potomac seemed to have risen into the atmosphere. There were pigs in the streets. Mud, and people shouting; everywhere the litter of construction and the long faces of men whose financial dreams were ruined. He followed a trail that led from a newspaper advertisement to a handbill to a poster to the new Smithsonian building. When the carriage let him off he confronted a mass of stone, wings and a cloister, battlements and a host of towers. He made his way to the main entrance and found himself in the Great Hall.

The beautiful display cases being built in the galleries behind the rows of columns caught his eye, as did the mounds of crates near the finished cases, but he moved past them toward the stairs at the hall's far end. People streamed at him, busily talking; hundreds of people who passed the tall windows and were lit by beams of muddy, late afternoon light, shadowed by the columns, and then set gleaming again. A river moved against him, parting with murmurs of apology. He was carried forward by a fantasy that he'd stand beside Zeke and, after pulling Annie and Tom to safety, tell his version of the story. Just once, in these august surroundings, he'd justify himself and Dr. Boerhaave and Ned, all of them, everyone.

The staircase looked like a waterfall. He fought his way up the inside railing, knowing all the time where this river of people must have its source but praying he was wrong. At the rear of the apparatus room, a few people trickled past him; he slipped past the hydroelectric machine and the pneumatic instruments, the Fresnel lens and the big battery. He drew a deep breath and passed through the wide door into the lecture room. The room was empty. The oval skylight above the speaker's platform shone down on an empty podium. The curved rows of seats spreading out in the shape of an open fan were empty; the horseshoe-shaped gallery above was empty as well. A poster attached to a pillar announced Zeke's lecture: 4:30 to 6:30 P.M., in this room, on this day. It was just past six now, yet somehow he'd missed it.

Where was Zeke? Where were Annie and Tom? The room was as big as a theater and held perhaps fifteen hundred seats; he could imagine Zeke's voice resonating from the smooth plaster walls as Annie and Tom went through their paces under the skylight's false sun. He sat for a minute and caught his breath, before making his way back downstairs again. Now the Great Hall was empty as well. Bewildered, unsure where to go next, he moved slowly. At the end of the hall nearest the stairs, the galleries were empty. Farther on, neat stacks of wood and panes of glass, sawhorses and boxes of workmen's tools sat between each pair of columns. Then he passed rows of half-built cases, rising in three tiers from floor to ceiling but without their glass doors or hardware; beyond them were a few rows of finished cases. A Negro carpenter adjusting a door on one of these looked up at him.

"May I help you?" he asked. "If you're having trouble walking . . ."

Erasmus looked down at his feet. "I'll be all right," he said. "It just takes me a little longer."

"Take all the time you want," the carpenter said, tapping the brass hinge. "So many people at that lecture, you were smart to wait until the room emptied out."

"I missed the lecture," Erasmus said, and moved on. Zeke and Annie and Tom could be anywhere, he thought. At any hotel, at anyone's home. He stared blankly at a mountain of crates, considering what to do next. Then realized what he was looking at.

Back home he'd read in the newspaper that Congress had appropriated money to build these cases, which were meant to house specimens from the expeditions of the last two decades. The centerpiece, he'd read, was to be the collection from his old Exploring Expedition. Stuffed in the Patent Office for fifteen years, mislabeled and poorly displayed, the specimens were to find a home here. He'd been thinking about other things when he read that; it had hardly registered, although once this would have been the most important news in the world. Now it didn't seem to matter where the things on which he'd wasted his youth ended up.

On the crates were labels, apparently meant to go on the doors of the cases once they were filled. He bent over one and read it wonderingly.

Case 71.

Collections made by the U.S. Exploring Expedition in the Feejee Islands . . . Cannibal Cooking Pots.

The Feejees are Cannibals. The flesh of women is preferred to that of men, and that part of the arm above the elbow and the thigh are regarded as the choicest parts. So highly do they esteem this food, that the greatest praise they can bestow on a delicacy is to say that it is as tender as a dead man.

Vessel for mixing oil . . . Fishing Nets of twine, from the bark of the Hibiscus . . . Flute of Bamboo, and other musical instruments . . . Paddles . . . Mask and Wig worn in dances . . . War Conch, blown as the sign of hostilities . . . Fishing Spears . . . War Clubs . . . Feejee Wigs . . . Native Cloth, worn as a turban on the head . . . Feejee Spears . . . Feejee drum made of the hollow trunk of a tree.

He leapt back as if he'd been burned. He both could and couldn't remember those objects, and the young version of himself who'd helped gather them. Two members of the Expedition had been killed by those Feejee Islanders. He hadn't taken part in the retaliatory raid, but he'd known what was happening. From the ship he'd seen the smoke from the burning villages and heard the rifle fire. Wilkes had argued that man-eating men deserved any punishment he might inflict, and although Erasmus had hated Wilkes's harsh ways with the native peoples, in this case part of him agreed. But that had been before Dr. Rae returned from the arctic with the first news of Franklin's fate, and those hints of mutilated corpses and human parts found in the British cooking kettles. Before Joe told him about the British boot.

He moved uneasily among the other crates. There were signs describing corals and crystals, cuttlefish and prawns: *Notice the Sea Mushroom*, one directed. How could he notice anything, with the objects locked inside their crates? He tried to imagine the ranks of display cases finished and gleaming: each case numbered, each shelf labeled, each item on each shelf tagged. How many miles of shelving, if he put every shelf from every tier of every case end to end? On those shelves would be thousands— tens of thousands—of specimens. Snakes and fossils and shards of wood, canoes and skulls and feathers and slippers all jumbled together. Stuffed dogs, stuffed fish. Exotic birds, gannets and toucans: *The Booby is so stupid that he will sit still and be knocked on the head.*

When all the specimens were arranged, this would be the largest collection in the country. Everything the biggest, the only, the best. Already there was a meteorite here, squatting dumbly behind two crates: *The largest specimen in the country, obtained at Saltillo. When found it was being used as an anvil. It is thought to be of lunar origin.* Behind it, the sign on another crate: *Human Skulls from the Feejee Islands, New Zealand, California, Mexico, North American Indians &c. One of the skulls is of Vendovi, the Feejee Chief and Murderer.*

Erasmus imagined Zeke striding past these crates with Annie and Tom and a crowd of followers, ignoring everything that didn't touch directly on him. He hadn't been so different himself when he was Zeke's age. Vendovi, whom he'd only glimpsed briefly, had killed one of the expedition's seamen and then been taken hostage by Wilkes in return. He and Erasmus had been on different ships, and Erasmus had hardly thought about him; hardly noticed when Vendovi was carried ashore at New York, to die the next day in the hospital. How had that person turned into a skull, and how had the skull landed here?

None of these skulls, none of those days, had entered into the version of the Exploring Expedition he'd recounted to Dr. Boerhaave when they'd first met. Perhaps he'd been ashamed even then. All the skulls but Vendovi's had come, he was almost sure, from burial grounds; other men on other ships had gathered them. Not he. Was it worse to capture a Feejee chief and let him die in a strange land than to tear an Esquimau woman from her home and exhibit her to curious strangers? Vendovi's death pained him now, but then he'd hardly noticed it. He'd gawked at the Feejee Islanders as if they were apes. As Zeke gawked at the Esquimaux, but with less enthusiasm and a colder eye. One more sign caught his eye:

Case 52.

The identical dress worn by Dr. E. K. Kane, the celebrated American Arctic Explorer, and brought by him to this Museum. We quote the following from the account of his travels:

"The clothing or personal outfit demands the nicest study of experience. Rightly clad, he is a lump of deformity, waddling over the ice, unpicturesque, uncouth, and seemingly helpless. The fox-skin jumper, or kapetah, *is a closed shirt, fitting very loosely to the person, but adapted to the head and neck by an almost air-tight hood, the* nessak. *Underneath the* kapetah *is a similar garment, but destitute of the hood, which is a shirt. It is made of bird skins, chewed in the mouth by the women until they are perfectly soft, and it is worn with this unequalled down next the body. More than 500 auks have been known to contribute to a garment of this description. The lower extremities are guarded by a pair of bear-skin breeches, the* nannooke. *The foot gear consists of a bird-skin sock, with a padding of grass over the sole. Outside of this is a bear-skin*

> *leg. In this dress, a man will sleep upon his sledge with the atmos-*
> *phere at 93 degrees below our freezing point. The only additional*
> *articles of dress are, a fox's tail held between the teeth to protect*
> *the nose in a wind, and mitts of seal skin well wadded with*
> *sledge straw."*

What was this doing here? The one thing Zeke might have noticed, even envied; Erasmus could see now why Zeke had come here on his honeymoon trip. Why he'd found it so crucial to curry favor with the Smithsonian's officials and scientists and to give his lecture not in one of Washington's theaters but in the glorious lecture room above.

This was Zeke's chance, his time to shine. In July another expedition had left England in search of Franklin and his men: Captain McClintock, aboard the *Fox*, headed with Lady Franklin's support for Boothia and King William Land. He meant to complete the search that Zeke had started but bungled—and if he succeeded, all Zeke's feats would be eclipsed except for his retrieval of Annie and Tom. They were his Sioux Indians, his two-headed infant in a jar. Zeke, Erasmus understood, had a tiny slot of time in which to make his name, a window between Kane and McClintock.

Erasmus poked at the crate, but it was solidly built and he could see nothing inside. He tapped it lightly with one of his sticks; then he hit it more strongly. By the time a hand clamped down on his shoulder he was braced on one stick and whacking with the other, as if he might shatter the thick pine boards and find his own life trapped inside.

"You must stop that," the carpenter said. "Right now. What's wrong with you? Are you ill?"

His skin was black, much darker than Annie's. Erasmus could think of no excuse. Weakly he said, "I had a fever earlier this year. I think it's come back."

"It rises off the river," the carpenter said. "It's running all over the city. The arctic woman and her son were so sick they had to stop the exhibition before it was done." He led Erasmus to a low box and said, "Sit down for a minute. Calm yourself."

"You saw them?" Erasmus said.

"Not the exhibition," the carpenter said. "But I saw the explorer come in with them, and I saw them leave. Four of the scientists who work here were carrying her. Another had her little boy."

"Do you know," Erasmus said, "did you happen to hear— where did they go?"

"To one of the towers, I think," the carpenter said. "Where the young men stay. The assistant scientists—they're just boys, some of them. When they aren't out in the field the director lets them stay in the empty rooms up in the towers. All day they sort and label their bones and then at night they drink too much and slide down the bannisters and run footraces here in the hall. They make a mess of things. I've told the director he can't expect me to work like this but he refuses to discipline them, even though last week they broke one of my doors . . ."

"Could you take me there?" Erasmus asked.

"I don't speak to those men." The carpenter fingered one of Erasmus's sticks, as if checking the quality of the work. "And I won't go near their rooms. But I'll tell you how to get there."

ERASMUS RESTED AT every landing, pinching his nose against the odor of sewer gas that seeped through the walls and permeated the staircase. He was in the largest of the main building's towers, a narrow rectangular oven that soaked up the sun's heat. On each landing paneled doors confronted him. These led, he supposed, to hot boxy rooms, and in those rooms were—what? Fervent young botanists and paleontologists, heaps of dusty equipment, spare books; concerns he couldn't imagine. He wished the carpenter had been more explicit. He heard laughter above him, and climbed another flight.

The three men he glimpsed through a half-open door were arguing too passionately to see him. Fossil dogs, fossil wolves; for a second Dr. Boerhaave's voice seemed to float across the surface of their discussion. *Large groups of plants and animals share a common morphology, a unity of plan. These plans exist as ideas in the mind of God, who expresses them differently from age to age. Individual species may disappear, but the blueprints persist, with variations; variant forms of the Form.* A wiry man in his early twenties leaned forward and said, "Cuvier doesn't even contest the existence of man during the epoch of the giant mammals."

"The question," said the red-haired man next to him, "is whether the associated human bones should be assigned equal antiquity with the dog bones found among them, and the hippopotami and extinct bears . . ."

Erasmus leaned inside the door. "Excuse me," he said. "I'm sorry to interrupt, but perhaps you could help me."

"A visitor!" the third young man said. In his hands he held something that looked like part of a human pelvis. "Come join us."

"I'm looking for Zechariah Voorhees," Erasmus said. On the windowsill a tumbler of whiskey caught the light, casting golden rays over bones and books and the huge-canined skulls of Asian swine. The room had the feel of a clubhouse, chaotic and busy, and for a moment he was reminded of the Toxophilites who'd sent the *Narwhal* off with such a splash.

"You're a friend?" asked the red-haired man.

"A colleague," he said; thinking, *Brother-in-law?* "I missed the lecture, but I heard the Esquimaux were taken sick. I was hoping to help."

"He was here a minute ago," said the man with the pelvis in his hand. "But I think he went to fetch the doctor."

"Where are *they*?" Erasmus asked. "The Esquimaux." If these were the men who'd helped carry Annie and Tom, they seemed mightily unconcerned about them now.

"Follow me," said the man. He looked curiously at Erasmus's feet, but asked nothing as he led the way to the next room over.

Erasmus knocked, pushing the door open when no one answered. Inside the stuffy room, Annie lay on one narrow cot and Tom on another. A desk and chair and a litter of dirty clothes filled the rest of the space. On the desk was a precarious tower of flat stone slabs, and in the chair a pale young man, already balding, who looked up when Erasmus entered.

"I didn't hear you knock," the pale man said. "You'll have to excuse me, I'm nearly deaf."

"May I come in?" Erasmus said, enunciating clearly. "These are my friends."

"Whose friend?" the man said, cupping his hand to his ear.

"Annie's friend," Erasmus shouted. He made his way past the desk, pushing socks and linen aside with his sticks. Annie's eyes were closed, but she stirred when Erasmus touched her shoulder. "Tseke?" she said.

"Erasmus. Do you remember me?"

Her skin was very hot. A coarse sheet was pulled up to her chin; when Erasmus turned back the corner he saw that she was naked beneath it, filmed with sweat. Hastily he covered her and checked on Tom. Unclothed as well, he lay on his side, staring at his own hands.

"Where is Tseke?" Annie whispered.

"He's coming," Erasmus said. He turned to the pale man. "Who undressed them? Whose room is this?"

"It's my room," the man answered. "I'm Fielding, I work here. The explorer who lectured this afternoon is an acquaintance of mine. His Esquimaux collapsed during the lecture—the heat, we think—and he asked if they could rest here until the doctor arrives. She undressed her son and herself, after Zeke left. I stepped outside. Of course. You know them?"

"I'm Zeke's brother-in-law."

"You know Zeke!" Fielding said.

"Yes!" Erasmus shouted again, exasperated despite himself. He couldn't imagine why Zeke had left Annie and Tom in the care of a man who couldn't hear their requests. "Where *is* he?"

"Next door," Fielding said. "With the others."

Through the wall Erasmus could hear the young men's voices. "He's not," he said. Then he gave up trying to explain and concentrated on Annie and Tom. He found a jug of water near the door and dampened his handkerchief, dabbing at Annie's face and Tom's face and hands. Fielding hovered, polite but useless. "Do you suppose they're really sick?" he asked. "The fellows next door told me they were just overheated."

"You have eyes—look at them."

Fielding shrugged and stepped back to his desk. "I don't have much experience with women and children," he said. "I'm in here all the time . . . the other scientists never want me to drink with them and we disagree about almost everything." He lifted a thin slab of stone, pointing to something that looked like a crinoid. "What *I* think about this," he said.

"Please," Erasmus said. "Not now." He heard feet pounding up the stairs, and then Zeke was in the room.

"Where have you been?" Erasmus asked, just as Zeke said, "What are *you* doing here?" After glaring at each other for a silent moment, they both bent over Annie.

Annie was someplace hot and dark, streaked with red, filled with noise and the smell of blood. She was a seal who'd come up for a breath of air and met a bear; the bear had been waiting and she was caught by surprise; there was a blow and then burning. She tried to heave herself back in the cool water but she was being dragged across the ice. She was being bitten. She was being eaten. She moaned and turned and opened her eyes and her son was staring at her. The worst thing about what was happening to her body was the way it kept her from protecting him. But her journey must mean something, her reasons for coming with Zeke must be true.

The piece of peculiar ice her mother had seen had turned out to be a thing called *mirror*; more were on the ship, and in the building full of dead insects and birds. She and her son had inched up to those mirrors, stared into them, touched each other's reflections. In the room below, before she'd stumbled and fallen and been unable to rise, she'd seen herself reflected in the watching people's eyes. She'd been sent here like a shard of splintered mirror, she thought, to capture an image of the world beyond her home.

"Annie," Zeke said. "Can you hear me?"

"Is the doctor coming?" Erasmus asked.

Annie heard their voices but not their words. The strangers' language left her and she longed for someone to say her real name and speak to her in real words, but these large figures murmured incomprehensibly. One was Zeke, a walking finger who pointed at her and then turned into the barrel of a rifle. The rifle had brought her tribe meat and fed the children. But the rifle was a finger and the finger was Zeke, who had not understood his connection to the other fingers, the hand, the wrist, the body that was her tribe. The body that had once been her. When she coughed a bullet seemed to enter her lungs.

Her son asked in their shared language if they could go home now. One of the bears took the other by the shoulder and both stepped out of view, leaving only a white figure, a little white fox, behind. The fox put his paws on a piece of stone. A fox might follow a bear, waiting for scraps from the kill. She closed her eyes again. At home, she thought, her body would be wrapped in skins and carried away from the huts, then laid on the ground with a rock for her pillow. Around her someone would place her soapstone cooking pots, each one broken into pieces, and her needles and thread and her *ulo*, all she'd need for her life beyond. Over her body a vault of rocks would be built. Over her jawbones the wind might play a song.

"He's here," Zeke said. "Right behind me." He turned and beckoned to the doctor; Fielding tiptoed away.

Brisk and gray-haired and competent, the doctor felt Annie's pulses, rolled down her lower eyelids, and slid his arm beneath her covering sheet. "Enlarged liver," he said. His hand crept beneath the cloth. "Enlarged spleen." He moved over to Tom and repeated his investigations, asking Zeke how long these people had been away from their home, where they'd been staying, when their symptoms had first appeared. He made a note when Zeke described the site of the Repository.

"Near a river *and* a creek?" He felt the sides of Annie's neck. "Most likely it's a miasmatic bilious fever," he said. "Normally you'd see a yellowing of the skin, but of course on them . . . you can see, though, the way the whites of their eyes have yellowed."

"Can I move them?" Zeke asked.

"Carefully," the doctor said. "And not far." He rummaged in his bag, pulling out boxes and vials. "Preparation of Peruvian bark," he said. "Decoction of boneset as an emetic, a calomel purgative to relieve congestion of the liver, a diaphoretic in an effervescing draught—we'll try to break the fever with these. Then they need to rest in a clean, dark, well-aired room."

"I talked to a friend here in Washington," Zeke said. "He's willing to let us stay with him for a few days."

"Not one of those young men," Erasmus protested. "They're hardly more than children."

Zeke shook his head. "Someone else," he said. "A physical anthropologist who's in charge of a whole section—he has a big house a few blocks from here, servants, spare rooms. His children are grown and his wife is very . . . tolerant. He's had Indians from the Andes staying with him before."

"That sounds suitable," the doctor said. "I can call on you twice daily there. I want to bleed them now; this almost always helps." He looked down at Annie and Tom. "Race does modify the action of remedies, though."

Erasmus leaned against the desk, watching as Zeke held the basins and lancets and helped the doctor spoon a dark brown liquid into Annie and Tom. He had a real affection for them, Erasmus saw.

Afterward Annie and Tom looked more comfortable. "Go out for a bit," the doctor said. "I want to listen to their bowels."

In the narrow hall, with the stairwell yawning below them, the two men regarded each other. "I can't believe you brought them here in this condition," Erasmus said. "You have to cancel the rest of the tour."

"I already have," Zeke said. His hair was glowing like a helmet. "Did you come here just to tell me that? I know they're sick, I'll take care of them. I'm not a *monster*."

Erasmus had planned to say something about the conditions in the Repository, which Alexandra had described to him; about his impressions of the Philadelphia exhibition; about Lavinia, left alone so Zeke could trot around accumulating fame. Then he thought of the way Annie's first words, whenever he saw her, were always "Where is Tseke?"

"Let me stay with you and Annie and Tom," he said. "I want to help them."

"There's nothing you can do to help," Zeke said. "I'll be with them, though." He peered over the railing, apparently fascinated by the zigzagging flights of stairs. "You can visit them all you want, when they're better. But you can see for yourself how sick they are. You're not a doctor—what can you do?"

He reached over and flicked one of Erasmus's sticks with his thumb. "You belong at home," he said. "You always did."

The stick rose, until the tip was pointed at Zeke's right knee; Erasmus couldn't help this, his arm did it, it had no connection to him. "*I* belong at home?" If the stick swung, at just the right angle, Zeke would topple, topple. "I'm not the one . . ."

"Stop worrying," Zeke said. He leaned over and pressed on Erasmus's forearm, pushing the stick back to the ground. "At least until they regain their health, I'm done with this tour."

Behind them the door opened. "I'm finished," the doctor said. "If you'd like, you can come back in."

"I want to talk to Annie," Erasmus said to Zeke. "I want her to tell me what *she* wants. Let me see her alone for a minute." Without waiting for an answer he backed into the room.

"Annie?" he said. "What can I do for you? Tell me how I can help."

"Tseke?" Annie said yet again.

"*Erasmus*," he said.

She opened her eyes. The whites were filmed with yellow—as was the rest of her, he thought, peering more closely at her face. It wasn't true what the doctor had said; the sickness glazed her normal color and gave her a slight greenish tinge, as if she'd been dusted with lichen spores.

"Oh," Annie said. "You."

Over the windows the curtains lifted, reaching toward the bed. She turned her head into the breeze and closed her eyes. "Go home," she said faintly.

For a minute more he gazed at her. She said nothing else. Perhaps she had gone to sleep. Tom too had his eyes closed; the curtains lifted and fell, lifted and fell, refusing to give Erasmus an answer. He gave up and returned to the hall.

"It's you she wants," he told Zeke bitterly. *You Lavinia wants*, he thought. "She keeps asking for you."

"I'll take care of them," Zeke said. "I promise."

He ran a thumb over his bushy eyebrows. Erasmus stood before him, hot and miserable. Not a breath of breeze moved through this windowless hall.

"I need her," Zeke said. "I've learned a lot from her, she's been helping me with my book." He bit off a fragment of thumbnail and dropped the shard down the stairwell. "It's going to be good," he said. "Personal, a sort of adventure tale—my encounters with the Esquimaux, my last vision of the *Narwhal*. It's going to be like Dr. Kane's book, only more interesting, more dramatic."

Erasmus's stomach knotted and rose. Why were they talking about this now, with Annie and Tom lying sick next door? They had never talked about anything, not Dr. Boerhaave's death or Ned's nose or all that might have been prevented if only Zeke hadn't been determined to head north. And now, now . . . *my encounters, my vision.* The lecture in Philadelphia had been shaped exactly this way. Erasmus said, "Why would you write an account that pretends all the rest of us weren't there?"

"You're all in it," Zeke said. "But no more than you deserve to be. Minor, minor characters."

"I haven't written about *you*," Erasmus said. "I didn't think that would be fair."

"What's fair?" Zeke said. "Was it *fair* that you abandoned me? Is it *fair* that I have nothing left, except the story I tell? You can't know what it was like for me up there. Coming back to the ship, finding you'd all walked out on me: it was very—*clarifying*. I learned who I could depend on. No one. No one but myself. You . . ."

The contempt in his eyes was shocking. "You're *nothing*. Not in the book. Not to me."

In his hands Erasmus felt the walking sticks dancing, as if the floor had metamorphosed into the open sea. "I may be nothing," he said. "But at least I don't destroy whatever I touch. What you're doing to Annie and Tom . . ."

Zeke stretched his arms over his head, opening and closing his fingers. "Go home," he said. "No one needs you here. I'll take care of Annie and Tom."

ANNIE WAS IN a room. Her son was in another; Zeke came and went between them. At home the *angekok* sought his visions in a hollow hidden in thick ice grounded on the shore; she pulled the white curtains of the canopied bed around her and imagined ice. The doctor came; the man who owned this house came. The servants, as fearful and disdainful as those in the house to which Zeke had first brought her, sponged her body and brought her food, which she didn't touch. The doctor forced pills and liquid between her teeth, some kind of poison. No one would listen to her. Not the doctor, not Zeke; not even Erasmus, who'd asked what she needed but then turned his back and disappeared when she'd said, *I want to go home*. Wasn't that what she'd said? Her body would never go home now and she must do what she could for her son. A white cloth over the bed, white cases over the pillows; she had little time; she worked. The great power, the *angekok* had once told her, comes only after struggle and concentration. By the strength of her thought alone, she must strip her body of flesh and blood and be able to see herself as a skeleton. Each bone, each tiny bone, clear before her eyes. Then the sacred language would descend, allowing her to name the parts of her body that would endure. When she named the last bone she'd be free; her spirit could travel and she could watch over her son. She burrowed under the white cloth and squeezed shut her eyes, beginning the terrible process of shedding her flesh. Let me be bone, she thought. Like the long narwhal spines at home, the walrus skulls, the delicate ribs of the seals. White bone.

* * *

THE LESS ALEXANDRA worked on the thing she most loved, the more her family appreciated her. The easiest days were those on which she didn't try to work at all. When she stopped looking so fiercely for a moment she might call her own, when she stopped rushing through her household tasks and simply gave into them, the days had a reasonable rhythm. And it was lovely, in a way, when her family thanked her—yet at night she weighed those thanks against the nagging sense that she'd wasted another set of precious hours. Her family won during the days of Erasmus's absence. But as soon as she saw him again, she regretted every lost minute.

At the engraving firm, he told her Annie and Tom were sick. Which was terrible, but at least their condition had forced Zeke to stop the exhibitions. Zeke was looking after them and would soon bring them home, where he'd settle down to work on a book that was almost done, and in which Erasmus had no place.

"In his book," Erasmus said, "I am—he said I am a *minor character.*" He peered over Alexandra's shoulder. "That's excellent," he said. "*Our* book will be beautiful. You've caught the gills and the scales exactly."

They spent long hours at their desks, working in a kind of splendid trance. Erasmus wrote ten, twelve, twenty pages a day; Alexandra's drawings accumulated and when they visited Copernicus they found the second painting done, and two more started. Around them the firm was humming, as if their frenzy were contagious. Humboldt concluded negotiations for the plates for a new encyclopedia, which seemed more than usually lucky as businesses elsewhere closed. Pleased with themselves, they all gathered one afternoon in the main office to celebrate over a drink.

The brothers, Alexandra saw, had settled into a new relationship. Perhaps it was their enforced proximity, or the way Erasmus worked so hard, with such clear purpose, and never complained about the small corners allotted to him. Or perhaps Linnaeus and Humboldt, cast for years as the steady, uninteresting middle brothers, were secretly pleased to be doing favors for the eldest. Linnaeus, in particular, seemed to relish his new role. He gave Erasmus frequent advice, visited Lavinia three times each week, no longer criticized Alexandra's work.

He was with Lavinia now; they lingered over their sherry while they waited for him. There would be an awkward moment, Alexandra knew, when Linnaeus would report that Lavinia was fine, but that she still didn't want to see Erasmus. It would be awkward, but it would pass. At six-thirty Linnaeus entered the office. Waving away the glass Humboldt held out to him, he flopped down in an armchair, very pale.

"What is it?" Erasmus said. "Is she—unwell, again?"

"Zeke is back," Linnaeus said. "He walked in right after I got there." Then he drew a long breath.

"Annie is dead," he said. He rested his hand on Erasmus's arm; Alexandra had never seen them touch before. "She died two days after you left."

"She's dead?" Erasmus said. "How can she be dead?"

Linnaeus closed his eyes and then took the glass Humboldt offered again. "I know," he said. "It's horrible. He brought Tom with him; he's recovering but still very frail."

Alexandra thought of Annie and Tom as she'd last seen them in the Repository. Shouldn't she have known—shouldn't they all have known—where this was heading? "But Lavinia and Zeke will take care of him," she said. "Won't they? They'll find a home for him, at least until he's better and can be returned to his family."

"Lavinia's very upset," Linnaeus said. "She asked Zeke who was more important to him, her or those Esquimaux. If you'd heard her voice—it was terrible. And then, and then . . ."

"What's *wrong* with her?" Erasmus burst out. "He's just a little boy, and now he's lost his mother. You'd think she'd remember what that was like."

"That's not the worst of it," Linnaeus said. "She had one of the maids settle Tom in the Repository; he's to sleep there with only those two dogs for company. Zeke didn't even try to stop her, he said he'd do whatever she wanted."

"Zeke can't," Erasmus said. "Can he?"

Linnaeus curled his lip. "I suppose he can do anything he wants. He claims he was nursing Tom in Washington; I'd like to see him nurse anyone but himself. Then he admitted he'd stayed a few extra days, to take care of Annie's remains."

"He had her buried down there?" Erasmus asked.

Linnaeus gulped at his drink. "There was no burial," he said. "No body, even. There are men at the Smithsonian who—who do this sort of thing. I don't know how, I don't want to know how. I think the man Zeke was staying with had the idea, he knows about bones and skulls. Zeke gave him his permission and he, they, *someone* prepared and mounted her skeleton for the museum. Zeke stayed to oversee it."

Erasmus groaned, and Alexandra thought about Toodlamik's bones and skin. Then about Annie as she'd first seen her, leaning against the windowpane until the sash was raised and she reached, so gratefully, for the air.

"He did it for Lavinia," Linnaeus continued. "Or so he claims. The skeleton's to go in a glass case in the hall across from Dr. Kane's exhibit, with a plaque about Zeke's expedition. You know how he is, he thinks this will make him famous. Everyone will want to buy his book and then he and Lavinia won't have to depend on his father's generosity, they won't have to worry about anything again."

"Is that what he's thinking?" Humboldt asked.

"I don't know. But Lavinia said she didn't care what happened to Annie's remains, she knew all about Zeke and Annie and she'd never been fooled, she wasn't *stupid*."

Humboldt raised an eyebrow and Copernicus said, "Surely we're not surprised by that? He spent six months in her company, after better than a year without any female companionship. Didn't we assume . . . ?"

"I don't know what *you* assumed," Linnaeus said. Alexandra could not help glancing at Erasmus; what had she assumed about him? "I assumed that he'd honored his commitment to Lavinia, and that Annie was just what he said. A member of the tribe that saved his life. If she was ever more than that, why would he be so unfeeling as to exhibit her bones?"

"Nothing," Erasmus said, "has ever gotten in the way of Zeke's ambitions."

She was gone, he thought. They'd hardly had the chance to know each other. For a minute Linnaeus's words drifted past him. When he could bear to listen again, Linnaeus was still discussing Zeke's plans: returning Tom to Washington, arranging to have him cared for by someone associated with the Smithsonian. Someone who might be willing to take Tom in and educate him.

Copernicus turned to Erasmus. "You have to do something."

"I know," Erasmus said. He reached for Linnaeus's hand. "It's not your fault."

"We're all at fault," Copernicus said. "You should have fought back when Zeke returned, and not let him persuade everyone that you acted wrongly on the voyage. We shouldn't have doubted you. And you and I should have refused to leave our home."

"I know," Erasmus repeated. They'd doubted him? "I know." He stared out the window, toward the river and his lost home on the opposite bank.

FROM THAT HOUSE, in the gathering twilight, Lavinia was gazing back. Somewhere, perhaps along the creek, Zeke was pacing through the haze that had carried the fever to Annie. And somewhere else, she imagined, her brothers were together. When had they ever put her first? Copernicus had traveled across the continent and Erasmus had sailed to both ends of the earth; neither had ever asked if she minded being left behind, alone and waiting for them. What had Erasmus given her? Her mother's walking shoe; a few odd books and lessons; a promise, which he'd broken. *Erasmus let me down*, Zeke had told her. *When I most needed him.* Because of Erasmus, he'd had to go north alone; because of Erasmus he'd ended up staying with Annie's family, bringing Annie home.

Outside the window the shadow of Annie rose before her, as it did every night at this time: piercing dark eyes, the smooth skin of her arms and throat, the quiet voice Zeke seemed to have found so alluring. Annie had been helpless here, completely dependent on Zeke—and what man could resist that? Her very existence had set Lavinia in the wrong. But she'd been patient, so patient, willing Zeke to turn away from Annie by the sheer force of her own desire. She had won him back, only to see the hurt and disappointment in his eyes as she turned away from the dead woman's son. Was it so awful, after their long separation, to want a scrap of normal life?

She'd stopped praying when Erasmus first returned without Zeke, started again with the help of Browning, stopped again when Zeke came home and her pleas were answered. Now she folded her hands across her waist and prayed she might be carrying a son.

11

The Nightmare Skeleton

(October 1857–August 1858)

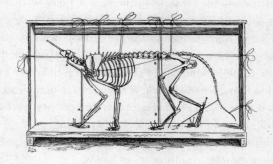

These are the qualities which are required to make a first-class collector: He must have a fair general knowledge of zoology, especially the vertebrates. He must be a good shot, a successful hunter, and capable of great physical endurance. Then he must be a neat and skillful operator with the knife, and conscientious in the details of his work, down to the smallest particulars, for without this quality his specimens will always be faulty and disappointing. In addition to all these requirements he must be a man of tireless energy, incapable of going to bed so long as there are birds to be skinned, and who, whenever a doubt arises in his mind in regard to the necessity of more work on a specimen, will *always give the specimen the benefit of the doubt.*

— W. J. Holland, *Taxidermy and Zoological Collecting* (1892)

*H*e woke to their sounds in the dark: whispers, rustlings, something dropped. In the moonlight the portraits above him shimmered, faces caught behind panes of glass like dead men peering through the ice, and at first he thought the sounds came from them. But there were footsteps moving his way. The two black dogs beside him rose and bristled; he sat upright on the mattress of caribou skins, terrified but determined to be brave. They had come to kill him, he thought. Zeke and his wife, who talked about him as if he weren't present or couldn't understand them. They wished him dead, as his mother was dead, and had chosen this night. They were leaning over him, while the traitorous dogs said nothing.

"It's all right," the woman said. "Can you be very quiet?" He could hear the dogs snuffling at her hands.

The man said, "We need to take you from here, so you won't be hurt. Will you come with us?"

Tom said nothing. He recognized the woman as the one who wasn't Lavinia; the one whose garment his mother had worn the first day here. The man was one of the brothers but he could never tell them apart. Then the man reached out and Tom knew him as Copernicus, from the bright painty tang of his hand.

"Tom?" Copernicus said.

He wasn't Tom; his real name was his secret and he'd never speak it among these people. Two days ago he'd decided to stop speaking altogether. But he rose to his feet when Copernicus asked; he walked from this building so full of death; he sat where they placed him and felt the ground slip as if he were on a sledge. Two other brothers appeared, but one stayed only briefly. In and out of other doors, other rooms, some still and others moving; he slept when he could, ate now and then, said nothing. The walls rattled, the floors shook, trees moved past him and then more buildings. His clothes were taken and other clothes put on him. Erasmus was here, he knew Erasmus. Sometimes he dozed against his shoulder.

The landscape changed and changed again, but it was never the one he wanted. The people so close to him talked in low worried voices, but also sat still for long stretches. Where was Zeke? Somewhere else: farther and farther away, he hoped. His people had a name for Zeke, a chain of soft syllables that meant *The One Who Is Trouble.* To his face, they'd said the syllables meant *The Great Explorer*, and Zeke had smiled and nodded his head and done his best to repeat them.

He had plans for Zeke. Tucked into his jacket were bones he'd stolen from the place where Zeke had caged him: a bird's curved ribs, a serpent's spine, a mouse's foot. He needed more. When he had enough he would make a *tupilaq*, a nightmare skeleton built from bones of all kinds of creatures, wrapped in a skin. By the edge of some water he would set it down and say the secret words; then the *tupilaq* would come alive and swim across any form of water, no matter how far. Blank-eyed it would swim up to Zeke, disguised as a familiar animal; sleek fur, smooth ears. Perhaps it would travel as a deer before allowing itself to be killed. After Zeke slit down the belly and parted the flesh he'd find all the wrong bones, connected in all the wrong ways. Then he'd die.

That vision kept Tom quiet as he traveled. This wasn't like the journeys he'd taken with his people, moving happily behind the dogs to another hunting ground. This was like the later journey, the days in the box moving over the water. They moved over land now, but he was still confined. When he could, when Erasmus would let him, he hung out the windows and filled his lungs. There were trees, and then mountains. Then very large mountains and air so cool and fresh it almost made him think of home.

When it rained he held his hands out to catch the water. Resting on the top of the sky, he believed, was the land where the dead lived—a place of light and warmth and abundant game, feasting and song and dance. His mother was there. She'd abandoned her body so that she might watch over him; those men who came later, to take what was left, had only made visible the process she'd begun. Light from the land where she'd gone shone through holes in the sky, appearing as stars. Water fell through those holes from the rivers; that water was rain. Each drop that touched his skin was a message from his mother.

The movement stopped. The door was opened from the outside. When he stepped down and saw a man missing part of his nose, his scream was the first sound he'd made in days and it rang in his own ears. He pitched forward and crouched on the ground with his arms over his head, and would not be moved.

EVEN WHEN THEY reached the cabin on the Ausable River, no one could convince Tom to open his eyes. His arms wound tightly around his knees, his eyes screwed shut, his mouth sealed, he sat without moving where Copernicus placed him, on the small, red-blanketed bed.

"Has he been like this the whole trip?" Ned asked.

"Not quite this bad," Erasmus said. He touched Ned's shoulder. "I'm so glad to see you." Then he turned to Tom again. "He hasn't said a word since he was taken from the Repository."

Ned made coffee for the tired travelers and quietly, with the boy in the background radiating a distress that no one could soothe, they caught each other up on the events of the past few weeks. Erasmus told Ned how Linnaeus had driven the carriage to their old home, although he'd do no more than that; how Copernicus and Alexandra had tiptoed into the Repository and swept the boy away. Each of them had told a separate lie, he said.

Copernicus had told his companions he was heading west. Alexandra, during a terrible quarrel with her siblings, had said she was taking a position teaching drawing at a female academy in Cincinnati. Erasmus, knowing the way Zeke thought and imagining how he'd set about searching for them, had purchased passage for two on a ship bound for Liverpool; it would take some time before anyone discovered that they hadn't arrived.

"I think we've covered our tracks," he told Ned. Although his feet had prevented him from taking an active role, the plans had worked smoothly so far, and they were his. "But none of this could have happened without you—how can I thank you for all your help?"

"It's not a problem," Ned replied. "I told you I'd help any way I could, and I meant it."

He bustled around the small kitchen, avoiding the knees of his guests. "I've found a house for you, about a mile from here," he said. "It's pleasant, and quite isolated, but it won't be ready until tomorrow. We'll have to stay here tonight." He watched his guests look around his tiny home. "I'm sorry," he said. "But it'll be all right. I've borrowed some extra bedding from the hotel."

"Of course it will be fine," Alexandra said. Her dark hair and strong features reminded him of his sister, Nora, as did the way she leaned toward the boy every few minutes and stroked his back. "You were good to take us in like this. And it's wonderful to see you well, after you were so sick in Philadelphia. I understand you have a fine job now?"

"It's good enough," Ned said. How could he tell her that he was in danger of losing it? The time he'd had to take off, while he searched for a house to lodge his guests; the flurry of letters arriving at the hotel, which had made the owner suspicious; the letters he'd had to write back and the supplies he'd had to purchase: all this to help a boy he'd never met. The tone of Erasmus's letters had been so distressed, though, and the tale he'd told so upsetting, that Ned could not deny him anything. *I failed his mother*, Erasmus had written. *I can't fail Tom.*

Ned walked toward the grubby, silent boy, the source of all this trouble. Searching for some words Joe had taught him before their trip to Anoatok, he introduced himself haltingly in the boy's language. To his surprise, Tom opened his eyes—and then his mouth, as if he might scream again at the sight of Ned's nose.

Ned had no more Esquimaux phrases, but Erasmus had written that Tom could speak and understand English. He thought about his own arrival at Grosse Isle, when he was just a boy himself: when he and his brother had been torn from their fevered sister and packed like cattle on a crowded barge, then shipped upriver and cast on the kindness of strangers. Who hadn't been kind, and hadn't spoken any language he could understand. The rippling, incomprehensible flow of French, which he'd never heard before; the English so different from the English he knew; and never a word of Gaelic, never a taste of home. Never a story he could recognize, nor a person willing to take responsibility for him. He looked into Tom's dark eyes, reading there *help. Can you help me?*

"We were on the ice, in a great storm, in terrible weather," Ned said. He tapped his eroded nostril. "In the darkness the *innersuit* appeared from behind the rocks and swept me away to their hiding place. They took my nose and forced me to stay with them, but I prayed for strength and at last was able to escape them. When I was returned to my people, this man"—here he pointed to Erasmus—"this man, who was our *angekok*, did magic and my nose was returned to me. But a piece was missing, a scar by which the *innersuit* let it be known that I was once captured by them."

Tom unwrapped his arms, straightened his legs, and reached forward to touch Ned's nose. "It is painful?" he asked; the first words he'd spoken since leaving Philadelphia.

"Not anymore," Ned said. "Will you eat something?" From the cupboard he pulled a tray of roasted ducks he'd prepared at the hotel.

"The *innersuit* tried to take my mother," Tom said. "But she conquered them." He bent over the tray.

"What now?" Ned asked Erasmus.

Erasmus lowered himself onto a chair. "I don't know," he said. "We've gotten this far, and that's something. Thanks to you we have a place to stay. The rest—I don't know yet."

While they talked Tom finished the first duck and started on a second, pushing aside the baked bones; the heat made them brittle and ugly, useless to him. But around the walls, just as in the place from which he'd come, there were also skeletons: bat, fox, serpent. Later, after everyone had gone to sleep, he would steal a bone from one of the bat's wings.

THE HOUSE NED had found for them was drafty but large, set amid a stand of hemlocks at the base of a mountain, not far from the trail that led to North Elba through the meadows. Six days a week, drawn by Tom's lonely eyes, Ned took a long detour on the way to the hotel and breakfasted with the little band of runaways. As he got to know Tom better, he brought a clasp knife, a hatchet, rabbits' feet. On his days off, he took Tom for rambles in the forest. Erasmus asked several times if he'd like to join their household, but he preferred to keep his own place. After his time on the *Narwhal* he'd sworn he would never again share living quarters with people not his family.

"Would you think about it?" Erasmus said. "Anytime you wanted, we'd make room for you." Ned brought strings of fish for breakfast, but continued to say no.

While the weeks slipped by, Erasmus tried to understand what he should do next. He walked and thought, thought and walked—a pleasure that had grown unfamiliar. At least they were safe here. With the snowshoes Ned had made for him he could cast his sticks aside; the broad netted platforms restored his lost toes and as long as it snowed he was free. A few miles from the house, he might have been in another country. The forest was dark and unbroken; he saw wolves, deer, panthers, loons: *okipok*, fast ice. Snow glazed the fields and sealed off the mountain peaks. All around him, in every tree and stone, he felt Annie and Dr. Boerhaave. Once he stood in the meadows, after a snowfall, and in the moonlight saw the dark abrupt peaks casting shadows onto a plain that resembled a frozen sea. The shadows took the shape of his dead friend's face, and then of Annie's.

Sometimes he met a trapper, and once he stumbled on a hermit's cottage, but away from the river valleys all was emptiness. He could see why Ned had been drawn back here; the settlers kept to themselves and asked few questions. Remembering Ned's evasions, he invented an ice-fishing accident to explain his feet, and also new identities for his little group. Even Copernicus wasn't well enough known to be recognized here in the wilderness, so he didn't bother to change their names. But to the people he met when he fetched supplies, he lied cheerfully. He claimed they were from Baltimore; that he was a journalist and his brother a painter, who'd both spent years out west. The boy with them was an Indian, whom they'd adopted. And Alexandra was his wife. He paused over that: his wife? Copernicus's wife? Then chose what seemed most believable.

Through the astounding cold of winter, he and Copernicus and Alexandra worked as they had at the Repository, writing and painting and drawing. Copernicus built a small easel for Tom, and gave him brushes and paint; Alexandra gave him paper and pencils. They taught him how to read and write.

"Show me how to make my parents' names," he demanded, and Alexandra wrote NESSARK in large block letters and, not knowing his mother's true name, ANNIE. Tom gripped a pencil in his fist and covered sheets of paper: NESSARK ANNIE NESSARK ANNIE NESSARK ANNIE ANNIE ANNIE. Around the names he drew hundreds of stubby birds. He ignored the brushes Copernicus gave him but he liked the paint, and after the first messy experiment Copernicus stocked up on turpentine and gave Tom a smock that covered his clothes. Tom painted with his thumbs, feathering the color with delicate strokes. The same scene again and again: an icy white plain, a jagged cliff, some low dark lumps that might have been huts, smaller dark dots. Two-legged dots and four-legged dots: people, dogs. Erasmus said, "This must be his version of Anoatok." Alexandra, watching Tom's efforts, said nothing but one night drew a carefully simplified dog and left it on Tom's bed.

He slept in the last of the square chambers lining the lofty main room in which they cooked and ate and worked: one, two, three, four boxes. Four single beds; four people sleeping alone. When Tom went into his room for long stretches and closed the door the others tried to grant him the same privacy they gave each other. They had to do this, Alexandra thought. Otherwise they couldn't have lived in this odd, interesting, almost communal way, as if their new home were a miniature New Harmony. Although the local people believed them a family, they weren't: they were four people sharing a house and chores and work on a book, the three adults also sharing responsibility for the child. Why was this so different from living with her brother and sisters and nephew and niece? Yet it was; every moment she felt as if she were inventing her life. Tom copied her dog drawing again and again, adding harnesses and linking these with a tangle of traces; later, with her help, he drew a sledge. He needed her, she thought. In a way her family didn't. But he made no demands.

She wrapped two shawls around the man's overcoat she'd purchased in the village and went out by herself for long walks across the meadows or along the deer paths winding through the woods, exulting in the astonishing cold and the dry snow whipping her cheeks. On the pair of snowshoes Ned had given her, she tromped the trail along Slide Brook to the South Meadows Brook. No one asked her where she was going or when she was coming back. She chopped wood for the stoves and took her turn cooking and wrestling with the laundry, but because Erasmus and Copernicus shared these tasks they felt like pleasures. At home, she thought, she'd felt like a servant doing similar work: because that had been Browning's household. Browning's home, somehow, in which she and Emily and Jane and even Harriet were guests. Here no one *expected* anything. There were rules, lists, things that had to be done—but they all had to do them.

Each morning she woke with a jolt, electrified by all she wanted to do and purely amazed at herself. Where had she gotten the nerve to confront her family and tell such enormous lies? Sneaking up the dark walk to the Repository, Copernicus beside her, she'd pushed open the door as noiselessly and confidently as if she'd been a criminal all her life. Kidnapping: that was the word for what they'd done, at least in some people's eyes. She'd known just what to say to Tom, just how to bundle him up and slip him into the carriage—as, here in these forbidding woods, she knew how to find her way along the streams without getting lost, how to gather wood, how to stoke the stove. She knew how much sleep she needed, which proved to be very little; how, even, to navigate her way through her feelings toward the two brothers. She kept to her own bed, although she sensed she would have been welcome in either of the two rooms flanking hers. For a while, which she knew wouldn't last forever, she enjoyed the delicate, teasing tension that kept the three of them afloat like a raft.

None of them knew where they were going next. They would finish the book, they agreed. Or as much of it as they could. After that—after that was a blank page Alexandra couldn't imagine.

When Erasmus had first approached her with his plan, she'd volunteered to help rescue Tom, and then to help care for him while she completed the drawings for the book. She hadn't been able to think any further than that. Now the drawings were halfway done.

A letter arrived, which Erasmus read aloud as they sat eating venison stew. *Zeke has spoken with the police*, Linnaeus wrote. *As if Zeke hadn't kidnapped Tom from his home to begin with. And named you and Copernicus as suspects, but not Alexandra. When I agreed to help I didn't expect to be left in such an uncomfortable position. Don't you think you should explain yourself to Zeke?*

Erasmus made a face, and Alexandra looked into her bowl. If this was a kidnapping, what were the words for the other things they'd done? The mess they'd left behind in Philadelphia, their angry families, Erasmus's tangled investments, which were all that supported the four of them yet were still confused—these things were difficult, yet the book was growing swiftly. Around them were mounds of manuscript that Erasmus read to her and Copernicus at night; mounds of drawings she pinned to the walls for the brothers' inspection and comments; two more of Copernicus's giant paintings. Each bird and seal and cliff that Erasmus and Dr. Boerhaave had captured in their notebooks, each whale and swarm of plankton, found a home in them.

"That's it," Erasmus said as each corner of Copernicus's paintings emerged. "That's what it looked like."

All of them, Alexandra thought, could envision the book clearly now: the design, the type, the way the drawings and paintings would fall among the words. Beside them Tom watched and listened, making his own words and pictures. He drew his mother, he drew his father, he drew walrus hunts and polar bears. He waited for Ned's visits. The snow piled up until everything around him was white and almost looked like home.

Sometimes Ned took him deep in the woods, where the traps

were set. They caught beaver, muskrat, rabbits; when they found a fox caught in one, growling and gnawing its frozen paw, Ned let Tom kill it. Tom stood on the fox, as he'd seen his father do, pinning its head and feet and then pressing his hands down on its chest so hard that its heart stopped and it died. Alexandra drew the way he skinned it with Ned's knife and staked the pelt out to bleach and dry. Erasmus and Ned cleaned the bones, reassembled them, and taught Tom their names. From a second fox, they allowed him to keep the leg bones and the skull.

"It's wonderful what he's learning," Ned said to Erasmus. "But how much longer can we keep him here like this?"

That morning Tom had woken to the sound of water dripping: not his mother, seeping through the sky, but icicles shrinking on the eaves. Something happened inside his eyes, as if the fog that had wrapped him since leaving his home had lifted. He gazed at Ned; at Erasmus and Alexandra bent over their tables; at Copernicus busy with a huge painting of the shoreline across the water from Anoatok. He said, "I want to go home."

Erasmus wrote two more lines and set his page aside. He looked up at Tom. His father, he remembered, had once looked at him with exasperation and said, "Can't you get over *anything*? Why do you have to lock yourself up here, just because things haven't gone the way you wanted?" All this time he'd been waiting for his next move to be revealed to him; here was the point of all his lies and lists. "I'm taking you home," he said. As if this was what he'd always meant to do. "As soon as the season is right."

LINNAEUS WROTE AGAIN:

Last week they went to Washington, to attend the ceremony at the Smithsonian; the collections of the Exploring Expedition have all been arranged in the Great Hall, and with them Annie's skeleton in a central display case. Zeke was given some sort of award but I don't know the details. Humboldt and I and our families are fine and we hope you are too, but I wish I didn't have to lie to everyone.

Zeke knows you didn't arrive in Liverpool, but no more than that—I don't think he <u>wants</u> to know more. After he contacted the police, he figured out that it cast a bad light on him and Lavinia if you were suspected of wrongdoing. Now he or someone else has started a rumor that Tom, ungrateful boy, has signed on as a cabin boy on a merchant ship. But really no one is interested in Tom's fate anymore. Everyone is talking, instead, about Zeke's book.

The bookshops sport great stacks of The Voyage of the Narwhal. At a dinner at the Laurens' last week a woman bent toward me and, with great seriousness, began describing the differences between the Arctic Highlanders and the Netsilik, just as if she knew what she was talking about. I have to tell you it's a most interesting work—vivid, well-written, full of adventures. Are you surprised to hear you play a very minor role in it? As do your shipmates. Captain Tyler, Mr. Tagliabeau, Robert Carey and Sean Hamilton visited the city briefly, to settle some question of wages with Zeke's father. They aren't happy with the way Zeke portrayed them but said it's no more than what they expected. When I told them you'd sailed for England they asked me to thank you for forwarding the letters to their families and to tell you they bear you no grudge—they profited from their sealing voyage and leave soon on another whaling ship. Also they said you'd want to know that the Greenlander called Joe is in Denmark, preparing reports for the missionary society and writing something about the Anoatok Esquimaux and their folktales. Is everyone writing a book?

Lavinia hardly speaks to me or Humboldt and I think is very unhappy. Zeke's father is having financial troubles and had to give up his plans to build them a house; and although Zeke should make plenty from his book there are apparently some debts we didn't know about. If I hear from you, she says, if I have a way to contact you—how awkward this is!—would I ask if you would consider letting her continue living in your house for the next year or two, or until you return: when are you returning? "Remind him of what he gave me when I was ten," she says, which I hope means more to you than it does to me. She knows we don't *like Zeke but reminds me that she loves him. What does she mean by love, I wonder?*

ERASMUS MADE ARRANGEMENTS. There would be no special ship this time, no provisions to arrange, no men to interview. After several inquiries he settled on a reliable whaling firm in New London, and a captain whose ship was due to leave mid-May and who didn't mind conveying paying passengers to Godhavn. The rest of the journey he must make on his own, but he'd settle the details in Greenland. Annie was gone; he couldn't bring her family her bones and couldn't imagine how he'd explain this failure. But he could return Tom to them. One last chance; he understood his luck. He wrote to Linnaeus, giving Lavinia permission to stay in the house indefinitely. His father's house; their father's house. On the ice, before everything had changed, he'd once built a model of it—and that was how it now existed in his mind. A small thing, blank-windowed and closed and cold. Let her stay there with Zeke.

He sat down with Copernicus. From the beginning Copernicus had refused to commit himself beyond the next week or month: one painting at a time, he'd said. He'd finish as many as he could. Still Erasmus had hoped he could convince Copernicus to come north. "If you could see it for yourself," he said. "The ice, the light, Tom's people in their own place . . ."

"It's not what I want," Copernicus said, startling him.

In the room's farthest corner, so absorbed in drawing bowhead whale that the men might have assumed she wasn't listening, Alexandra made a dark stroke she hadn't intended and then bit her lip. Of course Copernicus would go, it was his nature always to be going somewhere. His luck to be offered all the chances. Almost she rose, so the brothers could talk privately. Ned came into the room with a muskrat skin and paused as he heard the discussion; when Copernicus gestured for him to stay, Alexandra kept her place as well.

"I know it's hard to understand," Copernicus said. "But I can't take in one more thing. The West is still in my eyes, and the visions of the arctic you gave me, and now these mountains—this is an amazing place. As wild as the West, in certain ways, and changing so quickly—I could paint for the rest of my life and never get it all down. I'll finish what I can before you go, but I have to capture what's *here* as well."

"Are you sure?" Erasmus said. When they were boys, he remembered, a delegation of Indian chiefs had paraded through Philadelphia on their way to Washington. Even then, Copernicus had flown to his notebook and captured their spirits on paper. "Tom and I could use your help."

"I know," Copernicus said. "And I'd love to see those places for myself someday. But I'm here now, and my eyes are full. I have to get this place down while I can. Ned's going to help me."

Who would help her? Alexandra wondered. Never Copernicus, or not more than he already had. He might believe he was staying here in these mountains, but soon he'd be wandering again, alone again. She turned her gaze from him and back to her work. Erasmus turned as well, not toward her—she felt as invisible, among their swirl of plans, as Lavinia had once felt among her brothers—but toward Ned.

"I was wondering if you might like to come with *us*," Erasmus said to his old companion. "With me." His left foot throbbed and he reached down to rub it.

"I'm going to be Copernicus's guide," Ned said. "I can take him down the rivers and through the lakes, and we'll make camps in the woods. I know the area well. He'll paint. I'll hunt and cook. It will be good for both of us."

He didn't say that Copernicus had offered him a higher wage than he received at the hotel; nor that he had a plan of his own.

He'd saved some money and meant to save more. As they traveled the mountains, he hoped to find a site suitable for a small hotel of his own. A resort, not just for hunters but for their families, where there might be healthful outdoor recreations and indoor comforts. Where a fleet of guide boats might glide like gondolas up to sturdy docks, and take those who were adventurous, but not so strong or skilled, down the braided streams. On the side, he thought, he might establish a small taxidermy firm.

"I've always tried to help you," he said to Erasmus.

"You've been a huge help," Erasmus agreed. He tried to smile, he tried to show his gratitude. On the *Narwhal*, he remembered, Zeke had asked for company on his last trip north and been refused. Had that felt like this? To Ned he said, "After all you've done—you must do what *you* want."

Through the winter Ned had been plagued by a dream, which he kept to himself. In it he and Zeke and Dr. Boerhaave were lost again among the maze of pressure ridges. Dwarfed by the treacherous heaps of ice they spun in circles, chopping passageways only to discover their own tracks on the far side. Cold and hungry and weak, then weaker, they climbed and fell, burrowed and heaved, and never got anywhere. The dream was endless and without resolution; its only saving grace the fact that in it, the moment never arrived when Dr. Boerhaave slipped beneath the ice. Now he looked into his surviving friend's eyes.

"I can never repay you," he said. "For all you've taught me. But when we got back from the North, I swore I'd never set foot on a ship again." He stretched the muskrat pelt in his hands, turning the fur side toward Erasmus. "Tom asked me for this," he said. "Is that all right?"

"Of course," Erasmus said absently. As Ned ducked into Tom's room, Copernicus said, "I feel a bit like him."

"Like Ned?"

"I've traveled too much already."

Alexandra crosshatched a shadow. Imagine being able to say that, she thought. *Too much*; when all she'd ever felt was *Not enough*. He was wrong about himself, he'd always be in motion. No woman would ever hold him more than briefly. In the village, she knew, the shopkeeper's daughter slipped from her family's home late at night to meet Copernicus in the woods. Because he never brought her to this house, they all pretended it wasn't happening.

"I need to stay put," Copernicus continued. "I need to *work*. It's wonderful that you're going, though. And not just because of what you're doing for Tom. It will help the book."

"Will it?" Erasmus asked. He'd almost grown resigned to the idea that he couldn't finish it before he left. Alexandra's drawings were nearly complete, strong and accurate; the paintings were like windows onto the world he'd once glimpsed and he'd be happy with whatever number Copernicus finished. But the text itself was missing something. As he thought this Alexandra, so quiet while they talked, rose and slipped out the back door and into the sheltering trees.

"People live there, along with the plants and animals," Copernicus said. "If you could bring their way of life into the narrative . . ."

Erasmus wrote the firm in New London, letting the captain know he'd need only two berths; while he waited for his sailing date he packed and made lists and mused over Copernicus's advice. *Carl Linnaeus*, their father had said, *proposed a separate species of man, possessed of a tail and inhabiting the antarctic regions.* Erasmus had seen for himself that no one, tailless or otherwise, lived near the South Pole. *Beyond the north wind live the Hyperboreans.* Those he'd seen, but hadn't seen clearly. He felt, still, that he'd been right to leave himself out of the story; he was a minor character after all. Not just in Zeke's story, but in the stories of Ned and Annie and Tom, even Copernicus and Alexandra—he was only the wave that rocked the boat. Yet he'd omitted from his book not just himself, but the Esquimaux.

Observing people wasn't his business; even on the Exploring Expedition, the work of the linguists and anthropologists had made him uneasy. Instead he'd cultivated a kind of reserve. He had not, like Zeke, invaded an Esquimaux tribe; he hadn't, as had his dear Dr. Boerhaave, tried to record their way of life before it vanished. Thinking himself virtuous, he'd averted his eyes and studied the plants and animals instead.

But perhaps he'd simply been afraid? As if, by not passing judgment on the people he saw, he'd hoped to avoid having anyone pass judgment on him. The best thing might be never to visit such places—but he *had* visited, the damage was done; and he had to visit again. When he returned Tom to his family, he might watch everyone. Women, patiently scraping and chewing skins. Men with feet encased in bears' paws, bent over a seal's breathing hole; children swooping nets through clouds of dovekies. He might talk to them. Would they talk to him?

ON APRIL 26, late at night, Alexandra walked into his room. Twenty-two buttons down the front of her gray dress; she unfastened the first six, as simply as if she were shedding her dress for her painter's smock. Erasmus undid the rest. The first sight of her bare shoulders struck him like his first sight of the ice—how could he have forgotten that? He ran his thumb along her collarbones. Never would he forget this. He was leaving soon; she might be staying here or going somewhere new; she hadn't revealed her plans. Perhaps, as she'd told her family, she might be a teacher. Against her thighs, under her hands, with her tongue touching the base of his neck, Erasmus felt his life pulsing and streaming. Up north, when he was lonely, he could unfold this night against the sky. He wound Alexandra's hair around his palm and pulled it like a curtain over his eyes. Alexandra thought with surprise: *Oh, it was this.* This pleasure that bound Lavinia to Zeke, no matter what.

Later that night Erasmus gave Alexandra the little slab of screw-studded leather, which he'd carried all the way from Boothia and failed to share with his first friend. He opened his hand, he released it. She rested the sole on her bare stomach, with the metal points touching her weightlessly. How delicious, the contrast between the cool metal and his warm hand.

"It's for you," he said. "Something to remember me by."

She walked the points up her skin. She'd meant to enter this room weeks ago, as she'd also meant to make, separately, another request. Two different things, one not necessarily linked to the other. But she'd waited too long and now everything was happening at once. If she waited longer, though, she'd lose it all. "Take me with you," she said. "Instead of Copernicus."

Erasmus was silent. Once she'd pried him out of his desolation by pretending to need his company at the Academy of Sciences. Not for months had he understood what she'd done. "I'm so glad you're here," he said finally. "This—us together like this—I've wanted this for a long time. But you don't have to feel *bound* by it. I promise I'll be back. And if you happen to still be free then . . ."

She sat up impatiently and pressed the scrap of leather back into his hand. "I *want* to go," she said. "Don't you understand? It's what I've always wanted. When you were gone I read Parry's journals out loud to Lavinia, all the time wishing I could be where you were. And since you returned and we started work on this book . . . I want to *see*. I want to travel, I want to see everything."

A strand of her hair wound down her neck, across her left breast, unfurling over her ribs. Lovely, lovely. He gazed at her, then down at the graying hair on his own chest. "*Look at me*," she said. "I didn't come here to try to trick you into taking me, or shame you, or anything else. I wanted this, to touch you like this—but that's something different from wanting to go north."

She bent her knee, placing his hand above it on the inside of her thigh. "Any terms," she said. "You choose the terms. If you don't want us to be . . . to be together like this, we don't have to. I'll go as your assistant, your friend. Anything."

IN THE ROOM they shared for those last few weeks, Alexandra moved one hand along the curve of Erasmus's ribs. Next door, she heard Tom rustling in his bed. All the time they'd wasted—they might have made their way to each other months ago, but only when Tom had cracked a channel in Erasmus's heart could she sail in. Of course she would take care of Tom, she owed him everything. They would marry, they'd agreed, before the ship sailed.

"What are you thinking about?" she asked.

"How slow I am," he said.

Outside their door Copernicus painted. An extra painting, not one they'd planned—but the story Erasmus had told him months ago, about the underwater world he'd glimpsed when he fell through the ice, had suddenly seized him. He was anxious to finish, so he could begin painting the mountains around him. But for the moment he focused purely on the layer of ice, white on top then darkening to green and gray, lit by rays of sun pouring through a giant crack.

"How slow to make crucial decisions," Erasmus said. "To sense what's going on around me. I think how long it took me to understand Zeke, how I almost missed being friends with Dr. Boerhaave, how Ned had to force me to lead the men from the *Narwhal*."

The bottom of the ice was covered by a rich field of algae, on which infant fish and small crustaceans grazed. Three belugas, glowing and pale, occupied the lower left corner; a walrus, hanging vertically with its flippers swaying, was just about to surface. There were schools of capelin and swarms of jellyfish; murres he'd caught flying through the water. Copernicus pushed the stepladder to the right, so he could work on the narwhal whose tapered horn skimmed the walrus's flippers.

"How I was too late to save Annie," Erasmus said.

"Zeke moves quickly," Alexandra said. "Do you want to be like him?" She touched his chest.

"I almost missed *you*," Erasmus said. The gentle rasp of Copernicus's ladder against the floor was the sound that sent both them and Tom to sleep.

Tom dreamed a darker version of the scene Copernicus painted. The same ice, humped and shattered, but twilight rather than streaming sun; cold October rather than brilliant July. He dreamed a scene that preceded Zeke, at first as if he were dreaming simple history. His mother's brother left the camp with his sledge and six dogs, hoping to hunt seal on the thickening sea ice although the weather was bad. He left and didn't return. In Tom's dream, as in real life, a fog arose, and a terrible wind, which trapped them in their huts. When they were able to search for the lost hunter, they followed the tracks of the sledge until they vanished. In the moonlight a round area of new ice, surrounded by broken blocks, marked where the hunter had fallen through. The men chopped through it, widened the hole, and prepared the lines and harpoons and the sturdy bone hooks.

In his dream, Tom was no longer a small boy watching, but one of the men. In his arms he felt the pull of the line, and the gentle shudder of the hook as it bumped against something and then caught. In his back he felt the weight as he joined with the others, pulling up first the sledge and then, one by one, the dogs still tangled in their traces. On the traces he saw the marks of their teeth, where they'd tried to free themselves. Laid head to head on the ice, the dogs froze solid instantly. His hands grew numb as he coiled the line and sent the hook back into the water.

In his dream he could see everything, all he'd only been able to imagine when it happened; beneath the ice he saw the hook touch a booted leg. As if it were alive, the hook bounced three times along the leg and then caught the ankle. Gently, gently. He was the hook; he was the line; he was the strong body above, pulling delicately. He was the woman wailing as the boot broke the surface of the water, and he was the man watching as the body was born, feet first, from the sea. Feet, legs, hands, chest, head. The mouth was open in a terrible grimace, the fingernails broken where they'd clawed the edges of the hole. The body, laid out on the ice, glazed and stiffened and turned pure white. Tom bent over the face and saw not his uncle, but Zeke.

The sight jolted him awake; around him were only walls. At the foot of his bed lay the cache of bones and the muskrat pelt that would someday be his *tupilaq*. He turned so his head was near them. The place he had fled, and would never return to again, was called Philadelphia; and in that place, unaware of his fate, Zeke was sleeping. The sunny, golden length of him sprawled across the sheets, one arm almost touching the floor, one foot sticking off the mattress, bobbing as he dreamed of Annie.

Not Annie as she'd been in this house; not Annie as she'd been in Washington; not, not of her skeleton gleaming through a glass display case. But Annie as she'd been in Anoatok, utterly strange and utterly herself. She was smiling at him beneath a bird-filled sky. The life he'd lived with her and her family was the life Erasmus's father had taught him to seek; his dream shifted and he was part of that family, the true son, the son Mr. Wells had always wanted. The four sons of his body were only boys, listening wide-eyed to tales of bees brought back to life when covered by a fresh-killed ox's stomach. None of them had understood, as Zeke had, that those tales were natural history and not science. Surely that was what Mr. Wells had meant to teach him?

A FEW MORE times, in the drafty house, the four companions slept and woke. Then they were gone. Into the woods went Copernicus, easel and paintbox strapped to his back and Ned at his side: just for the summer, he said, just for the brief months of buttery, tree-filtered light. Erasmus and Tom and Alexandra set off for the coast. Later that summer, they'd learn that McClintock's *Fox* had been caught in the ice of Melville Bay during their own winter in the mountains. Swept twelve hundred miles south in the moving pack, the *Fox* had started north again as soon as the ice released it—headed, Erasmus knew, for exactly the place he and Zeke had explored. He guessed McClintock's crew would meet the same or similar Esquimaux and find their way to King William Land as he and Zeke had not. Driving a sledge bearing a red silk banner embroidered by Lady Franklin herself, they'd find relics and bodies and evidence, returning to the glory that might have been his.

But by the time all this happened, he wouldn't care. He'd be in Greenland, after an easy trip during which no disasters happened and no one died. A Scottish whaling ship ferried the three of them from Godhavn to Upernavik; after that came a Danish fishing boat, and then a skin-covered *umiak*. They had little luggage, and weren't much trouble. Past cliffs and glaciers and low gravel beaches strangers guided them: *where the geese nest; where the goblins hide; where the ice cave grows beneath the ledge.*

Erasmus took no notes: he would do that later. Beside him, though, Alexandra drew in a larger version of the black-bound notebooks she'd been filling since she was a girl. The sights she saw resembled those she'd first glimpsed in Erasmus's green journal and then reconstructed with his guidance: and were also completely different. She lay on gray rocks, eyes level with a tuft of tiny, bladder-shaped blossoms. In Philadelphia she'd drawn these twenty times but only now saw what Erasmus hadn't captured: each flower was really a calyx, inflated and striped and deceptive; the true petals were hidden inside. The stems, the texture of the rock, the ice, the sky, the streaming clouds—they looked one way to Erasmus, another way to her. Also—*also*, she thought, *it was everything*—they were themselves.

Erasmus watched her draw. Nothing she rendered was new to him, yet each stroke of her pencil—he had bought her special pencils, Dr. Boerhaave's pencils—was like a chisel held to a cleavage plane: tap, tap, and the rock split into two sharp pieces, the world cracked and spoke to him. Annie spoke to him each time it rained, Dr. Boerhaave when the wind blew; Tom was silent much of the time but Erasmus could hear the language of his body as he strengthened and straightened and breathed the air and ate the food he'd missed.

They found Tom's people late in August. Against the hills beyond Anoatok were two-legged dots, four-legged dots, which Tom was the first to spot. He ran up the rocky shore, Alexandra and Erasmus following more slowly but still steadily: Erasmus had grown used to his feet and regained his balance, casting aside his walking sticks for a single ball-headed cane. As he approached the dots turned into figures, and faces appeared. Among that small crowd moving toward him were Tom's father—which one was he?—and men who'd hunted and talked with Dr. Boerhaave. A tall man in a worn fur jacket stumbled forward, stretched out a hand, pressed Tom to his chest and then lifted him into the air.

Sometime later, the people moved toward Erasmus and Alexandra, and Tom made introductions: Ootuniah, Awahtok, and the three other young men whom Erasmus remembered visiting the *Narwhal*; Nessark, Tom's father, who had known both Dr. Boerhaave and Zeke; the *angekok*, who wore around his neck a thong strung with long teeth. A few more men and then, behind them, shy women and children. Alexandra took four steps and stood among them, bending so the children could touch her hair. One of the women touched the back of her hand and she turned it, offering her palm; the woman rested three fingers there. Erasmus felt that touch in his own hand but he kept his gaze on the men before him, repeating each name, burning each face into his mind. When it was time, speaking slowly, waiting after each phrase for Tom to repeat the words in a language he was just beginning to grasp, Erasmus explained to them what he knew of Annie's death.

As he spoke Nessark clasped his son's shoulders, nodding but saying nothing, looking down when Tom continued to speak for some time after Erasmus had stopped. Two geese flew by, and a swarm of murres. The *angekok* stepped forward to speak for Nessark and the rest of the tribe but for a moment said nothing at all; only the birds' thrumming wings broke the silence. Erasmus lowered his eyes and waited. He would be judged now, he thought. Alexandra's presence by his side had altered every other aspect of this final journey, but she couldn't spare him this. He might not be forgiven. He looked up again and caught the *angekok*'s stern gaze. When he spoke, Erasmus could hear in the words only the sound of running water and an echo of the wing beats.

The *angekok* paused so Tom could translate. They did not blame Erasmus for the loss of their sister's body, Tom said. *Their sister*, Erasmus thought, looking from the boy to his judge and back. *Tom's mother*. He would never be Tom again, that had never been his name; to which of those syllables did he answer? He himself, the *angekok* said, had determined that the tribe should guide Zeke out of their country; and he had permitted their sister and her son to leave them. His fault. His left hand folded around the teeth swaying on his chest. On her voyage of discovery, he said, she had been betrayed; when the poison took hold she had left her bones, so that she might save her son. The *angekok* pointed toward Erasmus's feet—so small, he said. Who had taken the rest? He gave Alexandra an *ulo* and Erasmus an amulet of little bone knives, with which to cut through bad weather.

Still later the *angekok*, after speaking with the boy, led him down the shore and across the worn floes leaning against each other like drunken soldiers. At the water's edge the boy handed over his collection. A skin laid flat against the ice, a bone laid here and another there; the *angekok* folded the pelt around the ill-sorted shards, chanting as he tied the bundle with a thong.

A few years later, as Zeke floated in the Rappahannock River, his face and chest above the blood-ribboned water, his shoulders bumping the hundreds of men who struggled, like him, to cross to the other side, something like a muskrat would brush his hands and Copernicus—drawn by the chaos, drawn by the wounds, always in movement but that day painting furiously on that bank—would see those dark shapes intertwine and wonder what they were. A war would have started by then, obscuring the arctic in people's minds as if it were no more than legend: *here are the hinges on which the world turns and the limits of the circuits of the stars.*

But for the moment Erasmus and Alexandra stood on the shore, peering down at the water as the boy who had led them here knelt and slipped the bundle in.

Author's Note
and Acknowledgments

Most of the background characters in this novel—including Titian Peale, Charles Wilkes, John Rae, John Richardson, Elisha Kent Kane, Sir John Franklin and his crew, Louis Agassiz, Samuel Morton and the other naturalists and philosophers mentioned, as well as Ootuniah, Awahtok, Nessark, and the other Smith Sound Inuit who befriended Dr. Kane—are historical persons. The foreground characters—including Zechariah Voorhees, Erasmus Wells, Alexandra Copeland and their families, as well as Dr. Boerhaave, Ned Kynd, the crews of the *Narwhal* and the other ships mentioned, and Annie and Tom—are invented.

I'm indebted to the journals and memoirs of many nineteenth-century arctic explorers, particularly those of George Back, John Barrow, Edward Belcher, Alexander Fisher, John Franklin, William Godfrey, Charles Francis Hall, Isaac Hayes, Elisha Kent Kane,

William Kennedy, George Lyon, Francis McClintock, Robert McClure, Sherard Osborn, William Edward Parry, Julius von Payer, John Rae, John Richardson, James Clark Ross, John Ross, Edward Sabine, Frederick Schwatka, William Scoresby, and Thomas Simpson.

Also helpful were many more recent books about the arctic in the nineteenth and twentieth centuries, especially Pierre Berton's *The Arctic Grail*, George Corner's *Dr. Kane of the Arctic Seas,* Richard Cyriax's *Sir John Franklin's Last Arctic Expedition*, Ernest Dodge's *The Polar Rosses,* Peter Freuchen's *The Arctic Year* and *Book of the Eskimos,* Sam Hall's *The Fourth World,* Chauncey Loomis's *Weird and Tragic Shores*, Barry Lopez's *Arctic Dreams*, Jeannette Mirsky's *To the Arctic,* Vilhjalmur Stefansson's *Arctic Manual*, and Doug Wilkinson's *Land of the Long Day*.

Anthropological and ethnological works by Asen Balikci, Franz Boas, Jean Malaurie, Samuel Morton, Richard Nelson, Gontran de Poncins, and Knud Rasmussen; William Elder's *Biography of Elisha Kent Kane*; Matthew Maury's *The Physical Geography of the Sea*; William Rhees's *An Account of The Smithsonian Institution, Its Founder, Building, Operations, Etc.*; W. J. Holland's *Taxidermy and Zoological Collecting*; and George Glidden and J. C. Nott's *Types of Mankind* provided other useful background. Stephen Jay Gould's *The Mismeasure of Man* steered me toward the work of Nott and Glidden; William Goetzmann's *New Lands, New Men: America and the Second Great Age of Discovery* provided initial information about the Exploring Expedition. The lines Erasmus Wells remembers his father reading to him are paraphrased from Pliny the Elder's *Natural History*.

I'm indebted to the Macdowell Colony, where I wrote the first lines of this novel; and to the Guggenheim Foundation, for a fellowship that enabled me to complete it. My thanks as well to Dave Reid, Charlie Innuaraq, Mathias Qaunaq, Limach Kadloo, and Joelie Aulaqiak of Pond Inlet, for showing me the beauties of the floe edge. Douglas M. Orr Jr. introduced me to the ballad "Lady Franklin's Lament"; Mark Sawin, of the University of Texas at Austin, shared with me both the bibliography of his research into the life of Elisha Kent Kane and his excellent master's thesis, "Raising Kane: The Making of a Hero, the Marketing of a Celebrity" (1997).

Wendy Weil and Carol Houck Smith offered constant support and the best kind of criticism; their help was invaluable. Peter

Landesman's thorough, perceptive comments guided me through the final draft. Without Margot Livesey, who was with me throughout the entire voyage, there would have been, as always, no book at all: my deepest thanks.

NOTE ON THE
ILLUSTRATIONS

The decorations at the beginning of each section and chapter are copies of engravings from G. Hartwig's *The Polar and Tropical Worlds* and from W. J. Holland's *Taxidermy and Zoological Collecting*. The two-page advertisement for Dr. Kane's *Arctic Explorations* in the chapter "Toodlamik, Skin and Bones" is reproduced from William Elder's *Biography of Elisha Kent Kane*. The engraving on the title page is from Francis McClintock's *The Voyage of the* Fox *in the Arctic Seas*.

'A delightful and surprisingly touching novel. The plot is high-spirited, enjoyable nonsense – rather like Wilkie Collins crossed with Nancy Mitford . . . But this literary bagatelle has unexpected depth and emotional resonance. It is written with winning and warming affection . . . it is both frothy and unexpectedly emotionally powerful'
Caroline Moore, *Sunday Telegraph*

'A dispassionate, yet affectionate study of the country-house, *Upstairs Downstairs* set-up whose death knell was sounded by the Second World War . . . Teresa Waugh brilliantly evokes the hermetically sealed world of the village estate, where the postmistress listens to everyone's telephone conversations, an umbrella is an object worthy of retrieval when mislaid and Annie can't imagine anywhere without elms'
Jane Charteris, *Literary Review*

'*The House* is beguiling and astringent, a celebration not a lament'
Matthew Dennison, *Country Life*

'Teresa Waugh introduces us to the rougher side of country house living at the end of the second world war . . . Within the powerful framework of *The House* an odd, sinister story is told through the diaries and letters of four of the six characters . . . It's a compulsive read and very funny'   Clayre Percy, *Spectator*

'A superb comic melodrama unfolds through the diaries and letters of four main characters'   Val Hennessy, *Daily Mail*

Teresa Waugh was born in 1940. This is her eighth novel, and she has translated numerous books from French and Italian. She lives in Somerset and was married to the late Auberon Waugh.

By Teresa Waugh

The House
A Friend Like Harvey
The Gossips
Sylvia's Lot
Song at Twilight
An Intolerable Burden
Waterloo, Waterloo
Painting Water

THE HOUSE
A NOVEL

Teresa Waugh

PHOENIX

A PHOENIX PAPERBACK

First published in Great Britain in 2002
by Weidenfeld & Nicolson
This paperback edition published in 2003
by Phoenix,
an imprint of Orion Books Ltd,
Orion House, 5 Upper St Martin's Lane,
London WC2H 9EA

Second impression 2003

A CIP catalogue record for this book
is available from the British Library.

ISBN 0 75381 722 5

Printed and bound in Great Britain by
Clays Ltd, St Ives plc

For Michael and Alistair

1945

Sydney Otterton's diary

Yesterday afternoon we buried my father in the awful family vault. There aren't many places left in it – one for myself and a couple more. All Priscilla says is, 'Don't you dare put me in that frightful place.' I think she despises my family and wouldn't want to be buried with them, which isn't altogether surprising, considering the way my dreadful mother has treated her. Then we all drank rather a lot and when I went to bed I dreamt I was back in the Western Desert.

In my dream it was as though I were in some safe haven, yet missing the excitement of a line of German shells bursting only thirty or forty yards away, missing the beauty of the desert and missing my comrades in arms. On waking, I was reminded of a time on leave in Cairo when four of us had smartened ourselves up and gone out on the town, initially full of high spirits, only to find them soon flagging. That night none of us slept and, on comparing notes in the morning, we discovered that we had all been kept awake by thoughts of the desert, of its incredible beauty, and by visions of tanks and armoured cars and all the heroic and sordid incidents of battle. We were not used to being safe. Waking this morning, I thought long and hard about what we had all been through only so very recently – North Africa, Italy, Normandy – and I wondered how any of us would ever manage to settle back into anything like a normal existence. I know that for a long time to come I will miss the thrill of war and the companionship it brings. Nothing will ever be quite like it again.

Back in the safety of England, I was hardly expecting my father to die so suddenly. After all, he was still comparatively young. My first reaction was one of irritation; it was inconvenient of him to die now, just when I was hoping to be selected to stand for Parliament and so to start a new life. Perhaps I am anaesthetised by war, but I feel quite indifferent to his passing. I have seen so many young men die, that the death in his mid-sixties of my father, with whom, in any case, I never got on particularly well – my mother saw to that – leaves me quite unaffected. But at least it means that *she* won't go back to the house. It will be Priscilla's and mine and we will be able to move in with the children and make it our own safe haven.

Mind you, we'll probably need a haven if the Bolsheviks get in – which most people seem to think they will. Even Priscilla says she's going to vote for them. As for me – if I go into politics now, it'll have to be the House of Lords.

It's funny how often I thought of Cranfield when I was abroad, especially during those last months in gaol in Germany. I used to play games in my mind, counting the rooms and imagining that there was one I had never discovered which was always somewhere between the white stairs and the West Room. Like it or not, a house like Cranfield Park works its way into one's system; it can't fail to become a part of one, regardless of whether or not one has been happy there. As it is, it was built by an Otterton, back in 1730 – admittedly with a Jamaican heiress's money. I don't doubt he married her for her dowry and probably made her very unhappy. She died young and they say her ghost haunts the house. Perhaps she lives in that undiscovered room between the white stairs and the West Room, pacing up and down from dawn to dusk.

JUNE 25TH

There's no damn money and Priscilla isn't sure she wants to live in the house. She says we can't afford to and that it reminds her of my parents. I'm having nightmares every night about my mother, the war, money, ghosts, undiscovered rooms. You name it.

I'm sure I will be able to persuade Priscilla to change her mind in the end. She will grow to love the house. I know she will. I will make her. Of course she can't see it the way I do and keeps complaining about the mess. She says it's full of junk and that my parents had no taste. I've told her she can do what she likes with it when we move in, arrange it as she pleases. She just says that the war has changed everything and that anyway the house is too big. Of course the bloody thing's big but I have no intention of spending the rest of my life in a cottage.

As soon as all the public records which have been stored there for the duration of the war have been taken back to Chancery Lane or wherever they belong, I'll get Priscilla to come round the house with me again. It'll look different then – and better. She's quite right about the place being full of junk – things which have been accumulating for generations. We'll have to sort it all out somehow and store away what we don't need. It's not as if there weren't plenty of room.

I bought a golden Labrador puppy this afternoon. She's called Peggy. Priscilla was rather annoyed, but the children are pleased.

JULY 5TH

My mother, thank God, has announced that she intends to go and live abroad. She doesn't say where, but I should imagine she ought to be ashamed to show her face round here after the way she has manipulated my father into leaving all his free money to her. No doubt she would have got the house too and the farm in Essex if they hadn't been entailed and then she would certainly have ended up leaving the whole lot to a cats' home.

Peggy is making quite a nuisance of herself, chewing up everything in sight. Priscilla is still unwilling to commit herself to moving into the house. I told her that Peggy wouldn't be so much under her feet there. Anyway, I mean to send the puppy down to the keeper's cottage and get Summers to train her.

Letter from Annie to her sister, Dolly

JULY 6TH, 1945

Dear Dolly,

Thank you for your letter. I'm sorry I have been so long in writing, but what with one thing and another I have been very busy. What with the relief of the war being over and now that her son is safely back, Mrs Gower has got all sort of plans. We've been spring cleaning the house from top to bottom and turning out all the cupboards.

I went home last week-end. Father was his usual self and very pleased to see me, but I think he misses you all, not that he complains. You know Father.

Now listen to this. While I was there the new Lord Otterton came to see me. It was at about six o'clock on Saturday evening. I have to say that I had a feeling he would be around before long. Anyway he must have heard that I was home for a few days. Father was down at the milking shed and I was ironing a few of his shirts when there was a knock on the kitchen door. Mister Sydney (as was) always comes round to the back door. I don't doubt you can picture him. He had this naughty little puppy with him which came straight in and made a huge puddle right by my feet. His Lordship just laughed and said, 'I want to talk to you Annie,' then he started on about his father dying and the house and his mother. He was going on alarming about his mother, calling her every name under the sun. I didn't say a thing, mind, but you can hardly blame him. No one's got a good word to say for her. I reckon his late Lordship is well out of it. It seems that the new Lady Otterton will only move into the house if I go with them. I told his Lordship that I'd have to think about it, but I could see he was full bent on persuading me. He's never been one to take no for an answer. To tell the truth, I can't quite make up my mind what to do. I'm supposed to return to Mrs Gower's on Sunday. Although I would like to come back here eventually, I don't want to leave the Gowers suddenly and neither did I really mean to leave so soon. I've been with them a long time and they've been good to me. I didn't mention anything to Father when he came in from milking. I wonder what you think? Then, of course, there's always Bert to consider too.

I hope Fred and the children are keeping well.

Love from
Annie

Sydney Otterton's diary

I saw Annie at the week-end. If only she would move into the house with us, I feel everything would be all right. It's just a question of persuading her to leave those wretched Gowers. I've always been fond of Annie ever since I was a boy when I used to play down at the farm with her brothers and sisters. I'm sure Priscilla likes her too and I think that if she agreed to come, it would make all the difference. When I saw her she was ironing Jerrold's shirts and wouldn't give me an answer, but just giggled and said 'We'll see.'

7

Letter from Dolly to Annie

Dear Annie,

Just a quick reply to your letter. I think the idea of your going to live at Cranfield is very exciting and it would be lovely for Father to have you nearby. But don't do anything too hasty, you know you have been with the Gowers for a long time. It's a decent job and you have been lucky to be with such good people. Then of course there's Bert to worry about! But that's up to you! To tell the truth, Fred and I never really thought that Bert was good enough for you.

Fred and I were thinking that if you do go to Cranfield, you ought to keep a diary about the goings on at the house. The *servant's*-eye view! We enjoy all your letters and read them over again. When all's said and done, you always were the bookish one and the one who should have stayed at school. I expect you would have done too, if Mother hadn't died and left you with the rest of us to look after. Who knows, your diaries could make you a fortune one day! And you could become a famous writer!

Fred and the children are well. Little Fred is growing up so fast that he's always hungry and it's sometimes difficult in these hard times, what with rationing, to give him enough to eat.

I enclose a letter for you to pass to Father to save on the postage. Let us know when you have decided what to do.

Love from
Dolly

Annie's diary

Fancy Dolly thinking I should keep a diary! Well, to tell the truth, it won't be the first time, not that I ever managed to keep it up for very long before. I can't get the house out of my mind. Why the house, I wonder, when I might be expected to be thinking of Bert or Father? I know Father would like me back at Cranfield Park to be near him as I'm the one he's always relied on since Mother died and am really the one who replaced her. Besides, he's very much alone now the others are all married. But it's not Father, it's the house that I keep thinking of, and the idea of living there, upstairs on the top floor I presume. Perhaps my room will look out over the copper beech avenue, down towards the farm where I grew up and where Father still lives. We used to go into the house at Christmas time only, when there was always an enormous tree in that huge marble hall with presents for everyone on the estate. Something for the children and a bottle of port for Father. I used to wonder what the rest of the house was like and I still do. I suppose it must be ever so grand inside, but cold, I should think. The girls that worked there always thought it rather frightening, but that could be because of her Ladyship. They say she drugs herself and shuts herself away in a darkened bedroom all day, shouting at anyone who crosses her. She and his late Lordship moved out during the war and lived in what they called the Dower House. She's still there now although they say she's going away soon which I should think will be a relief for everyone. She hardly ever goes out, but I have seen her from time to time stalking around the place, striding by with a long, forked stick, her pointed face as white as death and looking through you as if you were nothing. And when his Lordship was alive, they said he was afraid of her. No wonder Mr Sydney carries on so about her.

The house is very big indeed and none of my sisters has ever wanted to work there. They say they think it is haunted and they'd be frightened to live in. I see it differently. It's rather like the centre of our small world, the centre of everything we have known since childhood, a place full of mystery that draws you to it despite all the unhappiness that has gone on inside and despite its imposing, even forbidding front. I can imagine a kind of independent life there. I would have a big room, and if Lord and Lady Otterton really need me so badly, I'm sure I would be able to do things my own way without any difficulty.

To go back to Bert, the trouble with him is the usual thing of course. He wants me to marry him. But I'm certainly not going to do that and end up spending the rest of my life in a horrid little tied cottage with an outside w.c. and rising damp in the kitchen. No fear. He thinks I must want children by my age, and I do love children, mind, but what he doesn't understand is that I spent my youth bringing up my brothers and sisters after Mother died and I don't want to be doing all that again. And Bert, well, he's nice enough but he's a rogue really. A bit of fun, but a rogue. Not half as good-looking or as hard-working as Father. My father is one of nature's gentlemen.

Sydney Otterton's diary

Nobody can think of anything except the results of the election, which we won't in any case know until next week by which time they say they should have collected all the armed forces' votes from abroad. Priscilla carried out her threat to vote Labour because, she says, she really believes they will do something about housing and unemployment. She seems to be beguiled by the popular phrase, 'Labour can deliver the goods.' She must have been reading the *Manchester Guardian*. Anyway, it rather looks as if the Bolshies will have carried the day, although some people still seem to think that Winston could get back in with a majority of as much as eighty.

I still haven't heard from Annie about whether or not she'll work for us, although I think I've persuaded her, but she may have cold feet about telling the Gowers she wants to leave. I saw Jerrold this morning down at the farm and he said she would be coming home again at the week-end, so I'll look in and see her then. I've already told Priscilla that she *is* prepared to come, so I hope she won't let me down. Priscilla definitely does like Annie very much (I've verified that) and is, I think, beginning to envisage living in the house, despite her misgivings.

We spent the morning at the house yesterday and began to go through some of the things, to decide how it would be possible to arrange everything. There is such a lot there, some magnificent things of course, but a good deal of rubbish too. I never really knew that one half of it existed. It was a funny feeling really, going through so much stuff – some of which is so familiar and some of which means nothing to me – and realising that it's all mine now.

Priscilla says (and I suppose she's right) that if – always 'if' – we move into the house, we'll have to do something about the kitchen. She says that these days we can't expect to find people who are prepared to carry food up to the dining-room from the basement, and that, in any case, the food in my parents' day was 'perfectly filthy' because it was always cold. But I don't know what she has in mind.

The basement is a problem in itself. The only part of it that is even remotely presentable is the flat in the corner where the caretaker from the Public Records Office lived during the war, and even that is pretty dilapidated. The rest is dark and damp with the plaster crumbling off all the walls. I suppose we'll manage somehow, but even I sometimes think that I'm biting off more than I can chew. Not that I'll admit that to Priscilla.

Letter From Zbigniew Rakowski to Lord Otterton

1 Robin Hood Way,
Wimble-on-Thames,
Surrey.
JULY 20TH 1945

Dear Lord Otterton,

On perusing this letter you will no doubt cast your hands up in dismay when you discover that it comes from an unknown, humble writer who begs you of your generosity to bear with him a while and to listen to his modest story. My name, as you will observe, is Polish and I was born under Austrian rule in the town of Przemysl in South Eastern Poland, where at the time my father practised as a doctor of medicine. When I was but a mere boy of some ten summers, my poor mother died and my father, appalled by the Russification of Eastern Poland and wishing his only son to be educated in neither Russian nor German, decided to move to London where, in the early years of this century, he was fortunate enough to be able to establish a small practice and to educate his son.

You will doubtless be familiar with the role played by Przemysl in Eastern European history. Having been founded in 1340 on a trade route from Ruthvenia to Poland and, later, in the 15th and 16th centuries, having served as a frontier post to defend the country against invasion from the Tatars and Hungarians, Przemysl is a town full of significance to which its many elegant and interesting medieval and Renaissance buildings bear witness. It is a hill town, occasionally beset by mists and rain, but I will not trouble you further with details of this kind, having mentioned them only that you might appreciate from whence my lifelong passion for history sprang. My purpose, then, in writing to you, could you but indulge me one moment longer, is to beg of your kindness, permission that I, in my humble capacity as a chronicler of facts, might consult some documents which I believe to be in your possession.

In recent years research has led me to concentrate my modest endeavours, such as they are, on eighteenth-century England and thus I am now engaged on a study of the Whig aristocracy in that century. It is my belief that amongst your family papers you may have some letters from many distinguished figures which might be of help to me in my researches. Yours is, indeed, an illustrious family.

I beseech of you, in your kindness to an impecunious widower, to accept the enclosed copy of my most recent work which I send as a token of my deepest respect. In it you will find a complete list of the earlier works which it has been my privilege to publish.

Pray, Sir, excuse a mere scribbler from daring thus to intrude upon your time.

I remain, Sir, your humble and obedient servant.
Z. A. Rakowski

Sydney Otterton's diary

JULY 22ND

Annie has agreed to give the Gowers a month's notice and to move into the house with us. Hurrah! We couldn't manage without her. Priscilla is attempting to appear aloof, but she, too, has agreed. Not because of me but because of Annie.

Despite her affected aloofness, Priscilla has of course taken charge of everything to do with the move, which is just as well. She's very competent and doesn't allow herself to be pushed around. The more she takes charge, the more I feel the house will get into her system and the happier she will be to move in.

The children were all very excited when they were told the news. I took them to see the house this afternoon and showed them round. Even little Georgina appeared to be delighted and not at all discountenanced by the size of the place. I think the children must have been to the basement flat once or twice during the war, but otherwise they've probably never been inside the house at all, except as babies before the war. Jamie wasn't born until '40 so he wouldn't have been there then anyway, and Georgina who was born in '38 certainly wouldn't have been old enough to remember it.

Annie's diary

JULY 22ND

Father was delighted when I told him that I'd made up my mind to come home, to live in the big house and work for the Ottertons. His whole face lit up and his blue eyes twinkled more than they have done for a long time. He kept on saying with a smile, 'So I'll have my Annie back again.' That always sounds funny to me of course because of Mother's name being Annie. But I was glad to see Father looking so happy. As I say, he must be lonely at times now all the others have left home, but with me only two hundred yards away up the drive, it will be different.

Neither Bert nor the Gowers took it quite so well. Mrs Gower did say that when she heard that the late Lord Otterton had died, she was frightened that the new Lady Otterton might try to steal me. I felt like saying that I was hardly an object to be stolen but I thought I'd better mind my p's and q's, so I said nothing. It's funny the way the gentry when they employ you seem to think that they own you. In any case Mrs Gower was quite distant with me for a few days after that. Then she melted and began to say how much she would miss me which I dare say she will. Mind you she's been good to me over the years.

As for Bert, he worked himself up into a right tizwas. But of course he was only thinking about himself and worrying about who was going to wash his shirts and who was going to cook his Sunday dinner for him. He didn't like it at all when I said he'd better start to do a bit of cooking himself. And surely he could learn how to sew on his own buttons. But I began to feel quite sorry for him at one point so I took away a couple of pair of socks that needed darning.

Of course Bert's mother always spoilt him, waited on him hand foot and finger so that when she died he didn't know how to do a thing for himself. Bert's worked for the Gowers ever since he left school, in the garden and around the place. He stayed on in that same cottage after the death of his father who was head gardener there for years, and then again when his mother died. She was the scullery maid in days gone by. Because of all that I didn't quite dare tell him that I have an idea that I might be able to persuade his Lordship to take him on. There's an empty cottage down at the farm, just next to Father's which would do Bert nicely. I don't know if they have anyone in mind for it and, in any case, I'll have to have a think about what job he could do. I don't know if they need another farm hand, or an under-gardener perhaps to replace that lazy Stanley. I'll have a word with Father. He knows everything that goes on. Not that he'll give anything away, mind. Father is a very careful and peace-loving man. He hates any kind of trouble and doesn't like to interfere so I'll have to look how I go about it. Then, when I know how the land lies, I'll talk to Bert, by which time he may be beginning to miss me.

Georgina's exercise book

Yesterday Father took us to see the house were we are going to live. It is very very big and red. He showed us the stairs and the hall. There are lots of pictures and things and a stufed bear in the hall. Father says we can have it in the nursry. Nanny is leaving and we are getting a guvernis.

Sydney Otterton's diary

Priscilla is busy interviewing governesses for the two younger children. She's delighted to be getting rid of Nanny who she says has a face like a horse and with whom she has never got on. She wants the children to learn French, so she's interviewing French governesses and is keeping on old Major Doubleday from the village who's been coming in to teach them the three r's. I nipped out of the back door when I saw him coming this morning. He's like the Ancient Mariner. Once he gets hold of you, you can never escape. In his imagination he's never left India; it's Poona this and Ootie that, and what do I think of the Mahatma? And he remembers this and he remembers that and he remembers what happened when they passed the Government of India Act, and what do I think about the Punjab and what about the Muslim League? He really is an awful old bore who has a way of asking you a question in order to answer it himself at great length. But, according to Priscilla, he's an excellent teacher and Georgina certainly seems pretty good for her age at reading and writing. Anyway, I had to get away from him. I wanted to go down to the farm to see the vet who was coming to look at one of the carthorses which has gone lame.

Somehow we're going to have to beg, borrow or steal the money to buy a tractor before much longer. I'm still having nightmares.

A frightful bloody fool of a Pole came to lunch yesterday. He's writing some sort of history book and wants to look at a few family papers. There didn't seem any very good reason to refuse although it's rather a bad moment for him to turn up. Priscilla was very keen to let him come; she rather likes these writer fellows and got quite cross when I described him as an old humbug. She says she knows all about him and he's very well regarded, but even she could hardly deny that he's ridiculously affected and pompous, addressing everyone as 'Sir' and 'Ma'am' the way he does, and speaking in the most pedantic drawn-out tones. But you have to give it to him that to some extent he seems to be sending himself up all the time. In any case Priscilla played up to him, laughing a lot at his facetious jokes, and I could see that he was quite delighted by her. I told him what I thought there was in the way of papers and he has agreed to come back after we have moved in, but Priscilla still insisted on walking up to the house with him after lunch to show him the muniments room which for the moment is still under dust sheets. He's like a kind of gnome, all buttoned up in a worn-out jacket, with the utility label showing on his floppy sun hat.

I had to go and see the agent about the farm. It's running at a dreadful loss and we seem to be employing an awful lot of people. God alone knows how we'll ever sort it all out. I hate the thought of sacking men who've been here since before the war, but with the agricultural wage at around £8 a week, I can't see how we can afford to keep them all on, and I don't suppose things will get any easier under Mr Attlee. Everywhere I look there are problems; the stables are falling down, the cottages are all in a bad state of repair, the horses are lame. Sometimes I think that life in the Western Desert was simpler. Even the prospect of living in the house seems daunting when I wake at night, and yet it's the only thing that's really keeping me going. Priscilla is being wonderful about it and I daren't tell her that I occasionally get cold feet. She seems to think we'll manage with a butler, Annie, a cook, a governess and daily help from the farm and the village. She's probably right, but it seems odd when I remember all the people my parents used to employ. Butlers and footmen, tweenies, scullery maids and God knows what. Mind you, they all caused a lot of trouble. I'll never forget when my crazy old father discovered that the footman had been in bed with the butler. He worked himself up into a terrible rage and I can see him now, banging that big gong outside the dining-room with all his might and yelling, 'There are buggers in the house!' The pair of them were out by lunchtime the next day, poor devils, and I'm afraid I think the police were informed.

Zbigniew Rakowski's notebook

JULY 30TH

Lunched with Lord & Lady Otterton. I think they have papers which will be invaluable for my research, and I am kindly invited to return in the autumn by which time they will have moved into what at first sight appears to be a forbidding great barrack of a place. There was a good deal of talk about the new government. Lord Otterton who, having been captured in Normandy, spent the last few months of the war as a prisoner in Germany, regards what he chooses to call the Bolsheviks with a jaundiced eye. She, on the other hand, is delighted that they have been elected and voted for them herself. I sat on the fence. His Lordship and her Ladyship are in fact a most unlikely couple. He is small and dark with a round head and a round face, quite foreign looking, with a raunchy humour and displaying mostly a devil-may-care attitude. At times, though, he appears almost unsure of himself, glancing around with huge, dark, almost negro eyes, trying to catch an approving look from her Ladyship's hyacinth-blue ones.

We ate rabbit and stewed gooseberries. A more or less daily fare, her Ladyship told me, whilst proclaiming their luck at having the farm to live off in these hard times of rationing. She is tall and willowy, elegant with light brown hair tied loosely in a bun at the nape of her neck, a large nose and, despite her youth, a commanding presence. She clearly prides herself on her good taste and, unlike his Lordship, she appears to have some interest in literary matters. They live at present in the grounds of Cranfield Park, in a small gabled house with hanging tiles (a bailiff's house perhaps).

After lunch Lady O. insisted on walking with me to the big house. His Lordship seeming relieved to entrust me to her capable hands, mumbled something about having to go and see someone about something and quietly departed with a cat-like tread. We had walked up the rutted drive for barely a couple of hundred yards when, suddenly, around a bend, across a handful of fields, the great house appeared at an angle, large, oblong, a warm gleaming red, against a background of heavy summer woods. A first impression of this noble structure is never to be forgotten.

Built in around 1730, the house was designed for the second Lord Otterton by the Palladian architect, Giacomo Leoni. The exterior displays an exquisite reticence of decoration on which much of its beauty depends, but on entering the marble hall, a forty-foot cube which rises to take in the first floor of the house, the visitor will catch his breath at the magnificent opulence of this Palladian dream. Here is some of the finest plasterwork in England, but, as her Ladyship was only too ready to point out, gesticulating dramatically with her hands as she did so, the recent incumbents had little, if any taste. They had carpeted the magnificent white marble floor with heavy Persian and

Turkish carpets and furnished the room with, as her Lady-ship said, 'every conceivable bit of junk'. At present the carpets are rolled up and the 'junk' is covered with dust sheets. When she moves into the house, Lady O. plans to empty the hall, to leave it alone in its splendour that the proportions, the plasterwork and Rysbrack's two marble chimney-pieces on opposite walls may speak for themselves.

I must confess that it was a delightful afternoon I spent with Lady Otterton. She took endless trouble in showing me around the house, a tour much enlivened by her wit and charm. When we reached the muniments room (or the Red Drawing-Room as it is properly called), where I have been invited to work, she showed me a locked cabinet containing family papers which she assured me would be put at my disposal. The Ottertons, she told me, were not a literary family, indeed she regarded them as somewhat Philistine in their leanings. Their humour was slapstick, their occupations unrefined, their intelligence pedestrian, but for all that, she trusted that I might find something of interest for my researches among their papers. And for all that, they had caused this perfectly extraordinary monument to the eighteenth century to be built.

I had much to ponder over on my bus ride home. And I have much, I feel, to look forward to. The locked cabinet in the Red Drawing-Room is indeed full of promise. By September I shall need my muffler and my mittens, but I nevertheless envisage spending many a rewarding hour in that dark red room, beneath its delicate stucco ceiling. In truth, I also nurture a hope that I may have the chance further to enjoy some hours of her Ladyship's company. The Ottertons of today threaten to be quite as intriguing as their Whig ancestors.

Back home in my own modest abode in Robin Hood Way, I turned on one bar of my electric fire, for despite it being July, the evening was chilly, and made myself a cup of tea. Having eaten so royally at luncheon, I had no need of tea or supper, but took up my book immediately, only to find that Athens of the fifth century B.C. which had so engrossed me only twenty-four hours earlier, no longer had the power to enthral me. My mind kept returning to that great red house, that marble hall and to her Ladyship's hyacinth-blue eyes.

Annie's diary

Today her Ladyship took me around the house. I was quite fascinated. Even the rooms on the top floor where I shall have my room and where the children will live, seem huge to me, most of them with black patches on the ceiling where the water comes through when it rains. My bedroom which is not really as nice as the one at the Gowers' is, thank goodness, a little smaller than some, but next to it I will have my own sitting room. I don't have that with the Gowers. At the moment, everything's in a dreadful mess and needs a thorough cleaning. There is a huge landing on the top floor with a great, long table (I think they call it a refectory table) in the middle and a little spiral staircase going up onto the roof. We can have a washing line on the roof and dry the clothes there. From outside, it looks as if the roof is flat, but when you get up there, you find rows of small pointed roofs running parallel to each other, down which the rain flows into a series of gutters. It's an extraordinary place, that roof. I would never have imagined it to be like that. Round the edge is a stone balustrade much of which is broken. It would be very dangerous to allow the children up there.

The children's rooms, the governess's room and the nursery (or rather the schoolroom) all open onto the landing, from one side of which a long passage leads off to the other end of the house, to the servants' rooms and what will be the

21

butler's flat. Mind you they haven't found a butler or a cook yet. Or a governess for that matter, as far as I know.

There's one very funny thing at the end of that big landing, against the outside wall. At first I thought there were just two large bookcases sticking out into the landing space to form some sort of a corner cupboard. Up to a point I was right. Well, I couldn't help laughing when her Ladyship made me look a little closer. One of the walls is filled with real books, but the other one is made up of false ones and there's a door in them that you certainly don't notice at a distance. And all this to hide the fact that there's a w.c. in there. And in one of the rooms on the first floor, there's a bath inside a wardrobe and another w.c. in a big chest. You open up the lid and then you open the two front doors and Bob's your uncle! So long as no one's in a hurry!

It's going to be an awful job sorting everything out. At the moment there are things piled up everywhere, some of which have to be stored away and some which just need putting in the right place. Her Ladyship has all her own ideas. She wants everything moved around. Mind you, it looks as if no one has cared for the place for donkey's years. I think his late Lordship probably just gave up, it all being too much for him what with her shut in her room all day having hysterics. Mister Sydney says he can't ever remember seeing his mother on the top floor. She had no idea what went on there. It'll certainly take some cleaning up and they'll need to get the men in to move the furniture.

They're going to put a kitchen in one of the corner rooms on the first floor and have the dining-room off it, which is a darn good thing, if you ask me. I don't think I for one would stay if I had to spend any time down in the basement. That basement is more like something out of a Victorian slum than anything in a gentleman's residence.

When I got home and told Father about it all, I think he was quite horrified. He'd prefer to live in the bothy with an outside w.c. and a tin roof I shouldn't wonder, rather than up at the big house. But he never said anything. Typical Father. He just looked and smiled. I asked him if he thought they needed any extra men on the farm. Again he just looked, but I reckon he knew why I asked. And when I mentioned the empty cottage next door, he said he knew no more about it than I did, except that it wasn't in very good condition and he wouldn't want to keep a cow in it. Father loves his cows.

I've got till the end of the month with the Gowers and then I'll be back, staying with Father for a week or two before we move in and while we get the house in order. I still haven't dared tell Bert that I'd like him to come here. I'll have to find out if his Lordship will give him a job before I say anything.

AUGUST 6TH

After I'd cooked Bert's tea, he started on about me leaving. Why wouldn't I marry him and stay put? In that dingy, damp old cottage, cooking his tea and darning his socks for the rest of my days? I've heard it said that they don't marry you with the same face they court you. So why would Bert be any different? In the end, I made the mistake of telling him that he might be able to get a job with the Ottertons and come too. That didn't please him one little bit. It crossed my mind then that he would be afraid to leave the place where he's always been and the cottage where he was born.

Georgina's exercise book

AUGUST 6TH

We are getting a French mamzel when we go to the big house. She came to see Mummy yesterday and is very fat and old. Mummy speeks French to her so we cant understand. Mummy thinks she is *marvlous*.

23

Sydney Otterton's diary

Priscilla seems to think she's found a suitable governess. The old bat didn't look much fun to me but Priscilla who interviewed her for quite a long time, says she has excellent references. I think I've found a butler through a fellow I used to know at Sandhurst whom I bumped into the other day in London. Priscilla doesn't like the sound of him and thinks my pal is just trying to offload him. In any case he's coming to see us next week. So you could say that in one way the house is filling up, almost coming back to life even before we've moved in. The public records have nearly all been taken back to London now, so when that's done, we'll be set to go.

AUGUST 8TH

The Americans have dropped an atom bomb on Japan. It should mean the end of the war in the East, but I can't get it out of my mind. I dreamt I was driving round the farm in a tank with bombs dropping on every side.

AUGUST 11TH

They've dropped another bomb on Japan.

AUGUST 20TH

Thank God for Priscilla. Now she's really got the bit between her teeth about the house. She can't wait to move in and I feel that without her I would be totally useless. There are so many problems that I sometimes don't know where to turn. Of course we haven't got probate yet, so I've no idea what the death duties will be. The thought of them makes me ill. Whatever happens, we'll have to sell something and borrow huge sums from the bank as well. I'm sleeping badly and drinking a lot.

The house is beginning to look quite empty since Priscilla really began to move everything around, and an army of cleaning women is due to move in any day under Annie's stern eye. We should be in by mid-September. Then I think I'll feel better. I'll put the Essex property up for sale as soon as I can. But no one has got any money. Perhaps I'll feel better when I know the worst where death duties are concerned. But it won't be good news and it's not as if Mr Attlee's likely to make things any easier for the likes of us.

I wish my mother would go away. She's been talking about going ever since my father died, but she's still here. At least I have managed to avoid seeing her for some time.

I might go up to London and see Tony one of these days. He's a bit like me and can't get used to being back in civvy street. For years our day-to-day experiences in the war were everything to us. The war was all that mattered. The time in the desert haunts me especially. More than Italy, Normandy or being in gaol. It was such a strange and different life, one which no one who was not there can begin to imagine. It's so difficult now to concentrate on tumble-down cottages and widowed mothers, sales and governesses and solicitors. I sometimes feel like two people, almost as if the life I am leading back here is unreal, and that the real me has been left behind in a sandstorm with my Honey tanks in the Djebel. I also want to get hold of Johnson and take him on here. I somehow feel I can't really manage without Johnson. Life is incomplete without him. His flat, north-country manner and limitless courage made him the best troop sergeant we had in the desert, and I was damn lucky to have him as my driver. I shall never forget him on the day poor old Bill Martin was killed, opening the driver's hatch, standing up there without any cover and yelling at me, 'The buggers are trying to murder Mr Martin.' And they succeeded.

Georgina's exercise book

I am having a 4 posta bed. Mummy says it is only an ugly one and there is a lavatry inside the book case on the landing. Nanny has gone and Mamzel is here. She has got to teech us French. Boring. She looks at you with horrid eyes. Jamie thinks she is a german spy but Mummy says she's swiss. Lucky Thomas is at bording school so he wont have to see her much.

Zbigniew Rakowski's notebook

There is a distinct chill in the air in the Red Drawing-Room, which is compounded indeed by Lilian Otterton's icy stare as she gazes down from Laszlo's fine three-quarter-length portrait of her which hangs above my left shoulder. Lord O. speaks openly and scathingly about his mother, a woman who, to judge from her portrait, would not be out of place in a tale of Gothic horror. I do not like to feel her eyes upon me as she silently fingers her long necklace and as I peruse letters from Horace Walpole, Newcastle or Pitt, for the cabinet, once unlocked, has revealed a wealth of treasure. On the wall beside the portrait of Lady Otterton hangs its pair. The late Lord O. is far less mesmeric than his spouse. An ordinary-looking man in whom the artist has captured an expression which reveals both pomposity and hesitancy, even a certain brazen determination not to apologise. While I sat there, I was repeatedly tempted to allow my attention to wander from my work, to look up again and again at this strangely haunting couple who for so many years presided over this great mansion, allowing it quietly to decay under their stewardship. As I scrutinised their faces I attempted to divine their natures and through them to understand the present Lord O. who, together with his mother's dark looks and full mouth, has inherited his father's broad brow and slight build. But from whence came his jaunty manner and iconoclastic humour which at times amounts to insolence almost?

At luncheon, between mouthfuls of rabbit and vegetable marrow, I looked discreetly at Lord O. with the same question in mind. We lunched in the new dining-room on the first floor. The old dining-room on the ground floor, re-decorated as it was in 1801 for the Prince of Wales, is now no more than a museum, richly dark, heavy with mahogany furniture and louring family portraits.

There were present at luncheon with us, the three young Ottertons. Two pale boys with floppy locks, the older of which is due to return to his preparatory school at the end of the week, and a solemn girl with a round face like her father's and a bow in her hair. There is a Swiss woman employed to take care of these children. I did not like her in the least and wondered at Lady O. having thought to employ her. She speaks in the silvered tones of a practised hypocrite and has no light in her eyes. There is something soft and cruel about her, like a cat waiting to pounce. I fear for the children in her care, but then, I am nothing but an old fool with no understanding of the young and an over-active imagination which has only been enflamed by my morning spent watched over by the late Lord O. and his lady.

Lady O. was as gracious and as delightful as ever. She asked me kindly about my morning's work and I, in turn, congratulated her on the wonderful transformation she has so swiftly effected of the house, turning it from an exotic, dusty warehouse into an elegant abode. She seemed much gratified by my praise. Her eye is sure and her style unmatched. With the delicacy of her certain touch, she has most especially resurrected the hall in all its glory. Gone are the tables and chairs and carpets that could only have confused the eye, distracting it from the stupendous beauty of the proportions and the details of the carving. One chimney piece depicts the sacrifice to the goddess Diana and the other the sacrifice to Bacchus. Many an hour I would wish to spend in the now uncluttered beauty of the hall, gazing at these two admirable pieces of work.

Around the walls of the hall at the level of the ceilings on the rest of the ground floor there runs a narrow ledge, and opposite the front door, above this ledge, is a row of window embrasures through which it is possible to look down on the hall from a gallery running the length of it on the first floor. Her Ladyship told me that there is one small monkey of a man on the place (the estate carpenter, it would appear) who volunteered to skip fearlessly along this ledge with a bucket of soapy water and a scrubbing brush, in order to clean away the years of encrusted dirt. As he performed the task the whole household, with bated breath, admired him from below. His antics have earned him considerable recognition with the children for whom he has now become some kind of hero. The funny thing about him, Georgina opined when asked, was that he kept a small round hat on his head throughout the performance. For the most part at luncheon the children were seen and not heard, as was the governess.

After luncheon I thanked the Ottertons as graciously as I knew how for their kindnesses to me and, having confirmed that I would be more than grateful to return next week, I withdrew downstairs back to the Red Drawing-Room and to the uneasy company of Lilian Otterton and her husband. I expected to let myself quietly out of the house later in the afternoon and to wend my weary way home. It was a great surprise to me then, when about an hour later, the door of the muniments room suddenly opened, causing me, I have to admit, to start. Lady O. had come to see how I was getting on and to ask me if I was comfortable, whether I was warm enough or whether I would like Annie, her maid, to bring me a cup of tea. I thanked her profusely and explained that I had brought a thermos of tea with me. In these times of rationing, I feel that it is enough to be kindly invited to luncheon and that the least I can do is to provide my own tea.

Lady O. did not then immediately retire, but expressed an interest in my work. She flatters me by clearly having read the book I sent his Lordship. She did not know, she said, what papers the cabinet held and would be most interested to find out. So it was that instead of pursuing my research, I spent the next hour explaining to her Ladyship the contents and context of some of the letters which I had already seen before lunch. It was a delightful hour the memory of which I shall treasure.

At home I spent a quiet and thoughtful evening and, having a good deal to dwell on, felt contented in my own company, yet, as I eventually climbed the stairs, wearily carrying my old stone hot water bottle under my arm, I pondered on the fact that although I have much reading to do and my notes to sort out during the intervening days, next Tuesday seems so very far away.

Sydney Otterton's diary

SEPTEMBER 25TH

Priscilla is furious with Peggy. She's threatening to ban the poor puppy from the house since it made a mess on the Aubusson carpet in the saloon and that bloody old fool Rakowski went in there without looking where he was going and walked in it. She didn't think it at all funny when I suggested that she ban Rakowski. I don't know what he was doing in the saloon in the first place. Apparently he went in there to admire the tapestries, when I thought he was meant to be getting on with his work in the muniments room. Priscilla seems to be so taken by him, she's forever showing him this and showing him that and laughing extravagantly at his jokes. I'm not sure I really trust the fellow. But I suppose Priscilla did have a right to be annoyed; after all she spends hours on her hands and knees mending that carpet and anyway I was already in bad odour because I'd gone and bought an African grey parrot called Julia. She lives in my dressing-room.

Annie's diary

Her Ladyship's not at all pleased about the parrot. His Lordship has got it stuck in a great big cage in his dressing-room. It makes a dreadful mess, throwing seeds around and dropping them outside the cage on the floor. Her Ladyship says it will encourage mice and rats, but he just grins. Mind you he always has liked animals, but her Ladyship grumbles because she says he doesn't know how to look after them properly since Peggy made a mess in the saloon and *that* Mr Rakowski walked in it. We had the devil's own job trying to clean the carpet which is a very old and precious one, according to her Ladyship.

Anyway what with the new parrot and the new butler, this week has been all go. Mr and Mrs Cheadle moved into the flat with two children on Wednesday. Mr Cheadle looks like Mr Punch to me, with a bright red nose. As for Mrs Cheadle, I can't quite make her out. She doesn't say much and isn't prepared to work in the house. If you ask me, she looks a bit downtrodden, with black hair tied in a tight knot at the back of her head and an unsmiling, grey face. The children seem nice enough. There's a well-mannered girl who goes to the grammar school and a little boy. Then there's another girl who won't be here for long. She's married to a G.I. and is waiting to get to America. I don't much like the look of Mr Cheadle to tell the truth. I'd say that he was a bit too keen on the bottle. Her Ladyship snorted when she saw him. I heard her tell his Lordship that *she* should have been allowed to interview him before he was hired and that she'd very much like to know why he left his last place.

I was rather hoping his Lordship might have taken Bert on as an odd-job man but now it turns out that he has found someone who was in the war with him. I think he was his Lordship's driver and his Lordship is full bent on having him. Although he's more than likely soberer than Mr Cheadle, I don't think Bert would have been quite up to the job of butler, even with me supervising him. In any case, I wouldn't have wanted him living in the house.

SEPTEMBER 30TH

I can't say I'm really missing Bert. I know he wants me to go up there on my weekend off, but I think I'll have to make some excuse. If he won't come down here, he may have to find some other woman to do all his washing and ironing and darning. If he's lucky, he may find someone who is even prepared to marry him.

Father asked me at dinner time how I was getting on up at the house. He's obviously pleased to have me here to cook his Sunday dinner but I think he's surprised at my liking living in that great big cold house. I certainly have a kind of feeling there of independence in a way that I haven't properly known before. I have made my own rooms quite nice really. Mrs Gower gave me a lovely clock as a leaving present which I've put on my sitting-room mantelpiece and Mr Sydney has let me have some nice water-colours of the house. It's a little cold to be sure, but I see to it that one of the chars lays the fire for me every day. There's a huge old lift with a pulley in one corner of the house which is used, among other things, for bringing the logs up from the basement. I caught the two children trying to play in it the other day. In fact I don't suppose that even if he were here, Master Thomas who has gone back to school now, would be strong enough to pull it up with all three of them inside. I didn't want to tell his Lordship or her Ladyship what the children had been up to because I knew they would be for it. And I certainly wouldn't tell Mamzelle. She'd murder the pair of them as likely as not. All I did was to ask them if they were *supposed* to be playing with the lift. They knew darned well they weren't. Master Jamie just gave me an old-fashioned look and off they both went. I expect they'll be worrying in case I tell their parents.

Georgina's exercise book

Anie found us playing in the lift. I hope she doesn't tell Father. Mamzel killed Jamie's pet mous. She squoshed it behind the cubord to punish him. We think she's horrid. She says she is a frend of Queen Mary but Mummy says there must be some mistake. She says she's got a foto of some fairys which we can see if we are good. Jamie said it was a bluddy lie so she squished his mous.

Sydney Otterton's diary

OCTOBER 1ST

I saw my mother yesterday and told her that I had decided to take my seat in the House of Lords. I really don't know why I bothered to tell her, perhaps just for something to say. She of course just gazed at me with her usual cold, unfocused stare. I wish I didn't have a mother and I wish the one I have would bloody well go away. She keeps saying she is going abroad and when she does go, we may at least be able to get something from letting her house.

When I come across my mother unexpectedly as I did

yesterday, walking stealthily through the hall like some ghastly predator, I feel as if I've been kicked in the gut. Give me the Bosch any day. I don't know what she was doing in the house, but Priscilla, of whom I have a feeling that she may even be a little wary, would have been furious if she had found her. Why is it that I would far rather come under enemy fire than confront my witch of a mother?

Georgina's exercise book

Mamzel chucked a French book at us this morning because we dont understand it. Major Dubbleday is much nicer. He makes us do sums and reading. He tells us a lot about India. Jamie wants to go there. We dont dare tell about the mous. I dont think Mummy would believe us.

Zbigniew Rakowski's notebook

If I were truthful, I would surely be obliged to admit that my weekly visits to Cranfield Park have begun to take over my life. My research there is proving to be both fruitful and interesting, but it is Lord and Lady Otterton themselves and the peculiar world which surrounds them that I find most deeply fascinating. It is as if I had entered an unreal country peopled with mad hatters and white rabbits, a country somehow divorced from the rest of the world, in which all the rules are different and where the bizarre holds sway. It is not just Lord and Lady O. who create this atmosphere, but the extraordinary galaxy of characters by whom they have managed to surround themselves, the apparently hermetically sealed society in which they all exist and the way they interact with each other, all somehow absorbed into the house and all in some curious manner dependent upon it, enclosed as they are in its all-embracing vastness. The children seem as natural and as normal here as they would be in any suburban villa or tied cottage, blissfully unaware of the strangeness of their surroundings, regarding their home, and no doubt their parents, as quite run of the mill. It is as if they and everyone else in it were part of the house, or at least belonged to it, just as the pictures on the wall and the Mortlake tapestries do.

I have not yet had the opportunity to make the acquaintance of Lilian, Lady O. whom I am told inhabits a dower house on the estate, and perhaps the occasion may never present itself, but as I sit in the Red Drawing-Room, watched over by her and her somewhat quaint-looking husband, I find my thoughts only too frequently wandering from a proper contemplation of the second half of the seventeenth century, from the scandals surrounding Wilkes and from the scurrilous behaviour at the time of one George Otterton, to the consideration of the house as it now is and of the peculiar assortment of people living there.

I have already said that Lord and Lady O. seem to me to be quite unsuited to one another, and the more I see of them, the more persuaded I am of the rightness of this judgement. In another, but similar fashion, I perceive Lord O., in his heedless quixotism, as being quite unsuited to the elegance of the surroundings in which he finds himself. Some might call him vulgar, as many of his ancestors have been, yet his quite unusual wit and maverick disposition would make of this a misnomer. Imagine a man laughing at a puppy fouling an antique carpet; imagine him furthermore laughing at a humble guest who has the great misfortune to step into the deplorable leavings of this unenlightened hound. Her Ladyship and her faithful maid, Annie, were fulsome in their apologies, and came rushing with newspaper for my shoes which I had so carefully cleaned that very morning, and with soapy water for the carpet.

Her Ladyship is, of course, ever delightful, intelligent, courteous and witty. Annie, her maid, appears to hold a position of the greatest importance in the house since she is undoubtedly in the confidence of both his Lordship and her Ladyship. She, I would wager, is the power behind the throne. She it will be who, in the years to come, hires and fires. She is a good-looking woman of about forty years old with a firm tread, a quiet confident manner and a twinkle in her hazel eyes. There is nothing at all servile about Annie and, whilst being clearly relied upon and liked by Lady O., she appears to share a conspiratorial sense of fun with Lord O. I even suspect that I caught her, bucket and cloth in hand, exchanging a humorous glance with him, which I will find hard to forgive, although to me she is always the personifica-tion of good manners. Or do I on occasion detect an underlying irony in her tone?

The butler who, I believe, should by tradition be the head of such a household as this, is not a man I would trust, and he is, I would opine from my superficial observation of the situation, somewhat in awe of Annie. He shambles around the table when he waits at luncheon and I aver that on one occasion, I heard him hiccough in my left ear as he offered me the dish of baked apples. It would be fair to describe his breath, emanating as it does in uneven gusts from a mouth half open, as rank, if not putrid. Her Ladyship, I fear, is a little short with him, almost haughty, although she can hardly be held to account for this, since the man is clearly wanting in refinement and must test the patience of one so well-bred as she. His Lordship looks unconcerned and would no doubt have found the hiccoughing tremendously droll had he been aware of it, since he clearly appreciates the incongruous, not to say the grotesque, and the Hogarthian appearance of his butler may well be an added source of amusement to him.

With this cast of characters, the children, the governess

and others with whom I am as yet unfamiliar, who can doubt the fascination that this household has for me? Who can doubt that, as I return to my labours on a Tuesday morning, I feel a little elated, curious and somewhat excited to know what may have happened during the past week, and eager to divine the future? What is going to happen next? What indeed?

Her Ladyship has made a sitting-room for herself in a corner apartment. It is a delightful room, known, on account of the magnificent scenes of the chase depicted on the eighteenth-century English tapestries adorning the walls, as the Hunting Room. This is one of the most delicate rooms in the house, and the smallest on the ground floor. When I had finished my work yesterday, I was most kindly invited to partake of a cup of tea in that exquisite room. As I crossed the threshold a little warily, I felt obliged to enquire as to the whereabouts of the recalcitrant cur. 'Ma'am,' I ventured, 'I tread in trepidation lest his Lordship may have allowed his young dog to step this way before me.' The dog, she assured me, was under no circumstances allowed in the Hunting Room.

Over tea, Lady O. enquired kindly about my writing and appeared to be particularly interested in the modest novels I have penned. I made a mental note to bring her, on my next visit and in the nature of a grateful offering, my most recent work of fiction. We then became engrossed in what was, for me, a most stimulating discussion of the merits of various new writers, when, all of a sudden, the door burst open and in came his Lordship, preceded of course, by his bounding puppy dog. I saw the interruption as a sign that the time had come for me to take my leave.

Annie's diary

My room is really looking very nice. Her Ladyship found a pretty faded blue brocade bedspread in the old linen press on the back stairs. I think she hardly looked at it, but handed it to me, saying it was for Mamzelle who had been complaining that she didn't have one. I didn't much care for the one on my bed so I gave that one to Mamzelle and kept the blue one for myself. It goes much better in my room and it can't make any difference to anyone else. Beside my clock on the mantelpiece, I've got some photographs of the Gower family in a nice leather frame they gave me, and one of Father in his Sunday best, taken at one of my sisters' weddings. Yesterday afternoon I went for a walk. It was a beautiful day and I picked some autumn leaves which I have put in a jug on the table. Her Ladyship has done a beautiful arrangement in a large white urn she's put on a tall column in the hall. She takes endless trouble with the flowers and they are always lovely and very natural.

Now I have had a letter from Bert. He must be really missing me because he even suggested that I should find out if there is a job for him here, just as if the idea was all his own and that I hadn't suggested it in the first place. The only trouble is, I think he may have left it too late. I suppose he could have had Mr Johnson's job, but nothing would make his Lordship get rid of Mr Johnson when he's only just arrived. In any case his Lordship seems to spend half the day lolling about down in the boot room, talking about the war with him. Mr Johnson thinks the world of his Lordship and says he was very brave, which I don't doubt. They remind you of a pair of schoolboys when they're together. Of course his Lordship must be the younger of the two by a long way.

I quite like Mr Johnson. He comes from Yorkshire and is very blunt, but he likes a joke and seems to get on with his work despite his Lordship talking to him all the time. And he had a thing or two to say about Mamzelle. She was very rude to him, expecting him to clean her shoes as if she were the lady of the house. He soon told her where she could get off and advised her to clean her own b— shoes. I couldn't help laughing to myself about that.

As for Bert, I'm not quite sure yet what to do about him. I certainly won't answer his letter for a day or two. I can't think about him at the moment anyway because I've got too much on my mind. There's Lilian, Lady Otterton, for instance. She gave me the fright of my life the other day.

I'd just been in my sitting-room, doing some ironing for her Ladyship and was about to take it down to her room when I heard someone walk past down the passage. At first I didn't think twice, but supposed it was Mr Cheadle or Mamzelle or one of the children, but then I looked at the time (it was half past eleven in the morning) and I realised the children would be doing their lessons and, by rights, Mr Cheadle should have been in the butler's pantry, cleaning the silver or getting ready for lunch. In any case I felt a little unnerved because I thought the footsteps stopped for a moment outside my room. Now, if there is one thing I don't like, it is the idea of being watched or spied on. After a moment I decided to open the door and see who it could be, and there she was, as white as a ghost, walking back towards me down the passage. I said, 'Good morning, M'lady,' and she just stared at me, leaning forward a bit, with her head on one side, and after a long time said, 'Ah, Annie. I thought it was you. I should like to talk to you some time.' Then she turned on her heel and walked slowly away along the corridor towards the schoolroom. I don't know if she went in there, or if she just went downstairs and left the house. Neither his Lordship nor her Ladyship mentioned anything about her having been here, but if his Lordship had seen her, I'm sure we would all have heard about it.

Yesterday afternoon when I came in from my walk I found a note pushed under my door. I have no idea how it got there unless *she* has been back again. It crossed my mind that Mr Cheadle could have put it there but he says he didn't. Not that I would necessarily believe anything he said. I went into the dining-room the other day for her Ladyship, to fetch a handbag she had left in there and I caught him drinking port straight out of the decanter. He put the decanter back on the sideboard as quick as winking when he saw me and began to polish it with a grubby handkerchief. Then he said he was very busy, as if I had gone in there on purpose to get in his way. I didn't say anything and I won't say anything.

So I found this note in Lilian, Lady Otterton's spiky handwriting, written in purple ink. She has summoned me to go and see her one afternoon but she doesn't say why. There will be no need, she says, to tell anyone that she has been in touch with me. I'm wondering whether I ought to tell his Lordship or her Ladyship, but it would only make them angry. Her Ladyship says her mother-in-law is a terrible woman and that because of her, Master Sydney (as was) had a dreadful childhood. Mental cruelty, her Ladyship calls it, and then she says there was no love and no discipline. She doesn't have to tell me about that, and as for mental cruelty, the poor lad used to be whipped by the servants for nothing if *she* was in one of her tempers. Everyone on the place knew about it and we all felt sorry for Master Sydney, and for his late Lordship for that matter. I think most of us would forgive Master Sydney anything.

Perhaps I'll wait and see what Lady Lilian wants before I say a word to anyone. Mind you, I can't say I'm looking forward to going to see her. It crossed my mind to pretend I never found the note. If she gave it to Mr Cheadle, I could get away with that, but not if she put it under the door herself. I thought of going down there this afternoon, but it

39

was a lovely afternoon, so I decided to go for my usual walk instead. I may go tomorrow.

It was raining today, so I still haven't been to see *Lilian* as I stayed in to write a few letters instead, and to mend a couple of Father's shirts. I think that rather than go this week, I'll talk to Father about it on Sunday and see what he says. He's very wise, but then he doesn't say much.

Georgina's exercise book

OCTOBER 30TH

We don't see are grandmother very offen. She is fritning and looks quite like a wich. Jamie says she's spooky. Mr Dubbleday makes us learn tables *all the time*.

Sydney Otterton's diary

OCTOBER 30TH

The best thing to have happened lately is the arrival of Johnson. I don't know how long he will stay though, because he keeps talking about emigrating to Australia. I would have thought he might be a bit old to think of doing that, but he says there is nothing for him in this bankrupt country, and he seems pretty resentful about the war which he was damn lucky to survive. He certainly had one or two close shaves. He feels that it took the best years of his life and that he received scant thanks for his efforts. Then he came home only to discover that his woman had deserted him for a German P.O.W., so with no wife and no family to tie him down and only a sister he never sees in Skipton, he has nothing and no one to keep him here. I'll miss him dreadfully if he goes. It's bloody useful having him about the place as, not only is he able to do almost anything from stoking the boiler and mending the car, to plastering and wiring, but if I get a pair of parakeets I've seen, he is going to do up an old Victorian birdcage I've found in the basement. It's a magnificent thing shaped like a pagoda with a fountain for the birds to drink from. I haven't told Priscilla about that yet. I think she would be rather annoyed. As it is, she thinks I spend too much money on animals and too much time talking to Johnson. He's someone to talk to about the war so we are bound to spend quite a lot of time reminiscing, but Priscilla insists that I'm preventing him from doing his work, besides which she thinks I've got enough animals. She seems to think that animals stand in the way of my doing other things which she regards as more important. It's true to say that she does work very hard to keep the house going. I sometimes feel quite useless beside her. Despite her earlier reservations, it is quite clear to us all that she loves the house and it is quite clear to me that without her, it would never have been possible to make the move. She is wonderful. Only last week, she had the brilliant idea of hanging two of the Barlows on either side of the double doors between the hall and the saloon, where they fit exactly and counterbalance the windows opposite. That huge ostrich and the cassowary with the monkey on the pedestal behind him both look as if they were made to go there. Perhaps Priscilla thinks that with so many painted animals, we don't need real ones. I like both.

Still no sign of my mother leaving. And not only has she not left, but she has taken to wandering around the house whenever she feels like it. I've told Cheadle not to let her in. I've no idea what she wants, whether she just wants to help herself to a few things, which I somehow doubt, or whether there is some more sinister motive. I can't help blaming her for the fact that I'm finding it so difficult to settle down. I know it's partly because of the war, but still, it's strange because I was so sure that if and when we moved into the house, all my restlessness would disappear and I would begin to be able to concentrate on it and the farm. The truth is, there are just so many problems involved in both, that it's hard to know where to begin. And yet the thing about the house is that it acts like a kind of drug so that when I'm feeling really hopeless, I'll either have a gin and tonic, or I'll walk round it, drinking in its atmosphere, looking in long-forgotten cupboards, climbing up to the roof to admire the view. It gives me a peculiar sense of freedom and an extraordinary feeling of security although God alone knows why when the rain is coming through everywhere, so much plaster is crumbling and there are damp patches in half the rooms. If I concentrated on the dilapidation, I'd want to shoot myself, but then Priscilla has got the ground-floor rooms looking splendid. Better than they ever looked in my childhood. She instinctively knows how to hang the pictures and arrange the furniture to best advantage.

I've proved my legitimacy and had my writ of summons and am beginning to look forward to taking my seat in the House; perhaps things will get better then and life will seem more real. At the moment nothing appears to be solid or permanent and I sometimes feel as if I were only a figment of my own imagination.

Annie's diary

NOVEMBER 4TH

I couldn't get Father to say much at dinner-time about what I should do about *Lilian*, but I got the idea that he didn't really want me to go and see her. Then Father has always been one, as I say, to walk away from trouble. He admits as much himself. In fact he frequently claims that he makes *tracks*, as he would say, at the first sign of an argument. All I could get

42

out of him was that I should remember who my employers are and who is not my employer. That's right, I suppose, but then in one way, I'm quite curious to know what she wants. And then again, I don't want to find her suddenly wandering about outside my room, which I probably will if I don't obey her. His Lordship says he's told Mr Cheadle not to let her in, not that that will make any difference. She'll come in through the basement or any way she wants. In any case, I doubt she'd pay any attention to Mr Cheadle. As a matter of fact, I wouldn't mind seeing the pair of them together. Mr Cheadle with his big red nose and all that nasty spittle in the corners of his mouth, and her Ladyship with her white face, black hooded eyes and ghostly stare.

The other day Mr Cheadle wanted to know what the matter was with Lady Lilian. He had the nerve to ask me if she drank. I wasn't saying anything. Talk about the pot calling the kettle black.

Zbigniew Rakowski's notebook

There is no doubt about it that the house has a hold over each and every one of these people. And dare I suggest that it is even beginning to exercise a mysterious control over myself. I who regard myself as beholden to no one, enslaved to nothing, a poor immigrant from a beleaguered country to which I shall now probably never return. I have ever seen myself as unattached, impartial and have indeed considered this to be a peculiar advantage, most especially so to one of my chosen profession: a writer, and most particularly a historian must needs retain his detachment. Yet now, here I sit, eternally, it seems, watched over by Lilian, Lady Otterton, and what do I do under her very nose, under her disapproving eye? Instead of working as I should, instead of poring over and examining minutely the wealth of letters which have so fortunately fallen into my undeserving hands, the study of which would be so richly fruitful for my *œuvre*, instead of doing thus, I spend the time fantasising about the lives of the present Lord and Lady Otterton, dwelling (a little too lengthily, some might even submit) on the contemplation of her Ladyship's periwinkle eyes, as the French would say, her swan-like neck and sparkling wit. I, poor, humble gnome that I am, am hardly used to the attentions of so fine a lady, nevertheless, when at home last week, I was not a little disconcerted to discover on checking through my notes for the Whig aristocracy, that these are far too generously interwoven with musings on Cranfield and, as one might say, those who sail in her. Yet here in the Red Drawing-Room, do I find myself once again at their mercy.

It has however crossed my mind that whilst I am at work, it is possibly no waste of time to make notes on whatever it is about the place that might capture my attention. It is not beyond the realms of possibility that I might, at some later date, consider using not merely the historical notes I have collated, but also the material I have recorded with regard to the present day. Thus I might use it in creating some slight work of fiction. Perhaps even, the thought passes through my mind as I write, a murder story. This is not a genre at which I have so far tried my hand, but everything in this house is conducive to thoughts along these lines. *The Corpse on the Carpet* might I entitle my work. Or perhaps, *The Body in the Bathroom, Bloodstains in the Boudoir, Murder in the Mansion, Death in the Drawing-Room* . . . The imagination races. In my thick-coming fancies I can already see that blood-stained Aubusson carpet, and Annie, always Annie, quiet and enigmatic, laughter in her eyes, a bucket of cold water and a cloth in her hands, ever ready to wipe away the evidence of something about which she knows far more than she should. Indeed, with a study of the Whig aristocracy and a murder story simultaneously researched and published in the same year, I could truly claim to have killed two birds with one stone, and, no doubt, would be the less impoverished for it.

I have to confess to having perhaps been a little too extravagant in my thoughts whilst I was at work in the muniments room at Cranfield yesterday morning. At lunch Lord Otterton appeared to be very much concerned with taking his seat in the House of Lords and consequently most of the conversation turned on that subject. As I looked at her Ladyship, I could not help but recollect the ugly imaginings that had been mine so shortly before, as I envisaged her poor mangled body spread-eagled on the Aubusson carpet in the saloon, her blood so mercilessly spilt. So strong was my emotion at this remembrance, that it almost behoved me to take her hand and reassure her that she was of course in no real danger. But she quite naturally was unconcerned and certainly appeared heedless as she chattered gaily about his Lordship's arrangements or offered me a second helping of rabbit. After lunch, somewhat chastened by the contemplation of my own impertinence, I returned to the muniments room and was able to concentrate on some very interesting letters of Horace Walpole's which can only be of great benefit to my work in hand.

Annie's diary

There's a dreadful row going on between Mamzelle and Mr Cheadle. I'm not saying anything, mind. It's all about a tray which has been left on the table on the landing outside the schoolroom for four or five days now. Mamzelle says that it's Cheadle's job to take it back to the kitchen, but he just calls her every name under the sun and refuses to take it. I've seen the children giggling about it. I think they must hate that Mamzelle because she's never very nice to them. To tell the truth, I think she's as mad as a March hare. She's always so polite when she sees her Ladyship, but I can't help thinking that her Ladyship must see through her soon. I feel really sorry for the children. She fills them up with a lot of funny stories. The other day Georgina asked me if I believed in God. Now I wasn't telling anybody about whether or not I believe in God, so I just asked her why she wanted to know. And she came out with an extraordinary story.

That Mamzelle took the children for their walk one afternoon and they ended up going into the church. Now she told the children, that if they were very very good and went behind the altar with her, they would be able to see God. See God, my foot! But, on the other hand, if they were wicked, they wouldn't be able to see Him. Only good people could see God. So they all went behind the altar and of course they didn't see any god, or gods or goddesses, but that terrible woman fell on the floor and began to wail and to chant, claiming that she had her arms around God's ankles. Apparently Master Jamie whispered to his sister that Mamzelle was a b— fool and that she was only pretending, but I think Georgina was really worried that she might not be able to see God because she was too wicked. Then on Thursday morning her Ladyship happened to ask me to take the horologist to the schoolroom where there's a grandfather clock, and there was Mamzelle, for some reason telling the children that she had a photograph of some fairies she might or might not choose to show them. I felt quite foolish standing there and I can't imagine what Mr May can have thought. In future he is to come once a week to wind all the clocks in the house. Anyway, I was given to understand that Mamzelle was supposed to be teaching the children French, not telling them a lot of twaddle about fairies. I can't help noticing that most of the time, the children escape from the schoolroom as soon as they can and disappear somewhere in the house. Then it can be very difficult to find them and I've seen that woman pounding up and down the stairs shouting for them, purple in the face and puffing. I dread to think what happens when she finds them. I doubt she'll think it very easy to control Master Thomas when he gets back for the holidays. I should think he'd play her up something awful. And serve her right, to my mind. Anyway, I wonder what the outcome will be about the tray. I'm certainly not going to take it down for any of them.

In fact, I find there's something creepy about both Mamzelle and Lady Lilian. It's hard to know which of them is the worst. In the end I did go and see Lady Lilian. I went one afternoon like she said, not that I wanted to, so I put it off for a while. When I arrived at the back door, I found Doris, her maid, in the kitchen. She's a queer one that Doris with her scrawny figure and long face and all that, what I call common, peroxide hair. I wouldn't be surprised if the pair of them didn't dope themselves together. So Doris looks at me when she opens the door as if I had no business there. Well I could tell Doris a thing or two and I could tell her, furthermore, that my father has been at Cranfield far longer than she has so she needn't think she can come one over me. Doris came shortly after Lilian and his late Lordship were married. I seem to remember that her Ladyship always had difficulty in keeping servants which was hardly surprising. No one could ever understand why Doris Batty stayed so loyal. Two of a kind I suppose.

I expect her Ladyship must have heard someone at the back door, or else she heard voices, in any case, there *she* was, all of a sudden, in the kitchen. 'Ah Annie,' she says, just like she did when I met her in the corridor. Then she beckons me with her bony finger to follow her through to the front of the house. I don't know who is supposed to do the cleaning there, but I couldn't help noticing that the house was in a dreadful mess. We went into what must be her sitting-room. There were papers, old envelopes, dirty glasses and half-filled ashtrays everywhere and so many ornaments and so much furniture that there was hardly room to swing a cat. Never mind cats, as I came into the room, a fat old corgi with one eye growled at me from an armchair covered in dog's hair. Her Ladyship sank down into a great big sofa, stretched out a thin white hand and slowly stroked the cushion beside her. I felt quite a shudder run down my spine when she said, 'I'd like to have you next to me.'

I wasn't going to sit next to her on that darned sofa and have her stroke me, not for all the tea in China. Instead, I sat on an upright chair opposite her and as I sat down I heard the floorboards creaking outside the door. I have very sharp hearing and I wouldn't mind betting my bottom dollar that Doris was out there eavesdropping. I needed some Dutch courage so I just kept thinking of Father, and him saying, 'Remember who your employers are.' I thought of Dolly too and her telling me to keep a diary.

And all the time she goes on stroking the cushion beside her and sort of staring through me without ever smiling. Then she suddenly says in a grand voice, 'I'm leaving here you know.' Then she starts to tell me how ill-used she's been by Master Sydney after all she has done for him. She adored her son, she said, worshipped him. Not that I believe a word of it. And now, she told me, he had turned against her, and all because of his wife. She narrowed her eyes when she said that. 'And you work for her Ladyship, I gather,' she said icily and all sarcastic. I wanted to get up and walk out. To tell the truth, I began to wish I had never gone to see her in the first place. Anyway, the long and the short of it was that she wanted me to spy for her and to send her what she called a regular 'bulletin', only she pronounced it as if it were a foreign word, for which she would see that I was 'handsomely rewarded'. I could hardly believe my ears, but then, after all the talk there's been about her, I shouldn't really have been surprised. I said I wasn't sure I ought to do that, and then, as I was leaving, she caught hold of my wrist, pushed her face right up to mine and said, 'Do as I tell you child,' before adding mysteriously, 'There are things to be looked for.' Then she pressed a piece of paper into my hand on which I later discovered she had written the address of her bank! I couldn't get out of the place quickly enough and, as for the expression on Doris's face as she saw me out again through the back door, well, if looks could kill!

Sydney Otterton's diary

On Tuesday I took my seat in the House of Lords. They were debating demobilisation and on Wednesday Lord Methuen spoke on the preservation of historic buildings. I can hardly have been the only person in the place who felt a knife turning in the wound when he said that present-day taxation makes the occupancy of large country houses virtually impossible and that if they are to survive, they will have to be put to a new use.

It was a funny feeling really, being there, stepping into my father's shoes in yet another way. His was a modestly distinguished career and there are a lot of his friends still in the House who were kind enough to put themselves out to welcome me, the new boy. I certainly felt like a new boy but hope that as time goes by, I shall be able to live up to my father and to achieve some minor success myself.

On Tuesday the House rose at around half past five and then two pals of my father's, old Bodger Florey and Bumpkin Exebridge, asked me to go and have a drink with them; they both seemed far more concerned about the inconvenience of sitting in the Royal Gallery while the Commons occupies the Lords, than they were about affairs of state. No doubt it'll be a year or two before the lords get back to the Lords and all the bomb damage to the Palace of Westminster is repaired. I hate the sight of bomb-flattened London, it's terrible to see. So, feeling a bit flat after swearing my allegiance to King and country in such high-flown language and then listening to Bodger and Bumpkin banging on about nothing much, I decided to go round and see Tony. He was his usual cheerful self and we went out on the town. I'm afraid we got dreadfully drunk and I slept some of it off on his sofa before driving home in the small hours. Priscilla was not best pleased.

The next day I had a bloody great bill from my solicitors for nothing much that they had done, as far as I can see, and then, on Thursday, I had an unbelievably gloomy meeting with my bank manager. The farm in Essex still hasn't found a buyer. I have to admit that in the Lords that afternoon, I found it pretty difficult to listen to what was being said; my mind kept on returning to my appalling financial situation and wondering how the hell it's ever going to improve. No wonder I feel like going out and getting drunk with Tony. In actual fact I was glad to get back to Cranfield, despite Priscilla's frosty welcome. It is a private haven for all the problems that attend it.

A most extraordinary thing happened while I was in London on Thursday, and perhaps it was because of this that Cranfield felt so safe on my return. It was Annie who reported seeing a furniture van outside the Dower House when she walked down to the farm to see her father after lunch. When she got back she told Priscilla who made a few enquiries and discovered that my mother had just left, like that, without so much as a word to anyone, presumably taking the monstrous Doris with her. God alone knows where she's gone, but it feels to me as if a huge black cloud has lifted. I don't expect to hear from her for some time and certainly hope not to. Of course Priscilla is immensely relieved too and has quite forgiven my earlier misdemeanours.

I asked Annie if she had seen my mother at all recently. It

struck me that she gave me a funny look, but all she said was, 'Now you know I wouldn't have anything to do with *that* Lady Otterton.' My mother is the sort of woman who might easily have tried to put Annie against us or even to take her away. But then she doesn't know Annie as I do. Annie is a very intelligent woman and I trust her completely, even if she is a bit of a dark horse. She's always stood up for me which my mother probably knows and which is why my mother would, I suspect, so love to destroy her and to turn her against us.

Letter from Annie to Dolly

NOVEMBER 25TH, 1945

Dear Dolly,

I'm sorry to have been so long in writing but I think you can partly blame yourself for not having heard from me. Do you remember telling me that I ought to write a diary? Well, that is just what I have been doing and I'm afraid it rather puts me off letter-writing because I feel I've already said everything there is to say in the diary. Mind you, with all the goings on here, there is a lot to tell. Besides, there is something odd about the house that makes me want to keep a diary.

Lilian, Lady Otterton has left Cranfield at last. She didn't even tell his Lordship when or where she was going, but I think we are all very relieved now she has gone.

Bert is quite cross with me because I haven't been back to see him since I left the Gowers. I expect I'll go up there before Christmas, but what with one thing and another I've been very busy.

There's a Mr Johnson come to work here now. He was in the war with his Lordship and seems very nice. He comes from Yorkshire.

Father is keeping well as I hope you and Fred and the children are. Do write soon with your news.

With love from
Annie

Sydney Otterton's diary

It wasn't possible to get the shoot off the ground this year, but I should very much like to get it going again next year, if only in a modest sort of way. Whatever happens, one of these days I'll have to face up to doing something about Summers. I suppose he spends his days breeding ferrets and killing rabbits, but with precious little to do during the war and pheasant shooting suspended, I think he just got idler and idler. I sent Peggy to him for a while; he was supposed to house-train her and train her as a gun dog, but I rather think he failed on both those counts. Despite their having been left in peace for the last few years (or perhaps because of it), there are precious few pheasants around. My father used to raise quite a lot of them before the war but the stock is sadly depleted, and, as for next year, well I certainly haven't got any spare cash to spend on putting pheasants down. I don't like Summers's sly look, and never have. The children do a very good imitation of him riding his bicycle with both knees pointing outwards at a ridiculous angle. But I'll have to be careful how I handle him, because his mother-in-law, his wife and his sister-in-law all work in the house and Priscilla, who finds all three of them invaluable, doesn't want them upset. I sometimes panic at the thought that all these people, whether I like it or not, are dependent on me. I can barely afford their wages and I'm not at all sure how to cope with them, especially people like Summers who were employed by my parents before the war. I can't just kick them out. Thank God for the likes of Annie and old Jerrold who loves his cows, and for Johnson.

Annie has found someone called Miss Wheel whom Priscilla has employed to do some sewing. God knows where she hails from, but she sits all day with a sewing machine in a room on the top floor, cutting up old curtains and making them into new ones, fabricating cushions out of my grandmother's wedding dress and covering dressing-tables with worn brocade. Priscilla is delighted with her. Although she joins us for lunch and is round and smiling and rosy, she never speaks but to say please or thank you, and she reminds me of some sort of benign sorceress, working away silently in an upstairs room. What happens to her in the evenings, I have no idea. Apparently she is to be with us for a fortnight and may return again at a later date. From where, I wonder, did the all-powerful Annie whistle her up?

I feel a bit more cheerful since I've started going to the Lords. If I stay here all the time, I begin to panic about everything as I see myself drawn daily further into a quicksand of debt and decay. Then I go to London, spend a bit of money, which cheers me up, go to the Lords, see a few friends, and come back here refreshed.

Zbigniew Rakowski's notebook

DECEMBER 4TH

This evening I find that there is a great emptiness in my crabbed old soul and indeed I have no difficulty in divining the cause of this most gnawing malaise. Love is like a canker that eats into man's very being and where that love must be hidden, subsumed, suppressed, there must be exquisite pain. For the last two months and more, I have had the good fortune to be a regular visitor to Cranfield, there quietly to pursue my researches not only into the past, but also into the present. There I have repeatedly eaten rabbit and gooseberries and stewed apples at the table of one who must be the most elegant, the wittiest and the most intelligent lady in the land. Lady Otterton has graced me with her friendship, she has been so kind as to listen to the meanderings of a dreary old Pole, nay, she has laughed at my jokes, encouraged me in my work and inspired in me a passion quite unsuited to the occupancy of my old frame. If I am to be truthful, I must admit to having lingered over my work in the hope of prolonging my tenuous relationship with this most enchanting lady. But, alas, and woe indeed is me, the time has now come to an end when I can reasonably expect to continue to visit Cranfield on a regular basis.

With her usual kindness, Lady Otterton, when I bade her farewell this evening, assured me that I was always welcome to return should I require any further examination of the Otterton papers. 'And I do wish you would call me Priscilla,' she added. I, with a lump in my throat, could only reply, 'Thank you, Ma'am.' 'Any time you like,' she added vaguely so that I was unsure as to whether she referred to my calling her by her first name or to my continued visits. She insisted that she would be delighted to hear how I was getting on with my book and begged me to keep in touch which I, with some degree of presumption perhaps, take to be an invitation to write to her. This I shall surely do since there would certainly be no harm in the exercise and the correspondence would unquestionably allay, if not entirely alleviate the ache in my poor shrivelled heart.

For it is with a truly heavy heart that I now contemplate the long winter ahead, shut up as I shall be in my small hovel, with no outings in view, but the occasional visit to the public library, the occasional trip to town, there to pursue my researches, and the twice-weekly bicycle ride to the shops. To make matters worse, at this time of year the day barely breaks ere the night draws in. Similarly, in the fanciful mood in which I find myself, I imagine a weak winter sun rising within me to spread its watery light over the rejuvenated landscape of my soul, a light to be so soon, so swiftly, drowned by darkness. I know that I am an old fool whose brain has probably been addled by years of loneliness, and it is this loneliness which provokes me to write as I do, for what is there to look forward to now, but the Christmas visit of my bossy daughter with her mewling child and tiresome husband? Why should I not indulge myself a little with flights of delicious imaginings?

But it will not be only her Ladyship whom I shall miss, for I shall miss the house itself, that large mass of red brick, so deceptively clumsy at first sight, so subtly elegant on further examination. Only the monstrous *porte cochère*, that clings to the front of the house with the tenacity of a misshapen barnacle to the side of a boat, destroys the simplicity of the original design. It was most unfortunately put there in late Victorian times by the present Lord Otterton's grandfather, so that her Ladyship's carriage might in inclement weather drive right up to the front door. In order to make way for this horrible protrusion, Leoni's gracefully balustraded steps were removed and placed incongruously below the *porte cochère*, where they appear to be at a loss as to their purpose.

How can I, after so short a time, have come to love this magnificent great house almost as though it had become part of me, or I of it? I shall even miss the late Lord Otterton and his lady, watching over me as I work, for I have begun to feel at home in the Red Drawing-Room where I had made a comfortable corner for myself and which seemed to welcome me anew each week as I arrived. Of the hall, I will surely dream.

Letter from Annie to Dolly

Dear Dolly

This afternoon the tree was put up in the hall. Just as it used to be before the war. It took three men to fix it in place. I couldn't help thinking of you and Wilfie and Cis and the others, and of days gone by. You should have seen his Lordship. He was all smiles. I don't think I have ever seen him look so happy. He seems much more cheerful since his mother left, and I can't say I blame him. He must feel that at last the house is really his.

I'm not sure how they would have managed without Mr Johnson. He was the one who worked out what to do, with his Lordship walking around behind him in a right state of excitement, talking about mending tanks and saying that anyone who could mend a tank, could find a way of putting up a b— Christmas tree! Mr Johnson didn't say a word mind you, but just got on with the job. He looks like a very strong man.

I'll write again after Christmas and tell you all the news. I just had to tell you about the tree. Father is well, but I'm worried about what will happen when he retires next year. He'll certainly miss his cows, but I suppose he'll spend more time in his garden.

Happy Christmas & New Year to you all.

Love from
Annie

Sydney Otterton's diary

Our first Christmas in the house. God knows how Johnson and the others managed to fix the tree, but they did. The children were thrilled; they'd never seen anything like it and Priscilla managed brilliantly with the decorations and the estate party on Christmas Eve, and everything else for that matter. With two huge fires lit on either side of the hall, the place looked wonderful; you could have said it was just like old times except that it wasn't because my mother has at last been exorcised. It was like a proper, old-fashioned family Christmas such as I have never seen. Quite a lot of drinking went on, but then you'd expect that at Christmas. I think Priscilla was very pleased with how well she'd managed on a shoe-string and by how much everyone seemed to appreciate it all; in fact she was so pleased that she even melted a bit towards Peggy and allowed her into the library on Christmas Day. I reckon old Jerrold had a tear in his eye when he thanked me for his perennial bottle of port. He wished me luck. I don't care to think about him retiring which I'm afraid is due to happen at the end of this year and will be just one more problem. But never mind, I've decided to go into the New Year feeling optimistic. I can't help thinking that one way or another it will all work out, and in any case, it's hardly worth being kept awake about death duties night after night when it looks as if it will be months or possibly years before we even get probate.

1946

Annie's diary

Everything here seems to have been running quite smoothly since Christmas. There don't seem to have been any silly rows with Mamzelle, like the one about the schoolroom tray. Lord knows how long that tray stayed on the landing. It was her Ladyship who took it down in the end, making it quite clear as she did so what she thought of both Mr Cheadle and Mamzelle. I don't suppose the pair of them have addressed a word to one another since, though. No one can stick Mamzelle. Even Miss Wheel, who is a very kind person, was quite put out by her when she was here. She thought she was cruel to the children. And as for Mr Johnson, he just pulls her leg whenever he sees her. He generally says something about his being no more than a bootblack and she looks ready to burst a blood vessel.

Of course there was one thing that didn't work out very well over Christmas and that was my visit to Bert. He was quite upset that I hadn't been up to see him sooner, although he must understand that what with the bus fare, the train fare and then another bus fare at the other end, it costs me quite a bit to get there. It was different when I was coming back from there to see Father, because Mrs Gower used to pay my fare. I suppose I should be sorry for Bert as he is quite lonely. He won't go down to the pub for company because he says it's a waste of money, so he sits on his own in that cottage every evening and all week-end. In any case, he brought it up again about getting a job at Cranfield and I didn't know how to discourage him although I tried. I don't want Bert hanging around me for the rest of my life. I told him that if he was lonely, he'd better get along on and find someone else. But he didn't like the idea and then, blow me down, if he didn't ask me when Father was due to retire. So now he's thinking of applying for Father's job, which I call a bit of cheek. I doubt he knows one end of a cow from the other. Anyway he wasn't very pleased with me by the time I left, so perhaps he'll change his mind.

Mr Johnson is talking about going to Australia. He says they haven't enough people over there, so they're encouraging British ex-servicemen to emigrate. It'll be a shame if he goes though, because he's a very nice man and a hard worker. I expect his Lordship will do his best to dissuade him, but he keeps telling me about these assisted passages the Australian government are offering. He says it would only cost him £10 to get there and when he got there, they'd find him a job. It all sounds like so many castles in the air to me, and I've told him as much.

Then this morning I had a nasty shock. As I say, things have been running quite smoothly since Christmas. His Lordship and her Ladyship have been seeing eye to eye and even Peggy seems to have come to heel, but this morning I had this horrid letter from *Lilian* with which she enclosed a cheque. I was just thinking that we had all really begun to forget about her and to behave as if she didn't exist, but of course she's out there somewhere making her wicked plans. I know it's awful to think of such a thing, but I honestly suspect that his Lordship would be quite glad if she died. His Lordship's cousins came up to stay over the New Year and Mrs Coppleston (that's his Lordship's first cousin) said to me, 'Annie, my aunt is an evil woman, you must never do anything she asks.' It was almost as if she knew what was coming. But she said she could tell me a thing or two about his Lordship's childhood which would make my blood curdle. And I don't doubt it.

I really don't know what to do about this letter. I could show it to his Lordship, but then it would only cause an awful to-do. Or I could tell her Ladyship or wait till I see Father and discuss it with him. That is what I will probably do.

Meanwhile I'll keep it with this diary locked in a drawer in my bedroom. I don't want it to be found by any prying eyes. There are so many people around in the house all the time that you can never be sure. That dreadful spiky, violet handwriting on the envelope. I knew at once it was from her.

JANUARY 16TH

Father, who doesn't usually say much, thinks I should tell his Lordship about his mother's letter, but I'm not quite so sure that it's a good idea. He also says that I must return the money at once, which of course I have already done. I had to send it to the bank in London which is where the letter came from and the only address she gives. I'm just a bit worried about what she'll do next when she finds out what I've done. Father doesn't think I should answer her letter at all. 'Just you keep out of trouble my girl,' was what he said. He claims that nothing Lilian, Lady Otterton might do would ever surprise him. He didn't think Cranfield was going to be shot of her as easily as all that. She'd be haunting the place for a while to come in his view. He didn't think she could ever have been a happy woman and she could certainly not have been happy at Cranfield, and yet the place seems to have as strong a hold over her as it does over everyone else. I never heard Father talk so much.

Georgina's exercise book

JANUARY 16TH

Mamzelle is horrid and we hate her. She's allways nasty to Jamie because she hates him so she broke a baloon he got at Christmas on perpous. She spent ages sqashing it on the bed with her hands and then it burst in her face. Jamie laughed. He is very daring. We wish she would go because she spoils everything. Thomas told her she was fat so she ataked him with the toasting fork and stopped him having tea. I think Annie hates her to. We like Annie best. She's nice to us.

Sydney Otterton's diary

My spirits have been wonderfully buoyed up since Christmas; even the eternal grey weather has failed to get me down. The house is looking better than I can remember it and Priscilla is happy, permanently occupied with further improvements; the children are jolly, and everything seems to be getting better. In spite of rationing which I suppose will last for ever, we've had several friends to stay, each bearing pathetic little parcels of butter and sugar, and the house is alive again. But best of all, I've lost my mother. I haven't heard a squeak out of her since she left. I don't even know what country she is in. For all I know, she's still in London. The only address I have for her is care of her bank, not that I have any desire to get in touch with her. Perhaps this is just the lull before the storm, although I can't quite imagine what kind of a storm it will be.

I'm hoping to get a loan off the bank for a tractor which would make a hell of a difference to things here. It's time those two old horses were put out to grass, although I'm afraid it may have to be the knacker's yard for them. It'll be sad to see them go, but we can't run a place like this these days on two old mares, one of which goes lame every time there's a bit of harrowing to be done.

Of course there are still problems but all of a sudden I feel better able to face them. Not, in fact, that I really want to face up to the problem of Cheadle whom Priscilla wants me to sack because she says he's always drunk. I'm not entirely sure that's fair although he obviously does have a weakness in that direction. He seems to do his job and, after all, he's only been here for a few months so I feel I ought to give him a chance, despite the fact that I couldn't help noticing the port disappearing with amazing rapidity over Christmas. His daughter, who's having a baby any minute, is being taken off next week to a camp for G.I. brides at Tidworth where she'll have to stay until they can arrange some kind of transport to America for all these women. Poor old Cheadle, he looked quite red-faced and rheumy-eyed about it when I saw him this morning. I could hardly give him the sack on top of that.

Never mind Cheadle. I think that old Swiss cow in charge of the children is the one who ought to be shown the door. Priscilla doesn't believe the things the children say about her, but Annie said to me darkly yesterday, 'And her Ladyship doesn't know the half of it.' Priscilla says that children always invent things and that it would be very difficult to find anyone else suitable.

Another problem is the kitchen garden. Denman came to me the other day saying we needed another gardener. He says we can't possibly manage with just him and Stanley. He says the whole thing's gone right downhill since before the war when there were six gardeners. When I told him I couldn't afford to employ anyone else, he remarked sourly that he wasn't getting any younger which was manifestly the case as he limped away, muttering about his arthritic hip. I went and had a look at the garden later. It didn't look too bad to me, but as Priscilla remarked sharply, January is hardly the right time to be looking at gardens. I saw Stanley leaning idly on a fork, complaining that the ground was too hard to dig and in fact I did feel a bit sorry for poor old Denman. The garden used to be immaculate when I was a child and it must be sad for him to feel it getting out of control. Perhaps Johnson would lend him a hand. Johnson can do anything. They'll manage somehow between them.

I've been giving quite a lot of thought to my maiden speech in the House, not that I intend to be making it just yet, although I'm pretty sure it'll be about agricultural labour since that is a subject close to my heart.

Mr Cheadle's daughter went off at the beginning of the week. She's got to stay in a camp with all the other G.I. brides until she eventually goes to America. Mrs Cheadle is very upset. Mind you the woman hardly ever speaks to me, but I bumped into her on the stairs yesterday and she blew her nose loudly and looked as if she had been crying. Or perhaps she has just taken to the bottle like her husband.

Mr Johnson thinks that Mr Cheadle beats his wife and that the reason Mrs Cheadle was crying is that her daughter is her only ally. Mr Johnson wouldn't put anything past Mr Cheadle. He says he's told his Lordship that Cheadle helps himself to bottles from the cellar. The trouble with his Lordship is, he doesn't really want to know. He just laughs and goes off with that dog of his. It makes her Ladyship wild.

I haven't heard another word from *Lilian*, but I dread the post every day because I somehow don't think she is going to leave it at that.

Letter from Zbigniew Rakowski to Priscilla Otterton

1 Robin Hood Way,
Wimble-on-Thames,
Surrey.
FEBRUARY 3RD, 1946

Dear Priscilla,

It is, Ma'am, with a degree of trepidation that I take up my pen to write, for I fear that you will only find it in your heart to despise a bewildered old man who in his senescence, is obliged to admit that despite the most generous help afforded him by yourself and Lord Otterton, he has merely frittered away the hours and not therefore advanced as he had hoped in the work in which he is engaged. I have written some twenty thousand words of a work which should run to at least one hundred thousand and which is due with my publisher by the autumn. I fear that I have been side-tracked and thus have been engaged on a work of a more frivolous nature about which I will not bore you at the present time.

The expression of my gratitude to your good selves for the kindness and forbearance with which you received a tedious old man when you had but barely arrived at Cranfield, can only ever be inadequate. When, Ma'am, I wrote to thank you, before ever the evils of the festive season descended upon us, the fruits of my research were fresh in my mind and thus I hoped to be full of vigour with which to undertake the task in hand. Perhaps it was a visitation from my daughter which sapped that vigour. She is a good Catholic woman, and a conscientious person of little imagination who sees it as her painful duty, once or twice a year, to travel from her home in Liverpool to call upon her sad old widowed father, to instruct him about his diet, his clothing and any other matters which she considers as pertinent to his well-being.

Let me not however make excuses, for the fault, dear Brutus, is indeed not in our stars, but in ourselves, that we are underlings.

I have now, I fear, Ma'am, to implore of you to be merciful to me in my incompetence, for I have to admit that I have failed to make sufficient notes concerning some of the papers in Lord Otterton's possession: there are in truth one or two matters which I must clarify if I am to do justice to my subject. I hesitate to bother Lord Otterton with what for him must be so trivial a matter, for he is a busy man, and thus it is that I humbly turn to you with a request that I might, at some date suitable to yourselves in the not too distant future, be allowed to return to Cranfield, further to examine the aforementioned papers.

I have the honour to remain, Ma'am, your humble and obedient servant.

Z.A.R.

Sydney Otterton's diary

Rakowski's written to Priscilla asking to come back again. God knows what he needs to do that for. I was surprised that he took so long over those papers in the first place and fully imagined that he might have almost finished his book by now. Anyway Priscilla's quite delighted at the prospect of seeing the old humbug again. She's written back and asked him to lunch in a couple of weeks. Well I won't be here; I'll be in the House of Lords which I don't doubt will please him, as I suspect he's much more eager to see Priscilla than he is to get on with his book. She gets very cross when I say so, but in fact I think she's quite flattered by him. He's a wily old devil and I sometimes wonder what he's up to, nosing about the place. Annie giggles whenever I mention him and says, 'I reckon he rather *likes* her Ladyship.' Annie's regarded him as a comic figure ever since he walked in that dog mess in the saloon.

Extract from Zbigniew Rakowski's work in progress

. . . As a faint breath gurgled in her throat and a thread of saliva tinged with blood trickled from the corner of her Ladyship's beautifully formed mouth, she turned her hyacinth-blue eyes to look at the masked face of her would-be murderer who, in an instant and with a flamboyant gesture, defiantly ripped the stocking from a distorted face, to reveal the

*dreadful truth of an assassin's identity. But there was not merely breath
in her Ladyship's body yet, but courage to feign death and strength
enough for her survival.*

*'It was you,' she whispered faintly as the door closed behind the fleeing
figure of her assailant.*

*Confident in the assumption of a deed well done, her attacker had
swiftly withdrawn the dagger from the wound in her side, thus allowing
the blood to gush and flow until it formed a dark, sticky puddle on the
Aubusson carpet on which she lay, spread-eagled and lovely. The
murderous villain then placed the dagger in the lady's outflung lily-white
hand so that she might be thought to have inflicted the wound upon
herself, and tip-toed quickly from the room, blissfully unaware that the
blood-stained weapon had miraculously failed to attain a vital
organ . . .*

Georgina's exercise book

Mamzelle has been packing all day. She says she's going to
stay with the King and Queen. Poor them. Annie took us for
our walk this afternoon and we picked snodrops. She says
she's not shore the King and Queen know Mamzelle.
Mamzelle says there very sorry for her plite. When I told
Mummy she just said What Bosh!!!

Sydney Otterton's diary

At last it dawned on Priscilla that that bloody Swiss woman
was barking. Thank God she's been sent packing. I think
what finally persuaded Priscilla was the woman banging on
about a mixture of fairies and the Royal family. She was

certainly never really convinced of how nasty the old bag was to the children. I also suspect that Priscilla was reluctant to admit to her own bad judgement and to having hired such a lunatic. The woman definitely gave me the creeps and reminded me more of my mother than of anyone else. In any case the children seem much more cheerful with the new French governess who's tiny and looks like an old wizened walnut under a thin grey bun.

But we've still got Cheadle although I haven't dared tell Priscilla that I found him in a stupefied slumber, snoring his head off on the pantry floor the other morning. I got out of the room before he woke up but I must have disturbed him because a moment later when I was still in the passage outside, he came to the pantry door and I heard him say, 'Who's that? Can't you see I'm busy?' Priscilla would be furious. She was pretty cross with the way he announced dinner on the evening the Bishop and his wife came to discuss the future of the cathedral. He put his head round the saloon door, as drunk as a newt, and said, 'Your din-dins is ready M'lady.' It was incredibly funny because that's the way he talks to Peggy when he feeds her. I suppose Priscilla is right and we ought to get rid of him but he doesn't really do much harm and I can't face the bother of looking for someone else. There are so many other problems that need solving.

I've written to my mother, c/o her bank, telling her that since she has left the Dower House and emptied it of furniture, I presume she no longer wishes to lay any claim to it and that unless I hear from her to the contrary within a month, I will set about letting it. Of course I haven't heard a word from her as yet. And Priscilla has come up with another good idea for raising a little cash. She thinks we could make a viable flat on the first floor, with the West Room as the main bedroom. We don't really use that part of the house and there's a bathroom there already and a smallish room that could easily be made into a kitchen. Whoever lived there could use the white staircase and the back door in the basement and we would hardly ever see them.

Priscilla is incredible. I don't think anyone else could have anything like her energy and enthusiasm for reviving the house. She is full of good ideas and without her I would be absolutely done for. She's always trying to enthuse me about things and to encourage me and to dissuade me from thinking things are impossible. She can also be quite sharp, but I suppose that's a good thing. Annie laughs and says, 'Her Ladyship keeps us all on our toes.' She probably needs to especially now, as I'm afraid I haven't managed to keep up all that good cheer I felt after Christmas. I had quite a lot to drink last night and felt a bit better, but then I felt like hell this morning. Priscilla says I'm incompetent, that I drink too much and that I ought to concentrate on one thing at a time. I hope she realises that I couldn't begin to manage without her, although I don't think she quite appreciates how bloody difficult it is to try to run this place with no money. Neither do I think she quite understands about the war. I don't see how anyone can just come home after all that and get on with life as if nothing had happened. Johnson feels the same. Thank God for him is what I say. He reminded me only the other day of the camel I'd had shot for the men's Christmas dinner back in 1940. We were advancing to Saunnu and one of the fitters had just shot some kind of wild cat which one of the men who was a butcher in peacetime, skinned for the officers' dinner. To shoot the camel was strictly against orders, of course, and I got into a bit of hot water with my colonel afterwards, but as I saw it, it was those boys' first Christmas away from home and they might have been going to be killed the next day, so why couldn't they have some mild jollification at the expense of a camel?

Still, I can't blame the war for my inability to sack Cheadle. In an awful sort of way, I think I'd miss him if he went because he provides so much entertainment. You never know what the fellow's going to do next.

Georgina's exercise book

The new mamzel is much better than the old one. She's very little and Jamie is nearly as tall as her. She keeps a huge bottel of green stuff in the schoolroom cubbard. She's allways taking spoonfuls of it for her cough. It must be good because she never seems to cough. She is French.

Zbigniew Rakowski's notebook

I should indeed be ashamed to admit, even in this my personal notebook, how gladly last Thursday morning, despite the bitter cold, I set out for Cranfield, how light was my tread, how full my heart. Her Ladyship, I trust, is unaware that an old man's heart can be so vulnerable. Sighing like furnace, with a woeful ballad made to my mistress' eyebrow did I travel. Or rather, should I say, if I were completely honest, with a woeful tale of murder. Once my novel which I shall have the temerity to dedicate *To Priscilla* has been accepted by my publisher, I shall feel that I have in some degree freed myself from the stranglehold of my sweet passion and thus will be able to continue to work on matters of a more a serious nature. I do not at present wish to tell Lady Otterton what it is that I am writing for fear that she might well misinterpret my intentions and might also hesitate to invite me so willingly to Cranfield in the future. She will, I feel, when the book is published, be both dazzled by its jauntiness and flattered by the content. However, I fear that when I wrote to her, I let slip that I had not recently been devoting my efforts entirely to Whig history, and at luncheon on Thursday she, not unnaturally, with her usual spirit of enquiry, was curious to know what it was that I had been writing.

I think she was not a little displeased by my reluctance to discuss my novel with her. I surmise, however, that she guessed it to be a work of fiction in which I am involved, as, laughingly, but with a touch of hauteur, and an autocratic glance from those blue eyes, she remarked that she sincerely hoped that 'we' weren't all in it. It is extraordinary how vain the general public is; the least of human beings has but to meet a novelist once, to presume himself of sufficient interest to be instantly transposed to the pages of fiction. Of course in the case of Lady Otterton, she has every right to make such a presumption. I laughed inwardly as I looked at her across the luncheon table, chastising the children for not eating their cabbage, and imagined her as she has recently been in my mind's eye, *spread-eagled and lovely*, her blood staining the Aubusson. Then for a moment I felt a twinge of pity. How could I treat her so? But then the true artist must have a heart of stone and thus I must not be moved, but stick to my original plan.

There is a new governess; a small French woman with bright eyes and a brusque manner. She looks very old indeed and is, I trust, kinder than her predecessor who is to be immortalised in my novel.

To be frank, I practised a minor deceit in order to return to Cranfield on Thursday. I needed, for the purposes of the book I am engaged upon, to examine more closely the saloon and its furnishings. I was, furthermore, uncertain as to whether, between the Green Silk Room to the north and the Red Drawing-Room to the south, there were two of those beautiful mahogany doors, one behind the other, or if there was only one, set deep into the embrasure of the wall. I had entertained the idea of my murderer lurking for some while between two doors. To be sure, I can, in a work of fiction, design the doors and indeed the furniture to my own liking, do precisely as I please, but there is something about

Cranfield so magnificent and so imposing, that I would feel it an impertinence to tamper in any way with Leoni's great design, or indeed with the arrangements made inside the house by Priscilla Otterton herself.

Once again, I was aghast at the splendour of the hall with its fine proportions and the beauty of its plasterwork ceiling. Opposite the main entrance, a handsome pair of double mahogany doors open into the saloon through which can be seen French windows that in summer must be wonderfully opened onto a graceful flight of stone steps, and beyond them the garden and the lawns across which can be seen an incongruous, slanting may tree. One of the charms of this house is that, for all its grandeur, it has the capacity to accommodate the simple and the ordinary. The fine marble busts of negroes over the main doorway of the hall and the doors to the saloon had temporarily escaped my memory. Her Ladyship tells me that they were put there as a tribute to the Jamaican heiress whose money built the house. How bewitching a house it is! What a hold it appears to have over those mere mortals who pass through it. We mere mortals who, destined so soon to become dust, will be long gone before Cranfield crumbles. For, saving a bomb or an earthquake, Cranfield will surely survive to exercise its enchantment over generations as yet unborn. I wax lyrical, but I shall surely have to find some further reason for returning there. Bother the Whigs, I need to look again and again at the house and, indeed, I need to know what fate befalls those who live there now. I note that the drunken butler is still in residence.

Fortunately for my purposes, the doors are as I had imagined them. I shall have no trouble concealing my killer.

Annie's diary

It is bitterly cold in the house, or, as Father would say, it's cold enough to freeze a brass monkey. I reckon the only place where one could keep really warm would be in front of one of the two big fires in the hall. They're kept burning all day in this weather, but of course you would only freeze the minute you stepped back. Mamzelle is complaining about having chilblains for which she takes cough mixture. I couldn't help laughing when her Ladyship told me that she thinks Mamzelle has a peppermint liqueur in that bottle. All I can say is that she's a good deal better than the last governess and the children seem to like her more.

I've been helping her Ladyship get some rooms ready on the first floor to be let as a flat. The main bedroom is a huge, icy corner room with two windows on one side looking down across the lake and another two overlooking the garden. Because the floor has been raised to make room for a sunken bath, the windows come right down to the ground, which, I have to admit must be lovely in the summer. I couldn't help laughing when her Ladyship first showed me where the bath was. It is completely covered by floor-boards forming a lid that is lifted by means of brass handles which hook back to hold it to the wall.

Goodness knows who we'll ever get in that flat. I told his Lordship that I thought they'd better wait until the weather was a bit warmer before trying to find a tenant. I can't imagine anybody moving in there now. They'd probably freeze to death. We are quite lucky on the top floor really with the rooms being smaller and the ceilings a bit lower, although the school-room's big enough and cold enough. When I was in there the other day, the children were pushing each other about in front of the fire, trying to get near it. I told them that if they weren't careful, they'd fall in one day and then there'd be hell to pay. I didn't add, especially if it happens when Mamzelle's been at the cough mixture.

Mamzelle's only been here a couple of weeks, but she is forever telling me about this thing and that thing that she thinks needs fixing. Yesterday, it was a snapped sash cord in the window, and the day before it was a door with a broken latch. I thought Mr Johnson could mend both those things, but she won't have anything to do with him. I don't know why unless it is because she's taken a rather sudden fancy to the estate carpenter. Perhaps she broke the window on purpose! I wouldn't be surprised as Mr Kipling's always up there, laughing and talking to her on the top landing. I shouldn't wonder if she lets him have a drop of her cough mixture from time to time.

MARCH 8TH

There's a lovely picture on the paper this morning of the banana boats arriving here for the first time since before the war. I should think we could do with a banana or two each, what with the state of rationing. I thought that was all supposed to be getting better now, but rations have just been cut back again to what they were in the middle of the war, with only seven ounces of margarine each a week. I suppose we're lucky to be here with all the extra things off the farm, not that I fancy the idea of eating squirrel pie which is what the government is busy telling us to do. You won't catch me taking to that. No fear. Mamzelle takes the children out every afternoon to look for dandelions to make salad for their tea. There'll be plenty of them around, I should think, but she says they're not quite ready yet, not sweet enough. Would you believe it!

Letter from Annie to Dolly

Dear Dolly,

I wonder if you saw the picture on the paper yesterday morning of the banana boats arriving. I thought to myself, what wouldn't I give for a banana right now? To tell you the truth, I wasn't in the least bit bothered about bananas, not until we couldn't get them.

When I was writing my diary last evening, it crossed my mind that I should really have been writing to you instead, because you would be so interested in all the goings on. One of these days I will have to give you my diary to read to make up for all the letters I haven't written.

Anyway, I think I ought to tell you that I had another letter from Lilian, Lady Otterton this morning. I don't know what makes her so sure that I won't mention anything to his Lordship. I suppose I'll have to if she goes on, although Mr Johnson advises me to do nothing. Least said, soonest mended, is what he says. She didn't send me any money this time. In fact, I thought the letter was downright rude. She said she was disappointed in me and she wanted to know where my loyalty lay. All this in her dreadful spiky writing.

I only told Mr Johnson about it because he knows his Lordship well, is fond of him and would be on his side. Besides he (Mr Johnson) is a very kind man and sensible.

Father's really looking forward to your bringing the children to see him, but what with Easter being so late this year, it seems a long way off still.

Wilfie and Ethel came over for the afternoon on Sunday which was nice. Father was pleased to see them and they both looked well.

Love from
Annie

Georgina's exercise book

Mamzel makes us eat dandylions, but aksherly there quite nice. She says they eat them all the time in France. And they eat snails. Ugh!! Jamie wants to try them. He would. She's been caching them in the garden for him. There are some new people in the flat but Mummy says were not allowed to bother them. Ive seen them in the garden. They are very odd and have a big dog and a funny name and don't smile.

Sydney Otterton's diary

Priscilla's found a very rum fellow with an equally rum wife, to live in the flat. They answered an advertisement she put in the *Surrey Advertiser*. I suppose we won't have to have much to do with them, so it doesn't really matter what they're like so long as they pay the rent. Apart from anything else, they've got a pretty strange name. He says it's Channel Islands, but I'd have thought it was more of a bogus crook's name. Legros dit Courrier. It's certainly a new one on me. To be fair to her, Priscilla doesn't think much of the so-called Legros either, but unfortunately people weren't falling over themselves to live in vast, freezing-cold rooms in the corner of a dilapidated stately home. Legros looks like some kind of robot as he walks, staring at the ground in front of him and without appearing to move any other part of his body but his legs. He has bright brown, dyed hair in a thick mat, like a wig, over his head (it probably is a wig) and a very high colour. I should think he must be nearly seventy. In any case, he looks as if he might die of apoplexy any minute. Mrs Legros is one of those faceless women whom you cease to be able to imagine once they are out of sight. For all I know, she does cease to exist once she's out of sight. She walks silently beside her husband (if he is her husband), always holding on to the leash of their vast Pyrenean mountain dog and never looking up when you speak to her. The only thing one can't help noticing about her is the make-up which she cakes all over her face.

Priscilla thought it a bit odd when she took them round the flat in the first place because when she asked them where they'd been living before, they wouldn't answer. She's convinced that they have some kind of shady past, in which case, perhaps we shouldn't have let them have the flat. Let's just hope they don't rob us. I asked Annie what she thought about them, but she only giggled and said they were most extraordinary. Johnson was pretty annoyed about them and told me that they looked like trouble and that if he had a house, he wouldn't want to share it with them. Then he started saying something about Australia again, which depressed me.

Julia is beginning to talk which annoys Priscilla. She says that there are enough human beings talking nonsense without parrots having to join in. I think she's really annoyed because Julia gives a passable imitation of Priscilla calling my name. The children think it's very funny which I suppose she finds even more annoying. Annie's minding her p's and q's, as she would no doubt say.

I spent an evening with Tony MacIntosh in London last week. I couldn't help feeling rather sorry for him. He's completely on his uppers, without a bean to his name and with an ex-wife and a child to support. He's found some sort of a job in the City but earns a mere pittance. It crossed my mind that I might be able to help him by letting him have a room on the top floor here until he sorts himself out, but I haven't mentioned it to Priscilla yet, not that I can see why she should object. Tony is one of my friends she has always liked.

Letter from Bert Farthing to Lord Otterton

Cinder Path Cottage,
Battle-by-Stitch,
Sussex.
APRIL 5TH, 1946

M'lord,

Please excuse the liberty I take in writing but I would like to apply for the job of cowman as I have heard that Mr Jerrold is to retire soon. I am single, forty-two years old and have been working here for Mr and Mrs Gower since I left school. Mr Gower would give me a reference.

I am hard working and in good health and I look forward to hearing from your Lordship in the near future.

Yours respectfully
Albert Farthing

Annie's diary

APRIL 7TH

I don't know what has got into Bert. He's gone and written to his Lordship asking for Father's job when he retires. His Lordship showed me the letter and wanted to know what I thought about the idea and I think he may have wondered if I had anything to do with the matter, which of course I assured him I hadn't. But I had to be tactful although I wasn't quite sure what to say. For one thing Bert had no business writing that letter without consulting me, and, for another, I doubt he knows a darned thing about cows. I haven't dared say a word to Father yet. Apart from anything else, he doesn't really like his retirement being mentioned and what is more, he loves his cows and wouldn't want them to be looked after by anyone who didn't know what they were doing. For my part I'm not really sure whether or not I want Bert here. I have been getting along quite nicely without him, but then when I think about him, I do feel sorry for him, all alone in that cottage. But one thing's for certain. If he comes here, it's not going to be like it was before. To some extent I came here to get away from being his housemaid. In any case I doubt I would have the time now, what with all the work there is here, and Father and Mr Johnson's washing to do and one thing and another. Of course I could just tell his Lordship that Bert would be no good with the cows and that would soon queer his pitch. I might have a word with Father.

I think I am going to have to write a letter to *Lilian* (just a short one mind), saying that I am very sorry but I can't help her. That may put a stop to her writing to me. It's begun to bother me, seeing her writing on the envelope. I think it would be easier than telling his Lordship about her letters because he might easily go into a towering rage and he might anyway think that it was all somehow my fault. He might suppose that I'd already been talking to her before she left here or that I had told her something that I had no business to. Nothing makes his Lordship angrier than the thought of Lilian, Lady Otterton, and, there's no denying it, but he has a nasty temper when he's roused. I wouldn't want to tell her Ladyship either. I think it would only cause trouble as there always seems to be a row when the subject of Lilian comes up. I think her Ladyship accuses his Lordship of not standing up to his mother. He just says that her Ladyship really doesn't know what his mother is like and that he has had to put up with her spite and her moods, her lack of reason and her tantrums all his life. It makes me quite sad to think about it. He was a dear little boy, we all loved him on the farm, and we knew that *she* was downright unkind to him. It's his late Lordship who should have stood up to her, if you ask me, but then, they say he was terrified of her. The butler before the war was a Mr House from North Devon where Lady

Lilian's family came from, and he had a story or two to tell. Perhaps she's gone back to Devon. No one knows where she is, except the bank I suppose. All I can say is that it would certainly give me the heebie-jeebies if I suddenly bumped into her around these parts.

I didn't want to say anything to his Lordship or her Ladyship about Mr and Mrs Legros either for that matter. But I can't say I like the look of the pair of them. I heard her Ladyship say that it didn't really matter what they were like because she wouldn't be having very much to do with them, but Mr Johnson is really annoyed. What he says is that his Lordship must be out of his mind to have a pair of b——s like them in the house. I think he thinks that they'll steal all the silver and pictures and God knows what, and he has decided to make it his personal responsibility to watch what they get up to. Mr Johnson says that he sometimes thinks that life made more sense in the Western Desert than it ever does at Cranfield with what he calls this 'daft bunch'. I'm afraid he's still thinking about going to Australia. I hope he changes his mind. Perhaps he's too old to go now.

Sydney Otterton's diary

APRIL 10TH

The daffodils are all out. I've always loved Cranfield at daffodil time. So much so in fact, that I remember dreaming about it once when I was in Cairo on sick leave recovering from dysentery and lying in bed sweating in some grimy hotel. I kept falling asleep and then being woken up again by a damned fly landing repeatedly on my face. Every time I went back to sleep this dream recurred. Just a simple dream that I was at home down by the lake and the daffodils were in bloom. Priscilla just laughs when I tell her about it. I think she imagines I've invented it, but I can't think why. She says

I'm ridiculously sentimental, which doesn't stop her from filling the house with huge bowls of daffodils and saying that she's never seen lovelier ones than those in the field sloping down to the lake, 'fluttering and dancing in the breeze,' she says. *She* is allowed to quote poetry.

A peculiar thing happened yesterday afternoon. I'd been down to the farm to have a word with Jerrold about this and that and I was walking back up the drive with Peggy and looking across at the daffodils and down at the lake and wishing that I had enough money to dredge it and to renovate the old boathouse that's lurking there, mouldering among the bamboos, both of which things are sadly low on the list of priorities, when Legros appeared, buttoned up in a British warm and wearing an Anthony Eden hat. He had with him his wife, equally unsuitably dressed for a country walk, who was, as usual, hanging on for grim death to that huge hound leashed to a chain. The two of them were coming up from the lake, out from what is literally an impenetrable jungle of overgrown weeds and shrubs. There was something eerie about the way the pair of them suddenly materialised from nowhere and, heads bent, walked on up to the house without apparently having noticed me as I watched them from the drive above. As I went on up the hill and into the house through the front door, I was wondering what exactly it was that made the appearance of those two with their great white dog seem so sinister. I had the instinctive feeling that they had not wanted to be seen and that they had been snooping. But what on earth is there for them to snoop about down by the lake? Anyway as I crossed the hall, I thought I heard voices in the saloon, so I went over and opened the doors, expecting to find Priscilla and curious as to whom she might be talking, but there was no one in the saloon, although the door to the left, leading to the muniments room, was just quietly and mysteriously closing. I quickly nipped back into the hall and out of the other door, expecting to meet whoever it was coming through the library since there is no other way out. Sure enough, as I stepped into the library, I heard a low, ferocious growl and there was that damned white dog, lowering its huge head and baring its horrible teeth at me, with Mrs Legros hanging on to the lead as tightly as she could with both her hands. Legros stood beside her with his hat still on, which I have to admit he had the good grace to remove as I appeared with Peggy idiotically cowering at my heels.

The Legros have no business whatsoever in the library, let alone the saloon and they must have felt embarrassed by my finding them there. As for me, I have to admit that I was rather shaken by the sight of them and pretty angry, so I asked them what the bloody hell they thought they were doing and added rather unceremoniously that I didn't want them or their effing dog wandering about the house. Legros apologised obsequiously and made some ridiculous excuse in that flat whiny voice of his about the dog having slipped its leash and run away from them. I didn't believe a word of it and furthermore I don't trust the bugger a yard, with that broad, expressionless face of his and those shifty eyes.

When I told Priscilla what had happened, she was furious and pretty concerned about what they might have been up to. I did look round after they'd gone to see if they'd nicked anything but nothing seemed to be missing. I can only imagine that they were casing the joint. Priscilla was a bit worried that I might have been rude to them because she says that if I was, it would only put their backs up and make matters worse. I decided not to tell her exactly what I'd said. Then she calmed down and began to persuade herself that they had been telling the truth about the dog all along. Johnson's furious about the Legros and I'm beginning to think he may have a point.

Jerrold's due to retire in the summer, so I wanted to ask him what he thought about my taking on Annie's friend, Farthing. I know he didn't want the matter discussed but in the end, I got him to admit that he wouldn't want to hand the herd over to anyone who wasn't used to cows. So I'll let it go at that. After all Bert Farthing already has a job, and there'll be plenty of people coming out of the forces any minute, crying out for work on the land. I might even be lucky enough to find a decent cowman among them. What I can't quite make out is whether Annie really wants me to employ Farthing or not, and one thing we simply cannot afford to do, is to lose Annie.

Another problem is that you can't get a tractor for love or money. Apparently they're making plenty of them, but they all go abroad, along with the combines and the beet lifters that are made in this country. So this winter the poor landgirls will still be having the job of pulling by hand all the mangels and sugar beet that the government encourages us to grow. If ever there was a filthy job . . . then that is jolly well it.

Georgina's exercise book

Mummy stands on the landing and talks French all the time to Mamzelle. They talk for ages and ages and I dont no what they are saying. Now Mummy wants us to colect snails for her. She says she knows what to do. Im not going to eat them. So there.

Annie's diary

APRIL 15TH

Now there's an awful kerfuffle going on about the snails. You won't catch me eating snails, mind, but her Ladyship and the children and Mamzelle have brought dozens of them in from the garden and her Ladyship says they're going to be delicious and that Mamzelle knows all about them. Well she may, but what about poor Mrs Laws in the kitchen, trying to get on with her work? There's a great big wooden box right there on the floor ready for her to trip over, and full of darned snails crawling around in flour which is supposed to clean their insides out. Mrs Laws says that when she came down to the kitchen this morning, they'd got out and were walking all over the place, up the walls and along the draining board, and then his Lordship found one on the stairs which he thought very funny, but her Ladyship was furious. She said Mrs Laws ought to have known better. She should have put a lid and a heavy weight on the box to keep them from escaping. Mrs Laws was livid. She said she thought Mamzelle was supposed to be in charge of snails. In any case she's refusing to cook them and I can't say I blame her. Her Ladyship just said that nobody should look a gift-horse in the mouth in these hard times. Never mind the gift-horse's mouth, I'm not putting any snails into my own. That's for sure, and no one's ever called me fussy. Her Ladyship was in there in the kitchen this morning, pulling the wretched snails off the walls and off the oven door and carrying on alarming, talking about the French and how wonderful they are and how stupid the English are, just as if she wasn't English herself. Well I never noticed the French were so wonderful in the war, but I didn't say a thing. Now her Ladyship says the snails have got to stay another week in that box and then she'll cook them herself.

Mamzelle and Mrs Laws don't get on at all well which only makes matters worse. I suppose Mrs Laws has caught on to the fact that Mr Kipling spends half his time up in the school-room talking to Mamzelle. I feel sorry for Mrs Laws. We had enough trouble finding her and I know she's got Lorraine settled at the village school, but all the same, I doubt she'll stay if she has to spend her time chasing snails. I felt like telling her Ladyship she ought to be tactful, see.

I don't know what to do about Bert. Nothing I suppose, but I think he'll suspect me of not putting in a good word for him with his Lordship. In fact his Lordship asked me point blank what I thought about Bert coming to work here and that was after he said he'd already asked Father. Father never said a word to me, mind, but I doubt he would have encouraged the idea. I certainly didn't know what to say to his Lordship because the more I think about it now, the less I like the idea. I'd have thought Bert would have got used to being without me by now in any case. Then his Lordship mumbled something about not needing him to look after cows, but he might be wanted in the garden.

I haven't written to Lilian, Lady Otterton yet. I don't know why I keep putting it off.

Sydney Otterton's diary

MAY 5TH

Those bloody Legros are beginning to get on my nerves. I went down to the farm yesterday afternoon in my old van and when I wanted to come back, I couldn't get the damn thing to start so I walked up to the house with Peggy and went to look for Johnson who was taking a mowing machine to pieces in the back yard. He said he'd go and see if he could do something about the van for me. Then, feeling generally fed up, I went to the Japanese room, gave myself a gin and tonic, shut the doors and sat down to brood. Some of the cottages on the farm are in such dreadful condition, I can't imagine any man being prepared to live in them, let alone one with a wife and family. I don't see any way round it as I don't begin to have the money to do them all up. There'll have to be some kind of government help, particularly if what they want is to boost agriculture and encourage people back onto the land. Then I went on to think about my poisonous mother and, not unfairly, as far as I can see, to blame her for everything, all of which immediately made me want another drink and then I began to worry about Bert Farthing and Jerrold and Annie and the kitchen garden. We certainly need more help there. The whole place is overrun with docks and ground elder and I really don't see how poor old Denman can manage any longer without a bit more help. I was wondering about giving Farthing a job in the garden and then I just went back to worrying about the cottages again. There seems to be no way out.

It was about half past five and I was sitting there engrossed in my thoughts with Peggy, who's become quite biddable at last, lying peacefully at my feet, when all of a sudden I heard footsteps coming from the Palladio room next door. Priscilla had gone out for the day to see her aunt, so I supposed it might be Johnson coming to say he had mended the van, or that drunken fool, Cheadle, coming to help himself to a drink, but as I got up to go and see who it was, I heard soft voices. Who on earth would Johnson or Cheadle have been talking to? Just as I opened the door on my side, someone else opened the door on the ballroom side, and there I was, standing nose to nose with the nightmare couple and their dog. I have to say that it was a great pleasure to see the horrified looks on both their faces and to see them jump out of their skins. A sly expression momentarily crossed the old boy's face which reminded me uncomfortably of someone else, not that I could think who, but I thought he might be about to have an apoplectic fit. Pity he didn't. I was so angry and I suppose I'd had a drink, so I just bawled at them to get out, while Peggy stood beside me, ludicrously wagging her tail at the Pyrenean brute which was growling in a menacing fashion.

Thinking about it afterwards, I decided that they must have snooped about and seen that neither my van nor the car was anywhere around, so presuming that Priscilla and I were both out, they thought they could have a field day. I'm also certain that they must know that I use the Japanese room as my own private study and that I have my desk and all my papers in there.

Priscilla made me angry when she got back because she would keep going on about my shouting at the Legros, and complaining about my temper. Anybody would lose their temper with that grisly pair prowling around. I think they ought to go, but Priscilla says we can't do without the money and, because they were the only people who answered the advertisement, she's convinced that we'd never find anyone else. She didn't think it at all funny when I said I'd rather meet a fucking snail on a staircase than that pair of monsters in a ballroom. This morning she brought the subject up again rather coldly. She said that she would have to go and appease them because I had obviously been so rude and then she announced that she was sure they had a perfectly good excuse. After all, it was only natural for them to be curious about the house and they were probably only having an innocent look at the plasterwork. If they were so interested in the plasterwork why didn't they stay in the Palladio room or the hall? And, if they're so interested in plasterwork, why, as they walk, do they both always stare so fixedly at the floor?

Zbigniew Rakowski's notebook

JULY 25TH

These are bleak times indeed. Only few weeks ago we were being threatened with bread rationing, and now the latest news from Mr Shinwell is that we do not have enough coal to see us through the winter. With day after day such woeful tidings, imagine, amidst the ensuing gloom, my joy at the unexpected arrival by the morning post of a delightful letter from my *Beatrice*, my *Laura*, my very own *donna angelicata*, the

89

exquisite blue-eyed angel of my dreams. Lady Otterton bids me lunch at Cranfield next week. She wishes to introduce me to Lord Otterton's aunt who may have some papers which could be of interest to me. Alas, if only she knew how slowly *that* work is progressing, whilst *Bloodstains in the Boudoir* comes on apace, and will indeed be shortly finished.

I hastily wrote a note accepting her Ladyship's kind invitation, so that now an old man's life suddenly seems worth living again. Indeed I have concocted a plan whereby it may be possible for me to continue visiting Cranfield on a more or less regular basis for a while at least, but I shall wait until I have broached the matter with Priscilla before allowing myself to become too hopeful. This I think I shall do by letter after I have lunched there. I will not, I do not think, as yet, discuss my detective novel (*roman à clef* that it is) with her, for it has to be admitted that in the small hours, I have begun to toss and turn, to ask myself quite how her Ladyship will react to my little *bétise*, my humble *jeu d'ésprit*. Will it tickle her as it is designed to do? Will she see it as my own modest *Divine Comedy*? My hymn of love to Priscilla? At times I fear that once she has read it, she may banish me for ever from her sight, but surely not. Surely she will be flattered. Surely with her unique humour, unparalleled wit and peerless powers of perception, she will receive my dedication for what it is, an act of homage. Nevertheless, I will not discuss it prematurely.

Extract from Zbigniew Rakowski's work in progress

. . . The governess crept stealthily up the oak staircase, the murder weapon concealed beneath her cardigan. At this hour of day she felt confident of meeting no one. Her ample body quivered as one pudgy foot caused a polished board to creak ominously beneath her weight, and, unnoticed, a silvery hairpin slid from her white bun and fell to the floor,

landing noiselessly on the red patterned carpet that covered the centre of the stairs.

She knew exactly where she would deposit the blood-stained weapon, where indeed it would be quickly found and to the best possible effect. His Lordship, she thought, narrowing her pig-like eyes, will hang for this, and I, with my hand on the Sainte Bible, *will swear to his guilt . . .*

Sydney Otterton's diary

Priscilla asked Rakowski to lunch the other day because she wanted Aunt Lettice to meet him. He looked even smaller and more gnome-like than ever, but otherwise he was his usual self. You can't help quite liking the fellow despite all his humbug because, although he's always playing some damn silly part, he seems to know it, and he can be quite funny. Anyway he was obviously tickled pink to meet Aunt Lettice and she was quite delighted by him and said he was *moost* interesting. He seems to be taking an awfully long time to write his wretched book. It even crossed my mind that he might be spinning it out as an excuse to keep coming back here. Not only does he always gobble up his lunch, but he is obviously completely infatuated with Priscilla.

We're still being haunted by the Legros although I have to admit that I haven't found them snooping around the house again. All the same I hate the feeling of their presence.

I've finally agreed to take Farthing on to help in the garden as from next month, and on the farm if needed. He came to see me and seemed a decent enough sort of fellow. He's going to move into that almost derelict cottage next door to Jerrold. He seemed satisfied with that and is quite ready to do a bit of work on it himself, but I've said I'll get Kipling to have a go at it first and then Johnson might give it a lick of paint. He appeared to be quite pleased and is definitely keen to come. He's certainly got a good reference from the Gowers who will obviously be pretty sorry to lose him. Funnily enough, Annie hasn't said a word about it. Next week I've got a possible cowman coming to see me and Jerrold hasn't said much about that either. I think it'll break his heart to retire. As a matter of fact he looks as if he could go on for another twenty years.

Tony came down from London last week-end. He's certainly got his problems too, so I ended up offering him a room here. After all we've got this bloody great barracks of a house, half empty, and commuting to the City would be easy for him from Cranfield. He seemed very interested by the idea and is going to think about it, although I'm afraid Priscilla was doubtful about how well it would work out. Perhaps she gets fed up with the pair of us sitting up all night, reminiscing about the war, particularly about jollifications on leave in Cairo. Last week-end I suppose we did bang on a bit about the time we were on reconnaissance at Alamein when, with absolutely no warning, our jeep suddenly sank chassis deep into the sand. A huge Bedouin caravan had just arrived and as we were trying to get the jeep out, these great big white sheep-dogs began to attack us. Luckily the Arabs were very friendly and called the dogs off, but we had a nervous moment. Perhaps that bloody Pyrenean sheep-dog of Legros's reminds me of those dogs, which may be why I take such exception to it.

It's funny but it still seems that in spite of the discomfort, the fear, missing one's wife and so on, life was easier crossing the desert in a 'Honey' tank, than it can ever be in peacetime. I think Tony feels much the same. For one thing, we've seen too much, and feared too much, and lived on our nerves and, luckily for us, survived, but we can't put the whole damn thing behind us just like that, which is why, at the moment, everything seems to require such a monumental effort. In comparison to what we went through then, nothing now seems worthwhile or even very real. Our sensibilities were heightened in those days, now they are dulled, and at times one can feel almost despairing. Thank God for people like Johnson and Tony. Without them one might feel one was going quite mad at times.

Georgina's exercise book

We were playing in the garden and Thomas was anoying me because he said I had to be a german and be killed and I was crying. Then a car came and two men got out and asked for mr Legro. We were terryfied and Thomas took them to find Father. Jamie said they were germans who wanted to murder Father.

Annie's diary

AUGUST 16TH

There was a terrific to-do here yesterday afternoon. It was about three o'clock when I left by the back door to walk down to the farm. I had a letter to post and I was going to look in on Father. I'd just seen the children from my bedroom window. They were all three playing quite happily in the garden, but as I came out of the house, I found Thomas talking in rather a grand way, I thought, to two policemen. They were pulling his leg a bit, but when they saw me, one of them asked for Lord Otterton. I wasn't sure if his Lordship was in, but I directed them round to the front door. Thomas went striding off with them, ever so keen to know what was up, I don't doubt. I did wonder myself what they wanted, but, to tell the truth, by the time I'd posted my letter and got to Father's, I'd forgotten all about them. I was more worried about Father.

His Lordship has told him that when the new cowman and his family come, he will probably need Father's house, which is fair enough, I suppose, and the cottage at the lodge is plenty big enough for Father on his own, but it's not in a very good state of repair and Father will hate it after being in the same place all these years. He was looking a bit down in the dumps, but he didn't say much. 'It's drier where there's none,' is what Mother used to say when we children complained that the bread was stale. I rather think that that's the way Father sees most things in life. He's never been a great complainer. He never even said much when Mother went, but just turned to me instead. He used to say, 'You're my Annie now.' Poor Father, I reckon he must have been lonely at times.

He did ask me how I felt about Bert coming to Cranfield. I just told him that it won't make any difference to me, so he didn't say any more, only that he hoped they'd manage to make his cottage fit for human beings. Then he took me out to his garden to admire his marrows and his sweet peas. Father always loves his sweet peas.

By the time I got back up to the house, it seems that I'd missed most of the drama. Her Ladyship told me later to keep out of his Lordship's way because he was in a thundering rage. Apparently the police had been and after they'd spoken to his Lordship, they went along to see Mr and Mrs Legros and, blow me down, if they didn't arrest Mr Legros, but no one is saying what for. Her Ladyship was dreadfully worried because of the children. She hadn't wanted them involved, but then they'd been there when the police arrived and young Thomas had been marching around the house with them, looking for his father. Well somehow they were all sent packing back up to the school-room and Mamzelle was told to keep them inside for the rest of the afternoon although it was a lovely day and Thomas was full bent on looking for tadpoles. Her Ladyship said it was too late for tadpoles and he wouldn't find tadpoles anywhere in August. I'm not sure she was right, mind.

Anyway no one seems any the wiser about why the police took Mr Legros away. Apparently Mrs Legros was in floods of tears and quite hysterical. She left for the station soon after, in a taxi with that darned great dog. Her Ladyship doesn't think we'll see her again. She told me she didn't want me talking about what had happened to anyone. 'You know me,' I said to her. Now would I say a word? Well I certainly wouldn't say anything to Mrs Laws or the Cheadles, but I did have a word with Miss Wheel. She's back for a week, using the sewing machine in my sitting-room. She's covering a sofa with some old curtains her Ladyship found, and mending the curtains in the Peacock Room. It's wonderful what she can do and I'm certain she wouldn't be one to repeat anything.

I saw his Lordship when I went to turn down the beds. He wasn't in a rage then, in fact he looked as if butter wouldn't melt in his mouth. He probably wanted me to clear up the birdseed that blasted parrot had scattered all round his dressing-room. Anyway he asked me if I'd heard about the drama and what had happened to Mr Legros. He was chuckling about it as if it was the funniest thing that had ever happened. 'Do you know, Annie,' he said, 'I always hated the b——.' Then he went on about various times he'd found him prowling around the house with Mrs Legros whose face was as white as the dog's. Then he was stalking round the room, imitating the pair of them. You couldn't help laughing. Her Ladyship was quite annoyed when she came in. 'Annie,' she said, 'don't you realise this is quite serious?' And his Lordship said, 'Don't blame Annie.' I just quietly left.

I expect her Ladyship's worried because they might have stolen something and because she let them have the flat when his Lordship never wanted them here in the first place. Mr Johnson is sure to know all about it. I wonder what he'll have to say.

Sydney Otterton's diary

Priscilla's desperate to find someone else to take the flat now the Legros dit Courriers have gone. I presume we really have seen the last of them. I expect he'll be behind bars for a while as the police apparently had a list of charges as long as your arm. Of course they still owe quite a lot of rent, but judging by the fact that, as she left, she was begging us to lend her the train fare to London, I don't suppose we'll ever see a penny of it.

I do feel sorry for Priscilla though, because, to be fair, she took a lot of trouble to make that flat half-way decent and it was hardly her fault if a pair of crooks turned up to rent it. We haven't found anything missing yet, but I can't help feeling that we may before long.

I was talking to Johnson this evening and he told me something which has left me feeling a bit uneasy. Everybody in this village knows everyone else's business, partly because the post office is a centre for gossip, and partly because of the telephone exchange. If you ring someone and the line is engaged, the people at the exchange tell you that Mrs So-and-So's talking to her mother or her auntie . . . And as if that weren't bad enough, it now appears that the postman who empties the box at the farm has told the postmistress in the village that he's surprised by how many letters he collects from that particular box which are addressed to my mother. He'd heard that my mother and I didn't get on, so he took it upon himself to wonder who could have been writing to her. I think he was quite right to wonder. I would certainly like to know who, on this place, is busily keeping in contact with her, and why. I haven't written to my mother for months and Priscilla certainly wouldn't write to her. Of course the postmistress would love to know too, but where she made her mistake was in talking to Johnson about it. Even if he knew, he'd never tell her. He won't even tell me who he thinks it is, because, he says, he can't be certain.

Annie's diary

I was quite cross with Mr Johnson yesterday. We were having a cup of tea in my sitting-room and I'd just sat down to enjoy my one cigarette of the day. I always have my one cigarette with my cup of tea in the afternoon. Anyway, he looked at me as bold as brass and asked me if I had been writing to Lilian, Lady Otterton. I looked at him and I thought to myself, now, there's no good you gazing at me with those big brown eyes of yours, and making suggestions like that.

Of course he knew that *Lilian* had wanted to pay me to spy for her, but he must have known perfectly well that I would do no such thing. Furthermore I'd already told him so. Of course, like all men, when I gave him a piece of my mind, he tried to sweet talk me. 'Go on Annie,' he says, 'don't take on so . . .' I couldn't help wondering, though, why he was asking me about *Lilian* all of a sudden. Then he told me this long story about the postman who empties the box at the farm, finding all these letters to Lilian. Neither of us could imagine who on earth might be writing to her, but it's horrible to think that someone here is spying on us all. Mr Johnson is determined to find out who it is, even if it means putting off going to Australia, he said, with a twinkle in his eye. If you ask me he'll never get to Australia. In any case he'd do better to stay here.

It wasn't until I got to bed last night that I suddenly remembered that when I did eventually write to Lady Lilian, which I should have done way back, I posted the letter down at the farm. In fact, I'd been putting off writing and keeping my fingers crossed that she had forgotten about me when I suddenly had another nasty little note from her, written, I reckon, when she was out of her mind with drink or the Lord knows what! It didn't make very much sense as far as I could see. I don't know why, but I never mentioned that note to anyone, not even to Mr Johnson. I just tore it into little bits and put it straight down the w.c. Then, ever so quickly, I wrote a letter back and posted the wretched thing at the farm last week. I think it must have been the same day that the police came for Mr Legros. And now I don't want to tell Mr Johnson about that letter or he'll think I was fibbing yesterday. In my head I have been going over and over what I wrote and cannot imagine that anyone could read anything into it that was not meant to be there, yet the whole thing worries me. I only wrote the one perfectly innocent letter of which I made and kept a copy and which certainly doesn't explain who has been sending the others.

Letter from Annie to Lilian, Lady Otterton

Cranfield Park.
AUGUST 15TH, 1946

M'lady,

Thank you for your letter. I hope your Ladyship can appreciate that I am unable to give you any information about what passes at Cranfield. I am employed by the present Lord and Lady Otterton about whose private affairs I know nothing and to whom I owe my loyalty. Please do not ask for any further help from me.

Yours faithfully,
Annie Jerrold

Georgina's exercise book

Father wants to by us a pony but Mummy says there too xpensive. Mr Kipling is always in the school-room making mamzel laugh. He likes her cough mixcher and is always winking and pretending to cough. I hope we get a pony.

Zbigniew Rakowski's notebook

AUGUST 30TH

To what folly does an old man descend when his ancient frame is shaken as mine is by a passion more suited to the lusty heart of a younger Romeo? When I lunched earlier this month at Cranfield, so dazzled was I by her Ladyship's magical presence and so flattered by the kind attentions of Lord Otterton's gracious aunt, that I failed to remember to take my umbrella home with me. When I left my hovel in the morning, rain threatened, but the radiant sunshine of Priscilla's dazzling personality soon chased the clouds away, leaving a bright, light afternoon and a hyacinth-blue sky to match, need I say it, her Ladyship's sapphire eyes.

I did not think that Annie could reasonably be asked to make a parcel of so unwieldy an object and (let us not deceive ourselves about the matter) I somewhat relished the idea of an excuse to return as soon as I might to Cranfield, and thus I wrote to Priscilla to thank her for the delicious rabbit pie of which we had partaken, suggesting that I might, in the not too distant future, call to collect my carelessly mislaid umbrella. I have to admit that it was not without a little disappointment that I received her Ladyship's reply. Gladly she welcomed me to collect my umbrella at any time convenient to myself, insisting only that I inform Annie of my intentions. There was no invitation to share further exquisite ragouts of *oryctulagus cuniculus*, of carrots and turnips, only, or so it felt to my sick heart, instructions to collect my possessions and *scram*. Ah me, they are not long indeed, the days of wine and roses.

However, I did not wish to hasten too soon back to Cranfield, but rather preferred to relish the anxious days of sweet expectation leading up to my visit and carefully to plan it in such a way as to increase the likelihood of an encounter with the object of my dreams – nay, of my desire. So it was that yesterday morning I betook myself to Cranfield. It was about midday as I walked from the station up through the village to the park gates, bearing my small basket in which I had packed a book, my sandwiches and a cushion, for I thought to find a pleasant spot within sight of Leoni's *capolavoro* where I might sit and picnic and indulge my fancy.

As I walked up the drive and rounded the bend to see the great house away across the park, stark and red against the dark green, heavy summer background, I was reminded of my first visit to Cranfield just over a year ago. Such is the hold that this place has exerted over me since that very first day that I, a formerly sagacious old man, have been metamorphosed. I have become foolish and fanciful, but not for one moment do I regret my folly, for now I do not, as I did formerly, suffer from tedium nor from the inevitable *ennui* of the sceptic. Now there is excitement, intrigue and joy.

Yesterday, as I sat on my cushion under a tree, eating a fishpaste sandwich and gazing across at Cranfield, I could not be sure whether it was Priscilla or the house which truly held me in thrall. I had encountered no one on the drive, nor was I observed as I picked my way through nettles and thistles and up a gentle slope to the middle of a small field where a lone oak peacefully spreads its boughs. The day was hot and sultry, lazy insects hovered around my picnic, bold, daytime rabbits lolloped in and out of the hedgerows, some long-faced Guernsey cows stared soulfully at me across a rusty iron fence and somewhere a thrush sang. I was in an idyllic setting at an idyllic moment. When I had finished my picnic, I returned to the drive and walked on up it towards the house. At one point I came across a hundred tiny frogs crossing the road, leaping, hopping, jostling one another, heedless of the flattened bodies of their many peers so recently squashed by a passing vehicle, as, full of hope, they hurried on towards their destination.

Perhaps Annie had seen me approaching from a window, for no sooner had I reached the front door than there she was with my umbrella held out towards me. She did not suggest that I come in, but merely commented on the warmth of the weather and wished me good day. I can only say, that of a sudden I felt forlorn and unwilling to return immediately from whence I came. Thus it was that before betaking myself back to the village by way of the front lawn and the path that leads through the wood to the church, I wandered down towards the overgrown lake where I came across the three children attempting to capture frogs. The girl, Georgina, was, I noticed, in tears, bewailing her incompetence at the sport in hand. It crossed my mind to wonder if she might not be in danger of falling into the water and drowning, but considering her childish troubles to be none of my business, I simply doffed my sun hat, and went on my way.

Wishing to linger in the neighbourhood, for I was still hopeful of a chance encounter with her Ladyship, I found some trifling excuse to visit the village shop and post office where I happened to run into Mr Johnson. Johnson is a fine-looking fellow, a self-assured north countryman of some fifty summers, who joined the war with the 11th Hussars as a reservist and subsequently became Lord Otterton's driver. I have never been quite sure exactly what function he performs at Cranfield now, but his Lordship evidently holds him in the highest esteem and he in return is apparently devoted to his

Lordship. Perhaps his function is in some degree to act as a father figure to his indisciplined young employer.

I think that Mr Johnson was not immediately aware of my presence, for he was engaged in a curious exchange with a postman and the spinster lady who keeps the shop. I could not help but remark that, even in this warm weather, Miss Gooch, as she is called, was wearing her usual grey, knitted mittens. Her poor hands are twisted with arthritis. The postman stood between her and Johnson, one elbow leaning casually on the counter, with his hat held behind his head between the thumb and forefinger of his other hand, thus permitting himself to use the ear-finger, not for the purpose for which it was named, but rather with which to scratch his balding pate. After a moment, Miss Gooch, sensing my presence, interrupted the conversation to wish me good afternoon. It was then that Johnson first noticed me, but not before I had partially divined the nature of the discourse in which the three of them were involved.

It would appear that they had been discussing calligraphy. Mr Johnson, in possession of various samples of hand-writing, was, to my amazement, being advised by Miss Gooch and the postman as to whether or not they were familiar with any of them. 'I seen that one,' I heard the postman say ungrammatically, as he continued scratching his head in the manner I have described. Miss Gooch meanwhile looked a little puzzled. She is a gentle old lady who always wears her snowy hair tied into a roll at the nape of her neck by a blue ribbon attached around her head. This ribbon and her overall both seem designed to match the thick rich, waxy blue of the paper bags used by grocers everywhere. Despite her spectacles, she appears to be a little short-sighted and so was bent like a small mouse over whatever it was that Mr Johnson had placed on the counter, her grey paws placed carefully side by side.

I may be an old man, but as a professional writer, it is ever my business to observe. It sometimes occurs to me that whatever quaint mannerisms may be mine, they have the effect of bamboozling others as to my real nature. Thus I do not suppose for one moment that it crossed the mind of either Johnson or Miss Gooch that I was even remotely aware that what they were involved in was no ordinary commercial transaction, yet, as soon as Johnson became conscious of my presence, he hastily snatched up various pieces of paper and stuffed them into his pocket. He gave me a somewhat cursory nod and a flat, north-country 'good-afternoon', before swiftly leaving the shop with a few muttered words to Miss Gooch and a sidelong glance at the postman. A rather flustered Miss Gooch then hastened to attend to my requirements.

On reflection, there was something so strange about the whole episode, that it was as if I had entered the pages of my own novel. *The Poisoned Postmistress*, I instantly thought, or perhaps *The Soldier Servant's Revenge*. But what, I wonder, can verily lie at the root of all this mystery?

I haven't yet put my new proposal to either Lord or Lady Otterton. I shall do so forthwith, as indeed I must.

Georgina's exercise book

AUGUST 30TH

Yesterday Mr Rkofsky cort us down by the lake. Were not supposed to go there becaus me and Jamie cant swim. Thomas said it was all right becos he could save us if we fell in and he wanted to get some frogs to put in mamzel's bed. Acsherly we only got one and it escaped. Mamzel was livid. She said she saw us out of the window and we wernt on the lawn but we said we were. Mr Rkofsky looks funny. I think hes very old. He's got a beerd and a sun hat and talks like an old old man.

Annie's diary

I cannot understand how Mr Johnson knows that I wrote to Lilian, Lady Otterton. Of course he may be simply guessing, but it's most peculiar him being so sure. Naturally I've said nothing, I've only told him that he has no idea what he's talking about. 'Now come on Annie,' he says. 'You can come clean.' He makes me quite cross, and to tell the truth, I suspect he's being difficult just because of Bert's arrival which will have put his nose out of joint no end, I should think. Anyway all he can think about these days now the football has started up again for the first time since the war, is winning the pools and dashing off to the other side of the world. Thousands of people were so excited about the football, that they all turned out the other day in the pouring rain to watch some match or other. As for me, I'd sooner stay at home and do my ironing, or go for a quiet walk through the fields.

His Lordship's been in a bad mood lately too, so, between the pair of them, I've been pretty fed up. Mr Kipling hadn't finished the work he was supposed to have done on the cottage by the time Bert appeared, which is hardly surprising, since he spends all day up on the school-room landing with Mamzelle, laughing and giggling. Anyway the fuss about the cottage made his Lordship see red although he just thinks it's funny about Mr Kipling and Mamzelle, so he doesn't say anything to Mr Kipling but lets him get away with murder. It's a wonder what that man sees in Mamzelle, if you ask me, but I couldn't help laughing to myself the other day when I heard Mrs Kipling say that she was welcome to have the lazy so-and-so for all she cared.

Then there's Father who's staying on till October now because his new cottage isn't ready either, and, in any case, he's all of a dither about moving. Not that he ever complains, but I can tell. And naturally he's worried to death about his blessed cows. We don't know anything yet about the man his Lordship has taken on, but Father thinks the yield is sure to go down as soon as he retires. And I don't doubt it.

Bert's been at me too of course, because I haven't been seeing him as much as he would like, but I told him that what with Father and one thing and another, I haven't the time. I don't think he's cottoned on to Mr Johnson yet.

Sydney Otterton's diary

SEPTEMBER 15TH

Blasted Kipling is never anywhere to be found although Priscilla tells me he spends half his time in the school-room with that French woman who apparently calls him *le petit homme au châpeau rond* and fills him up with *crème de menthe*. I don't know what Mrs Kipling has to say about it, but I should think he must be pretty desperate if he's after Mlle. She must be twice his age. Anyway, it's quite annoying because he hasn't finished the work he's supposed to have done on Bert Farthing's cottage, so Bert's living in something like a slum. The window frames are all splintering and the whole place is riddled with rot. In fact Bert's been pretty good about it and has been doing some work on the place himself. Priscilla gets cross because she says she can't think how I commanded a regiment or led a column across the desert, if I can't even sort Kipling out. What am I supposed to do? Go up to the school-room and tell the pair of them to stop boozing?

Johnson's making a bit of a nuisance of himself at the moment too. I don't know why he has to go on so much about all these letters he says someone's been sending my mother. I don't want to hear any more about it, but he's determined to get to the bottom of it. He told me point blank that he didn't think it had anything to do with Annie. It's never ever crossed my mind that she might be involved in any way with my mother. Now he wants to know if I can find a sample of Legros's handwriting because the nosy postman has a theory that the letters have stopped. It's ridiculous to suppose that I can control who writes to whom. In any case whoever it is that was writing could be posting their letters somewhere else for all I know, or care. You can't go around suspecting the Legros; the frightful pair didn't even know my mother.

Much more to the point is my maiden speech which I'd rather given up thinking about but which I will be making some time in the autumn. Obviously it'll be about what most concerns me which is the agricultural industry and housing. Everything to do with all that is chaotic at the moment and I'm sure I'm not the only landlord with such insoluble problems on my hands, even if I am the only one with an estate carpenter who spends his time poodle-faking with a geriatric governess.

In fact I find that with the House of Lords not sitting at the moment, I become quite restless spending all my time here. Perhaps it's just because nothing ever seems to be settled and Priscilla who does so much so well makes me feel pretty useless at times. I can't help thinking things will get a bit easier once we do finally get probate, whenever that will be. At least, then, I'll have some idea of how things stand.

I thought of buying a horse and a pony for the children but foolishly mentioned it to Priscilla who announced categorically that I couldn't afford either. There doesn't seem to be much point in living in a place like this if you can't even have a horse, and the children were delighted by the thought of a pony but now we'll just have to see how things go next year.

One good thing is that Priscilla has found a respectable widow who certainly ought to be a better bet than the Legros to take the flat. But on top of that particular success, she's begun to get really very fed up with Cheadle. She insists that he has to go, and I can't deny that he was absolutely blotto when Priscilla's aunt came to lunch. He couldn't begin to walk in a straight line and at one point I really thought he was going to fall over, but I still can't help feeling sorry for the old boy. With that great big red hooked nose of his, he looks more like my parrot than anything else, and I don't suppose for a moment that he'll find another job very easily. Mrs Cheadle looks like a real martinet; she probably cracks a whip at him to keep him in some sort of order. No wonder the poor fellow has taken to the bottle, living with a woman like her. I've promised Priscilla I'll talk to him at the end of the week but I can't say I'm looking forward to doing so, although I suppose I'll have to. After all, I know Priscilla has a point; apart from anything else the bugger's getting through my port at a terrific rate.

I've been having rather unpleasant nightmares lately so in order to put off the hour of going to sleep, I've been sitting up late and consequently drinking rather a lot myself which may explain why I'm not very much in Priscilla's good books at the moment.

Annie's diary

SEPTEMBER 19TH

Mr Johnson told me in the end how he knew I'd written to *Lilian*. Apparently he's been talking to the postman who empties the box at the farm. I wasn't very pleased with him and haven't spoken to him for a week which not only serves him right, but is just as well because it's given me a chance to see a bit of Bert who's feeling rather down in the dumps since coming here. I told him it was his own damn fault. No one asked him to move. It's hardly surprising if he misses the cottage he's lived in all his life which, in any case, is a darned sight nicer than what he's living in now. That cottage has been empty for any number of years so no wonder it's full of damp and falling to bits. He wasn't very pleased either when I made it quite plain that we weren't picking up where we left off. 'Oh, Annie,' he said, 'I only came here because of you.' 'More fool you,' I said. It's not that I mind keeping him company of an evening from time to time, but he needn't think I'm being his unpaid housekeeper-cum-wife. He can look elsewhere for a fool who's prepared to play that part. I don't really know why I didn't stop him from coming here in the first place. Mark my words, there's bound to be trouble.

There's a new person coming into the flat which her Ladyship's very pleased about. We've had to go and clear it up behind the Legros. They left a shocking mess and it took Mrs Kipling and Mrs Summers all morning to make the place look half respectable. You'd have thought it hadn't seen a duster since before the Legros moved in. The oven was covered in grease, there was some sour milk left in the Frigidaire, the bath and the w.c. were filthy, there were dog hairs all over the place and there was even a bowl full of stinking dog food in the middle of the bedroom floor. It was quite peculiar. Considering how neat and tidy the pair of them always looked, you would have thought that Mrs Legros would have been most particular. Her Ladyship and I were just taking the loose covers off the chairs to get them cleaned when Mr Johnson turned up to see if her Ladyship needed him to mend anything or move some furniture. I just let him get on with it and didn't pay him a blind bit of notice, although I did hear him say he'd take all the rubbish down, and there was plenty of that. I doubt the Legros had so much as emptied a waste-paper basket during the whole time they were here.

What with one thing and another, I sometimes wonder how long his Lordship and her Ladyship will be able to keep going here. There seem to be so many difficulties in every quarter, not to mention all the personal intrigue that goes on and, if his Lordship doesn't give Mr Cheadle the sack shortly, I think there'll be a hell of a to-do. I keep my mouth shut but

I do know Mr Johnson said something to his Lordship about all the empty port bottles that were put out last week. He didn't say anything about Mr Cheadle though, but only passed a comment. His Lordship can draw his own conclusions, but I think he'd have a bit of a shock if he went and looked in his cellar which is supposed to have been well stocked since before the war. I really don't know why his Lordship keeps Cheadle on. Either he can't be bothered to do anything about finding a new butler, or he really thinks the whole thing is just funny. And I wouldn't put that past him. He always thinks everything is funny.

Sydney Otterton's diary

SEPTEMBER 28TH

I sacked Cheadle yesterday morning. All Priscilla could find to say when I told her was, 'High time too!' Of course she's right up to a point but when I thought he was about to blub I couldn't help feeling sorry for the miserable old so-and-so. For one thing, it's impossible to imagine what will happen to him now. I don't suppose he could stop drinking if he tried, so even if he gets another job, he won't keep it for long. He's probably been at the bottle all his life and you can hardly blame him for that, with a wife like his. Well I soon stopped feeling sorry for him when he turned on me and called me every name under the sun. Luckily Johnson was around down in the basement after that. I don't know what he was doing, but he found Cheadle in a terrible rage, getting ready to pour all my best port down the drain as an act of revenge. Johnson managed to calm him down and when he told me about it later, he said that even he felt sorry for Cheadle. The man's got a wife and two children still at school and now he'll have nowhere to live. I felt so guilty about it that I started drinking rather earlier than I should have myself.

After that I began thinking about my mother again. I suppose that when one is a child whatever happens seems normal since it is the only norm one knows, but by Jove it was peculiar living on the top floor of this house with a mad mother who either screamed at one or ignored one and of whom I was certainly afraid. The servants were terrified of her too. I used to lie in bed at night petrified lest she should decide to come roaming around the house seeking whom she might devour. Sometimes she would come into my room and stare at me crazily without saying anything and then turn and leave as suddenly as she had come. At other, rarer but in some ways more awful times, she would put on a tremendous show of acutely embarrassing and quite artificial maternal concern, boasting to whoever was around about her marvellous son. The very memory of her mad, vacant stare is enough to make me shudder. I can't think why my father didn't have her locked up, as she occasionally threatened to do to me when she disapproved of something I'd done.

I suppose that I initially came to understand how mad and bad she was when I used to be sent to stay with my cousins in Devon. Their mother was so kind and sweet and always appeared so concerned for me when the time came to pack me off back home. Nowadays the more I think of my father living in this house with a woman like that, the more I pity him although I can't really forgive him for having been so weak. I remember now, that whenever she was out or away, which wasn't very often, he would become quite a different man. He would relax and become mellower, laughing a lot. He made good jokes, but beyond that, I don't think we ever had a serious conversation. I think we were wary of each other. Now that it's too late, there are a lot of things I would like to be able to ask him.

Thomas went back to school last week which was just as well as Mlle can't begin to control him, but all the same, I couldn't help feeling a pang when I saw him go. He was quite subdued, not at all his usual cocky self. In fact he looked quite forlorn as he got into the car and I couldn't help wondering what the future held for him, or indeed what there will be left of this place by the time I kick the bucket. Nothing, I should think, to judge from the way things are going. The other children both seem remarkably jolly as if they didn't have a care in the world. Mlle has them out there every day picking food from the fields and hedgerows – dandelions, blackberries, sorrel, mushrooms, wild carrots. She'll be feeding them on bird's-nest soup before she's through.

Johnson's still going on about those letters to my mother and his latest idea is that they definitely were from the Legros. I told him not to be a bloody fool. How could the Legros have anything to do with my mother or know anything about her, let alone how to get in touch with her? And in any case, what would they have to say to her? They came out of nowhere and, according to someone, had been living abroad in Switzerland all through the war. Anyway, he says that when the flat was cleared out after they left, he found some samples of their handwriting in the dustbin which he then took up to the Post Office where both Miss Gooch and the postman swore that it was the same as the writing on the envelopes addressed to my mother. If you ask me the whole thing's getting quite out of hand, but Priscilla is a bit uneasy about it all and can't quite dismiss the thought of Legros. In any case, I don't see that there's very much we can do about it either way since the fellow's probably in jug by now.

Georgina's exercise book

SEPTEMBER 29TH

Poor Thomas had to go back to school. He says its beastly and they beat you all the time and give you no food. Weve started lessons again. Major Doubleday is boring. He makes us do spelling and tables all the time. Mamzel makes us talk French at tea. Jamie just giggles.

Sydney Otterton's diary

I don't know what Johnson expects me to do about the blasted Legros. Everyone's talking about the Nuremberg verdicts and all he can think about is Legros, as if the fellow were some sort of monster on a par with Goering or Ribbentrop. He even seems to think that I ought to write to my mother and ask her if she knows anything about the Legros. I've told him that that would be perfectly pointless because, subject as she is to insane delusions, she'd only lie. She might not even answer my letter. As far as I can see, the sooner the whole matter is forgotten, the better. Priscilla thinks that Johnson has a point for once. She thinks that if we were being spied on by a crook, we ought not merely to try to find out what has been going on, but to make it absolutely clear to my mother that we won't put up with any more of it. She also thinks that the Legros must have stolen things from us and that we should go through everything very carefully to see if anything is missing. There is so much junk in this house and there are so many pictures and snuff-boxes and trinkets everywhere that probably even I don't know exactly what we've got. Besides everything has been moved about so much since before the war that it's impossible to remember where some pieces of furniture are, let alone all the damn bibelots. None of the best things appear to have been touched, some of which would have been easy to take. I somehow don't think that whatever the truth about them may be, those Legros were thieves.

Rakowski is back again. I must say I was even quite pleased

to see him. But no doubt not as pleased as Priscilla. She makes a lot of fun of him behind his back but I think, like me, she finds him funny and unusual, besides which he flatters her a lot and makes her think she's very clever. She is perfectly clever, but she gets fed up with me because I'm so unintellectual and is furious when I tease her for reading French books. In fact I rather admire her for being able to, but I'm not going to say so. Anyway Rakowski and she bang on together about Proust and Gide and Flaubert which seems to make them both happy. Funny thing about Rakowski is that, for all his affected mannerisms and all his archaic turns of phrase, he's not really intellectually pretentious. Probably because he has such an acute sense of the ridiculous which he depends upon to present the ludicrous image he does of himself. An image behind which he hides so that none of us probably knows the real Rakowski. Anyway he's back again. I wonder what he'd think if he knew that at one time Johnson suspected him of being the secret letter-writer. But he's apparently been exculpated. Johnson saw him in the Post Office one afternoon which, for some reason, he found very suspicious. I can't imagine Johnson having a good word to say for Rakowski whom I've often heard him refer to as that 'pansy writer'. Next to Legros, he'd probably be most delighted to see him incriminated.

This time the pansy writer has an idea that he wants to write a history of the Otterton family. Of course there are masses more papers for him to go through here and my aunt, who took to him when she met him at lunch, has been, as she would say, *moost* enthusiastic about the idea. She has got quite a few family papers and she not only knows a great deal about the family, but, despite evidence to the contrary, she firmly believes that the Ottertons are the greatest blessing that the Good Lord ever happened to bestow on this country. They're certainly a rum bunch which is probably what appeals to Rakowski about them. I don't really know what the fellow thinks he's doing, though, because he hasn't finished his book on the Whigs yet and, according to Priscilla, is being chased by his publisher.

Zbigniew Rakowski's notebook

So it is settled that I am to return on a regular basis to Cranfield. Lord and Lady Otterton and indeed his Lordship's gracious aunt, Lady Isley, have all encouraged me most generously in my new undertaking. Not wishing to put too high a value on my poor self as a writer, I am somewhat tempted to suspect that neither Lord Otterton nor Lady Isley felt entirely indifferent to what they may both have perceived as a flattering request on my part. They may have been not a little surprised that an old Polak such as myself should become so interested in a family abounding with rakes and turncoats, with angry men and eccentrics, that he would wish to devote some two or three hundred pages to their antics, not to mention the many hours required to research those antics. Whatever surprise they may have felt, however, they kept concealed and purported to regard it as only natural that their family should be of inordinate interest to anyone who might pause for one moment to consider it.

There are, of course, as well as the rakes and turncoats, one or two deserving members of the family whose deeds are worthy of recall. Not least of these is the great Sydney Otterton, the eighteenth-century Speaker of the House of Commons, renowned unlike, alas, too many of the family, for his integrity and devotion to duty, and who at the end of a long life, suffered a protracted and painful death which he is said to have borne with courage, good humour and breeding! I have to say that Lord Otterton is himself less anxious than his aunt to promote the respectable members of the family. He, with a wide grin, would rather dwell on one Tom

Otterton whose passion was to drive a four-in-hand and of whom it was apparently said that he possessed an infinity of wit that not too infrequently degenerated into buffoonery. Lord Otterton, I conclude, is more than likely sensible of an affinity with this character.

Although I am of the opinion that I will delight in the undertaking on which I will shortly embark, of course it is not the integrity and wisdom of Speaker Otterton alone, nor is it the tomfoolery of his descendants that draws me back and back to Cranfield, that house which has so infiltrated my soul as to have now become almost a part of my very being. My frivolous work of fiction is all but finished, yet I have decided that for the time being I must put it aside, most particularly because I sense that with my return to the house, I may feel the need to alter it and develop it in directions that had not hitherto occurred to me. As for my other work, I fear that I am still lagging behind with it. It will be long overdue before it reaches my publisher's desk but I mean to make a start on my further research whilst completing the work in hand. Perhaps I will allow myself a visit to Cranfield as a reward for finishing a chapter, thus providing my idle old self with a carrot when what I truly need may be a stick.

Priscilla, not altogether surprisingly, is somewhat sardonic with regard to my project. 'They're a very dull family, you know,' she says. 'Not one of them ever read a book and their taste has always been quite appalling.' 'Ah, but Ma'am,' I reply, 'they caused to be built one of the great houses of England, something of which they can be justly proud. Think Ma'am,' I begged her, 'of Rysbrack's exquisite chimney pieces, think of his garlanded grapes, of his sacrifice to Diana, his sacrifice to Bacchus, and let me hear no more of this nonsense.' 'I can only imagine that the Ottertons were very vulgar at the time,' she retorts, 'vying with other rich families as to who could have the biggest or the grandest house. Or as to who could spend most money. Cranfield was just an accident dependent on the circumstance. Consider,' she says, 'the monstrosity they would have built had good fortune attended them a hundred and fifty years later.' 'Ah, the ifs and buts of history,' I sigh. Yet no one is more carried away than she by the enchantment of the very house she affects to denigrate.

Letter from Annie to Dolly

NOVEMBER 3RD, 1946

Dear Dolly,

Thank you for your letter. I'm sorry not to have written for so long but we have been very busy here what with one thing and another and then I have been helping Father move as well. He seems quite happy at the lodge and says that it suits him at his age to have a smaller garden. Mind you he has already started digging it. He says that no one has looked after that garden since before the war. Well, I wouldn't be surprised because for one thing the house has been empty. It's not in too bad a condition though and the w.c. is just by the back door. I wish it was inside, but at least it's not right at the end of the garden.

The new cowman has come. He is a little red-headed man with a very big wife. They have several children who make a lot of noise and get on Bert's nerves next door. Bert has cheered up a bit which is just as well but I suspect he's really regretting having made the move. Not that he'd admit it, mind.

There's also a new butler. A Mr Mason. He and Mrs Mason keep themselves to themselves so I'm not sure what to think of them yet. I rather think his Lordship misses Mr Cheadle, for all his faults, and the children are always singing a song he taught them about a brown-faced sailor. Rather a drunken song, if you ask me. Not that I've said so.

His Lordship has bought a pink and white cockatoo which lives with the parrot in his dressing-room and makes a frightful darned mess and a lot of noise. Her Ladyship was none too pleased when that put in an appearance.

The house is very cold and we are all hoping that we don't have too hard a winter.

Well that's all the news for now. Give my love to the children.

Love from
Annie

Sydney Otterton's diary

NOVEMBER 29TH

Having spent the evening with Tony, I got home pretty late last night and needless to say have an almighty hangover this morning. I think he's agreed to come and live here after Christmas. I know he likes the idea and only hesitates for fear that it might not work out and we might regret it. Priscilla agrees with me that it's an easy way to help an old friend and that, in any case, it would be nice for us to have him here. He can pay a peppercorn rent, if he feels like it.

I'd been at the House of Lords all afternoon where they were debating the rise in the divorce rate. The Lord Chancellor kept talking about a tidal wave of divorce sweeping the country, but, as Tony said, what else can you expect? He came back after the war to find his wife disappeared, as no doubt hundreds of other men did (Johnson for one) and I don't really see what the government or any other government can do about it. In my view it would be quite impossible in any case for a man to come back from fighting or from being a prisoner of war and to pick up with his wife as if nothing had happened. Apart from anything else, you've hardly seen each other for six years.

Anyway next week I've got my maiden speech to make, which is causing me a lot of trouble. I know what I want to say but I want to be sure of doing it well, but still, I don't quite understand why the prospect of standing up and saying what I have to say seems rather more terrifying at times than the thought of a line of German tanks. I'll be glad when it's over.

Zbigniew Rakowski's notebook

DECEMBER 10TH

Today I visited Cranfield for the last time this year. It was bitterly cold in the Red Drawing-Room despite a small electric heater with one bar that Annie very kindly saw fit to provide me with. Next time I go there I shall remember to take a rug to wrap around my knees. I doubt that I could gladly suffer such cold again, even for a glance from her Ladyship's blue eyes or for the pleasure of lunching with her.

Lord Otterton at luncheon was much concerned with the House of Lords and his maiden speech which he apparently delivered with aplomb yesterday afternoon. He seemed quite elated by what had clearly been a success for him. I enquired as to the subject on which he had addressed the House. It was indeed a subject that must be dear to his heart, concerning the housing of the rural labour force and the renovation of old cottages, which he claims would be considerably more economical than the building of new houses. I feel that to a certain extent we were treated to a repeat performance of yesterday's speech, with his Lordship ending his oration with a flourish of sentiment, for we, he says are merely trustees for the future, whose duty it is to protect the beauty of our villages and countryside and not destroy them with indiscriminate building for which future generations will curse us. Lord Otterton appeared to have the full support of his consort in this matter.

So I shall not now return to Cranfield until the New Year but hermit-like will withdraw to my small dwelling where I shall slave over the final chapter of the Whigs, interrupted briefly only by the annual Christmas visit of my poor daughter and her tedious husband. At least I shall have the consolation of knowing that it will be easier for me to keep the frostbite at bay in my small room than it ever would be in the Red Drawing-Room at Cranfield.

Sydney Otterton's diary

DECEMBER 10TH

Priscilla is wonderful as usual. God knows how she keeps this house afloat as well as being so very nice and encouraging as she was to me about my speech which, I have to say, went off very well. Several people congratulated me about it afterwards so that I felt quite pleased with myself. It seemed like the first thing I'd done at all well since the end of the war, so that all yesterday evening and this morning I was quite fired up by the prospect of some kind of continuing political involvement.

Then old Rakowski came to lunch and asked how the speech had gone and by the time I'd talked about it to him and gone through the whole thing again, I suddenly felt very flat and deflated. It's freezing cold and quite impossible to keep this place warm. I know we're lucky to have our own logs, but we need coal as well, so let's hope we have a mild winter as it appears that the country's already running out of fuel.

Poor Priscilla's keeping an amazing smile on her face and doing her very best about Christmas which is a nightmare that none of us can afford. I admire her energy and her level-headedness. It's hardly surprising if she gets a bit fed up with me at times as I seem to go from the heights to the depths without any warning. A depressing letter from my solicitors this morning didn't help either. I'll be glad when Christmas is over.

Georgina's exercise book

No more lessons. Goody-goody gumdrops! Thomas is coming home tomorrow and theirs only a week till Christmas. Goody-goody gumdrops!

1947

Georgina's exercise book

Poor Thomas had to go back to school today. He looked sad and now he's gone me and Jamie have to start lessons. Boo-hoo. We prayed for snow so we'd get snowed in and he wouldn't have to go but it didn't work. Jamie's always singing a briliant song Mr Cheedle taught us about the brown faced sailor lardy dardy da. Father thinks its funny but Mummy says its silly. Anyway Mr Cheedle's gone and now we've got Mr Mason who is boring. Mamzel keeps teaching us French songs about o clair de la looner. I heard her singing them to Mr Kipling and he was laughing. Father's got a friend called Tony whose come to live with us. He's awfully nice.

Annie's diary

I can truly say I have never been so cold in all my life. What with the fuel shortage and now a shortage of food as well, it'll be a wonder if any of us ever survive this winter. The meat ration was reduced again yesterday from one and tuppence worth a week to a shilling's worth and now they're even talking of rationing bread. No one's going to be getting very fat with that.

Mr Rakowski was here yesterday, working away in the Red Drawing-Room with a rug wrapped round his knees and a hot-water bottle which I filled up for him a couple of times by his feet. I can just see him struggling on and off the bus with that great heavy stone thing under his arm and his rug and all his bits and pieces of paper. He was wearing mittens while he worked but he told me that by the time he left at three o'clock, he thought he might have frostbite on his fingers. Never mind frostbite, but I'm sure he'll have chilblains. His fingers looked blue with the cold. I said that I wondered at him venturing out in weather like this. 'Ah Ma'am,' he says, 'but a man has a living to earn.' You can't help laughing.

It's just as well really that Father has moved. The lodge with that tiny kitchen is much easier to keep warm than the other house was, but I don't like the idea of him at his age having to go outside to the w.c. in the dark in this freezing weather. I would hate to think of him slipping on the ice and breaking something and then lying there alone all night. I told him to keep a chamber pot in the bedroom but he pretended he hadn't heard. He just sat there with his eyes twinkling and never said a word. I know he hates to admit that he's getting any older. He doesn't think much to the new cowman, but then he wouldn't, would he? And he certainly disapproves of the thought of a new milking machine. What he says is that it's always been the case that a cow needs milking by hand, and it always will be.

Mr Johnson annoys me. He's still talking about Australia as if he was likely to be off there any minute. 'I'd be on that boat tomorrow if I could,' he says. Then he goes on about it being summer over there and he laughs and looks a bit soppy and says, 'Wouldn't you come with me, Annie?' No fear, I told him. Wild horses wouldn't drag me to the other side of the world, summertime or no summertime. Then he says he's not talking about wild horses but kangaroos. 'Think of all that sunshine, sweet Annie,' he says. I quickly told him not to 'sweet Annie' me and that it would soon be winter again as like as not, once we got there. So then he goes on about the blasted kangaroos. Now I ask you, what would I want with kangaroos? I suppose he's just pulling my leg because I'm sure he's too old really to think of emigrating, although he does say he's applied for the papers. But I have to admit, I was a bit worried when his Lordship asked me the other day what I really thought about Mr Johnson going to Australia. 'I don't know what I'd do without him, Annie,' he said. 'You know he was my driver during the war.' Well, we all know that. Then his Lordship goes on praising him up to the skies, saying you don't find many like him, so brave and trustworthy and loyal. On and on he goes. He thinks the world of him. All I could say was that I couldn't imagine him going, and his Lordship looked quite relieved. 'You do your best to persuade him to stay, Annie,' he said. Well, I'll do that, whatever happens.

Zbigniew Rakowski's notebook

As her Ladyship's faithful Annie would say, it is cold enough to freeze a brass monkey and has indeed been so for many days. The good Annie was kind enough to replenish more than once the hot-water bottle which I had had the foresight to take with me on my last visit to Cranfield. Without it I fear I might, like Captain Scott, have been found huddled up and frozen to death despite the fire which had been generously kindled on my behalf in the Red Drawing-Room and which made not the slightest difference to the icy temperature in which I found myself. It is quite hard to imagine how all those good people survive in the Arctic conditions which they are obliged to endure in the house of my dreams. They have plenty of wood from around the place to keep the fires burning, but it is coal or coke that is needed if any heat is to be given out, and with the crisis deepening in Mr Shinwell's newly nationalised mines, it hardly seems that there be very much of either commodity available for any of us in the near future. For myself, I feel that I will be obliged to wait until this cold spell is over before returning to my labours at Cranfield. I trust the wait will be of but short duration.

With the departure of the inimitable Cheadle, the atmosphere in the house has changed a little. The new man has an expressionless face and cold eyes behind which I felt I discerned a hint of mockery. I should like to watch him more closely for there is something about him that makes me feel a touch uneasy. He came, while I was at my work, ostensibly to put a little something on the fire, but in truth, I am of the opinion that he came to check up on me. I did not care for the way he glanced at me, nor indeed did I care for the insolent manner in which he addressed me, instructing me to leave everything as I had found it.

Priscilla bears up wonderfully under what must be very difficult conditions. She, with her indefatigable energy, her wit and efficiency, manages to radiate a special warmth and to enliven the very house with her vigour. I shall miss her during my absence, as I always do. She laughs at me for wishing to write about the Otterton family, so that occasionally I am minded to ponder once again on how she will react to my trifling melodrama. She in fact has asked no further questions about it of late and has perhaps put it from her mind.

Sydney Otterton's diary

FEBRUARY 12TH

There's been an almighty bloody snowfall. The drive will be completely impassable unless they've managed to get the horses harnessed to the snowplough, which I doubt as most of the men will be snowed into their cottages. In fact what we could really do with at the moment is a confounded tractor. We can't even get out of this house as the snowdrifts come to half-way up the front door. Tony and I started to give Johnson a hand to dig a way out of the back door, but we didn't get very far because there was nowhere to go but into another drift. The telephone lines are down and, according to Mlle who heard it on the wireless just before the power was cut off, half the rest of the country is without power or fuel. Luckily Priscilla has quite a supply of candles and there's a certain amount of wood stored in the basement, but God alone knows what we'll do if this lasts for long and it certainly doesn't look like thawing yet. Things were bad enough during the cold weather in January what with Kipling risking his life every other day, climbing into the most impossible places to unfreeze frozen pipes with his blow-lamp, while that bloody fool of a Frenchwoman shouted from below, '*Bravo, le petit homme au châpeau rond!*' which only served to drive him on to further dare-devil exploits. And now with this lot, all I can say is, heaven help us when the thaw does set in and every vulnerable part of the roof gives way, which it surely will.

Despite the fact that Priscilla has always hated the snow which she says gives her a headache, there's a very jolly atmosphere in the house as we all feel ourselves to be in a state of siege. It's almost like being in gaol again. Johnson and Tony and I had a bit of a booze-up in the Japanese room to warm us up after our failed attempt to escape. There wasn't any booze in gaol but Johnson remembered a time in the desert when we thought we'd captured some whiskey off a retreating column of Italians, but it turned out to be scent which was part of their rations. That was a bitter disappointment. Then there was another time when we had better luck. I'd been on sick leave and was going back to join my squadron right in the south when our truck broke down, luckily not far from the rear echelons of the Indian Army Service Corps. The Indians were very kind, they entertained us in their dug-in tents, put us up for the night, mended the truck and sent us on our way. When we reached the squadron the next day, I found they'd also loaded us up with a whole lot of all the things we most valued, like beer, tea, sugar, tinned milk, tinned fruit and even some whiskey.

'Now here we are in t' bloody snowstorm without any Indians,' says Johnson. So then we spent some time discussing in a rather frivolous fashion whether we'd rather be in a snowstorm or a sandstorm. No conclusions were reached although all three of us agreed that at times we couldn't help missing playing fox and geese with Jerry in the desert, and yet we all three still have nightmares about it. Well all nightmares are obviously pretty confused, so that I sometimes dream that I'm at Villers Bocage, or back in gaol, having abandoned the Regiment to be destroyed by Rommel somewhere in Egypt, and that I can't escape and I panic, and everyone else is dead, and then of course I wake up in a bloody awful sweat. One of the worst things about being in gaol was not knowing what had happened to the Regiment and particularly to the rest of my Division after I was captured at Villers Bocage, although occasionally new prisoners would arrive bringing news from outside.

11 P.M.

There didn't seem much chance of getting out today so I was scribbling in my diary just after lunch when all of a sudden the power was reconnected for a few hours, which means that we have at least been able to hear the news. The weather forecast is dreadful, with no let-up in sight. In some parts of the country the R.A.F. is dropping food parcels for people and livestock in isolated villages, all the coal trains are stuck in twenty-foot drifts and the troops have been called in to help clear the main roads. All this with the country teetering on the verge of bankruptcy.

Anyway the good news is that they managed to get the snowplough harnessed down at the farm and they've begun to clear the drive where, luckily, the drifts don't appear to be too bad. In the end Johnson succeeded in digging quite a path from the back door, but I still fell into a snowdrift up to my waist because I couldn't find the damn drive. All the same I was able to get down to where the plough was and give the men a bit of encouragement. Of course they had to stop what they were doing by four thirty because of lack of light, but if it doesn't snow again tonight and if the wind doesn't get up, they should be able to go on in the morning from where they left off. But whatever happens, conditions will be pretty treacherous because of these sub-zero temperatures.

Annie was worried to death about old Jerrold on his own at the lodge and insisted on making her way all the way down there to see him. Priscilla told her not to come back tonight, so we don't know how she got on although I think Johnson went with her to make sure she was all right. I hope they've got some heat in that cottage, although I know Annie'll look after Jerrold somehow. I'm not sure about murder, but I don't doubt she'd steal for him. I must admit, it was a sad day when he retired. The new man seems like a decent fellow although of course the yield dropped as soon as Jerrold went. It'll be right down now, with this lot, and that's for sure.

There's one thing about Cranfield in the snow which always strikes me, though, and which, however dejected one may be and however appalling the circumstances, serves to lift the spirits. I was bowled over by it again this afternoon as I walked back up from seeing the horses pulling the plough. I have heard people describe the house as severe, even plain. Those who don't use their eyes sometimes dismiss it, superciliously comparing it to a red-brick jam factory. Why jam, I shall never know. But the truth is that when the snow lies on the ground, especially as thick and sparkling as it is at the moment, those bricks shine, each with a rosy warmth of its own. The whole great house glows and I, for one, know that I'll never want to leave it. This evening it was particularly inviting as I walked back up the hill for there was another power cut, but in some of the windows candlelight flickered.

Georgina's exercise book

Our prayer was answered and it snowed but poor Thomas is at school. I bet he's playing snowballs. It's terribly cold and I've got chilblains. At first I wanted to go out in the snow but now I hate it and were allways being made to go out. We keep falling in it and we get wet in our boots and my gluves stick to my hands and it makes you cry. Mamzel says it gives her a cough so she keeps on having that green medcin. She says it keeps her warm. Mummy says snow gives her a headache and Father says the countrys going bankrupt which Mamzel says means we havent got any money. We cant have lessons because Major Doubleday cant get here so Mamzel gives us extra French and tells us how nice it is where she lives in some mountains with lots of snow and cheese with holes in it. The kettle takes ages to boil on the fire and Mamzel says that's because we arent alloud enough coal.

Annie's diary

FEBRUARY 28TH

I don't know how we're going to manage if this dreadful weather goes on much longer. Her Ladyship let me have a couple of days off to go and stay with Father. Luckily Mr Johnson came with me because we found Father climbing up a ladder with a blow-lamp, trying to unfreeze an outside pipe and Mr Johnson was able to do it for him while Father and I held the ladder. Never mind climbing a ladder, the walk was bad enough, with the pair of us slithering all over the place, and then when we reached the bend in the drive we couldn't tell where to go next. The snowplough hadn't managed to get that far, so we just had to guess which way to go, which meant we kept falling into drifts. I was soaked to the skin by the time we got to Father's. He was pleased to see us both and teased me a bit. He wanted to know what we had to laugh so much about in these hard times. Mr Johnson had a good torch and a stick but I didn't envy him walking back on his own after tea while I remained inside. Father's managed to keep his kitchen quite warm and I think he would have liked me to stay more than a couple of days. Perhaps he feels a little nervous on his own under these conditions, but he must know that I can't spend all my time at his place although I do try to go and see him as often as I can. I have my work to do. What with all this snow and ice and all the slithering about and the power cuts and one thing and another, I'm beginning to see why Mr Johnson's so keen on Australia after all.

Sydney Otterton's diary

Priscilla says the children are becoming obstreperous, which she puts down to the bad weather and the fact that Double-day has either been snowed in all winter or his car hasn't been able to start, so they've hardly had any proper lessons although she's been reading *Our Island Story* to them and making them learn poetry by heart to keep them quiet and Mlle's been giving them geography lessons about the Haute-Savoie or wherever she comes from. And after yesterday's snowfall, it looks as if nothing's about to change in a hurry. As it is, the whole country seems to be at a permanent standstill. I've hardly been able to get to London for the last six weeks and Tony's been stuck at Cranfield too, worrying about whether he made the right decision by coming here in the first place. The initial euphoria which we all felt when we started getting out the snowplough has all but evaporated.

Tony and I tend to sit up late by candlelight and reminisce about the war and drink, which only annoys Priscilla and doesn't really help us much either, even if it momentarily alleviates the depressing feeling of us all being trapped.

The trouble is you can't make any plans because of the weather and in addition to that, I can't make any plans because of my financial situation. We still haven't got probate which I had really hoped would have come through by now, and we still haven't got a tractor although the bank has promised me a loan to get one as soon as I can, but since tractors are like gold dust these days, we may have to wait for some time yet.

The good news is that they're re-raising the Regiment which since the war has been too short of numbers to function. A bit of peacetime soldiering with the territorials won't come amiss. Tony's pleased about it too. It'll involve one evening a week up in St John's Wood, one camp probably in the summer and the odd weekend I should imagine.

MARCH 31ST

I cannot think why we so longed for the thaw. The floods everywhere are dreadful and this morning the ceiling fell in in one of the top-floor bedrooms. We've got buckets out catching drips in almost all the upstairs rooms and this morning I received a letter from my solicitors saying that at last we have got probate. The sum I owe in death duties is formidable by any standards. Priscilla, when I told her, immediately began to make practical suggestions about what we could sell to raise some money and was quite encouraged by the fact that long-term, low-interest bank loans are available to people with death duties to pay. All I can do is put the letter to one side and not think about it, which won't do me any good, I know that. Whatever happens, I'll have to go and see both the bank and the solicitors at the end of the week, so I suppose I'll have to face up to the situation whether I like it or not.

The other bit of bad news this morning was that Johnson came to me and told me that he is more or less definitely going to Australia. I couldn't believe my ears because I think I've been telling myself that it was all a pipe-dream of his. But he's convinced that there's another, brighter life out there for him, and who can blame him? He said he's *hud inooff* of this effing country and there's not much he'll miss about it. We shook hands and I wished him well although I had a lump in my throat. Johnson's been one of the best friends I ever had and I told him so. He laughed that dry laugh of his and said, 'You'll be all right, M'lord, you've got this lot to look after.' Then he said, 'but mind you don't drink too much,' and left the room. It was as if we'd said goodbye to one another then and there, but of course he'll be here for another couple of months until he's got everything fixed for certain.

Letter from Dolly to Annie

APRIL 2ND, 1947

Dear Annie,

I don't know what we would all do without you if you went to Australia, especially Father. He was so glad when you came back to live at Cranfield and I'm sure that you being there has made all the difference to his retirement. Of course the rest of us come to see him whenever we can, but you must understand how hard it is to get away when you have a family, not to mention the expense. I appreciate that what with them being nearer, Wilfie and Ethel manage to get over rather more often than we do, or than Elsie does, but then of course you've always been Father's favourite, ever since Mother died. People say you've almost been a second wife to him.

You will have to make your own decision, but what about

Bert? Have you thought about him? What would he say if you suddenly disappeared off to Australia with this Mr Johnson of yours? Now Annie, let me give you a piece of good advice from a younger sister, which is that they never marry you with the same face they court you. What would happen to you if you got all the way to Australia and Mr Johnson turned out not to be the man you thought he was? You would be stranded out there with no family and, never mind the assisted passage out, how would you be able to afford the passage home? I don't want to hurt your feelings but, at your age, it is unlikely that you will be having any children, so you could find yourself in a really lonely position. And how do you know that you would like Australia anyway? The children have been asking if Auntie Annie would have to walk on her head if she went there. Well, in some ways you might feel that you really were walking on your head with everything being so unfamiliar and there being snakes and things.

In the end, though, the decision is yours, but please don't make it without bearing in mind everything I have said. I haven't discussed the matter with anyone else and only told the children that you wondered what it would be like living in Australia. I certainly didn't suggest you would really be going there. If you do as I advise, no more need be said about it to anyone. Don't break poor Father's heart.

Love from
Dolly

Annie's diary

I am not at all pleased with Dolly who has written me a most interfering letter suggesting that I am about to abandon

Father and go hurrying off to Australia. If I meant to go to Australia, I wouldn't need to ask Dolly's permission, I would just go whether she liked it or not. I did mention in a letter that the idea was quite tempting, but I hardly expected her to take it seriously. I suppose she didn't like the thought because she was terrified that if I went, then she would have to come and see Father a bit more often than she does. It's all very well her talking about the family and what it costs to get here. We all know about that, but she doesn't live so far away and I can't count how many months it is since she took the trouble to come. Some of my brothers are better than her, but you would think a daughter might think to bother about her old father. And what has Father ever done to deserve that kind of treatment I would like to know? She goes on about me being Father's favourite. Well, if you ask me, that's hardly surprising, and I reckon she must be jealous.

As for Australia, I think Mr Johnson has at last understood that nothing on earth would make me go there. Leave Cranfield? Not me. Not even for *his* big brown eyes. But it's nice to have been asked I suppose. Of course I'll miss him when he goes. Life won't be at all the same without him and I expect this huge house will feel quite empty with him gone. His Lordship will be altogether lost too. That's for sure. Nobody knows the countless things he does about the place. He gets a bit funny though if I ask him to write and tell me what Australia's like when he gets there. The other day he even looked quite angry and said pretty bluntly, 'If there's anything you want to know about Australia, you can come and see it for yourself, sweet Annie.' If he won't stay here for me, then I don't honestly see why I should go dragging all over the world for him, ironing his shirts and cooking his dinner. They're all the same in the end. And then there's Father. I could never leave Father.

Zbigniew Rakowski's notebook

I did not think in January when I very nearly caught my death of cold at Cranfield, that my absence from the place that haunts me daily, would be so long enforced due to the Siberian conditions of our English winter. It is truly remarkable, I am inclined to think, that I, at my advanced age, should have managed to weather the storm (if that is not too facile a metaphor) and survive this fearful winter. Relentless hardship combined with the severity of the cold has carried many poor souls back to their Maker, causing unimaginable problems for undertakers caught in snowdrifts and for grave-diggers who were naturally prevented by circumstances from fulfilling their function. Fortunately for my dear daughter, I did not add to the confusion by joining the queue of corpses in the morgue. She, I fear, would have been sorely distressed, would have wrung her hands and told her beads. No doubt her tedious husband would have dealt efficiently with my demise.

But enough of this self-indulgence, for I wish not to die, but to live. So, not only did I weather the storm, but I am delighted to be able to say that I also managed during my prolonged incarceration in Wimble-on-Thames, to put the finishing touches to the *Whig Aristocracy* so that the manuscript is now with my publisher who appears to be both pleased with it and enthusiastic about my proposed history of the Otterton family.

Yesterday, at last, I returned to Cranfield, my passion for the house (and dare I say, for the chatelaine?) quite unabated, my curiosity concerning both its past and its present as alive as ever. Ah, but what did I find? The daffodils, crowning glory of Capability Brown's gently sloping incline to the lake, had, after so harsh a winter, not surprisingly hesitated to show their gentle faces to the elements, thus they were not yet, as might have been expected, nodding their heads in sprightly dance, but were merely in bud. 'Daffodils are late this year,' were the words with which Lord Otterton greeted me.

Yet it was not the absence of daffodils which I found distressing, so much as the atmosphere inside the house itself. Having, over the past two years, witnessed Cranfield rise, as it were, from the ashes under Priscilla's divine guidance, I was mortified to feel that it had somehow not come through the winter quite unscathed. I cannot say exactly to what I attributed this sensation. Perhaps I merely garnered it from the conversation of my hosts which was, in my opinion, unusually pessimistic. There was a woebegone look about the place, the carpets seemed noticeably more threadbare, the pictures in greater need of cleaning, and in the air there hung a depressing feeling of poverty. Although it is abundantly clear that living at Cranfield must be quite a struggle for Lord and Lady Otterton, formerly the atmosphere has been one of carefree optimism, of living for the day, with the wise Priscilla, doubtless less profligate than her husband, forever rising to the occasion as gracious hostess. Tuesday's budget, however, had no doubt done little to lighten the tone of the moment. His Lordship was bitterly cursing the fact that the Chancellor of the Exchequer has increased the price of a packet of twenty cigarettes by one shilling, so that he is now obliged to pay three shillings and fourpence for his Craven-A.

Nevertheless, I do not believe that it was the price of the Cravan-A alone that cast a blight over Lord Otterton's mood, for he lightly let fall that he has recently received a long-awaited demand for death duties. He only said, 'I can't pay them,' and laughed. I feared then for him and for the house and most of all for my *donna angelicata*.

It is very difficult to imagine what would happen to the Ottertons were they to lose, or for some reason beyond their control, be deprived of their essential framework which is

Cranfield. Of course they have not always lived at Cranfield and although I met them before they moved into the house, that house was already, as far as my perception of them was concerned, almost as much a part of them and of their reality, as were her Ladyship's hyacinth-blue eyes. From my own observation, I can only fear that, deprived of his house and estate (dilapidated though they may be), feeling quite lost and insubstantial, and knowing not whither to turn, the temptation to surrender to Bacchus in order to boost his morale or, as the case might be, to drown his sorrows, might be too great for Lord Otterton to resist. In what kind of house might he live? In what English county? Would he not appear naked, dispossessed of all that is his, unsurrounded by the aura that a great house, however decrepit, bestows on one so at ease in it, one who has never, for a single moment since earliest childhood, doubted that he will grow up to inherit it and who has imagined no other path in life to be open to him? There must have been times during the war when his Lordship feared for his life, but nonetheless, knew to what he would return in the event of his survival. Such certainty must shore a man up, must give him confidence and infuse him with a sense of knowing who and what he is.

As for the beautiful Priscilla who has brought so much of herself, of her imagination, her intelligence and energy to bear on reviving the house, on transforming it from a dusty furniture repository, and home, or so I am told, of a deluded dope fiend, into a family dwelling, tattered but treasured, full of mirth and life and hope, how could she now bear to be torn from its elegant surroundings? How could she bear to abandon the Aubusson to decay, how could she suffer, now she has grasped them so adequately, to relinquish the reins of power, to leave that miraculous place quietly to decline?

This winter has already taken a toll of the house. How many empty, uninhabited winters could it withstand as rain and melted snow seeped through every conceivable part of the roof, as frost gnawed into the brick and the stone, as, blistered from the summer's sun, the unpainted sills crumbled, as the damp rose from the basement, the ivy crept up the walls, its tendrils working their way through broken panes to invade the inside of that lovely house? I see the eighteenth-century French flock falling in sheaths from the walls of the Palladio room, I see mildew spreading its way across the Mortlake tapestries in the Saloon whilst the ever-invasive moth gnaws its way through the delicious tapestries in her Ladyship's own Hunting Room. It would not be long before mice and rats and bats became the proud verminous inheritors of this lordly mansion, whilst my poor Priscilla eked out her existence in some suburban villa to which she was unsuited by both birth and temperament, her children mewling and puking at her feet whilst Lord Otterton tremblingly replenished his whiskey glass. How could she bear such a fate? Surely she could not, but would instead, one spring morning as a ray of hope filtered through cloudy skies, pack her few things and flee to the protection of an old but faithful admirer . . . How her delicacy would lighten my hovel, her wit awaken Robin Hood Way, her style set Wimble-on-Thames on fire! Ah me, what folly to be old and fanciful! Yet, after my recent visit to Cranfield I could not help but wonder whether the Ottertons would be able to cling on and whether they would still be there in a year's time, say. Or two.

Once again as I was bent over my researches in the Red Drawing-Room, I was made uneasy by the repeated intrusions of the man, Mason. He came, quite rightly, to announce that luncheon was served, but came, I felt, in what can only be described as an insinuating manner. He enquired, most unnecessarily, in my opinion, as to which drawers I had opened and as to whether or not I had left the room at any time during the morning. Later, in the afternoon, he appeared again, this time with nothing further to say than that he wondered whether or not I was still there. Having, I can only surmise, persuaded his Lordship to be rid of the picaroon Cheadle, Priscilla appears quite unconcerned about the faceless Mr Mason. He does not serve at table in a state of extreme intoxication, but moves his large frame quietly and with dignity around the dining-room which I suppose is all that she requires of him. Nonetheless, it is my intention to watch him, just as he watches me, and just as he doubtless watches the other members of the household. It is hard to imagine what may or may not lie behind this attitude of his and I am surprised that it appears to have gone unnoticed by the Ottertons who both smile at him and address him in a light, *dégagé* tone as if there were no problem attached to his incumbency.

For my own part, I am at present simply buoyed up by the promise of the hours to be spent working at Cranfield and the prospect of many interesting and no doubt delightful conversations to be held with Priscilla. Who can tell what the future holds for any of us?

Sydney Otterton's diary

APRIL 25TH

I thought after I'd seen my solicitor the other day that we really had reached the end of the road. I came away from his office thinking that if there were a handy bridge, I might just as well jump off it, but then I thought that to survive having my tank blown away from under me in the desert, only to jump off a bridge in peacetime seemed pretty futile, so instead, I came home and went to look for Tony who'd just got back from London. Tony was very sympathetic when I told him what blasted Littlejohn had said, which was, that taking everything into account, I ought to consider the estate bankrupt. He also said he couldn't see how I would ever be able to pay the death duties and that, for his money, the best thing I could possibly do would be to sell up and clear out.

Where, I asked him, is the bloody fool who's going to buy a damn great barracks of a place with a leaking roof like Cranfield in times like this? Oh, he says, some rich American. It would certainly have to be a bloody fool of a rich American. In any case, what rich American would think of settling in this country at the moment? We aren't allowed to light a coal fire or a gas fire from now until September, rationing is worse than it ever was in wartime, there are no building materials and there's no agricultural machinery, if you buy an egg, it's usually bad and cigarettes cost 3s./4d. a packet. Apart from anything else, I just couldn't sell up. I couldn't do it. Talking to Tony cheered me up a bit even though he doesn't have any good news to bring back from the Stock Exchange, but he did encourage me to hang on and we ended up agreeing that things can really only get better. I may even have to go and see Aunt Lettice. She might help. Perhaps she would be able to lend me some money.

Priscilla has this idea that we should have a sale. She's certainly right about the house being full of stuff we could sell. Not that we'd probably raise an awful lot of money because no one has any money to spend these days. But still, it would be something.

MAY 1ST

Priscilla and I spent the whole week-end going all round the house trying to decide what to put in the sale. We spent hours going through an amazing amount of dust-covered rubbish and occasionally falling on a long-forgotten treasure. Luckily Priscilla has a good eye and knows probably rather better than I do, what is what. Too bad if we have to sell one or two decent pieces because we need the cash, but, on the whole what we're flogging is masses of Victorian junk which unfortunately won't go for much, and some later, pre-war stuff. Most of the unused servants' rooms on the top floor are crammed with things, many of which I don't remember ever having seen before, and still I haven't found the undiscovered room of my dreams, about which I dreamt again only the other night. Perhaps it really is only a fantasy. Considering all the trouble Priscilla has taken over the house since we moved in, I thought she probably had a better idea than I did about what there was, but even she was amazed by some things we turned up.

God knows if my parents ever really knew what they had stuffed into the far corners of this house, and then during the war a lot of things must just have been stacked away any-old-how to make room for the public records when they were sent down here. All the really good stuff downstairs is entailed, so none of that will go in the sale because I couldn't hock it even if I wanted to.

Then this morning the people came from the auctioneers; a very excited, wispy little mouse of a man with bat ears and a quick, quiet voice, accompanied by a callow youth barely out of school who told me he'd just missed the war. I thought how green he was compared to all those boys in North Africa, but for all his inexperience, he kept interrupting the mouse in a most opinionated fashion. We went round the house again showing them what we wanted to sell and occasionally Mouse pounced greedily on something he'd seen and which we had no intention of flogging. I thought, thank God for Priscilla who's not only got a good eye, but is firm and determined. In fact we did give way over one or two things, but nothing important. But we're not nearly through yet. Mouse and his boy will be back again tomorrow with their little books of tickets, sticking lot numbers on everything and anything they can get their hands on.

MAY 8TH

When I got back from the House of Lords quite late last night, I found Priscilla still up in the Hunting Room, writing letters. Sometimes she's quite cross when I get back but she looked surprisingly pleased to see me and even a little relieved. She told me she'd been feeling very uneasy all evening on account of the fact that she'd been shopping in the afternoon, and just as she was coming out of the International Stores, who should she see disappearing down the High Street, but the Legros. Usually she comes back from the International Stores talking about some ruddy Uriah Heep of a grocer who's managed to charm her with his oily manner, but this time, she was so worked up about seeing the Legros (or thinking she had) that she even refused to laugh when I made a joke about her beloved grocer who's always trying to let her have a little more than our rations allow. I wanted to know how she could be so sure it was the Legros, if she only saw their backs. She said they had the dog with them and that she would have recognised that dog and the way they walked with it between them anywhere. I suppose it probably was them. But what if it was? If they're not in prison, they've got to be somewhere and I can see no very good reason why they shouldn't still be living around here.

I told Priscilla that it was unlike her to be so worked up and that I couldn't imagine what had got into her. I said that as far as I was concerned the Legros were past history. After all, they must have been gone for at least six months and there hasn't been any trouble of any kind since Mrs Arbuthnot moved in. I only hope she stays. Anyway then Priscilla began to get quite annoyed because she said she hadn't finished telling me what had happened and that the thing she had found most disturbing was the fact that she'd stood outside the grocer's shop, watching the Legros walk down the hill and just as they reached the bottom of the High Street, Mrs Mason suddenly appeared, walking up the pavement towards them. Priscilla swears that Mrs Mason not only acknowledged them, but stopped to speak to them. I told her that that had to be rubbish because the Legros left here long before Cheadle did and that there was then a gap of about a month before the Masons came, so they couldn't conceivably know each other. Anyway I don't see how

Priscilla could possibly have told from that distance whether or not it was Mrs Mason, although, I have to admit that it is a bit odd if what she says is right. But I can't help feeling she imagined it all.

Zbigniew Rakowski's notebook

Both Lord and Lady Otterton were to be away on my most recent visit to Cranfield, and thus it was that I left home armed with a thermos of tea and some sandwiches for my luncheon. This I had intended to consume in the Red Drawing-Room during a short break from my labours, but the late spring having turned to summer almost overnight, I decided instead to take a walk in the grounds and to find an agreeable seat in some bosky corner of the garden where I could enjoy my simple picnic whilst admiring the south front of the house. That façade, with its stone pilasters and its swags above the first-floor windows, is unquestionably the most delicate of the four and the most Italianate. Below it there lies an elegant little formal garden which provides a delightful framework for the house when viewed from that side.

Forlorn though I may have been on account of Priscilla's absence, it was not without a slight spring in my tread that I walked past the Maori meeting hut (a hideous carved wooden edifice imported by Lord Otterton's grandfather from New Zealand where he served a term as Governor) and on up the slope of the lawn to a white-painted seat happily placed beneath two tall wellingtonias. Here I could sit, peacefully gazing on the lovely old house, its bricks now a rosy pink in the dancing sunlight, whilst I sipped my tea and consumed my usual fishpaste sandwich.

As I sat, I mused on past generations of Ottertons,

eccentric, flamboyant men and women, the vagaries of whose careers I had that very morning been studying, and attempted to picture them in this their proper setting. The Prince of Wales was a frequent visitor to Cranfield since it made a convenient stopping place on his journey from London to Brighton. Thus I envisaged Prinny, *embonpoint* and florid, trotting briskly up to the West front (so elegant then, before the addition of the monstrous Victorian *porte-cochère*), his brougham drawn perhaps by a dappled grey mare with arched neck, curly mane and flowing tail, snorting imperiously as the coachman up front is barely able to restrain her from breaking into a canter. Or perhaps, accompanied by Mrs FitzHerbert and some Whig crony, he might have travelled in a landau harnessed to four shiny black steeds haughtily tossing their heads and frothing at the nostrils. Then I turned to imagining the dark-eyed heiress from Jamaica whose money, a century earlier, had been used to build the house. Had she, two hundred years ago, wandered on this very lawn, admiring the same Italianate architecture that I now admired, yet heavy at heart, unloved and forlorn, missing the sunlit island home of her childhood as she stood, a diminutive figure in a silken gown, beneath grey English skies?

With such fond romantic thoughts as these was my foolish old head filled as I slowly munched my sandwiches under the wellingtonias, when all at once my reverie was interrupted by the sight of a dark-clad figure advancing towards me across the grass. I did not instantly discern the wooden features of the butler, Mason, but as he drew nearer, he looked straight at me and, at the same time, hastened his step, so that just as I recognised him, so did I realise that his intention was to seek me out. He then walked right up to where I sat and, with a gracelessness born of egalitarianism, but without what may be called a with-your-leave or a by-your-leave, stationed his not insignificant bulk on the seat beside me, pushing my thermos unceremoniously out of the way as he did so.

'Picnicking, I see,' were the words with which he first addressed me.

I fear that good manners did not then prevent me from instantly, but inadvertently, moving a little away from the man, towards the edge of the seat. But I soon recovered what I would like to think of as my natural aplomb and wished him good-afternoon, whereupon he rudely, and without more ado, waved an arm airily around and asked me my opinion of what he vulgarly referred to as 'this set-up'.

'Such houses as these,' he next saw fit to remark, 'are an anachronism.' He then went on to explain to me that there was no place for them in today's world. Since we were all equal, no one should be allowed to live in a house that was any bigger than anyone else's. In his view the stately homes of England should be nationalised and turned into council flats or conceivably used as palaces for the people, whatever such palaces might be. 'This monstrosity,' he said, jabbing a forefinger in the direction of Cranfield and with a sudden edge of anger in his voice, 'is a great redbrick blot on the landscape, a witness to all the injustices of the past.'

I am obliged to admit that as the man spoke, I was stunned into silence. With my solitary peaceful picnic so rudely interrupted and my fanciful thoughts abruptly banished, I had some difficulty in turning my full attention to the angry substance of the butler's diatribe. All history, he informed me, is nothing but the process of creating man through human labour, and in his struggle against nature, man finds the conditions of his fulfilment . . . the dawn of consciousness is inseparable from the struggle . . . man has irrefutable proof of his own creation by himself . . . On and on he went, quite carried away by the class struggle and how man becomes an alienated being in a capitalist society. I was not clear as to whether his favoured solution to all these wrongs lay in perpetual revolution or in one almighty conflagration; and neither, I consider, was he. He talked of the freedom which would come when the proletariat eventually succeeded in eliminating the bourgeoisie, thus producing a classless society, and he talked repeatedly of the oppressor and the oppressed, whilst allowing me no opportunity to reply. Coming as I do from a country that has suffered considerably from oppression throughout the ages, I felt that I might have something to contribute to a dialogue on the subject, but the man spoke uninterruptedly, as one possessed, almost as though he were oblivious of my presence, punching the air with his fist, as if attempting, by his rhetoric, to incite to action some imaginary crowd gathered on the lawn beneath us, or perhaps wishing only to work himself up into further flights of hyperbole. Yet I felt sure that his purpose in crossing the lawn that day and walking up the slope to where I sat, was to seek me out and to impart his bitter philosophy to me. He cannot have been unaware, as he spoke so passionately of history, that I was, in my own humble way, a historian, to some extent a maker of history since the version of events which I pass on to my readers constitutes but one man's perception of the truth. Perhaps I should have been bolder and made some valiant attempt to interrupt the flow of his discourse but, to be perfectly frank, as he sat there next to me, taking up so much space, I felt contaminated by his presence so that all I could wish was for him to depart.

Eventually, in my desperation, I gathered up my few things and with my customary apologetic manner, excused myself, saying that I had to return to my labours, thus, I added as a light-hearted quip which quite passed him by, to continue the process of creating man. He did not rise from the seat as I made my way back down the slope, but merely remarked in a gruff, unmannerly way that he would look in and see me sometime.

Much have I puzzled over this episode during the days since it occurred. Many aspects of it are to me quite incomprehensible; for instance, how, I ask myself, does this unmitigated villain imagine that he is going to achieve his dreamed-of revolution by working as a butler (most servile of all occupations) to the Ottertons? And what indeed did he hope to gain by informing me, humble pen-pusher that I am, of his political leanings? Does he not suppose that I will inform both Lord and Lady Otterton of his crude intrusion on my picnic? The imagination reels at the thought of what his intentions might be. Does he mean to burn the house down, to engulf his Lordship and her precious Ladyship in flames as they lie sleeping, or will he open the doors to allow the farm workers, armed with their scythes and pitchforks, to invade, to rip the tapestries from the wall and smash Rysbrack's masterpieces into smithereens? Yet how, one wonders, would that advance his cause? For the present, I remain dumbfounded by the whole episode but have decided that I will not instantly report it to Lady Otterton. I think indeed that I shall wait to see what happens next, wait until I can ascertain what precisely it is that the butler wants of me. Wait and watch.

Sydney Otterton's diary

MAY 17TH

Just as I was beginning to think that everything was completely hopeless and that there was nothing any of us could do that would make any difference, things started to look up. For one thing the arrangements for the sale are going ahead quite well, and it's all rather exciting. Then yesterday, at long last, a tractor was delivered which my very generous aunt has offered to pay for. The sun's shining too, so that what with one thing and another we'd all be feeling pretty cheerful if it weren't for the bloody awful fact of Johnson's departure at the end of the month. Priscilla thinks Annie's in love with him and she may well be right, although I thought Bert was Annie's so-called 'young man'. It will be bad enough losing Johnson, but I don't know what the hell we'll do if Annie decides to go with him. She's Priscilla's right-hand man, so to speak, and as such, she more or less keeps the show on the road. Not that Annie's mentioned a thing about Johnson or Australia to us, so Priscilla may have imagined the whole thing, but, according to her, Annie hardly ever goes to see Bert these days.

Annie's diary

MAY 31ST

So Mr Johnson has gone and left us. I somehow never really believed it would happen. He's sailing from Southampton on Monday and wanted me to go down there and wave him off. I certainly wasn't going to do that, and I told him so. Not on your life! I said. I've got work to do and I can't keep taking days off to go trailing down to Southampton, never mind the cost of the fare there and back.

It's a funny thing though, but when he said goodbye, I suddenly began to wonder what it must be like out there with all the sunshine and the wide open spaces and jobs for everyone. But then all these promises of a golden future never meant very much to me. Life's too hard for most of us and nothing wonderful ever drops into your lap as far as I can see. Well Mr Johnson dropped into mine, but he didn't stay for long of course. I told him I was sure he'd be back before he could say Jack Robinson. He only laughed a dry sort of laugh and stood there with his head on one side, looking at me with those big brown eyes of his. I can see him now. 'Sweet Annie,' he said in his flat Yorkshire voice, 'I'm not coming back. The sooner you get that fixed in your pretty little head the better.' 'Pretty little head, my foot!' I said. Well, he's not such a bad-looking man himself. I don't think I could wave him goodbye though. 'Not watch me sail out of

Southampton Water leaning on the taffrail and waving?' he said. 'My, you're a hard-hearted one.'

Now no one can call me hard-hearted, not after the way I've looked after Father, and Mr Johnson made me quite cross saying that. I had to turn my back as he left the room and the last thing he said was, 'If you ever change your mind, Annie, I'll be waiting for you, but we're neither of us that young any more, so don't leave it too long.'

I must say that I don't feel very happy at the thought of having to spend my days off with Bert from now on. But I expect I'll mostly go down to Father's. Father was funny about Mr Johnson. He wanted to know what all the talk was about Australia, and then one evening he said, 'If you want to go to Australia, Annie, don't you stay behind on account of your old father.' I can't imagine what made him think that I'd be going to Australia, unless Dolly had something to do with it. Then he went and said, 'I'll be able to manage, so long as you write home every so often.' He's a good man, my father, and I don't think I could ever leave him, any more than I could leave Cranfield which has been home for me all my life, even when I was away working for the Gowers. I'd miss the beech trees and the old elm on the corner of the drive and the walk down to the lake, and I'd miss the daffodils in spring and the primroses in the Big Wood and the cows lying down in the field because they know when it's going to rain. I can't imagine kangaroos having half that amount of good sense, and as for the wide-open spaces, well the park is good enough for me. I can stand by the bend in the drive and look out over the fields and the woods and not see another house and I can stare for ages out of my bedroom window across the gardens and the lake and never wish for a better view. I told Mr Johnson repeatedly that he would miss England. 'Never,' was all he would say. And then he'd go on about this country having done nothing for him and start again about all the wonderful things that would be waiting for him in Australia. The assisted passage out was only costing him

£10 and when he got there, they'd find him a job and it would all be marvellous. Well, we shall see.

Sydney Otterton's diary

Johnson finally left last week. I wished him the best of luck but secretly hope he'll be back again before long although I very much doubt it. He'll probably make a go of it and all I can say is that, if the other immigrants are worth half of Johnson, then Australia's not doing badly. I think Priscilla may have had a point about Annie who's been in a filthy temper ever since Johnson left and is not at all her usual amenable self. She didn't even take much interest in the sale which is quite unlike her. She generally wants to know everything about anything that's going on.

In fact Priscilla was quite wonderful the way she organised the sale. She took it all right out of my hands and made most of the decisions. We planned on using the avenue for extra parking, at least we hoped it would be necessary although with the appalling state of petrol rationing as it is, we weren't sure that anyone would turn up at all. We also had to hope it would remain dry or someone would be bound to get stuck in the mud. As it turned out, we were lucky with the weather and the extra parking space was definitely needed. The auctioneers set themselves up in the hall, with the lots stacked around them and in the saloon behind them. I'm not sure how many chairs were put out, but they were all taken and there were plenty of people standing as well. I recognised half the village and was amused to see old Doubleday bidding 8s./6d. for a po cupboard. Perhaps the fellow is growing incontinent with age.

On the two days before the sale half the county must have turned out to view. I think that over the years, what with my parents cutting themselves off the way they did, the house had become such a place of mystery to everyone in the neighbourhood that they were all eaten up with curiosity about it. A good many people certainly came without the slightest intention of buying anything in the first place. All the same it went quite well; with nearly four hundred lots, the average price of the better ones being somewhere in the region of eight or nine guineas, we managed to raise nearly three thousand pounds. Considering there's so little money around, I think we must have been quite lucky to get that. At least it's something in the kitty. Not nearly enough, but a little.

So, one way and another, I was feeling on pretty good form the other afternoon when I bumped into Pammie in St James's. I hadn't seen her since the war but she didn't seem to have changed at all. She was her usual jolly self and all the more so, on account, according to her, of the fact that her divorce from Archie had just become absolute. I must say, I always thought of Archie as a very moderate fellow and could never understand why she married him in the first place. Anyway we had dinner together and what with one thing and another I didn't get back till the morning. I'm afraid Priscilla thinks that the Lords sat late and that I spent the night in my club.

Georgina's exercise book

You have to go to the hall to get cool because its so boiling hot but weve still got to do lessons which is boring and we cant collect snails because Mamzel says they only come out in the rain. I hate Mr Mason because he's allways creeping around behind us and he tries to tickle Jamie. I told Mamzel and she said I was silly and that she likes mr Mason much more than Mr Cheadle. When Jamie told Mummy she said hed imagined it and when he told Father Father just said why didn't Jamie run away because he can probly run faster than mr Mason anyway. Jamies jolly rude to Mr Mason but I think he is a bit fritened of him to.

Sydney Otterton's diary

It's unbelievably hot which is very welcome after the winter we had, but of course they're already complaining about lack of rain on the farm. When I was down there yesterday I found that one of the men had seen fit to have a bonfire in this weather and had burnt the snowplough because it was taking up too much room in the old stables. Of course I immediately knew it had to be Goodfellow who'd done that. No one else could be such a bloody idiot. When I asked him what the hell he thought he'd been thinking of, he just said, looking at me moronically and scratching his head, 'Seeing it's so hot, I didn't think you'd be needing it again, M'lord.' I could have strangled the bugger. I was already in a pretty bad mood because the two old horses, both of which had been around a long time, went off to the knacker's yard in the morning. We've kept Violet who's got a few more years' work in her and who may well come in handy despite the tractor.

The children gave me a tortoise for my birthday. I've called it Adelaide although I haven't the first idea how to sex a tortoise. I don't know what the matter is with the children at the moment. They keep on complaining about Mason and saying they're frightened of him. Seems a perfectly decent fellow to me and anyway I don't see that they have much to do with him. Priscilla says they're getting bored and it's time they both went to school. Although I'll miss them, it'll be quite a relief not to have to keep bumping into old Double-day on the stairs. I always say he's like the Ancient Mariner, quite impossible to get away from and you have to listen to him banging on about India and Gandhi and the pros and cons of partition as if he, and he alone, held the solution to the problems of the sub-continent in the palm of his hand. Priscilla says he's taught the children very well up to now and that when they do go to school, they'll both be well ahead for their age. I suppose old bores like him are good at teaching because they don't mind saying the same thing over and over again.

Annie's still not her usual self. I'm sure she's pining for Johnson. I asked her the other day how she thought Bert was getting on and if he likes being here. She barely gave me a civil answer.

Zbigniew Rakowski's notebook

The family is away and without its presence a strange aura of unreality hangs over Cranfield. I sense a sultriness about the park as I walk up the drive from the bus stop to the house. The trees seem bowed down by the weight of their heavy, dusty August foliage, in the air there is a stillness and the earth, after so hot a summer as this, is dry and caked whilst the fields are a colourless brown. I pass a mournful Guernsey herd clustered beneath a gigantic elm, tails swishing languidly in a vain attempt to disperse the flies. The atmosphere in the house echoes the melancholy outside. There is a silence about the place and many of the shutters are closed partly because there is no one at home and partly, I would imagine, in order to protect pictures and tapestries and carpets and fine furniture from the glare of the mid-day sun. I do not doubt that the butler who, in the absence of the Ottertons, must fulfil the role of guardian or caretaker, delights in not having to bother to open and close the shutters, or indeed to wait upon his employers. How he spends his day is a matter for conjecture.

Since that dreadful afternoon when the man, Mason, sought me out to harangue me as I sat innocently enjoying a sandwich, I have not found it easy to banish his odious image from my mind. On subsequent visits to Cranfield, I have carefully observed his demeanour and have not been in the least delighted by anything I have seen. He too is watchful and, since that day on the lawn, has taken to addressing me in a quasi-subservient, quasi-threatening and, to a certain extent, conniving manner as though he and I shared some guilty secret which gave him power over me. Indeed we do share a secret but certainly not one which causes me to feel the slightest twinge of guilt and if the man has the temerity to think that he has any hold over me at all, he is bound to be sorely disappointed. I am somewhat tempted to the view that his fanaticism leads him to see things in the narrowest possible way and that because of it, he has little, if any understanding of those around him; thus he has quite mistakenly presumed to win me to his cause and, without having paused to wonder what my nature might be, has decided to co-opt my help in perpetrating his nefarious campaign, howsoever he might choose to do so. This morning when I reached the house, he had the impertinence to claim to be delighted by my arrival, flinging the great front door open and welcoming me as if he were Lord Otterton himself and master of all he surveyed.

I would gladly have been left to find my own way to the Red Drawing-Room with which I am, not unnaturally, only too familiar, but Mason saw fit to accompany me and to watch over me while I unlocked the cabinet where are kept the papers on which I am at present working. 'Should you find something of particular interest,' he addressed me with a sly grin, 'I have no doubt that you will let me know.' I am still at a complete loss as to what, if anything, I might find among the family papers that could be of any possible interest to the man.

Priscilla, accompanied by the good Annie, has taken the three young Ottertons to spend a few days beside the sea in Cornwall. The French governess has returned to her native land and his Lordship, or so Mason told me with a snigger, has been busy in London, but takes the night sleeper to Penzance this evening to join his family. I did not know, nor do I wish to dwell on what Mason might have intended to suggest by his snigger. If he was implying what I can only suppose that he was, then I would very much like to know by what means he is privy to his Lordship's secrets. Rather, I suppose him to be a person of mischievous intent who will stoop to any depths to undermine those who house him and pay his wages, thus to further his vile purposes and to bring his longed-for revolution one step nearer.

My little foible of a detective novel which so absorbed me a while ago has lain for some months now, untouched in a drawer of my desk. Little does Mason know how it is the very baseness of his behaviour which causes me to turn once more to that work. When I first wrote it, I cast the demon governess in the role of murderess, for such a wretch as is Mason had not yet entered the scene. But now, of an idle moment, my mind is unavoidably drawn back to that melodrama for there can be no doubt but that there is a part to be played in it by that detestable man. Having temporarily mislaid one of my notebooks, without which I feel denuded, I am sorely tempted to take a few days' respite from my serious work and return to that novelette and to tinker with it awhile.

Perhaps it was the unwonted atmosphere that hung about the house, or perhaps I should blame my carelessness on the fact that the butler's disagreeable behaviour did much to disturb my usual equanimity, but whatever the case, I was most distressed to discover on my return to Robin Hood

Way, that I had absent-mindedly left one of my notebooks behind. I can only imagine that I accidentally locked it away in the cabinet with the family papers that I had been perusing, once I had finished with them. I do not know if there is any key to the cabinet other than the one which Lady Otterton entrusted to my keeping before her departure for the Cornish coast. In any case, I would not be inclined to ask the butler to forward my notebook. I would wish neither to be indebted to him in any way, nor to have him involved in my affairs. Had Annie been at Cranfield and in possession of a key to the cabinet, I feel sure that she would have forwarded the troublesome object to me at my home, but as it is, I will have to suffer from the consequences of my own folly and do without that notebook until I next return to Cranfield.

Letter from Annie to Dolly

Sennen Cove
Cornwall
AUGUST 4TH, 1947

Dear Dolly,

I expect Father will have told you that her Ladyship wanted me to come to Cornwall to look after the children for a week. We are having a lovely time and the weather is good apart from one day when there was a terrific storm and we watched the lifeboat put to sea. The children were very excited. I'm so glad her Ladyship asked me to come because I feel the change is doing me good. I love Cranfield, as you know, but there has been so much going on lately that it can begin to get you down.

We are staying in a hotel right on the beach. It has rather a noisy bar where all the fishermen come in the evening. Of course his Lordship finds that very amusing and is himself the life and soul of the party! There's one fisherman called Double George (his real name is George George) who they all think is wonderful. Double George has a very nice-looking son who is going to take the children mackerel fishing.

Father said that you would be coming over to see him while I am away. I hope you found him well. Did he tell you about the time back in June during that very hot weather when Goodfellow burnt the snowplough? You couldn't help having a laugh, but his Lordship was in a right tizwas.

Love from
Annie

Georgina's exercise book

Mamzel has gone to France and she's not coming back. That horrid Mr Mason went into Thomas's room in the middle of the night when Thomas was in bed and looked at him. Thomas says he wasn't fritened and Mr Mason was in his butler's sute. Then Tony came along and said What the bloody hell do you think you are doing Mason or something and Mr Mason went away. Jamie wants to hach a plot to kill Mr Mason because he thinks hes a spy. We've got someone Mummy says is a holliday guverness now. She's called Tiz and is very nice. Yesterday she showed us how to disect frogs. I wish we could go back to the seaside.

Annie's diary

If Mr Johnson has heard the latest news he'll certainly be glad to think he's left the country. Things seem to be going from bad to worse. The meat ration has been cut again and Mr Attlee warns us that we can only expect more cuts and more restrictions. We're all right here at Cranfield really because of the extra things we get off the farm like rabbits and the occasional pigeon, but I do sometimes wonder why I didn't decide to go to Australia too. Of course I would have missed Father and he would have missed me I know, but then he would have got used to it without me and I would have written every week and surely the others would have looked after him. I haven't heard a word from Mr Johnson, not that I would have expected to yet, but I wonder if he sometimes thinks about us.

The children have an atlas in the school-room and I had a quick look at it when I was in there the other day. Georgina wanted to show me a map of India because she and Jamie want to go there when they're grown up. That Major Double-day has been teaching them all about it and Georgina's been learning some poem about India which she wanted to recite to me. Anyway I had a quick look at Australia on the Q.T. because I wanted to see where Mr Johnson was. I know that after all those weeks at sea he was due to land in Perth. I suppose he got there safely and I hope he wasn't seasick. Mind you when I suggested before he left that he might be seasick, he was quite put out. If he wasn't seasick in a troop ship during the war, he had no intention of being sick in peacetime. But I simply don't know if he's still in Perth or not. He may have been found a job anywhere in Australia and it's a big place.

Now that Mamzelle's left, Mr Kipling spends his time hanging around the kitchen and getting under all our feet. I rather think he's got his eye on Mrs Laws. I suppose Mrs

Kipling's used to his carryings on, but I can't imagine how he gets his work done and he's supposed to be doing a lot of extra work now that Mr Johnson's gone. That's until the new man comes. He can be quite funny though, Mr Kipling, especially when he gets on to the subject of that so-called cough mixture Mamzelle kept up in the school-room. To tell the truth, I think he was tickled pink by her taking such a fancy to him.

There's a new governess, her Ladyship calls her a holiday governess, who's here until the children go to school in the autumn. I somehow don't think she will want to have anything to do with Mr Kipling, though. She's very young and nice-looking and I wouldn't doubt that she has a young man of her own somewhere.

I had a letter waiting for me from Mr Rakowski when we got back from Cornwall. He wants me to look out for one of his notebooks which he has mislaid although he thinks he may have locked it up in the cabinet down in the Red Drawing-Room. I've had a look for it and I've asked Mr Mason if he's seen it but neither of us has come across it. It would be unlike Mr Rakowski to mislay something like that, I should think. He is a most meticulous person.

Sydney Otterton's diary

SEPTEMBER 5TH

It seems quite incredible that the war has been over for two years and the country's still in such a bloody awful mess. There's no fuel, no petrol, no coal, the miners are on strike and only a few weeks ago people were queuing in the streets of London for potatoes. My own affairs are in no better shape and as a result I swing between moods of extreme elation and near desperation and I've begun to have night-mares again.

There's some suggestion that it may be a good idea to get rid of the dairy herd and have sheep instead, but God alone knows if that will really work. Or we may keep the cows and have a few sheep as well. Whatever happens, it always seems to involve enormous outlay and very little return. If we want to keep the cows, we'll have to try to keep abreast of the times and install an electric milking machine. And where the hell does the money come from for that? At least we've got the tractor now and that does make a lot of difference. Thank the Lord and Aunt Lettice.

I found some excuse to go up to London yesterday, hoping, I suppose, to avoid thinking about my problems. I spent the evening with Pammie who was her usual cheerful self, crowing about her alimony and boasting about some coat she'd bought. It looked like a perfectly ordinary coat to me, but she just laughed and said that she was amazed I hadn't heard of the New Look. Nothing ever seems to get Pammie down and I have to say that after a couple of hours with her you can't help but feel your spirits lifting. I got back quite late to find Tony and Priscilla deep in some serious conversation in the Hunting Room. They looked almost surprised to see me. The three of us ended up having a drink together, then Priscilla went off to bed and Tony and I sat up till all hours. He told me that he, too, has been suffering from nightmares lately, then he started to bang on about the children's new governess to whom he appears to have taken a great shine. I didn't tell him that I'd been seeing Pammie but just laughed and said that, for my part, I was rather sorry to see the old Frenchwoman go. She must have been as ancient as the hills, but she was very spirited and she made me laugh with all her dandelion salad and snails. The poor woman hadn't been back to France since before the war and she couldn't wait to leave and make way for the lovely Tiz.

Then of course we started to get maudlin about Johnson and wish he'd never left and that led to reminiscing about the war and that kept us up most of the night which at least prevented either of us having nightmares for once. I still don't understand how we can be expected to throw the experiences of the war off just like that and get on with things as if nothing had ever happened. Tony feels the same. Sometimes I look back on those years and begin to see myself as if I were a completely different person to the person I am now. I seem to have been far better suited to leading a column of tanks across the desert than I am to dealing with the everyday problems of the estate, which is rather a pity, because the everyday problems are what I will have to deal with if we are to stay on here for much longer. And I sometimes wonder for just how much longer we will be able to hang on.

Priscilla, who, after all, was the one who hesitated to move into the house in the first place, is far more sanguine than I am at times. Perhaps that is because she has put so much energy into the place and, no doubt because of that, she has really grown to love it. She has certainly given it a face-lift and brought it back to life in a remarkable way which even I could never have imagined. After all, the house as I knew it in my childhood was always pretty gloomy because of the brooding presence of my mother and because of my father who was afraid of her and consequently permanently on tenterhooks when she was around. But you could always escape to some far-flung corner and there was always the dream of that imaginary room which I never found. I think our children now probably have that same feeling of being able to escape that I had as a child, down the back stairs or into the basement or the Blue Corner Room or to the West Room before we made it into part of the flat. I used to love the West Room with that sunken bath and the view across the lake to the temple. Anyway, no one ever knew where one was or what one was up to.

One rather odd thing came out of my conversation with Tony last night, which was that he wanted to know what I thought of Mason. I can't imagine why everyone is always going on about Mason. He seems like a perfectly harmless individual to me. He doesn't down all my best port like Cheadle did and he seems to do his job without much problem, but it struck me that Tony went on in rather an annoyingly insistent way, wanting to know what I *really* thought about him. I told him I didn't *really* think about the fellow at all. Then he said to me, rather pompously, 'Well, Sydney, I think you should.'

I had no idea what he was getting at, so this morning I asked Priscilla what she thought about Mason. To tell the truth, it occurred to me that she reacted a bit oddly to my question. She seemed to hesitate as if taken aback by it, then said, 'I don't like him, if you must know, but I can't tell you why.' Then she quickly changed the subject. I wasn't quite sure what she meant. Did she mean that she didn't know why she disliked him, or did she mean that she had cause to dislike him, which for some reason she could not tell me?

Letter from Priscilla Otterton to Zbigniew Rakowski

Cranfield
25.9.47

Dear Z.A.R.,

Thank you so much for your most amusing letter which arrived this morning and for the three others that I'm afraid I haven't yet acknowledged, but I have been very busy lately with the school holidays and one thing and another. Thomas went back to Westfields on Thursday, taking Jamie with him for the first time and at last I have found a moment to get back to the mountain of letters on my desk.

Annie tells me that she has looked everywhere she can think of for your lost notebook but has not been able to find it and Mason claims not to have seen it either. We cannot look in the cabinet as the only key is the one you have, but I feel sure that when you next come, you will find your notebook there. I hope that its loss hasn't been too much of a bore for you. You know we are all looking forward to reading your final assessment of the Otterton family. I'm sure you will manage to make them as interesting as anyone could, although I'm afraid that, as you must have realised by now, they are rather a Philistine bunch.

I know that although you occasionally write them, you don't often read novels, but I wonder if you have read the novels of Henry Green? A friend recently recommended *Loving* to me. I would be interested to know what you thought of it.

We look forward to seeing you as usual for lunch on Tuesday next, 30th September. I am sorry that no one was here to look after you when you came last.

Yours ever,
Priscilla

Zbigniew Rakowski's notebook

OCTOBER 1ST

How lucky I consider myself to be during these hard times, when so many people have so much to put up with, to have my benighted existence blessed with such joy as my visits to Cranfield inspire perforce. It has been some time since the crowning joy of lunching with the exquisite Lady Otterton was mine. I had occasionally corresponded with her during the summer months as she is kind enough to say that my frivolous missives amuse her, but she, poor lady, has been so occupied by family duties that she did not, until most recently, have the time to respond. Unimaginable was my delight last week on perceiving her distinguished handwriting on a letter delivered to me by Friday's second post. Indeed I felt quite like a schoolboy as, with trembling hand, I inserted the paper-knife into the envelope to slit it open. I have not, I fear, read *Loving*, the novel by Henry Green to which she referred in her most amiable letter, although I am familiar with and have admired other works by the same writer. *Loving*. Yes, *Loving*. Loving as I do, I hastened to the Boots library on Saturday morning only to discover to my chagrin that they did not have a copy of the desired book, thus I would be unable to discuss it with Priscilla when next I saw her. Not unnaturally, however, I asked that they reserve the book for me, a request that I shall now be obliged to withdraw since, in her very great kindness, Lady Otterton lent me her precious own copy of *Loving* when I lunched at Cranfield yesterday.

Lord Otterton was not present at luncheon and since the children are now all at school and there is no longer a permanent governess, it befell the odious Mason to wait on her Ladyship with only my humble self for company. I could not but wonder what the man (if he was listening to us) made of our literary conversations, nor of the laughter we enjoyed, for I have to admit that, delighted to be back once more at Cranfield, partaking of the familiar rabbit stew and fired up by a quite unexpected *tête-à-tête* with my *donna angelicata*, I found myself to be on quite spirited form. There can be no doubt that there were moments when I was absolutely convinced that the butler, in most un-butlerlike fashion, attempted to catch my eye. I, of course, withstood his invitation.

It was not indeed until later in the afternoon that I had occasion to exchange more than a polite good-day with Mason. After luncheon her Ladyship kindly proposed that I take a stroll with her in the garden before returning to my labours, an offer which I was only too glad to accept. She is turning her attention particularly to the small formal garden by the South Front of the house which she intends to fill with roses.

However, not long before I was due to leave in order to catch my bus, and as I was somewhat anxiously searching once again through the drawers of the cabinet for my lost notebook (for I had, to my consternation, failed to find it on my arrival in the morning), the door of the Red Drawing-Room creaked open and who should appear, but the monstrous Mason, of course. And what did he have in his hand, but my precious notebook which, with his face contorted by the vilest leer, he held out towards me? Without a word, I crossed the room to where he stood and put my hand out to take the book, at which point, to my unutterable amazement, he withdrew his hand and whipped the note-book behind his back.

'You should not be so careless,' the dreadful man said. 'If you leave your notes around in this fashion, how can you be sure that someone won't read them?'

Were I of a different disposition, or of a different age or build, I feel I could have struck the man.

'My notebooks can be of interest to myself alone,' I said with all the dignity I could muster, 'since they contain only my notes for the work I have in progress.' I looked him straight in the eye, daring him to betray that he had read more than my scribblings about the Otterton family, that he had pried into my very heart and was thus privy to the secret flights of an old man's fancy. But what a senseless old dunderhead am I? For who but I would ever be so foolish as to intersperse his working notes with what other men confide only to a diary? I do it and have always done it because, for me, my work is my life, as is my love for Priscilla, and here the two go inescapably hand in hand; yet from that dreadful moment, as he and I stood there in the doorway to the Red Drawing-Room, I could no longer doubt that Mason knew of my passion for Lady Otterton, and that should the need arise, he would use that information to bring about my downfall.

It was hardly surprising that I was unable to sleep last

night, so consumed was I by hatred of the loathsome butler. I lay awake and attempted to read *Loving* which *she* had so enjoyed, but I soon found that I was turning the pages without having absorbed one word of what was written. Such a blight has Mason cast over Cranfield, that I shall never again, so long as he is butler, be able to go there with an easy heart, nor enjoy the pleasant, *dégagé* atmosphere to which I have become so accustomed.

I did not, however, allow the man to suppose for one instant that he had dismayed me in the slightest. I merely insisted that he hand over the notebook which he was of course obliged to do (having, no doubt, already perused it at his leisure), whereupon I thanked him graciously and enquired as to where he had found it. Her Ladyship, I informed him, had expressly told me that when asked, he had denied all knowledge of it.

'Aha,' he had the insolence to rejoin, 'I only found it after I had spoken to her Ladyship.' I could not help but notice that he pronounced the last two words in the most satirical manner imaginable.

All night I turned the matter over in my mind and it is my considered opinion that on my previous visit to Cranfield, that man sneaked into the Red Drawing-Room whilst I was answering a call of nature and impudently helped himself to my notebook, with what purpose in mind, I cannot imagine. I am, nonetheless, forced to conclude that what he found must surely have delighted him and indeed been more than he had any reason to expect, for I am indeed a very foolish fond old man. It always seemed most unlikely that I, who am normally so particular, should have muddled my own notes with the Otterton papers, and have put them without realising it into the cabinet. It is likelier by far that, not noticing that one was missing, I gathered my notebooks together and restored them, thus incomplete in number, to my basket before leaving the house.

I am intensely exercised by the incident, concerned as to

what will be the outcome and consequently quite unable to concentrate on my work. One way or another, however, I shall see that the butler reaps his punishment.

Letter from Annie to Dolly

Dear Dolly,

I do hope that you will find a way of getting down to see Father soon as he has not been at all well lately. He is very tired and lacks energy even for his garden and is not at all his usual self. He won't see the doctor which is an added worry. I wonder if you would be able to persuade him. He certainly won't listen to me.

What with one thing and another I am finding myself very busy at the moment. I think I told you that Jamie has gone off to boarding school and Georgina is now at day school, so there is no longer a governess. I have to get Georgina ready for school in the morning and give her her tea when she comes home. She leaves her bicycle at the station and catches the train to the next stop down the line. As you know, I have always liked children so I am very happy with this arrangement. Georgina laughs at me because I say that I would really have liked to have been a nurse. It's not too late, she says. But I'm afraid it is. Then of course there's the extra washing and ironing.

I hope to see you soon at Father's. Give my love to Fred and the children.

Love from
Annie

Georgina's exercise book

Sometimes it seems funny without Jamie or Mamzel but I like Annie looking after me. Schools alright and I like going by bike to the station but if its raining Tony usherly takes me in his car. Only the car often doesn't start and he has to get out and what he calls crank it up which takes ages. When I get home I rome about the house and no one knows were I am. Ive found lots of good books in a shelf on the back stairs and I'm looking for a secret room. Father thinks theres one somewere and he's allways singing us songs about annie get your gun which makes our Annie laugh. I hate Mr Mason hes such a spy.

Sydney Otterton's diary

I had a most disturbing letter from my mother out of the blue today. I felt quite sick when I saw her handwriting on the envelope which, I observe, was posted in London, but the only address it gives is, as usual, the address of her bank. Nothing from her could possibly be good news and all she seemed to want to do on this occasion was to accuse me of stealing some of her possessions. She claims that a few pieces of furniture belonging to her were left here and that furthermore, according to her informants, I have had a sale and sold them. She is threatening me with some kind of legal action which is of course barmy as I certainly haven't sold anything which belongs to her, unless she plans to lay claim to the po cupboard old Doubleday bought for eight bob. Of course she's barking mad, not that that helps, and all this means is that I will find myself running up a whole lot of unnecessary lawyers' bills on top of everything else. She's also complaining about my having let the Dower House which she seems to think is hers by right. She certainly took all the furniture out of there when she left, some of which, I have no doubt was mine.

I bought a pair of Java finches last week to add to all the others in my dressing-room. Priscilla thinks they are a dreadful waste of money, and I think she tries to encourage Annie to complain about the mess, but they cheer me up and anyway I think Annie likes them, although she says that Mrs Summers won't go into my dressing-room because she's frightened of the parrot. Anyway the new finches make much less mess than Julia who not only talks quite a lot now, but can also imitate the noise of a vacuum cleaner, so someone must do the hoovering. Priscilla was furious when I told her that, because she thinks Annie does it, and it's not fair on Annie because it's not her job.

I don't know what to do about my wretched mother. I'm sure there's trouble in store.

Annie's diary

Georgina is very pleased at the moment because the government has announced that we're going to be allowed extra sweets over Christmas which is all very well when you think that only a couple of weeks ago they cut the bacon ration to one ounce a week. Perhaps things will get better next year. It's certainly high time something changed, although Princess Elizabeth's wedding was nice. Georgina and I looked at all the pictures in the papers and in *Picture Post*. The Princess had a beautiful dress and Princess Margaret Rose made a lovely bridesmaid.

And still not a word from Mr Johnson. I couldn't resist

asking his Lordship the other day if he had heard anything. I was clearing up after all those darned birds of his when his Lordship came into his dressing-room, grinning. 'That's very good of you Annie,' he says. 'Now don't you tell her Ladyship,' I said. 'She'll be furious with me.' Her Ladyship has forbidden me to clear up after the birds. So then I asked about Mr Johnson and I thought his Lordship gave me a funny kind of surprised, half-sad look. 'No Annie,' he said, 'I haven't heard a word. Not a word.' Then he wanted to know if I'd heard anything. I said no, I certainly hadn't and just got on with what I was doing. I can see me spending half of Christmas nursing poor Father who is still poorly and the other half with Bert, listening to him moaning on at me about wishing he'd never moved and complaining that I don't see enough of him. Perhaps Mr Johnson will send a Christmas card. The new man, Bob, isn't half as much fun as Mr Johnson was and not so nice-looking either. But then, handsome is as handsome does, as Father would say.

1948

Annie's diary

What with one thing and another, I'm quite thankful to be into the New Year. Perhaps things will begin to look up a bit. Her Ladyship was wondering this morning if I'd had time to turn the collars on some of Thomas's old school shirts, so as to hand them on to Jamie. 'Well,' I said to her, 'you know what Christmas was.' It was one thing after another, what with the Christmas tree and the estate party and me helping her Ladyship with all that, and his Lordship roaring about and saying he couldn't afford any of it and carrying on alarming about Lilian one minute, and worrying about where the blasted tortoise was hibernating the next. Then there was the holiday governess who did less than nothing to help. She was very nice-looking, mind, but she could hardly speak a word of English and she spent most of the day lying in bed complaining about the cold. She should have been here last year if she wanted to know about the cold. Meanwhile the children were running wild all over the house and when her Ladyship asked that Francine what the matter was, she apparently just burst into floods of tears and said she had lied and she wasn't a governess at all but an out-of-work actress. Her Ladyship can be quite sharp at times, so she told her that she hoped she was a better actress than she was governess. In the end the young woman went back to France early which was just as well, but it meant that I was left with the children most of the time, not to mention all the washing and ironing and darning that that involved. Then on Boxing Day I had the most dreadful sore throat and his Lordship was going shooting with Mr MacIntosh upstairs and a few other friends and there was an awful hoo-ha at tea time because there weren't any birds. Never mind birds, I thought. He's got enough birds in his dressing-room, dropping seeds everywhere and attracting mice and all he can do is talk about putting pheasants down and starting up the shoot again properly, and her Ladyship isn't too pleased about that because she says he can't begin to afford it. And then, there was Father, not complaining, mind, but not at all his usual self. And Dolly came over with Fred and the children and she wanted to know if I had heard anything from Mr Johnson which is none of her business. Then she made me quite cross by saying that she expected I was really glad to have decided not to go to Australia. Really glad, my foot!

Bert wasn't too cheerful over Christmas either. I didn't particularly want him to come round to Father's on Christmas evening, but Father insisted. He said I wasn't being kind when the man was all on his own with no family. Me not kind? Well, I gave in and let him come, but he just sat there in the corner looking down in the mouth until Dolly started up about Australia and then he looked as if he was about to strangle me. He left pretty soon after that and went on home. 'Why won't you marry me Annie?' he said on New Year's Eve. 'Oh, come on, Bert,' I said, 'I thought we'd gone through all that.' Then he has the nerve to say to me, 'Oh, I know why. It's because your heart is in Australia.' 'Never you mind Australia,' I told him.

I've still got a rotten cold and her Ladyship's talking about the collars on the children's shirts. She ought to know that I won't forget them and they'll be done in time for the children to go back to school next week. Things might calm down a bit then.

I'm rather surprised that none of us has heard a word from Johnson since he went to Australia. I sometimes wonder if Annie wishes she had gone with him but perhaps he just never asked her to. She's a bit funny about him though and doesn't like it if you ever mention his name. In any case, it's certainly just as well for us that she didn't go. And now Priscilla's talking about taking the Golden Hind to Paris and going to stay with friends near Montluçon later on this year. She's got some scheme whereby we give pounds to our French friends when they come over here and they give them back in francs when we go over there. I'm not terribly keen to go myself but Priscilla loves the place and speaks the language and anyway always wants to go abroad.

I stopped at the village shop yesterday for some cigarettes and bumped into old Doubleday who, having just heard the news about Gandhi, had on a very long face of course. He's such a damn know-all about everything to do with India, that he insisted on telling me that he could have seen it coming. Then he urgently required me to agree with everything he said, as if my agreement somehow had the power automatically to confirm his rightness and the wisdom of all his opinions. The funny thing was that I'd hardly got home when Georgina came in from school and the first thing she wanted to know was why Gandhi had been shot, and was it true that they were going to burn his body on a bonfire. She was very pleased when I told her I'd been talking to Doubleday about it. If he taught them nothing else, he certainly taught those children about India and the British Empire. Even little Jamie informed me at Christmas that the new coins would no longer have *Ind. Imp.* on them.

All this nonsense with my mother is still going on. She remains quite convinced I've stolen and sold some of her things despite the fact that I've sent her the auctioneer's catalogue asking her to identify anything she claims as hers. If it could then be proved that some object or other was hers, I would have to pay her for it. But of course she makes absolutely no sense and is now threatening to come down here and go round the whole house. I'm terrified of her coming while we are out or away and have given the servants strict instructions not to let her in. Priscilla is very brave and prepared to meet her head on but what Priscilla doesn't fully realise is just how unreasonable my mother is. If you cross her she either narrows her eyes and with a wave of her hand dismisses what you've said as something not worth saying, or she flies into a towering rage.

Tony brought a very pretty girl called Lavinia down for the week-end. He seems quite keen on her but the poor devil is so hard up I can't see him marrying again in a hurry. I rather liked her but Priscilla wasn't so sure because she didn't think she was very bright. Anyway we're all so used to Tony being here now that I can't imagine what it will be like without him if he moves away.

Bloody awful time of year, but at least it's not as bad as it was last year and luckily we haven't needed the snowplough yet, although of course we had the buckets out on the upstairs landing again the other day when it rained so hard. Much as I love this place, I sometimes feel the need to get the hell out of it. Still, the weekly drill night helps. Once I've got through all the paperwork which naturally falls to the Colonel's lot, there's always a pretty jolly get-together in the mess to look forward to afterwards.

Then there's Pammie who is usually ready to cheer me up. She's a bit of a good-time girl, I suppose, which is perhaps why she enables one to forget one's worries for a while. And she doesn't demand anything beyond a good time. I dread to think what Priscilla would say if she knew about Pammie. I couldn't do without Priscilla. She does her best to keep me up to the mark but I'm not sure she realises quite how difficult it is to do anything when everything is such a muddle. Sometimes she makes me feel as if I am totally useless. Perhaps she's right.

Zbigniew Rakowski's notebook

FEBRUARY 11TH

I had not been to Cranfield for some time and so, despite the fact that I feared the chill of the Red Drawing-Room, it was not without a certain thrill of expectation that I set out yesterday morning armed with a rug for my knees and a stone bottle for my feet, the which I trusted I would be able to prevail upon the good Annie to fill for me. I would not venture to ask such a service of the dreadful butler. Indeed I would be reluctant to ask one single favour of the man whom I half hoped might have been dismissed during the intervening weeks. I say 'half hoped', for I am forced to admit that one part of me wished once more to clap, as the saying goes, my eye upon the monstrous man. This no doubt because of my inordinate curiosity as to what it is that lies behind his strange and peculiarly immodest behaviour. I would like to know exactly what it is that the scoundrel is after. It would also interest me to know from whence he hails. How is it that Lord Otterton came to hire such a devious, deceitful man to be his butler? Has he not noticed that there is something profoundly disturbing about the man's presence in his house? What references did Mason have? Did he formerly work in some ducal residence from which he was dismissed? Did he then blackmail his Grace into giving him a good reference? Anything is possible and it is my intention to discover the truth. Quite how I will set about it, I am not as yet sure. Neither am I decided as to the wisdom of confiding my doubts about the man to her Ladyship. It is hardly my place to criticise the servants in a house where I have been made nothing, if not greatly welcome.

'Aha . . .' Whenever he opens the front door to me, the impertinent fellow has, I note, taken to greeting me in this fashion. On this most recent occasion, there followed an even more impertinent, 'It is none other than *our* Zbigniew.' I do not know by what criterion the butler has abrogated to himself the right to address me by my Christian name which he pronounces, either through ignorance or with the specific intention of sneering, I know not which, as Spig-new. I felt the hairs on my neck prickle as I struggled to control my temper, not quite sure whether it was this *Spig-new* or the awful use of the possessive pronoun which most enraged me. However, if I am to discover anything, it is in my interest to remain calm and on apparently good terms with this vile creature. 'Good morning Mr Mason,' I politely rejoined.

I was of course too proud to ask the man to fill the bottle for my feet and lived all morning in the hope that Annie might appear as she usually does to offer me a cup of tea. Yesterday, there was no sign of her and I cannot but suspect that this was somehow Mason's doing. So my poor feet froze although I was glad of the rug I had brought with which I managed to keep my legs and knees tolerably warm. Luncheon was a hurried affair since both Lord and Lady Otterton had to rush away about their various occupations punctually in the early afternoon. It was perhaps because of this that they both appeared a trifle distracted. I myself felt not a little uneasy being waited upon in a servile fashion by the man who, only a few hours earlier, had had the temerity to address me in such very different tones.

It was my intention to catch an earlier bus than usual home after luncheon, thus I was already engaged in carefully gathering up my possessions when the butler came sidling through the door, bearing aloft on one hand, just like any caricature of a butler, a large silver salver on which, to my horror, I discerned not one, but two cups. 'I thought our *Spig-*

new might welcome a cuppa,' he remarked as he oiled his way across the faded Persian carpet. Oh the vulgarity of the creature!

To my astonishment, the man's insolence did not this time enrage me, rather I sensed a thrill of excitement run through my old veins. It flashed across my mind that if I should partake of tea with the butler, I might make my first hesitant steps towards unravelling something of the mystery which surrounded him. This was an opportunity which I should at least not overlook. Mason deposited the salver on the table at which I had been working and, as he drew up an exquisite Louis XV *fauteuil* for himself to sit upon, asked me in a patronising manner whether or not I had remembered to lock the cabinet. 'I am sure you would wish to leave everything as you found it,' he added with a leer. Then, taking a seat on the *fauteuil* and tweaking his trousers at the knees as he did so, he gave me an almost humorous look which sent a chill right through me and said sweetly, with his head on one side, 'And be sure to take all your notebooks.' How I loathed the man!

How I detested the way he perched upright on the chair whose delicate, worn tapestry deserves in its decrepitude to be protected from the pressure of the human form, and most particularly so from the grotesque posterior of the infamous Mason. Knees placed firmly together, he sipped his tea from a bone china cup, crooking his little finger and simpering, for all the world like an elderly spinster at a clergyman's tea party. As I looked at the man, I decided that he was deranged. Quite deranged. But here, I thought, is at least something of an opportunity. I must make of it what I can.

'I think you must have been here now for over a year,' I opined with a hint of enquiry in my tone. 'Might I ask where you worked before?'

I instantly noted the man's body stiffen almost impercept-ibly and there was a moment's hesitation before he replied with a question of his own. So I was not wrong in supposing that he had something to hide. Neither was I wrong in thinking that he had read my notebook which I so carelessly allowed him to purloin, for with his question which was so vulgar that I do not care to repeat it, he made it abundantly clear that he needed my help and that he would not hesitate to use blackmail in order to obtain it. So as to ascertain what I wish to know about the man and to discover the secrets of his nefarious plot, it occurred to me that for the present time at least, I should appear to go along with whatever the treacherous scallywag might suggest. Ultimately of course, he may act as he wishes, for the worst he can do is to cover an old man in shame, reveal his folly and have him banished for ever from the presence of his loved one. All of which things, I trust I would bear like a man.

Perhaps I should not have been totally surprised when Mason then told me that he was looking, on behalf of a person or persons unknown, as he chose to put it, for some important private letters which had gone missing in the house during the upheaval created by the war when the late Lord Otterton and his Lady moved out to the Dower House, leaving Leoni's triumph free to accommodate the nation's historic treasures sent there from the Public Record Office. Since, as he surmised, I had not only free access to the family papers, but in addition the ear of *his Lordship* and *her exquisite Ladyship*, which words he pronounced with such derision that I was barely able to contain my anger, he was satisfied that I was the person best placed to aid him in his search for the missing documents.

Thinking of these things, I am brought to mind of a day, not last summer, but the summer before when, in the village store, I came across Lord Otterton's driver, Johnson, a decent, apparently admirable man who used to work about the place, but who has since left to go, or so I am told, to the Colonies. There was then, as I recall, some intrigue concerning letters. I do not know what letter and nor do I know what the outcome of the affair was at the time. I only know that letters were involved and that they were in some mysterious way causing concern in certain quarters. I seem to remember that I made some reference to the incident in my notebook at the time. I must verify whether or not that was one and the same notebook that Mason temporarily purloined and from which I later observed he had carefully removed one or two pages in such a way that I was not at first aware of his perfidy. He left me yesterday like a trout with a fly hanging over my nose and refused on that occasion to enlighten me further, telling me only in a free and easy, off-hand manner that he would keep me informed. As I finally left the Red Drawing-Room yesterday afternoon, I sensed the presence of Laszlo's Lady Otterton looking down from the wall so that I could almost feel her cold eyes on my back, following me out of the room. I have much to think about in the days that lie ahead.

Sydney Otterton's diary

FEBRUARY 15TH

I really haven't been making much of a go of anything lately which is probably why Priscilla is pretty fed up with me. I suppose the Regiment provides some sort of occasional discipline and to a certain extent so does the House of Lords which I do attend regularly and which has the added advantage of making me feel I'm doing something vaguely useful, if only by just going there. At home things seem much more difficult. There's the problem of the sheep for which we took out another enormous loan and which look as if they're not going to be very successful. I've never known animals have so many bloody diseases. If they don't have maggots, they have rotting feet and if their feet don't rot, they probably get scab, besides which, at this time of year they need an awful lot of fodder and that gives them intestinal troubles. Another minor inconvenience is that Peggy has taken to chasing them so I have to keep her on the lead when I go anywhere near where they are. I'm not sure that the man we've got looking after them knows a thing about what he's meant to be doing and I have a nasty feeling that instead of there being a pot of gold at the end of the road, the whole experiment is going to turn into an expensive failure. I keep thinking that sheep look wrong here in any case. They don't seem to have enough room and consequently need pampering, quite unlike the huge flocks I remember seeing in Australia before the war. Those sheep were apparently much more capable of looking after themselves even when they were lambing. Priscilla said it was a bad idea in the first place to go in for sheep, but since she doesn't know the first thing about farming, there didn't seem to be any very good reason why I should listen to her on the subject. She kept saying that she just had this feeling that it wouldn't work and it looks as if she was bloody well right.

On top of that there's been an outbreak of foot and mouth at Sharpe's farm down the road, so I'm just waiting for that to spread to us. We've got buckets of disinfectant by every gate, but I was coming up the drive only yesterday and I caught that idiot Goodfellow climbing a gate, obviously without having dipped his feet in the stuff which was right there under his nose. Thank God I never had him with me in an armoured car at Gubi or anywhere else for that matter.

Last night I woke up in an almighty sweat from one of those awful nightmares where you're trying to stand up and run and your limbs won't move. I got out of bed and went to talk to my birds in my dressing-room, thinking that that would rid me of the shakes. It didn't do much good because when I went back to bed about half an hour later, I fell into a restless sleep as soon as I'd turned the light off and the dream immediately recurred. I feel sure that that particular dream must result from the time my entire squadron was knocked out at a place called Belanda in a hilly part of the desert. After a few enemy reconnaissance planes had been over, everything had seemed perfectly calm and the attack in the early morning came very suddenly. I remember spending the whole of the rest of that day walking or running in the sand with a few other survivors. We were being chased and fired at by enemy tanks and kept dropping flat so as to hide in a hollow. God Almighty knows how we survived. I remember lying in one such hollow with one of my men and saying to him, 'It looks as if we've had it this time.' He didn't answer and it wasn't till later that night, after we'd been picked up and he'd been treated for burns that I realised he hadn't been able to speak because his lips had been sealed together by fire as he jumped from our burning tank. Of course we must have been terrified at the time, but it was all part of the day's work and one didn't have time to think about being afraid. Yet now, in a quiet country house in peacetime with nothing more to worry about than a few mangy sheep, it all comes back to haunt me. I don't understand it. It's not as if Cranfield isn't where I want to be. In fact it's so much part of me that it sometimes occurs to me that without it I wouldn't really exist although I also think sometimes that I'd like to burn the whole place down and be completely free of it. I wonder how Johnson's getting on in Australia. Perhaps he did have a point, going there to get away from it all. It certainly occasionally occurs to me to envy his being able to start from scratch. Starting again like that, a man is left with the raw material of nothing but himself or what he has made of himself.

Of course if I had been blown up by the Bosch, I wouldn't have to worry about the sheep or the cows, or the roof leaking, or my mother and death duties and the farm cottages and the fencing. That's another thing about sheep, the buggers break out of everywhere and contrive to do the most unbelievable amount of damage in no time.

Georgina's exercise book

When I got back from school I couldn't be bothered to do my home work so I just romed about the house looking for that lost room that Father and I can't find. Mrs Arbuthnot was just going into her flat and she said would I like a sweet. Mummy says we cant bother Mrs Arbutnot but I said yes because I think the hiden room is somewere in her flat. Mrs Arbuthnot laughs a lot and calls you dear and is very nice. She's got white hair and is old. She says Cranfield is a *maaarvlous* place and she thinks there probebly is a secret room but she says its not in her flat. She wouldn't know. I bet horrible Mr Mason knows were it is. He's so nosey. He was on the back stairs landing yesterday rummijing in a drawer and he jumped out of his skin when he saw me and began to tell me off for coming upstairs. I wish Jamie or Thomas was there. They would be rude to him. I didn't dare. He looks so frightning. I think he hates us.

I didn't know Mr Rakofsky was here and he made me jump when I went into the hall this afternoon. He was standing so still in front of one of the fireplaces and he sudenly turned round and said good afternoon mairm. He said he was looking at the fireplace because he loves it and did I love it. I said I loved the hall and he said a lot of stuff about the hall and a lot of stuff about looking for some boring old papers. I think he's funny. He's more intrested not nosy like Mr Mason and I think he likes us but I think he likes the house even more.

Zbigniew Rakowski's notebook

Yesterday afternoon I encountered the girl, Georgina, in the marble hall. I surmised from the beret on her head and the satchel on her back, that she was just returning from school. She informed me that she loved the hall at Cranfield which did not surprise me. The child must by now be nine or ten years old and no doubt the spirit of the place is already deeply embedded in her consciousness. She told me that she often roamed about the house looking for a secret room which she has not yet found. She wondered if I might know of such a place. I told her that I did not but proceeded to talk to her at some length about the beauties of the hall in which we stood. I spoke of Rysbrack and of the fine plasterwork ceiling, of the magnificent proportions and I even expostulated on the beauty of the shining mahogany doors. The poor child must have found such discourse tedious but she was good enough to listen politely to an old man's prattle.

I then suggested that she might miss her brothers who are away at school, but although she assured me that she looked forward to the holidays and to their return, she was, I opine, glad to be able to advise me that she never felt lonely in the house, there being so many places to hide and so many things to find. What sort of things did she find, I wished to know. 'Oh, books,' she said, 'and pills. Once Jamie and I found some old pills in a drawer in the Green Silk Room and we tried them but they weren't very nice.' I looked somewhat startled for, although I would not of course have mentioned the cause of my alarm to the child herself, I could not help but wonder what poison her depraved grandmother might have left lurking in some forgotten corner. She laughed, nevertheless, at what must have been my obvious concern and said that I was like her mother (oh, the bitter-sweet innocent words of childhood!) who had been quite *frantic* when she heard of the incident. 'She made us swear never to eat anything we found lying about again.' I did not wonder at poor Priscilla's distress.

Before we parted company, it did occur to me to ask Georgina in as casual a tone as I knew how to muster, if at any time during the course of her investigations she had come across any old papers or letters. 'Oh,' she replied with a jaunty air, 'there are papers and bits of letters everywhere but they're awfully boring.' I felt at that moment obliged to enjoin her to keep her parents informed should she discover any further *awfully boring* papers which, although of no apparent interest to her, might well be of some interest to adults. I then humbly informed her that I was writing a history of her family (a fact with which she assured me she was already familiar) and explained that for this reason, I myself might be interested in her findings. I think that she was not displeased by the suggestion that she might be enrolled to play the part of a minor sleuth. I cannot deny that I was somewhat delighted by her parting shot, whereby she directed me not to seek the help of the butler. 'Mr Mason is too nosy,' she said, but I was also not a little distressed to hear her add, 'Anyway I think he hates us.'

In fact Mr Mason left me in peace yesterday. Or that is to say comparative peace. He refrained from taking tea with me and attempted to put no further pressure on me. Last time I saw him, he had had the temerity to tell me that time was on our side. I should take things slowly and quietly observe. The revolution would come in due course. He must, in my opinion, be a very stupid man for he appears to take no account whatsoever of the fact that I myself may not be wholly incapable of independent thought, nor that I might have some loyalty to Lord and Lady Otterton who have so kindly acted as my patrons over the last two years or so. How can he believe that the contents of my snivelling notebook can really be held as a threat over the head of a man of even the slightest integrity? Yet, I do declare that that is just what he does think. And so the game goes on with myself as deeply involved as he is, for I am determined to find whatever it may be that he seeks before he does so and to use it against him, and I am equally determined to discover how it is that he has come to be involved in such a fashion in this peculiar affair.

I become increasingly convinced that Lilian, Lady Otterton has a good deal to answer for. It is my intention gradually to ingratiate myself with the repulsive Mason, thus to gain his trust with a view to wheedling a little more information out of the man. What a truly splendid stroke of luck to have encountered the child who may prove to be an invaluable, hidden ally.

Annie's diary

Bert was quite full of himself yesterday evening because he had won 7s./6d. on Sheila's Cottage which won the Grand National. He never usually has a bet, only one on the Grand National and one on the Derby, just like me, not that I've ever been so lucky, although I think I did once win two bob on the Derby, but that was years gone by. In fact he made me quite cross because he straight away started to say that if his good fortune was to last, he would soon be able to afford to get married. I do wish he would take no for an answer. I was so put out that I left quite soon after I'd cleared up his tea. In any case I was fairly tired and didn't want to get to bed too late.

What with Easter being early this year, the boys will be back for the holidays in a day or two and that will liven us all up a bit. They'll be running around all over the place, acting the giddy goat and will be sure to get into trouble with his Lordship before long, with him in his present mood. He's not been very happy at all lately and he flies off the handle at the slightest thing. We all know that when his Lordship's in a bad mood it affects everyone. Not that he's ever been anything but nice to me. But then I've always been very fond of him ever since he was a little boy, and I know that what with *Lilian* and one thing and another, he's had a dreadful time. I expect he's worried about the foot and mouth, but I'm quite sure it's not just that. I think he's got his mother on his mind again now. It's terrible the power that woman had over her family – she used to have his Lordship and his late Lordship quaking in their shoes. I reckon Lady Isley was the only one that never took a blind bit of notice of her.

They say that when his Lordship was seventeen or eighteen his mother was so angry with him over some incident or other that she tried to persuade the doctor to certify him and have him locked up in a lunatic asylum. She could never bear not to have her own way, besides which she was always said to bear some deep resentment against his Lordship. I've always thought it must have been something to do with the baby she had earlier that died. Perhaps that was what sent her off her head in the first place. All the same, what sort of woman would try to put her own son away? If you ask me she was the one that wanted locking up. Under the circumstances, I feel you can hardly blame his Lordship if he's a bit difficult at times. Mr Johnson always said he was marvellous in the war, very brave and he kept everyone's spirits up. Mr Johnson thought the world of him. Well, they thought the world of each other.

I often wonder how Mr Johnson is getting on. It's funny that he never wrote.

Her Ladyship says she can't wait to get away from us all. She's going off to France for a week as soon as the children go back to school and she says that once she has crossed the Channel she will be able to forget all her worries. 'I'll leave them behind for you, Annie,' she said to me. 'I know I can trust you to see that everything is properly looked after while I'm away.' Well, I thought to myself, I should certainly hope you can trust me. And there'll be Miss Wheel for company. She's coming for the inside of the week to mend some of the old curtains. I look forward to seeing Miss Wheel.

I expect Mr Rakowski will be here during the week as well and I know her Ladyship likes me to look in and see that he's all right. I always used to take him his tea in the afternoons, but lately Mr Mason seems very keen to do that. I don't know quite what's going on between those two. They shut themselves up together in that Red Drawing-Room for hours. Lord knows what they have to talk to each other about. I should hardly have thought that they were each other's cup of tea. In fact I'm beginning to wonder about Mr Mason. There's something about him that I don't quite like, not that I can put my finger on what it is exactly. There's something not altogether nice about the way he keeps turning up in odd places. I mean what business could he possibly have had to be going through the books in the bookcase on the top landing? And another time when the children were out with the governess I saw him coming out of the school-room. He looked a little surprised to see me and when I remarked that the children were out, he said something about a tray and having to take it down to the kitchen. Well that was odd because he certainly didn't have any tray in his hands, or anything else for that matter. It reminded me of the time the old mamzelle and Mr Cheadle had argued about who should take a tray downstairs. There was a tray that time of course because we all saw it sitting on the landing table for days on end.

Georgina's exercise book

We all hate Mr Mason. Thomas says he is evil. When he goes to bed he puts a chair against the door to keep Mr Mason out and sleeps with a water pistol by his bed. We are planning our revenge but when we told Mummy we hated him she just said don't be silly but Tony looked very kind and said he quite understood the children. I don't think Mr Mason has any rite to go barjing into Jamies or Thomas's room. Why can't he stay in his own room. And he's always looking for things. Ive started to look for things for Mr Rakofsky. It's quite fun but I don't know what I'm supposed to be looking for. Perhaps there is some treshure in the secret room. Anyway I pretend I'm a detectiv and I hope I find something before Mr Mason does because I think he would steal it and do a midnight flit like the man in the story we heard on Children's Hour.

Father has bought us a pony called a strawberry rone. It's quite pink with a black main and tail and I can't catch it or make it go when I'm on it. Thomas and Jamie galop like mad. Thomas is going to put a stink bomb in the pantry to annoy Mr Mason. I hope he dares.

Letter from Annie to Dolly

Cranfield Park.
APRIL 30TH, 1948

Dear Dolly,

I know you will be glad to hear that Father is looking up a bit, both in health and in his spirits. I think the warmer weather and the arrival of Spring have done him a lot of good. His being able to get back out in the garden has been a blessing.

He's been in a terrible state about all the weeds coming up and everything else that needed doing. I'm sure that won't be any surprise to you. As a matter of fact Bert did a bit of digging for him a while back so the place wasn't in too bad a way.

It'll be ever so quiet here for a bit now as the boys have gone off back to school and her Ladyship left for France this morning. She was all over the place. I'd done her packing and her suitcase was ready in the hall but first of all she couldn't find her passport and then she nearly left her handbag behind. Meanwhile his Lordship who was supposed to be driving her to London, was standing there laughing and saying it was a good thing she didn't have to get a squadron of tanks across the desert which made her furious. Anyway you would never believe what happened next, in fact no sooner than they were out of the door. I just went up to the kitchen for something and there was Mrs Laws with a funny look about her, I thought. She was standing there with that Lorraine by her side, holding her by the hand. It crossed my mind that the child should have been at school and then I wondered why on earth the woman was wearing her hat and coat at that time of day. 'Where are you going Mrs Laws?' I said. And then I realised she had a suitcase standing by her side. 'We're leaving Annie,' she said. 'We've had enough.' And all that without so much as a with your leave or a by your leave. I dread to think what his Lordship will say when he gets back. Never mind her Lady-ship. Anyway the pair of them have gone and the Lord knows how we are going to manage without a cook. I wouldn't wonder if Mr Kipling didn't have something to do with it.

Miss Wheel is here which is company for me in the evenings.

No more news for now so I'll finish. I hope you are all keeping well and I look forward to hearing from you soon. Give my love to Fred and the children.

Love from
Annie

Zbigniew Rakowski's notebook

As I trod the now so familiar path to Cranfield yesterday morning, enjoying the sweet scents of spring that filled the air, admiring, as I rounded the bend in the drive, the magnificent view of the house, so square and bold and yet so peaceful, at one with its surroundings, roseate against a background of tall, almost black wellingtonias and the newly sprung vivid green of the beech leaves, little did I imagine that a dramatic afternoon lay ahead.

Lady Otterton was, I of course knew, in France, enjoying as I hoped, a well-deserved visit to relatives. I picture her in some crumbling château whose pale *boiserie* and faded *toile de Jouy* are the perfect framework for her slender, aristocratic figure. I even imagine the washed-out blue of the cloth on which a little shepherdess, seated on a swing, hangs from the bough of a leafy tree whilst sheep graze at her feet and lambs gambol around her. I see Priscilla, seated no less elegantly on a cream and gilt *fauteuil*, conversing flawlessly in the language of Racine. But enough of that. I also knew that Lord Otterton would not be at home and that I was therefore not bidden to luncheon. Thus I had with me, as is my wont on such occasions, my picnic and my thermos. I hoped as I admired the gently sloping beauty of the park and mused on Priscilla's visit to France, that on such a pleasant day as this, the indescribable Mason would not interfere too grossly with my labours, although I was quite of the opinion that the time had come for me to oblige myself to pass some little time with his odious personage, if I was to progress at all in my investigations which, I was forced to admit to myself, had remained somewhat static during the preceding weeks.

By midday what had been a promising, fine morning had clouded over and there was a hint of rain in the dark clouds as I glanced out of the Red Drawing-Room window across the long lawn to where a hawthorn tree surprisingly leans and spreads its knotty branches. Not far to the right of it stands an old oak, more suited perhaps to the grandeur of its surroundings than is the little hawthorn. I have often wondered how and when these two trees came to be planted and had thought to take my rug and sit under one or the other to partake of my picnic, thus to admire for a change the East Front of the house.

In the event, however, I decided to eat my sandwiches speedily at the table where I work, to lose no time and thus to take an earlier than usual bus home. Like the weather, my mood had clouded over and, feeling weary, I did not for once feel equal to the task of battling with mystery or with Mason. When nature's own egalitarian had opened the door for me in the morning, he had not appeared to be quite his usual cock-a-hoop self. (I can think of no better way to describe this man's generally self-satisfied manner.) Rather he brushed me aside with a 'No one informed me that you were coming today', as if I were some tiresome encumbrance, and neither did he intrude on me all morning. Instead it was the good Annie who came to see if I was in need of anything. She, I am always glad to see. When I enquired on this occasion if all was well, she informed me of the disruption caused in the household by the sudden defection of the cook. His Lordship was in London and had not been seen for a few days and she was much concerned as to what her Ladyship's reaction would be when she returned to hear the bad news. Annie told me that she could not help but like the cook, yet, in her view, it was all wrong for anyone to leave in such a way without so much as a word to anyone. To have one's work interrupted for a while by Annie with her chatter is always a pleasure. She is, in my view, not only an honest woman, but shrewd, good-looking and humorous besides. I do not doubt her discretion for, as she herself is ever at pains to inform one, she likes to mind her p's and q's.

It was quite early in the afternoon when I collected my

belongings and made for the hall with the intention of leaving by the front door, and perhaps of lingering for a usual brief moment on my way, to admire yet again the nobility of the whole.

As I lingered in the hall, Mason suddenly burst through the door from the opposite side. He was walking fast, his hands clenched by his chest with his elbows sticking out behind him; on his face he wore an expression of concentrated urgency and, as he hastened towards the front door, he appeared to be completely oblivious of my presence, so that I was able to step swiftly back into the doorway at the back of the hall, from which I had emerged, and to stand there quietly without having been observed. Imagine then my amazement on seeing the treacherous butler advance towards the front door. Just before disappearing from my view into the porch, he stopped for a moment, still, as if to collect himself, and there he remained for a fleeting instant, straight as a die, pulling his shoulders back, smoothing his hair with both hands which he then proceeded to rub unctuously together before hurrying into the porch where I imagine he flung the door open, for I heard him instantly utter an unmitigatedly fawning, high-pitched 'M'lady!'

My heart missed a beat since, not unnaturally, my first thought was for Priscilla. Could she conceivably have returned early from her crumbling château? But just as the thought flitted through my mind, I became aware of the fact that under no circumstances would Mason have addressed the Lady Otterton that I know in such sycophantic tones. Nor indeed would his behaviour before he opened the door have remotely resembled that which I have described. The man's manner when addressing Priscilla can indeed be obsequious, and usually is, but nevertheless, I have observed a certain wariness in his attitude towards her as though, like an animal, he senses danger in her presence. When talking to Priscilla, Mason is very much on his mettle.

I held my breath as, from the sheltered alcove of my

doorway, I then observed a slight woman dressed in black and mauve step from the porch that so defiles the West Front of the house, into the hall itself. Having passed so many hours seated beneath Laszlo's painting, I would anywhere have recognised the chilling figure of Lilian who now appeared, a little older than in her portrait, but otherwise just as though she had simply stepped down from the confines of the gilt frame which normally keeps her so safely incarcerated, to stand there before me, in flesh and blood, so tiny in the whiteness of the vast hall. Even from where I was, I could easily discern the pale face and hooded eyes, the straight nose, the pointed chin, the black, black hair (no doubt artificially aided by now in the depths of its colour). Round her neck she wore a long chain, just as she does in her portrait.

She raised an arm to wave autocratically towards the door on the side of the hall opposite me. As she did so, her sleeve fell back down her forearm to reveal a delicate wrist such as I would have expected to find on a porcelain figurine only. 'I'll go upstairs first,' she said grandly. 'See to the men, will you.' And with that she swept out of the hall by the far door. No sooner had she disappeared than Mason went back at once to the porch, from whence he immediately returned accompanied by two burly men attired in workmen's overalls. 'Come with me,' he commanded and without further ado, the three of them followed in the footsteps of the ghost-like Lilian and, as she had, disappeared from my view.

So alarmed was I by what I had witnessed, that I needed a moment to recover my equilibrium before daring to venture out on my journey home. At the same time, I was hesitant to remain in the house for fear of coming face to face with the dowager lady herself, yet, for the moment, I felt that there was no alternative but to withdraw back into the Red Drawing-Room from whence I had come, there to ponder on what my next move might be and perhaps, if I am honest, to ascertain that Laszlo's Lilian was still in her frame, that

Lady Otterton had not stepped out of the picture, and that what I had seen was no fantom, no creation of my heat-oppressed imagination, but a living, mortal being.

After some moments of consideration, and having re-assured myself that the painted Lilian was unquestionably still in her rightful place, I determined that what I had seen was enough; certainly enough for me to have a far greater hold over Mason than he could conceivably have over me merely on the evidence of a few paltry pages expressing the drooling fantasies of a frail old man. Eventually, on leaving the house through the basement and the back door, I was fortunate not to encounter a soul, but since my departure I have been quite unable to rid my mind of what occurred yesterday afternoon and am fearful as to what the eventual outcome of that dramatic event may possibly be. I lay awake last night, haunted by the idea that I, a cowardly old fool, may well have betrayed my good patrons by failing to spy (for spying it would indeed have been) on the further activities of her Ladyship and Mason, not to mention their burly accomplices. Yet at the time, it did not seem right that I should snoop. Snoop, ah yes, snoop. What an ugly word that is!

Georgina's exercise book

MAY 4TH

A very frightening thing hapenned when I got back from school this afternoon. No one was about so I was just roming around as usual. I was in the galery looking down on the hall when all at once the front door bell rang. It was like a really spooky story and I was spying up above. First disgusting Mr Mason came running all bisily to the door and then in came guess who? GRANDMAMA!!!!! Who's not aloud here *at all*. Mr Mason looked as if he knew her and she just marched in looking like a witch with two great big workmen behind her.

I bet she knows Mummy and Father are away or she'd never have dared come here. I stayed spying for a long time even though I was afraid she might see me. After a bit these great big men started to carry fernicher out of the door. They were stealing our things! Father will be livid! Aksherly it was very frightening. Then Annie found me and was cross because she said she didn't know where I had got to. I asked her if she'd seen Grandmama but she wouldn't say. I'm writing this in bed after lights out but no one will know because I bet they're only thinking about Grandmama and what Mummy and Father will say.

Annie's diary

I don't know what in the Lord's name her Ladyship will say when she gets back, and as for his Lordship, well, I should think anyone would be afraid to be near him when he finds out about what went on this afternoon. I'm afraid there'll be a bit of bad language. Anyway I can't get hold of him in London because there's no answer from the number he left. Luckily Mr MacIntosh came back quite early from work so I was able to tell him about what Lilian has done. I was really glad Mr MacIntosh was here. He was very kind and said I wasn't to worry and that he would go on trying to get hold of his Lordship for me this evening. I told him that it wasn't me who let Lady Otterton in just when his Lordship and her Ladyship are both away and he said he knew I wouldn't do a thing like that.

The Lord above knows what she's taken. She even went into her Ladyship's bedroom and emptied the contents of one small chest of drawers all over the bed and I had only this week relined those drawers and tidied them beautifully. Then these dreadful men came in and Lady Lilian told them to take the chest down and put it in their lorry. And that wasn't the end of it. There's no knowing what they didn't take. I was standing there saying that her Ladyship was away and Lilian just looked through me with that awful stare of hers and said, 'Oh, it's you. Simply do as I say, will you.' Then she dismissed me and there was nothing at all that I could do but stand there and watch her ransacking the place. I never felt so dreadful in all my life.

I don't know how she managed to get in unless she found the back door unlocked which Mr Mason thinks she must have done. Mr Mason says that Mr Rakowski left earlier than usual and that he saw him going down the basement stairs which means that he must have gone out through the back door and left it open. Mind you, I can't help feeling that there's something a bit funny about that. Mr Rakowski always goes out through the front door. I think he likes to admire the hall on his way. I've often seen him there just gazing up at the ceiling. Once he was even stroking the doors. It must have been on one of Mr Mason's days off because I remember I was going through to the Japanese Room to close the shutters and draw the curtains. And I know it must have been winter because fires were burning in those two big fireplaces and it was already dark although Mr Rakowski was still there. I remember he stopped me and said, 'Don't hurry through, Ma'am. You should stop to look at these chimney-pieces.' And I said something about not having any time to stand about staring at things because I had my work to do, and he laughed and said, 'Ma'am, pray feel the exquisite texture of these peerless glossy doors.' 'I don't know about peerless,' I said, 'but I have to say I've always liked the look of them.' Then, blow me down if he didn't say that I ought to keep a diary because according to him I'd have a fascinating story to tell. I never said a thing mind, but just gave him a look on the Q.T. and thought to myself that he was the one who was supposed to be the writer. Of course I've heard it all before. The servant's-eye view, my foot! So I left him there stroking those darned doors and went on to do my work. Then Bert goes and tells me, as if he knows a thing about anything, that some people love wood. And well they may.

So if Mr Rakowski didn't leave the back door open, which I doubt, how did Lilian get in? I have my suspicions. For one thing I didn't like the way Mr Mason was so sure that he'd seen Mr Rakowski leave early and I didn't like the way he talked about it, so fast that no one could get a word in edgeways, just like the children when they are telling fibs. Before long, I thought, you'll be swearing to me on the Holy Bible that you *saw* the poor man leaving the door open.

The other thing is that I was worried to death about Georgina. I didn't know where on earth she'd got to after she came back from school. She's supposed to come and find me when she gets in and I am always around waiting for her, but she loves to go off, roaming around all over the house so that it's quite impossible to find her. I didn't know what would happen if she came across her grandmother helping herself to the furniture, not to mention emptying her mother's drawers all over the place without so much as a with-your-leave or a by-your-leave. I thought she would be quite frightened. Besides, I didn't think that, as a child, she ought to know what was going on. Luckily I found her wandering along the gallery above the hall. I can't imagine what in the Lord's name she was doing there. Just mooching about was what she said. Mooching about, my good Lord! Where did she find an expression like that? I asked her if she wasn't supposed to be doing her homework. Oh no, she said, she only had a tiny bit to do. Anyway, never mind that, at least I was able to get her up to the schoolroom before she realised that there was anything funny going on and we managed to sit down and have our tea quite peacefully. I was really pleased to have Miss Wheel there with us. She was a great help with Georgina.

To tell the truth I don't know how I managed to get

through the rest of the evening. There was me trying to get in touch with his Lordship on the one hand and trying to get Georgina to bed on the other, worried sick about what had happened. Thank the Lord for Mr MacIntosh. I didn't know whether to mention Mr Mason to him. He knows just as well as the rest of us do that no one is allowed to let Lilian into the house and he must wonder, like I do, exactly how she did get in.

Sydney Otterton's diary

I have never been so angry in my life as I was when I got home on Thursday and saw with my own eyes exactly what my mother had been up to. Mason denies having let the bloody woman into the house in the first place and poor Annie swears that she knew nothing about it at all until she found her ordering the contents of Priscilla's drawers to be tipped out onto the bed by two great thugs. It appears that Rakowski was here that day and he is being blamed by some-and-some for having left the back door open when he went. But that doesn't really ring true to me because my mother, after all, turned up here with a ruddy great furniture van, which she wasn't likely to have done if she had any doubts about being able to get into the house. Besides, someone must have told her that both Priscilla and I were away. She would never have been able to do what she did if either of us had been at home and she must have known that.

The children hate Mason, Priscilla thinks there's something funny about him and Tony mistrusts the fellow, but I've never had any problem with him. He's a dull dog as far as I can see, an impassive sort of man who says very little, a pretty typical sort of butler who does his job adequately and doesn't seem to have caused any trouble so far. I don't know why everyone's got it in for him. Annie won't commit herself but I'm not sure she's very keen on him either. In any case why the hell would he have let my mother in when I was away after I had specifically told him not to? He had absolutely nothing to gain from doing so, but the sack.

I find it quite impossible to understand what exactly motivated my mother to take what she did. She could have taken a good many things of much greater value. Perhaps she felt that she had a claim on that chest of drawers of Priscilla's which she emptied out because once upon a time it was, I think, in her room. But still that doesn't make an awful lot of sense. It's a pretty enough piece of furniture but my mother has masses of stuff which she took from the Dower House and I can see no very good reason beyond sheer malice as to why she should have decided to take that in particular. According to Annie, she not only took what she wanted, but she also wandered all around the house ordering cupboards and drawers to be opened for her.

However she damn well got in, I really don't see why Mason was unable to prevent her from taking things away. I have to say, he doesn't seem able to give a very good account of himself.

It's hardly surprising if Priscilla who doesn't cry easily was in tears when she came back from France. She said she'd had a wonderful time and getting home to find that Mrs Laws had walked out wouldn't have bothered her in the least because she was such a rotten cook, but it was horrible going into her bedroom knowing that it had been ransacked by my mother. I don't really know what to do about it. I suppose I could send my mother a lawyer's letter but I know for certain that it won't make any difference at all. I'm not prepared to take her to court and although I could threaten her, she's so mad that I don't think it would have any effect on her. What we have to do, is to find out how she got in and who told her that Priscilla and I were away. I wonder if Rakowski knows a thing or two.

Georgina's exercise book

I don't dare tell Father that I saw Grandmama ariving at the front door. He's in a really bad mood and I think hed be livid with me. Mummy was crying when she came home and I think it was because Grandmama had stolen her things but she sent me back to the schoolroom and said it was nothing to do with children. If I told Mummy what I saw she'd be livid too and say what was I doing in the galery and why wasn't I doing my homework and it was none of my bisness and stuff like that. I bet Mr Mason told a wopper because I heard Annie say to Miss Wheel that Grandmama came in through the back door which I know she *DID NOT*. I wish Jamie was here he's very good at spying. I wish Mr Rekofsky would come back again. I like him.

Annie's diary

It was awful when her Ladyship got home. I felt real sorry for her. She's never been one to go crying but when she found out about what had been going on, she just burst into tears and I can't say I blame her. I even felt like crying myself when I thought of all the trouble I'd taken to tidy those drawers. But her Ladyship wasn't a bit worried about Mrs Laws because she said she'd been a rotten cook all along. Mind you she's never said anything like that before, but of course she was full of talk about all this French food she'd been eating. Mrs Laws, she said, was very Anglo-Saxon. I wasn't sure what she meant by that but then she went on about Mrs Laws not wanting to cook those wretched snails. Well I must admit that I was on Mrs Laws's side about that. Not that I would have said anything.

His Lordship came back from London with this great big pink cockatoo called Brylcreme to add to the menagerie in his dressing-room. It seems to be the only thing that brings a smile to his face these days, not that her Ladyship or anyone else was particularly pleased to see it and poor Georgina is quite terrified of it. I think she pretends not to hear his Lordship calling her in case he's going to ask her to help him clean out the cage. As a matter of fact, I think her Ladyship was more annoyed about the arrival of *Brylcreme* than she ever was about the departure of Mrs Laws. What with Brylcreme *and* Lilian, you couldn't help feeling sorry for her.

I still think Mr Mason had something to do with Lilian coming here last week. It's at times like this that I miss Mr Johnson. He would have known what to do and he would never have let that woman into the house or allowed her to take away the furniture. I can't help remembering how he kept an eye on those Legros when they were in the flat and he was convinced they were up to no good. Well I hope he's happy now, standing upside down in Australia with all those kangaroos. It's funny that he never wrote.

As a matter of fact, I have an idea that her Ladyship thinks Mr Mason's got something to do with what went on too, but, how can it be proved? She says, 'Annie, his Lordship won't listen to me if I criticise Mason. I can't tell you why,' she says, 'but there's something about that man I don't like. What do you think?' Now I wasn't going to say a word. 'And what's more, Mr MacIntosh can't stand the man,' she goes on. 'Oh,' I thought to myself. I'm not saying anything about Mr MacIntosh either.

Sydney Otterton's diary

My mother-in-law is here for the week-end driving poor Priscilla nearly mad so I've shut myself away for a while in the Japanese Room. Priscilla bears a good deal of resentment against her mother, with reason perhaps, but she doesn't look very happy when I suggest she tries mine for a change. One thing though that has cheered me up lately is my new cockatoo. It's absolutely beautiful but I'm afraid it does make a bit of a mess. Priscilla wasn't at all pleased to see it and even Annie looked at me 'askance', as she would say. 'Now then, M'lord,' she said, 'whoo' (with a drawn-out 'o') 'do you think is going to clear up the mess?' I just laughed because I know she won't mind doing it for me. After all, what's the hoover for? Sometimes Georgina can help, but she keeps saying she's frightened of the bird which is absolute nonsense.

As a matter of fact I've had rather a good idea. When I was going around the house to see what damage my mother had done, I found a lot of old beds stacked up in one of the unused servants' rooms and I thought I'd get Kipling to use the springs to make an aviary for the birds in my dressing-room. When I told Kipling what I wanted, he gave me a sly, somewhat insolent grin and said, rather as if he was putting me in my place, that he was busy mending the struts in the greenhouses at the moment. He was supposed to have finished that job months ago but he tells me the weather has prevented him from getting on with it. I know exactly what the weather has been like. I wish Johnson was still here.

I've sent my wretched mother a lawyer's letter to complain about her thieving and telling her to keep out of the house. I've told her that if she comes back and takes anything else which isn't hers all hell will be let loose. I don't suppose it will have any effect at all and was probably just a waste of money (more cash in those greedy lawyers' pockets), but I felt that something had to be put on paper about what had happened. And I still don't know what she was after. It can't have just been the few pieces of furniture which she took and which she certainly didn't need. She even took a rickety old bit of white-painted rubbish from one of the servants' rooms. I'd also like to know why she went round the house opening and shutting drawers and cupboards as if she was looking for something. What in God's name could she have been looking for?

Priscilla is adamant that I ought to sack Mason but I can't really see why. She almost gives me the impression that she's frightened of him, but as far as I can see he hasn't done anything wrong and he totally denies having had anything to do with my mother getting into the house. I can't help feeling that he must be telling the truth because if he weren't, someone else would probably have seen something and would have said so. In any case he could never be certain that he hadn't been seen, so one might imagine that if he were lying, he'd be a bit more uneasy. I think Rakowski's coming here some time next week, so when we see him, we might just ask him if he went out by the back door that day and left it open, for which crime he is endlessly being held responsible.

Zbigniew Rakowski's notebook

MAY 20TH

It was certainly not without a degree of trepidation that I made my way to Cranfield on Tuesday morning. It was indeed some time since I had had the undiluted pleasure of conversing (let alone lunching) with Priscilla. Thus, but for the unsettling events of my last visit, I should have been walking with a spring in my step, anticipating with excruciating delight her Ladyship's account of her visit to France. I had already, in the solitude of Robin Hood Way, envisaged her seated in the dining-room at the head of the handsome mahogany table, heedless of the vile Mason as he hovered around and bent to hand her the rabbit stew, her manner, as ever, vivacious, her fine eyes shining as with histrionic gesture, much wit and a vivid turn of phrase she described her experiences in the crumbling château in the *Allier*. But eagerly as I dwelt on the prospect of Priscilla's conversation, I could not rid myself of the dreadful, intrusive thought of the treacherous Mason, not simply waiting at table as is his business, but listening, watching, deceiving. It did at times, however, cross my mind to wonder whether I might not find on my return to Cranfield that the sinister creature had been dismissed. I was not entirely sure that this would be the most desirable outcome and somewhat doubted that I would in fact discover it to be the case, since I felt convinced that he must have denied any responsibility for having allowed Lady Lilian to enter the house. Lord Otterton has never made a secret of the fact that he has forbidden the servants to open the door to his mother. On my frail shoulders, then, lay the burden of knowledge, for I alone had witnessed the door being opened, I alone had heard the butler's sycophantic cry of recognition and I alone had observed the violet-clad dowager sweeping into the hall.

Not only was I uncertain as to whether I should find Mason still at Cranfield, but I was not sure either as to the wisdom of informing Lord and Lady Otterton of all that I had seen. I was and am of course aware that I have a duty towards the Ottertons, but it is difficult for me to be sure as to the way in which this duty might best be fulfilled. To have told what I knew would inevitably have brought about the butler's dismissal which would in turn prevent me from making any further discoveries concerning the mystery at the heart of the matter. As things stood, I was of the opinion that I alone was in a position to unveil something of the truth, having, as I would do, should I remain silent, a unique hold over the obnoxious servant. Yet, for all my deliberations over the past days, I was, as I walked up the drive, still undecided as to the path I would take.

I rang the bell, and even as I did so, standing beneath the hideous *porte cochère* built so vandalistically and yet so lovingly in 1876 by his Lordship's grandfather in order that his lady wife might not alight from her carriage in the rain, my mind was in a turmoil as to how I should proceed. I held my breath as I heard the door being unlocked from the inside for I did not know whether, as it opened, I would be confronted by the awful Mason himself, by Annie in his stead, or perhaps by some newly appointed butler. Strange to say, it was not in fact without some degree of relief that, as the great door swung open, I instantly discerned the familiar if repulsive features of the unspeakable Mason. He did not look in the least dismayed to see me, thus confirming me in my belief that he had been completely unaware of my presence at the back of the hall on that terrible afternoon. I said nothing beyond a polite good-morning, considering it only wise to bide my time before in any way confronting the brute or even allowing him to suspect that I might have something distasteful awaiting him up my sleeve.

So concerned was I with the drama in which I had unwittingly become involved that I was, on Tuesday morning, most unfortunately, quite unable to attend to the work which is my business and the sole reason for my continued presence at Cranfield. I decided that should Mason seek me out in the Red Drawing-Room before luncheon, I would, at that early stage, say nothing, for I wished there to be no unnecessary complications when I conversed later with Lady Otterton and indeed with Lord Otterton, should he be present. It occurred to me that it was not beyond the realms of possibility that either his Lordship or indeed her Ladyship might wish to enlighten me as to the events surrounding the dowager Lady Otterton's recent monstrous behaviour, and under the butler's vigilant eye, I not unnaturally hoped to assume an air of polite interest and mild amazement, for I knew that he would be watching carefully and listening closely to everything that might be said. It is always a matter of surprise to me that, unless they address their servants directly, expecting them then, as the saying goes, to 'jump to it', the upper classes presume those self-same servants to have no ears at all.

As we sat down to the luncheon table we spoke of France; indeed as I unfolded my linen napkin and placed it on my knees, I enquired of Lady Otterton as to how her French trip had been. Somewhat frivolously perhaps, I even took the mild liberty of suggesting to Priscilla that I had imagined her staying in an elegant, if conceivably somewhat dilapidated château. Laughing gaily at my presumption, she nevertheless assured me that I had not been wholly wrong in what I surmised. 'It wasn't quite as dilapidated as Cranfield,' she jested, 'but in some ways less comfortable. The French don't have sofas, you know.' She added that she never found it very easy sitting for long periods, making *petite conversation* on those upright Louis XV or Louis XVI chairs, thus confirming the image I had had of her perched on an elegant *fauteuil*. But, as I had anticipated, we were not long at table before Lord Otterton himself turned to the subject of his mother.

'Mr Rakowski!' he addressed me earnestly, fixing me with his big brown eyes as he did so. 'Have you heard what my poisonous mother did while Priscilla and I were both away?' I did my very best to appear quite natural whilst sensing the unnerving presence of the butler hovering behind my chair with a dish of new potatoes.

'Pray, what did she do?' I enquired, carefully thus avoiding giving a direct reply to his Lordship's question. I was then told in no uncertain terms of Lilian's unforgivably deranged behaviour as, according to her son, she forced her way into the house in order to help herself to whatever she chose and, in his words, 'drove off with a bloody great cartload of my possessions.'

Completely unperturbed, the butler, forever with his dish of potatoes, leant to wait upon his Lordship.

'No one knows how the hell she got in,' said Lord Otterton as, with a nodded acknowledgement to Mason, he helped himself to the potatoes. 'Mason here didn't know a thing about it until she was half-way down the drive with the booty. Did you?' His Lordship turned to address the butler.

'Not a thing, M'lord.' Mason, still holding the dish, straightened himself up and looked his employer right in the eye as he lied. May the devil take the wretched man's soul!

'I don't suppose you were aware of anything?' Lord Otterton turned to address me. 'I think you were here that day.'

Now indeed was my chance to wipe the odious complacency from the butler's face, but as I have implied, I considered that too sudden an onslaught might ultimately result in no more than a Pyrrhic victory. Nevertheless I was at pains not to tell an untruth and consequently was careful to remark that, as is my wont, I had been occupied for the greater part of the day in the Red Drawing-Room which I had not left even for luncheon since, with the weather being changeable, it had struck me as unwise to venture into the garden where both I and my sandwiches would have risked being rained upon. There is nothing I dislike more than a damp sandwich.

'You didn't hear or see anything on the way out?' Lord Otterton then asked, but fortunately continued without waiting for me to reply. 'There is some suggestion that she may have come in through the back door and the basement, but you usually leave by the front door, I imagine?'

'Ah,' I was eager to reply, 'on this occasion, Sir, I left through the basement, but I can assure you that I encountered not a soul.' I further denied any suggestion that I might have left the door open behind me. The basement door has a

Yale lock on it and I would, beyond any question of doubt, have seen to it that I closed the door properly behind me. However, as I explained myself thus, a flash of intuition informed me that the two-faced butler had unquestionably attempted to lay the blame for Lilian's intrusion at my feet. I wondered if he had left it at that, merely implying that I, a careless old man, had absent-mindedly omitted to shut the door, or had he additionally suggested that I, miserable ageing writer that I am, forever prying needlessly into the affairs of others, was in cahoots (as the Americans say) with the dowager Lady Otterton. Was I, appallingly, under suspicion of treachery? Am I to be Mason's scapegoat? We shall see about that. Caution, I inwardly told myself, should rule my every action.

It was not until quite late in the afternoon, indeed shortly before I was intending to collect my things and leave, that I heard the door of the Red Drawing-Room open quietly behind me. I had not seen the butler since luncheon and had been asking myself what his next move might be. Would he come to torment me, or did he prefer to leave me, as he no doubt hoped, in a state of nervous uncertainty, thus further to have me, as he supposed, in his power?

The door creaked cautiously open. I affected to ignore the intrusion, hoping, by my insouciant demeanour to put the butler just a little on his mettle. On hearing what resembled a faint whimper rather than a whisper, I turned my whole body slowly round in my chair, to be confronted amazingly, by none other than the child, Georgina. I gazed at her for a moment solemnly over my half-moon spectacles. 'Good afternoon, Ma'am,' I said as she hesitated in the doorway. Two untidy pigtails stuck out from under her navy-blue beret which she wore at what can be described only as a raffish angle with the badge over her right ear. She was dressed in a blue-striped summer frock, with her customary brown leather satchel hanging loosely from one shoulder. My stern gaze appeared to do little to set the poor creature at her ease.

'Pray close the door and tell me how I may help you,' I continued, for I discerned from the tentative look on her face that she was not surprised to find me at my work, but had in fact sought me out.

The child shut the door as I had bidden her and slowly, with an undisguised degree of embarrassment, came towards where I sat. 'Mr Rakowski,' she began, 'Mummy says we're not allowed in here when you are working . . . Actually, I don't think we're supposed to come in here at all . . .'

'Never mind,' I interrupted, for I was curious indeed to know what had brought her. I informed her that I had finished my labours for the day and assured her that, as far as I was concerned, she was invited in and that I was delighted, indeed flattered by her visit. She stood rather awkwardly beside the bureau on which my work was spread out in front of me, fiddling with one of her pigtails in a fashion that I surmise was quite simply due to nervousness. I looked at her. She did not, I thought, resemble her mother.

'How, Ma'am, may I be of assistance to you?' I then enquired.

Did I remember, she wanted to know, ages ago asking her to look for some old papers? I was careful to reply that although I was aware of the conversation to which she alluded, I had not precisely instructed her to search for papers, but had merely enjoined her, should she come across any diaries or bundles of letters in a drawer or cupboard, to be so good as to inform her parents of that discovery.

She appeared to pay little attention to what I said, but continued in her own vein. 'I think,' she said, 'that everyone in this house is looking for something.' Then, as if she had gained confidence with speaking, she turned to look me straight in the eye and asked not a little fiercely, 'Can you keep a secret?' I naturally assured her that it would indeed be a sorry story if I, at my stage of life, were not able to do such a thing. 'Ah, dear Ma'am,' I sighed, 'many is the secret that I shall take with me to my final resting place.'

'You see,' she continued, heedless of my deliberations, 'an awful thing happened not last week, but the week before and you must absolutely swear on your word of honour not to tell anyone . . .' I placed my right hand solemnly on my heart as she hastily proceeded with her tale. 'Mummy and Father would be livid if they knew because I was supposed to be doing my homework, but I was in the gallery above the hall and the bell rang and I saw horrible Mr Mason,' here she narrowed her eyes, 'go to the door and let in my grand-mother. And do you know,' at this point the young lady contrived to sound immensely grand, 'that my grandmother is not allowed here at all because she's been so beastly to Father?'

Imagine my confusion on suddenly being apprised of the fact that I had not been alone in witnessing Mason's treachery! I immediately understood that this unexpected information could not but add an altogether new dimension to my dilemma. But my first reaction was to be wary, for I wished to be quite certain as to whether or not, from her vantage point in the gallery, Georgina had been able to discern the smallish figure of an old man standing in the shadow of the doorway at the back of the hall. I considered it unlikely since, in order to see me, she would have been obliged to lean right out over the hall, thus revealing her presence to anyone below. After considerable, careful en-quiry, I was able to satisfy myself that she had indeed been unaware of my presence and that she, as I had until this moment, believed herself to have been the only person to witness her grandmother's arrival.

I thought to question the young lady as to why she had chosen to entrust a stuffy, elderly gentleman such as I with this important information, for it occurred to me that her parents would surely overlook her minor disobedience in their gratitude at discovering the truth about Mason; yet I was not entirely sure that it suited my own purposes to have the child intervene, and thus it behoved me to hesitate before encouraging her to approach Lord or Lady Otterton with her story, something which she herself was, in any case, loath to do. However, as she continued speaking, one aspect of the matter, an explanation for which had so far eluded me, was clarified. What, I had been wondering, was the connection in her child's mind between the arrival of her grandmother and the conversation she and I had formerly held concerning old, lost papers.

In singularly animated mode she described to me how she had come across the vile Mason rummaging, as she thought, guiltily, through drawers on the back stairs; this, in a far from unintelligent manner, she connected to the fact that he, now revealed to be her grandmother's accomplice, was searching for something on Lilian's behalf. Did I know, she asked me, that Lilian had gone through the house with what she referred to as a fine toothbrush, looking for something and no one, not even her father, could imagine what. She had overheard her father talking about it to Mr MacIntosh.

I have to confess that whilst the child spoke, I was growing a little nervous as to what part I was to be called upon to play in the whole proceedings. And to think that all the while I have here in the drawer of my bureau a little work of my own imagination, *Death in the Dining-Room* or whatever, which begins to appear more trivial every day when compared to the real intrigue at Cranfield!

Before the young lady eventually took her leave of me to return to the schoolroom and, no doubt tea and cucumber sandwiches under the watchful eye of the good Annie, we had agreed that I would reveal her secret to no one and that she would institute a search in every conceivable nook and cranny. Should she find anything that might be of interest, she insisted that she would bring it to me, despite my assurance that I would be under a moral obligation to inform her parents of any such discovery. In my heart I did not, and do not, for one moment imagine that anything will result from her childish search. I am, nevertheless, only strengthened in my desire to ascertain the nature of the truth concerning this most mysterious intrigue, thus perhaps to reveal myself to her Ladyship as a knight in shining armour galloping to her rescue from the least expected quarter.

Sydney Otterton's diary

I haven't heard a damn thing from either my mother or her lawyers which I suppose is just as well. What with the foot and mouth which, by the grace of God, we seem to have avoided, I have managed to put her right out of my mind, although I don't suppose for a moment that she will allow it to stay that way for very long. Priscilla has come to the conclusion that my mother's only motive in coming here was to make a scene and cause us as much trouble as possible because, for one thing, she thinks that my mother is horribly jealous of her and bitterly resents her living at Cranfield. I suppose she may well be right up to a point but my mother's desire to make everybody else's life a misery goes back far longer than any resentment she may have of Priscilla. Of course there can be no doubt about it that Priscilla is yet another person whom she somehow sees as being in her way. But it's impossible to say what my mother's way is or where, if she were to be satisfied, it would lead. Her trouble is that she sees the entire world as being in some sort of conspiracy against her and so she is full of hatred, resentment and spite. I find it quite strange when someone (say a man of my age) talks about his mother with anything approaching affection. To have had a remotely reasonable or fond mother, even one that occasionally appeared genuinely to like one the least little bit, is completely outside my experience.

Priscilla now thinks that Rakowski must have left the back door open, despite what he says, and she has decided that my mother has no ulterior, hidden motive for her actions. She says she's just mad and bad and probably does whatever comes into her head for no good reason. Perhaps this line of thinking makes things easier for her. In any case, she says that my mother probably decided on a whim that she wanted various things from Cranfield so she just came and helped herself, and more than likely took a spiteful pleasure in throwing Priscilla's things about at the same time. Funnily enough, when I do think about it, and about the way she apparently went through a whole lot of cupboards which simply could not have contained anything of interest, I'm beginning to suspect that she may well be looking for something that she really doesn't want us to find first. It crossed my mind that she might even think that my father left a last will hidden away somewhere which might have benefited ourselves. Perhaps he did. God alone knows!

Anyway, what with the House of Lords and the T.A. and problems over the sheep and the British Legion jamboree and everyone on the committee squabbling about the best ways to raise money for the new cathedral, I've had enough to think about without bothering about my mad mother. And what with the dock strike looming, Nye Bevan and the new health service, the row about capital punishment and, on a more cheerful note, the Olympic Games, you'd have thought that even she could have found something else to think about, but then she's never ever been aware of anything or anyone outside herself so that all of those things will pass her by as if they never were. I sometimes wonder how it will all end up.

I saw Pammie on Thursday evening and consequently came home quite late. She made me laugh because she was in such a fury about the government having what she regarded as the impertinence to suggest that women should wear shorter skirts because the so-called New Look is unpatriotic in its extravagant use of material. Pammie drove ambulances in the war with, she says, doodlebugs dropping all around her and that, she says, ought to be proof enough of her patriotism. I thought both Tony and Priscilla would be amused by that, so when I got back and found the pair of them having a drink together in the Hunting Room, I just pretended that I'd seen Pammie in the street and she'd told me all this. Tony laughed but Priscilla gave me a long, hard look. She probably doesn't trust me and I can't say I blame her, but we were married very young, then came the war, then after the war came the house and everything that that entails. I don't really see that a fling on the side with Pammie is the end of the world, but I couldn't help feeling a bit of a rat all the same.

Then Priscilla started to go on about Mason again. In fact I thought she'd given up on that one. I can't keep sacking butlers, after all, she made me sack Cheadle which was probably quite right in the end, although, I must say the fellow was far more amusing than Mason. In fact I sometimes wonder what's happened to the old scoundrel now. I suppose he's drinking his way through some other poor so-and-so's cellar. Anyway I keep telling Priscilla that I can hardly just ask Mason to leave for no other reason than that her Ladyship doesn't like the look of his face. Then Tony joined in, talking in a very reasonable voice and making me rather annoyed. What the hell's it got to do with him? They've both got some damn fool theory about the fellow being sinister. I always thought it was in the nature of butlers to be either drunk or sinister. The butler my parents had before the war was permanently plastered.

I don't know what Georgina's up to these days either. She's plotting some secret of her own but I suppose it's pretty harmless. She keeps coming and asking me if there are any locked rooms in the house, or any secret passages or whether there's any piece of furniture with a secret drawer in it and she wants to know where I would hide something if I really didn't want somebody to find it. At first I thought that she'd just been reading some children's adventure stories, but she's so insistent and looks so earnest that I'm beginning to wonder if there isn't more to it. She says she's got a list in some exercise book or other of all the best places in the house to hide things. I've asked her what on earth she wants to hide and all she says is, 'Aha, wouldn't you like to know!'

Georgina's exercise book

I keep forgeting to look for the stuff for Mr Rakofsky. I've tride to ask Father were he thinks is a good hiding place but he wont tell me. Mr Rakofsky wont say what he thinks about Mr Mason but I'm just sure he's on our side. I wish Jamie and Thomas were here. I think Grandmama was proberbly looking for some hidden mony because Father hasn't got any mony and she doesn't want him to have any and she's rolling in it. Its very hard looking for things here because the house is so big. I haven't even found the secret room yet. Perhaps the mony is in there. I hope Grandmama didn't find it when she came here. Mr Rakofsky says things about letters but I'm sure its mony or treasure they're looking for. What would Mr Mason want some boring old letters for?

Letter from Annie to Dolly

Cranfield Park
JULY 4TH, 1948

Dear Dolly,
It was nice seeing you and Fred and the children when you came over to visit Father last week. Little Fred is a good boy. He has grown so much since Christmas that he'll soon be as tall as his father. Of course Father was thrilled to have you all over for the day and I was glad that you were able to see

for yourself how much better he is. I am writing this in his kitchen on Sunday afternoon while he is in the garden tying up his dahlias. He has a beautiful show of them this year. I hope you made sure to admire them last week, although I'm not certain they were quite out yet.

I wonder how you will all manage what with the meat ration being cut back again. I do think of you. We are very lucky here with all the rabbits and the odd pigeon but I'm not sure about the pheasant her Ladyship gave to Lord and Lady Williton last week-end. When Ellen (that's the new cook I think I told you about) went to put it in the oven, she discovered that it was crawling with maggots. Her Ladyship just said that there was nothing else to give them and that it didn't matter because it was all meat anyway. Then she washed the bird out with vinegar and made poor Ellen cook it. Ellen said she was glad that no one expected her to eat it. It didn't make her half sick, she said, to dish the darned thing up. As far as I know Lord and Lady Williton are still alive!

Do write when you have a moment. Things go on here much as usual despite the hoo-ha about Lilian, Lady Otterton, and I'm sure we haven't heard the last of her. I can't think what she wanted, coming here like that. And between you and me and the gatepost, I wouldn't be at all surprised if it wasn't Mr Mason who let her in. The trouble is that no one knows.

Love from
Annie

Annie's diary

JULY 24TH

Georgina broke up on Wednesday and the boys came home at the end of last week for their eight-week summer holiday. My good Lord, I could do with an eight-week summer holiday myself what with all the goings on! Tiz has come back to see to the children. She is a very nice person and I think everyone was pleased to see her including Mr MacIntosh. He was smiling all over his face when she turned up! Mind you, she is very nice-looking. His Lordship has bought the children another pony, a black one called Billy which he bought off the gypsies. Her Ladyship thinks it's really foolish of him to have bought it from the gypsies because she says it's a bad-tempered animal and you can't tell where it's come from or how it has been treated. I hear it all from both sides but I don't pay any attention as it's nothing to do with me. His Lordship says the ponies will keep the children occupied during the summer, and off he sends them, down to the farm to clean the tack. But Bert saw them at the stables the other day and he said they certainly weren't cleaning any tack. He says they spent the whole afternoon swinging on the stable doors and clambering among the hay bales. I wouldn't doubt it. They aren't going to the seaside this year because her Ladyship says they can't afford it, so I hope the children don't go getting into too much trouble.

Letter from William Johnson to Annie Jerrold

'Cranfield',
Coolgardie,
W. Australia
APRIL 2ND, 1948

Dear Annie,

I was going to write yesterday but then it was April 1st so I thought you might think it was a practical joke after all this time. Don't think that I don't miss you, Annie, and that I'm not still waiting, it's just that I didn't want to write until things were settled.

When I got here, they sent me up to this place 350 miles inland from Perth called Coolgardie. Years gone by it used to be a gold mining town, but now it's mostly pastureland round about. They gave me a good engineering job with the railways and put me up with several others in some sort of a Nissen hut. There are plenty of kangaroos which I'm sure you would like if you saw them, and acacia trees everywhere.

Now I don't live in the Nissen hut any more because, dearest Annie, I have built my own bungalow. It isn't very big but there's plenty of room for two. I couldn't think what to call it so I just called it 'Cranfield' after the old place back home. It's not quite as grand, but at least the rain doesn't come through the roof.

Give my regards to his Lordship and tell him that I often think of the good times we had together in the war.

I don't know how long this letter will take to reach you, but I will keep waiting.

Love from
Yr. Bill Johnson
P.S. I think about you every day.

Annie's diary

AUGUST 9TH

Mr Johnson was the last person I was thinking about yesterday afternoon when the second post arrived. I'd been to see if Father was all right after the dreadful gale we've had. There were trees down everywhere in the park with one across the drive and Father had lost a tile or two off his roof. He said he could fix them himself, but I didn't want him getting up that ladder so I told him to wait for Bert. Bert will do the job in no time. It's no good waiting for Mr Kipling. You could wait a month of Sundays for him. So I'd just left

Father's to come on home when the postman turned in under the lodge. He wanted to know if the tree had been cleared from the drive which it had more or less, but I said I'd take the letters all the same to save him the trouble. There's not usually much that comes in the afternoon post, only his Lordship's *Hansard*, but there wouldn't be any *Hansard* at this time of year, so I was a bit surprised to see the postman at all, but not half so surprised as I was when he handed me this letter with the envelope covered in all these great big foreign stamps and addressed to me. At first I couldn't think what the devil it could be. Then I realised that the stamps were Australian. 'My good Lord!' I thought to myself. I wasn't going to open the letter there and then with that nosy postman sticking his head out of his van and grinning at me like nobody's business, so I just put it in my bag and took it on back up to the house with me. I thought I'd read it quietly when I had a bit of time to myself.

Well, well, well, so there's Mr Johnson still wanting me to go out there and join him in Australia. I could hardly believe my eyes when I read his letter, and me thinking all the time how hard-hearted he was just going off like that and never writing. My first thought was, well, I've got over you now, so it's no good cropping up again just because you feel like it and talking about bungalows and kangaroos. Then I couldn't help thinking that it was nice to be asked and nice to know that there was somewhere else I could go, if I felt like it. Never mind it's the other end of the world. I shall think about it for a while before I answer and the Lord knows how long it will take my answer to reach him because I couldn't help noticing that that letter of his had taken nearly four months to get here.

I haven't said anything to his Lordship or her Ladyship.

Gerozina's exercise book

We got taken down to the gates to watch the Olympic runner running to London with a flaming torch which comes all the way from Greese. Everybody cheered.

Its always pelting. Father was going to take us out in the pony trap yesterday but it absolutely pelted all day so we couldn't go. We were all mucking around in the room with the state bed in it were we are not aloud and we herd someone coming. Thomas and I ran away in time but Jamie hid in the great big wardrobe in their. Thomas and I saw Mr Mason on the landing and he said he'd tell our parents on us. Luckily he didn't catch Jamie because when Jamie was in the wardrobe his foot went through into a sort of hiden draw underneath. It wasn't his forlt. Anyway what do you think he found? As they say in storys. He found this huge great bundle of letters. We were very excited but they looked very boring and were all adressed to someone called Doris. Worse luck there wasn't any money in them. I asked Mummy when Mr Rakofsky was coming and she just said why are you always asking about Mr Rakofsky? We've hiden the letters under a floorbord in Thomas's room.

Sydney Otterton's diary

I sometimes feel that nothing around here ever improves. Whatever you do goes wrong. Sheep, cows, crops, there's always a problem and nothing makes any money. My bank is forever hounding me and if it weren't for Aunt Lettice's help,

I don't suppose we'd still be living at Cranfield. It's an unending struggle. Priscilla is brilliantly resourceful. I don't know how she manages. She gives me quite a lot of stick for not pulling my weight, but what can I do about the cottages for instance? We had managed to get some repairs done at last, then that gale in August blew half the roofs off again. One thing that did cheer me up was the King opening Parliament last week. It was the first State Opening since '38 and it certainly made some of us feel that things were beginning to return to normal. Afterwards Priscilla and I spent a jolly evening with the Willitons.

Funny how empty the house seems when the children are all at school, particularly at this time of year which is always pretty gloomy anyway. There's something the matter with Annie too. I can't make out what, but Priscilla too has noticed that she's not her usual self. Priscilla thinks it may have something to do with old Jerrold being ill again. He was so much better in the summer but apparently he's gone downhill lately and Annie must be pretty worried because she's always adored her father. After her mother died, everyone said she used to look after him like a wife and she took care of all those younger brothers and sisters too. It's a mystery why Annie has never married. After all, she's a good-looking woman. Priscilla says she thinks it's because Annie sees herself as being above the likes of Bert, but I used to think she was keen on Johnson before he went to Australia. I often wonder how he got on and I sometimes wish I could go and join him out there one day, throw this lot in and start a new life. I might leave my clothes on a beach somewhere and let people think that I'd swum out to sea and drowned. I wonder what Priscilla would do? I sometimes think she might go off with Tony. Perhaps she will anyway. She'd probably be a good deal better off with him than with me in the end.

Annie's diary

Jam rationing has come to an end. Not that bought jam is anything like homemade and in any case the quality is nothing like it was before the war. Princess Elizabeth has had a son but they haven't announced his names yet. I expect they'll call him Albert or Bertie after the King, but then perhaps that's a bit too German for these days.

Poor Father is not at all well again. I'd like to know how I could possibly go off to Australia and leave him now, even if I wanted to. I wrote to Mr Johnson by Airmail so I hope he will have got the letter quite quickly. I said I was downright surprised to hear from him after so long and I told him about Father and that otherwise everything was much the same here as when he left. I couldn't help adding that we all miss him. I still haven't told his Lordship that I've heard from him. I must do soon. I sometimes think about that bungalow though. You can't help laughing at it being called Cranfield. I don't suppose it's much like this Cranfield.

Things are quite quiet here at the moment. Her Ladyship's been busy with one thing and another, like the Red Cross and St Dunstan's, but his Lordship has been spending so much time in London and the children are off at school. This year seems to have flown by though, and it won't be many weeks now before they're all home for the Christmas holidays. Then her Ladyship's bound to be all over the place what with the estate party and the puddings and the cake and the Christmas tree, not to mention the wrapping up and the rest of the whole darned caboodle to boot.

1949

Zbigniew Rakowski's notebook

It has been some months since my last visit to Cranfield during which time I have indeed been quietly and most studiously sitting here at home in Robin Hood Way, concentrating on my history of the Otterton family. On the couple of occasions that I returned to the house during the summer and early autumn, I saw no one. That is to say that on both occasions the family was absent and on both occasions it was the good Annie who opened the door to me. Thus the drama of last spring with Lilian, Lady Otterton's arrival and all the monstrous Mason's devious dealings had perforce retreated into the background of my imagination.

I have to confess that I am not entirely displeased with the work on which I am at present engaged, for during the winter months I have made not inconsiderable progress, drawing together the threads of the disparate members of this family to reveal, as I trust, some kind of homogeneity. I have become quite engrossed in the earlier Ottertons and of some of them, trimmers and rapscallions though they may be, I have even grown inordinately fond. There was one Lord Otterton who so disliked the sight of his plain spouse's face that he caused a screen to be placed on the dining-room table, that he might not be obliged to look upon his wife as he dined. The screen was of a variety that could be raised or lowered at wish and he was frequently heard to shout at the footman, 'Higher, you damn fool, higher, I can still see her Ladyship's face.' Such a character as he, uncouth and ribald, living as he did, surrounded by great architectural magnificence, cannot but attract my attention and fascinate me. Did the beauty of his surroundings in no way gentle his condition? Did he not wish to stroke those silken mahogany doors or gaze in wonder at Rysbrack's masterpieces? Did he not look in awe at his surroundings? Sometimes I marvel that such a house as Cranfield can have been built by a family who produced so many Philistines. Or, am I perchance a little unjust? Perhaps the exquisite nature of her surroundings so highlighted the said Lady Otterton's ill-favoured countenance, that the contrast between their beauty and her ugliness made it unbearable for his Lordship to dwell upon her features. Who is to know? What is sadly not in doubt, is that she was an heiress whose fortune must, at least momentarily, have caused his Lordship to disregard whatever aesthetic sensibilities he may have had. But where, the present Lord Otterton may sigh, is that fortune now?

As for my little work of fiction, that too, has been relegated to almost forgotten territory, although I am in no doubt that as soon as the family history is completed, I will feel the urge to return to it, for with what reluctance will I eventually be obliged to turn my back on Cranfield and its inhabitants, both of which have done so much to thaw an old man's chilly heart, to lighten for him the burden of age and to restore in him a zest for life? For so long now have I been engrossed in Cranfield that its absence will surely create a void.

Crowned as it is by a forlornly crumbling balustrade, the house, when I returned to it yesterday, struck me as melancholy indeed, almost forbidding beneath the louring grey clouds. The winter hedgerows, appearing to have taken their cue from the skies above, seemed themselves to be devoid of colour. Beyond them, a solitary, leafless oak, under which I had picnicked one summer, its bleak black branches reaching to the unyielding heavens, stood desolate and abandoned amongst the brambles of an unkempt field. It seemed to me, as I walked up the drive, that for this particular family of aristocrats, even without the intervention of their treacherous butler, Nemesis was at hand.

I need hardly say that, despite the door being opened to me by the odiously servile Mason, I had no sooner entered the hall and gazed aloft once more at the incomparable plasterwork of the ceiling, than my spirits soared again. Referring as I do (and rightly so) to Mr Mason's odious servility, I am nevertheless obliged to confess that, at the sight of the man, although my hackles, so to speak, rose, I felt a not unwelcome surge of blood in my veins, a tremor of almost youthful excitement provoked, no doubt, by my coming face to face once more, and after so many months, with my enemy – nay my quarry. The hideous man was still employed at Cranfield then!

What work I had in mind to do I was able to accomplish quite speedily and was therefore more than ready to be invited to the dining-room for luncheon when I eventually heard the summons from the gong at the foot of the oak staircase. After the usual quiet Christmas spent at home, interrupted only by the customary brief visit from my daughter, her husband who remains as tedious as ever and their pale child, I was delighted by the prospect of a little company, particularly of course, company that included the lovely Lady Otterton. There was, as it so happened, a not inconsiderable gathering already assembled in the dining-room when I arrived there. Lord and Lady Otterton were both present with their three children and a young governess; Lady Isley and Mr MacIntosh were also present. Lady Otterton welcomed me most cordially, saying what a long time it had been since I last lunched at Cranfield. I was indeed honoured to be placed beside Lady Isley who showed ample interest in my work and was kind enough to say that she could barely wait for me to complete it. Lord Otterton was his usual jovial self, iconoclastic and bawdy of humour, thus in his buffoonery reminding me once more and not a little of one or two of his ancestors with whom I have lately grown so familiar.

So concentrated was I on my conversation with Lady Isley

and so eager to hear what she had to say to me, that I scarcely paid any attention to the butler as he handed around the food. I did however notice that the young Georgina appeared at times to be looking at me across the table in a somewhat concentrated fashion, gazing at me earnestly as though wishing to attract my attention. I was just a little disconcerted at the thought of what she might wish to confide in me. She might conceivably, as I very well knew, have something of value to say, but she might equally have only childish prattle to convey. I had intended to collect up my papers and leave as soon as luncheon was over, but decided instead to idle away half an hour or so in the Red Drawing-Room just in case the child saw fit to seek me out for, all of a sudden, I felt myself once more immersed in the excitement of what I had begun to think of as last year's drama.

Despite all that has gone before and despite my renascent interest in the peculiar goings-on at Cranfield, I could not have been more surprised, *bouleversé* indeed is the word that springs to mind, than I was by the information brought to me by the two children that afternoon. Shortly after luncheon I was quietly reading a book at the table I am accustomed to use for a desk in the Red Drawing-Room when there was a hesitant knock on the door accompanied by some kind of unintelligible murmurings and a stifled giggle. There were further giggles in response to my invitation, 'Pray enter!' On this occasion the child, Georgina, was escorted by the younger of her two brothers, James, a humorous-looking boy who, if my ears do not deceive me, is commonly referred to by the sobriquet 'Jamie'. I rose to my feet to greet the young people as they advanced gauchely, nudging each other with their elbows and still, or so it seemed to me, nervously verging on the edge of laughter. It was not for me to enquire as to the object of their mirth. 'Ma'am. Sir,' I merely said, addressing them with a little bow in my customary manner, for who should say that *politesse* be reserved for adults alone? 'How can I be of assistance to you?'

At my few short words, the pair of them, incapable of composing themselves any longer, burst into a crescendo of futile, childish laughter. When this at last subsided, I was not displeased to hear them both apologise, which apology all but set them off again on a further wave of hilarity, but Georgina, managing to pull herself together, so to speak, began to explain the reasons for their having sought me out. Thomas, she opined, should have come with them too but he had gone out shooting with their father. 'Thomas was with us when it happened,' she explained mysteriously, 'and anyway, it wasn't Jamie's fault but we daren't tell because Mummy and Father would be livid.' The children had gone, or so it transpired from the girl's somewhat incoherent and, to say the least, unchronological account of the events which had occurred during the summer holidays, to the state bedroom in order that Thomas who had acquired an early fascination with history, might enact the part of Henry VIII at the Field of the Cloth of God, with the four-poster bed necessarily serving as the King's tent. Thomas was perforce to portray Henry VIII in their game. 'I always have to be the enemy,' Georgina explained crossly. 'Indeed, Ma'am,' I spoke, as I hope, in tones expressive of my understanding of her plight, thus to encourage her to continue with her tale. At her side James, having quite regained his self-control, occasionally interrupted to agree with her or to urge her to further disclosures, remembering nevertheless to reiterate that whatever had happened was not his fault and that I must promise not to tell their parents of the occurrence.

Naturally I was and am in no position to connive with the children against their parents, nor would I conceive of doing so, but by the time it was eventually revealed to me that, as a result of the children's disobedience, a pile of hidden letters had come to light which since last August has been residing under the floorboards of Thomas's bedroom, I was of a mind to suggest that should the letters which the children sought to hand over to me, then be passed to their parents which, I hastened to explain, was inevitable, it would be politic to suggest, without resorting to a falsehood, that they came from under Thomas's floorboards. In truth, I was surprised that neither Georgina nor James had fallen upon this way out of their difficulties, the art of deceit being in no manner alien to the childish mind.

'We don't think the letters look very interesting,' James advised me with a touch of bathos in his tone. 'They're all to someone called Miss Batty.' The pronouncement of which name reduced the boy once more to a state of helpless mirth.

'Actually,' young Georgina interjected in the blithest of tones, 'we haven't really read them.' It was not her wish, or so I surmised, to allow her brother to cast an air of despondency upon the proceedings; rather, she wished to keep me on my proverbial toes, eager for delivery of the secret bundle which she hoped would reveal a thrilling tale of intrigue, and death no doubt. She meanwhile would be cast as some precocious latter-day Sherlock Holmes of Cranfield Park.

Most unfortunately, considering the time that has already elapsed since the discovery of these letters which may indeed prove to be of as little consequence as Master James suggests, neither of the children thought that they would be able to retrieve the bundle without the help of Thomas and it was therefore not possible for them to hand them to me yesterday afternoon. Conscious of the fact that my behaviour might be regarded in certain quarters as somewhat dubious, I hastened to tell Georgina that I would be returning to Cranfield two weeks hence. This, I am forced to confess, would not be strictly necessary for the purposes of my work, but curiosity as to the contents of the *letters to Miss Batty* tempted me to behave in a way that is totally out of character. For what indeed am I, a humble scribbler, friend of the family, entrusted with the family papers and given the *entrée* to Cranfield Park, doing, making secret pacts, and entering into puerile alliances with the children of the house? Is it not my duty to refer them at once to their parents, or indeed to inform their parents of their discovery if they persist in refusing so to do?

My mind goes back not only to the unpleasant incident when the wretched Mason sat with me on the lawn, spouting his unequivocal revolutionary views and sneering at his employers, but also to the remarkably unpleasing sight of the man rubbing his hands unctuously together before opening the front door to the mauve dowager. I truly feel that, because of my hold over Mason, of which he is as yet unaware, I am in the singular position of being able to discover something which may well be of considerable assistance to the Ottertons, and it is with this in mind that I allow myself to fall in with the peculiar commerce of these two young scallywags at the risk of being thought to deceive those I seek to serve.

Georgina's exercise book

Thomas and Jamie have gone back to school but I've got the letters under my bed and Im going to give them to Mr Rakofsky tomorrow. They were in my jersey draw but Annie saw them when she was getting my school uniform reddy and said Whats all this rubbish then? She had them in her hand and I just grabbed them and she said not to be rude. I told her they were something I had to do for school but I don't think she even looked at them but just said 'Well don't keep dirty bits of paper in your clothes draw.' Phew!!!

I took the letters to school in my satchel for fear that Annie would find them and gave them to Mr Rakofsky when I got back. He said 'thank you mam' very grandly and put them in his basket. I think he is a bit exited but all he said was 'I shall peroose them at my liesure.' I'm dying to know if there really good. Jamie thinks there boring.

In spite of the filthy weather, the eternally leaking roof and all the other problems, none of which seems to have been satisfactorily resolved (nor, for that matter is likely to be), I have been feeling in pretty good form lately. Priscilla and I are going to Copenhagen next week-end. When the Jørgensens invited us, I didn't think Priscilla would want to go. She hasn't been very pleased with me lately and who can really blame her? Perhaps I was beginning to think that she wasn't even prepared to put up with me for much longer and, all I can say about that is that I couldn't survive here (or anywhere else for that matter) without her. She makes this whole place work, in so far as it works at all. Aunt Lettice thinks she's marvellous, and I'm sure that everybody on the farm and in the house likes and respects her, although I expect they're quite frightened of her, but then so am I when it comes to the point. I often wonder if she really will run off with Tony, but then that would probably only create more problems than it would solve. Tony hasn't got any money and she could hardly run to his flat on the top floor. Perhaps in the difficult circumstances of our marriage, we are doing as well as can be expected. In any case I'm really pleased about Copenhagen. We haven't seen the yolly Yørgensens since before the war and neither of us has ever been to Denmark. Priscilla keeps talking in a sing-song voice about something she says is called *smørrebrød* and which she claims is all they ever eat in Denmark. She's already started telling me to go steady on the schnapps.

I haven't seen Pammie for a while which may be just as well. In fact, I think she's got another feller. The thing about Pammie is that, being what you might call a good-time girl, she's quite keen on sheckles, in which commodity I am remarkably deficient. Anyway I've been in the Lords most of the time, keeping myself out of trouble, and I've managed to prevent myself from getting too gloomy as well. One thing that's probably helped to keep me cheerful is that I haven't seen the bloody bank manager for a while, but I can't imagine that happy state of affairs lasting very long.

A world without a bank manager or my mother would be a truly wonderful place. I could even bear all the recurring nightmares if those two weren't lurking in the background. Although when the nightmares come, I wake up sweating like a pig and with my heart pounding, I have in some peculiar way grown almost attached to them. It is as if I feel them to be necessary, not so much because I don't want to forget the war, but because they remind me that the war was real. People sometimes talk about the war now as if it never really happened, or at least as if it were somehow all over, ready to be forgotten, and yet if you walk about London you can't fail to be devastated by the bomb sites which are a permanent reminder of the Blitz and all the lives lost. I don't know why we weren't more frightened than we were at the time. It's all the belated fear that visits me now at night I suppose. Then I think of some of my friends, the poor sods who died and who aren't even here to feel afraid.

I often suspect that the Regiment is the one thing that keeps me sane at all. I always look forward to my one night a week with it. In a way those evenings are a kind of escape but at the same time they provide some sort of balance to life and, if they have served no other purpose, they have certainly made the transition from war to peace at least more comprehensible. For six years the war seemed to be everything; it was our entire existence and sometimes it still feels that way even though it's been over for nearly four years now. You can't just put it behind you, and neither in a way does one really want to. Most of the others feel the same and several of them have told me that they too suffer from nightmares, which they generally treat as a laughing matter.

As for my mother, there's absolutely no knowing when she will suddenly make herself felt again. I've never been able to work out what in God's name she could have been looking for last year when she marched in and turned everything upside down. Perhaps she found whatever it was. In any case, she's gone remarkably quiet since then. The extraordinary thing about her was that she ran this place as a hospital during the First World War. I was too young to know much about it then, but, on looking back, it's quite impossible to imagine her doing anything of the kind. As I grew up, I can remember her either lying in bed, doping herself to the eyeballs, or mysteriously appearing at meals, only to cause a tremendous scene. She must have made a terrifying matron. There's no member of the family I have ever spoken to who has a good word to say for her. Aunt Lettice maintains that when she married my father she was thoroughly spoilt, very selfish and already half mad, but that she really began to go right off her rocker after her first child died. She always told me that if that child had been a son and had survived, she would never have had another one. That would have saved me a lot of trouble!

Sometimes when I think back on what the house was like before the war, I am amazed at what Priscilla has achieved. Then, for all the lavish way of life and for all the servants, the atmosphere was one of holy dread brought about by the brooding presence of my mother and the perpetual fear of her rages and her irrational orders. My poor old father who, at the best of times could be incredibly funny and very good company, was generally reduced to a gibbering wreck by her and consequently fewer and fewer people came to the house. Now, with Priscilla and Annie and the children and the great fires in the hall and friends to stay and my parrots and Peggy, it's turned into the real home it ought to be, despite rationing, the leaking roof and the mice keeping you awake at night. Priscilla blames me for the mice which she claims wouldn't rampage nearly so freely if it weren't for my birds. I suppose she could be right. Annie certainly sides with her on that one.

Tony and I have been doing a bit of rough shooting at week-ends and we even took the boys out once or twice over Christmas. There are plenty of rabbits and the occasional pigeon but I'm afraid that pheasants are few and far between. I certainly can't afford to start putting any down, but neither, come to that, can I afford to go on paying a keeper so I'm coming round to the idea of forming a syndicate which would be the only possible way of getting the shoot off the ground again properly. Perhaps I'll look into that after we come back from Denmark. One thing at a time is what I say although Priscilla complains that I never stick to any of them.

Letter from Horace Pink to Doris Batty

7 Back Alley Lane.
JUNE 25TH, 1910

Dear Miss Batty,

Please excuse the liberty I take of approaching you and allow me to humbly thank you in advance for being so kind as to read this letter. I am sure that a fine woman such as yourself must realise that the unfortunate recent events at Cranfield Park have given rise to what you might call a lot of talk. Being as you're the one what's so close to her Ladyship you must know what really went on. I myself have some information her Ladyship would give a king's ransom to know and I am of a mind to advise you of the said information for a consideration. Since I lost my position I am not exactly flush and a small consideration would come in handy.

You will find me residing in lodgings at the above address where I could meet you at your convenience on any day that you could arrange a ride into town.

I remain her Ladyship's trusty and obedient servant,

Yrs. Very Sincerely
Horace G. Pink

Zbigniew Rakowski's notebook

Considering the baffling circumstances which have constantly attracted my attention at Cranfield, not to say distracted me from my work, nothing could have been more instantly intriguing than the remarkable parcel of letters handed to me by Georgina Otterton on a colourless January afternoon in the Red Drawing-Room. I had not arrived at the house that day until after luncheon, hardly wishing to impose myself upon the Ottertons under anything resembling a false pretext and had indeed been feeling uncomfortable throughout the afternoon, even somewhat fraudulent, having no great business to attend to among the archives that day. I found myself impatiently and not infrequently glancing at my watch, anxious for the hour at which the child might return from school and not a little apprehensive lest she forget the arrangement by which we had agreed to the handing over of the *letters to Miss Batty*. However, I need have had no fear, for young Georgina appeared most promptly in the half dusk at four o'clock and, without more ado, she extracted from her somewhat tattered school bag (for I have noticed that children these days have a tendency to drag their bags along the ground behind them in a most unmannerly and, one would have thought, uncomfortable fashion) an even more tattered bundle of brownish envelopes. I carefully wrapped them in a sheet of newspaper which I had had the foresight to bring with me, placed them in my basket and assured the young lady that I would take the greatest care of them and that I would peruse them at my leisure. I further felt the obligation to add that there would inevitably come a moment when I would be compelled to inform her parents of her discovery. This information she accepted with good grace. I fear, however, that as I packed away those letters, the shaking of my infirm old hand could not but have made manifest even to the most obtuse observer, the emotion the occasion had aroused in me. For at last I had my hands on what I presumed to be unread letters concerning the Otterton family. It was not until I reached home that I discovered the date of those letters, but whatever the date, here was a biographer's dream come true. A secret cache of letters had come to light and fallen miraculously into this old scribbler's hands!

Need I say that during the days that have since elapsed, I have to the most irresponsible degree neglected the work on which I am supposed to be engaged in order to concentrate on the amazing evidence that has so inadvertently landed in my undeserving lap? The letters, not unnaturally, raise a few questions which I am not immediately able to answer. Who for instance is, or was, the nefarious Mr Horace Pink? Miss Batty, I can only surmise, must have been Lilian, Lady Otterton's personal maid.

At a glance, from the moment I cast my eyes on the very first of Master Pink's odious missives, I was instantly aware that what I had unwittingly unearthed was a case of the basest and most vile blackmail.

I have now perused the letters with the greatest care and with my accustomed attention to detail, and have furthermore transcribed them into a notebook for my own keeping. Now it is, alas, my unquestionable duty to hand the offending documents over to Lord Otterton. I shoulder this responsibility, not with any pleasure, but rather with a deep sense of foreboding, for the contents of the letters, the discovery of which so excited me, are of such an unpleasing nature that the reading of them will but cause the greatest distress to

Lord Otterton. So unpalatable indeed are the contents, that it has even crossed my vacillating old mind to place the lot of them on a bonfire. But my training is that of a historian whose whole being recoils at the suggestion of suppressing evidence, burning papers, hiding the truth. Besides, there is the not inconsiderable element of the children's awareness of the existence of these papers. It is not inconceivable that one of them will one day enquire as to the contents of the bundle they so fortuitously (or not so fortuitously) discovered or may even wish to know of its whereabouts. These papers, I have constantly to remind myself, do not belong to me and it is as much as my honour is worth not to hand them over to their rightful owner, whatever the outcome may be. In my greedy desire to be the first to cast an eye over newly unearthed documents, I have perhaps already overstepped the mark, even betrayed the trust of my benefactors whilst inadvertently putting one foot in a quagmire.

Sydney Otterton's diary

There was the usual pile of rubbish waiting for me when we got back from Denmark. Bills, a bloody awful letter from the bank manager, complaints from the tenants about the condition of their houses, a letter from Mrs Arbuthnot saying she was leaving because she finds the flat too draughty in winter. She says she's been very happy here and that she loves it in summer because of the view. Cold comfort to me! Then there was this barmy communication from old Rakowski. I was rather surprised by that because he usually conducts all his affairs to do with Cranfield through Priscilla with whom he has been conducting a lengthy (and no doubt on his part verbose) correspondence for years. He wants to see me on my own as he says he has something of 'the gravest importance to communicate', which he wishes to do in the strictest of confidence. He accompanies this, as is his wont, with a good deal of metaphorical bowing and scraping. I can't imagine for the life of me what the fellow has to say; after all he's been coming here for so long now that he can hardly suddenly have turned up some new piece of shady family history with which to scandalise us. Perhaps the great Speaker of whom we are all so proud will turn out to have been a bugger. But who cares? In fact, I've often wondered how Rakowski's managed to spend quite so much time as he has among those archives. I should think he must know them all back to front by now. Perhaps he just uses them as an excuse to come and fawn at Priscilla's feet, but it annoys her when I say so. In any case, he's quite an entertaining old boy and if he wants to come and see me he can, but I can't believe there's any urgency, so I've dropped him a line suggesting a day next month. As a matter of fact I couldn't help laughing at Priscilla because, for all her indignation when I tease her about Rakowski, when I showed her his letter she was quite incensed that he had written to me instead of to her.

The trouble with going away is that you forget all your troubles and then when you get back, they always seem to have multiplied a thousandfold. It seems unfortunately to be a fact of human nature that people love to greet you with the news that there's a tree down in Beggar's Bottom, the tiles are off the gardener's cottage, the cows aren't giving enough milk and that a mouse has given birth to four babies in the bread bin, which babies it has subsequently eaten. That last piece of information sent Priscilla wild. I wouldn't have liked to be in Ellen's shoes, whose lame excuse was that it must have been a very strong mouse to lift the lid off the bread bin. Annie thought it all very funny and was, I suspect, quite pleased to see Ellen put on the mat.

Poor old Annie's been a bit down in the dumps again because of Jerrold's health. He seemed so much better in the summer but, according to her, he's had some sort of lapse while we've been away. So I expect the mouse in the bread bin provided a bit of a distraction.

A yolly good time was had by all with the yolly Jørgensens who were extremely lavish with their schnapps. An enormous amount of it was drunk which no doubt added to the yeneral yollity. Anyway I certainly wouldn't mind going back there one of these days yust to get away from this lot for a while.

One thing that does cheer me up is the arrival of Otto. I simply couldn't resist him when I found him in the local pet shop yesterday afternoon. I don't know how old he is but they told me he was about three months. Surprisingly enough, young otters are quite easy to train and there's no doubt about it, but this one is an amazingly friendly little chap, so that even Priscilla who usually complains about my animals, has been won round to him. I took him out for a walk in the garden this morning and he was already following me like a lamb.

Annie's diary

MARCH 6TH

I sometimes think you might as well live in Whipsnade Zoo as at Cranfield Park. But you can't help quite liking his Lordship's otter. Even her Ladyship walked down to the farm with the pair of them the other day. But then her Ladyship doesn't have to clear up the mess it makes in the house. His Lordship just laughs as usual.

There's no two ways about it, but poor Father has taken a turn for the worse since Christmas. I always say that it's the winter that does him in. It brings back the bronchitis every time. Perhaps if we get some warmer weather when the spring eventually comes, then he'll look up a bit. It's funny how often all through the winter I've been thinking about Mr

Johnson's letter and how, if I had wanted, I could be in Coolgardie with the kangaroos now. Well I didn't want. No fear. There are enough animals here in what her Ladyship calls his Lordship's *menagerie* without anyone needing to go all the way to Australia to look at kangaroos. I wouldn't be surprised if we didn't have kangaroos here in the garden before long, to judge by the way things are going.

I wouldn't say a word to anyone mind, but when the weather's bad I can't help sometimes wondering what it would be like in Australia, and when Bert gets on my nerves, I tell him that for two pins I'd be off. But I've always said I couldn't leave Father and I certainly wrote and told Mr Johnson as much. In fact I told him he was plain daft to go on thinking that I would or ever could come and join him. Even if he has called his house 'Cranfield', I doubt it would be very much like home.

Mind you, it was pretty quiet around here with his Lordship and her Ladyship away, which was just as well as it gave me a chance to go down and spend more time with Father. But it's all go again now they're back, what with Otto, and guests to stay every other week-end and his Lordship going on talking all the time in what he says is a Danish accent. It sounds plain silly to me but it makes him laugh and even though it annoys her, I've noticed it sometimes makes her Ladyship laugh too. To tell the truth I was really glad to see them back because what with them both out of the way, I was a bit worried that Lilian, Lady Otterton might put in an appearance since she seems to have some downright peculiar way of knowing what's going on here most of the time. I was particularly anxious because no one has yet explained satisfactorily how she got in last time. Not to my satisfaction at any rate. But I have my suspicions. And I don't think Mr Rakowski is to blame either. Mr Rakowski is a gentleman. I am quite sure he would never dream of leaving anyone's back door open.

I haven't liked what I've seen of Mr Mason at all while his

Lordship and her Ladyship have been away. Not that I was ever very fond of him, come to that, and I know the children don't like him in the least little bit. I have a suspicion that Mr MacIntosh isn't all that keen on him either. Mr MacIntosh is always very kind to me when Lord and Lady Otterton are both away, coming and finding me every day to ask if everything is all right. He was ever so considerate that afternoon when Lilian did come and you can't help feeling that he's someone who will always back you up. I shall be really sad to see him go if he ever leaves Cranfield, not that he looks like wanting to leave at the moment, as far as I can see.

Mr MacIntosh said to me only the other day, 'Now, Annie, you don't want to bother yourself about Mason.' Then he gave me a rather old-fashioned look and said, 'If you ask me, his days here are numbered.' I think that must be because of her Ladyship. She hasn't said much lately but I know that she used to go on to his Lordship about Mr Mason and about how she never trusted him. I can't stand the way the man's for ever snooping. Wherever you come across him, he's always opening a drawer or looking in a cupboard. The Lord knows what he's after. Apart from that, he's quite unfriendly and never has been one to pass the time of day with you.

MARCH 12TH

Goodness gracious me, what a hoo-ha there was this morning! There was her Ladyship all dressed up, as smart as anything in her Red Cross uniform, ready to go off to her meeting while his Lordship was putting that darned otter on a lead and planning to take it God knows where. And what was Annie Jerrold doing? Picking up the birdseed the wretched parrots had thrown out of their cages all over the dressing-room floor, while one of the cockatoos was sitting on a picture frame, only making matters worse by screaming its head off. Her Ladyship was in a very brisk mood, telling his Lordship about this, that and the other that needed doing and wasn't he worried about that bird which was going to ruin the picture frame and please would he not waste Annie's time by asking her to clear up after his wretched animals. And his Lordship was messing around all the while with the otter which isn't supposed to be in the house anyway, and saying Annie didn't mind. And Annie said nothing.

Anyway all at once, there was this terrific din of pounding feet and a banging on the door and in burst Mr Mason. I couldn't think what had come over the man, barging in like that and it took me a moment to take in what he was saying. Then I realised he was talking about a burglary. At that point even his Lordship had to stop fooling around with that otter. Well his Lordship went to ring the police and her Ladyship had to go off to her meeting. When the police came, there were two of them and they spent the whole morning interviewing everyone in the house and asking if we'd seen or heard anything, which of course no one had, so they decided the burglar must have come at night. The funny thing was, he didn't take anything, only the coronets which were kept in glass cases in the Red Drawing-Room. Whoever it was had thrown something through the Red Drawing-Room window and then must have put a ladder up to it to get in.

His Lordship was swearing and blinding about it like nobody's business although in the end he decided it was quite funny because according to him the coronets weren't worth a tinker's cuss because they were only made of base metal and a bit of old velvet. The burglar probably thought they were made of gold so he must have been downright disappointed. I just hope he doesn't come back and take something that is valuable. Anyway, what with the otter and the burglary and the police, today was quite a day. And I don't know what we're going to do about Ellen, she's been quaking in her shoes at the thought of burglars ever since the police came, and seems quite sure that next time they'll be wanting to murder her. Why her? I really don't know. She already thought the house was haunted, so perhaps she won't be with us much longer and then we'll have to be looking for another cook.

Sydney Otterton's diary

Clothes rationing ended yesterday which seems to have resulted in a great deal of rejoicing in certain quarters. Georgina, much to Priscilla's annoyance, is demanding a velvet dress like one some other child has, but I'm not sure she's going to get it, rationing or no rationing. Meanwhile my coronets are probably sitting at the bottom of the lake since the police regard the whole burglary as remarkably suspicious. For one thing they think it was an inside job with the window having been broken from indoors, and for another, they can't understand why the burglar took nothing except the coronets, although, of course he may have been interrupted by someone or by something even if no one seems to know anything about it, or to have been around to interrupt him. As a result the police have pretty well lost interest, but as far as we're concerned, suspicion inevitably falls on Mason, but there is absolutely no hard evidence to point to him. Tony has a theory that Mason has always been very resentful of us and that he might have taken the coronets to cock a snook at us. The only thing for him to have done with them then would have been to dispose of them as quickly as possible, and the nearest and best place in which to dispose of them was the lake. It would be one thing, if we were looking for a dead body, but I'm damned if the lake needs dragging for the sake of two tin coronets. In any case it all seems pretty odd to me because I can't really see what Mason, or anyone else for that matter, could hope to gain by such tomfoolery. However, I've told Mason to make sure that the shutters are closed on all the downstairs windows every night in future. He looked at me with his dead eyes and said, 'Yes, M'lord,' as cold as ice.

Annie's looking pretty gloomy about her father who seems to be going downhill, poor devil. Those were the days, when he was cowman. Nothing has been quite the same since he retired; in fact it's a pity he's not feeling a bit better at the moment or he might have been able to help out in the present crisis. Apparently a lot of funny things were going on while we were in Denmark, but no one said anything till a couple of days ago when all the men on the farm began to complain about some sort of dreadful wailing that they claimed was coming out of Wilkins's house all day long. Apparently Bert, who lives in the next-door cottage, said it went on all night as well, and Annie who's been down to see Bert, was full of it. She says it was like some kind of terrible howling and everyone thought Wilkins must have been beating up his wife. Anyway, yesterday Priscilla decided to find out what the hell was going on, only to discover that the noise made by the pair of them was quite horrific. So the upshot of it is that both Wilkinses have been carted away to the local looney bin by men in white coats and I haven't got a cowman. Or a coronet, come to that! According to the quack, they're suffering from some weird kind of lunacy known as *folie à deux* which seems to have manifested itself on this occasion in a bloody awful din. Anyway Bert's taken over the milking for the moment until I can find someone else. I'm frankly amazed by the unexpected things that manage to crop up one after another to put a spanner in the works; so much so that I'm more than ever convinced that it's a great deal easier to lead a column of tanks across the desert than it ever can be to run a country estate. I somehow thought that when we got rid of the sheep which were a short-lived and totally uncommercial experiment, things would miraculously begin to get better, but that hardly seems to have turned out to be the case, although I can't deny that whatever else may happen, I'm damned glad to have seen the back of those moth-eaten creatures. At least I don't have to worry about them any longer.

I must admit that what with the wailing Wilkinses and the stolen coronets probably having been thrown in the lake, I thought I'd heard it all. Then along comes Rakowski with his piece of newly discovered family history. To tell the truth, I hadn't really given him a thought since I got his letter saying he wanted to see me. I'd imagined that all he wanted was to discuss some nit-picking detail about the house or my great-grandfather which would be unlikely to make what Annie would call a ha'p'orth of difference to any of us. He's a tidy, meticulous little fellow, Rakowski, and fastidious to a fault where detail is concerned, which is why it vaguely occurred to me that he might want me to put him right over some minor incident about which I would, in fact, most probably know considerably less than he. Anyway, having refused to come to lunch, he turned up here yesterday morning with a bundle of letters. Priscilla had gone off shopping in a bit of a huff because I think she was annoyed at the old boy wanting to see me on my own, and by the time she got home, I'd left for London.

Rakowski started telling me some long rigmarole about how the children had found the letters and handed them to him which struck me as pretty odd. I can't think why they didn't give them straight to me or Priscilla. As it turns out, it would have been better for them not to fall into the hands of an outsider, although, I have to say, I'm quite sure Rakowski is an honourable fellow. I am convinced that he is most unlikely to mention the contents to anyone other than myself. He maintains that the children, having found them, never bothered to read them, assuming them to be of little interest and that they only handed them over to him as part of some sort of game. As a matter of fact, I'm quite surprised that they'd ever spoken to him other than to say good-morning or good-afternoon.

Then of course Rakowski wanted to know if I knew who Horace G. Pink and Miss Doris Batty were. He may be the soul of honour, but he is also a nosy little beggar. After all he could have handed me the letters without having read them, or he might have discreetly claimed not to have read them, even if he had, but that would have been more than his curiosity could bear, because he also wants me to fill in the missing details for him. In fact I couldn't help him about Horace Pink, but, as for Batty, well enough I know the fiendish Batty! Monstrous woman. She was my mother's lady's maid before I was born and as far as I know, she's still with her now. If there was one woman I hated more than I hated my mother and of whom I was more afraid, it was Batty. When, as a child, I displeased my mother, it was always Batty who was told to take the cane to me. Or the riding crop. Whatever came to hand.

Without explaining the exact contents of the letters, Rakowski told me that I would find their tone profoundly distasteful. He implied, without however being specific, that an element of blackmail was involved. I would advise you, he said, to lock the letters away where no prying eye can see them. Then, very much to my amazement, he rather pompously informed me that whatever I chose to do with them was entirely up to me. He would, he said, enquire no further. He then began somewhat raffishly to talk beside the point, dropping a few heavy hints as he did so. He, as a historian, would never recommend the burning of letters or family papers, however insignificant those papers might appear to be. Indeed, in his humble opinion, the burning of historical evidence was a moral crime, 'dastardly behaviour, Sir!' Some people, he conceded, did not hold these views and would rashly and indiscriminately burn anything which they supposed might bring themselves or their families into disrepute. He banged on for quite a while, then Mason appeared with the drinks tray. In fact, I thought Rakowski gave Mason rather a funny look, perhaps because he suspected him of listening at the door, which, had he been, would not have surprised me in the least. Anyway, the old boy accepted a glass of sherry from the salver that Mason, with a basilisk stare, offered him, and having downed it remarkably quickly, took his leave.

I don't know if it had anything to do with Mason's furtive, darting eyes, or if it was in response to Rakowski's overt warnings, but I was careful to lock that parcel of letters away in my desk, and to pocket the key, rather than leave it as I generally do, in the keyhole. I had no time to read the letters before leaving for London, but I did have time, thank God, for another large gin and tonic.

Letter from Horace Pink to Doris Batty

7 Back Alley Lane.
JULY 10TH, 1910

Dear Miss Batty,

Seeing as how I have not had the pleasure of a reply to my earlier communication with yourself, I have it in mind to approach you again. I am of the opinion that you did not fully understand the nature of my request. There is information what I know about that would put your precious Ladyship's pretty little nose out of joint. For a consideration I would be prepared to discuss the aforesaid intelligence with a view to it not going no further.

You will appreciate that it is the loyalty of a humble servant which prompts me to approach you over this matter. I would not like to see her Ladyship, nor yourself neither, get into a mess on account of what I knows. I would of thought that as one what is still in her Ladyship's employ you, yourself, Miss Batty, might of been inclined to be as trusty a servant to her Ladyship as is

Yr humble and faithful freind
Horace G. Pink

Sydney Otterton's diary

Christ Almighty! I don't know what the hell to do about these awful letters of Rakowski's. I wish to God I'd never set eyes on them. For the first time in my life, I've even begun to feel a little sorry for my mother, although not for Batty. That woman deserves to be hanged! And to think that my mad mother still employs her, probably, I now suspect, because she's been blackmailed into doing so.

Priscilla, surprisingly, is rather less shocked than I am. Perhaps because it's not her family which is involved and also because she so loathes my mother that she most likely believes her to be capable of anything from a white lie to genocide. Of course she also rather likes evidence of my mother's perfidy (as if any more were needed) in order to shore up her strongly held opinions, and perhaps, even to explain my own lack of filial sentiment. But in fact we don't yet know the truth of the matter. In my opinion, if there is any truth at all in Pink's filthy allegations, then Batty has to be the guilty party. I remember from my childhood how evil that woman was. I'm even beginning to think of my mother as a victim in Batty's clutches. Whatever one feels about her, there must be certain things of which one can never believe one's own mother to be capable.

One thing I have discovered is the identity of Horace Pink. It wasn't very difficult. I only had to ask Jerrold. He's a man who keeps his own counsel, but he's also always had his ear to the ground and I was certain (quite rightly as it turned out) that he would remember the name of anyone who had ever worked in the house or on the estate, so I went down to see him. The poor devil was looking a bit green about the gills, but sure enough, he did remember, although he scratched his head for a while and complained about time running on before he came up with anything. Then he said that there'd definitely been a Horace Pink at Cranfield 'years gone by'. A footman who hadn't lasted long, he seemed to think. But he couldn't put a face to him, nor could he remember exactly when he was here, but he thought it might have been around the time I was born, or even a few years earlier. Of course Jerrold never knew why he'd left, nor what had happened to him later. Or if he did, he wasn't going to say. I need to ask someone who actually worked in the house at the time but I couldn't at first think of anyone whose whereabouts I knew, except for Batty, and she's about as likely to answer my letters as she was Horace Pink's. Anyway, it suddenly crossed my mind that I could drop by the almshouses and look in on old Nanny McFee to see if she knows anything. Priscilla's always going on at me about not going to see my old nanny often enough, so she should be delighted to hear that I'm going tomorrow afternoon. Not that I'm really sure of what use it will be to learn very much more about Pink. The fellow may well be dead, for all I know, or in prison. For that matter he may still be blackmailing my mother. Perhaps he can afford to live in a stately home by now, which may well have something to do with my being so bloody broke all the time.

Annie's diary

MARCH 28TH

Bert quite got on my nerves when I was cooking his tea yesterday evening. He would go on about how this horse he had his money on in the Grand National fell at the third fence which according to him he shouldn't have done. Just because he won 7s./6d. last year, he seems to think that he's going to win something every year. Well, I told him not to be so sure. He ought to know better than to think he can count on any darned horse in the Grand National. Anyway he would carry on so, that I had to make it quite plain I could think of better ways to spend my Sunday evenings than cooking his tea and listening to him complaining about a horse. For one thing, I could have been down at Father's, but my little sister is stopping with him for a week, so I took pity on Bert for once. I think Bert's quite full of himself now, what with him taking over the milking which he seems to think impresses me, just because of Father having been the cowman. I reckon that Father was a better cowman than Bert would ever be in a month of Sundays. Never mind the milking, he's as pleased as Punch too about the Wilkinses being carted off, poor things.

I never heard such a noise in all my life as those Wilkinses were making next door last time I was at Bert's, and I can't help admitting that last night I was downright relieved to know they'd gone away. Bert saw them leave. He said it was terrible. First of all some relations came to collect the children who were all crying and not wanting to go, and kicking up an awful shindy and then an ambulance came for the parents and they were both wailing like nobody's business. I told Bert that I always thought there was something funny about those two. They never did look you in the eye, either of them.

His Lordship went to see Father the other day. I wasn't sure if it was just a friendly call or if there was something he particularly wanted to talk to him about. Father wasn't saying anything. Only that he was real glad to see his Lordship. I suppose it might have had something to do with this Horace Pink his Lordship keeps wanting to know about. The funny thing is that the name rings a bell to me for some reason, not that I can think for the life of me who he might be. But if he worked here when his Lordship was a baby, I wouldn't have been much more than seven or eight years old so I wouldn't have known anything about him. After all we never went into the house in those days, although Mother would have known the people who worked there because she used to go up once a week to collect and deliver the mending from the servants' hall. One thing I learnt from my mother was how to mend and how to darn. I'll always think of Mother doing the mending, either for all of us or for the big house.

And it's just as well I did learn how to darn, what with all the sheets and pillow-cases and socks that I have piled up at the moment waiting to be mended. There's been so much going on lately what with the burglary and Father, and one thing and another, that I've got quite behind.

Sydney Otterton's diary

MARCH 31ST

I've been brooding all week about Horace Pink and his filthy correspondence. I'm not yet at all sure what I want to do about it. I suppose I could just put all the letters in a parcel and send them to my mother, or, come to that, to Doris Batty c/o my mother, via the bank, but I'm not convinced that that would be the best solution. For one thing, I'd like to know if Pink is alive or not because if he is, he may well still be living off the proceeds of his blackmail and to tell the truth, I wouldn't mind seeing the fellow in gaol. If he's dead, I suppose that casts rather a different light on things. If I find that he is dead, I might simply throw the letters on the fire, although I wouldn't mind letting Batty know first that I have discovered her secret, and leaving her to sweat a bit.

Priscilla, for once, is as undecided as I am about what we ought to do next. She came up with the idea, though, that these letters may have been what my mother has been looking for so desperately. After all, she presumably knew of their existence, and must have been incensed at Batty leaving them around for someone else to find. I can't imagine why Batty was such a fool. Or why the bloody hell she kept them at all when they could only have incriminated her. I suppose she's a very stupid woman and perhaps she thought that if she kept them, she might eventually be able to get the man for blackmail, or, more than likely, use them in some vile way for her own ends.

Nanny turned out to be very useful. She moaned a bit about my never coming to see her, but then when I asked about Pink, she quite cheered up. She never knew what happened to him in the end, or even if he was alive or dead, but she certainly remembered him quite clearly as the second footman. But that was before I was born. Nanny left after my mother's first child died and went to work briefly for another family before coming back to look after me. Pink, she remembers, was at Cranfield when she first arrived. He sounds like a very moderate fellow. According to Nanny, the servants' gossip was that on his days off he used to dress up in women's clothes, stays and bloomers, the lot. She heard that from the butler and she says she wouldn't wonder if it was true. She never liked the man because he reminded her of a spiteful schoolgirl, but there was something about him which made it difficult not to notice him. He was a small man, pale and dark and what she called foreign-looking, with a narrow mean little face, a huge nose and small black eyes. Looked like a Spanish rat, she said. The sort of man who, according to her, was always there when he wasn't wanted, forever turning up in unexpected places, poking his nose into other people's business, looking at you askance. Nanny said that she always thought he had a thing about Batty. I was a bit surprised by that, I have to admit, but she insisted that Batty had been a good-looking woman in her day. She couldn't remember why Pink left, although she thought there might have been some kind of scandal that might have involved Batty. But then it all happened immediately after the baby died when everyone was in a bad way and she, of course, was leaving too. 'It was a dreadful thing when we lost that baby,' she said. 'It happened on my day off, and when I came back, the poor little thing was gone.' Funnily enough I had never heard her mention it before. Then she began to cry and to tell me that in all her years as a nursery-maid and then a nanny, that was the only one she'd lost.

Letter from Horace Pink to Doris Batty

7 Back Alley Lane.
AUGUST 7TH, 1910

Dear Miss Batty,

I do not doubt that you yourself, Miss Batty, must be enlitened as to the fact that since leaving Cranfield Park I have been unemployed which is not a comfortable position for an honest man what is innocent to of fallen into. I have been most patient with yourself and with her Ladyship who I hoped would of sent me some small consideration by now in the lite of the information what you must have told her I knows of.

I was interested to read in the newspaper last week as how the doctor what poisoned and dismembered his wife was arrested on a ship going to Canada. I expect he and his accomplice was both hoping to go scot free whereas it now transpires that the pair of them will as like as not swing for it. Have you ever considered how a man, or a woman come to that, must feel standing on that there trap door waiting for the noose to be slipped ever so gently round his acursed neck?

I remain, Miss Batty, as ever
Her Ladyship's devoted servant and your loyal friend
Horace G. Pink

Sydney Otterton's diary

Priscilla and I have reached a point where we are really having to ask ourselves quite seriously how much longer we can manage to stay here with things going as badly as they are. The results of the local council elections have certainly put a smile on the face of the Tories, but I don't think my circumstances will alter much even with a change of government. This government seems to be getting into deeper and deeper trouble every week and perhaps I ought to feel some sort of sympathy for them since my affairs appear to be in very much the same sort of state as the country's as a whole. For all the loans and concessions on agricultural land, and for all Aunt Lettice's immensely generous help, I'm beginning to think that I will never be able to pay the death duties or work my way out of the morass of debt and decay in which I find myself. Most people (especially my bank manager) are of the opinion that I'm raving mad even to consider trying to go on living in Cranfield. Sometimes I try not to think about what will happen and then I go off to London and get drunk and see Posy and she gives me hell and calls me a two-timer and then I have another drink and come home and go to bed and wake up in the small hours sick to the gills and in a bloody awful panic.

My nightmares have taken on a new, rather macabre dimension. I'm either in the Western Desert, or at Villers Bocage or somewhere in Italy and I've got this baby with me and I have to save it from the enemy whose lines are forever advancing, and the turret of my tank jams and under their tin hats every single German has the face of Doris Batty. It's extraordinary that anything quite so ridiculous can cause one to sweat so much.

Tony and I had lunch together the other day in London

because he very kindly offered to go round to Somerset House with me to see what we could find out about Horace Pink. We looked up his birth certificate and discovered that he was born in Bermondsey in 1885 which means that he's only in his mid sixties, if he's alive, which I imagine he is since we didn't find a death certificate. I'm beginning to think that my only possible line of action is to approach my mother and Batty directly which I am certainly loath to do. Otherwise I burn the letters. After all, those letters must have been lost for years and have only been found by chance. Of course it would be one thing if they had never been found, but having come to light, they cannot be entirely ignored. All the same, I think I'll do nothing for a while, nothing always being the easiest option and anyway I've got plenty of other things to think about, not to mention a couple of weeks' soldiering at Lulworth coming up soon. There's nothing like playing with tanks to take one's mind off one's troubles.

Georgina's exercise book

MAY 6TH

Everybody's in an awful bate these days which is very boring of them. Mummy keeps saying we haven't got any money and Father's always shouting. I think he's cross with the government about something. Mr Rakowski never comes any more and I bet he went and lost those letters and stinky Mr Mason's still here. I wish he would go. No one likes him and he's still always snooping.

JULY 19TH

Its better now the hollidays are here and Thomas and Jamie have come back from school. Father says we can take a picnic to the big wood in the pony trap tomorrow. We've got a French governess for the holidays. She's jolly young but she's going to be a nun so we're supposed to be good.

Letter from Horace Pink to Doris Batty

7 Back Alley Lane.
AUGUST 16TH, 1910

Dear Miss Batty,

Not having received no reply to my former letters, the situation has considerably deteriorated. As you know I am unemployed and consequently I who am an honest gentleman, am having a awful deal of trouble rubbing two pence together as you might say. I find as I am obliged to write to you again to beg of her Ladyship's mercy that she might send me a consideration in view of what I knows. I think you should understand that I have evidence of the facts what the police might be interested in.

I await your gracious reply,
Yr ever faithful friend
Horace G. Pink

Zbigniew Rakowski's notebook

SEPTEMBER 4TH

Pine. Indeed I do for the beautiful Lady Otterton. She of the hyacinth eyes. It is now some six or seven months since I last visited Cranfield and since I handed Mr Pink's offending letters over to Lord Otterton. I have in all honesty had no good reason to return there in the interim, for I can barely claim to require any further access to the Cranfield archives. I

261

have done all the research that I need, and have furthermore, during the course of these last months, managed to progress so considerably with my work that I am in truth nearing its conclusion. I have on occasion exchanged the briefest notes with Priscilla who has been so kind as to inform me that she looks forward to my returning to Cranfield in the near future since she feels that it would be most unfortunate were we to lose touch. She has, she avers, enjoyed our luncheon-time discussions. I am indeed more than gratified by her sentiment.

There yet remains the unsettled business of Mason. Alone in Robin Hood Way, I have dwelt at length on the perfidy of Mason, and on what appears to me now as my own defective handling of the matter and my own inadequate dealing with the information that I have. I have had no communication with Lord Otterton since that sunless morning in February when I handed him Pink's nefarious correspondence, nor, for that matter, did I truthfully expect any. No doubt his Lordship has dealt with the letters according to his own lights. I meanwhile am left with the uncomfortable thought that Lilian, Lady Otterton, in cahoots, as modern idiom would express it, with the repulsive Mason, was probably looking for the letters which so inadvertently came into my possession. Such a supposition leads me to ask a good many questions regarding the nature of Mason's employment and the degree of knowledge he may or may not have concerning the Pink letters. I have indeed become a very slow old man, both vainly deluded and cumbersome in my thinking. Overwhelmed in my dotage by a foolish passion for a lovely lady, not to say over-excited by the faintest suspicion of Gothic intrigue, I have perhaps not acted as I should have done, with such prudence and sagacity of which I could reasonably have been proud.

If, as I half suspect, Lord Otterton is still in ignorance of the part played by Mason, and if Mason is still employed at Cranfield, I am inclined to think that the time has surely come for me to apprise the Ottertons of everything of which

I am aware. Indeed the time is long past when I should initially have done so and, mulling as I do over the events as they occurred, I find myself somewhat confused in my own mind as to why I acted then as I did. I can only surmise that at the time I felt that the hold I had over Mason would eventually enable me to unravel his dark secret which, I am now of the firm opinion, must have revolved entirely around the lost letters. Thus I have this morning penned a letter to Lord Otterton begging him to allow me to call at Cranfield to discuss one or two important matters with him. I have not intimated what these important matters might be, leaving him to suppose that they are most likely connected with *The Otterton Family*, towards the conclusion of which work, I reiterate, I am now drawing, and with which I am not wholly displeased. I cannot but dwell on the fact that the end is nigh for, satisfied although I may be with the work, it will surely be with a heavy heart that I survey the vacuum into which its completion will condemn me to live, unless I return, as I have often intimated that I might, to my unfinished little crime novel, the which, in my heart of hearts, I know on reflection can of course, for reasons of loyalty, never be published. But no doubt it will nevertheless provide me with a little *divertimento* during the lonely days that must inevitably lie ahead.

SEPTEMBER 19TH

Today I lunched once more at Cranfield. I was deeply touched to receive a gracious note from Priscilla written, as she was kind enough to explain, in response to my letter to his Lordship, which had arrived during his absence in Scotland where I gather he had repaired with friends on some sporting venture. She suggested that I come to see his Lordship in the morning and insisted that I stay to luncheon since, she maintained, she has missed my regular visits and both she and Lord Otterton would very much like to hear how I am progressing with the family history.

My initial reaction was one of dismay since it occurred to me that once I had divulged my knowledge to Lord Otterton, which eventuality would inevitably occur before luncheon, I might very well be no longer *persona grata* at their table, around which table, to make matters worse, there would presumably be lurking, *coûte que coûte*, the abominable Mason. How would Lord Otterton react to the information that I had witnessed the butler opening the door to his violet-clad mother all those months ago? Would it not be natural for him to enquire as to the delay in my keeping him informed? Would he not inevitably see me as party to the dreadful dealings? It is hardly surprising, that with this in mind, I therefore set out for Cranfield on this occasion without my usual lightness of step, and not without a little trepidation.

As after so many months, I once more wound my way up the drive, and as the great house hove into view, reminding me suddenly of a gigantic liner in a sea of green, my heart gave a lurch at the realisation of what that house had come to mean to me and of what she must mean to those who sail in her. How all our imaginations are captured! Even the children's own awareness appears to be woven inextricably into the warp and the weft of the life of the house, from which they would seem to see their own young lives as being inseparable.

Yesterday, after many months of denial, the government devalued the pound and I could not but reflect as I walked on towards the house, that like the country, Lord Otterton most probably teeters on the edge of bankruptcy. For how much longer would he and his exquisite consort be able to continue in the aristocratic style, albeit threadbare, to which they are accustomed? I felt a sudden sinking of the heart as it occurred to me with a peculiar rapier-like certainty that this, for whatsoever reason, might be the very last time I would be invited to my beloved Cranfield.

It would be no falsification to add that when, a few

moments after I had rung the bell, the front door was opened by none other than the detestable Mason himself, still employed to wait upon the Ottertons and to hand sweet-meats to my Beatrice, I again felt a sickening shock to the system, which resulted partly from my having had no contact with the man for months and partly from a sense of guilt, that were it not for my delay in acting, the dreadful creature should surely have been given his cards many weeks ago. And yet, who else had I expected would open the door? There was nothing for it but to steel myself to the encounter and thus I instantly straightened my back and looked hard at the brute, confident in the knowledge that, although my days at Cranfield might be numbered, so indeed were his.

Lord Otterton received me in the Japanese Room where he offered me a glass of sherry and invited me to sit down before a blazing fire. Much as I did not like the thought of the inevitable reappearance of Mason bearing a drinks tray laden with decanters of sherry and gin and no doubt bottles of tonic for what I have observed to be his Lordship's preferred tipple, I was glad of the offer of a little something which I felt could not but give me Dutch courage for the task in hand. A task, the performance of which I had, over the past days, many times rehearsed.

Since no situation ever eventually bears the least resem-blance to that which has been previously imagined, it remains a mystery as to why men and women are ever wont to concern themselves with such unavailing rehearsals. Not surprisingly, Lord Otterton did not react in any way for which I might have prepared myself. After a few brief pleasantries concerning the weather and his recent visit to Scotland, I gently broached the matter of Pink's letters and then, emboldened by my sherry, informed his Lordship that I had some further distressing news for him. Whilst I perambulated around the subject, trying, I fear, to justify my delay in coming forth with the aforementioned information, I noticed his Lordship's large dark eyes wandering away from my gaze, anxiously seeking the corners of the room, as if it were he, not I, who had something to fear. He stood up and with hunched shoulders, but without a word, strode to the table where Mason had left the drinks tray and swiftly replenished his glass. It crossed my addled old mind that the contents of the letters must have shocked him so profoundly, that now he dreaded what I might have to say next. Eventually I came to the point.

His Lordship was standing in front of the fire and, as I finished speaking, he said not a word, but loured at me in apparent incomprehension before, without tarrying even to put down his tumbler, he crossed the room on his cat-like tread, flung open the door (another of those fine mahogany doors) and without so much as a moment's hesitation, without pausing, *même*, to close that door, he left the room. I, quite at a loss, appalled to say the least, at what I might have unleashed, leaped nervously from the armchair in which I had been seated and stood where his Lordship had been standing in front of the fire, knowing not what to do. To go or to stay? To be or not to be . . . ?

It seemed to me then that I remained a long while in a surreal state of suspended animation in front of that fire. In the silence that appeared to have been occasioned by Lord Otterton's sudden departure, I had the impression that I was alone, all alone in that great mansion, that it and I were both anachronisms which might at any given moment be swept up together by some supernatural whirlwind, blown away, disintegrated, annihilated and finally consigned to nothing more substantial than the fallibility of human memory, which I suppose is where we belong.

When the whirlwind came, it was not quite as I had anticipated it would be. It manifested itself rather, in the form of such a thundering and a shouting from the hall, such an exchange of oaths, such a bawling and such a *hollering* (for want of a better word), as I have never before experienced. My immediate reaction was to cross to the door and gently close it, for it was indeed no business of mine to be eavesdropping.

I stood for some time at the window, gazing out over the formal rose garden, up the grassy slope to the Victorian grotto beneath the trees, and back along the top of the bank to the dark wellingtonias under which I had been partaking of a humble sandwich on that fateful occasion when I was first approached by the perfidious Mason. It seemed so long ago that all at once I was shocked by what appeared to me to have been my own inertia. The dreadful whirlwind of noise which the mahogany doors themselves were unable to block out, and that reached me even as my back was turned, should long ago have blown over, had I behaved as I ought to have done. Had I not been blinded by an old man's hopeless love and by the romance of Cranfield itself.

Later Priscilla came to find me. No doubt, she said, I was aware that there had been something of a rumpus, but we had better have luncheon all the same. Luncheon was an uncomfortable meal. His Lordship scowled and spoke little, her Ladyship made some attempt to converse, asking me my opinion of André Gide in whose *Journal* she is at present engrossed. There being no Mason to wait at table, we helped ourselves from the sideboard to rabbit pie and mashed potatoes, followed by stewed plums.

Sydney Otterton's diary

SEPTEMBER 23RD

I can't imagine that many people were taken completely by surprise when, none too soon, and after a massive amount of twisting and turning, umpteen denials and a good many outright lies, Stafford Cripps finally announced the devaluation of the pound. Apparently, so as to stop the news from leaking out early, and after the Chancellor had acquainted them with the new exchange rate, the leaders of the Opposition were locked up for hours with a whole bunch of lobby hacks in some government offices or other. Next the banks and the Stock Exchange were closed. What with all that and the milk ration being cut again, the entire country appears to be in a terrible state of turmoil. My blasted cows, under Bert's aegis, are certainly doing nothing to help boost the milk supply at the moment, but in my present circumstances, I really don't want to have to employ another hand, so I'm just hoping that Buttercup III and her pals will soon knuckle under. According to Annie, Jerrold's pretty fed up with what he's been hearing about it all, but then Jerrold blames everything that goes wrong with the cows on the electric milking machine and nothing anyone can ever say will change his mind on that score.

So what with all that going on, I'd almost completely forgotten about Rakowski wanting to see me again, when along the bloody old fool comes with another well-timed bombshell. I cannot understand why the hell the blithering imbecile never told me before about Mason and my mother. He spun me some futile rigmarole about why he didn't say anything at the time, none of which seemed to make very much sense to me. All Priscilla says is that she told me so, which she didn't. Well, I know she never liked Mason although she always refused to say exactly what it was that she objected to about him, but she certainly didn't suspect him of having anything to do with my mother, as far as I know.

Anyway Rakowski came and sat himself down opposite me in the Japanese Room, gibbering and talking nonsense so that I hadn't the faintest idea what he was getting at, then all of a sudden he made this bloody silly announcement about having seen Mason open the door to my mother. I just looked at him sitting there bolt upright in his mittens with a scarf tied round his scraggy old neck, fingering his little goatee beard, and the sight of him made me so angry I couldn't speak. I couldn't imagine what the fucking idiot thought he'd been up to all this time, squatting in the bowels of the earth, writing some damn silly book, talking about literature to Priscilla and pretending to be everybody's friend. He even tried to bring the children into it somehow. I think at the time it was my intention to go and find Priscilla, anyway for some reason I simply left the room, only to walk straight into Mason who was coming across the hall to announce lunch.

I was so angry when I saw him that I just bawled at him and told him to f— off there and then. In fact in the end I managed to get a surprising amount of information out of that bugger. I think he must have been completely taken by surprise when he met me. In any case, I thought the man must be right off his head to judge by the way he started to bellow back at me, calling me a parasite and yelling about man's struggle against nature and the evils of capitalism and how it served me right if my coronets were rusting at the bottom of the lake. It was where they belonged. As for me and my family, he said he'd like to see us all, along with Annie (poor Annie), cleaning the lavatories on Waterloo Station. I've never seen a man so disturbed, purple in the face, his eyes swivelling in his bloody head and his jowls quivering. He was almost foaming at the mouth and I doubt that my mother would have been very pleased with her henchman if she could have heard the way he talked about her so that even I felt obliged to defend her. Anyway, I saw the man again in the evening when he appeared to have come to his senses although in some ways he was almost odder than he'd been in the morning. I told him that in fact I never wished to clap eyes on him again although before he left I wanted an answer to one or two questions. Most uncharacteristically he kept wanting to shake my hand and to tell me that we were 'mates'. I've no intention of being his mate.

Priscilla was annoyed with me for getting so angry. She goes on about it being undignified and she keeps saying that it would be more 'telling' if I kept calm. Or some such bloody rubbish. But she also says that I seem to have to get angry before I'm prepared to sack anyone, which to my mind is a perfectly reasonable sequence of events.

I don't know what Mason thought I could do to him beyond sacking him, which I had already done, but when I saw him before he left, when he kept on wanting to shake my hand, I had the overwhelming impression that he was terrified of something. Which, I imagine, is the only reason why he was prepared to tell me as much as he did.

I have to say I was amazed when he announced that Mrs Mason and the awful Mrs Legros dit Courrier are sisters, although when I thought about it later, a bell rang somewhere in the back of my mind. Then of course Priscilla reminded me of how ages ago she'd seen the two of them waving or nodding at each other outside the International Stores. In fact I do remember her telling me something of the sort at the time, but I didn't pay any attention which perhaps I should have done. Priscilla says I never pay any attention to anything she says which is absolute cock, and, in any case I don't really see what difference it would have made in this instance if I had. After all you can't stop people nodding at each other in a public place nor can you count it as evidence of appalling treachery if they do. Priscilla says we could and should have found out all about Mason months ago which would have saved us from being spied on for all this time in our own house. I have to say the thought, first of those creepy Legros with that bloody big dog of theirs and then Mason snooping around is pretty unpleasant. I do remember being delighted when the police came and removed Legros. The ruddy flat's been empty for ages now, but perhaps it's just as well with people like the Legros around.

Like every other feckless coward, Mason is a man of little loyalty. He told me that Legros who was planted here in the flat by my mother (and I have yet to find out exactly what the connection there is), later tipped him the wink to apply for the job of butler, but after I'd sacked the bugger, there was nothing bad enough that Mason could find to say about Legros.

'Now that you and I are mates, M'lord,' says Mason, clinging onto my hand with both his sweaty mitts, and trembling like a jelly, 'I think it only right to tell you that my brother-in-law, that is to say the *wife's* brother-in-law, is a crook.' Thank God he let go of my hand at last, in order I suppose to draw himself up before going on in his vile wheedling tone to call Legros every name under the sun, from a forger to a paedophile. 'And,' he said, his eyes rolling in his head like a madman, 'he's out to smash the capitalist system.' All of that would have been bad enough without the fellow, who's much taller than me, having to bend over me and push his revolting great face into mine so that I caught a gust of his stinking breath that almost made me gag. What with the Wilkinses at the farm and the Masons in the house, I began to think I was doing a public service by running a looney bin.

How I long for Johnson and the voice of sanity, not that he'll ever come back from Australia now, but funnily enough, he was the one who was initially on to the Legros. I don't know why we never listened to him at the time.

The luckiest thing of all is that none of these idiots bribed by my mother ever found what they were presumably sent to look for, and instead, by some miracle the children were the ones to discover Pink's letters. I don't think I have been told the whole truth about that either, but then that is the least of my worries. One thing that I am quite curious about though, is how much Mason or Legros knew about what they were looking for. But that isn't something to which I could easily expect an answer. I certainly didn't want to hear much more about Legros, but Mason insisted on telling me with peculiar satisfaction combined with a spiteful snigger that the man is back inside. 'To think what the wife's sister has been through,' he added sanctimoniously, rubbing his hands together and then pursing his lips. It struck me that neither the wife nor the wife's sister had shown any great perception in their choice of husband.

The funny thing is that now, in retrospect and with the Masons gone, I find that it's Rakowski who really makes me angry. I was rather fond of the fellow and always quite pleased to see him when he turned up. He's an affected old booby, a bit unctuous at times and obviously besotted with Priscilla, but he's unusual and he's got a sense of humour and up until this happened, I always thought he was on one's side. Now I feel that he has just been watching us, or looking at us like specimens under his microscope. For two pins he'd pull all our wings off. Merely to think about the fellow makes me reach for the gin. I've told Priscilla that I don't want to see him here again. I don't give a toss about his ruddy book. He can finish it as he pleases but without any further help from me.

Letter from Annie to Dolly

Cranfield Park
OCTOBER 2ND, 1949

Dear Dolly,

As I write this I am sitting at Father's kitchen table, with Father having a quick forty winks in the armchair by the stove. I'm worried about his cough which seems to be getting worse rather than better and am sure that it cannot be helped by the coke fumes that come billowing out of that stove. The whole house smells of coke. All the same he seems to be in quite good heart and never complains. To tell the truth, he thinks about nothing so much as his Michaelmas daisies!

There's been terrific goings on at the house recently what

with Mr Mason getting the sack. I think everyone was pleased when that happened. If you ask me he was a nasty piece of work. Anyway, it turned out that it was him who let *Lilian* in last year against his Lordship's orders. Mr Rakowski, the gentleman who is writing a book about the family, saw him opening the front door to her, but no one seems to know why he kept quiet about it until now. Well you can imagine what a fury his Lordship was in when he heard!

Bert is still managing the cows and very pleased with himself about that. I expect he's hoping his Lordship won't find another cowman. Father grumbles about it and worries about his cows and goes on alarming about the electric milking machine. He says that Bert's not the right man for the job anyway and that if his Lordship wants the yield to go up, he'd do better to hire an experienced cowman.

Father's just woken up and will be wanting his tea, so I'll stop now. Give my love to Fred and the children.

Love from
Annie

Georgina's exercise book

SEPTEMBER 29TH

The boys have gone back to school and it's quite boring. I was helping Father feed his parrots and he was awfully angry with Mr Rakofsky. He says he can't come here any more and it's all something to do with those letters we found. I admitted that we'd found them and given them to Mr Rakofsky and Father was quite cross and said we should have given them to him. He wanted to know if we had read them but I told him they looked boring so we hadn't and he said they were nothing to do with us anyway. When I asked what they were about he got really annoyed and said 'None of your b—y bisness!!' Then he said something about children having little minds and I know he was only trying to bait me so I said he was lucky that I helped him with his birds. Then he got in a better mood.

I'm really sorry about Mr Rakofski because he was very nice to us and I liked him. I'm sure he hasn't done anything wrong and I wish Father would let him come back. I asked Mummy when he was coming again but I think she smelt a rat. She said something like 'What's that got to do with you?' and I said I dunno but I like him and she said 'He comes here to do his work and he doesn't want children interrupting him all the time.' That was very unfair because I never interrupted him *all the time.*

Zbigniew Rakowski's notebook

OCTOBER 4TH

Alas another bleak Tuesday dawns without the prospect of a visit to Cranfield. I no longer remember how it came about that my outings to Cranfield always took place on a Tuesday, but since the very earliest days of my association with the Ottertons, that has ever been the way. My history of the family is all but completed and indeed I should be engaged in writing those final pages now, rather than in yielding to these my feelings of despair and bitter disappointment.

Only yesterday I received a most courteous note from Priscilla. Ah, how my cracked old heart missed a beat when I recognised her fair firm hand on the light blue envelope, but how dashed were my hopes when I read what she had to say! She wished me to know that she shared her husband's incomprehension at what she chose to call my 'secretive' behaviour and she was indeed appalled that I had endeavoured to involve the children in what she referred to as my machinations. She was, she claimed, at a loss to discern to what ends I had acted as I did. She and Lord Otterton had, she opined, regarded me as a friend and had both enjoyed my company on the many occasions I lunched with them, which made it all the more painful for them to realise that I had not been straight with them. Straight indeed. She wished me luck with the *Ottertons* and assured me that she and Lord Otterton were looking forward to receiving a copy of the book when it is eventually published. She then reminded me, in a manner that I can regard as nothing less than insulting, that I might be so good as not to forget to send Lady Isley a copy as well. She closed her missive with the chilling observation that our paths might cross again at some future date.

This hurtful letter left me in such a distressed state that I was quite unable to concentrate on my work for the rest of the day. How unjust I found it, for I had only acted out of love for her and loyalty to her family, tempered, as I now see, by vanity, for it was not young Georgina, but I who so fondly saw myself as a latter-day Holmes. What folly indeed to suppose that I, brittle-boned old buffoon that I am, had the makings of a great detective, that I would be able to solve the imponderable, unmask the treacherous, kill the dragon and save my Beatrice, to the echoing applause of her family. Let *dithering nincompoop* be the words inscribed on my tombstone, for now this dithering nincompoop finds himself, by his own hand, destined to a disappointed and cheerless future, bereft of the delights of Cranfield, of rabbit pie and mahogany doors, of Georgina and Annie, of Laszlo's scornful Lilian and Rysbrack's sacrifice to Bacchus, of Lord Otterton's extravagant humour and exquisite eccentricity, but most surely bereft of the joy born of friendship with Priscilla. *Freude, schöner Götterfunken* . . . Ah me! If only . . . the saddest words indeed.

Sydney Otterton's diary

Priscilla and I have had a long discussion about these ruddy letters of Pink's and for once we seem to be more or less in agreement as to what we ought to do, which is, thank God, nothing for the moment. As Priscilla points out, they were written nearly forty years ago and have probably lain undiscovered under the floorboards for nearly as long. They raise a hell of a lot of questions, some of which don't bear answering and we both feel that it would be madness to act rashly which, in Priscilla's eyes, would include burning them. For my part I would happily burn them, but she has made me promise to keep them till after Christmas and then to think again. I vaguely thought of putting them back under another piece of old floorboard and leaving them there for future generations to discover but Priscilla has taken them and locked them away with her jewellery in her bedroom safe.

One of the things that worries me about the blasted things, is not knowing who else has read them. Priscilla is sure that Rakowski must have. He had them long enough as far as I can make out, although he never really came quite clean about exactly when they were found. I refuse to discuss the matter with the children although Georgina volunteered that they never read them. She could of course be lying but I do in fact believe her.

Then there remains the problem of Mason and the Legros and the whole network of spies imposed on us by my mother. How the hell can I ever employ anyone again without suspecting them of being in her pay? And what do I do about that bunch of crooks out there? What do they know? Or think they know? Priscilla says ignore them. Forget all about them, she says, because they can't do us any more harm. But I sometimes think that the only way to put a stop to all this nonsense would be to send Pink's letters to my mother and let her got on with it. And I sometimes think that the vile creature Batty deserves whatever she might have coming to her.

Anyway, it's agreed that we won't think about it all again until after Christmas. And God alone knows where we will be by then. In the debtors' gaol I should think, judging by the way things are going. Never mind Pink's letters and my mother, there are far more important things to think about at the moment, like how long we can seriously consider going on here. Priscilla has begun to think quite a lot about the Dower House, which is a relief in some ways because I'm afraid that if we had to leave here, she might take that opportunity to leave me. The Dower House would certainly be a possibility for us as the tenants there only pay a pittance and in any case their lease is due to come up for renewal in the New Year. Even Aunt Lettice, the one person who more than anyone else would hate to see the Ottertons leave Cranfield, is beginning to think that we will eventually have to decide to move out. You could say that under the circumstances, the sooner we do so, the better. Or perhaps we'll hang on until after the election before we decide, not that I can really see what difference that will make to my affairs either way.

Zbigniew Rakowski's notebook

TUESDAY, NOVEMBER 15TH

Woe is me, for it is forever Tuesday and I am forever banished. *The Otterton Family* is with the publisher who has been kind enough to say that he is delighted with it and who now pesters me to know what my next project will be. I am quite unable to consider any further undertaking at the moment, so heavy is my heart, so great the void that surrounds me. The book I have dedicated, with her permission, *to Priscilla*. How well I remember humbly begging her, in those now far-off halcyon days, graciously to accept this mark of my respect and admiration! How well I remember too, her obvious delight at the suggestion, for she was, I dare opine, somewhat flattered by the notion. I have not seen fit, under the present circumstances, to withdraw this badge of my esteem.

So here I sit, alone in Robin Hood Way, twiddling my thumbs as it were, dreading once more the long winter ahead, the advent of Christmas and the arrival of my daughter with her tedious husband, who will no doubt regard it as their bounden duty to 'cheer me up'. I feel myself sinking into a terminal state of depression for the world no longer holds any gladness for me; I anticipate nothing now beyond gradual decay, a loosening of the muscles, a stiffening of the joints, a dimming of the light, a numbing of the senses and a softening of the brain. Ah, Beatrice, to what have you reduced me? Even my little novel, my so-called *divertissement*, has lost its savour.

Annie's diary

DECEMBER 15TH

I was quite surprised yesterday morning when, along with a letter from Dolly, the postman delivered this Christmas card from Mr Johnson. A lovely card mind, but I never thought to hear from him again after what I wrote last year, telling him downright cruelly that I would never dream of going to Australia, not for all the tea in China. Not that he went on about me going there any more but he did enclose a short letter, saying that he was getting on all right and that although he never regrets his decision to leave this country he sometimes misses it. He quite made me laugh, saying it's the drizzle he misses most and what he called 'them soft grey days'. The drizzle and the elm trees. Never mind the drizzle, I would definitely miss the elm trees myself. He says he still often thinks about Cranfield and would like to hear how his Lordship's getting on. He ended up by saying that he's come to consider himself quite a good cook, but he does occasionally wish he had someone to share his bungalow with. I suppose that was a bit of a dig at me, but then I reckon that by now he must have given up any hope of seeing me again. He certainly should have, although I don't mind writing back and telling him all the news, but I think I'll add (just to be on the safe side) that neither do I have any regrets about staying here in spite of the grey skies and the drizzle.

We still haven't got a new butler, or a cowman come to that. I sometimes think his Lordship is frightened to take on anyone new after all the trouble there's been. In any case, it means that I have a lot of extra work trying to make sure things get done properly and seeing to it that the dailies clean the silver. When there are guests Bert smartens himself up and comes in to wait at table. I reckon he's a darned sight better at that job than he ever is at milking the cows. He certainly seems to enjoy taking everything over. Father was furious when I told him. He wanted to know who on earth had ever heard of a cowman waiting at table? Well, I told him, times are changing. He said there was no doubt about that.

Poor old father he's not at all well, always coughing and spluttering and finding it hard to get about. It breaks my heart to see him like that, not that I think he's really lost interest in life, nor, come to that, has he lost the twinkle in his eye. When I complain about the winter, he just laughs and says, 'Now don't you go moaning on my girl, for it won't be long afore the snowdrops is up!' He seems quite sure that when the snowdrops come up, he'll begin to feel better, and then, he says, there'll be the daffs and before you can say Jack Robinson it will be time for him to prune the roses again.

1950

Sydney Otterton's diary

An abysmal meeting with my bank manager on Friday only confirmed what in fact I already knew which is that we are going to have to leave this place. The farm accounts are like something out of *Alice in Wonderland*, completely topsy-turvy. The only thing about them that is abundantly clear is the fact that we are losing money hand over fist.

Priscilla and I went over to lunch with Aunt Lettice and had a long talk with her just after Christmas. Even she was beginning to think that things couldn't quite go on as they are, and that was before this last disastrous meeting with the bank manager. There's no possible way in which I will ever be able to pay off the death duties and keep my head above water, never mind run the farm, start up the shoot (even to do it as a syndicate will require an injection of capital which I don't have), pay the servants, keep the bloody roof on the house and pay the school fees. I've already had to sell most of the houses I had in the village, the tenant farmers are buying their farms and it's still costing me an arm and a leg to try to keep the cottages here in any sort of condition for human beings to live in.

It seems to me that, much as I shall feel a failure having to move out, perhaps it will be a relief finally to have made the decision to go. And to tell the truth, that decision is now all but made. I just need to sleep on it for a little while longer so as to accustom myself to the idea before I announce it to the world.

The new butler moved in immediately after Christmas, which might be a bit awkward, but at least I had the foresight to warn him that we might not be here for ever and that if we did move out he might consider staying on as caretaker since we wouldn't want to leave the house empty. He seems like a decent enough fellow with a wife who doesn't say much and a pair of grown-up children.

There's the election coming up on February 23rd but I know perfectly well that not all the elections in Christendom would make a pennyworth of difference to my state of affairs.

It's funny about Priscilla. She was so reluctant to move into Cranfield in the first instance, but now of course, partly because she's done so much for the place, she loves it and feels tremendously sad at the thought of moving out. All the same, I regard her as infinitely more practical than I am, so I feel sure that she must have faced up to the reality of the situation long before I did and so of course knew that we would inevitably have to go. She is quite keen on the thought of the Dower House and declares very positively that we are lucky to have somewhere so nice to move to. She's also talking about having another sale which would make sense and raise a bit of money too, and then she talks about our opening the house to the public.

I, on the other hand, sometimes think that if we are to leave the house, we might as well sell up altogether and go somewhere else. Be shot of Cranfield, lock, stock and barrel: start again from scratch. Excise the past which would most likely be impossible because, for one thing which I don't think Priscilla can ever fully understand and, silly though it may sound, the house is like a part of myself. That's probably why I feel so strongly. It's in my blood for whatever reason. It always has been and always will be but I can't tell if that's because of the hall which is about the grandest and most beautiful one in England, or because of the mean little dark back stairs leading to the basement where I used to hide as a child, or if it's because of the top landing where I went to play and to escape my mother's wrath. I had a bloody awful childhood I admit, but there were always the servants who were invariably kind to me and I think sorry for me too. I remember an old cook we used to have, feeding me on little cakes, and the butler who'd take me to the pantry when I was only about twelve years old to ask my opinion on a bottle of my father's port he had seen fit to open. In those days the house, too, felt like a friend. It was certainly a place of refuge. So for whatever reason, I love it. I love the way it stands; I love its solidity, its grace, the welcome it extends, the treasures in conceals and I have, to boot, always assumed that I would end my days here. In the Western Desert I often dreamt about it, sometimes about that imaginary undiscovered room, or just that I was standing in the hall or the saloon with friends, brother officers who might never even have been to Cranfield, and laughing, always laughing, because, despite my monstrous mother, the house has never struck me as an unhappy place. It has too great a character of its own to be affected by one or other of its temporary custodians.

My family built Cranfield. To have to abandon it now after they have owned it for two hundred years must be a mark of defeat and the thought of seeing it standing here empty day after day while I struggle on with a failing farm and an ailing bank account seems infinitely depressing. But Priscilla is amazing. She just turns her mind to the opening of the house and sees it as an enjoyable challenge rather than a miserable reverse. Or perhaps she's just trying to buoy me up. In any case we haven't yet decided exactly what to do in the end. Whatever happens, I suppose we'll have a furniture sale and that awful ass of a mouse from the auctioneers will be back again, delighted by my misfortune and twitching to get his hands on all my possessions.

Annie's diary

I can't really make out what's going on at the moment. His Lordship seems to be in a bad mood all the time. Not at all his usual self and her Ladyship has barely spoken to me since Christmas. I was drawing her bath this morning and only asked her which dress she wanted ironed for this evening when she quite snapped my head off. I thought to myself, you don't have to talk to Annie Jerrold like that just because things aren't going your way, but I didn't say a word. I've got my own problems to dwell on, what with Father and one thing and another, and then there's Bert starting up all over again about getting married. If I had as many pounds in the bank as I have had proposals, I'd be a rich woman by now.

It was only the other day I wrote to Mr Johnson to thank him for his card and to tell him all the news. I simply hadn't had a minute to sit down and write before but I knew he would be glad to hear about his Lordship and perhaps even be quite surprised to learn that the family is still living in the big house. After all, it was never any secret that his Lordship was broke. 'Don't you realise, Annie, I'm stony b—y broke,' he always used to say from the very start. Anyway I couldn't help adding that Mr Johnson ought to be back here right now as we have had nothing but the grey drizzle he loves so much for the last three or four weeks. And him out there in all that sunshine. Never mind sunshine, I could do with it being a little less muddy under foot. And fancy them not having any elm trees in Australia. I can't imagine anywhere without elms.

Georgina was asking about Mr Rakowski the other day. I can't for the life of me think why she's got to be so interested in him, but she's forever wondering why he never comes here any more. I told her that I supposed he'd finished his book, not that that was a good enough reason for her. Now I don't mind admitting that I like Mr Rakowski and always have done. He was very nice to me and a perfect gentleman, not that I wanted to say anything to Georgina about his Lordship being so furious when he discovered about him knowing all about Mr Mason and not saying a word. I, for one, doubt we'll be seeing much more of Mr Rakowski in the future. As it was, I thought Georgina gave me a funny look and I wondered if she knew more than she should when she immediately said that she was very pleased Mr Mason had left. She says she hated him. I've told her not to go on about hating people but she says she doesn't care because she and Thomas and Jamie all hated him and he was disgusting. I'm not quite sure what she meant by that but I told her that none of them need think about him any more since he's gone now. All she says is, good riddance to bad rubbish.

Mr Marshall, the new butler, seems quite a nice man and his wife is a much friendlier person than Mrs Mason ever was. She asked me in for a cup of tea soon after they arrived and told me all about her family.

Zbigniew Rakowski's notebook

FEBRUARY 14TH

Ah me! I note the date: Saint Valentine's Day! The day on which, according to ancient legend, every bird 'chooseth a mate', for neither Valentine the bishop nor Valentine the priest, holy martyrs and wise men both, manifested, in so far as we can tell from the relevant hagiography, the slightest concern for worldly passion or romantic love. I too have finally turned my back on such things for what use is it to me now to dream of hyacinth eyes and fine aristocratic looks, to ache for witty repartee, to yearn for rabbit pie? These things are not for me. Priscilla has made it quite clear that I have served my purpose, that in the end I have not pleased her and she no longer has any use for the funny, ageing little Pole who used to come to Cranfield and talk to her about literature, praise her good taste and laugh so gaily at her wit. Thus, mortified by what I now see as an old man's gullibility, have I consigned a once-precious bundle of letters senselessly tied up in hyacinth-blue ribbon to the flames.

I have finished my book and my publishers have not refrained from badgering me continuously to know what I will write about next. Before Christmas my spirits were so low that I never envisaged putting pen to paper again, but now I feel my own gloom, rather than being reinforced by the gloom of an English February, has gradually turned to scorn and from scorn it is but one short step to anger.

My daughter came fleetingly as usual for Christmas and, as I had predicted, attempted to 'cheer me up' with little anecdotes about her life in the north, about her neighbours and their imperfections. I enquired of her, not without a measure of sarcasm which I fear she did not detect, how it felt to be the only sane person in her village. My daughter bears, I fear, a strong resemblance to her late mother. The late Mrs Rakowski was a dour woman, pretty enough and demure in youth, whose limited imagination was responsible for her turning as the years passed into a narrow-minded, puritanical person, addicted to her religion and profoundly contemptuous of the foibles and weaknesses of her fellow beings. Thus she found her cantankerous husband, whose writing she rarely read, a trial, and her daughter an irksome duty. After a long illness, bravely borne as they say, she was relieved to shuffle off this mortal coil and to die in the odour of sanctity. To this day many is the rosary said by my daughter with a view to shortening the duration of her mother's stay in Purgatory and hastening her arrival in the land of milk and honey, there, I suppose, to take her place among the congregation of saints from whence she will look down at those less fortunate than herself, confirmed in the rightness of her belief that the greedy, the mean and the adulterous should perish, or like Dante's Paolo and Francesca, be buffeted about eternally in a stinking wind that keeps them forever apart. The late Mrs Rakowski, as I learnt to my cost, was nothing if not uncompromising.

It was not, however, without a flicker of pleasure, that I noticed for the first time a streak of rebellion in my young granddaughter, the which, I cannot but surmise, must denote an awakening intelligence and a desire to question some of her mother's assumptions, not to mention the platitudes that spring so readily from her father's lips.

The child went so far as to display a certain curiosity with regard to the scribblings of her old grandfather, and so fired was her imagination by the no more than pallid description of Cranfield and its inhabitants with which I regaled her, that she repeatedly requested further information as to the lives of the children, the age of the house, the size of the rooms, the pictures on the walls. No admonition from her parents who, showing no interest whatsoever in the subject themselves, pressed her to refrain from asking so many questions, could silence her. She desired even to know my opinion with regard to the rights and wrongs of people living in such large houses in these post-war days of hardship. Equality, she informed me, was what the war had been all about. She then went on to declare with what I deemed to be an incipient and indeed precocious revolutionary zeal, that the fathers of some of the children with whom she is at school are unemployed.

For once, I am forced to admit, that number one Robin Hood Way felt disagreeably empty after the three of them had left. Not that my son-in-law's departure could ever be anything but a solace to me. The man, a tax collector whose every utterance is greeted with nods of approval by his unquestioning wife, is both opinionated and preternaturally ignorant, and it is therefore a sorry truth indeed that neither my daughter nor her dreary husband could ever be in possession of the wherewithal to 'cheer me up' in the slightest degree, but I am forced and certainly happy to admit that where they failed, my admirable little granddaughter succeeded. The child has come a long way from being the silent, pallid creature I remember and I shall henceforth look forward to seeing how she is to develop.

So with the young lady and her cheerless parents back in the no doubt equally cheerless north, and provoked by the memory of the child's most pertinent questions, I have sat brooding, nay pondering on my experiences at Cranfield over the last few years. I have considered every aspect of my relationship to the house which I will always hold in deepest affection and to the family with whom I became so defencelessly involved. Alone in my front room in Robin Hood Way I have castigated myself out loud for the folly whereby I permitted myself during those years to lose all judgement, to abandon reason and to dream. And that, all for the love of a lady . . . Priscilla is undoubtedly a fine woman in many ways; legion will be those who have fallen, or will fall for her charms, beguiled by her wit and dazzled by her looks, as indeed was I, yet I am firmly of the opinion that at some point it behoves realism and rationality to take romanticism by the hand so as to lead it resolutely away. For me that moment has now come. And as I suggested earlier, scorn is but a short step away from anger. I fear that scorn has, not unnaturally, resulted from my contemplation of Priscilla's high-handed behaviour whereby, true to the traditions of a *grande dame* such as I fear she considers herself to be, she has taken me, a poor humble foreigner, squeezed all the juices from my soul and thrown away the husk.

Lord Otterton, on the other hand, I regard as a likeable, engaging scallywag, a ribald man, a chancer, what-you-will, an indisciplined person not to be taken too seriously on any level. I am told that he fought bravely in the war, the which I do not hesitate to believe and for which reason I am bound to admire him. Originating, as I do, from a country which for generations has been fought over, divided and subjected to the whims of its predatory neighbours, I would be the first to hail the intrepid man who fights for his country's freedom and certainly I have no reason to doubt Lord Otterton's considerable courage, not to say his daring, even his bravado. It would hardly surprise me if his experiences of war, culminating as they did in prison, had not made him unable or unwilling to adjust to the humdrum demands of everyday life in peacetime. Not that his life strikes this humble observer as being of a notably humdrum nature, nor as one deserving sympathy. Whatever his privations may have been, he does not know and has never known, as my own poor dear father did, the rigours of total displacement, he has not suffered the loss of home, of country, of friends, nor has he had to abandon the daily use of his native tongue, a far more grievous wrench than it is commonly supposed to be. No, the Ottertons, despite whatever qualities they may possess, have, I fear, come to deserve my scorn.

Thus, as I sit twiddling my thumbs, has my mind returned to the little *divertissement* with which some years ago I fondly teased my brain. I have now taken from the drawer of my bureau the manuscript of that sometime tale of murder, adultery and betrayal, conceived, as it was, of an intelligence clouded with romantic dreams. Despite, or perhaps on account of my altered mood, it strikes me once more as being infinitely full of possibilities and, with this in mind, I have begun to rewrite it, to reshape it indeed according to my present pragmatic view of things. It is to be a humorous, not to say witty set piece, a precise account of life at Cranfield, incorporating all the drama, all the hatred, all the passion, all the weaknesses of the family who still, although who can guess for how long, inhabit that captivating place. Once again, as I pick up my pen, I feel the sap rise in me and the creative urge is reawakened.

Annie's diary

I can't help worrying about Father's health. We had all hoped that with the winter nearly over he might begin to feel a bit better, but every time I go to see him, I feel he's spiralled down even further. He never complains of course, just the same as usual, but he's looking so tired and thin and his cough never lets up so that sometimes when he's gasping for breath, I think he's going to choke to death. Worst of all, he seems to have lost interest in the garden. It was all I could do on Sunday afternoon to persuade him to put his overcoat on and poke his nose out of doors just to take a look at the daffodils which were all in bud, and the japonica which was quite covered in bloom and which he's always loved. Mind you, I think he was quite pleased when I picked some of it and put it in a jug on the table in the kitchen for him. 'Japonica,' he said. 'Now that was always your mother's favourite shrub. "Promise of Spring" she used to call it.' Well it's only another week before the first day of Spring now, but you'd never believe it, not to see Father huddled over that dusty old coke fire. Other years he'd have been out and about, digging the garden, pruning his roses, anything but sit indoors with the mild weather we've been having these last few days.

Then there's his Lordship telling me that he can't afford to stay at Cranfield any longer, not that that entirely surprised me. 'Annie,' he says, 'we can't go on. I've tried to keep the show on the road but I'm afraid the party's over now.' Then he says no one knows yet so, 'don't go spreading it around.' See me spreading anything around. 'Now who on earth would I tell?' I asked him. He says, 'I think we'll go to the Dower House. You'll come too, won't you, Annie?' I told him it only seemed like yesterday that he was calling on me down at Father's, begging me to come to work for her

Ladyship, and there was me trying to get on with the ironing and that darned puppy was piddling all over the floor. I asked him what he was going to do with his *menagerie*. 'Oh,' he says, as bright as a button, 'take the animals with me of course.' I can picture her Ladyship's face when she sees all those parrots and the otter, not to mention the giant squirrel he's just been and bought, all moving house with her. She can't stand them as it is, and then the other day there was poor Georgina crying because the squirrel had bitten her. All his Lordship did was laugh and say it didn't hurt. I dare say it didn't really, but I wouldn't fancy being attacked by a huge great squirrel whether it came from India or not. I can't think what his Lordship wants with an Indian squirrel after all the trouble they've been having on the farm and in the kitchen garden trying to keep the ordinary grey squirrels down. I've told him that I for one am not going near the blasted creature, not for all the tea in China.

So what with this and that, it's hardly surprising if I haven't been sleeping much lately. For one thing, I know for sure that if we move out of Cranfield, it will only give Bert an excuse to go on at me again about getting married. I doubt he'll ever take no for an answer, but of course being in the Dower House won't be the same as living here. Not that I can make up my mind about anything until her Ladyship's said something to me and she hasn't said a word as yet. All the same, I couldn't help looking around my room this morning and thinking how I would miss it and particularly how I would miss the view from the window, out over the lawns and the park to the distant hills. I can spend hours just staring out of that window. Georgina who's always learning something by heart knows a poem about the sheep and cows, and us having no time to stand and stare. She laughs when I go on about it. I tell her it's just like me, I don't have half enough time to stand and stare and then she tells me the poem was written by a tramp. I should have thought he had plenty of time to stand and stare, if anyone did.

I wonder what will happen to Mr MacIntosh if we leave Cranfield. I'll miss Mr MacIntosh and I should think her Ladyship will too. As a matter of fact I expect we'll all miss Mr MacIntosh.

Sydney Otterton's diary

The government was defeated in the Commons for the first time yesterday and it doesn't look as if it will be able to survive much longer. People can talk about nothing else although I have to admit that my mind has really been on other things. We've at last made the firm decision to move to the Dower House in June, taking Annie with us I hope.

I was rather surprised by Annie's reaction to leaving Cranfield. She knows I haven't got a brass bean to my name, but it made her very cross when I told her we would definitely have to go. Then when Priscilla talked to her she was apparently quite huffy and announced that she wasn't saying what she would do. I'm sure she will come with us. For one thing, where else would she go? And for another, she's got her father here. Poor old Jerrold, I fear he may not be long for this world. Then there's Bert too of course.

There can be no doubt about the hold the house has on us all. Everyone's unhappy about the turn of events, even Georgina was in tears when Priscilla told her we were leaving. She says she doesn't like the Dower House at all. In fact she says she hates it. In a way, I've felt much better about moving since our plans became more definite and since we made them known publicly. Although to begin with I played with the idea of going right away to Shropshire or somewhere, I'm glad Priscilla convinced me of the folly of that line of action. I need to be near London, not only for the House of Lords, but for the Regiment too, that is, so long as I remain with it. I also happen to know that I couldn't in fact really bear to be far from Cranfield which is after all where I belong, if any of us belongs anywhere. It was just that at one point I found the idea of living here, but not in the house, unbearable as if it would have been a daily reminder of my inability to manage my own affairs with any degree of competence at all.

We're going to hold another sale before we go, but we'll do it through Sotheby's this time, and then we're planning to open the house to the public. Priscilla is full of how I'd be too illiterate to write a guide book, so she intends to do it herself which suits me because I'm quite sure she's right and that she'll do it far better than I could. She's also very busy thinking of how to do up the Dower House and talking about getting Miss Wheel back on board to make the curtains. In a way it's all quite exciting. I'm thinking of building a large aviary in the garden for some of my birds which Priscilla says is a waste of money. She didn't think it very funny when I told her that my motto has always been, 'Spend your way out!' Anyway, as I said, we'll be saving money on so many things when we do move, like not hiring some bloody fool to wind the clocks once a week, that I don't see why I shouldn't have an aviary.

Then we rather changed the subject because she suddenly wanted to know what on earth we were going to do about those damn letters from that frightful fellow, Pink. In fact I hadn't given them a thought for months. Not since Priscilla locked them away in her safe. Anyway, she rather flew off the handle, saying that before I spent my way into the debtors' gaol, she would like to know what to do about those blackmailing letters. She said she'd been thinking about them lately and that it bothered her having them in her safe. She wanted to be shot of them, certainly before the move, and as far as she was concerned she had finally come to the conclusion that the best possible thing to do with them was to send them to my mother, care of her bank. We would probably never hear another word about them and at least the ball would be in my mother's court where it belonged. And, talking about balls and courts, Priscilla may think my aviary is a waste of money but she's full bent on having a tennis court at the Dower House. I expect she will get her way. Not that I ever intend to play tennis. The last time I went anywhere with a tennis racquet was when I smuggled some love-birds back to England from Australia before I was married. All the way home on the boat I kept them in a tennis-ball box with holes punched in the side and when we reached Southampton I swanned off the boat with the box tied to a racquet as if I were Fred Perry himself. No one asked any questions.

In the end I told Priscilla to do what she liked with those letters. I don't want to have to think about them and wish to God we'd never found them, so I suppose she will send them off to my mother which may, as she suspects, mean that we never hear any more about them, or it may create one hell of a shindy. She is convinced that if we either burn them or keep them we'll never be shot of interference from my mother who, she says, must have been looking for the letters all this time. Why else, Priscilla wants to know, did she come here that time when we were away, and why was she always trying to pay people to snoop on us? She must have known of the existence of the letters and have been living in dread lest they were found.

Georgina's exercise book

It is very sad because we have got to leave Cranfield. When Mummy told me I cried and she said not to be silly because it didn't matter to me but it does and I do *not* want to go. Jamie and I wont have anywhere decent to hide from the grown-ups in the horrid old Dower House which is a silly house anyway with gohsts in it I bet. And Thomas will be absolutely furious because he thinks he's going to live here when Father's dead and turn me and Jamie out. No one is at all pleased. I'm sure Annie wants to stay because she looked really sorry when I asked her what she thought. She's not happy anyway because her father had to go to hospitle today and he's very ill. I may have to go to boarding school after we move which is another thing I do *not* want to do, but Mummy says children always have a wonderful time and they have no idea what grown-ups have to put up with. It seems to me that grown-ups always do what they want like moving house whenever they feel like it and dragging the poor children behind them. I don't think Father really wants to go but he says he's going to build a special aviery for the birds at the new house and he's looking forward to that. I hope we don't have to take that vile squirrel which bit me with us. But I suppose we will.

Extract from Zbigniew Rakowski's work in progress

How fondly did the beautiful Hyacinth imagine herself to be a liberal and intelligent woman unfettered by the customary assumptions, not to say prejudices of her class. With her beauty and natural wit, it was in truth not impossible for her to persuade those of lesser birth or lesser understanding that she was indeed what she wished to appear, a generous-hearted, open-minded Renaissance princess. Yet she ruled her stately home with a rod of iron and, it was she, rather than her jocose if irascible, nay volatile husband who, like the Queen in Alice in Wonderland, *dispensed justice, mercilessly banishing old favourites, beheading, so to speak, the innocent, promoting the vain and treacherous, ever confident in the rightness of her own judgement. It was hardly surprising then, that there were those of her entourage who would gladly plot her downfall, even some of those closest to her might have wished to be rid of this turbulent high-priestess . . .*

Letter from Annie to her sister Dolly

Dear Dolly

You left so soon after the funeral yesterday that what with one thing and another I hardly had a chance to see you, but I did want to say how glad I was that you were able to get over to see Father before he passed away. He went very peacefully and I am sure it was a blessed release for him even though I feel that nothing will ever be the same again. I've spent so much time with him, particularly recently, that I know I will miss him terribly. I was very fond of Father.

Of course I knew there was bound to be trouble from Bert. Can you believe it, but he has already decided that he would like to move into Father's cottage! What a cheek, I thought to myself, even though I'll grant you that it's much nicer than his own. No doubt he would like to have me there with him, but what with the Ottertons moving out of the big house in June, I have other things to think about. Her Ladyship goes on at me about going with them to the Dower House. We'll see, is all I have told her for the moment.

I'll be going up to the churchyard at the week-end to see to the grave.

Give my love to Fred and the children.

Love from
Annie

Sydney Otterton's diary

APRIL 15TH

The British Legion do in the village last night was full of nosy buggers wanting to know every damn thing about our move.

Old Doubleday and one or two others were overflowing with disingenuous sympathy for my impecunious state, blaming the Labour government, but no doubt behind my back rubbing their hands in glee at the thought of my misfortunes. Somehow the news has got about that next year we are planning to open the house to the public and three quarters of the retired majors in the Home Counties want to be at the door with their wives selling tickets and showing the *hoi polloi* around, whilst commiserating with me about the horrors of letting the public into one's home. It took the wind out of their sails when I told them I was rather looking forward to it.

It's only a few weeks now before we move and, funnily enough, I've very quickly become accustomed to the idea. We've been spending a good deal of time going round the house and choosing what furniture and pictures to take with us and what to put in the sale. All the better and larger things will of course have to stay here to be put on show. The Dower House under Priscilla's aegis is beginning to look very nice indeed and it'll certainly be warmer and a great deal more comfortable than Cranfield is in our present circumstances. This morning we took the children to see how it was getting on and even Georgina was quite excited by the prospect of her new bedroom. The one she's in at the moment is certainly falling apart. The rain came in above her bed last winter and the wallpaper which must have been put up at least fifty years ago has almost come away from one wall. Thomas was quite happy too. And so he bloody well ought to be since Priscilla has seen to it that he has one of the nicest rooms.

And it's perfectly true that the whole idea (which I didn't find at all appealing at first) of opening the house has begun to take quite a hold with me. After all we won't be the first people to do it, and as far as I can see, it's just another way of keeping the roof on the bloody thing.

Old Jerrold was buried on Monday and there wasn't a dry eye in the place. He was part of my childhood and a thoroughly good fellow for whom I had a great deal of affection. I will miss him and will certainly feel that Cranfield won't be the same without his quiet wisdom and watchful eye. Priscilla had a soft spot for him too and keeps claiming that he was very good-looking. You could have fooled me. He had a nice, friendly face, but as far as I was concerned, he was just a very decent country sort of man and a damn good cowman.

Annie, not surprisingly, has clammed up and is very unhappy so it's no good asking her about her plans at the moment. 'I was always very fond of me father,' she told me yesterday in an understatement typical of her. And that's about as far as she will commit herself. Priscilla, who has now decided that Annie is tremendously insular and would never ever want to go abroad, was once afraid that she might run off to Australia with Johnson, not that I ever thought she would leave here as long as Jerrold was alive. In fact not long ago she told me that the one thing she would like to do if she won the football pools, would be to travel. She'd particularly like to go to Italy. Why Italy, I have no idea. Anyway Priscilla obviously hasn't got it quite right for once.

I still think Annie will stay with us in the end, although she may easily decide to move in with Bert and marry him. Poor old Jerrold was hardly cold in his grave before Bert formed up to me to say he wanted Jerrold's cottage, which was what made me think he and Annie might be planning to get married. I wouldn't have put it past Annie to have told Bert all along that she wouldn't marry him until after her father died. For one thing she would never have put up with living where Bert is now. Annie quite likes her creature comforts. Priscilla always says that Annie's room is warmer and more comfortable than her own. In any case I can't really see why she shouldn't look after herself. If she doesn't no one else will. Anyway I haven't made up my mind what to do about Bert yet which may in a way rather depend on what Annie decides to do.

Priscilla finally got me to send those bloody letters to my

mother. I just enclosed a note with them to say that they had turned up and that I would be grateful if she would be so kind as to return them to Batty. Not surprisingly, I haven't heard a word, but at least I suppose my mother may now decide to leave us alone, although half of me feels that we should have burnt the wretched things and been done with them. I rather think Priscilla, who's always got an eye for a story, still has a sneaking curiosity about the whole Pink/Batty saga and longs to know the truth of it. For all the high-faluting literature she reads, I've often caught her with her nose in a Margery Allingham or a Raymond Chandler.

Annie's diary

It's hard to believe that it's already a month since poor Father died. I don't think I'll ever get used to his not being here. I'm always thinking about him and about how he was in days gone by when he was young and fit. It was different when Mother went somehow because for one thing there was Father then and for another, I didn't have time to think about anything then but getting along on and looking after the family. I certainly never had time to stand and stare. Not like the sheep and cows. I don't like going down to Father's place now, although I've had to go and tidy up his things. And I certainly don't fancy living there with Bert. Bert gets on my nerves the way he always thinks he'll be able to make me do whatever he wants in the end so long as he wants it badly enough. Well, all I can say is that he doesn't know Annie Jerrold if that's what he thinks. I decided to drop Mr Johnson a line just so as to let him know about Father. Now I always thought Mr Johnson a very nice man and I know he liked Father. He and Father got on very well together.

I also thought Mr Johnson would be interested to know

how the move was coming along and I'm certain he'd like to hear all about the family and about Mr MacIntosh. Mr MacIntosh was talking to me only yesterday morning. They'd all just come back from church and were in the saloon. I was looking for his Lordship because one of his parrots was out of its cage, sitting on a gilt picture frame up there in his dressing-room, attacking it with its beak. It was making a dreadful mess. Anyway I think his Lordship must have been reading the lesson because there he was, prancing up and down laughing and going on about Nebuchadnezzar and a burning fiery furnace and her Ladyship was telling him not to be foolish and Georgina was giggling and then he started to recite some rhyme which her Ladyship said was unsuitable for children. Of course I wasn't paying a blind bit of attention, I'd only come to say about the parrot. Then just as I was leaving the room, Mr MacIntosh came over and asked me how I was. He said I must be missing Father. He's ever so kind, is Mr MacIntosh. Anyway, he then went on about how sad all these changes were, and leaving Cranfield was like the end of an era. He'd loved living here, he said, but he was looking forward to his new cottage in the village. I've got an idea that it's one of his Lordship's he's bought. He said I was to make sure and go and see him there when he's settled in, which I most certainly will, if I'm still here.

I haven't yet said anything to her Ladyship about staying on indefinitely although she will keep telling me about the bedroom I'm to have at the Dower House, which I have to say is very nice although of course it doesn't have the view. To my mind neither she nor his Lordship seems to think that there is anywhere else I could go. Well, we shall see about that. I haven't said a word about Bert and Father's cottage even though his Lordship was trying to sound me out about it the other day. I said to his Lordship, 'It's your cottage, you must do as you please with it.' I thought to myself then that it was a darned good thing I knew how to mind my p's and q's.

I don't know what he's going to do about Bert and I've no idea who else he might want to put in that cottage.

Georgina's exercise book

Yesterday afternoon I was just mucking about down by the lake after school when I saw this really spooky person. When I told Mummy about her, she said I was being silly because the public footpath goes past the lake so there's nothing odd about anyone being down there. I still thought this woman was spooky. She was very old and ugly and she gave me a vile look. I didn't want to talk to her because she gave me the creeps but when she gave me this vile look she said something about 'I'm on an erand child.' I hate people who call you child. We're not alloud to call them woman. I don't know what she was doing. I wish Jamie or Thomas had been there. I told Annie about her but she just said not to worry. These days Annie's in a bad mood and doesn't talk nearly so much. She probably doesn't want to move and nor do I but Mummy's made my new room look pretty so I suppose it will be all right in the end. I'm aloud to choose the wallpaper and I'm having some of the stuff out of my old room. I began to sort of exagerate a bit about that spooky woman to make Mummy believe me but I think she just decided I'd made the whole thing up. Perhaps it was a gohst but I think it looked too sort of solid.

Letter from Zbigniew Rakowski to Priscilla Otterton

1 Robin Hood Way
MAY 26TH, 1950

Dear Priscilla,

It is not without considerable misgivings that I tremblingly submit for your and Lord Otterton's generous scrutiny the enclosed humble offering, the fruit of my protracted labours at Cranfield. How sincerely do I hope that you will look charitably on these pages and that in them Lord Otterton will be pleased to recognise some of the more picturesque members of his family into whom I have attempted to breathe new life. I hope that it will not be with a jaundiced eye that he views the juxtaposition of saint and scoundrel and that both you and he will derive at least some pleasure from the perusal of this volume.

To work at Cranfield was as great a pleasure as it was a privilege, its beauty will perpetually nourish my imagination and I shall forever cherish my remembrance of the place. It was with a great sense of doom that I learned of your intention to abandon it to trippers, but I now take this opportunity to wish you every success as you venture to open your exquisite house to what I fear may prove to be an undeserving public.

It remains only for me to thank you both for the notable forbearance with which you permitted me to pore over the Cranfield archives and for the generosity with which you so graciously extended your hospitality to a lonely old pen pusher, one who is now engaged in the writing of a mere novel which dwells, with, I pray not too heavy a hand, on the darker side of human nature.

I remain, humble chronicler of the Otterton family
yours most sincerely
Z.A.R.

Sydney Otterton's diary

For some reason which I don't understand I have started having nightmares again. I had begun to think that I had got over them, but I've had some horrible ones recently. Last night I dreamt we were landing in Salerno Bay, except of course it wasn't Salerno Bay as I remember it, it was more like Woolacombe and my legs had been shot from under me so I couldn't think how I was going to run up the beach. Then of course I woke up in a dreadful sweat. In fact when we did get to Salerno in real life, I and another young officer had a lucky escape. We'd landed under cover of darkness and were horrified when dawn broke to see the destruction around us. Village after village had been reduced to rubble and as we progressed we came across huge numbers of dispossessed and wounded civilians, men and women, old and young, and there were everywhere piles of dead cattle and horses, lying on their backs, killed by the shelling. Anyway, just after breakfast I was sent out with this other fellow to reconnoitre and after a few miles we found a blown-up bridge where the pair of us came under a salvo of German artillery fire. We dived for cover and crept back, I can't imagine how, to where I had left my driver in the scout car, fully expecting to discover that he'd been blown up. In fact he too had, by some miracle, been missed and had accelerated back to take cover round a bend in the road. Despite the passage of time, these images still haunt me and I imagine they always will.

Anyway everyone else is pretty cheerful this morning what with the sun shining for the Whitsun week-end and petrol rationing ending at the same time. People have been queuing at the garages since before midnight so I should imagine the whole world will be on the roads over the Bank Holiday.

I have a niggling feeling of unease somehow connected to

my mother and Pink and Batty and the fact that I haven't heard so much as a squeak since we sent off those letters. I don't really see why we should have heard anything, but instinctively I feel that such a shock as they must have given my mother (assuming her to have received them) would have provoked some kind of reaction from her – if only rage and, as is common knowledge, she's not one to keep her anger to herself.

This morning's post brought a copy of Rakowski's book, dedicated to Priscilla and enclosing an unctuous letter to her of course. I thought it rather lacked his usual humour but he's probably still feeling hard done by or uncomfortable about the bloody silly way he carried on. The book looks all right and is decently illustrated with a few well-chosen pictures of the house, the Speaker and so forth. Priscilla has requisitioned it for the moment and seems quite to have forgiven Rakowski his sins. She's decided that the old fool is just a bit of an ass, that he wasn't really thinking about what he was doing and that we ought to take a lenient view considering the trouble he went to over the book. For all I know she'll be asking him back for lunch again before long. That's all right by me. I hold no grudges even though it may strike me that there remain a couple of things he has manifestly failed to explain.

Annie's diary

JUNE 2ND

A funny thing happened yesterday afternoon just as I was coming back from seeing Bert. It must have been about half past four and as it was such a lovely day, I thought that instead of walking straight up the drive, I'd go the long way round, down through the field to the lake, over the bridge and up the path to the house. There's a dreadful blanket of duckweed on the lake so that it hardly looks as if there's any water in it at all, but there must be because I saw a heron standing on a bit of old tree that's fallen across the surface and, as Father would have told anyone, where there's a heron there are sure to be fish. So I was simply standing there, just like the sheep and cows, staring at the heron, wondering about the fish swimming about down there under all that weed and thinking what a shame it was that his Lordship would probably never be able to afford to drain the lake and clean it out. As it is you can only walk along one side of it at the moment. The other side where the old boathouse is, is completely overgrown with bamboo and elder and brambles, you'd barely know there had ever been a path there. In fact you can scarcely see where the boathouse is any more because it's almost hidden behind what look like giant rhubarb leaves. It must have all been so different years gone by when there were dozens of gardeners and no doubt swans and lilies on the lake as well. Anyway I was just looking at that darned heron when I suddenly noticed something sticking up out of the water underneath the branch on which he was standing. Blow me down if it didn't look exactly like a lady's shoe. Then I thought it must be a bit of old wood stuck at a funny angle, not that I could be quite sure, but as there was no means by which I could have got round to the other side, I just stood as close to the edge as I dared and squinted at this thing from across the water. Of course I couldn't see it very well, but I'd eat my hat if that wretched bit of wood didn't turn out to be someone's shoe in the end. Anyway there it was for all the world to see, pointing up through the duckweed some of which clung to it in greenish streaks. I was just wondering how in the devil's name it got there when there was a rustling in the undergrowth behind where the boathouse is and a trembling in the bamboos as if they'd been caught by a sudden gust of wind. Well there certainly wasn't a breath of wind yesterday. I can vouch for that. In fact it was so warm that I'd taken my cardigan off and was carrying it over my arm. To be honest I felt a bit nervous, almost as if I'd seen a ghost. Anyway the heron must have felt the same because it suddenly rose from the branch and flapped away towards the lower lake which, if you ask me, is in even worse condition than the upper one. To be perfectly frank it's no more than a swamp now.

As I walked on up to the house I tried to put what had happened out of my mind and began to think about the move which is only a couple of weeks away now. The house looks ever so grand standing above you against the dark trees as you come up from the lake below and I suddenly felt really sad at the thought of leaving it. Not that I'll be going far yet as I've agreed to start off at the Dower House with her Ladyship and just see how it goes. His Lordship was overjoyed when he heard I'd decided to stay, for a while at least, I said. 'Neither of us would be any good without you, Annie,' he said.

It was lovely and cool inside the house and I was on my way up to my room when I came across Georgina sitting cross-legged in a corner on the half landing with her nose in a book. I was surprised to see her because her Ladyship was supposed to have gone to collect her from school and take her to buy some new shoes. 'My Good Lord,' I said to her. 'I wasn't expecting you back so early and now you'll be wanting your tea.' Well her Ladyship had fetched her from school but had decided against going shopping so they'd come straight home. Georgina explained all this, and then gave me quite a turn by saying that as she'd supposed I was at the farm she'd started to walk down the drive to meet me but had got scared, as she put it, because she'd seen some peculiar woman coming up onto the drive from the overgrown side of the lake. So she'd run back to the house to hide. I couldn't make head or tail of what she was talking about at first, but she can be quite obstinate and was absolutely full bent on telling me that she'd seen this woman snooping around the lake before. As a matter of fact I do remember her saying something of the sort a little while back but I didn't take much notice at the time. Anyway this time I wanted to know what that woman looked like, but all Georgina could tell me was that she was very old and very ugly and rather frightening. I never mentioned a word about the wind in the bamboos mind, but I did say that she really must tell his Lordship or her Ladyship, especially now she's seen this person twice. She says she told her Ladyship the first time and her Ladyship said she was imagining things, so she doesn't want to say any more, besides which she seems to think she'll get into some sort of trouble. What for, I can't make out, but then Georgina always thinks she's going to get into trouble for nothing.

As a matter of fact I wondered if the woman she'd seen might be the wife of the mad cowman we had for a while after Father retired, come back to pester us. I reckon she was pretty well as strange as her husband, that Mrs Wilkins, but I don't suppose the pair of them remained locked up for all that long. Or perhaps she has escaped from the asylum. But of course I didn't say any of that to Georgina because I didn't want to frighten her any more. I have decided though, that if she won't tell her parents, I will certainly have to say something myself. We don't want lunatics roaming around the place just when we're moving. And we don't want another burglary either, thank you very much.

Georgina's exercise book

I saw that horrible spooky woman again this afternoon. Annie says I've got to tell Mummy and Father but I think they'd just say I was silly. Mummy wasn't intrested when I told her the first time. The witch woman gave me another vile look just like last time but she didn't say anything because

309

I ran away too soon. I think Annie was a bit frightened when I said she'd been snooping about down by the lake but she would *not* admit it. She just kept saying, 'Now then Georgina you tell your parents what happened.' And Annie will *not* say who she thinks this ugly woman is or what she thinks she's doing. I think she could be a kidnapper but as Father says he hasn't got any money he'll never be able to pay the ransom. I bet I'm going to have nightmares now.

Sydney Otterton's diary

JUNE 5TH

Bert found my mother's body on Saturday morning. Apparently Annie had been talking to him about a shoe she thought she'd seen in the lake. Something about the way she went on about it made him curious, so as soon as he'd finished milking the cows that morning he went along to investigate. Now I expect the poor blighter wishes that he'd never been near the place. I suspect that no one had been near the lake for a couple of days, during which time the body had somehow floated right up against the bank and it was lying there half exposed when Bert found it. All I can say is thank the Lord Georgina never found it. She's always playing down by the lake. The police came and I had the unpleasant task of having to identify the body which they say must have been in the water for two or three days. Now there's going to be a hell of a lot of trouble. For one thing there obviously has to be a post-mortem so we can't yet arrange a funeral, and for another there are going to be a great many questions which will have to be answered.

I am of the opinion that my mother did herself in, possibly as a consequence of receiving the Pink letters, or perhaps for some other reason of which we are unaware, but then both Annie and Georgina swear that there was someone else involved. Georgina actually saw a woman near the lake on Thursday afternoon whom she describes as old and ugly and on that same day Annie thought not only that she saw a woman's shoe poking out of the water but also that someone was moving about in the bamboos behind the boathouse. That naturally had to be told to the police, which of course means that we are now all about to be involved in a possible murder enquiry. But it goes without saying that if my mother did decide to kill herself she would, without any question of doubt, have chosen to do so in the way most calculated to cause us the maximum possible distress.

The worst of it is that I can't see how I can avoid telling the police about the letters. If I honestly thought I could get away with it, I'd say nothing. None of us wants all that horror from the past dragged up, what with the stuff about the dead baby and so forth. But on the other hand, if Batty killed my mother, I don't see why I should let her get away with it. I loathed my mother, but that isn't a reason for allowing that filthy bitch to murder her. Priscilla thinks we'll all be under suspicion but, as I told her, I at least should be off the hook. I can hardly have killed my mother for gain since, not surprisingly, it appears she's left all her money to a cats' home. She told me long ago that that was her intention and my lawyers are in possession of a letter informing me that I have no expectations from her. Not that that has prevented the police from giving me a pretty unpleasant grilling and I don't doubt that there will be more of the same before we're through. All the servants have to be questioned and all the farm workers. Poor innocent Bert has been given a dreadful time and the only one that seems to have disappeared into thin air is Batty.

Priscilla in fact is absolutely furious about the whole thing which, rather untypically, she sees as an evil omen for our move. 'All the same,' I heard her say to Annie, 'as far as my mother-in-law is concerned, she won't be any loss.' 'Well no one was very fond of *that* Lady Otterton,' Annie replied.

For some reason best known to herself Annie thinks that the woman Georgina saw must have been the mad cowman's wife, but although Georgina isn't much good at describing her, I'm still convinced it was Batty. I can't think of any reason why Mrs Wilkins would want to come back and haunt us.

Bert really has been given a thorough going-over by the police when all he's done is to come across a dead body floating in the duckweed and come up here as green as grass to raise the alarm. I was in the bath when he arrived. Apparently he was out there for ages, banging at the back door, ringing the bell and hollering for help. Marshall eventually heard the din, let him in and brought him up to the hall. Then I think Annie heard something going on. I suppose she heard Bert's voice and must have wondered what on earth he was doing here at that time, so she went down to see what in God's name the shindy was about. By the time I got to him, the wretched fellow was sitting on a hall chair with his head in his hands, shaking from head to foot and saying he'd never seen the like of it in all his born days. It took me a moment or two to make out what it was he had seen and I have to say that when he told me, I was at first quite unable to take it in. All I could think of in some sort of totally irrelevant way, was that after all this I'd have to let the fellow have Jerrold's cottage if that was what he really wanted, and that that would mean having to spend a bit of money on his because I can't imagine anyone else being prepared to live in it as it is.

In any case, we're all in some bloody awful sort of limbo at the moment, waiting, as far as I can see, for the police to lay hands on Batty. The sooner they find her the better.

Georgina's exercise book

The grown-ups didn't want me to know about Grandmama being drowned in the lake but they had to tell me which was sucks to them because this police woman wanted to ask me about that creepy old witch I saw. I think the witch probably murdered Grandmama but Annie says I've no bisness saying such things. The grown-ups are going about with very long faces and always stopping talking when they see me. And Mummy just keeps saying 'pas devan' which she thinks I can't understand but I can. So this police woman was very nice and she kept on asking me what the witch looked like and what colour was her hair and stuff like that and then she said she didn't want me to be upset. Actualy it's very exciting!! I wish Jamie and Thomas were here but I heard Mummy say the other day something about it being just as well the boys were at school. I hate the way grown-ups always think children are a nuissance.

Annie's diary

JUNE 8TH

Father wasn't a man of many words but, if he said it once, he said it a hundred times that Lilian, Lady Otterton meant trouble. If you ask me he never liked her from the word go and I think he felt quite sorry for his late Lordship having to put up with her. Now fancy her choosing to go and drown herself in the lake just now, what with us all busy moving out of the house, and her Ladyship's having so much on her plate and his Lordship with plenty of things to think about. I reckon she did it on purpose just to spite them. I think it would be a darn good thing if the police could find Miss

Batty and get the whole thing sorted out once and for all. I reckon that woman knows what happened. Then perhaps the rest of us might be given a little bit of peace and quiet. There's Mrs Marshall up there in the butler's flat, she's quite indignant, saying that when Mr Marshall took the job here he was supposed he was coming to work for a respectable family, he certainly hadn't expected to be questioned like a common criminal. I thought to myself, oh Lord, they'll be off again before you can say Jack Robinson and his Lordship will be looking for another caretaker. The police have been all over the place for days now. It's much worse than when we had the burglary.

You can't help feeling sorry for Bert. It was such a dreadful shock finding her Ladyship's body like that. He's really shaken up still and has been questioned over and over again by the police. As if Bert would go pushing anyone into the lake! And if he did, where would be the sense in his rushing up to the house to tell us all about it? Mind you, I've no idea what took him down there in the first place. He says it was something to do with my talking to him about a shoe and the wind in the bamboos which made him wonder what had been going on, but really, I think it was just that it was a nice fine morning so once he'd finished with the cows, he felt like a bit of a walk. It's beautiful at that time of day with no one about, and peaceful, especially down by the lake. I expect he went there almost automatically, never mind the shoe. Come to that, it chills my bones just thinking of that there shoe and of me only standing on the bank in the sunshine with my cardigan over my arm and not knowing what on earth I was looking at. His Lordship's convinced Miss Batty was involved and I have to admit now that it was probably her that Georgina saw on the drive. I don't know why I was so set on its being Mrs Wilkins.

Sydney Otterton's diary

They've done the autopsy and established that death was by drowning so at least we can bury my mother now. There'll have to be an inquest of course and I suppose the verdict will be accidental death. There's been no suicide note and no sign of Batty for the moment, not that I imagine she will find it very easy to lie low for long. She may well have killed my mother but how can we ever know? I turn the thing over and over in my mind, sometimes feeling relieved that my mother is dead, sensing the removal of an enemy and of a whole area of spite directly mainly towards me, but I'm always appalled by the manner of her death and the uncertainty surrounding it, and yet in some sort of way I can almost feel sorry for her, which was something I never did when she was alive. Batty now surfaces in my dreams. I've seen her being taken prisoner with me after the Normandy Landings and I've seen my mother driving a Honey through the desert, searching the barren landscape for water to drown in, with hundreds of flies settling on her arms and her face. My God, will I ever be shot of these dreams?

In the midst of all this Marshall came to see me yesterday morning to give me his notice. He said that Mrs Marshall didn't care for what he referred to as the police presence in the house. I asked him who the bloody hell she expected to find in the house after a three-day-old corpse had been discovered in the lake. We were hardly likely to be entertaining King Farouk and Rita Hayworth. As he left the room and just as he was closing the door, he said, 'I can appreciate that you're upset, M'lord.' Patronising bugger. He had the nerve to add graciously that he'll stay until he finds another job. I never really thought he was much of a fellow. I gave myself a large gin and tonic after that.

According to Priscilla, Mrs Wilkins who came under

suspicion for some reason, is out of the bin and living with her children in a council house up the road. The husband's still inside but she's apparently perfectly all right, in which case she must have been a bit put out on coming back from visiting her mother in Basingstoke to find P.C. Plod on her doorstep, wanting to know if she'd killed my mother. I had to tell Annie. She's been convinced all along that Mrs Wilkins had something to do with it all. I can't think why unless it's because Bert whipped her up against the woman when she was wailing in the cottage next door to him. I imagine that it was only because Annie mentioned her to the police in the first place that they bothered to go looking for her.

JUNE 10TH

Batty's turned up at last. Stark staring mad, if you ask me. Thank the Lord Priscilla was here at the time. I don't know how the hell I would have dealt with her on my own. In fact Priscilla had just come back from the village shop and was taking her shopping out of the car round by the back door when she heard a kind of wail or whimper. She looked round and who in the devil's name should she find standing by her shoulder, but Batty. One thing about Priscilla is that, although she can get quite worked up about minor things and quite carried away at times, when there's any kind of real crisis she always manages to remain magnificently calm. She brought Batty into the house and met me crossing the hall with the dog. The undertaker had been to see me and I'd been showing him out. A bit of a Uriah Heep of a man who'd been full of unwelcome condolences, bowing and scraping and saying how sorry he was and it being not so many years since he had the honour of burying his late Lordship. I couldn't wait to get rid of the fellow.

Anyway the last thing I was expecting was to turn round and find Batty walking across the hall with Priscilla. In fact Batty, as if nothing untoward had occurred, stopped to admire the flowers Priscilla had arranged in the big vase on top of that pillar in the hall. Very nice flowers, but I had no intention of standing and discussing roses with Batty, the woman I have most hated all my life. The mere fact of seeing that woman makes me feel queasy because she instantly evokes so much of the fear and horror of my childhood. I can still see the expression on her face when she used to take a birch to me or a belt, or whatever she thought would inflict most pain on a small child. But Priscilla said later that one look at her now was enough to make anyone realise that she had finally completely taken leave of her senses and whether or not she had been before, she was clearly now certifiable. Priscilla even went so far as to say that she could feel sorry for her because she was wandering around like a lost soul in hell. I told Priscilla she'd feel rather differently if she'd known her as I did.

Anyway the long and the short of it was that Priscilla called a doctor and the police and while we were waiting for them all to arrive, we managed to get the beginnings of an explanation from Batty about everything that has happened. It was difficult to make much sense of what she said because she became appallingly distressed whenever my mother's death was mentioned. I thought that must mean that she'd pushed her in the lake, but Priscilla, who fancies herself as an amateur psychologist, is convinced that the woman was in love with my mother and that with her dead, the bottom's fallen out of Batty's world.

Letter from Annie to Dolly

JUNE 11TH, 1950

Dear Dolly,

I'm sorry I was unable to come up and see you last week-end but as you must have gathered, it's been one thing after another here what with Lilian, Lady Otterton falling in the lake and Miss Batty disappearing and poor Bert finding the body, and us being supposed to move house. The funeral is on Tuesday but it's not to be a big affair. Do you remember all the things we used to hear about Lilian and the way she carried on? Well I know we shouldn't speak ill of the dead, but I can't imagine his Lordship is going to miss her very much. Now no one can say I don't miss Father. I think of him every day that passes and there are all his roses blooming in his garden and him not here to see them. It breaks your heart.

Would you believe it now? Who should turn up yesterday but Miss Batty? And, if you ask me, there's more to it all than meets the eye. We haven't heard the end of it yet. You mark my words. Well her Ladyship called the police who'd been looking for her and they stayed here questioning her for hours, but then in the end she was taken away to the lunatic asylum.

I hope we will be able to get back to normal again once the funeral is over. There's going to be a lot to do what with all the packing up. We shall see what happens after that, but I will let you know as soon as I can get away to come and see you.

Give my love to Fred and the children.

Love from
Annie

Zbigniew Rakowski's notebook

JUNE 10TH

If truth is to be my helmsman, I am forced to admit that it was not without the faintest tremor of excitement that I read in the press of the retrieval of Lilian, Lady Otterton's body from the weed-infested waters of Capability Brown's once limpid lake at Cranfield. What discovery could better have suited my mood just as I handed the finished manuscript of my little *divertissement* to my publishers? My publishers are not only delighted, but, dare I say it, tickled pink, by my new *œuvre*. It is full of lust and envy, hatred, guilt and pride, all couched in a veneer of exquisite refinement. The tale is a simple one of betrayal and murder, but told, I trust, in a vein such as to carry the reader light-heartedly on, whilst ever ensuring that beneath an apparently frivolous surface, there lies an awareness of the baseness that is mankind.

I deemed it only suitable that I should pen a line to Lord Otterton, to commiserate with him on the loss of his mother, but I was not able to distance myself from the remembrance of the manner in which he was wont to refer to that lady, under whose daunting portrait and disdainful eye I worked for so many contented hours. However I acquitted myself with a brief acknowledgement of the distress the circumstances must have afforded him, wished to be remembered to Priscilla and, at the same time thanked him for the kind words he had written to me on receiving *The Otterton Family*. I did not consider it suitable to inform him of my latest work which, *D.V.*, will be published in the Autumn. I fear that this little tease may not delight the Ottertons quite so much as did my lively and scholarly account of their eccentric ancestors. I can only hope that before they lay eyes on that little volume, I may have the opportunity of discovering the truth behind Lilian's death from her of the hyacinth eyes. Alone in my humble dwelling, many are the hours I spend pondering what might be the connection between those blackmailing letters that passed through my hands and the subsequent, recent, fearful events that are reported to have befallen at Cranfield. If I am not very much mistaken, her Ladyship has of late taken a more lenient view towards me and, appreciating, as she surely does, my interest in the family, she might, perhaps, even be so gracious, were we to meet, as to inform me of the outcome of the drama which has occurred.

Sydney Otterton's diary

We buried my mother this morning in that bloody awful vault. There's only one place left in it now. For me I suppose. We took Thomas out from school but didn't think the other children needed to attend. Apart from ourselves, one cousin, Aunt Lettice, a couple of the older men from the farm and my mother's solicitor, there were one or two representatives of local organisations and that was all. Aunt Lettice said that as the door of the vault closed behind the coffin, she felt it was a blessed relief, not, as is usually the case, for the one who had died, but for those of us left behind. We went back to the house and had a few stiff drinks, then everyone left except for my cousin and Aunt Lettice who stayed for lunch. And that, I suppose, will be the last lunch party we ever hold at Cranfield. I felt like blubbing. Not for my mother but for the house. Next week we'll be in the Dower House.

Tomorrow morning I've got the local chief bobby coming to see me. He seems to think I'd like to know exactly what they managed to get out of Batty, which indeed I would. It sounds as though they're not going to charge her.

Letter from William Johnson to Annie Jerrold

'Cranfield',
Coolgardie,
W. Australia
MAY 9TH, 1950

Dear Annie,

Thank you for your letter. I was very sorry to hear about your father. He was a good man and I had a great respect for him. You will miss him very much. I was also interested to hear the news about his Lordship. Please remember me to him. I often think about the war and all the good times we had together.

To go by what I hear the old country is in a bit of a mess at the moment so I think I did the right thing by coming here.

Now Annie, why didn't you write sooner? I waited a long time but I was lonely you see and I don't know how to put this, but when I met Sarah, she was lonely too. Her husband was killed a year ago in a mining accident and she was all on her own. They'd come from Yorkshire like me and it was nice to meet a lass from Yorkshire and talk about the places we both remembered. Sarah didn't have no children and I didn't have no one either, only you, and you said you would never come so Sarah and I got married Christmas time. You'd like Sarah. She keeps the bungalow nice and tidy and feeds me well. I think I've put on weight since we married.

I've still got the photo you gave me Annie, of you in your father's garden holding a great big bunch of daffodils and I'll never forget the jokes we used to have together and your laughing eyes.

Love from
Bill

Sydney Otterton's diary

JUNE 15TH

The Chief Constable, a man with the good old-fashioned name of Wapshott, came to see me yesterday morning. Priscilla found him rather annoying because she said he was too smooth and too good-looking for his own good, but as far as I could see he was a perfectly reasonable fellow. I think she took against him because she decided he was arrogant. She also said he was delighted to be at Cranfield. I didn't see why he shouldn't be. It's a damn nice place and we won't be here for long now so he might as well have made the best of it. In any case, the man wasn't really that interesting. It was what he told us that really mattered. He was here for quite a long time and I think almost as amazed as we were by the whole sorry story.

The first thing he told us, which I have to admit rather took the wind out of my sails, was that within the next few days, they would be taking a team down to the lake to look for Pink's body which, if Batty is to be believed, lies there in a shallow grave. He then, to my considerable relief, announced that it was most unlikely there would be enough evidence of any kind to justify a charge of murder. The question arises as to whether Batty is or was criminally insane. Whether or not she is in any condition to be charged with manslaughter is another matter. It's not that I wish Batty well. In fact nothing would give me greater pleasure than to see her behind bars, but I think Wapshott and I both feel that some skeletons are best left in their cupboards. My mother's dead, Pink, it appears, is dead and Batty's locked up in a loony bin where she's likely to remain for some time. Of course Mason and Legros and various others of my mother's henchmen are still out and about but I can see very little reason why they would wish to return to haunt us now.

No one can be quite sure that Batty in her present condition is capable of telling, let alone recalling, the truth, but it appears that by the time she turned up here, dropped, as it happens, by Mason with whom she'd been in hiding since my mother's death, she was so confused and so indi scriminately angry with everyone, that she didn't mind what she said to anyone. Nevertheless, not surprisingly, it took them a long time to make much sense of what she was saying.

Funnily enough Priscilla was obviously on the right track about Batty because, according to the trick-cyclist at the bin, she had a pathological obsession with my mother whose death has consequently left her completely unhinged. Such was her obsession that she had difficulty in separating her thoughts and her actions from those of my mother. She seemed to think that the two of them were activated by one mind, all of which sounds pretty rum to me although, when I was a child, in a funny sort of way, I did see them as peculiarly united. I wouldn't be at all surprised if my father didn't feel the same.

As to the baby that died, there is some doubt as to whether Pink ever had any real evidence to suggest that either my mother or Batty had anything to do with its death. Batty swears that neither she nor *her Ladyship* would have ever done anything to harm what she apparently referred to as 'the mite'. Who knows? And who knows what gave Pink the idea that he could blackmail them? And why did they react as they apparently did to the blackmail unless they had something to hide? But I really didn't want to question Wapshott too closely about any of that. He, I suspect, wants to let sleeping dogs lie almost as much as we do. But of course things may change once they've exhumed Pink. In any case, if Batty is to be believed, and there's no one else who can tell us anything different, she eventually agreed to meet Pink down by the lake where she thought they would be out of sight in the boathouse. She claims that my mother never knew of the meeting. That again is something about which we shall never know the truth.

Of course, all this happened forty years ago now, so even if she was perfectly clear-headed, Batty's memory would have been likely to play her false after so long. But what she does claim to remember is meeting Pink under the bamboos and going with him into the boathouse with the intention, I suppose, of coming to some kind of agreement with him. Perhaps my mother had even given her money to pay him off. All she is able to articulate now, apparently, is that she just wanted to give him a talking to. Once they were inside the boathouse, he drew a knife and began to threaten her. For some reason a lot of tools had been left in the boathouse, probably left around by some lazy so-and-so who had been doing a few repairs down there. Anyway, Batty, in self-defence, grabbed a hammer with which she hit Pink on the side of the head.

Pink was a small man, but it is still difficult to imagine how Batty managed all alone to drag his body out of the boathouse, up the slope further into the bushes and there, with the help of whatever tools she'd found, to bury him in the shallow grave where he presumably remains to this day but which is shortly to be disturbed. A surge of adrenalin would, I suppose, have given her extra strength.

It is unclear as to whether or not my mother ever knew what had happened, whether or not she was indeed an accessory after the fact, but it is my belief that she must have known and that the weight of it all, from the baby's death to Pink's, only served to intensify her dependency on Batty and on heroin.

Whatever else she did or didn't know, she must at least have known about the letters which for obvious reasons she was so desperate to find. Batty claims to have hidden them in a succession of places. Why she never destroyed them I can't think, unless she thought that she herself might one day want to use them against my mother. She apparently thinks she hid them in some cupboard just before the war, which I told Wapshott couldn't be true because the children had found them under the floorboards on the top landing. In any case when the war came and my parents moved out of the house to make way for the public records, she never took them with her. She thought she knew where they were and that no one would find them, but when my father died immediately after the war and we came to live here, she and my mother began to panic. Of course we moved all the furniture around so she no longer knew where she thought she had put them. Perhaps she just lied to my mother because she never really wanted my mother to get her hands on those letters. Anyway that was when all the fun started and all the snooping.

We were sitting in the Japanese Room and at a certain point, before Wapshatt had even touched on my mother's death, a glacial silence suddenly descended. Even the smooth Chief Constable was briefly discountenanced. It was as though an evil gust of wind had all at once blown through the room, wrapping its icy fingers around each of us in turn. For a moment I wanted to be shot of Cranfield and everything it represents, but then I can hardly blame the house. I looked nervously at Priscilla who was looking at the floor and back at Wapshott who was running his long fingers through his lank hair. I stood up nervously and rang the bell for Marshall to bring the drinks tray.

Annie's diary

JUNE 17TH

His Lordship was in a dreadful state after that policeman came to see him the other morning. Cursing and swearing all over the place and talking about his b— mother and b— Doris Batty. I reckon he'd had one or two drinks by the time he came up to change for dinner just as I was drawing her Ladyship's bath. I wasn't feeling too happy myself but I wasn't saying anything about that. Anyway he heard me in the bathroom and he came in to tell me that he thought it was a darn good thing they were moving out. He'd had enough of everything. Mind you, I think he was just being awkward. I told him not to take on so but he wasn't going to listen.

'How would you like it Annie,' he said, 'if you'd had my mother?' I couldn't help laughing at the very thought of it, but his Lordship wasn't seeing the funny side. They don't know, he told me, whether she killed herself or if Batty pushed her in the water. Then when her Ladyship went to have her bath, he followed me into the bedroom, and there was me trying to lay out her Ladyship's clothes for the evening and him striding up and down in a dreadful state.

Now Miss Batty wasn't likely to admit to murder was she? I have no idea what he was going on about, but he kept saying that it was all because of some letters he'd sent to his mother. Her Ladyship wasn't very pleased to find him still there when she came out of the bathroom. 'Oh Sydney,' she says, 'do go and get changed.' Lady Isley was coming to dinner and we all know how punctual she is. Anyway his Lordship went off to his dressing-room still mumbling and swearing.

Sydney Otterton's diary

Priscilla kept on telling me this morning that I had bad blood from my mother's family. That may well be the case, but it didn't seem to occur to her that if I have bad blood then so do her children. Perhaps she thinks theirs is diluted, but I reminded her of an ancestor of hers who took a pig onto the roof of his house and then threw it down as a punishment for not admiring the view. He can't have been all that sane, but Priscilla didn't think it funny. No one seems to think anything funny any more. Even Annie. She's been really down in the dumps for the last few weeks. God alone knows why.

Of course I can't think about anything except my mother at the moment. And the more I think about her, the more confusing I find everything. I know that I was right in thinking that Mason and Legros were planted here in order for them to find those incriminating letters. What no one will ever know now is the degree of my mother's guilt and although I was initially convinced that she had killed herself, I am now not so sure. What on earth, one wonders, were she and Batty doing down by the lake? They must have gone there as a reaction to receiving the letters from me and I can only imagine that they went to see if Pink's grave had been disturbed. It may or may not have been the first my mother heard about Pink's death or there may even have been some incomprehensible reason of her own whereby she followed Batty to the lake that day. After all my mother was certainly quite as deranged as Batty, so who can say what her reasons might have been? Batty of course says that my mother slipped on the bank, fell into the lake and drowned and that she, Batty, was powerless to save her. That may well be true. The only problem is that Batty appears to have been involved in rather too many unexplained deaths.

One of the most unsettling aspects of the whole affair, is the connection between Batty, the Legros and Mason. All right, so Mrs Mason and Mrs Legros are sisters, and we knew that, but as if that weren't enough, it now turns out, according to Wapshott, that Batty is Legros's sister. And Legros, who uses five or six different names, has a record as long as your arm. He's spent a good deal of his life in and out of gaol and has repeatedly been in trouble for sexual attacks on young children. The police suspect Mason and Legros of being part of a ring involving sexual molestation of young boys, not that it's so simple to pin anything on them. I felt quite uneasy when Wapshott told me about that because I couldn't help remembering the violent reaction the children always had to Mason and how they always called him disgusting. I thought they were being silly at the time and I paid no attention, but now I wonder if he tried something on one of them. it wouldn't surprise me. There have always been a lot of buggers around and children are easy prey because they never tell. I can remember a gardener I used to avoid like the plague.

Priscilla quite rightly says that we've just got to try and put all this behind us now and concentrate on the move, the sale and then, opening the house to the public next year. But there remains the grisly problem of the exhumation of Pink's body which may result in some kind of case against Batty. And that will make it quite impossible for us to put the whole thing behind us for a while. Aunt Lettice, needless to say, is quite delighted by the whole saga. She finds it *moost* interesting. Probably more interesting than anything else she's heard for a long time.

Georgina's exercise book

When I got back from school today my bed had been taken away because it's going in the sale. I wanted to take it to the Dower House but Mummy said it was too big which made me very sad. I wonder who will have it next. It's our very last night in the poor house and I've got to sleep on a mattress in the peacock room tonight. Father and Mummy seem quite excited about everything and Father's laughing rather a lot and Mummy keeps saying, 'You're such a fool Sydney,' and laughing too. Yesterday she said, 'Your father has so many ideas that one of them must sometimes be good.' Father was really pleased about that. But Annie's not in a good mood at all. In fact she's been in a bad mood for ages now. Perhaps she feels like I do that nothing will ever be the same again. After the summer holidays I've got to go to boarding school and Thomas has got to go to public school and no one seems to know if Annie is even going to stay with us. When I asked Mummy about Annie she told me to mind my own business. Anyway my new room's all right, but it's really boring compared to my old one which I will never forget for as long as I live.

Annie's diary

There's no doubt about it, but his Lordship is as cheerful as a cricket. He seems to be really pleased about the move. He's been hanging pictures all day and moving the furniture about in his study and in his dressing-room. I was expecting him to be quite depressed about moving, but I reckon it must be a weight off his mind to have left the poor old house. Perhaps what with all the recent goings on, he was reminded too much of the past so he'll be glad to have moved out. After all he must have some horrible memories of years gone by which he may feel won't be troubling him so much now he's left the house.

It's funny to think of the Marshalls up there all alone on the top floor. I rather think they wish they hadn't given their notice now. I wonder who his Lordship will find as a butler and caretaker. We haven't had much luck with butlers so far what with Mr Cheadle and then Mr Mason. Her Ladyship always hated Mr Mason but she never said why and I've wondered if it wasn't something to do with Mr MacIntosh. Mr Mason may have known something he had no business knowing. Anyway Mr MacIntosh has gone now, too, not that he's very far away. Only in the village.

I never said her Ladyship hadn't given me a nice room. I expect she thinks that if I have a nice room, I'll want to stay. Well I'm not going anywhere now, so that's that. Not that I've said a word to anyone.

Sydney Otterton's diary

Priscilla went charging off to see old Rakowski this morning. His daughter rang on the day we moved to say he'd had a stroke and was in hospital. I couldn't really see why she rang us but Priscilla felt sorry for the old boy so she agreed to go and see him. Apparently he's not too bad but his daughter thinks he won't be able to go on living alone so she wanted to know if Priscilla knew of any reasonable old people's home in the neighbourhood.

I'm surprised by how glad I am to have moved. For one thing the Dower House is a very decent house and for another, in some peculiar way, I almost feel as if nothing has changed. The house is still there for me to see through the trees every time I step outside the front door, and what with the grant from the Ministry of Works which we're hoping to get for the roof, the future is looking up for Cranfield. Priscilla seems quite happy too. Only Annie remains moody. I can't laugh her out of it.

1995

POSTSCRIPT

I first went to Cranfield on Easter Monday three years ago. Easter was late that year and with the sun shining throughout the Bank Holiday week-end, England was briefly the loveliest country in the world. John Major had surprisingly just won a fourth successive Conservative victory at the polls, and for the first time a woman was about to become Speaker of the House of Commons. The country was so changed from the one inhabited by my grandfather during the years immediately after the war when he used to spend so much time at Cranfield, that I doubt he would have recognised it.

It seems likely that my grandfather never returned to Cranfield after his first stroke early in 1950. All I do know is that when he moved from the Edwardian terrace house at Wimble-on-Thames where we used to spend Christmas during my childhood, to a residential home for the elderly, surrounded by laurels and rhododendrons and situated in a sprawling village three miles from the gates of Cranfield Park, Lady Otterton was briefly good to him, visiting him at comparatively regular intervals until the dreadful day when she discovered how he had lampooned her and her family in *Hyacinth's House*. *Hyacinth's House* was the last book he ever wrote, and in it he describes Cranfield just as clearly and with just as much passion as he does in *The Otterton Family* or in his own private diaries. The characters in the book were as easily identifiable as was the house.

Unfortunately after my grandfather moved to The Laurels, he only recorded a few rare details of his daily life. Perhaps he found writing difficult or perhaps he had entered a period of deep depression. On the few occasions I visited him there, I felt that he had changed and although he appeared to be pleased to see me, he was never so talkative or so entertaining as I remembered him to have been earlier. I do, however, recall his once making a remark that led me to suppose that he regretted having alienated Lady Otterton. After all, he was a lonely old man who could ill afford to lose the few friends he had. 'Her Ladyship,' he remarked, 'was not amused by my little *persiflage*.' Then he said something about it having perhaps been a mistake to cast Annie as the butler. He would never have wished to offend Annie whom he regarded as an intelligent and worthy woman with a finely tuned awareness of the droll.

Although I remember, at a very young age, being fascinated by my grandfather's tales of Cranfield which, then, in my imagination, seemed to be just as real or unreal a place as Rapunzel's tower, it was not until four years ago when my mother died and I inherited his papers that I fully appreciated the depth of Grandpapa's romantic attachment to the house.

My mother's relationship with her father was such that neither he nor she appeared to show any real interest in the other. She steadfastly refused to read his books, claiming that, since he was a free thinker, they could not but contain blasphemous material. To her dying day she maintained that through his cold-heartedness he had sent her mother to an early grave. She dutifully visited him once, or perhaps twice a year and on Sundays prayed for his reconversion to the fold. Consequently when he died, she had many masses said for the repose of his soul, but never once had the curiosity so much as to glance at one page of the many notebooks he left behind. Lady Otterton attended the funeral.

When I came to think about it, it struck me as remarkably lucky that my mother had even kept those notebooks. She might so easily have burnt them or thrown them in the dustbin. But then she in turn died and I returned home to help my father sort out her personal effects. In the loft I came across a battered old leather attaché case marked with the initials Z.A.R., and on looking inside discovered it to be full of exercise books, every page of which was closely covered in my grandfather's neat, old-fashioned hand. Of course I knew my father would have no use for my grandfather's diaries, indeed that he would be glad to be rid of them. My father hates anything that he refers to as 'clutter', which for him includes ornaments, novels or keepsakes of any kind. He also dislikes my chosen profession. 'You're supposed to be the writer,' he said rudely. 'You had better take that rubbish away with you, or dispose of it.'

Initially I had a certain amount of difficulty in making much sense of what I read because of my grandfather's rather unusual habit of keeping what amounted to his personal diaries amongst whatever notes he was making for a work in hand. But as soon as I began to read the notebooks for the year 1945, my imagination was engaged; so much unexpected feeling did Grandpapa express and so vivid was his description of Cranfield and of the Ottertons, that I began to be as captivated by them as he had been. The more I read, the more obsessed I became until I finally decided that I had to investigate the family further. I had not only to go to Cranfield and to see it for myself, which was easily enough done, but I had also somehow to decipher the truth behind the half-told story in the diaries.

In a strange way, I felt my grandfather's spirit urging me on, urging me to ignore a biography of Piłsudski which had been commissioned and which I should have been researching, in favour of a story about a crumbling mansion and an improbable eighty-year-old tale of blackmail and possible murder. It was all quite unlike anything that I had been involved in before, or that had ever come my way, but it so aroused my curiosity that I decided to beg for an extension on Piłsudski, on the grounds that some new letters of his had come to light; in reality so as to pursue my researches into what I had come to think of, not as the Ottertons, but as *the house*, with a view to writing a book about it. A sequel to *The Otterton Family* perhaps, or to *Hyacinth's House*. Who knows?

In the event, the book wrote itself in the form of all the diaries and papers that so fortuitously came my way. My thanks are especially due to the present Lord Otterton for all the help he has given me, most particularly in so kindly allowing me access to his father's diaries. I would also like to thank Georgina Otterton for speaking to me freely and at length about her early years at Cranfield and for her generosity in permitting me to include in this work extracts from her childhood notebooks. I would like to thank Dolly Quick for the letters and diaries of her late sister, Annie, and for William Johnson's two letters. My attempts to trace Mr Johnson resulted in the discovery that he died of a heart attack early in 1974; his wife, Sarah, survived him briefly. I am grateful to Mr Johnson's niece, Carly Paine, for permission to publish Mr Johnson's two letters.

Of course there would have been no tale to recount without those people who lived at Cranfield and who in these letters and diaries tell their own stories. People with whom, over the last two or three years, I have become more familiar than I could ever have done had I known them in person. People whose lives and attitudes, like every one of ours, depended very much on the times they lived in and the attitudes of their day. All of them, in some way victims. All of them conditioned by Cranfield. I see the house as the protagonist of this tale. It is the house that shaped their destinies, directed their thinking and held them all entranced. For every one of them the house appears to have been of paramount importance.

So it was with bated breath that I made my first expedition to Cranfield. I had learnt that the late Lord Otterton, with the enormous support of his wife, struggled for several years to make a success of opening the house to the public and that it was eventually the good Lady Isley who came to their help and who, by generously endowing the house, made it possible for it to be handed over to the National Trust.

As a result of a huge grant from the Ministry of Works, the house was given a brand-new copper roof shortly after the Ottertons left, and in the heady early days under the National Trust, the ground floor and main staircase were entirely redecorated by a fashionable interior designer of the day and the basement was completely renovated, ready to house a shop and a tea room. With so much money spent on the house, with it saved for posterity, given a new lease of life as a piece of history, a museum, made into somewhere for holiday-makers to go on a rainy day, or somewhere to take a visiting mother-in-law or a guest from the Antipodes, I wondered how I would recognise the crumbling old house that had so enchanted my grandfather.

My first impression of the house was of its sheer size and of course of the redness of the brick. I could see at once, from the car park which had formerly, as I later learnt from Georgina, been a bulb park, that this was a house at which you needed to look carefully before you could begin to appreciate its grandeur or indeed its beauty. Yet I immediately felt familiar with it, as if it were an old friend. As I stood there in the car park, queuing at a wooden hut for my ticket, surrounded by rows of parked cars, off whose shiny red and green and blue roofs the sun glinted mockingly, was the house already beginning to work its ineffable magic on me?

I bought my ticket and began to wander slowly in the direction of the house. As I came out of the car park, with Cranfield standing at an angle to the left of me, I looked down across a field towards the lake. There should have been daffodils, although because of the early spring, they would already have been blown, but the daffodils so loved by Sydney Otterton and Annie were no longer there. All the same, as I looked over towards Capability Brown's lake, I could not but feel that I knew it already and I supposed that were I to walk down to its shore, I might encounter Annie making her way back from the farm, or there I might find young children at play. At the very least, I would see, protruding from the water, a rigid foot shod in delicate black calfskin. A pointed little shoe, I imagined, with a narrow strap across the front attached by a small round black button.

Involuntarily I shuddered, and then, like a dog emerging from the water, shook myself so as to bring myself to my senses. By profession I am a historian and therefore have no business fantasising about the ghosts of footmen, faded daffodils and murdered chatelaines. I had come to Cranfield in search of the truth, not to write a ghost story. I turned to walk up the short incline to the front door sheltered as it is by the Victorian excrescence, or *porte cochère*, built, as I knew, by Lady Isley's father, Sydney Otterton's grandfather. Even that was familiar to me.

Within a few moments, I would be inside the marble hall, gasping at the magnificence of the ceiling, awed by the beauty of Rysbrack's chimney-pieces. There, as I stroked the silken polished mahogany of the doors, I would conjure up the past, attempt to visualise the stark post-war era, imagine Sydney Otterton striding with his golden labrador across the great white marble floor and think of my grandfather, huddled fifty years earlier, in the cold of the Red Drawing-Room, concentrating, not as he should have been, on earlier Ottertons, but on Priscilla Otterton's blue eyes.

I was suitably impressed by the magnificence of the interior at Cranfield. As many have done before and as others will do in the future, I gasped at the hall ceiling. For all the money thrown at the house, for all the pseudo-eighteenth-century, fussy, ruched curtains, for all the elaborate and often jarring colours that betoken the exuberance of a runaway horse or a decorator out of his element, the house manages to retain its dignity and an aura of its past. I was reminded of something Sydney Otterton wrote in his diary about the house: It has too great a character of its own to be affected by one or other of its temporary custodians.

Since that first visit, I have returned on several occasions to Cranfield and on one occasion I was kindly shown behind the scenes and taken to the top floor where Georgina had had her bedroom. There was the school-room with the old wallpaper peeling off the walls, there was the landing I had already so clearly envisaged from the diaries, the lavatory concealed behind a bookcase, the spiral staircase to the roof and Annie's favourite view over the lawns and the park to the distant hills. Water dripped through the roof, just as it had done after the war, for the copper roof had been incorrectly laid and Cranfield was about to receive its second new roof in forty years, its original one having lasted for over two hundred.

The contrast between the grand downstairs rooms which the visitor normally sees and the musty old top floor seemed to summarise for me the history of the house and to encapsulate its essence as a home and a museum and as an integral part of British social history.

Only one act of vandalism truly made me weep and makes me weep again to think on it. Those silken mahogany doors have been painted cream, or fawn, or beige – and the paint dragged to produce a striped effect. How could anyone wish to stroke them now?

Elizabeth Rakowska Walters

1995